VAMPIRE'S MAGE

BOOKS 5-8

DEMONS OF FIRE & NIGHT

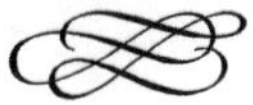

C.N. CRAWFORD

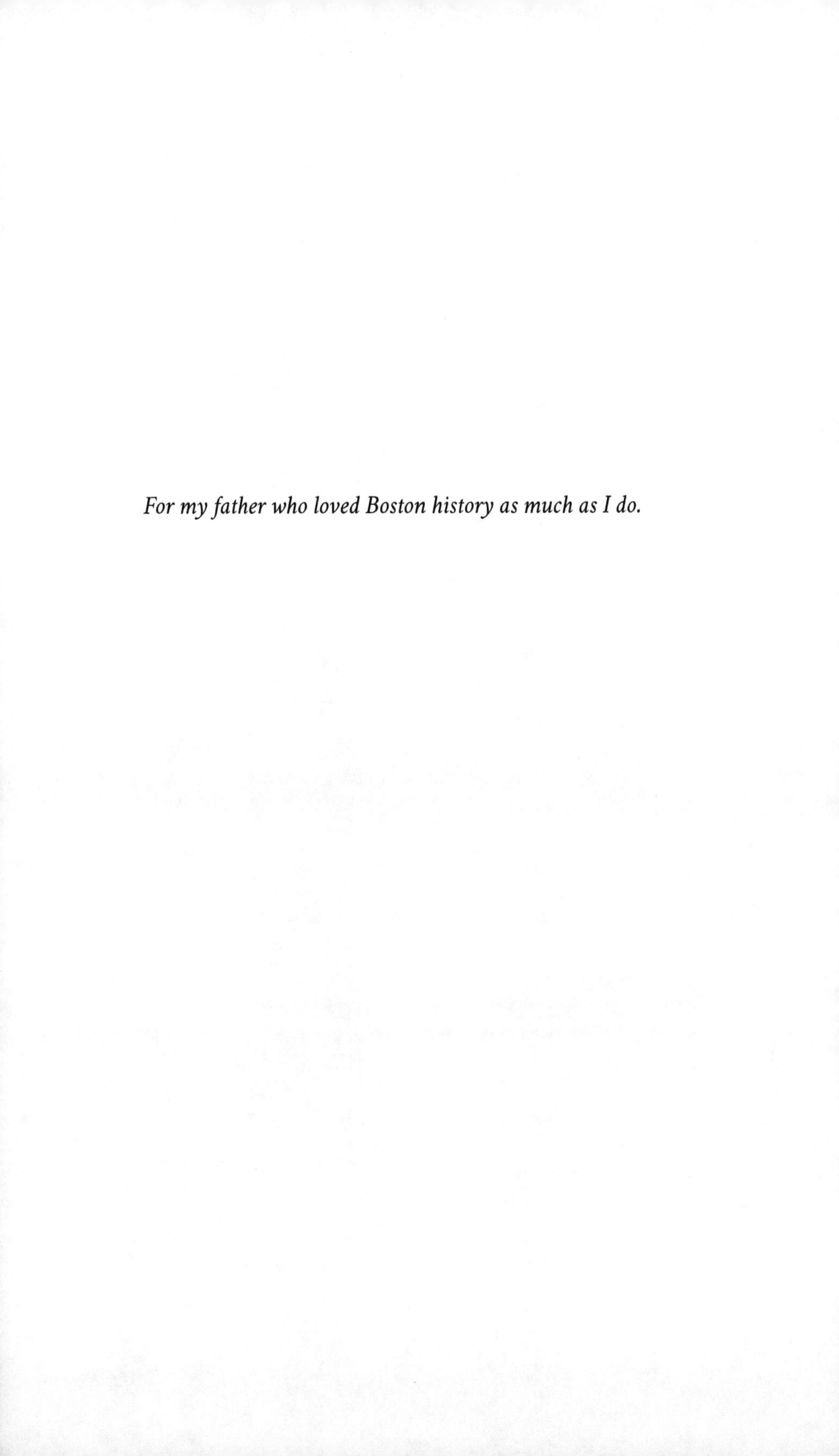

For my father who loved Boston history as much as I do.

MAGIC HUNTER - BOOK ONE

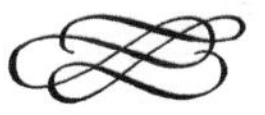

CHAPTER 1

$\mathcal{A}$ hard rain drenched Rosalind's black clothes, plastering them to her body like a second skin. Despite the downpour, she pressed on over the pavement, skulking past the library. Her thoughts roiled through her mind like the dark storm clouds above.

She really wasn't up for killing someone tonight.

Not someone, she reminded herself. *Something.*

Either way, she'd much rather be spending the night at one of the dorm parties—warm and dry, drinking cheap beer, flirting over red plastic cups. That was what most people did on a Friday night, right? Beer pong. DJs. Hook-ups with hot guys.

Sadly, none of that was an option tonight. *Someone* had to keep the demons from slaughtering Thorndike's student body.

The new iron walls built around the campus had failed to keep the monsters at bay, and two students had been killed in the past month. And to make matters worse for her, personally, if Rosalind screwed up tonight's mission she could kiss her life's dream goodbye. No more demon-hunting for her.

She pulled a hawthorn stake from her belt, whispering the Brotherhood's motto: *"Lux in tenebris lucet."* Light shines in the darkness.

Though right now she could barely see through the pouring rain.

She couldn't let the nasty weather stand in her way, though; she really didn't want to lose this job. For one thing, as a member of the Brotherhood, she belonged to an ancient and noble tradition of Hunters: the protectors of humankind. Not to mention that she got really nice boots out of the deal, and the Brotherhood kept her well-supplied with money and lethal gadgets.

While checking over her shoulder, she almost tripped over a collection of votive candles. A few skittered across the pavement. She scanned the shadows to see if she'd attracted any attention, but nothing moved.

As she pressed on, she mentally cursed the students who left all that crap lying around campus—as if candles or pictures of angels could scare away demons. Superstitions were for the desperate, a way of giving the illusion of control—not that Rosalind was in a position to criticize. No one in the world could pry her lucky ring from her finger.

Stake in hand, she continued on, striding past Thorndike's new mascot: a vampire effigy, sewn from black felt, impaled on a wooden stake. Some art students had thrown it together after a few local attacks, and the fabric sagged in the rain.

She hurried down a winding path, and thunder rumbled—almost as if nature wanted to ratchet up her nerves—like she wasn't stressed out enough.

Tonight's assignment wasn't just a low-level goblin or a boggart, like the usual jobs she'd had in the past few years. She was supposed to eliminate a redcap, a powerful demon of the mountain goddess.

Rosalind wasn't thrilled about the prospect. Redcaps couldn't live without human blood, and this one had slaughtered two cashiers in the Somerville Market Basket just yesterday, gnawing through their guts while shoppers stared in horror over packaged cupcakes and Twix bars.

Even aside from the supermarket murders, she had a good reason to be nervous. She'd already screwed up *two* assignments—both vampires—and now her whole future was on the line. One more failure, and she'd be kicked out of the Brotherhood—set adrift in the world of ordinary people who relied on angel pictures for protection. And she was fairly certain a redcap wasn't any easier to kill than a vamp.

She paused to survey the lawn, trying to get a sense of magic curling through the air. She let her body attune to the atmosphere's vibrations. This part of hunting was her strength. Many people could feel magic's frequencies, but Rosalind's skills went further. She could actually *see* magic—and smell it, too.

An aura tickled her skin, raising goose bumps. As it moved around her in smooth, blue waves, she shivered. The magic carried the briny smell of the ocean. *Not a redcap's aura. Fascinating—but not my target.*

She slipped into one of the alleys by the old theater, scanning the shadows. Her Guardian still hadn't told her where to find the demon, but she had a pretty good idea. If she were a redcap, she'd be heading for one of the frat parties on Wendell Ave. If a demon wanted to feast on nubile flesh, the drunk college students at those parties would be an easy bet.

At the mouth of the alley, Rosalind tightened her fingers around the stake, knuckles whitening.

She should focus on the positive. If she succeeded in tonight's task, she'd get her chalice—the pendant given to novices after their first big kill. But, after a string of failures, she couldn't shake the cloud of dread hanging over her, and she was just starting to catch a glimpse of a burnt-orange aura curling through the air...

Her phone buzzed, and she nearly jumped out of her boots. She yanked it out of her pocket. It was Josiah, her Guardian from the Brotherhood, texting her an update.

Redcap is heading for the Delta Theta Alpha house. Intercept him there.

With the fetid smell—like a dank cave—wafting into her nostrils, she didn't even need the text.

She hurried across the lawn. From the top of the hill, she scanned the row of frat houses until she homed in on the aura's source. *There he is.* A shiver crawled up her spine. Wispy copper tendrils rolled off him—the redcap's magic.

His red hat shone brightly under a yellow streetlight, glistening with gore. Crimson drops of blood dripped onto his zebra-print suit. Redcaps didn't normally wear clothes, and the sight was jarring to Rosalind—like she'd spotted a fox walking on its hind legs, dressed in a wedding gown. Perhaps the demon planned to blend in at a *pimps and hoes* party, and hoped no one would notice the human blood dripping from his hat.

Stalking along the sidewalk, she gripped her stake. With the two vamps, she'd hesitated. They'd looked so *human.* But this time, she needed to hit her mark. If she didn't, dozens of students would die. In fact, if the next few minutes didn't go the way she planned, the redcap would be dipping his hat into *her* blood.

He isn't human, she reminded herself. *He isn't even a person. He's a thing.*

One of these days, she'd just like to stay in, playing beer pong.

Gritting her teeth, she broke into a sprint. She pumped her arms harder, her breath growing ragged. If he managed to get inside the party, the slaughter would be horrific.

Her boots pounded the pavement, and the demon whirled, teeth bared. *Good.* The less human he looked, the easier this would be.

Twisting her torso, she hurled the stake at his chest with all the force she could muster, but his hand flew out and snatched it from the air.

His grin was a thing of terror.

Uh-oh. That's not how it went in training. She screeched to a halt, scrambling to grab the handheld flamethrower from her belt. The weapon wasn't much larger than a can of Coke, but it produced a three-foot flame that burned at 1,000 degrees Celsius.

Before she had the chance to blast him, the creature's hands were on her, gripping her wrists to stop her from accessing the arsenal on her belt. He was younger than most redcaps—his face elegant, his grasp iron-clad. Beauty and strength were just two of the weapons that demons had in their arsenal.

And what did Rosalind have? A bit of wood and some gadgets.

He inhaled deeply, licking his pale lips. "I like it when my dinner puts up a bit of a fight." His voice slithered over her skin.

Ugh. Even for a demon, this one was creepy as hell. Maybe it wouldn't be so hard to stab him.

She brought her knee up hard into his groin, and his pale eyes bulged. He might be a monster, but he still had nerve endings where it mattered. He loosened his grip on one of her wrists, just enough for her to wrench it free. She twisted her hips, bringing the full force of her palm into his Adam's apple. *Crunch.*

As he hunched over, gasping in pain, she grabbed another stake from her belt.

He was lunging for her neck, teeth bared, when she plunged the stake into his heart.

Or, at least, she'd been aiming for his heart. What she got must have been a lung, because he gripped his chest, stumbling back but stubbornly refusing to die. *Shit.* Josiah would be pissed.

As the redcap ripped the stake from his ribs, she pulled the flamethrower from her belt. The demon's eyes widened, and for the first time, she saw genuine fear.

Disturbingly human-like fear.

This caused an extra moment of hesitation on Rosalind's part, and the redcap had the upper hand again.

As he leapt for her, she pressed the button on the flamethrower, but it was too late. The demon knocked her to the ground. Almost instantly, his sharp teeth pierced her neck. White-hot pain exploded through her throat.

At this moment, on the edge of death, she could think of only one thing: *I am the worst demon Hunter in the world.* Pain blazed through her body.

The knife. She had a knife in her belt. *Come on, Rosalind. You got this.*

Just as she pulled it out, a pair of strong hands clamped around the redcap's head, twisting it sharply to the side with a sickening *crack.*

Her stomach flipped, and she shoved the demon off her. She stared, open-mouthed, as a black-clad Hunter sliced off the redcap's head with a sword in one shockingly swift motion. With a morbid fascination, she stared as the stranger plunged his fingers into the demon's chest. For one horrible moment, the air filled with the sound of crunching bone and tearing flesh. As the redcap's headless body twitched on the ground, the Hunter ripped out his beating heart.

Her first thought was: *Shit. I was supposed to kill the demon.*

Her second was: *How the hell could a human rip a heart out like that?*

When she glanced up at the Hunter, her body froze.

Not a Hunter. Not even close.

Despite his beauty, the man before her was twice as horrifying as the demon he'd killed. He was human, but not like her. A tattooed crescent moon, dark and sharp as a dragon's claw, marked his neck, and a raven perched on his shoulder. He held the demon's heart in his hand, crimson blood dripping down his arm.

A cold and silvery nocturnal power crackled in the air around them, old as night itself. Before her stood a shadow mage, and the aura unfurling from his body was ancient and terrifying.

He stared at her, his eyes cold and pale as glaciers, and dark shadows whispered around him. A pit opened in the hollow of her stomach. *He knows what I did, and he's here for vengeance.*

With a flick of his wrist, the mage tossed the demon's heart to the ground. Rosalind gripped her bleeding throat with one hand, grasping for a vial of iron dust with the other. Fear tore her mind apart.

Even as she reached for the dust, the mage was already whispering in a demonic tongue. His spell transfixed her in place, freezing her muscles. She couldn't move, and her mind screamed with pure panic.

As the mage spoke, his aura strengthened, permeating her bones.

Her blood roared in her ears, and she tried desperately to command her muscles to obey her. *This is it. He's going to compel me to bash my own brains out on the pavement.* And the one stupid, useless thought pounding in her skull was: *I haven't even achieved my chalice pendant.*

A powerful magic crackled over her skin as the raven fluttered around her. Rosalind flinched, waiting for the *coup de grace.*

But, instead of a death blow, she felt the sharp pain in her neck subside, and her arms relaxed, free to move. A shuddering breath slid from her, and she pulled her hand from her throat. He'd *healed* her.

Why the hell would a shadow mage heal a Hunter? Mages and Hunters were ancient enemies, and if he'd known what she'd done…

She locked the thought away. She had no idea if mage skills included telepathy.

As his magic caressed her skin, it occurred to her she'd never felt this aura before. It wasn't the briny scent from earlier. It was rich and earthy—and strangely sensual, as if it was licking her skin.

As she rose, she gripped the vial of aerosolized dust, holding his gaze. He stood at least a head taller than her, and something about his predatory stillness told her to *run*. Still, she schooled her features into calm. Showing fear to a mage would only provoke his bloodlust.

She swallowed hard, trying to gather her thoughts as she stared at him, stunned as much by his beauty as by his feral gaze. Slate-gray eyes, tousled brown hair, sharp cheekbones—he looked more angelic than demonic. How could a mage be so gorgeous? Magic was supposed to corrupt human bodies.

His gaze slid to her weapon. "Purgator dust." His voice chilled her skin. "You mean to burn the magic off me, after I just saved your life?"

She gritted her teeth. She knew one thing: he hadn't saved her life because he was a nice guy. But either way, she wasn't supposed to kill him. As humans, mages were to be taken back to the Brotherhood's Chambers alive. Of course, that assumed she actually stood a chance against him. In reality, he could probably pulverize her with a spell in a fraction of a second.

She tried to steady her voice, refusing to show submission. "It's my job to catch monsters."

She eyed his physique—pure, lean muscle, his forearms tattooed with a forest of magical symbols. Everything about his appearance screamed at her to get away—yet there was something oddly *familiar* about him. She'd seen those pale eyes before. And what was with his accent? Not American. Not English. Something older, that tickled the darkest recesses of her memory.

The raven—his familiar—perched on his shoulder, its dark gaze fixed on her.

"You think I'm a monster." The mage's tone conveyed only the faintest hint of interest. "Why am I not surprised?" With the bestial glint in his eye, he'd clearly lost his humanity long ago.

"Well, yeah." She didn't want to tempt his wrath, but there was no point lying to a mage. It would only make him angrier.

What was she supposed to do now? She'd just let a mage kill her target and cast a spell on her. And she had *no* chance of beating him in a fight.

She lowered her voice to steady it. "Do you kill Hunters like me?"

His gaze rooted her in place. "Hunters, yes. But not like you."

Her heart clenched, and she held the dust up to his face. He could have stopped her by now—broken her fingers, if he'd wanted to—but he hadn't. But he must know that, if she sprayed the dust, his torment would be excruciating.

"What are you talking about?" She'd gained mastery of her voice, at least, and it sounded far more confident than she felt. His comment had unnerved her, and she couldn't stop staring at him. The shocking contrast of his jaw-dropping beauty with the primal ferocity in his eyes seemed positively otherworldly. "You hardly seem human anymore." She hadn't meant to say that part out loud.

"And yet I just saved your life."

"I didn't need your help. I had it under control."

"That's not how it looked. He was gnawing at your jugular."

Don't show weakness, Rosalind. "I was lulling him into a false sense of security. I was preparing to attack." Her stupid hand trembled, and she hated that he could see her fear. He probably loved every second of her terror, relished the scent of her panic.

His eyes slid over her, landing on her ring—her good luck charm, and one she never took off.

"An iron ring," he said. "That's how you stay sane."

"What are you talking about?"

He slipped closer, his movements fluid, and adrenaline flooded her veins. *Run.*

But she couldn't run. Turning her back on him would mean instant death. She kept her feet planted on the ground, her heart racing.

Rivulets of rain poured down his skin. "I want to see what happens when you take it off."

It was more of a command than a request, but she knew better than to follow his orders. She had no clue why he found her ring interesting, but his intense scrutiny made her uneasy. Like he was peeling away her armor, or catching her coming out of the shower.

"I don't take it off. Ever. It's my good luck charm. Some people have votive candles. I have my ring to keep the monsters away."

"Doesn't work, though. After all, I'm here." He leaned closer, and despite the rain she could feel the warmth of his skin. She inhaled his powerful magic: air seared by lightning, a hint of sage and earth. She felt a strange wave of something like desire rolling off him, though she had no idea how she could sense that. He whispered into her ear, "You need to run, Rosalind. They're coming for you."

A shudder crawled up her spine as understanding began to dawn in her mind. He hadn't found her by accident—he'd come for her. But *why?*

She gripped the iron dust tighter, knuckles whitening. "Who's coming for me?"

"The Brotherhood. They want to watch the world burn, and you with it."

Ice closed around her heart. *No. He's lying.* "Why would the Brotherhood come for one of their own?"

"You're not one of theirs. I know what you are. And the Brotherhood will soon find it out."

He turned, slipping silently into one of the alleys.

With a shaking hand, she lowered the dust.

CHAPTER 2

osalind stepped out of the steamy shower, drying her dark hair with a towel. Josiah had been frantically texting her about meeting in the library for a post-mortem, but she wanted to stop by her residence hall first. The encounter with the mage had left her nerves ravaged.

Plus, it was kind of hard to rush to a work meeting when you knew you were about to get fired.

She slipped into a pair of jeans and a low-cut white shirt. The right outfit wasn't enough to get her out of this mess, but it couldn't hurt. She'd chosen her clothes strategically: the white represented purity—Josiah seemed turned on by that, and the low-cut top was just revealing enough to distract him with her cleavage. Only her weapon belt, complete with a loaded gun, ruined the sleek lines of her outfit. But there was no way she was leaving home without it.

She slid her knee-high boots on over her jeans. The iron-lined toes would come in handy if she saw the mage again.

As she leaned closer to the mirror, she pinched her cheeks, bringing out a blush, before glancing at the faint, white scars on her neck. The redcap's attack had been a *very* close call. She should be happy to be alive at all. Still, she couldn't shake the crushing disappointment of her failed kill.

Maybe she could persuade Josiah to bend the rules a little, to keep her on as a Hunter. She'd been *born* for this. Granted, she panicked when confronted with actual demons, but she'd get better if they gave her a chance.

She gathered up her hunting clothes and pushed through the bathroom door. The mage's terrifying warning—whatever he'd meant by it—whispered through her skull. As she walked through the hall, she blinked back tears, trying not to imagine the worst case scenario: exile from the Brotherhood.

She pushed open the door of her cramped dorm room.

Her roommate, Tammi, lay on her bed, playing music through her iPhone. As soon as she saw Rosalind, she yanked out her headphones.

"Rosalind!" Beaming, Tammi flipped her long, blonde hair behind her shoulders. As she took in Rosalind's grim expression, the smile quickly faded from her face. "What's going on? You look like you're about to cry. Is this about Josiah?"

"Sort of." She dropped her clothes on her bed. "I actually have to go meet him in Harvard Square to talk about some stuff."

Tammi crinkled her brow. "What *stuff*? Is this one of those conversations where you have to sit there and listen to him rehash all the reasons he dumped you? Because I would skip that if I were you."

"No. It's work-related, but probably just as painful."

"Oh, right. Your mysterious job that no one is allowed to know about."

Rosalind sighed. "Not for long. I'm pretty sure I'm about to get fired." She shouldn't be talking about this, but she was still so charged up from the encounter with the mage. It was hard to even think straight.

Tammi cocked her head. "Okay, *what* exactly do you do at night? Because I've been vacillating between *stripper* and *assassin* for a while."

Rosalind's phone beeped, and she yanked it out of her pocket. "Hang on a second. What the hell? It's Mason." Rosalind and her father didn't exactly have a close relationship. In fact, she only ever thought of him by his first name—when she thought of him at all. And he *never* texted her.

When she unlocked her phone to read the text, panic curdled her stomach. It simply read:

I tried to save you from yourself, but I can't protect you any longer.

Her breath caught in her throat. Did her father really know about her failure already? "This isn't good," she whispered. The last thing she wanted to do was talk to Mason, but she needed to find out what was going on.

"*What* isn't good?" Tammi asked. "You seem all dramatic."

Rosalind paced the floor as she dialed his number. His voice mail picked up. *Jerk.* It was just like him to send a cryptic, panic-inducing text and then shut off his phone. A cold sweat broke out on her forehead, and she threw her phone in frustration.

"Rosalind!" Tammi said. "You're freaking me out. What is going on?"

"Mason is an asshole." Rosalind picked up her phone from the pile of discarded clothes on the floor. Luckily, it hadn't broken, and she jammed it into her pocket.

Tammi unscrewed the top of a nail polish bottle and began painting her toenails. "You already knew that. But I'm guessing whatever you're upset about has to do with your father?"

"I don't even know." Rosalind took a deep breath, suddenly desperate to confide in her friend. "Can you keep a secret?"

Tammi stared at her. "Of course I can. Plus, I've told you my secrets."

Rosalind was the only one on campus who knew Tammi's original name: Marcus Robbins. Twenty years before, Tammi had been born into a boy's body. And while that part wasn't a secret, Tammi didn't want anyone knowing about her birth name. And she especially didn't want anyone seeing the photos of her awkward mullet phase.

Rosalind sat at the edge of her bed, just below her poster of a bearded Darwin. "I'm just trying to figure out where to start."

"Oh, just come out with it. Whatever it is, it can't be as bad as the time I had to tell my fundamentalist parents I was transitioning."

She raises a good point. Rosalind dug her fingernails into the duvet. "Okay. The thing is, I'm part of the Brotherhood. I'm a demon hunter. I was supposed to kill a redcap tonight, and I messed up." It came out in a rush. She already felt a weight off her chest.

"*What?*" Tammi knocked over her nail polish, and a pool of crimson stained her duvet.

"Josiah is my ex-boyfriend, but he's also my Guardian in the Brotherhood," Rosalind said. "He dumped me because the Brotherhood forbids novice and Guardian relationships. And I'm supposed to be reporting to him in about fifteen minutes, so he can fire me for screwing up."

"He can wait. This is fucking huge. I did *not* have you pegged as a Hunter. I wasn't even sure if Hunters were real. Can you even fight?" Tammi stood, her face flushed. "Start from the beginning. How long have you been a part of the Brotherhood?"

This really was a long story. "I became a Hunter at eighteen, but I've been in the Brotherhood since I was five. That's when Mason adopted me. The one good thing he ever did for me was introducing me to the Brotherhood. The order gave me stability and a sense of belonging—everything Mason failed to give me. I always thought a future with the Brotherhood was my destiny. I thought I'd be promoted to Guardian someday, leading a group of novices in the ancient tradition of the hunt. And then, tonight, I messed everything up. Again. They can't risk having incompetent people fighting demons. It's too dangerous."

"What happened?" Tammi asked breathlessly.

An image of the mage's cold, icy stare flashed in Rosalind's brain, and she shuddered. "I've already racked up two failed kills. Three, and you're out. Tonight, I was supposed to kill a redcap, but I let the situation get out of control."

"You let him get away?"

"Not exactly. He bit me."

"Holy shit, Ros. Why aren't you dead?"

"Because a really hot mage showed up, ripped out the demon's heart, and then healed me. And then I let the mage get away."

Tammi stared at her, open-mouthed. "Jesus, Rosalind." She pulled her hair off her face. "Look on the bright side. At least you made it out alive. And it can't be that terrible to get saved by a hot guy."

Rosalind flinched. "I don't think the Brotherhood will be so impressed with those things."

Tammi frowned. "Don't you think we should be making peace with the demons, or at least the mages? I'm just a little wary of the Brotherhood, since they don't do trials and all..."

Rosalind didn't need to hear this lecture right now. When demons were trying to feast on your guts, you didn't always have the luxury of putting them on trial. "Did the mages give us a chance to make peace when they murdered a hundred kids in Boston? Did that redcap ask for peace when he ate the two cashiers in Market Basket? The vamps have killed two people on campus in the past month. Tonight, this guy was going to slaughter ten times that."

"I guess so..." Tammi said doubtfully.

Rosalind could feel the blood rushing to her head. "The Brotherhood have been protecting humans from dark magic since the dawn of civilization. Without Hunters, demons would enslave us all. And the demons aren't going to wait around for us to put everyone on trial while they rape and eat their way through Boston's citizens. Demons don't respect weakness. We have to fight back."

Tammi sat on the edge of her bed, her brow furrowed. "Fine. But why you? Why can't you have a normal job? You're a computer science major. You have useful skills."

Rosalind shook her head. "Because the world needs people like me. Anyway, programming doesn't exactly light my world on fire. I'm not meant for a nine-to-five job. But since I'm about to get fired tonight, coding is probably back in the cards for me."

Tammi raised her brow. "Killing is the only thing that would make you happy? That's messed up."

"I still haven't killed anything. That's why I'm in trouble. And it's not that I *want* to kill anything. I just like being part of something important. And I like the sense of adventure. If I could choose any job in the world, I'd join Darwin's Beagle voyage. But until someone invents time travel and Victorian gender equality, I'll have to stick with the Brotherhood."

Rosalind's phone beeped again, and she scrambled to yank it out. It was Josiah again, demanding to know where she was. "Shit. I really need to go."

"If you get fired, come find me. There's a streak night planned. We'll get hammered and watch all the naked guys running around campus. You'll forget all about the redcap."

"I'll text you!" Rosalind grabbed her umbrella and rushed out the door, leaving her coat behind. There was no point wearing a low-cut top if you were going to put a coat over it.

And she'd need all the resources she could muster to face Josiah.

CHAPTER 3

With an umbrella in hand, Rosalind hurried through one of Harvard Yard's brick gates. She kept her eyes locked on the Brotherhood's towering command center: the Victorian brick building known as the Chambers.

It had once been a performance and lecture hall. Since the mage attacks in Boston, the Brotherhood had taken it over, refurbishing the interior at an astounding speed. It had been refitted with a combination of cutting-edge technology and old world grandeur, and it now acted as the Brotherhood's Massachusetts headquarters.

As she walked up the stone steps to a set of glass doors, she tried to pull her thoughts together. She'd need to project competence if she wanted to convince Josiah she was valuable to the Brotherhood.

She paused next to the small scanner by the door, lining up her iris with the blue circle in the retina scanner. When she heard the beep, she swiped her ID card, and the glass door clicked open. The Brotherhood were a little paranoid with their security measures, but you had to be vigilant when fighting blood-drinking demons.

Through the glass doors, she nodded at Martha, the rosy-cheeked security guard behind the desk, and hurried on to the central corridor. After scanning her retina a second time, she pulled open an oak door, its surface carved with Latin phrases.

The sight of the Great Hall always took her breath away. It was the most stunning part of the building—a cavernous, cathedral-like space modeled after a Roman amphitheater, with semicircular rows of benches surrounding a round stage. She often envisioned herself lecturing beneath its enormous stone dome about the history of witchcraft, instilling students with a sense of reverence for the Sanguine Brotherhood's history.

During the day, sunlight streamed through an oculus onto the lecture stage, illuminating the Guardians with pure white light. But now only pale moonlight lit the interior.

Her footsteps echoed, and she scanned the stone benches for her Guardian. For most, he'd be hard to pick out at all, but she was an expert at spotting tiny movements in the dark, and the slow rise and fall of his enormous chest drew her eye. As she caught sight of him, her heart quickened.

"Rosalind." His voice boomed through the hall. "I've been waiting for twenty-seven minutes. You're late."

"Sorry. I wanted to figure out what the hell I wanted to say to you."

He splayed his fingers. "How about the truth?"

He was definitely pissed.

She climbed the stairs, taking in his huge form, nearly as imposing as the Great Hall. The guy could deadlift five hundred pounds. She was still working on three hundred. *Let's just say I never want to get on Josiah's bad side.*

As she approached, he fixed her with one of his stony stares. "What happened? I've been worried sick."

"I'm fine." She sat next to him on the bench, its cold surface chilling her through her clothes. "But there was a complication."

He leaned in, his dark eyes intense. "Tell me."

"The redcap is dead, but I saw a shadow mage. He interfered. Technically, he's the one who killed the redcap. And he healed my neck wounds."

"Your neck *what?* Seven hells, Rosalind." He flicked on a small flashlight and inspected her skin. His face hardened. "You let a demon bite you. And then you let a shadow mage cast a healing spell. I'm going to have to purify you of any magical residue. Why did you allow that to happen? I've seen you fight. You hesitated, didn't you?"

He knows me too well. "The redcap looked human. I saw fear in his eyes."

"Need I remind you what demons have done to human kind? What they did to your birth parents?"

"You don't need to remind me. I think about it every day." It was something she and Josiah had in common. Vampires had slaughtered both their parents. But in Josiah's case, he could remember the event vividly. His trauma could make him a little intense on the subject.

"If given half the chance, that redcap would've chained you up in a dungeon. Demons don't have souls. They're pure predators. As a Hunter, if you hesitate, you die. You're lucky to be alive right now."

She hid her face with her hands. Her low-cut top wasn't working at all. "I know all this."

He pulled out his phone, flipping through his photos before shoving a gruesome picture in her face: a young man lying on the pavement, most of his neck missing. "This is what your redcap did yesterday, a few days after he killed the cashiers. The victim's name was Perry. A writer—recently engaged and planning his wedding. His fiancée lost her mind when we delivered the news."

Rosalind closed her eyes, suppressing the bile rising in her throat. "I know. He looked scared at one point. It threw me off."

Josiah's dark eyes flashed. "Do I need to show you the pictures of the cheerleading team the demons ripped apart two months ago? Since the supernatural world has gone public, they don't care about discretion anymore. They're murdering indiscriminately."

"You've mentioned it once or twice." *Shit.* She needed to keep her attitude in check if she wanted to keep her job.

"It's not just about vindicating human deaths. I want you to be safe. The Brotherhood isn't going to lose you on my watch. You're our strongest novice, and it's my job to guide you. Your physical training is fine. You need mental training."

Our strongest novice. He still thought that? "If you give me another chance, I won't hesitate next time."

"I want to hear about the shadow mage. Why was he there?"

Why *was* he there? "He was terrifying. Insanely powerful." Just thinking about his cold voice chilled her blood. "It was almost like he'd come to give me a message. He said he *knew what I was.* He said the Brotherhood will know soon, too." She shivered, thinking of the powerful thrill of his aura. "What do you think he meant?"

"I have no idea."

"He mentioned my ring. Something about how it keeps me sane."

"He obviously wanted to throw you off guard. And he did. Don't tell anyone about it until we know more. That's the sort of thing that leads to rumors." Josiah ran a hand over his buzz cut. "Tell me what he looked like."

"Beautiful, really. Smooth skin. Pale eyes. Brown hair. Tattoos—I saw a crescent moon."

"Magic deforms human bodies. He's obviously glamoured himself."

"Ah."

"Why didn't you spray him with dust? It would have seared the magic off him."

She shook her head. This was the truth she really didn't want to admit, but she owed Josiah an explanation. "With the demon, I saw fear in his eyes. And he seemed human. But with the shadow mage... *I* was afraid. I thought if he sensed I might hurt him, he'd murder me with his mind. His aura was immensely powerful. And when he first showed up, I was certain he was there for vengeance."

"Vengeance for what?"

A wave of guilt washed over her. "I mean, because of what *we* did in the interrogation room. His eyes looked so much like the inc—"

"You did nothing wrong in that interrogation room," Josiah cut her off. "The Brotherhood need us to act quickly. The mages have infested half of New England now, and something terrible is coming. Worse than the Boston Slaughter. If we show them weakness, they win. It's that simple."

A sigh slid from her. "Something is definitely coming. And I want to be on the side of the Brotherhood when it comes. It wasn't just the shadow mage on our campus tonight. There was a sea mage, too."

"Did you see him?"

She shook her head. "No. He must have been further away, but his magic smelled of the ocean."

He swore under his breath. "I shouldn't have allowed you to go out alone tonight."

The comment hit her like a slap in the face. "Of course you should have. I'm a Hunter. Going out alone is part of the job, and you know I can fight."

"Your combat skills are incredible, but mentally you're not battle ready. You can't let your emotions get the better of you." He shook his head. "You need to master your fear, or the demons will see you as prey."

She flinched. "We've been over this. It's why you singled me out for that special session downstairs." She took a deep breath. She had no clue why she'd made it out alive at all, and now, she just needed Josiah to get to the point. "So what's the deal. Am I fired?"

"The Chamber will review the case, but it's not as if you're the first novice to screw up. The Brotherhood won't want to lose you. You'll be giving them intel about two mages on the Thorndike Campus. No one else can sense them from so far away, or with such precision."

"I've had an excellent teacher." She exhaled slowly. He wasn't an unreasonable Guardian, and he always seemed to have her back. On top of that, Josiah was one of the best Hunters the Brotherhood had ever trained. Randolph Loring had promoted him to Guardian at only twenty-three years old.

Her relationship with him should have been awkward after the break up, but she'd quickly stopped thinking of him in a romantic way —even if his chiseled physique excited all the other female novices.

"It's not just your hunting skills that make you valuable," he said, eyes flicking to her neckline. "With your Computer Science degree, the Brotherhood will want you to work on their security systems." He pulled out a small, iron pendant, inset with rubies. "I still have your chalice."

"Next time."

His eyes met hers, and he handed it over. "Take it. You've earned it, anyway."

She forced a smile. It was sweet of him to try make her feel better, though she didn't deserve this. "Thank you, Josiah."

He pulled out an iron flask, etched with Latin phrases, and handed it to her—ambrosia, the sacred drink of the Hunters. "This will help clear you of the stain of magic."

She took a sip of the sweet liquid, and instantly her aching muscles relaxed. The stuff was addictive.

"Better?" He lowered his eyes. "You know I only had to end it with you because the Brotherhood wouldn't allow us to be together."

She handed him the flask again. "I know, Josiah."

"I'll still protect you."

Her father's message flashed in her mind. *I can't protect you.* "That reminds me." She pulled her phone out of her pocket, bringing up Mason's text. "Any idea what Mason is talking about?"

His brow furrowed, Josiah stared at the phone. "How should I know? Why don't you ask him?"

"He's not answering. He shut off his phone."

Josiah arched an eyebrow. "Great parenting."

"He's not really a… parent," she muttered.

"I have no idea what he's talking about, but like I said, I'm here to protect you. Get some rest. I'll let you know when you need to come before the Chamber."

The blood drained from her head as a horrible thought struck her. "Will I need to go in front of Randolph Loring and everything?" He was the flame-haired leader of the Brotherhood. His family's power stretched back centuries. The man was at least ten times as intimidating as Josiah.

"Relax. Randolph has better things to do than listen to a novice."

Rosalind rose, but Josiah touched her hand. "Don't think about the mage. Whatever he said to you, he was just trying to screw with your mind. And stay out of trouble tonight. If a mage has marked you for some reason, you need to stay hidden. You know how much they'd love to take you as a slave for their own disgusting purposes. He'll want to rape and feed on you. Or turn you into a monster like him."

She winced, thinking of how easily the shadow mage could lure someone into a trap. His beauty and sensual aura were all the weapons he needed. "I'll be safe. Thanks, Josiah." She curled her fingers around the chalice pendant.

"*Lux in tenebris lucet.*"

She smiled. "Light shines in the darkness."

As she left the Great Hall, she tried Mason again, but the call went straight to voicemail. At the sound of his clipped voice on the recording, her muscles tensed. It was hard not to remember him calling her an "abomination." Hard not to think of him tying her to a chair to beat her legs every time he lost his temper. She had no idea why he'd wanted to adopt her at all.

As she walked through Harvard Yard, she shoved the images from her mind and tried to imagine her life *before* Mason. Before the vamps ripped her life away by slaughtering her parents. She could remember only glimmers. Buttery sunlight. Someone patching up her knee. Toes sinking into the sand on a beach. Her parents giving her periwinkle and yellow wildflowers on her birthday. Her own face, smiling.

She could have sworn someone else lingered at the edges of the memories: a boy.

With a jolt, she remembered his eyes, pale and gray—not unlike the shadow mage's.

Chilled to the bone, she hugged herself tight.

Of course, it wasn't like gray was such an unusual color.

Yep. That mage definitely messed with my head.

CHAPTER 4

$\mathcal{B}$y the time she returned to Thorndike's campus, the rain had slowed to a light drizzle. Rosalind stalked across the quad, trying to sneak through the shadows undetected. She couldn't shake the feeling that someone was watching her. At least she had her weapon belt if the mage planned to stalk her.

Once inside her dorm building, she released a breath. Demons and mages could enter here, but their magic wouldn't work within the walls.

After the monsters had come out of the magical closet five years ago, Thorndike's buildings had been refitted with aura detectors that sprayed iron dust. At least the building would keep her safe from the lethal spells of a psychotic mage.

She strode down the hall to her room and unlocked the door. After pulling off her coat, she flicked on the light.

She gasped. Two men in black suits stood in her room—one thin, with impossibly long legs, and the other roughly the size and heft of an industrial fridge. *What the fuck?*

Instantly, her hand flew to her vial of dust.

Fridge smiled. "Well-trained, I see. But that won't work on us."

"We're from the Brotherhood," said the long-shanked one. "We don't use magic."

Her mind turned from confusion to horror. She really *was* in trouble. "I just saw my Guardian. I thought everything was going to be okay. What are you doing in my room? And where's my roommate?"

Longshanks tilted his narrow head, studying her. "Randolph Loring sent us."

Randolph Loring knew who she was? She wasn't sure if she should be flattered or terrified. "Is this about the mages? How did you hear about that so fast?"

Fridge licked his pale lips, edging closer. "I'm sure we will enjoy hearing about the other mages. But no. This is about *you*, Rosalind."

"I want to see Josiah," she managed. "I just gave him intel about two mages on campus. You should be hunting them."

"Josiah can't help you now," said Longshanks.

Fear crawled up the back of her neck. "Josiah is my Guardian. I need him here for this conversation."

Fridge smiled, his long teeth like a row of tombstones. "No. You don't."

She took a step back, her mind burning with panic. She shouldn't be afraid of her own people, and yet... "Why are you here for me? I haven't done anything wrong. There's a shadow mage *and* a sea-mage stalking the campus, and you're here harassing me."

Longshanks edged closer, and Rosalind took another step back—right into another body. A quick glance behind her told her the third person was a woman—a very large, muscular woman. Her heart clenched. There were three of them, trapping her in the dorm room.

"We know you're a mage," the woman whispered in her ear. "And I know you're not stupid enough to resist us."

A wave of horror slammed into Rosalind. *A mage.* Now *that* wasn't possible, even if she didn't know who her birth parents were. Unlike the other monsters, mages were made, not born. To become a mage, you needed to actually commit to learning magic. It could take years to learn Angelic, the magical language. It wasn't like it happened by accident. "You've made a mistake. I've never learned a spell in my life."

"The Brotherhood doesn't make mistakes," Fridge said. "Cuff her."

The woman gripped Rosalind's arms, and Rosalind's adrenaline surged. Once the Brotherhood had someone in their sights, they didn't tend to change their minds easily. She didn't know what they did with convicted mages, but she was pretty sure no one arrested by the Brotherhood made it into the daylight again.

Tammi was right about one thing: the Brotherhood didn't do trials.

A survival instinct—pure panic—blazed through the ancient part of her brain. *Run, Rosalind.*

Before the woman could finishing cuffing her, Rosalind reached back, grabbing the woman by her neck. She locked her arm around the woman's neck and, using her body weight as leverage, flipped the woman over her shoulder and onto the floor. Free, Rosalind rushed for the door to the hall, slamming it behind her.

By the time Fridge busted through, she'd pulled her gun from her belt, already loaded with silver bullets. She pointed it at the Hunter's head. The bullets were meant for werewolves, of course—not other Hunters—but they'd still kill a human.

Was she pulling the dumbest stunt of her life right now? Probably —but it was too late to turn back. She just needed to get down the stairwell, and out the door, then find a quiet place to get in touch with Josiah. He'd help her sort this out. He had promised to protect her.

Fridge paused at the edge of the doorframe, blocking in the others. He raised his hands, his face reddening with rage. "The mage has a gun."

"If I were an actual mage, I wouldn't *need* a gun. But like I said. I'm not a mage." It wasn't like she was going to *use* it on him, but he didn't need to know that. Slowly, she backed away from him, edging closer to the stairwell with her gun trained on the Hunters.

When she reached the stairs, she bellowed at the top of her lungs, "Streeaaaaaak niiiiiiiiiight!"

Within moments, hallway doors slammed open. Rosalind didn't wait around to watch her classmates strip off. She was already gunning down the steps. The horde of naked college students would cause just enough chaos to let her slip outside undetected.

With a racing pulse, she burst through the front doors, careening for one of the dark alleys between the campus's brick Victorian buildings. She knew exactly how to hide on the Thorndike campus, and slipped past some recycling bins into an unlit passage. From there, she could sneak through to the football field and jump into a cab.

She'd have just enough time to call Josiah—assuming he could help her at all. Maybe she'd just watched her entire life blow up before her eyes.

From the alley, she sprinted past the darkened, tree-lined tennis courts, heading for the football field. Fear blazed, giving her extra speed, until a rhythmic noise stopped her in her tracks.

Rotors beat overhead, and a circular light danced over the tennis courts. *Search helicopters.* Were they for *her?* When the light swerved over the football field, she saw men, swarming the grass in dark clothes. The light swerved again, and she caught a glimpse of flame-red hair, and the glint of an iron chalice pendant. A chill gripped her spine.

Randolph Loring. He'd come for her, leading the hunt.

Seven hells. What the fuck was going on? The Brotherhood had brought down their whole damn army, searching for her. Her body buzzed with panic. *This is all wrong.* She belonged *with* the Brotherhood—not fighting them. It was her destiny to become a Guardian.

Yet here was Randolph Loring, hunting her.

Tendrils of a cold, ancient magic tickled her body, and she whirled, nearly jumping out of her skin. Someone was coming right for her on a sleek, black motorcycle.

The shadow mage.

Her mouth went dry as he pulled to a stop beside her. "Get on the bike or you'll die."

She wasn't sure if that was a threat or a rescue attempt, but his commanding voice was awfully convincing either way. "I don't understand what's happening."

As if he'd tell her the truth.

"I already told you what's happening. They know about you. I told you to run, and you didn't listen."

She shook her head. "But—"

"You don't have time. You can come with me, or let the mage-Hunters murder you. Your choice."

She wanted to throw up. She couldn't believe she was even contemplating the advice of a shadow mage, yet Randolph Loring was hunting her. There would be no trial, no chance to explain herself.

Gunshots rang out, and an unholy pain splintered her shoulder. She screamed, instinctively dropping to a crouch, hands clutching the bleeding wound. The pain ripped her chest apart, taking her breath away.

I need to get the hell out of here before they slaughter me. Trying to block out the pain, she jumped on the bike and wrapped her arms around the mage's waist. With her face tucked in close to his leather jacket, she stifled a scream as he took off.

The helicopter swerved above, and another hail of bullets ripped through the night air. She flinched. She would die, slaughtered by her own people before she got the chance to defend herself.

The mage sped through a roundabout. A powerful wave of magic vibrated over her skin as he chanted a spell.

The gunshots fell silent, and the helicopter wavered in the night sky before careening off course. Was the mage actually controlling the goddamn *wind?*

Horror punched a hole in her gut. She'd just been shot by the Brotherhood and taken up with a powerful monster—one capable of murdering a whole legion of Hunters. Tears pricked her eyes, and she clamped them shut, trying to gain control. She couldn't let herself fall apart.

As they raced through Cambridge, the wind rushed over her skin, making her shiver. Or maybe she was shivering from the certainty that the rest of her life would be spent as a fugitive. She'd end up as the mage's sex slave, or a vamp's blood-bag, until someone decided to reap her soul for the god of night.

The searing pain in her shoulder stole her breath. *Think of some-*

thing calming. That was what she always did when the world seemed in danger of shutting her down. *The beaches in England, the hawthorns, blue and yellow wildflowers.*

It wasn't working.

Nauseated, she heard the sorcerer chant another spell—and gaped as both their bodies glimmered out of view. *Gods, the invisibility is a mind-fuck.*

That's it, then. She'd just hurled herself into the dark side, and now she couldn't help but second-guess her choice. Had Randolph Loring really come for her? What if this was some sort of test—one that she'd failed, wretchedly? Or what if it had been a horrible series of accidents, and she'd just thrown herself at a seductive shadow mage?

She should have gone willingly with the Brotherhood when they'd first arrived, but she'd panicked. They didn't evaluate the guilt of their prisoners, because they operated with one hundred percent certainty. To be honest, she'd never questioned them before either. The Brotherhood was always right, and the world needed them to act decisively or the demons would win.

At least, they'd always been right until now.

Now, even Josiah wouldn't be able to help her. Kind of hard to claim you were innocent of magic when you ran off clinging to a shadow mage's chest.

Her dark hair whipped wildly around her head, and the wind stung her skin through her blood-soaked shirt. The mage had offered to help her, but there would be a price. With mages, nothing was ever what it seemed.

She forced herself to block out the agony. They raced down Mass Ave, heading for Harvard Square—the location of the Brotherhood's Chambers. *Why the hell would he take her to the Brotherhood?* But as they wove through Harvard Square's congested intersection it was clear the mage had other plans. He was probably ushering her to his demon harem right now.

She felt sick. Her life was over, and she didn't even know why. Sure, she'd screwed up tonight, but she was innocent.

If anyone had answers to this catastrophe, it was the shadow mage.

She wanted to ask him everything he knew, even though he turned her stomach in knots of fear.

"Why do they think I'm a mage?" she shouted as they tore down Brattle Street.

He ignored her.

They zoomed past a row of old Victorian mansions before veering sharply left—heading right for wrought-iron cemetery gate. It swung open just as they approached.

At the sight of the gently sloping paths and marble graves, she shuddered with cold recognition. He'd taken her to Mount Auburn Cemetery. The place wasn't so much a graveyard as a full-blown Victorian necropolis—a walled city of the dead, complete with street names and towering mausoleums.

And this was the point where she'd learn how she would die.

CHAPTER 5

She ran through the options of what might happen in the next hour. Hanging? Impalement? Crushed to death by rocks? Like an idiot, she'd come here willingly—though her shoulder hurt so badly that death almost seemed like a mercy at this point.

Just as their bodies shimmered back to visibility, the mage pulled up outside a looming gothic chapel, its towering walls built from dark granite. He parked his bike in the shadows and turned off the engine.

She loosened her grip on his waist, grimacing at the pain when she shifted position. "What are we doing here?"

"This is your safe haven. Abduxiel Mansion." He stepped off the bike. "I'm going to heal your shoulder, and then you're going inside."

Rosalind gritted her teeth, crippled by pain. It felt like the bullet must have shattered her collarbone.

He moved closer. Gently, he tugged down the collar of her white shirt, exposing her wounded shoulder.

Pain ripped through her entire arm. If the agony from the gunshot weren't drowning out all other thoughts, she'd probably be running in terror from the mage right now.

As he traced his fingers over her flesh, he whispered a spell. His aura seeped into her body, drawing the pain from her shattered bones and caressing her skin. She glanced down to see her wound healing, and let out a long breath. Gods, it felt so much better. As if that weren't enough, the blood disappeared from her shirt.

She took a steadying breath as the mage covered her shoulder with her shirt again. Something about his proximity deeply unnerved her. Maybe it was the fact that he served the night god—just like the vamps who'd murdered her parents.

"What about the bullet?" she asked.

"Gone."

She still had no idea why he was helping her. "You even cleaned the blood out of my shirt."

"It would attract vampires."

She shuddered. "Thank you. I guess." He'd just saved her life, yet he was her natural enemy. Frantic thoughts whirled through her mind. "I don't understand what's happening. Why are we here? Why is Randolph Loring hunting me?"

At that moment, the chapel doors creaked open, and a man in a black robe motioned for her to enter. A dark hood cast his face in shadow.

"You're safe here," the mage said. "Orcus will look after you."

"You want me to stay in this mansion?"

"The Brotherhood won't be able to find you here."

The sight of the cleric tightened her chest. He looked like a grim reaper. In fact, he probably *was* a grim reaper. "Do I have a choice in any of this? Am I a prisoner?"

The mage's raven circled overhead, then landed on his shoulder. "You came here willingly, but I have instructions to make sure you're safe, which means staying in the mansion. Orcus will make sure no one hurts you."

Desperation warped her mind, and she struggled to string a coherent thought together. "I can't stay here. There's obviously been some sort of mistake. I'm not a mage. I'm a Hunter. When things have calmed down, I'll explain everything to the Brotherhood. I've never even *seen* a spell book." She suddenly felt a desperate need to convince him.

Dark lashes framed his pale eyes, and his unwavering gaze almost hypnotized her. "The Brotherhood execute people without trials, and they want to burn you," he said matter-of-factly. "You won't be able to reason with them. On some level, you understand that, or you'd never have come with me."

The night wind kissed her skin. "They execute demons. Not people. And they don't *burn* people anymore. That was just a medieval thing."

"The medieval ways are returning."

"I'm not a mage." Her mind raced with panic. What if this whole thing had been an illusion concocted by the demons to tempt her away from her true path? "I've never learned any magic."

Moonlight bathed his cheekbones and pale eyes in silver. "It doesn't matter what you are. It matters what they think you are."

"And I'm supposed to stay with the grim reaper." She had no idea who to trust at this point, but the shadow mage ranked pretty low on the list, and she couldn't see herself going out for Appletinis with the faceless reaper anytime soon. "I'm supposed to just take your word for all of this."

"You're supposed to use your own senses and capacity for rational thought. You saw the Brotherhood coming for you, and they shot you." He glanced away. "I don't have time for this."

"How can I trust my own senses when you have the power to warp them?"

His cold gaze slid over her, and as he stepped closer, her heart skipped a beat. "What purpose would that serve? If I wanted you dead, you'd be in the earth right now. If I wanted you to kill people, you'd be pulling out one of those knives and thrusting it into a heart."

Dread tightened its grip around her chest as she looked up at him. "Tell me why you helped me."

"Ambrose wants you alive."

"And who the hell is Ambrose?"

"You don't need to know that right now."

She bit the inside of her cheek to stop herself from screaming at him. She needed answers, and he was giving her nothing. She steadied her voice. "Okay, let's start with this: You know my name. You apparently know things about me. And who, exactly, are you?"

"Caine Mountfort. We've met before." He cocked his head, examining her. "Apparently, I didn't leave such a lasting impression."

Recognition flickered in the recesses of her mind—the boy with the gray eyes... "Did I know you in England? Before Mason adopted me?"

"England?" He arched an eyebrow. "Is that what the Brotherhood told you?"

She was ready to scream with frustration. "Yes, because that's where I'm from. I lived in England until a few of your vampire buddies murdered my parents."

He took a long, slow breath as if marshaling his patience. Something seemed to have unnerved him. "Look, I don't have the time or the inclination to delve into this with you. You must go with Orcus."

His habit of enticing her with hints while refusing to give a straight answer made her want to punch something. Her world had just been shattered, and the mage had answers he didn't care to share. And there wasn't a damn thing she could do about it—not when he had mind-blowing magic on his side.

A hot tear spilled down her cheek. "Can't you just answer my questions? What do you know about me? And why are the Brotherhood hunting me down? You and I both know I can't be a mage if I've never chanted a single spell."

He reached down, lifting her hand. At the touch of his strong hands, she felt a brief thrill from his magical aura, and it surged through her body like a jolt of electricity. What *was* that?

"Keep this ring on and stay away from the Brotherhood. You'll be fine." His gray eyes met hers. "Don't trust anyone. Not Orcus. Not me. Not your best friends. No one. That's all you need to know." He turned to leave.

Don't trust a bloodthirsty mage or the grim reaper standing behind me? Gee, you don't say. His evasiveness infuriated her. "Are you coming back here?"

"No."

"Where are you going?"

"You don't need to know that. Stay with Orcus." It was hard to ignore the ring of command in his voice.

Just like a goddamn mage to leave her question unanswered.

As she stood there like an idiot, he slipped into the cemetery's shadows. *My one chance at the truth—gone.*

"Come with me." Orcus's gravelly voice made her jump, and she nearly staked him. There was no way in hell she wanted to go into Abduxiel Mansion with Crypt Guy.

Scary as Caine was, at least he was human, and a hood didn't obscure his face.

His particularly stunning face.

The way she saw it, there were two options right now. Either the Brotherhood had made a mistake, or Caine had created this whole thing as an illusion. A cool breeze slipped over her skin, and she shivered.

What if Caine had glamoured demons to come for her? What if Longshanks and Fridge had been reapers spelled to appear human—

No. Magic didn't work in the confines of Thorndike's buildings. Plus, Caine had a point. If he wanted to control her, he could hypnotize her to do whatever he wanted.

Still, her heart clung to the possibility that this was all some sort of mistake. She pulled out her cell phone, and a message flashed from Josiah.

Where are you?

While Orcus cleared his throat, she frantically typed a message back to her Guardian.

Why are the Brotherhood after me? They say I'm a witch. I saw Randolph Loring. Did he come for me??

"Miss." Orcus touched her arm, his fingers cold and bony. "You must come inside."

She jerked her arm away from his touch, staring intently at her screen until a message popped up from Josiah.

Someone accused you of witchcraft. I don't know who. You must stay hidden until I can fix this. Don't use your phone again. I will find you. Lux in tenebris lucet.

The Brotherhood would track her phone. Panic clenched her heart. Even Josiah wanted her to run. Perfect, loyal Josiah, completely faithful to the Brotherhood, thought she should flee from the Hunters. He knew that once the Brotherhood had their sights set on a target, they didn't give second chances—no explanations, no trials, no pardons.

At least her Guardian stood by her.

She swiped open another message—this one from Tammi, who'd been texting her from a campus party.

Ros where r u... I'm getting drukeus I lost one of my shoes...

Good. At least the Purifiers hadn't involved her.

Rosalind hammered out another message.

Tammi—things have gotten weird with the Brotherhood. Josiah and I will sort it out. I'm OK, but I'll be offline for a while. Speak soon. XO

She shut off her phone, steeling herself for a night with Crypt Guy.

She turned, but she couldn't force herself to follow Orcus. In fact, there was no freaking way she was sealing herself up in a gothic mansion while Caine slipped off with her secrets. He'd implied her English roots were a lie, and then refused to explain. He'd known that the Brotherhood would come for her, but wouldn't say why.

He was the only person who had the answers she needed, and she would wrench them out of him if her life depended on it. *Which it does, come to think of it.*

Her entire world had just shattered, and she wasn't giving up on the remaining fragments without a fight.

She turned to the cleric. "I'm not coming in. I have more questions for Caine."

"You will come with me, Miss," he hissed, grabbing her arm.

A swift elbow to the jaw sent him sprawling in the chapel doorway, and she launched into a sprint over the grass, thundering up a grassy hill.

She wove through weeping stone angels and crooked obelisks, the gravestones jutting from the ground at odd angles like broken bones.

She tore past a row of stone crypts, and down a gently sloping hill. But she was running blindly, and had lost all trace of Caine. He'd slipped somewhere deep into the cemetery's shadows. She ground to a halt near a gently rippling pond, trying to attune her senses to the delicious tingling of Caine's magic.

A chilly wind rustled the leaves, and the moonlight shone on a tombstone's etching. *The Lord of Terror.* Even for someone used to hunting demons, she was getting the creeps.

The breeze brought with it the scent of thunderstorms and wet grass, and the hair rising on the back of her arms told her that a powerful aura lurked nearby.

She followed a winding path that led to the water, catching the smell of burnt air—Caine's magic. She just needed to home in on it.

She crept closer to the pond, drawn by his powerful aura. Anyone could sense magic, if they knew how to tune in to the right vibrations, but Rosalind could actually *see* it too. As far as she knew, no other Hunter had that ability. It was the reason she was born for the Brotherhood.

Goose bumps prickled on her skin as she drew closer to a row of mausoleums overlooking the water. Caine's sensual magic lingered around one of the crypts, nestled among the oak and beeches, pulling her closer.

As she rubbed her arms in the chilly spring air, she approached the arched crypt. Its door hung slightly open, and the crypt walls glowed, faintly silver. This was the one. Caine lurked inside; gods knew why. Probably the entrance to a personal dungeon.

The magic rippled off the stony walls in waves, skimming over her skin. It called to her, sucking her in like the gravitational pull of a black hole.

As she pushed open the metal door, it let out a loud creaking noise that echoed off a high, peaked ceiling. Empty. *What the hell?* He'd definitely come in here. She could still smell his magic and see the lingering glow.

Faint moonlight reached the interior of the crypt, highlighting marble walls and glinting off a deep pool of dark water in the center of the crypt. *What is a giant puddle doing in a mausoleum?*

A powerful aura rolled off it, smelling of ozone—Caine's magic. White-hot excitement surged in her veins. As with everything to do with mages, this mausoleum wasn't exactly as it seemed.

It was a portal.

Of course a mage wouldn't bother with a motorcycle when a portal could get him where he wanted instantly.

Her heart clenched. If she wanted to follow him through, she'd need to act now. Portals didn't last forever.

There was a chance this one would take her right to Caine, and she could confront him to get the answers she wanted. There was also the possibility that he'd fly into a lethal rage. Plunging through the portal meant crossing an obvious boundary. And if she angered him, she'd suffer a slow and painful death at his hands.

Then again, he'd obviously spared her life for a reason. It was just like Josiah said. She needed to master her fear to get what she wanted. And what she wanted right now, more than anything, was answers.

The shadow mage held the key not only to her present life disasters, but to her past. He was the only remaining thread to her golden childhood memories, before the demons had ruined everything.

She gritted her teeth. The idea of jumping into a cold pool of water at the bottom of a crypt ranked only marginally higher than spending a night with Crypt Guy. She twisted the lucky ring around her finger, wondering what Tammi would tell her to do. She was pretty sure what Tammi would tell her *not* to do, starting with "don't follow a psychotic mage through a pool of water in the bottom of a crypt." Tammi was practical like that.

But if Rosalind took the practical route, she'd never find out the truth about herself. She'd never find out if Caine knew something more about her past, or why everyone thought she was a witch.

After sucking in a breath, she took a step forward, and leapt into the icy water.

CHAPTER 6

She plunged deep into the frigid water, the cold piercing her skin. Immediately, she regretted her choice. The pool was far deeper than she'd expected.

Frantically, she kicked her legs to return to the surface, but the shock of the chill disoriented her. For a moment, she couldn't tell which way was up or down, and she flailed in the murky water, her pulse racing.

At last, her head pierced the surface; she tried to suck in air, but the frigid water had frozen her muscles.

Breathe, Rosalind.

As she blinked, waiting for the world to come in focus, she gasped. She was floating in a stone fountain, and her body shook from the cold. Above her, water flowed from the mouth of a stone woman in a torn dress. Rosalind clambered to the fountain's edge, hoisting herself out of the water onto a cobblestone street. The air smelled of jasmine and sandalwood.

Where the hell *was* she?

The force of the magical aura sickened her, seeping into her skull like a poisonous miasma. She doubled over, retching. Good thing she'd skipped dinner.

Freezing, she rubbed her arms, trying to catch her breath. Her white shirt now clung to her skin, her blue bra showing through the sodden fabric. *Great.*

She stood on a narrow lane, constructed entirely of stone. Pale moonflowers and gardenias hung from vines growing on the buildings that surrounded her, as though nature were trying to reclaim its domain.

But something drew her gaze upward: a steep-peaked castle stood on a high rocky hill, bathed in silvery moonlight. The towering gothic palace loomed over the land. *What the hell...?*

She couldn't breathe. She hadn't taken a portal to Caine's house, or even his dungeon. She'd transported herself to another world. Everyone had heard the legends, but she'd never believed them to be true.

Maremount, Mount Acidale, Lilinor... What if these mythical places were real? And what if she'd just leapt into one of the demon realms? If that were the case, she needed to get the hell out of here. Fast. She could fight one or two demons—in theory. But she wasn't ready to fight a whole demon realm.

Her imagination roamed free, and her mind spun with all the horrifying things she could remember about demons. Some killed fast, and others savored their victims' agony, plucking apart the sinews and muscle like artists of gore.

At this point, only two things were certain: she was a complete idiot for plunging through the portal, and she should have stayed with the grim reaper.

She hugged herself, overcome by a sudden urge to plunge back into the cemetery. But when she glanced back into the fountain, all the water had disappeared.

Her world tilted; it felt like all the blood drained from her head. What the hell had she just done? Sure, she was probably safe from the Brotherhood here, but she wasn't safe from anything else. In fact, she'd just thrown herself right into the monster's lair. She *really* needed to find Caine now, assuming he still wanted to keep her alive.

She swallowed hard and took a tentative step, her teeth chattering.

If she were lucky, she'd thrown herself into the mage's realm. *Which one is that? Maremount, maybe.* At least, that's what Josiah had once told her.

As she stepped over the damp cobblestones, cold fear washed over her skin. There was no sign of Caine in the city's dark shadows, and she felt none of his dark magic caressing her skin. She reached for the flamethrower at her belt.

She needed to master her fear and plan strategically, practically. It was what Josiah would tell her to do—at least, after he'd finished going apoplectic at her current situation. Gods, she wished he were here.

Think, Rosalind. Since Caine was a shadow mage, he was aligned with the night god. So were the vamps. Hadn't Josiah said something about a vampire kingdom? Lilinor, perhaps? If that's where she'd come, she would soon meet her parents' fate.

Mentally, she tallied the weapons in her belt. If she had to face vamps, her gun would be useless. Silver bullets were fantastic against some monsters, but silver was the night god's element. Contrary to popular belief, vampires and incubi actually *liked* silver. It made them stronger.

No, if this was Lilinor, she'd need her flamethrower, the one remaining hawthorn stake, and maybe the iron dust. That alone could cause intense pain to any magical creature.

She just needed to stop the damn shaking in her hands if she wanted to use a weapon.

She tiptoed over the old cobblestones. As she followed the narrow alley into a town square, she suppressed the urge to scream for Caine at the top of her lungs. He was her best chance at survival, but she couldn't draw attention.

She sniffed the air. Her ears pricked as something rustled nearby, and she pulled the stake from her belt, followed by the flamethrower.

Thud.

She spun, just as two pale vamps leapt to the street. A giant, ginger-haired man stood next to a raven-haired woman.

No hesitating this time, Rosalind.

"Well, look here," the man said. "A human, offering herself up to us."

"I can see her veins through that shirt, pumping blood," the woman said.

Rosalind pressed the button, unleashing the flames, and the vampires scuttled back, clothes blazing.

Someone grabbed her hair from behind, and Rosalind slammed her elbow into the monster's ribs before reaching for the stake. She spun, ramming the wood into another female vamp's heart. As the creature turned to ash, Rosalind snatched her stake from the dust heap.

"She murdered Domenica!" someone shrieked.

Rosalind whirled at the sound of footfalls, and jammed the wood into another vamp's chest.

They were on her like a plague of locusts, and before she could even get to her feet again, one of them grabbed her from behind, pinning her arms in a vise-like grip. He ripped the stake from her hands, then spun her around and slammed her up against the wall. Her back cracked against the stone. As he pinned her arms above her head, the vamp's sharp nails pierced her wrists. Revulsion spread through her. *This is how Mom and Dad died.*

The vamp's hair was long and black, flowing over his shoulders, and his eyes blazed blood red. "She's looking for someone strong. She wants me to keep her as my pet. She came here because she wanted it."

Rosalind burned with anger. The vamp's vise-like grip dug into her arms, and he pressed his body against hers. Vampires were lusty creatures, but the look in this one's eye screamed something more like "sex offender."

As he sniffed her neck, her legs flailed. Her kicks to his shins did nothing. His cold tongue shot out of his mouth, and he licked her neck, moaning.

Freaking vile. Rage exploded in her mind and she rammed her knee right up into his groin. She heard a pained grunt, and his hands loosened just long enough for her to free herself. She whipped the iron dust from her belt, spraying it on the small crowd of vampires.

Their screams pierced the quiet, and her stomach turned as the scent of burning flesh filled the air. Four vamps, blazing like torches—all except the raven-haired vamp, who turned on her again as his buddies turned to ash.

Her mouth went dry. The screams would only lure more vamps. How the hell was she supposed to master her fear in this situation? It's not like *any* human could hack her way out of a demon realm.

"What the hell is going on?" A deep voice interrupted from the shadows.

The vampire's head whipped around, and he gaped as Caine stepped into the moonlight.

Caine's voice was cold and steady. "Were you trying to kill this girl?"

"She belongs to me, sir." The vamp licked his lips. "She murdered five of Ambrose's soldiers. I'm going to play with her a while, and drink her slowly. I'd like to keep her as a pet."

Caine's raven circled his head. Ice tinged his voice. "Step away from her, Horace. Ambrose wants her alive."

Horace's lip curled. "But, sir. She came into our world. That means she *wants* to be my pet. She wouldn't have sought us out if she didn't want us."

"I already told you not to touch her." Caine flicked his fingertips at the vamp.

Horace's body lurched, his neck arching backward at an awkward angle. The silent square filled with the sounds of snapping and crunching bones, then Horace's agonized screams. When Caine lowered his hand again, the screams faded to a whimper.

Horace crumpled to the ground.

Rosalind gaped. *Seven hells. Remind me never to get on his bad side—if I'm not already.*

Caine crossed to her, his eyes flashing. In fact, he looked like he might rip her head off. "What exactly do you think you're doing here? Please don't tell me you've got everything under control again."

She straightened. "I'm looking for answers. My life just fell apart within the span of an hour, and I want to know why. You apparently know a thing or two about it." Her voice rose in volume. He scared the wits out of her, but she had nothing left to lose. And what good was living when your life was over? "I want to know who you are, and who I am, and why everyone thinks I'm a witch. And you're going to tell me." For once, she kept the tremble out of her voice.

Caine's predatory gaze slid over her transparent shirt, and she remembered what Josiah had told her: to someone like Caine, other humans existed only to satisfy their depraved desires.

"You can't stay here," he said. "We're going to see Ambrose. We'll talk on the way."

We'll talk. So he was going to tell her something. "And who is Ambrose?"

"The Lord of this realm. And considering you just slaughtered five vampires in his kingdom, he's just about the only person who can save your life at this point."

CHAPTER 7

Side by side, they crept through the city's winding streets. Caine's raven perched on his shoulder.

Rosalind suspected one thing: the angry set of Caine's jaw suggested he regretted saving her life, or that he might hypnotize her to choke herself to death at any moment.

"Are we in the vampire realm?" she asked.

"Lilinor. I suppose you cleverly deduced that by the presence of all the vampires," he said, his voice glacial. "How did you find me?"

The vampire's mythical realm wasn't so mythical, apparently. "I followed your magic."

"How?" he demanded.

"It smells like rainstorms, and it leaves behind a silvery shimmer."

He slid a disbelieving gaze at her. "You can *see* magic?"

"Yes. It's what makes me a good Hunter." She might have been overdoing the bragging, but something about his cocky attitude really irked her, and she wanted him to know she had her own talents.

"You didn't look skilled when I first met you."

Jerk. "My skills are not the problem. I just felt bad for the redcap for a fraction of a second. It's called empathy. Something that most people have, unless magic has sapped your humanity."

"That hesitation suggests a certain lack of skill. A lack of mastery over your own emotions."

Awesome. So even in the demon realm, I'm getting lectured. "Do we have to have this conversation?"

"You're the one who came after me for answers," he said.

"I want answers about why the Brotherhood think I'm a mage, not your analysis of my lack of skill." She shivered, rubbing her arms. Even if his arrogance grated, she should probably be a little nicer to Caine—she was completely dependent on him for her survival right now, and had to keep him happy. "Thank you for helping me."

Only the bird responded, with a puff of feathers.

"How do I leave Lilinor?" Rosalind asked. "What happens when someone gets to the boundaries?"

"Do you always chatter like this?"

She hugged herself, trying to stay warm in her waterlogged clothes. "I'm just curious. This is the first time I've visited an alternate universe. I never knew they were real before."

He cut her a sharp look. "There are no edges. When you get to the boundaries, you end up in another part of Lilinor. Only magic will get you from one world to another. That's why you need me."

She'd always wondered how the alternate universes worked, and the raw fascination almost suppressed her fear. This sort of information was *gold* to the Brotherhood—another bit of ammunition if she wanted to redeem herself. "Do you think space-time is warped at the boundaries by an intensely dense magical aura? Maybe shadow magic and light magic are magnetically attracted at a universe's edges. The aura is staggeringly dense there. That might explain why I felt so sick when I came through."

"Gods below. Are you still talking?" His bird twitched her wings and flew off. "You've even managed to bore Lilu."

Rosalind narrowed her eyes. "I had to fight a flock of vampires to get this far, and I endured a neck-licking from Horace. I realize it was immensely stupid of me to come, but can I at least get an answer or two? Starting with an exit plan?"

"There's no way out of Lilinor unless I create another portal. We must speak to the Vampire Lord first."

"You need his permission? Interesting. I thought you were powerful." Hunting for psychological weaknesses—not a lesson the Brotherhood taught, but one she'd learned from the mean girls who made fun of her clothes in middle school.

"I *am* powerful. I command Ambrose's entire army against the legion of light demons." His voice betrayed only the faintest hint of irritation.

"You've commanded an entire army, but you have to ask permission to make a door."

"A portal. It's not a door. And, more than that, the shadow demons have a hierarchy." Caine's attitude suggested he didn't bend easily to authority. He must struggle with his own rebellious impulses.

"I have more questions."

Caine pressed his fingers to his eyes as if trying to manage a migraine. "I deeply regret pulling the vampires off you."

As she followed him up the winding cobblestone road, she gazed up at him. "I need to know why everyone thinks I'm a mage."

"Fine." His pale gaze met hers for a brief instant. "But you're so ignorant, I don't even know where to start."

"Start from the beginning."

"For one thing, the Brotherhood are notoriously inept."

"No, we're not," she protested. Though obviously, they'd screwed up in her case.

"The Salem Witch Trials. The Scottish Witch Hunt... all the European witch crazes. The Brotherhood's rampant slaughter led to panic. That's why the magical lands were created in the first place."

That wasn't how she'd learned it, but she got the idea. He was talking about magical lands like Maremount—New England's own hidden land of mages.

"The real demons needn't have bothered, because your Hunter predecessors spent most of their time murdering the innocent. The Brotherhood—or the Purgators, as they used to be known—have been screwing up for thousands of years."

Of course, he saw things from the demon point of view. "When I said start at the beginning, I didn't really mean thousands of years ago."

"Almost none of the Brotherhood's victims were actual mages," he continued on. "The Hunters went after the poor, the weak, the desperate. The cranky and ill-tempered. Those who worshipped the wrong gods. Anyone they didn't like. Anyone who didn't fit in. If any real mages were among their victims, it was pure accident."

An extremely biased account. "So, assuming you're telling me the truth—" which, by the way, she really wasn't assuming "—what you're saying is that they've screwed up again with my case."

They passed a candlelit tavern, and she caught a glimpse of vampires packed inside, drinking from silver goblets.

"That's actually not what I'm saying. For once, they got it right."

A cold sense of dread snaked up her spine. Everything he said was pretty much the opposite of what she knew to be the truth.

Or what she'd *thought* was the truth.

And yet, somehow something about the way he spoke suggested *honesty.*

"I don't understand. How can I be a mage if I've never learned a single spell? No one is born a mage."

He led them up a narrow, winding lane. Steep-peaked stone houses towered over them at crooked angles. "That's true. Neither you or I came into this world as a mage. Neither did we learn magic in the conventional way. We both have your parents to thank for that."

A cold sweat broke out on her brow. He knew who her parents were. "What did my birth parents do? How do we know each other? Were you there when they died?" He wasn't her *brother,* was he? She remembered his gray eyes…

He paused, his gaze locking on hers. "We're not from England, for one thing."

"And where are we from?" Her voice was barely a whisper.

"From Maremount."

The ground wavered beneath her feet. She came from a land of *mages?*

She took a shuddering breath. "But I've been with the Brotherhood since I was five. I was too young to be a mage. They can't possibly blame me for a spell I cast when I was a little child."

When he stepped closer, she had to fight the instinct to step away. *Don't show fear, Rosalind.*

He touched her hand, and his energy fluttered over her skin—that strange, inexplicable thrill. As he lifted her fingers, he examined her ring. "Iron dampens the magic. If you take this off, you'll lose your mind. That's because you're possessed with an extra spirit. You have two souls. One is your own, and the other belongs to a mage, long-since dead. Your parents imbued us both with mages' souls. The spirits they gave us were supposed to grant us powerful magic, and your parents believed they could control the mages within us. It didn't work out. And without a lot of training, your mind will splinter. You won't be able to handle both souls."

She slipped her hand from his grasp, horror vibrating through her skull. For about the tenth time tonight, the world almost seemed to stop, and an overwhelming sense of vertigo flooded her mind.

Two souls? Her mind rebelled against everything he was saying. She was stuck in an unending nightmare.

She was a Hunter, but one corrupted by a dark magic. And her own parents had done it to her. If she took off the ring, she'd devolve into a predatory beast, like Caine.

She wanted to believe he was lying—just another mage trick—but in the darkest recesses of her mind she had the strangest sense that he was telling the truth.

"So that's what Mason meant about me being corrupted."

"You're not corrupted. You could have tremendous power if you accepted it."

"I don't understand." She could hardly breathe as her world crashed down on her. "Did vampires kill my parents?"

"No. Your parents sent you out of Maremount. They gave you to someone from the Brotherhood to keep your power in check. They probably paid someone to keep the magic hidden. To make sure you kept that ring on."

"Mason," she said, her pulse racing. "And all this time, my parents let me think they were dead. And they're alive in Maremount." Her voice broke.

"Please don't start crying."

She tried to force the tears back. "Why did they send me away?"

"They saw what happened to me."

Something in his tone told her not to ask what he meant—not now, at least.

No wonder Mason had never shown any interest in her. He wasn't really a father at all—more like a warden. Her stomach hollowed out. This was all too much to take in. "My parents ruined me."

Her drenched clothes hung like ice against her skin, and she shivered, trying to keep her teeth from chattering.

He looked her over. "We need to get to Ambrose before you freeze to death. Let's go." He turned, stalking up the hill.

Caine's revelation crushed her. She'd always imagined her parents as loving and kind, maybe other Hunters. Not demonic cultists who'd been paying someone to look after her, and who'd let her think they were dead. *Seven hells*. That wasn't how it was supposed to be. Her fingernails pierced her palms, but this time, she wasn't going to let herself cry.

She glanced at him. "Why is it that you're able to live with two souls? Why haven't you lost your mind?"

"Keep your voice down. You're going to attract a legion of human traffickers who will force you into one of the brothels."

Obviously, she needed to get this witch's soul the hell out of her body. And *then* she'd explain it all to the Brotherhood—how none of it was really her fault. If she exorcised the spirit, she could get her life back. After all, she was still human. "How do I get the mage out of me?"

"I think you need to focus on the problem at hand. You must have had ambrosia recently, because you smell like a Hunter. It marks you out as a demon's natural enemy. Any one of this world's inhabitants would love to keep you as a pet. And if you get even the slightest cut on your skin, the whole city will descend to feast on a Hunter."

She frowned. He was being dramatic. "That seems a bit extreme. And *you're* human. Why don't they kill you?"

"Never mind that."

The narrow street opened into a long esplanade dominated by the towering stone castle. Moonlight glinted off its sharp spires, and a silver portcullis barred the gate. Gargoyles leered from buttresses high above.

She had no desire to go through that gate, but apparently she needed to speak to the Vampire Lord. This was what her life had become.

Caine paused, touching her wrist. His fingers warmed her skin, sending a thrill through her arm.

"When we go in there, someone might attack." He reached for his back pocket, pulling out a hawthorn stake. "From what I saw earlier, I understand you know how to defend yourself."

"Believe me. I've killed plenty of vampires." And by "plenty," she meant the few she'd just killed.

Caine led her to the portcullis, and chanted a spell to lift the silver gate. When it cranked and groaned to the top of the entrance, he led her into a long hall. Ivory rib vaults towered high above them like bones and, within steep-peaked arches, the walls were painted a deep crimson. Since her parents were apparently mages, they'd be right at home in a place like this, Rosalind sure as hell wasn't. The look of the place sent a shudder up her spine.

As they walked through the hall, she caught glimpses of tapestries. Some were threaded with portraits of Nyxobas, the cloaked god of night. Others depicted horned demons with red eyes.

At the end of the hall, ornate wooden doors barred their path. Caine whispered another spell, and the doors creaked open into a great hall, its walls formed by what appeared to be human bones inset with sapphires, pearls, and moonstones. An array of silver weapons lined one of the bone-walls, and the air smelled of gardenias.

Vampires stood along the sides of the room, their shoulders rigid with military discipline. Horace stood among them. Of course, vampires easily outpaced humans.

Candles burned in chandeliers that hung from arches thirty feet above, casting a wavering light over the room. Horace's cold, dark eyes darted to Rosalind, and he flared his nostrils.

But Rosalind's gaze was most drawn to the stunning blond vampire in the silver throne: Ambrose, his face cold and beautiful as a renaissance statue. He didn't look more than twenty-five, but as a Lord he was probably centuries old.

As she followed Caine into the hall, her muscles tensed. Her little hawthorn stake suddenly seemed inadequate in a room full of vampire nobility.

Her eyes flicked to the rows of vamps. She could actually *see* their desperate attempts at restraint. Horace trembled visibly, working his jaw. Apparently, her ambrosia-filled blood smelled amazing—or maybe her second soul smelled amazing. Either way, she was a rabbit in the center of a pack of wolves right now.

As she straightened, she took a deep breath. She wasn't going to show fear. Human terror only stoked a demon's bloodlust.

But before she could take another step, Horace's rough nails clamped into her shoulders. For the second time that night, a demon's fangs punctured her throat, and pain lanced her neck.

CHAPTER 8

She snatched the stake from her belt and slammed it into his back. She felt a sharp tear in her neck as Horace ripped out his fangs, but he wasn't turning to ash. She must have missed the damn heart again.

Caine rushed forward, a silver sword in his hand, and swung for Horace, severing his head. Blood sprayed, and the body convulsed, twitching on the floor as though electrified. Fast as lightning, Caine reached down, ripping Horace's heart from his chest.

She stared as Horace's headless corpse blackened, turning to ash.

Sweet earthly gods. That was disturbing.

From his silver throne, Ambrose arched an eyebrow, his green eyes trained on Caine. "Did you just kill one of my favorite lieutenants? For a *human?*" His nostrils flared, and he sniffed the air. "One of Blodrial's followers, by the smell of her blood?"

Rosalind touched her neck, and her hand came away crimson.

"Rosalind," Caine said.

Uh-oh. Hadn't Caine said something about getting cut?

The vampires' bloodthirsty stares bored into her. A pregnant silence filled the room, broken by the low growling of ravenous vamps. They shifted, trembling at the effort of restraint. The pack of wolves was just about ready to feast on this rabbit.

Ambrose stood. "Control yourselves—"

From all around the room, the vampires lunged. Rosalind gripped the stake, crouching as a female vamp leapt for her. She thrust the stake upward, right into the vamp's heart. This time, she didn't miss, but another had already grabbed her from behind. She slammed her elbows into his ribs. She caught a glimpse of Caine cutting through a line of vamps in a whirlwind of silver and black, sword through bone. His jaw-dropping speed seemed almost otherworldly.

She whipped out the flamethrower, and as a hulking vamp leapt for her she depressed the button, unleashing a torrent of flames. Fire engulfed him, and his agonized shrieks turned her stomach. He flailed, screaming, until Caine sliced off his head in one smooth arc.

She glanced at Ambrose, but he was no longer in his throne. Her mouth went dry. He was right next to her, his fangs bared. Holy shit. She'd neither seen him nor heard him approach.

His green eyes locked on hers, and though her mind screamed *run,* her body wouldn't obey. The Vampire Lord was a perfect predator, freezing her in place with his penetrating gaze. She stood in stunned silence as he licked his lips.

"Ambrose," Caine spoke sharply. "Step back. That's Rosalind."

Ambrose growled, closing his eyes. His blond hair was unruffled—as if he hadn't just witnessed a massacre in his own home. He reached out, swiping a cold finger through the blood dripping down her neck. He licked it, moaning almost imperceptibly. "Heal her before I rip her little body to shreds. She tastes exquisite." He spoke with a clipped English accent. As he backed away, she saw that his eyes were a deep red.

Caine rushed to her, his body soaked with vampire blood. He looked like something from a nightmare. She had no idea how a human had managed to cut down a roomful of vampire nobility. Aside from Ambrose, only one vampire remained, a willowy female with dark skin.

Caine lifted his fingers to Rosalind's neck, sending a hot thrill through her skin—an almost addictive sensation. He closed his eyes, chanting in the Angelic language, and the sharp pain in her neck subsided. As her wound healed, the Vampire Lord's shoulders visibly relaxed, but his eyes remained fixed on Caine with a lethal glint.

"Why did you bring her here?"

"I didn't," Caine said. "She was supposed to stay in Abduxiel Mansion. Instead, she followed me through the portal."

Ambrose steepled his fingers. With his perfect lips and sharp cheekbones, he could have been a model. Just like Caine. It was almost as though vampire aristocracy was determined by sheer beauty alone; maybe that was why Caine commanded such respect around here.

Ambrose's eyes burned with ferocity. "You *let* her follow you here. A Hunter, who might tell the Brotherhood how to find us. And you see what's happened. Eight of my best advisors, slaughtered. Not to mention that Rosalind nearly died. Has your mind become muddled because of your familial connection?"

Familial connection?

Caine's mouth twitched with apparent irritation. "My mind is perfectly sound, Ambrose. I had no idea she'd be so stupid as to rush through a portal into a demon realm."

Now that is just insulting. "Okay, hang on a second," Rosalind said. "First of all, I'm not stupid. Apart from everything I've done tonight. But I was acting desperate because I needed answers. This is the first I've ever heard of this mage thing, and it seems that both the Brotherhood and the demons know more than I do about my two souls. And why do you all care if I live or die? No one has explained that to me yet."

The female vampire crossed to Ambrose, handing him a cloth. The Vampire Lord wiped the blood off his hands, green eyes locked on Rosalind. "Why did you come, girl? What exactly was your plan?"

"I wouldn't say I had a plan, as it were." She added that last bit to sound more formal. It wasn't like she'd ever spoken to a Lord before, even if he was a demon.

"Not a plan." His eyes roamed over her wet clothes, lingering on her transparent white shirt. "Just a desire."

She flushed. She could imagine what he was thinking. "Exactly."

"I can understand that." He licked his lips. "And what was your desire?"

"I needed to learn why the Brotherhood think I'm a witch. I needed to know where I came from. I need to know how to get my life back."

Ambrose cocked his head. "Your life back? Why would you want that?"

"I was happy."

He frowned. "No, you weren't. And now you know why you're important. You have the potential for great power, just like Caine. In fact, you've just seen him demonstrate a bit of that power, when he cut down half my Council."

Caine shrugged. "Horace was an ass, and he needed to be put down. I did you a favor. And now, I must return her to her own world. I'm going to need to open another portal."

"I hope that when you train Rosalind, you'll instill obedience in her even if the concept doesn't suit you." Ambrose's green eyes drank in Rosalind. "Her blood tastes of hawthorn bark. Funny, that."

How do I respond to a comment as creepy as that? It was an odd coincidence. "They're my favorite trees." It was the best wood for staking vamps, though now was not a good time to remind him of that. Anyway, it was more than that. Her best dreams took place in hawthorn groves, the earth carpeted by white petals. "The blossoms are pretty, and they bring good luck."

He stepped closer, staring into her eyes again. "Tell me, Rosalind. Do you dream of the forest?"

Another creepy comment, but—how does he know that? Can vamps read minds? "Yes. Often."

He edged closer, touching her neck, and she shuddered. Apparently, vampires weren't big on personal space. The candlelight flickered over his porcelain skin, and she caught a hint of his scent—burning cloves. "You will stay here tonight. I'll make sure you're safe. Tomorrow, Caine and Aurora will take you back to your world." He nodded at the willowy female. "I'm assigning them to protect you from the Brotherhood. Your behavior is unpredictable, and they will need to watch you closely."

"What?" Caine asked through gritted teeth. "I'm the General of your army. I just won a victory for you against the hellhounds in Uffern. And you want to put me in charge of minding a pedestrian girl?"

Asshole. It wasn't like she wanted to spend time with him either, but his tone was more than a little insulting.

Ambrose studied him. "If you don't like your new role, Caine, you shouldn't have brought her here."

Aurora didn't speak, but the rage contorting her face told Rosalind that she didn't like this plan any more than Caine did.

Rosalind narrowed her eyes at the Vampire Lord. "What do you get out of this?"

"Clever girl." Ambrose studied her. "Let's just say I'm protecting a personal interest. A mage with your powers could be useful to me some day. I trust Caine will be able to break your faith in the Brotherhood."

Apparently, Ambrose wouldn't be on board with her plan to exorcise the second spirit. *Best not to mention it now.*

Caine's gaze was pure ice. "She's impulsive, completely unprepared to practice magic, and deeply committed to the Brotherhood. It will be a long time before she becomes a functioning mage."

"You know she's not just any girl." Lifting Rosalind's hand, Ambrose examined her ring. "What happens when you take it off?" he asked her—but before she had the chance to respond, he slipped it from her finger.

She gasped, and her body exploded with an earthy, vernal aura. An ancient creature stared out from her eyes. A *thing,* taking over her body, one vein and muscle at a time. An overpowering scent of rotting leaves filled the air, and she stared into Ambrose's emerald green eyes, his skin pale in the flickering candlelight. Such a strange, perfect beauty, life and death in one vessel.

She wanted to crush him. The thing inside Rosalind made her reach for his face, but the Lord slipped out of her grasp.

Rage ignited her body, and her legs trembled. Someone screamed in her skull—a wild, unquiet mind inside her own, and it said only one word. *Ambrose. Ambrose.* It was the only word in her mind now, and the thing inside her drowned out her own thoughts.

The mage inside her wanted to touch his cool, pale skin, but he kept slipping away from her. His retreat only stoked her desire. The spirit wanted to rip his clothes from his body. Ambrose would burn with her, would feel her lust and her wrath stoking the flames of the funeral pyre. The mage forced her hand to Ambrose's neck, and some part of her screamed at herself to stop.

But that was the weak part.

Ambrose. She would shatter his bones, drink his blood, grip his pulsing heart in her fingers, she would glory in ripping out his entrails—

Someone else stood before her now, his hand on her waist, face gleaming like moonlight on water. His shocking beauty struck her dumb. The spirit didn't know his name, but lust and rage screamed in her skull, splintering her thoughts. Her body burned white-hot like a dying star, blazing from the inside out. Her skin blistered and cracked from the heat. She wrapped her arms around the stranger's body, quenching her blazing agony—

In an instant, the voices went still, and relief washed over her.

Rosalind. She was Rosalind, the Hunter, in control of her own body once again. Her arms tightened around Caine, and her body trembled, wracked by the remnants of pain. The spirit had gone. She glanced at her hand. Caine had slipped the ring back on her finger.

She wrenched away from him, clamping her hand over her mouth. She didn't want to puke in front of them.

Never again. She never wanted her mind to splinter like that again. She'd been in hell.

She dug her fingernails into her palms, clamping her eyes shut. She needed to get this insane spirit out of her body. The demonic force would completely shatter her.

Caine's arm encircled her waist, holding her up. "She isn't ready for that yet."

Rosalind straightened. She *really* hated looking weak, especially in front of the demons. "I'll never be ready for that. This thing inside me is a monster."

"What was it that the spirit wanted?" Ambrose's words slid over her like cold rain.

"I don't know," she snapped. She hated him right now for ripping the ring off her with no warning, and she had a strange feeling the mage inside hated him, too.

Her body wouldn't stop shaking.

This was why people shouldn't mess around with the dark arts. Her birth parents were obviously raving lunatics.

The vampire inched closer, running his thumb over her cheek, and she shuddered. His beauty was cold and empty.

She couldn't wait to get out of there. She wanted Josiah and Tammi more than ever.

"Never mind, little sparrow," Ambrose said. "Delicate little thing. You will stay in Aurora's room for the night. She can sleep elsewhere. She will be perfectly hospitable. Tomorrow, the three of you will leave." He shot a glance at Caine. "I trust you'll take good care of her. Don't let her out of your sight, or she'll betray us to the Brotherhood. She still believes in them. Begin teaching her as soon as you can. Once she's trained, she'll be quite useful to me."

CHAPTER 9

rained. According to Ambrose, she was a delicate little thing who required training and obedience. Rosalind wasn't stupid enough to argue with the Vampire Lord in his own kingdom, but there was no way in hell anyone was going to *train* her.

She followed Aurora down a dimly-lit hall. Stone vaults arched high above like a gray skeleton, intricately carved with moonflowers and stars. Candles flickered in jeweled sconces along the walls, casting dancing shadows over the marble floor. Gods, she really wanted to go back to her little dorm room. This place was creepy as hell, and she needed to run through this whole disaster of a night with Tammi.

Her mind reeled. Tonight, her world had been blown apart.

Whatever it took, she would rip this witch's soul from her body. She'd felt the thing's mind, its sickness—a demented spirit, one full of dark, twisted impulses. She wasn't going to give up her own body without a fight.

Aurora's heels clacked over the stone floor, and Rosalind glanced at her. The vampire wore a tiny red dress that hugged her body, and long silver earrings. She was gorgeous. While she didn't look like she wanted to tear into Rosalind's neck, appearances could be deceptive.

"All the other vampires tried to kill me, but you didn't."

"How perceptive of you." Aurora had a British accent, just like Ambrose.

"Why didn't you?"

"I have better self-control, and you were with Caine. I'm quite fond of him." Her eyes met Rosalind's. "I hope you don't try to slay him with your witch-hunting bollocks. You won't be able to kill him, but if you get a stake in him, I'll have to drain your blood."

Fantastic. Aurora already hates me.

"Of course not. He's human. I only kill monsters." She sucked in a breath. *Best not to mention the monster-killing thing again.* "No offense."

"None taken." Aurora halted before an oak door, pushing it open into an expansive bedroom. Moonlight shone through tall, stained-glass windows into an untidy room littered with papers, mounds of clothing, old cassette tapes, and eyeless dolls. A desk stood below the window, its surface covered with flasks of blood and bottles of amber liquid.

Aurora plucked a white dress off the floor, tossing it to Rosalind. "You can change out of your wet clothes. A white dress should be pure enough for you."

Aurora *definitely* hated her.

As the vampire lit candles around the room, Rosalind changed into the tight white gown. The thin fabric was practically sheer and not great for fighting, but at least she was no longer freezing. She draped her sodden clothes over a chair to dry.

Rosalind swallowed hard, glancing around the room. Oil-painted portraits hung all over the walls, but the subjects' eyes were scratched out. Interspersed among the paintings, someone had scrawled notes in the frantic, irregular scrawl of a serial killer. She caught a glimpse of a few words, *BlOoD* and *RaGe* among them. Instead of a bed, a coffin lined with red silk lay in the center of the room.

The room looked like a playground for the criminally insane. *Holy shit. This is who I've thrown in with.*

Aurora turned to stare at her. "What do you think of my room?"

Rosalind took a deep, steadying breath, her foot crunching on a cassette tape. "The paintings are… interesting."

For the first time, she saw Aurora's face brighten into a smile. "Do you like them?"

"Are the crossed-out eyes a vampire thing?"

"What? No. I made those when I was human. I was an art student at Goldsmiths before I died."

That was a slight relief. "Ah. And the handwritten notes, too?"

"I've been dead nearly thirty years, but I like to think of my art as avant-garde, you know?" Aurora looked her up and down. "Just be careful what you touch in my room, Hunter."

"I'm not exactly eager to rifle around."

Aurora narrowed her eyes. "Like, if you touch my Tears for Fears cassette tapes, I will rip your head off and light you on fire."

Rosalind's stomach lurched.

Aurora stared at her. "It's just an expression."

"I won't touch them." Rosalind nodded at the casket, her skin growing cold. "I didn't know vampires actually slept in coffins."

"Most don't. I just thought it was kind of cool, so I made a coffin. Only they're not so good for shagging." Aurora cocked her head. "I've never seen Ambrose take such an interest in a human before."

"I didn't enjoy his interest. He seemed a little off-key." *Insane, really.* Then again, everyone here was obviously slightly mental.

"He's six hundred years old, so he's a little old school; that makes him different. Like, when he was a kid, there was nothing to play with but a wooden circle and a hoop. Public executions were entertainment in those days. But he's sexy as hell, and he's always been good to me. And if anyone messes with him, I would feast on their heart."

Rosalind tried to force a smile. "Another vampire expression?"

Aurora blinked. "No. That was literal. Anyway, he said I'm supposed to be hospitable and shit. So what do humans drink?"

"Water is fine."

"We don't have that here." Aurora rifled around on the desk, bottles clinking. "I know!" She unscrewed a cap from a bottle labelled *whiskey*, pouring it into a silver goblet, then decanted a measure of blood for herself, topped with whiskey.

She handed Rosalind the bloodless goblet and gazed at her, raising her own. "To the dark side."

Rosalind lifted her drink. "To the… whatever." She didn't want to be rude, but she wasn't about to toast to the *dark side*. She took a sip, and the whiskey burned her throat.

"You know," Aurora said. "Vampires aren't as bad as everyone thinks. People think that we're horrible monsters, but we're not really. We're just like regular people."

Right—apart from all the slaughtering, and walls made of human skulls. Rosalind scanned the room, and her eyes landed on something that churned her stomach: fingers poking out from below a pile of clothes on the floor. "Is that a human hand?"

Aurora turned and snatched a severed hand from the floor. "Oh, yeah." She looked up at Rosalind, her face a picture of innocence. "But he was a very bad person."

Oh gods. Do I really have to spend the night in here?

"Are you hungry?" Aurora asked. She dropped the hand on the desk and rummaged through the papers, pulling out a half-eaten Snickers bar. "We don't really eat food, per se, but I took this off the severed-hand guy. He didn't look like he had any diseases or anything, so it's probably fine."

Rosalind's mind spun like a cyclone. She didn't belong here, yet she'd willingly plunged into a city of the dead. Maybe the demented witch's spirit had compelled her to do it. Either that, or she was a first-rate idiot like Caine had said.

Whatever the case, Rosalind was desperate for human company right now—even the evil kind. "Where is Caine?"

Aurora narrowed her dark eyes. "You're not going to try to hurt him, are you? It won't go well for you if you do. He's a bit full of himself, but he also happens to be the most lethal mage I've ever seen. As you could probably tell from tonight's slaughter."

"I won't try to hurt him. I just wanted to see another human face. Preferably one that's attached to a living body."

"Two doors down, past the portrait of Lord Byron."

Rosalind shivered. In a world of demons, she was forced to rely on someone as terrifying as Caine for an ally.

65

CHAPTER 10

*R*osalind walked down the hallway, pausing just after the portrait of Lord Byron dressed in some sort of orange turban. She knocked on the oak door, trying to figure out what she wanted to say to Caine.

She'd have to enlist his help to get the mage out of her body, but she couldn't ask him about the exorcism here. Even the gargoyles were probably spying for the Vampire Lord.

Was Caine really any better than the vampires, just because he was human?

As his footfalls crossed the floor, she half wanted to turn around and run back to the serial killer suite.

Caine pulled open the door, his hair disheveled and wet, like he'd just stepped out of a bath. Droplets of water beaded on his bare chest, and her eyes lingered on his muscled body. Tattoos covered his flawless skin: constellations, a raven, a moon cycle, and Angelic script.

Washed clean of blood, he now wore only his black jeans. She tried not to stare.

For the first time, she saw a flicker of a smile. "Rosalind. It seems the only thing that can rob you of your formidable powers of inquisition is the sight of me without a shirt on."

Cocky bastard. Why had she come here? She couldn't remember anymore. She just needed to keep her eyes on his face. "You're not my stepbrother, are you?"

Gods. Why had she just said that?

"Why? Is your delicate mind troubled by impure thoughts?" He leaned against the door frame, his gaze slowly trailing over her white gown, like he was memorizing every curve of her body. He smelled amazing—a fresh scent, like the earth after a rainstorm. "Don't worry. The vampires wouldn't begrudge a little brotherly love if that's what you're looking for. Unlike the Chambers, we don't judge here."

"Oh, please. First of all, that's disgusting. And second of all, you're not my type." She clamped her hands on her hips. "Can you just answer the question? Ambrose said something about a familial connection. I don't like the idea of being related to a man who's been completely corrupted by magic."

"I knew your parents, but we're not related. In fact, they would have been horrified by the thought. I was merely part of their experiment. When it didn't go as planned, our relationship was over."

"I see. If we're not related, why did they imbue you with an extra soul, too?"

"They wanted to make sure the spell worked before they tried anything on their own flesh and blood."

It was hard to decide the worst thing Rosalind had learned tonight: her exile from the Brotherhood, the mage in her body, or the fact that her birth parents were a couple of assholes. She couldn't take any more shitty news without completely losing her mind—assuming she still had a mind to lose.

She couldn't reconcile Caine's description of her parents with her happy memories of her early childhood, even if they were vague. "I don't understand. I thought my parents were loving. I remember when they gave me flowers and patched up my knee. And I think I remember you. There was a boy with eyes like yours."

"I'm sure you were happy. But things aren't always as perfect as you remember them."

She hugged herself. "We get out of here soon, right?"

"Yes. Before the sun rises. Aurora can't travel in the light. Go to sleep, Rosalind." There was that commanding tone again. "You only have three hours of rest before we move."

But she knew she wouldn't be sleeping at all. Not in the serial killer room, and certainly not with the news that a crazed spirit had infected her body.

Rosalind jolted upright, gasping for breath. After their rapid departure through another portal in Lilinor, they'd arrived in Caine's Salem apartment, twenty miles north of Boston.

When you hung around with creatures of the night, sunrise signaled bedtime. Now, the sunset streamed through the windows, washing the living room and kitchen in pumpkin light.

Despite its warmth, she shuddered, wrapping Caine's blanket tighter around her shoulders. She'd been dreaming of Mason. Her nightmares were no different from her memories. In her dream, he'd tied her to a chair, beating the bottoms of her feet with his leather belt, all the while ranting about corruption.

As if staying in a mage's apartment weren't bad enough, reminders of Mason had brought her out in a cold sweat.

It was so obvious to her now: Mason had known about the possession all along. It was why he'd always been so repulsed by her. When she'd first arrived, he'd started off reasonably nice—warm mugs of cocoa to warm her in the cold mansion, letting her watch TV as long as she wanted. But then he'd catch her drifting off, losing herself in thought, and something about her dreaminess made him angry. She understood now—it was the mage inside of her. He wanted to beat the magic out of her.

She straightened, pushing the blanket off her to survey the room. For a tattoo-covered mage who lived among corpses, Caine kept a surprisingly tidy apartment. Oak bookshelves, packed with alphabetically arranged poetry and spell books, lined one wall. Midnight-blue sofas stood on the bare wooden floors, and the tall windows overlooked one of the old colonial cemeteries, where the setting sun cast long shadows over the grass.

Four silver-framed mirrors hung on the rough stone walls. Of course he had four mirrors in one room. The guy obviously loved himself.

Rosalind glanced down at herself. The white dress Aurora had given her was crumpled from sleep, and her long hair was tangled into knots. She looked like a disaster, and she tried to smooth out her tangles

Footsteps sounded behind her; she turned to see Caine, his hair gently rumpled from sleep. He wore an undershirt that showed off his athletic form.

She had a bad feeling that the only way to get this mage out of her body would be through powerful magic—the kind that Caine had—except the Vampire Lord wanted her to remain possessed. Ambrose had some sort of big plans for her. What was the likelihood of Caine defying him?

She'd have to tap into his anti-authoritarian nature.

"I hope you slept well," he said. "Might as well get comfortable for a while since you're apparently staying here."

"I slept fine." There was no way she'd be staying, but she'd wait a moment before bringing that up. "I take it you're not thrilled about having me here."

He leaned against a granite countertop. "As it happens, I have better things to do than to train a novice Hunter in the dark arts. Especially a noble-born girl who will go into hysterics every time things get a little difficult."

Arrogant prick. Everything about him irked her. "That's fine by me, because I'm not actually going to train with you. I'll be out of here as soon as I get... everything sorted out."

"And what do you expect to sort out? Do you have a plan now? Or still just a desire?"

Her stomach rumbled. How was she supposed to come up with a plan with a stomach this hollow? "I have a strong desire for some food."

"I don't keep the house well-stocked. I'm not exactly the cooking type. When Aurora gets up, we'll go out somewhere."

"Is she your girlfriend?" Rosalind asked.

He arched an eyebrow, crossing to the living room. "No. Interesting that you asked though. I seem to recall you saying I'm not your type. I'm not sure that I believe you anymore. You've now inquired about our family affiliation and my relationship status."

She failed to suppress an eye roll. *The ego on this guy is unparalleled.* "You're probably glamoured, just like my Guardian said. Under your demigod facade, I'm sure you look like a beast."

He flashed a half-smile. "Is that so?"

She flushed. Why did he make her so nervous? She usually made men nervous, not the other way around. "It's basic witch-lore. Magic pollutes the body and turns humans into monsters."

"Demigod, was it? Tell me, what is the most impressive part of this beautifying spell I've woven? Do you think I did a better job on my face or my body with this—demigod spell? I'd really love to hear more."

Her stomach fluttered. *Shit.* Josiah hadn't been wrong about the disfigurement, had he?

She gritted her teeth. "Please tell me it's a spell. Because based on the number of mirrors around this place, I'm a little worried about what would happen if your ego grows any bigger than it already is."

"Can you blame me for loving something that's so—demigod-like?" He cocked his head contemplatively. "That phrasing is unwieldy. Let's shorten to *godlike.*"

"If self-love had mass, yours would create a singularity that would warp space-time and destroy the universe."

"Has anyone ever said you're charming when you talk about science?"

"No."

"Unsurprising." He folded his fingers behind his head, in all likelihood trying to give off the best view of his muscled arms. "If you don't believe me about the glamour, why don't you spray that purgator dust on me? If it's a spell, you'll see the real me. The demonic, twisted Caine that lurks below the surface, warped by magic."

"Since you have an aura, the dust will burn you."

"I can handle a little pain."

"Anything for your vanity, right?"

She snatched her purgator dust from the coffee table, pausing for a moment at the self-satisfied smirk on his face. This would hurt—a lot. What if the agony flipped a switch in his brain? He could slaughter her in an instant.

Still, maybe now was a good time to practice that whole fear-mastery thing. She had to get used to hurting the bad guys.

She strengthened her resolve and pushed the button. Shiny red dust poured from the canister, coating his skin. A flicker of pain registered on his face, though in reality he must be withstanding indescribable pain. All this to prove to her that he was pretty.

And, gods damn it, he was right. The guy was stunning, and it wasn't because of magic. She sucked in a breath. "Fine. We've established that you're not deformed."

He brushed the dust off his face. "I think we agreed on the term 'godlike.'"

Rosalind wanted to hide her face. This was mortifying.

As the last of the sun dipped below the horizon, Aurora strode into the room, clad in a tight silver dress. "What the bloody hell do you think you're doing to Caine, Hunter?"

"It's fine," Caine said. "I asked her to do it."

Aurora crossed her arms. "I don't even want to know."

Caine rose, visibly trying to manage the pain. He soaked a kitchen cloth in water and began cleaning himself off. "Would you like to help me clean off my body, Rosalind, since you're such a fan of my godlike physique?"

Gods, kill me now.

"I've walked into something really weird, haven't I?" Aurora said. "Please don't tell me you fed his ego."

With the dust washed off him, Caine smiled. "Our Hunter has spent a little too much time among the impure, and now she fancies a bit of shadow mage. Her mind must be corrupted like ours. Funny. I wouldn't have guessed a follower of the True God, not to mention one from lofty Maremount nobility, would be so easily warped. I suppose, in the face of godlike beauty, a little lust is only to be expected even in the purest of creatures. I wonder how far we can take that."

She shielded her eyes with her hand. *What an ass.*

She needed to get out of there before she gave in to temptation. The longer she stayed around Caine, the harder it would be to piece her life back together, to resume her life among the Brotherhood.

If such a thing was even possible at this point.

CHAPTER 12

"Speaking of becoming corrupted," Rosalind said. "I'm not letting you train me. I want to get this mage's soul out of me. The Brotherhood can't blame me for something that was done to me when I was a child. Once I have this thing exorcised, I can get out of your life."

"Uh-uh," Aurora said. "Ambrose said Caine's going to train you. So that's what's happening."

"You can't force me to learn something," Rosalind said.

"Actually, he can," Aurora snapped. "He has mind control abilities."

"I'm not going to hypnotize her," Caine said. "She'll go along with it willingly. What other options does she have?"

"Actually, I'm not going along with it," Rosalind said.

Caine stared at her. "Don't be ridiculous. You're completely irrational."

"I'm *irrational*? I just learned that I'm possessed by a lunatic spirit. I think it's perfectly rational to want it exorcised."

Aurora's face was stony. "You think the Brotherhood would take you back, after you spent time with us, using Caine's magic?"

"I'm still human. Humans have rights." Maybe the vampire had a point, but Rosalind couldn't even consider that option. She had no life outside of the Brotherhood—no future. "None of this has been my fault. I was only a kid when this happened. I have to make them see that. I don't want to be here, and you don't want me here. If you help me with the possession, we're done with each other for good."

As the room darkened, Caine chanted a spell to light the candles in the iron sconces around the room, then folded his hands behind his head. "You must understand that your actual guilt isn't the point. The Brotherhood convict whoever they want. Sometimes it's demons and witches, and sometimes not. Look outside the window. You can see where they pressed Giles Corey to death with a load of rocks during the Salem Witch Trials. The old man had never looked at a spell book in his life. Did that stop them? No. They had their sights set on him, so he was dead."

"He actually deserved it," added Aurora. "Not for being a mage. He was just an arsehole. Apart from that, Caine has a point."

"That wasn't the Brotherhood." Rosalind wanted to clamp her hands over her ears. It couldn't be true. The Brotherhood had to be certain of guilt, or it meant they'd been interrogating innocent people —even *killing* captives, according to Caine. The blood rose to her cheeks. "The Brotherhood know what they're doing. I've committed my life to them. I belong with them."

Caine arched an eyebrow. "The Brotherhood won't dig too deeply into extenuating circumstances. Any hint of magic is enough for them to stoke the flames of your funeral pyre."

"You're wrong," Rosalind said. She needed to remember what Josiah said. Mages would do whatever they could to mess with your head.

"They're barbaric," Aurora countered.

Rosalind's temper flared. The demons would love people to think that good and evil were merely subjective concepts with a whole lot of gray area. "*We're* barbaric? And what about you? I found a severed hand in your room last night. You drink human blood."

"So? Hunters drink inhuman blood," Aurora shot back.

"What are you talking about?" Rosalind asked.

"The ambrosia you drink," Caine said. "It's made with the blood of furies, kept as slaves against their will. You do worship a god of blood, you know. Honestly Rosalind. It's almost like you don't know anything useful."

"Why do you think vampires are so keen on Hunter blood?" Aurora asked. "Lucky for you, it fades fast, or I'd be taking a little nip from your wrist."

"And speaking of barbaric," Caine said. "Let's not forget that the Brotherhood have reinstated burning as a punishment for witchcraft."

No. They're lying. The Brotherhood didn't touch humans, and she'd never heard anyone talk about burnings or blood drinking.

Her mind was racing now. The mage had already muddled her thoughts, trying to lure her to the dark side.

She had to remember the pictures Josiah had shown her, the ravaged and burned bodies of the mages' victims. "Forget about the blood. Your people—vampires, mages, demons—they slaughter humans like prey, just for sport. You both know it. Look at what happened in Boston. Mages rampaged through a high school. They shot students with arrows. Burned them to death. For what?"

Caine nodded. "There are some sadistic mages out there. I won't deny that."

Somehow, this admission felt like a victory to Rosalind.

"Too bad the Brotherhood never manages to actually catch them," he added, "since they're always too busy murdering doddery old widows."

Rosalind had to stop herself from throwing the canister of dust at his head. Of course he was just screwing with her mind, but everything he said seemed to strike a chord. It was getting harder to believe the Brotherhood only went after the bad guys, when they were so busy chasing *her* down.

It was as though her whole future as a Guardian had just gone up in flames, even if she knew Josiah was looking out for her. "Whether or not the Brotherhood will take me back, I can't live with this mage inside my head. It's like having an invader in my own body."

"Some people would be thrilled to have that power, you know," Aurora said.

Rosalind didn't even want to think about the crushing, raging agony that had pierced her mind when Ambrose ripped off the ring. "What if the ring doesn't stay on me forever? What if someone pulls it off again, like Ambrose did? I was in hell." She shot a glance at Caine. "You understand, right?"

"Oh, I understand." He traced his finger over his lower lip. "But you need to get over it."

Arrogant prick. "And what exactly happened to you? What went so terribly wrong that my parents cast you off into the streets? You obviously lost your mind. Did you kill someone?"

Caine's body went still, and his eyes darkened to deep, black pools, as deep and vast as the cosmos. Shadows swirled around him.

At the sight of his pitch-black eyes, panic hit her like a fist. Caine wasn't just a mage. He was a *demon*, and she'd just pushed him into attack mode. Dread clenched her heart, and for a moment, she thought she saw the ghost of dark wings unfolding behind him. His predatory, midnight glare whispered into the darkest parts of her mind, *run.*

A moment later, his eyes cleared, and he rolled his neck.

She clasped her hands together to hide the shaking. She couldn't let him see her fear, even if she'd just come within whispering distance of death.

"I can't take any more of this," Caine said. "If I have to listen to her talk every night, I'd just as soon face the wrath of Ambrose. I want her out of here. Now."

Rosalind clenched her trembling fingers. Maybe she'd gone too far.

Aurora's eyes bulged. "You can't be serious. You're going to defy Ambrose?"

Caine's eyes flashed like storm clouds. "If I have to listen to her carrying on every night and asking me stupid questions, I'm going to murder her myself."

"So you're handing her over to the Brotherhood?" Aurora asked.

Caine shot Rosalind a cold look. "I will get you the information you need for your exorcism, and then you need to leave. I don't want to see your face again. Do we have a deal?"

Still rattled, she lowered her voice to steady it. "I swear on my honor as Hunter."

Aurora snorted. "Hunter honor. That's obviously bollocks."

"I'll take what I can get," Caine said. "And then we'll send her back to the people who want to kill her if that's what she really wants."

"You're acting crazy," Aurora said. "What if she tells the Brotherhood all about us?"

He stared out the window at the cemetery. "I'll erase us from her memory."

Rosalind didn't like the sound of a supernatural lobotomy. "I don't want you to erase my brain."

He leveled his icy gaze on her. "That's the deal. If you want the exorcism, take it or leave it. I can't risk you running back to the Brotherhood to tell them where we are. Even you must be able to understand that."

He had a point. "Fine." She didn't trust him, and didn't know what he might find in there. Maybe she could slip away just after the exorcism.

"You're both insane," Aurora said. "I'm going to make sure Ambrose understands this was done against my advisement."

Rosalind let out a long breath, still trying to hide the raw fear she'd felt at the sight of Caine's black eyes. "Is there some spell you need to find, to get this mage out of me?"

"This is beyond even me," Caine said. "We'll need to find the sybil."

Rosalind stood. "Great. Where do we find this sybil?"

"I don't know," Caine said. "But Jorge will. He's a vampire who runs Salem's blood bar."

"The blood bar is the only part of the plan that I can get behind," Aurora said. "Because I'm a little cranky before I have my evening drink."

Caine eyed Rosalind's outfit. "But you can't go in there wearing that virginal white dress. They'll eat you alive."

"Literally," Aurora said.

"What am I supposed to wear?"

Aurora looked her over. "I'll take care of the outfit."

Great. Not only were they muddling her mind, but she was going to start dressing like them, too. "Is that really necessary?"

Caine narrowed his eyes. "Unless you have a death wish, which I'm starting to think you do."

CHAPTER 13

osalind, sitting on the back of Caine's bike, wrapped her arms tight around him. They roared down a narrow Salem street, past crooked colonial houses, on their way to meet Aurora at the bar. Lilu trailed behind them.

A marine wind rushed over Rosalind's bare arms, and moonlight dazzled off puddles as they rushed past.

It was beautiful by the water, but she didn't belong in Salem with her arms wrapped around a mage's body. Her plan had been simple: become a Guardian and fight evil. Until now, her worst-case scenario involved leaving the Brotherhood to become some kind of software engineer. Maybe a computational biologist, to keep things a little interesting.

No part of her plans had involved donning a black leather dress, covering herself in fake alchemical tattoos, and straddling a sorcerer's motorcycle. But things didn't always go to plan.

Caine had cast a spell to cover her in magical markings that snaked around her arms and back, disguising her as a mage. It so happened there was a lot of exposed skin to cover, thanks to Aurora's outfit choices. Apparently, demons didn't like leaving anything to the imagination. As she sat on the back of Caine's bike, the short dress was hitched all the way up her thighs. At her insistence, she'd kept her own boots on.

As they pulled up to a rickety old pier, Rosalind spotted Aurora standing in the amber light of a streetlamp not far from the harbor. The low-cut back of her dress exposed a brutal network of scars.

Gods, what happened to her? It looked as though she'd accidentally exposed her skin to the sunlight and never healed.

As Rosalind stepped off the bike, she shuddered. Whatever had caused those scars must have been agonizing.

Aurora turned, eyeing Rosalind's outfit. "I told you that dress would suit you."

Maybe it *did* suit her. Rosalind hadn't failed to notice Caine's jaw drop when she'd stepped out of the room in the tiny black dress. Still, she felt exposed, and tugged the neckline up.

"But you've got to stop fidgeting," Aurora added. "You're acting like a pedestrian."

Rosalind frowned. "A pedestrian?"

"Ordinary people," Aurora said. "Those without magic. Boring. Stuck on the ground. Like you with that stupid iron ring. I told you. Stop fidgeting."

"This isn't how I normally dress. And there's no room in this dress for my weapon belt." Not to mention a bra.

"Only pedestrians need weapons," Caine said.

She *liked* her weapons. But even without them, a Hunter had other tools. Josiah had taught her to scan her environment for anything that was usable as a weapon. Ingenuity was the one area where Hunters had the upper hand. Iron dust could defeat magic, and Hunters knew how to fight the old-fashioned way: fists, broken bottles, big blocks of wood—whatever they could find.

In the cool sea air, goose bumps raised on her skin. Nothing stood on the wharf apart from a ramshackle, two-story house labelled *Sail Loft*. Weather-beaten and boarded with old wood, it must have been deserted for centuries.

She hugged herself. "That's where we're going?"

"Glamoured," Caine said. "Unlike me."

Rosalind paused, touching his arm. "I'm supposed to act like a mage, and they'll believe it?"

Caine nodded. "As much as you can. They'll know you're human by your scent, but they won't touch a mage. If they think you're pedestrian, things will become unpleasant fast. And if they discover you're a Hunter, you can expect an excruciating death."

"Fantastic," she said.

"That's why you should take the ring off," Aurora said. "What if a high demon comes in? Some of them could smell your Hunter blood even if you haven't drunk ambrosia in a day. A bit of real magic would protect you."

Instinctively, Rosalind tightened her hand into a fist. The whole point of this was that she'd never again have to suffer the wild, burning rage of the witch's soul, that uncontrolled animal mind that threatened to swallow her whole. "That is *not* a good idea."

"It's true. She's not ready for that yet," Caine said. "We'll just hope no high demons are there tonight."

Aurora arched an eyebrow. "You just want to hope? That's your plan? We should've left her at home."

"We can't leave her anywhere until I erase some of her memories," Caine shot back. "She could still run to the Brotherhood with everything she knows, in the hopes of making a deal."

Rosalind scowled. She really hated that whole memory-erasing idea. "I'm not taking off the ring again until I can get this spirit out."

Caine looked her over, his gaze lingering on her skin. "It's fine. With the tattoos, she can pass as a mage. As long as she can manage to refrain from lecturing everyone about morality for the next twenty minutes."

"We'll just go in and ask about the sybil, right?" Rosalind asked.

"No," Caine said. "You don't want to launch right into the sybil thing. It's never good to let vampires know you're desperate. It gives them power over you. We'll blend in, get some food, act like normal shadow mages, and then casually ask Jorge about the sybil."

"Little problem," Aurora said. "She doesn't smell like a mage."

Caine arched an eyebrow. "Mages don't have a smell."

"Yours is like fresh earth," Aurora said. "A bit of peat and some sage. I think that part belongs to you. But the magic has its own scent. Anyone who's conducted Angelic spells in the past several days smells like a lightning storm and singed air."

Rosalind furrowed her brow. "Are you telling me I need to smell like ozone?"

Aurora shrugged. "If you don't want the vampires to kill you, you need to smell like Caine. Or you need to take off the ring and do one little magical spell. Or we can leave you outside and chain you to the pier."

Rosalind's eyes widened. "I'm not just being stubborn. I'm afraid of losing my freaking mind. This witch's soul is like an inferno. It's completely warped, and I don't even want to know what it would do if I let her out. It wouldn't be pretty. I think in that case *I'd* be the one ripping out throats."

"Fine. So rub up against Caine." Aurora flicked a hand at the mage before staring at Rosalind again. "Don't look at me like that! You don't know how many pedestrian girls would pay good money for that."

"She's not lying," Caine said, with a small shrug.

Aurora sighed. "Bollocks. I fed the ego."

Rosalind took a tentative step and a deep breath. The thought of getting close to Caine sent her pulse racing, though she wasn't sure if that was because he was a demon from the shadow hell, or because he looked like a Greek god. "Rub up against Caine? You have got to be kidding me."

Caine flashed a half-smile. "Given your well-established appreciation of my beauty—"

"The scent is strongest on the neck," Aurora cut in. "And don't pretend to be disgusted, Rosalind. I can hear both your pulses racing."

Rosalind glanced away, cheeks burning, though she wasn't even sure why she cared what they thought. She was a Hunter, for crying out loud, and this was all part of a mission for the Brotherhood— albeit, a severely screwed up mission. Caine was just part of the job, a means to an end.

In the silence, the only sound was water lapping against the pier.

"Right. It's just a body. Just two bodies, coming together..." Had she really just said that out loud? *Rosalind, you absolute moron. Please stop talking.*

Aurora rolled her eyes. "Are you going to do this weird babbling all night? If I get any hungrier, your pedestrian smell will no longer be a problem."

Chilled by the ocean breeze, Rosalind rubbed her tattoo-covered arms. "Right."

"Because I would have eaten you," added Aurora for emphasis. "Not an expression."

"Yeah. I got that." Rosalind stepped closer to Caine, her heart thumping. Just part of her mission. Her shockingly, wildly fucked-up mission, completely unsanctioned by the Brotherhood, who wanted to arrest her. Or possibly kill her. This was the mission of a demon-infected Hunter gone rogue.

What would Josiah make of all this?

Aurora threw her arms up in the air. "Ugh. I'll give you two some privacy. I'm going in for a drink before I murder you both." She stalked away over the pier.

Rosalind stepped closer to Caine. Moonlight bathed his skin in milky light. With his tousled hair and sharp cheekbones, he really was stunning—obnoxiously so, in fact. As a mage, he was supposed to look like a withered hag... but if he was a demon, maybe that explained his otherworldly beauty.

He held out his hand, and she took it, edging closer to his body. Wordlessly, he lifted her wrist to his warm neck, pressing it against his smooth skin. In the night air, she could feel the heat coming off his muscled body, the blood pulsing fast in his veins. As she stood close to him, a strange thrill whispered over her skin, and she had to restrain herself from closing the last few inches between them.

He's not human, she reminded herself. *He's a predator.*

She cleared her throat. "I saw your eyes change earlier. When you were angry."

"Yes."

"It happens to demons. You're not human." It seemed an oddly personal conversation—yet she was standing here, pressing her wrist against his throat. Might as well get to know him.

"I'm half demon."

"What kind?"

"Incubus."

At that word, horror churned in her gut, and she snatched her arm away from him.

A look of confusion flickered across his features. "I'm not going to hurt you."

She swallowed hard, trying to shut out the guilty thoughts echoing in her mind. "Josiah told me that all incubi were brutal rapists."

He took a long, slow breath. "Josiah is wrong," he said softly.

She stared at him, trying to control the thoughts swirling in her mind. *But Josiah can't be wrong—because if he is, then I've committed a far worse sin than I thought.* "Are you sure?" she asked, her voice barely a whisper.

A mixture of emotions flitted through his gray eyes, hurt and anger among them. "Of course I'm sure. I feed off sexual energy. That's true. But I've never forced anyone against their will." The cocky smirk returned to his lips. "You've seen how I look. Why would I need to?"

Remorse tightened her throat. If Caine were telling the truth… She couldn't let herself think about what she'd done—not now. She was close enough to losing her mind as it was. "But some incubi must be evil," she said.

"Demons don't have the same concept of evil that you have, but if you're asking if some demons are rapists and murderers, the answer is yes. Just like humans."

She forced the guilty memories deep into her mental vault. If she pored over them now, she'd never make it out of this situation with her wits intact. "Are there many like you?"

He shook his head. "Not many, no. And even fewer succubi. Even mages hate the females."

"Why?"

"When succubi feed from humans, it's not quite as pleasurable as when incubi do it."

"Oh." She swallowed hard, moving closer again to press her hand against his neck. "I'm sorry I freaked out. I thought incubi were… evil." She drank in his clean, earthy scent, her eyes lingering on the flawless skin near his collarbone before drifting up to his full lips. They looked soft, and she couldn't help but stare. If he ever wanted to feed from her, she wasn't sure she'd be able to turn him down— assuming he was telling the truth about only choosing willing partners.

"You've been brainwashed. It's not your fault." He lowered her wrist. "There. It's not always so bad when you get close to the monsters."

Not bad at all—horrifyingly, disturbingly *not bad*. Obviously, the mage's spirit inside was leading her into dark, animalistic places, drawing her to other corrupted souls.

Okay, fine. The truth was that Caine was just hot as hell.

As she stepped away from him, she steadied her breath. *Keep your composure, Rosalind.* Somehow, the fact that he wasn't a real monster— that she actually *liked* him— was more horrifying than anything else she could have learned about him. It raised questions she didn't want to answer.

She followed him over the old wooden pier toward the bar, and the breeze lifted her hair. As much as she hated herself for it, his warmth had been delicious, and she could almost imagine what he'd look like without his—

Stop it. She clenched her jaw. She was on a Hunter mission, and couldn't get distracted by his beauty. And more than that, she now had a duty to report back to the Brotherhood what she knew about incubi. Of course, people like Josiah would say that Caine was a liar, but his voice had the ring of truth in it—not to mention the fact that he hadn't once tried to force himself on her, even though he could easily overpower her.

They reached the shoddy old door to the bar, and Caine yanked it open, revealing a room fit for vampire royalty. White stone swooped high above them, and candles blazed from ornate chandeliers. Vampires stood around, drinking blood from champagne flutes.

Or at least, they *had* been drinking moments before. Right now, they were all staring at Rosalind. In fact, it kind of seemed like the whole *wrist on neck* maneuver hadn't worked.

A tall, thin man stood behind an oak bar, his hand paused mid-pour. His fangs glinted in the candlelight. "Caine. Did you bring a Hunter into my bar?"

Shit. Was it the smell of her blood? She scanned the room for weapons. A marble fireplace with burning logs and silver pokers. Chandeliers, and champagne flutes all over the place. *I can work with this.*

"Jorge." Caine smiled. "Would I bring a Hunter into your bar?"

"She smells like a mage, but she's wearing an iron ring. And by the frisky glint in her eye, it doesn't look like she's been hypnotized."

Oh. So they did notice the ring.

Caine stared him down. "Of course she's a mage. But a bastard fire cleric put a curse on her, and now she has to wear the ring to suppress the spell or her whole body will go up in flames. And I'm quite fond of her body."

"I'm sure you are. I know your type." The bartender winked, returning to his blood Martini. "Fine. Keep the ring on. As long as you can vouch for her."

Apart from the fangs, the guy *really* didn't seem like a vampire. Vampires weren't supposed to wink.

Caine grabbed Rosalind's hand and led her to the bar. She shot him a quick glance. His features were relaxed. Impressive lying—a crucial skill in any mage's repertoire. *Is there a chance he'd been lying about incubi?*

Apparently, she was supposed to pretend to be his girlfriend. She could live with that if it meant she could get her life back. *All part of the mission.*

Caine led her to the silver bar stools, where Aurora was already knocking back a glass of blood.

Blood-drinkers and demons. This was her new crowd. She took a seat next to Caine, who leaned on the bar.

Drying a Martini glass, Jorge nodded at him. "What can I get for you? The usual?"

"The usual. And the same for my girlfriend."

Jorge nodded. "Two bourbons, and two dinners of food."

She turned to Caine, her stomach rumbling. She didn't have high hopes for the menu. "Two *dinners of food?*"

He leaned in to her. "He hasn't eaten food in several centuries. Don't expect anything amazing."

"What are you implying?" Aurora asked. "Vampires can't cook?"

He stared at her. "You tried to make me ramen noodles in a tea kettle."

Aurora shook her head. "What's the problem? That's what I ate when I was a human."

"I guess that's what happens when you die in college," Caine said.

Jorge filled two tumblers with bourbon, sliding them over the bar.

Rosalind cocked her head, glancing at Caine. "You don't drink blood?"

His eyebrows shot up. "Why would I drink *blood?*"

"I thought mages drank human blood. From skulls. But if you're an incubus..." She let the thought die out on her tongue. There was no way she wanted to vocalize that he gained power through sex.

"Right. Mages drink blood. Just like we all have to glamour ourselves to hide our deformities." He leaned in to whisper in her ear. "No. I'm pretty sure we've established that's bollocks. I'm gorgeous, and you're the blood-drinking human."

Shit. She'd forgotten about the ambrosia. Maybe it *was* possible. After all, Blodrial was known as the sacred god of blood. The Guardians were a little obsessive about the drink. It wasn't human blood, but—on the other hand—maybe trying to rationalize blood drinking was not a good sign.

Jorge dropped off two white plates, piled with food. At least, technically it was food: a pile of Swedish fish, two uncooked tortillas, a stack of American cheese slices, and a frozen pancake, artfully presented on a doily.

It was the most screwed-up meal she'd ever seen, but her mouth watered anyway. Hunger gnawed in her stomach.

With her fork, she lifted a tortilla, grimacing. Within the tortillas, candy hearts were stuck in a smear of jam. Red slogans emblazoned their surfaces: *Love Me, Hot Lips,* and *XOXO.* This had to be the weirdest quesadilla in the history of "dinners of food."

Caine handed her a blue heart: *Adore me.* "This one's for you. A reasonable suggestion."

"It doesn't seem fair to take that from you. I don't think I could ever adore you as much as you do."

"Give me your pancake."

"What?"

"There are only two edible things on that plate. The candy fish and the pancake. At least let me warm it for you." He reached over, spearing the pancake on his fork. After he chanted a quick spell, it thawed and toasted to a golden brown. He dropped it on her plate again. "Don't say I never did anything for you."

She nearly cracked a smile for the first time since the Brotherhood had come for her. The truth was, Caine *had* been helping her.

She just had no idea why.

She took a bite of the pancake. Sweet and fluffy. Within about twenty seconds, she'd chomped through the entire thing, before stuffing a handful of Swedish fish into her mouth. She moved on to the American cheese slices, and when she was unwrapping the final piece she looked up to find Caine eyeing her with concern.

"I don't think I've ever seen anyone eat that fast," he said. "I'm a little alarmed."

Aurora stared over her drink. "Unsettling, really. It reminds me a little of that time I saw Horace eat a truck driver outside a McDonald's."

"I haven't eaten in a full day." She was still grumpy, in fact. She whispered, "What do you think the chances are that a high demon will come in?"

He shrugged. "Fifty-fifty. Might be fun, really. But if it happens, you should get out of here. Let me handle it."

The arrogance on this guy. "What are you going to do, toast some waffles for him? Burn his bagel until he's cross?"

"You're still cranky." Caine handed her his pancake. "Have mine."

He glanced down the bar, catching Jorge's eye.

Smiling, the bartender sidled up to them. "How were the dinners?"

"Amazing, as always," Caine said. "We'll just need two more bourbons. Neat."

"No problem." Jorge pulled a glass bottle from the shelves, unscrewing the cap to fill two more glass tumblers. "I'm just happy to see you with a girl who isn't trying to murder you for once."

"Give it time," Aurora said.

Rosalind frowned. "Wait. Why is Caine always with girls who want to murder him?"

Jorge scratched his chin. "The vampire girls get obsessed with him after he screws—"

"We don't need to get into that," Caine snapped. "Has no one ever told you that bartenders are supposed to be discreet?"

Jorge furrowed his brow. "I've never heard that."

Caine scowled. "I don't know why I continue to be surprised whenever vampires fail to be empathic."

Jorge leered at Rosalind, waggling an eyebrow. "I'm perfectly empathic."

Given the way he was looking at her, she was pretty sure he thought "empathic" meant *horny.*

Caine knocked back his drink. "Speaking of my new girl—as you mentioned, she's not trying to kill me. Obviously, I'm quite fond of her for that reason. And there's that little curse. It's not a big deal, of course. But it would be nice to take that ring off her so she could use her magic again."

Jorge flashed a wolfish smile. "You want to get some of those kinky spells going?"

She nearly spat out the pancake. *What does that even mean?*

Caine nodded. "Exactly. So if we could figure out how to lift the spell…"

Grinning, Jorge leaned on the bar. "You need Sambethe. The sybil."

Caine swirled his drink. "And where would I find the sybil?"

Jorge let his eyes roam over Rosalind's body. Whatever "kinky magic" meant, he seemed to like the idea a little too much. "The sybil is allied with Borgerith."

"Ah," Caine said. "The goddess of the mountains. So she won't speak to us."

Jorge leaned in further, looking around the bar. "You can find her in Elysium. It's an underground club where demons get together, no matter what the alliances. Fire demons mix with night, rock mixes with sea. It's chaos. But you can't tell people. The gods wouldn't exactly approve."

Rosalind took a sip of the bourbon. "And where would we find—"

Something halted her sentence. A wave of shadowy magic rippled through the bar, crawling over her skin like spider legs. She glanced around. The magic was a deep red, the color of dried blood, and it smelled of moldering hemlock—a smell of death.

"Caine," she whispered. "We should go."

"Why? I haven't even finished my drink."

"Because something powerful is headed right here. Something deadly."

Caine studied her, but before she could get an answer out of him, the bartender's eyes flicked to the door, and his face went even paler. "Bileth," he whispered.

Rosalind turned to the entrance. In the doorframe stood a hulk of a night demon, his skin pale as moonlight and cheekbones sharp as razors. He must have been three hundred pounds of pure muscle, and horns grew from his skull. His eyes were empty, ivory pools.

A shiver ran up her spine. She'd seen him before—his portrait hung in Lilinor Castle. Every fiber of her being screamed at her to run. She'd read about high demons before, but she'd never seen one. And hadn't Caine said something about smelling her blood…

Caine slipped an arm around her shoulders, pulling her close to him. He whispered, "I'll handle this. Get out of here."

She was terrified, but she wasn't going to run from a demon. She was a Hunter.

The high demon cocked his head, sniffing, then licked his lips. His gaze slid over Rosalind's body, and Caine whispered, "Run. You too, Aurora."

Aurora was out the door in a split second. But Rosalind stood rooted to the spot. She was a Hunter, damn it, and this was her chance to prove herself. She wasn't going to leave Caine to fight alone.

On top of that, it wasn't like she could run that fast. Bileth would stop her in a second.

In the next moment, the high demon was before them. Caine squared off with him, muscles tensed.

The demon opened his mouth, revealing jagged teeth. "Is this Hunter with you?"

Oh, shit. Hadn't taken long for him to suss her out. His fetid magic coated her body, roiling through her blood like a poison. But Caine's magic was there, too, cool and silvery. With their auras blazing, the two demons seemed to be gearing up for a serious battle.

"Her? A Hunter?" Caine asked, obviously stalling. He glanced at Rosalind, his eyes burning into her. "She's a mage, and she was just leaving. Though now that you mention it, she may have accidentally ingested—"

Bileth gripped the mage's throat with both hands, and long, ivory nails pierced Caine's neck. Crimson tendrils spiraled from the demon's fingertips, wrapping Caine in a web that pinned his arms against his body, binding his legs, sealing his mouth shut to stop his magic.

CHAPTER 14

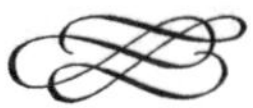

The silver glow around Caine began to weaken, and fear screamed through Rosalind's mind.

Bileth's power only grew stronger, and his red magic exploded from him like a dying star. He was about to murder Caine.

She grabbed Aurora's champagne flute, smashing it over Bileth's head. She plunged the fractured stem into his back.

His pale eyes swiveled to her as she grasped for another glass. This time, he grabbed her wrist, crushing it in a death grip. Holy hells, he was breaking her bones.

In another split second, he pinned both her wrists, black talons piercing her skin. He pulled her closer, so close she could smell the blood on his breath.

He smiled, and the sight of his long, white teeth made her shudder.

"I like touching your things, incubus," he growled.

Revulsion welled in her gut as his inky red magic swirled around her head. It coiled into her mind, whispering through her own thoughts, until her body was no longer quite her own. She gaped at him, her heart beating fast as a hummingbird's.

The demon released her hands, but she no longer controlled them. *Touch him,* a voice whispered in her mind.

She watched in horror as the demon's magic forced her to reach out for his chest, hands sliding over his skin. Revulsion rose in her throat as Bileth propelled her closer, forcing her arms around his neck until she was practically grinding against him.

As he growled, his magic forced her to lurch away from him. *Grab the broken glass.* Her hand flew out for a broken shard on the bar, and her blood roared in her ears. She gripped it hard, slicing open her flesh. Blood dripped onto the floor. The vamps gasped, scenting fresh blood.

Bileth forced her hand to her throat. She strained against his magic, her arm shaking. The shard pierced her neck, and pain ripped through her skin. She whimpered, concentrating on the magic that invaded her mind like a noxious ink. She needed to master her fear, to shove this magic out before he forced her to slit her own throat. She shivered, trying to push his poison from her body.

Nearby, Caine's tingly aura grew stronger, filling the room. It caressed her injured hand and healed the gaping wound. With a tremendous force of will, she cut a glance his way, watching as he ripped himself free from Bileth's magic. His body blazed with his pearly aura. In a split second, his knife pressed against Bileth's throat. At that moment, Bileth's magic completely snapped from her mind.

Caine's eyes—dark as an abyss, glinting with an ancient violence—sent a shiver up her spine.

His voice came out low and steady. "You know I hate to argue with you, Bileth. But she's a mage."

Bileth's body vibrated with barely contained rage. "Then where is her aura?"

"I'm not allowing her to use magic now. She was getting out of control."

"And yet I smell the god of blood. You're attacking *me* to save a Hunter?"

Rage bloomed in her chest. The way Bileth had controlled her body filled her with intense loathing, and she wanted to hurt him.

Right now, the demon's attention was on Caine. She needed to help the incubus anyway. If anything happened to him, she'd be responsible for his death.

With a racing pulse, she leapt onto the oak bar, then jumped for one of the chandeliers. She kicked her legs, swinging in a wide arc. As the air charged with Caine's nocturnal magic, she propelled herself to the next chandelier, clutching at the silver. Below, the vamps hissed.

"Rosalind," Caine shouted. "I told you to run."

Blazing candles tumbled to the ground, and hot wax spilled on her skin as she swung from one chandelier to the next, toward the fireplace. *What the hell was my game plan?*

With an enraged snarl, Bileth ripped himself free from Caine's grasp. "Hunter!"

The scent of rotting hemlock drew closer, Bileth's blood-red magic curling around her skin. Panic punched a hole in her chest. He wasn't fighting Caine anymore. He was coming for her.

She jumped to the ground, grabbing the silver poker. Hot anger burned through her, and she whirled. She threw it in a high arc as he lunged for her, and it pierced the center of his chest.

The demon froze, gripping the metal. He opened his mouth, and the chorus of shrieks that emerged from his throat turned her blood to ice. There wasn't enough time to consider how proud Josiah would be, because her attack had stoked the vampires' fury.

As she leapt over a table, Jorge jumped for her. She ducked, bringing her fist up into his groin. With a twist of her body, she kicked him into the fireplace. As she did, another vamp grabbed her by the hair, yanking her head back with a sharp snap. But the attack was short lived. Something had stopped the vampires.

She glanced at Caine who murmured, his body luminescent.

Bound by Caine's magic, the vampires lurched, bodies contorting in pain. The horrifying crunch of vampire bone echoed through the room. She released a breath. As long as he was chanting, he had the vampires under control.

She cut a glance to Bileth, and terror crawled up her spine. His dark, wide eyes were fixed on her, and he ripped the poker from his ribs. She needed to get out of here *now.*

Leaping onto the tables, she crashed through champagne flutes of blood in a frantic rush to the door. "Caine! Let's go."

His eyes met hers, and he broke his spell over the vamps.

Rosalind flew, bursting through the door, and Caine followed in a black blur.

Once outside, he flicked his wrist, and the door slammed shut. Enraged shouts reverberated through the walls as demons pounded on the door. Her heart leapt into her throat. Bileth was still in there, and it couldn't be long until he tore through the rickety walls.

Caine glared at her. "Do you realize that you just impaled one of the most powerful demons in the world? There was a reason I didn't slit his throat."

The blood drained from her head. This "master your fear" thing wasn't working out so well. Maybe she still needed to work on distinguishing bravery from flat-out stupidity.

This time, she wasn't going to wait for Caine's instruction to run.

She took off in a sprint over the pier, charging for the bike. Somehow, Caine was already there by the time she arrived, waiting for her on his bike.

She jumped on, gripping his waist. He revved his engine, peeling off into Salem's narrow streets. His magical aura rippled over her skin. Dizzy, she watched her body disappear as the street sped by below them.

She tried to control the shaking in her hands so Caine wouldn't notice. The way Bileth had controlled her mind made her sick. *That* was a demon's true nature—the reason that Hunters had been fighting evil for centuries.

She clamped her eyes shut. Here she was, clinging to a demon as though he were any different.

Caine roared through Salem's winding streets and up a dark hill—away from his apartment. Where exactly was he taking her? For all she knew, he could be dragging her to Nyxobas as punishment for assaulting Bileth. He could be sentencing her to the shadow hell.

Fear tightened her chest as they sped past tiny wooden houses on a tree-lined street. She still didn't trust Caine, and the recent display of his power told her just what she'd be up against if she stopped being useful to him.

He pulled off the main road into a parking lot, slamming to a stop near the wooded edge of the pavement.

Rosalind shot a nervous look to the darkened pharmacy nearby. *What the hell?*

He stepped off his bike, and she followed, taking a tentative step away from him. They were completely alone.

He stepped closer, casting a scrutinizing gaze at her neck. When he touched her skin with his fingertips, she flinched.

"Did Bileth bite you?" he asked.

"No. He didn't get that far."

"Good. If he had, you'd die an agonizing death in the next hour." He frowned. "But you realize you just got me barred from my favorite drinking hole when you lit the bartender on fire."

"I was revolted by Bileth's magic in my mind. It disgusts me that demons want to control humans' minds. We're just their toys."

"You think that's how I see you?"

The question caught her off guard. "I don't know yet."

"It should be obvious that I don't, or our interactions would be very different. Anyway, Bileth isn't an ordinary demon. He commands eighty-five legions, and he reports directly to Nyxobas. He's as ancient as the god himself, a fallen angel from the celestial wars several millennia ago."

She swallowed hard. "But you held a blade to his throat."

"That would be difficult to fix diplomatically, yes. But I've angered him before, and I could usually make amends by supplying him with expensive vodka and a particularly stunning courtesan or two. Plus, I've never actually stabbed him. I don't think he'll forgive impalement with a fireplace poker so easily. You should have run."

"I did tell you that something was coming. But you wanted to finish your drink. Plus, I wouldn't have made it out fast enough." She couldn't tell him the truth—that she'd needed to save him to atone for what she'd done.

"You had a second chance to run."

Her legs were still trembling, and the memory of Bileth's complete control still haunted her. "I wanted to hurt him. He deserved it. And anyway, I thought you needed my help."

"I don't see how that would be any of your concern. According to you, I'm a monster. And more than that, I told you I'd handle it." His voice had a razor-sharp edge; his eyes were dark storm clouds. "And I would have. Aurora ran when I told her to."

Despite the look of primal wrath in his eyes, irritation spurred her on. "I don't like being bossed around. You need to stop giving me commands. I'm not your soldier. And why couldn't you just tell people that Ambrose wanted me alive? Surely the Vampire Lord has some clout."

Caine took a deep breath, and his eyes returned to their normal gray. "It's not that simple. Ambrose doesn't want Bileth to know what he's planning."

"What's he planning?"

"You don't need to know that. Not as long as you still plan on exorcising the spirit."

Exasperated, she glanced around at the empty lot. "Can you at least tell me what we're doing in a parking lot?"

"Come with me." He stopped himself, taking a deep breath. "Please come with me, Rosalind." Turning abruptly, he marched up the thickly overgrown, rocky hill.

She followed, slipping on the steep, rocky slope as she scrambled to catch up. "Is there some sort of botanical emergency that needs addressing?"

"You should rethink your plan. About purging the mage's soul."

"And this rethinking needs to happen in the woods?"

Maples loomed high above them, blocking out most of the moonlight. They crunched over fallen leaves and twigs.

Caine led them up a steep hill into a grove of maple and poplar trees overlooking the parking lot. "In 1692, this is where the Brotherhood hanged nineteen people who had nothing to do with magic."

Another history lesson. "I'm not saying the Brotherhood are perfect. So they get it wrong sometimes, and they need to modernize.

But they're trying to protect humanity, and no one else is fighting the predatory demons like Bileth."

"The Brotherhood aren't perfect, and neither is the magical world. We've got that in common. The difference is that the Brotherhood is gaining an unprecedented amount of power. People are terrified of magic, and that means the Hunters no longer have any restraints. No more trials. No more mercy. They're starting to execute mages, and people they mistakenly think are mages. They want to watch the world burn. They want to watch *you* burn. And you want to run back to them. Do you have a death wish, Rosalind?"

Executions. Burnings. That stuff wasn't true, was it? "First of all, I'm human. They won't hurt me. Second of all, they don't burn anyone."

"Running back to the Brotherhood would be suicide."

Tears pricked her eyes. What good was her life if she had no home, no family? She didn't even know who she could trust anymore. "I don't see myself having a lot of options." She shook her head. "I don't understand what you want from me."

"You have a gift. You're meant to fight. Just like I am. And call me crazy, but I think you should fight the people who want to burn you to death. Your plan to throw yourself on their mercy is utterly stupid."

She cocked an eyebrow. "That's your mage-recruitment pitch? Calling me stupid?"

"I said your plan is stupid. Not you."

"You haven't explained why we need to be knee-deep in shrubbery for this conversation."

He stepped closer, fingers grazing her hand. His touch sparked her with a warm, electrical charge. *Must be an incubus thing.*

"Take off the ring." He winced as though in pain. "It is your choice to take off the ring, but I would strongly suggest that you do it. You need to see the magic that lurks under the surface—what the Brotherhood is so terrified of. Then tell me if it scares you, too. Because I've seen you fight. You're a warrior. Like me."

At the thought of taking off the ring, raw panic burned through her nerves. "What is it with you people and wanting me to lose my mind?"

"Like you said, you don't have a ton of options. The people you plan on running to for protection want to kill you. Now the demon world wants to kill you, too, and they will hunt you unless you convert. It's your one chance at saving yourself."

She narrowed her eyes. "How do I know I can trust you?"

"I've saved your life more than once now. And I'll be here now, when you take off the ring. If the spirit tries to hurt you, I'll put the ring back on. Just like I did in Lilinor."

The wind rustled the elm leaves, whipping her hair around her head. She couldn't bear the thought of that wild rage and agony. "I'm not doing it."

"Running away from your true nature won't keep you alive. You can't be scared of it."

"It's not my true nature. It's an invasive nature, just like Bileth's aura in my skull. And I don't want the magic to corrupt and deform my body."

Caine furrowed his brow. "I thought we'd established that my godlike beauty dispelled that myth."

"That's just because you're an incubus."

"No, it's because magic *doesn't* deform the human body. When will you understand that the Purgators are wrong about nearly everything?"

"I *felt* this thing corrupting me. I felt the evil when Ambrose yanked off the ring."

"You've been trained to fundamentally reject magic, and that's why it feels evil. You've been hiding from it for most of your life, and that means you're at war with it. You need to accept that it's a part of you now."

If he thought she could master this particular fear, he was wrong. The spirit's mind was the seventh circle of hell. Of *course* she was scared. Fear was a normal human emotion, absent only from demons and psychopaths. And while Caine fit at least one of those categories, Rosalind still felt a natural, human terror at the idea of losing her mind.

Even so, it wasn't like she'd admit to being scared. She had her pride.

She lifted her face. "If anyone should be scared of me taking off the ring, it's you, since I'm pretty sure this mage is a psychotic murderer. But if that's what you want, then fine. Just stand back so I don't rip your spine out through your throat."

Nice. I'm starting to talk like a vamp.

Caine smiled. "Don't get cocky. You speared one demon prince, but I'm not overly worried about my chances in a fight against you."

Now she kind of hoped the mage would do a tiny bit of damage. She sucked in a shaky breath, and slipped the ring off her finger.

CHAPTER 15

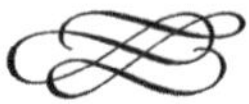

As soon as she slid the ring off, the second soul inside her opened like a flower, and another presence filled her mind.

"Druloch calls to me," it whispered. "I live within the tree's shadows."

Someone looked out at the world through her eyes, and sent energy through her legs, forcing her to run. Bright, silvery light pierced the oak leaves above her. Elms towered over the forest floor. In the bright moonlight, they cast long shadows—the woods' fingers.

The forest teemed with life. Hawthorn petals carpeted the mossy earth. Around the path, blueberry bushes grew, and wild fox grape vines climbed over trees, their branches full of sparrows and black-birds. The rich, peaty scent of the woods hung thick in the air. But there was death here, too, and sacrifice. Something drew her into the trees' shadows.

She slammed to a halt, feeling the vibrations of the surrounding woods. A flutter of movement caught her eye from a tangle of roots on the ground—black wings, a squawking bird. In the shadows, a crow ripped out a sparrow's entrails, and the tiny bird screeched in agony. The crow was eating it alive. Lost somewhere in the aura,

Rosalind felt sick. She wanted to wring the sparrow's neck to end its misery.

But the thing inside her relished the electrifying cycle of life and death. *In the dark parts of the forest, the strong feed on the weak.*

The spirit wanted to feed.

It forced her to her knees, and made her plunge her fingers into the ground. Vernal power coursed through her veins, and a green aura swirled through her body. This mage wanted her to bury herself in dark moss.

I'm in here, her mind screamed. *My name is Rosalind.*

The mage forced back her head, scanning the woods. Sage-colored algae grew on felled tree trunks. In the distance, an elk tore along a path. The trees' spirits breathed around her, trunks swelling like bellows, the air thick and sweet with their whispered breath.

Power charged her body, and the mage compelled her to rub the dirt over her arms and chest. The rejuvenating power of fertile soil.

Her mind shrieked with the invader's thoughts.

The hawthorns. The sharp claws of lust. The fire. You led me to the fire. You will burn.

Somewhere inside this chaotic mind, Rosalind tried to make herself stand. *Rosalind…* The name grew fainter.

Something was wrong. Rage tightened around her heart like a cinquefoil vine. The moonlight burned too strong, dazzling through the leaves, blinding her. The smell of burning flesh filled the woods. Within moments, agony ripped her apart, her skin burning, blackening, and cracking. Pain splintered her mind until the world tilted.

The mage was burning her body.

Something else needed to die to stop this. Her blood boiled, and around her, oak leaves blazed like candles, lit with the witch's fury.

Oh gods. The agony warped her mind. Someone was here. An agent of the night god. *Break his ribs. Rip his heart from his chest. Drink the blood to cool your flames.*

She leapt up from the ground, her pain blinding, and slammed into the mage, her fist ramming into his skull. After knocking him to the ground, she jumped on his chest, hands slipping around his throat.

But the flames faded, her skin cooled, and a long sigh slid from her. Now the pain was just memory. She could see him now—so beautiful, his eyes a pale gray. The mage wanted him, and now Rosalind wanted him, too. She ran her fingers over his chest. The spirit forced her to lower her mouth to his and lick his lower lip, pressing her body against him, burning with need as she kissed him—

He slammed the ring back on her finger, and the thing withered in her mind, its presence only a faint echo.

She was lying on top of Caine, her hands fisted into his tousled hair and her mouth pressed against his. His soft, warm lips were electrifying, sending a different kind of heat through her—one that she liked. She forced herself to inch back, and stared into his eyes, trying to catch her breath.

Caine's breath warmed her neck. He murmured, "Apparently, your spirit wanted to get her hands on me, but not for fighting."

Her dress was torn, hiked up to the waist. Heat warmed her cheeks, and she said the first thing that popped into her head: "This is why I don't wear dresses."

His eyes blazed with a pale light, and he trailed his fingertips down her back, leaving a trail of tingles. "If you're going to straddle demons in the woods, you might as well show a little leg."

Oh, gods. She'd just pushed him onto the forest floor and assaulted him. And he'd clamped the ring back on her finger. For an incubus, that must have taken an awful lot of self-control—or maybe she wasn't his type.

Caine glanced at the mud and dirt coating her body, and whispered a spell. As he spoke, his aura whispered over her skin. She watched the muck lift into the air.

As much as Caine's aura soothed her, the thought of the mage inside controlling her body made her stomach turn. She unclenched her fingers from Caine's hair, gazing into those glacial eyes. "You shouldn't have made me take it off. I don't want that thing inside me, forcing me to do things against my will. Just like Bileth."

He frowned. "Forcing you to do horrible things like kiss me."

"Exactly." Seven hells. If the other novices knew what she'd been getting up to, they'd celebrate her downfall. The golden Hunter, covered in alchemical tattoos and mud, straddling an incubus in the Salem woods.

His hand slipped around the back of her neck; at his touch, another electrical charge sparked through her skin. "And yet, I don't see you jumping off me very fast."

Shit. He was right. Embarrassment warmed her face. She leapt up, tugging down her hem. Though, really, it was probably a little late to reclaim her dignity now. "I don't know what happened. I couldn't stop the witch."

He propped up on his elbows. "You can't expect to master it right away. You need to be stronger than the spirit."

A ghost of that crazed blaze still burned in her mind. Her fingers trembled as she brushed the leaves off her dress. "That's not the kind of war I know how to fight. She's completely crazy. I'm not taking that ring off again. Not until I get the spirit out."

"She's absolutely not crazy. Jumping on top of me was the first sensible thing I've seen you do, and honestly the first time I've seen you enjoy yourself."

She shivered. Didn't he realize? The agony had been unbearable. "My body was on fire."

He flashed a smile, and she knew he was thinking of the kiss.

"I don't mean with lust. I mean my skin was literally charring, and so were the trees. My body was blistering with flames."

He arched an eyebrow. "When you were on top of me?"

"No, before that. I was angry. Enraged. And everything was aflame. And then when I—when the mage jumped on you, I guess she felt something else. The pain subsided, and it felt calm again."

"See? I'm magic." He rose, pulling a stray leaf from his hair. "Maybe the flames were a vision of your future if you give yourself back to the Brotherhood. I don't know what else it would be. Your spirit isn't a fire mage. Ambrose said you tasted of hawthorns."

Rosalind nodded. "She's a forest mage. That explains all the tree stuff. I should have felt it through her aura, but it's too intense for me to even think straight."

"My spirit worshipped Nyxobas. Yours was aligned with Druloch, the god who lurks in the woods' dark shadows."

"The mage was drawn to the darkness. Something about the cycle of life and death. But the flames were so strong. She must be using fire magic."

"It's not possible. There are three shadow gods—sea, night, and forest. They've been warring with the gods of fire and light for millennia. That means there's no way you're connected to fire magic."

The sea god. A chill whispered over her skin. She'd scented a sea-witch on the Thorndike Campus. Could that mage be connected to all this? Something told her not to mention it to Caine. It was entirely possible that Rosalind was responsible for yet another mage's capture, and she had no way of knowing if that mage had been evil or just another poor idiot caught up in things beyond her control. She wanted to change the subject. "I'm not well versed in the shadow gods and fire gods. I've only been taught about Blodrial, the one true god."

"Blodrial fell from heaven after the celestial wars, just like the others. The only thing that sets him apart is that he doesn't believe humans should speak Angelic."

Of course they shouldn't. She'd just seen evidence of what the Angelic language could do to a human mind. "Right. Because it's evil in human bodies, and it screws people up. Blodrial is right."

"He's against it because the gift of magic to human kind was the original sin that banished our gods from heaven. The gods are all trying to free themselves from their punishment."

She'd never heard this version before. "And what is their punishment?"

"The celestial gods—those who won the war, trapped them in matter. The shadow and fire gods are trying to gain freedom by collecting human souls, competing with each other. But Blodrial thinks he can repent by stamping out magic on earth. Erasing the original sin. None of them can accept their punishment, and we all lost something. Even humans."

"What did we lose?" She was grateful for the temporary reprieve from thinking about the flames.

"Ignorance. Knowledge comes with a price. When humans learned to speak the Angelic language, they also learned about something else —their own mortality. Pedestrians have a story about a snake and a fruit tree that covers that concept."

"Don't eat from the tree of knowledge, or you'll die."

"Exactly."

She rubbed her throbbing temples. This was all too much for her now. She didn't want to think about her own death, not after she'd felt so close to it just moments ago. "Okay. So you have no idea why I felt like I was on fire?"

"No idea. It never happened to me. I had a whole lot of rage and bloodlust, but no flames. Still, as long as you stay near me while you learn to control the aura, I can help. You said it didn't hurt when you were near me."

He still wasn't telling her the whole story. "Why are you and Ambrose so invested in my power?"

"Unlike the Brotherhood, we want you alive. Isn't that enough information for you?"

"No. It isn't. And I don't get it. How are you able to stay sane with two souls?"

"I had to accept the mage, and then bend him to my own will. I had to become stronger than him. Now I use his knowledge and power, but he doesn't control me."

Shuddering, she thought of her blackening skin. "If I don't wear the ring, she'll consume me from the inside out. I won't be me anymore."

"I won't let that happen."

She wanted to see Tammi and Josiah, and walk the halls of Thorndike University. She didn't want to live in a world where people casually tossed human hands onto the floor, and she definitely didn't want to live with a violent lunatic invading her brain, forcing her to do things against her will.

How could my own parents have done this to me? Magic had obviously twisted their minds into insanity. "I don't want to be a mage. I don't want to be like you. I need to at least try to get my old life back."

"The Brotherhood will not give you your life back."

"Josiah will help me. He's my Guardian."

"That's absurd. No one in the Brotherhood is trustworthy."

"*I'm* in the Brotherhood. And anyway, am I supposed to believe you're trustworthy? You still won't tell me what Ambrose wants me for."

Josiah simply *had* to help her. Even if she couldn't rejoin the Brotherhood, she needed to claw some kind of normal life back.

His voice grew cold. "Your Guardian obviously hasn't guarded you very well so far, but it's your own life if you want to throw it away. I hope the burning you endure at the hands of the Brotherhood is somehow less painful than the illusion of burning that so terrifies you. Though it's highly improbable."

He turned, striding down the overgrown slope, and she followed, trying to maintain her balance on the slippery rocks. At the bottom of the hill, Caine paused to look at a small, flowering shrub.

His hand hovered over a cluster of white flowers before he plucked them from the plant. Wordlessly, he handed them to Rosalind, then stalked into the parking lot.

She twirled the delicate stem in her fingers. Hawthorn blossoms.

CHAPTER 16

After they returned to the waterfront, Caine parked his bike under an oak. He climbed off, and Rosalind followed him across a patch of grass by Salem Harbor. The briny wind kissed her face, skimming over her tattered dress.

She had no idea what they were doing now. It wasn't like he'd filled her in or anything. But she had a bad feeling he might change his mind about his promise to help her exorcise the spirit. He seemed to think she was making a terrible mistake, but he wasn't the one who had to feel the flames when the ring came off.

He paused before a small gray stone in the ground. Chanting, he flicked his wrist. She gasped as a dark, steep-peaked house glimmered into view. She had to catch her breath at the illusion—or maybe it was the other way around. The house's invisibility was the illusion.

Caine opened a red door into a hall, warmly lit by candles. "My other home. The secret one." He motioned for her to enter, and she followed him into an ivory-walled hall. "Right now, you're the only person who knows this exists. Aurora will be only the second person. If you're still going to insist on rejoining the mage Hunters, I'll have to steal this particular memory from you before you leave. Or I'll have to kill you. Your choice."

Rosalind cocked her hip. "I don't really like the idea of you rooting around in my brain."

"What are you afraid I'll see?"

She toyed with her ring. *You'd slaughter me if you knew the terrible thing I did.* She pushed the thought away. "It's more that I don't particularly want brain damage."

"I'm an artist of dark magic. I'd leave all your computer science jibber-jabber intact."

"Mmm. Sounds like you really know what you're talking about." She frowned. "When are we going to see the sybil? Where's this nightclub?"

"We'll go tonight, once Aurora gets here. Hopefully, none of Elysium's patrons have heard about your little incident with Bileth." He motioned for her to follow him into a high-ceilinged living room. "In the meantime, let me introduce you to my parlor."

Parlor. It was a strangely old-fashioned New England word for a delicately beautiful place. Silvery wallpaper covered the walls, decorated with ethereal spider-web patterns. Midnight-blue curtains hung from bay windows overlooking the water, and candles burned in silver candelabra. The entire place was impeccably tidy. He probably had cleaning spells to do the work for him.

She sat on a deep blue sofa, smoothing out her tangled hair. She looked like a mess. At least the tattoos had faded from her skin, but her dress was hanging off her—probably shredded around the time she threw herself at Caine.

He sat next to her, and she glanced at him, trying not to stare at his beautiful features, his strong jawline and glacial eyes. "I think I might remember you. I remember glimpses from when we were kids. I remember someone like you on the beach. A young boy with gray eyes."

He eyed her cautiously. "I'm older than you. My memories are a bit clearer."

Curiosity bloomed in her mind. "What do you remember? What were my parents like?"

"Powerful."

He wasn't giving details, and she had the unsettling feeling they'd done something terrible to him.

A sigh slid from her. "I remember feeling loved. Even if my parents were witches, I felt safe then. But you weren't safe. They threw you out."

He gazed into the candle flames. "Nothing I didn't deserve," he said, so softly she barely heard him.

A lump rose in her throat. "You were just a kid."

"Is that so?" A muscle feathered in his jaw. "You don't think like a Hunter with all that empathy of yours."

"Maybe the Brotherhood isn't as bad as you think." She thought of Mason, making a mental correction. "Some of them are awful. But most of the Brotherhood made me feel like I had a home again. I felt valued, and important. I had a place among them. They give me a purpose."

"Is it worth your life?"

"They have to take me back. I don't have anything else," she said.

"That's quite a lot of faith you put in them."

"It's not so much faith. It's more like—"

"—A desire," he said. It was the same phrasing Ambrose had used, but on an incubus's lips, the word had an entirely different association. Her mind burned with the memory of his lips on hers, of her body pressed against his, fingers coiled into his hair.

But he'd put a stop to their kiss. It was stupid, but she almost felt the sting of rejection.

"You know when I kissed you earlier?" She flinched at her own question. *Shut up, Rosalind.*

His lips curled in a faint smile. "The image is fresh in my memory."

"I was just wondering, since you're an incubus…" Why in the gods' names was she bringing this up? She'd lost all her impulse control since she started hanging out with demons. "Why did you stop me? I thought incubi fed off—" She cleared her throat. "You know."

He arched an eyebrow. "*You know.* Is that what you call it in the Brotherhood?"

Her chest flushed. She had no idea why she'd gotten sidetracked by this conversation. She should be focusing on the sybil right now, and finding a way to piece her life back together. "You know what I mean."

He ran a finger over his lower lip, studying her. "Why did I stop it? Because you weren't in control. I can tell you it took a tremendous amount of restraint on my part."

Rosalind stared at him, entranced by the flickering candlelight dancing over his skin.

"Hello?" Aurora's voice broke the silence.

Rosalind let out a long breath, letting some of the tension uncoil inside her.

"Caine!" Aurora shouted from the doorway. "Am I invited in?"

"Of course you're invited in," he said.

Beaming, Aurora glided into the living room. "So *this* is the secret lair of the great shadow mage."

Rosalind arched an eyebrow. "Vampires can't enter without an invitation? I thought that was a myth."

"It is," Aurora said. "But I just feel awkward barging into someone's house. I mean, Lilu led me here—but she's a bird so it wasn't, like, a proper invitation with words. And I didn't want to be a third wheel in case you were banging."

"You're welcome here," Caine said. "Bileth won't find this house. He may track us to the waterfront, but we're invisible to him."

Aurora threw herself down on a chaise lounge. "I would have stayed to help with the fight, but I had a feeling you'd be doing that bone crunching thing, and I didn't want to get caught in the crossfire. You need to tell me everything that happened." Her eyes landed on an oak liquor cabinet, and within moments, she was across the room, rooting around the glass bottles. "I'll need a cocktail for this."

"Bileth knows I'm a Hunter," Rosalind said.

"How the hell did you make it out of there alive?" Aurora pulled out three Martini glasses, laying them on a tray. She filled them with whiskey. "You must've blinked your big eyes at him to charm him. Showed off a little of that perky cleavage."

"Not exactly," Caine muttered. "She impaled him with a fire poker."

Aurora whirled, the tray of cocktails in her hands. "She did *what?*"

"I'm a Hunter," Rosalind said. "I hunted him. I didn't know he was some kind of demon royalty. And I was worried about Caine."

Caine quirked a smile. "You were worried about me? I thought you were a Hunter. I'm pretty sure I'm among your intended prey."

Flustered, she plucked a cocktail glass off the tray. "Maybe, but right now you're my one hope at exorcising the spirit."

Aurora shoved a glass in Caine's hands, before downing her own in one go. She collapsed into a chair. "None of that matters now. We're all dead. For real this time. Did you know Bileth is known as 'The Scalpel' for the way he removes people's skin just for fun?"

Rosalind's stomach turned a flip. When Caine had been trying to convince her that demons and Hunters were somehow morally equivalent, he'd conveniently left out the bit about The Scalpel.

Caine traced his finger along the rim of his glass. "It's not a good situation. And, to make matters worse, we can't kill Bileth without provoking a major war."

"If you gave him the Hunter," Aurora said, "he might forget the whole thing."

Rosalind tightened her grip on the Martini glass. "You can't give me up. It wasn't my fault. I thought I was helping Caine."

Aurora arched an eyebrow. "You're really caught up in this fault thing, aren't you? Hasn't anyone ever told you that sometimes bad things happen to good people?"

"We're not going to give her to Bileth," Caine said. "Ambrose would never forgive it—and anyway, the Hunter is growing on me. At least in the rare moments when she's quiet."

Aurora was already refilling her drink. "You're directly defying Ambrose's orders to train her, so I'm a bit confused why you're suddenly worried about his forgiveness."

"I wasn't going to defy him entirely," Caine said. "I have a solution that meets Ambrose's needs as well as hers."

This was the first Rosalind had heard of this concept. "Wait. *What* solution that meets both our needs?"

"Ambrose wants the mage's spirit to survive," Caine said. "The spirit will simply need another body. And I have a willing host who would gladly accept this power."

"Who?" Aurora asked.

He sipped his drink. "Me."

Rosalind straightened. "I don't think that's a good idea. The mage's mind will break you. It was physically painful. Her body was on fire. And can you really handle another soul?"

Aurora glared over her Martini glass. "What do you care what happens to him? Once you run back to the Brotherhood, it will be your job to ram an iron spear through his heart. You get that, right?"

"I won't come for him, even if he doesn't erase my memories." It was the first time the thought had ever occurred to her, but as soon as the words were out of her mouth, she knew them to be true. Even if he was a demon, he'd done nothing but help her so far.

The longer she spent with the demons, the less she wanted to hunt them.

"Oh, really? You won't hunt him now, and he's growing fond of you?" Aurora's eyes raked over Rosalind's dress. "Did something happen between you two? And would that something have anything to do with the state of your clothes, and the fact that you both smell like you've been rolling in dirt?"

"Don't be ridiculous," Rosalind said.

Aurora rolled her eyes. "I was wondering how long it would take. At least maybe now that she's taken the edge off, she can relax a little and listen to some sense."

"It wasn't like that," Rosalind said. "We were trying to take the ring off to see what would happen."

"I get you. I haven't 'taken the ring off' in weeks and it's making me crazy." Aurora sloshed her drink.

Rosalind blushed. "I meant literally. My actual iron ring."

Aurora's face brightened. "Thank the gods. Taking that off is the first good thing I've heard you say since I've met you. You're going to let Caine train you, like Ambrose said?"

Rosalind tightened her fist. "It's not possible. There's something wrong with the spirit. She was on fire, and so was I."

But Rosalind was almost starting to see Aurora's point. With a demon lord hunting her, she needed the protection of someone powerful. Once she exorcised this spirit, there would be no more Caine and no more Ambrose.

Only the Brotherhood, who wanted her dead.

Her chest tightened. What if Caine and Aurora were right? What if the Brotherhood would never accept her innocence?

Aurora glared at her. "You'll be on fire if you run back to the Brotherhood, but I don't see that stopping you."

"Caine already made that point." She sipped her cocktail, which tasted of straight whiskey. "What is this?"

"A Manhattan," Aurora said. "Except I forgot the bitters and that other stuff, so it's just the whiskey."

Caine's eyes darkened, his body tensing to a predatory alertness. In a fraction of a second, he was at the window. "There's a Hunter nearby."

Josiah? Spilling her bourbon, she leapt up and rushed to the glass. She peered into the dim harbor walk, but she could see no one out there.

Caine stared. "He's not that close. He's prowling somewhere around Essex street, a few blocks away."

"What if it's my Guardian?" she breathed. "I haven't been able to contact him. I destroyed my phone when I went through the fountain."

"What if it's your executioner?" Caine asked. "Or what if they're one and the same?"

This was her chance to find out what the Brotherhood were thinking. What if they'd changed their minds, and Josiah had come to deliver the news?

She dug her nails into her palms. "I need to see for myself."

"You must have lost your mind," he said. "You want to show yourself to a mage Hunter?"

"Yes. I need to find out where I stand."

He pressed his palm against the window, studying her. "I'm not letting you go alone. It's too dangerous. Also, I can't risk you passing along information."

"Fine." She had no idea how Josiah would react to learning that she was actually *living* among the witches. There would be no way to hide it if he met Caine, whose entire body hummed with magic.

"I'll have to erase his memory after," Caine added.

"He'll never agree to that."

"I don't need him to agree."

She rubbed the bridge of her nose. "This Hunter could tell me what's going on with my case. Maybe they've forgiven it by now." If nothing else, she needed to know if Josiah might sell her out. She'd rather find out now than later.

Caine nodded at the door. "Let's go."

Running a hand through her wild hair, she followed him out his front door, and they stepped out into the cool spring air. The wind rushed over her skin as they stalked down a street lined with weather-beaten wooden homes.

Cringing, she cast a quick glance at her outfit. *Ugh.* She looked like some kind of vagabond stripper. "With all the magical spells at your disposal, I don't suppose you have one that could mend a dress?"

His gray eyes roamed over her body. "Of course I do. But I don't see the point. You look perfect as you are now."

A blush crept up her chest. Of course he'd say something like that. He was an incubus.

They turned the corner onto Essex Street, and she hugged herself.

Maybe the outfit didn't matter. There were only two possibilities for Josiah. Either he had faith in her, or he didn't. If he trusted her integrity, he'd listen to her explanation—even if Randolph Loring and the rest of the Brotherhood wanted her dead.

Just outside a crooked yellow home, a figure prowled through the shadows. While most people wouldn't have seen anything in the dim light, she was used to spotting movements at night. *Josiah.* She'd recognize those broad shoulders anywhere.

He'd come for her. A smile brightened her face, and she broke into a run.

CHAPTER 17

She wrapped her arms around him, but Josiah wasn't looking at her. His eyes were too busy burning a hole in Caine. Josiah's fingers wrapped around his flamethrower. "Did this monster hurt you?"

She touched her Guardian's wrist. "Josiah. Relax. He's been helping me."

"*He's* been helping you? A mage?" He spat out the last word like a curse.

Caine's face registered only disinterest. "Not just a mage. I'm an incubus if that makes you feel any better."

Rosalind flinched. *Shut up, Caine.*

"An incubus." Josiah's face reddened. "I told you about them. Has he touched you?"

"No," she said. No need to tell him what happened in the woods. "But I'm so happy you found me. How did you know where I was?"

"No one in the Brotherhood will tell me anything. Apparently, they think I might help you. And they're right, of course. I had to spy on Randolph Loring when he was speaking to one of his associates in the Chambers. They know you're in Salem, but they don't know where. I've been searching the streets all night." A deep growl slipped into his voice. "And here I find you, with an incubus. He needs to be put down."

"You seem cranky." Caine studied his nails. "I suppose it can't please you to know that an incubus is protecting your girlfriend when you failed to do so."

Rosalind glared at Caine. "I'm not his girlfriend anymore. He's just worried about me." She glanced at Josiah. A vein pulsed in his forehead. He was about to lose it. "Look. Caine is a demon, and he's got an ego problem. But I knew him when I was a kid. And he's going to help us sort all of this out, so I can get my life back."

Josiah studied her carefully. "You spent your childhood with an incubus? How is that possible?"

She took a shaky breath. This was it. This was the point when she'd learn if her Guardian would stand by her, even with her magic-tainted background. "He explained to me the reason Randolph Loring thinks I'm a witch."

"What is it?" Josiah asked.

"I'm not from England. I was adopted from Maremount. My parents were… corrupted by magic. They did something to me, but I was only a little kid. I didn't have a choice. I don't even remember it. And when they realized what a terrible mistake they'd made, they sent me off to live with the Brotherhood. With Mason."

A streetlight glinted off his dark eyes, and he brushed a strand of hair off her face. "What did your parents do?"

"They summoned a mage's spirit into my body. I'm possessed with it, even now. As long as I keep the iron ring on, it dampens the magic, and I feel normal. The true god protects me. But if I take it off, the mage takes over my body. She can make me do things I don't want to. She can turn me into a mage and force me to cast spells."

Josiah paled. "Are you sure this is all true?"

"Twice now I've had the ring off, just for a few moments. I felt her invade my mind. It's horrible. I was splintering, and my skin was burning."

Josiah glared at Caine again. "And how is a demon going to help you rid yourself of magic? And, more importantly, *why* would he help you?"

"I'm just a caring person," Caine said, his voice flat.

"He's going to help me find a sybil in one of the demons' clubs, and she can tell us how to exorcise it. Caine will absorb the spirit into his own body."

"He's doing it to gain even more power," Josiah said.

She sighed. "Probably. And if he doesn't exorcise the spirit, he's stuck training me under the orders of the Vampire Lord. He seems to find the idea kind of tedious."

Josiah's eyes bulged, and she half-wondered if he was having a heart attack. "The Vampire Lord?" Clearly, she shouldn't even mention Bileth, or her Guardian would hurl up his dinner.

She touched his arm. "Once I'm free, we can explain it all to the Brotherhood, that I'm cleansed again, and they can stop hunting me, right?"

Josiah stared at her intently. "I'll see what I can find out. Maybe there's some sort of precedent in the Brotherhood's history of exorcisms. I can tell you that I'll fight for you."

Relief washed over her. "Thank you, Josiah." She'd nearly forgotten to ask him the questions that had been burning in her mind for the past twenty-four hours. "Josiah. Have you heard anything about the Brotherhood burning people?"

The vein bulged in his forehead again as he clenched his jaw. "Did this demon tell you that? You can't possibly trust him."

He wasn't answering the question. "Does that mean there are no burnings?"

"Of course there are no burnings," he shouted. "Do you think I'd be on board with that? And I'm not leaving you here with an incubus. It's out of the question."

"What are you going to do?" One of Caine's eyebrows raised, as if faintly interested for the first time. "Take her to Randolph Loring before she's been exorcised? I suppose from where you stand, it's better to risk burning her at the stake than leaving her with an incubus who might get his hands on her. One of these things would irreparably crush your ego, while the other would just be a bit unpleasant. All that ash and blackened bone to clean up."

Caine just *had* to make things worse. *Asshole.*

Josiah's nostrils flared. "You're not even human. You're a depraved beast, and you belong in the shadow hell."

"I'm pretty sure I could steal your woman from there." Caine's voice was glacial.

"Stop it, both of you." The wind rushed over her bare skin, giving her goose bumps. Of course they hated each other. What had she expected? "I'm calling the shots here. I'm the one with the demonic possession, and I'll decide what to do with it. I'm sticking with Caine until we can exorcise the spirit. I don't know what's happening after that, or if the Brotherhood will take me back or hunt me to the ends of the earth. But I do know I can't live with this monster inside of me. I've felt it, Josiah. And if I don't get it out, it will torment me until I die. Caine says he can help me, and I believe him."

Josiah's eyes were desperate. "I forbid you to stay with him."

Rosalind clenched her jaw. "You're not listening. There's nowhere else for me to go right now."

Her Guardian jabbed a finger in her face. "Do not let him touch you. I'm not messing around, Rosalind."

Was this really the most important issue right now? "I won't let Caine near me." She touched Josiah's arm, trying to mollify him. "Please try to find out about my case—if the Brotherhood will take someone back after they've been cleansed. Or at least maybe they'll stop sending goons to arrest me so I can go back to Thorndike."

"Of course I will."

"Are we done here?" Caine asked.

"We're done," she said. "You don't need to erase his memory, do you?"

"Like hell he's—" but Josiah couldn't continue the sentence, because his face had gone slack.

She whirled to find Caine chanting, his hand raised.

"Caine!" Frustration simmered in her chest, and she shoved him. "He needs his memories to help me. And it's not like he learned anything that Randolph doesn't already know. You don't need to erase his mind."

Dead-eyed, Josiah turned, walking jerkily as though warring with himself.

What the hell is Caine playing at? Anger coiled through her, and she yanked out the iron dust, aiming it at Caine. "Stop fucking with him. He's here to help me."

Caine cut her a sharp look, and lowered his hand. "I didn't erase his memory. I just wanted him to leave. He was annoying."

Anger exploded in her skull. What was it with men and needing to dominate others?

But Caine was no ordinary man. Not only did he have this natural impulse for domination, but he had the means to exert complete control over others through his magic. "You just wanted him to know that you were in charge."

"It's better for him if he understands that."

She narrowed her eyes, losing patience. "Do you have some kind of god complex?"

"He must understand that he can't fight me, or he'll end up dead. He's not really on your side, Rosalind. He's only helping you because he's scared of what will happen if you get too close to the demons."

"Of course he's scared. He doesn't want me to get hurt."

"That's not what I meant. He's scared he couldn't satisfy you the way a demon could."

"That's bullshit. Just because you're an incubus you interpret everyone else with your own disgusting flaws. And maybe your mind-blowing arrogance clouds your judgment. You just met him, and you already think you know everything about him, based on a two-minute conversation? And I didn't even get to the part about how you lied about the executions."

"My judgment is clouded?" Ice tinged his voice. "That's a bit rich coming from someone whose defining characteristic is chronic wrongness, mixed with a staggering dose of condescension. You and your insecure boyfriend are so preoccupied by evil that you've entirely overlooked all the Brotherhood's transgressions."

He was a genius at mixing truth with lies, and right about then she was seriously sick of his shit. "I wasn't wrong about a high demon coming into the bar, but you ignored me, because you think you know everything."

"It's hard for me to value the opinion of a staggering hypocrite. You belong to an organization that believes in their own superiority over others, that uses torture as a tactic. You are completely blind to your own faults. But, of course, knowing how you were as a child that's not surprising. A superiority complex is in your nature."

"What the hell is that supposed to mean?" She shook her head. He was trying to distract her. "Never mind. The point is, demons thrive on control over humans. Just look at what Bileth did to me. The Brotherhood have their faults, but we don't hurt people just for enjoyment. We're not sadists. We act strategically. If some people get hurt, that's unfortunate, but we don't take pleasure in it."

"Whatever helps you sleep at night."

Angry heat warmed her cheeks. "We don't take away people's free will and force ourselves on others. That's a demon thing, because you are abominations. Even if you compel yourself to be nice most of the time, the facade will crack eventually. You can't help forcing your will onto others. You're corrupted." A part of her needed it to be true— needed the monsters to be real, for the lines between good and evil to be clear. But the other part of her despised the words coming out of her own mouth. She'd called him an "abomination," and "corrupted," echoing Mason's favorite insults.

He flinched. For a moment, his features looked so human that she almost forgot what he really was, but in the next instant his pale irises darkened into a fierce, animal glare. Silvery light swirled off him, and his true demonic form emerged.

CHAPTER 18

*H*is cold magic crackled in the air, the power washing through her in waves. The dreadful ghost of dark wings rose up behind Caine, beating the air with a freezing wind. The temperature dropped by at least ten degrees, and Rosalind shivered. Apparently, she'd hit a nerve.

Her body buzzed with nervous energy, and Caine's dark gaze rooted her to the spot. If it came down to a fight between them, would she have *any* chance of survival, or would it only be a matter of time before he hypnotized her to bash her skull into the street?

An unnatural stillness overtook his body, like a beast of prey waiting to pounce. "If I'd wanted to take away your free will, this night would have gone very differently."

Nearby, heels pounded on the pavement, and Caine's gaze cut away.

Rosalind let out a long breath, and turned to spot a tall, blonde girl struggling to run in high heels.

She frowned, straining her eyes in the dim light. "Tammi?"

The charged air calmed, and Caine's eyes cleared as the air began to thaw. "Please tell me that's not another Hunter. I can't take any more of your kind."

"Rosalind!" Tammi sprinted over. Her blonde hair flew wildly around, and her usually impeccable makeup streaked her face. After nearly crashing into Rosalind, she stopped to rest her hands on her knees. "That's it," she gasped. "My life is over. My parents disowned me years ago, and now I can't go back to Thorndike."

Panic coiled in Rosalind's chest, and she touched her friend's shoulder. "Tammi, what's going on? What are you talking about?"

Tammi straightened, still catching her breath. "I can't believe I found you."

"Are you okay?" Rosalind asked. "*How* did you find me? What's going on?"

"I've been following Josiah from a distance," she said. "He took the train here, and I trailed after him, but I lost him in the park. He walks fast. And by the way, I know way too much about him now. Did you know he reads billionaire romances? Am I babbling? I'm kind of jacked up on the excitement. I'm basically a fugitive now. From the law."

Rosalind's blood turned to ice. "What are you talking about?"

"Did you say billionaire romances?" Suddenly playful again, a smile played about Caine's lips.

Tammi's eyes landed on the incubus. "Oh, hello."

"Tammi, meet Caine. He's a demon, but he's helping me solve my… issue…" She'd gloss over the fact that she'd just called him an *abomination.* Clearly that was a bit much—even if he had hypnotized Josiah. "Anyway, what do you mean you're a fugitive?"

"Okay. We *really* need to talk. You would not believe the shit storm that's been going on since you left. The Brotherhood have been hounding me ever since you disappeared. They yanked me out of my art history final and then pulled me in for a bunch of interviews in the Chambers. During the last interview, I was interrogated by some asshole named General Loring—"

Rosalind's mouth went dry. "Randolph Loring interrogated you? The red-haired guy? What did he want to know?"

"If I've ever seen you conduct magic. If you had friends who used magic. And what were the names of all your friends? And did I notice if there were any deformities on you, signs of corruption by magic? And if I wasn't going to be helpful, they were going to arrest me and try out some of their enhanced interrogation techniques. And I don't imagine he plans to put me in the women's prison. I got kind of a fanatical vibe."

"Your friend is a great deal more sensible than you are," Caine said.

Anger ignited Rosalind's nerves, and something else, too. Guilt, maybe. This was the other side of that swift justice she'd been so quick to excuse. "But you haven't done anything wrong. How could they arrest you?"

"They called it obstruction of justice." Tammi wiped some of the smudged makeup from her cheek. "They're a freaking cult. I know, because I was raised by crazy fundamentalists. The difference is that my parent's church had a broken neon sign outside of it, and the Brotherhood have taken over half our country."

A wave of grief washed over Rosalind, yet something inside her wanted to cling to the gleaming image she had of the Brotherhood. "It's a war between good and evil. We're fighting to destroy monsters, like the demon who tried to control my mind not that long ago." That was the Brotherhood's explanation when their methods were questioned. In a war between good and evil, they must do whatever it took to win. Only the weak-willed complained.

"Nothing is that simple," Tammi said. "You can't divide people neatly into two different categories. I know that better than anyone."

Something clenched tightly around Rosalind's heart. "But you can divide humans and demons. Think about everything they've done to us. I've seen the pictures of the children they murdered—the school in Boston, the vampire attacks in Maine. That's what evil is."

Tammi cocked her head. "Demons kill humans. Humans kill demons. It's the same thing."

"It's not the same thing. We're fighting back. The demons want to use us and control our minds."

Caine's eyes flashed. "The only reason Hunters don't use that particular skill is that they don't know how. Have you asked Aurora how she got those scars all over her back? They're from one of the Brotherhood interrogation rooms before she escaped. They used iron and hawthorn wood to carve her up. Fortunately, she's oddly proud of the scars. Demons are no more evil than humans. Some of them just happen to be a lot more powerful."

Guilt tightened her chest. "I didn't know Aurora was in there."

Tammi placed her hands on her hips. "I'm confused. You told me Caine was helping you, but you also seem to think demons are evil."

"She did just call me an 'abomination,'" Caine said morosely.

Rosalind sucked in a sharp breath. "Okay. That was… a little harsh, I admit. I just thought you were being controlling, but you're not completely evil."

"I'm sorry, am I interrupting a lover's quarrel?" Tammi scowled. "Because I was talking about the fact that I'm a fugitive. It's kind of a big thing for me right now. All I'm saying is, the Brotherhood want to throw me in jail and torture me until I crack. So if that's not evil, I'm not really clear how we're defining that particular term."

Rosalind's tears threatened to break through the surface. Tammi was right—Rosalind just hadn't wanted to admit it. She still thought Caine was an arrogant jerk, but she didn't want him tortured to death, and she definitely didn't want her closest friend thrown in the Brotherhood's prisons.

Sorrow welled in her chest. What about all the innocent people who'd gotten caught in the Brotherhood's crossfire? Or what about people like *her,* corrupted by magic through no fault of her own, hunted down like she was some kind of murderer? The Brotherhood's reach had spiraled out of control. Even she could see that now.

Yet she'd been a willing part of this system, refusing to let herself think about the casualties and the collateral damage. After all, in a war between good and evil, anything was justified, right?

"I can see how the Brotherhood's methods are… problematic." She glanced at Caine. For once, he was keeping his mouth shut. Maybe he understood that her whole future was collapsing before her. "I suppose my loyalty to the Brotherhood is just another example of my chronic wrongness."

"It's really the primary example," he said.

Grief overwhelmed her, and she fought to keep the tears at bay. She'd been thinking of the Brotherhood as her family for so long. But maybe they were a severely dysfunctional, abusive family—not unlike Mason. And if they were coming after Tammi, it was time to move on. "I won't go back to the Brotherhood. I still want to protect humans and fight the real monsters." Suddenly exhausted, she rubbed a hand over her forehead. "Maybe the monsters aren't as easy to identify as I once thought. Only the really horrible ones, like Bileth, and the mage inside me."

Tammi crinkled her brow. "The what inside you?"

Rosalind glanced at her friend. "I'm possessed. By the ghost of a crazy lady."

Tammi narrowed her eyes. "That's what they told me in the church I used to go to."

"Yeah, but mine is a real possession. I have access to magic, but I can't use it without being possessed by a maniac. And not only that, but if I take my ring off, my skin starts burning, like I'm standing in the center of an inferno."

Tammi's eyes widened. "Holy shit, Ros."

"There was one way around that, if I recall," added Caine.

"I can't throw myself at you every time..." Flustered, she let her sentence trail off.

Tammi twirled a strand of blonde hair around her finger, eyeing Caine. "That doesn't sound so bad to me."

A smile played over Caine's lips. "I told you your friend was sensible."

When she thought of taking off her ring, panic blazed through her nerves. "Forget it. How soon can we go see the sybil?"

"You still want to do that?" Caine asked. "Even though you're starting to understand that the Brotherhood are wrong about every-thing—including that magic is evil—you're still running away from your own power like a scared child."

The way he spoke to her still irked her. "Yes. I want the exorcism. But if you need to hear it, you're right about the Brotherhood, Caine, and I no longer have a future. I hope that makes you feel better. You obviously like control over things, and now another thing is going your way." Still flickering between anger and a burning disappointment, she felt a sudden need to lash out at him again. "Out of curiosity, does anything ever not go your way, or do you just seduce or hypnotize your way into getting anything you want?"

Anger flashed in his eyes. "That's quite the statement from someone noble-born and raised in a mansion. I'm guessing this is the first terrible thing to ever happen to you and that's why you have no idea how to handle it."

"You're guessing wrong."

Caine studied her with an unreadable expression.

Tammi cleared her throat. "This conversation is fun and everything, but I can't really go back to the Thorndike campus without getting arrested, so...."

Rosalind touched Caine's arm. "Can she stay with us? Please? Just until we get the spirit out. Then we'll figure something else out, and we'll get out of your life."

"Another human to look after?" he asked. "It's not a good idea."

"What else is she supposed to do?"

He traced his fingers over his jaw, considering her plea. "Fine. At least she's more sensible than you are."

Tammi wiped away another tear. "And then what? Where can we go that the Brotherhood won't find us?"

Rosalind turned to her friend. "It's going to be okay. Josiah said he'd help work on my case. I know the Brotherhood are unreasonable, but Josiah isn't. He said he'd help look for a precedent. If they're not after me, they'll stop harassing you."

Tammi crinkled her brow. "You think Josiah can do that?"

"I can't guarantee it, but..." Her sentence trailed off. *It's the only option we have* just didn't sound very reassuring. She glanced at Caine. "How soon can we go to Elysium?"

"We can go as soon as you want." His cold gaze met hers. "But if you want to come with me, you'll have to learn to act submissive for a few minutes. The only pedestrians allowed in Elysium are there as courtesans to offer pleasure to the demons."

She crossed her arms. "You have got to be kidding me."

CHAPTER 19

*R*osalind wasn't sure which was worse: the fact that she was willingly going into the demons' night club—pretending to be a courtesan—or the ridiculous outfit Caine had created for her, using magic.

After studying her body to take her measurements, he'd transformed her ragged outfit into a tiny white dress. Now, she tottered along the road in six-inch heels, practically tripping over her own feet.

For a demon associated with pleasure, he'd created bizarrely sadistic shoes. Still, as he'd pointed out defensively, the heels contained actual stiletto blades in case things got messy, and the hair sticks pulling her locks into an untidy bun were fashioned from large hawthorn spikes, inset with iron. Perfect for staking vamps if anyone got bloodthirsty. As an extra precaution, she'd collected a vial of iron dust, now tucked in her cleavage. This time, she wasn't going into a demon lair totally defenseless.

Elegant in her slinky leather dress, Tammi had already mastered the art of walking in heels. In fact, her new ensemble had almost brightened her morose mood. As they walked, she smoothed her hair over her shoulders.

Draped with stunning silver jewelry, Aurora took a swig of something from a flask—blood, probably. "You sure it's a good idea to bring the pedestrians into these places? Demons get hungry. Shit. I'm hungry."

"We don't have a choice," Caine said. "Rosalind will have to meet the sybil directly to get the oracle."

"What about Tammi?" Aurora asked. "She could've stayed at your house."

"No way I'm missing a demon sex club," Tammi said. "This is the only good thing to come out of this shit show."

Caine wore dark jeans and a form-fitting T-shirt that showed off his athletic physique and his tattoos. Rosalind couldn't stop her gaze from lingering over his body.

"I'll make sure nothing happens to them," he said.

Rosalind stumbled over a stray brick, then righted herself. "I can fight, too. I've come prepared with several weapons. It's almost like no one is impressed that I speared a high demon."

"You can't even walk normally," Aurora pointed out. "The spearing was obviously pure luck."

"It's these shoes," she shot back through gritted teeth. At this point, she was almost hoping things got rowdy so she could demonstrate her real skills—not that she had any desire to run into Bileth again. In fact, a shiver inched up her spine at the thought of him. "Speaking of my amazing skill at spearing demon princes, Bileth won't be there, will he?"

"No chance," Caine said. "These types of places, where light and shadow demons mix, are completely forbidden by the gods. A high demon like him can't know this place even exists, or everyone inside would be cast into the seven hells."

"If they're risking that, the cocktails at this place must be amazing," Tammi said.

"While they go off to find their sybil, I'm going to get you a thyme-tini," Aurora said. "They are to die for. Not literally."

"If this place is for all kinds of demons, what sort of demon runs it?" Rosalind asked.

"A valkyrie named Mist," Caine said. "Try to avoid her. She can be —difficult."

That was probably an understatement, considering valkyries were ancient demons of war and death. The aristocratic demonesses not only collected souls for the storm god, but they could instill other people with battle-crazed wrath.

Tammi flipped her hair over her shoulder. "How, exactly, does one act like a courtesan?"

Caine walked with his hands in his pockets. "All courtesans have been trained by Arielle, a succubus. She has taught legions of humans over the years, and she's an expert in seduction."

"So, we're supposed to be seductive?" Tammi asked.

"Yes," he replied. "And, if you can, try to give the impression of underlying desperation and maybe some emotional issues."

Tammi touched her lips. "Oh, I've got all that covered."

Goose bumps covered Rosalind's arms, and she hugged herself. "Acting seductive wasn't exactly part of my training."

Caine's eyes trailed over her body. "You'll be fine. Just—try not to speak."

"Thanks."

Aurora took another swig before wiping the back of her hand over her mouth. "And if anyone asks, you two human courtesans belong to us. I'm claiming Tammi, since she's less stupid than Rosalind."

Ouch. "There's that classic vampire charm again," Rosalind said.

They turned into a small, tree-lined square dominated by a stone church built to look like a castle. Their footsteps clacked over the pavement, and the only other sound was the wind rushing through maple leaves. Rosalind hugged herself tightly, trying to control the nervousness buzzing through her body. She was about to step into a nightclub full of monsters, dressed as bait, with only a few tiny weapons.

Steeling her resolve, she followed Caine to a heavy oak door. As he chanted a spell, she felt the sensual touch of his aura, trailing over her skin like butterfly kisses. The sensation was extremely distracting, and she tried to focus her thoughts on her weapons. They'd be the key to saving her life—and Tammi's—if any of these demons tried to devour them.

The door swung open into a packed dance hall, lit by glowing balls of light. Rhythmic music blared, the bass vibrating deep in her body.

Waves of magic unfurled from the creatures inside, skimming her skin with red, periwinkle, emerald, nectarine, and gold. She'd never been around so many magical auras at once, and they rushed through her chest. Shivering with their power, she tried to pick them apart. She had a sense that some belonged to powerful hellhounds and vamps. Others belonged to simple nature spirits: wood nymphs and tree sprites. She couldn't get a read on their intentions, but her overall impression was that the creatures inside this club were here for one thing: pleasure.

The auras were intoxicating, almost overwhelming. She reached out to anchor herself, gripping Caine's arm. At his touch, her mind cleared again, and she could feel only his clean, tingling aura caressing her skin. *Interesting.* She hadn't known you could block out other auras with touch.

Caine turned to her, his eyes trailing over her dress. "You look perfect."

Embarrassingly, her cheeks flushed, and she glanced into the club. Aurora and Tammi were already pushing into the crowd, heading for the bar, but a small group had gathered around Rosalind and Caine. The human women wore a vivid collection of jeweled hot pants, corsets, glittering underwear, and fishnets.

Apparently, her own outfit was rather conservative.

A green-eyed beauty at the front of the group ran a finger down her ruby red bra. She had a perfect hourglass figure, and her eyes were fixed on Caine. "Are you an incubus?"

"How did you know?" he asked with a smile.

The woman flicked her hair over her shoulder. "I've never seen anyone so hot in my life."

A smile played over Caine's lips. "You obviously have good taste. Seeing as you're someone who knows things, do you know where I'd find a woman named Sambethe?"

She smiled, obviously thrilled at the chance to help him. "Yeah. She's the weird gray-haired lady. She's always in one of the booths back there." She pointed to a far corner. "She just sits there, hammering margaritas."

Gold lights pulsed over Caine's smooth skin. "You've been most helpful."

The woman took a step closer, eyes hopeful. "Are you looking for a human mate? I've been dying to meet an incubus. We all have."

He slipped his arm around Rosalind's waist, the bass vibrating through his skin. "I've chosen my courtesan for tonight."

Courtesan. She was a Hunter, damn it. Or at least, she used to be, back when her life had a point. She schooled her face into a wide-eyed expression that she imagined courtesans wore, mouth slightly open. She tried to ignore the flash of self-loathing.

The blonde frowned, casting a critical eye over Rosalind's body. "Her? Why? What's so special about her?"

Rosalind opened her mouth to defend herself before realizing that she'd been about to extol her own virtues as a courtesan. So she did the wide-eyed thing again. *Gods, kill me now.*

A wicked grin flashed over Caine's face. "She's beautiful, obviously. But more importantly, she's mute."

Rosalind's mouth clamped shut. *Jerk.*

Disappointed, the woman strutted away.

A mute, adoring woman—that would suit him. She gave his arm a squeeze that she hoped hurt just a little, but before they could move beyond the door's entrance, another woman approached—this one clearly a demon. Seven feet tall, she wore a metallic gown that shimmered over her body like liquid mercury. Translucent black wings rose from her shoulders, a stark contrast to her platinum hair. Gray eyes bored into Rosalind.

Caine inclined his head. "Mist. Thank you for welcoming us."

"I haven't seen you here in a while," she said, eyes still lingering on Rosalind. "I see you brought a human. I trust you know the rules here. The only humans allowed must be courtesans, trained by Arielle in the art of serving demons."

"Of course," Caine said. "Arielle gave me this one as a gift. She loves to serve my needs."

Rosalind cringed. The urge to roll her eyes was almost overpowering.

Mist scanned the length of Rosalind's body, like she was assessing a prize horse. "She looks surprisingly strong for a courtesan."

Caine slid his arm around her waist. "I chose her for that reason. I don't like my girls to break when I play with them a little roughly."

Rosalind bit down a retort. *This excursion better be worth it.*

"Well. Enjoy yourselves." With a last, lingering glare at Rosalind, Mist slipped into the crowd like her namesake.

Caine held Rosalind's hand, leading her further into the club. She tried not to stare at the demons and humans grinding against each other, or the nymphs gyrating in cages, wearing sequined pasties.

A few human men stood in archways, offering up their necks to female vamps, or following after them on leashes. All fairly pathetic from the human side of things.

As she and Caine pushed further into the club, Rosalind caught a glimpse of two female water nymphs wrestling in a sparkly liquid, surrounded by a crowd of leering male onlookers. The demons certainly had more exciting parties than the Brotherhood—she'd give them that—but she was completely out of place here.

She focused on forcing her features into an approximation of a "doe-eyed" expression, though she'd never really known what that meant.

Caine turned, frowning. "What are you doing with your face?"

"I was trying to look seductive." She kept her hand locked in his, anchoring herself to his aura.

"You look terminally alarmed."

Frustration simmered in her chest. "I told you. Acting seductive wasn't part of my training."

He leaned in close, his breath warming her neck as his aura gently licked her skin. "I can, of course, help you with that—one of the incubus talents."

Warmth radiated off his body, and she glanced at his full lips, slightly open. Her eyes trailed down his arms. His skin looked gloriously soft, but the muscles under them hard as steel. She inched closer, overcome by a sudden urge to pull him in for a kiss. *Get a hold of yourself, Rosalind. He's using his incubus magic.* "I didn't say you could do that."

"Do what?"

"Use your incubus seduction talents."

He whispered into her ear. "I'm not using any magic."

Her pulse raced. He *wasn't* using his magic, or she would have felt his aura strengthen. She swallowed hard, trying to gain mastery of herself. She wasn't going to fall for the charms of an incubus. "I knew that."

"You've got that seductive look now." He brushed a strand of hair out of her face. "Shall we continue on?"

She tried to ignore the heat tingling through her body. She was here for the sybil—not to enjoy herself.

As they approached the booths at the back, a human woman in an emerald-green corset held a tray over her head. A single margarita stood on it.

Caine touched the woman's arm, and she turned, flashing a stunning smile at him. Flame-red hair cascaded over her shoulders. "Hi, gorgeous."

"Hello. I need this drink." He plucked it from the tray.

"Oh." The girl's face crinkled in confusion. "It's for Sambethe."

"I'll bring it to her. And while you're at it, two Manhattans for us. Dry."

Looking him over, she licked her lips. "I'll be right there."

Caine threaded his fingers through Rosalind's, and wove his way to a darkened corner of the club.

In a booth, lit from above by glowing golden orbs, sat a white-haired woman in a stunning, coppery gown. Her frosty hair contrasted starkly with a smooth, creamy complexion. The woman's milky eyes landed on the margarita in Caine's hands, and she jabbed a finger at it. "Is that for me?"

"I brought it specially for you. My name is Caine." He took a seat across from her in the booth, and Rosalind followed, squeezing in next to him so she could anchor herself to his aura.

Sambethe snatched the drink from the table, extending a long, pointed tongue to lick the salt off the rim.

Caine leaned in close, peering at Sambethe from below his lashes. "Is it true that you are very discreet with your oracles?"

"Don't try to flirt with me, boy. I'm far too old for that." She lifted her drink. "You keep these coming, and I'll do whatever you want."

Smiling obsequiously, the red-haired waitress rushed over to the table, her tray laden with two Manhattans.

Caine leaned back in his seat, eyeing the redhead. "How did you get those so fast?"

She glanced away, blushing. "I took them off another waitress's tray. I thought you were more important."

"Well done," Caine said, snatching them from her tray. "Now, we'll need five margaritas."

Sambethe chuckled. "Now we're talking."

The waitress hurried away, and Rosalind turned back to the sybil. Was she still supposed to pretend to be mute? This was getting old.

Sambethe drained her cocktail. "We'll need a private space."

Caine closed his eyes, whispering an incantation. As his aura swirled through Rosalind's body, a black curtain closed around the booth's opening.

Sambethe's milky eyes swerved to Rosalind. "You can stop pretending to be a courtesan. I know what you are."

Rosalind's chest tightened. *Is that a warning?* "But you won't tell anyone?"

Golden light shimmered over the sybil's skin. "What do I care? I'm seven thousand years old. Ask your question."

Rosalind took a long breath. "I have another soul in my body. A mage's soul. If I take off this ring—" She lifted her hand. "—I plummet into a world of hell. It's like my mind is fracturing, and my body is on fire. I want to know how to fix it. How do I get the mage out of me?"

Sambethe held Rosalind's gaze for an uncomfortably long time.

"Hold on to your cocktails. This could get messy." She slid her own empty glass out of the way and climbed onto the table.

After throwing back her head, the Sybil began to sway and jerk. Her arms twitched to the rhythmic pulsing of the club's music. Then, with a frantic snarl, she hunched down to a crouching position, her head weaving around in the air like a snake's, her muscles taut. Her eyes locked on Rosalind's before she reached out to grip Rosalind's head. A powerful aura coursed through Rosalind like a mountain wind, clean and ancient.

"Blodrial's child, split in two." Her deep voice howled like a gale. "The mage, tormented by fire. Nyxobas's servant made her burn." Her head lolled, eyelids fluttering. "On a full moon, find the hawthorn grove. The spell belongs to Blodrial. Coat yourself in iron, and the incubus will chant. He will take on the extra soul."

Relief flooded Rosalind. They had an answer—a solution at last.

Sambethe threw her head back, sighing. She wasn't done. "The incubus will take on the extra soul. Three souls in one body. Two that don't belong together, shattered by broken love. Someone must be sacrificed. The incubus's body will sicken and die."

Horror slid through Rosalind's bones. *The incubus's body will sicken and die.* If Caine took on the soul, he would die? That was supposed to be the solution?

Sambethe's muscles relaxed, and she slid back into her seat just as the black curtain disappeared.

Rosalind dropped her head into her hands as panic clenched around her lungs. This had been her one hope.

Caine took a gulp of his drink. "Just to clarify, I will die if I take on the other soul?"

The sybil lifted her empty margarita glass, shaking it. "Seems that way."

Devastated, Rosalind trembled. This was it—her life was over. She lifted her eyes to the sybil, fingers tightening around her drink. "Is there another possible solution? Couldn't the soul go into the afterworld, where it belongs?"

The waitress sashayed over to the table, lowering the tray of margaritas, and Sambethe grabbed another. "No. It's stuck in a body until someone dies with it. That's your parents' fault."

"What about another person?" Rosalind asked, desperation eating at her.

"Who would want to take that on? You could force someone, I guess." The sybil rose, licking the salt off her drink as she shuffled out of the booth. "You kids have a lot to talk about. I'm going to dance."

The news knocked the wind out of Rosalind, and she could hardly breathe. She was ruined. And, with a wave of dread, she realized Tammi's life was destroyed too. Unless Rosalind turned herself in, the Brotherhood would hunt them both to the ends of the earth.

Her fingers tightened around Caine's arm. *Corrupted. For good.*

He eyed her warily. "I can feel your panic. You need to calm down. The other demons will be able to smell your fear."

She shot him a dirty look, then gripped her Manhattan and chugged it down in one go. "Of course I'm freaking out. I'm cursed. And Tammi's life is ruined too."

He leaned in close, his breath warming her neck. "You can't make a scene here. You're supposed to be a courtesan."

Anger burned through her body. "What difference does it make? My life is over. I might as well let one of these monsters drain my blood now. Then maybe the Brotherhood will stop coming after Tammi."

Caine narrowed his eyes. "Your life is not over, but it will be if you don't get a hold of yourself."

The weight of the sybil's revelation crushed the air from her lungs. "Tammi and I have nowhere to go. We can't escape the Brotherhood." She scanned the room, her eyes landing on the flame-haired courtesan, eagerly massaging the feet of a horned demon. "We'll have to become courtesans for real. I'll have to rub demon feet."

"Don't be ridiculous," Caine said. "You'd make a terrible courtesan. You're going to become a mage."

"You don't understand." Her pulse raced, and she couldn't keep her voice from rising. She needed to get a grip, but her world had just completely crashed down on her, and she could no longer control herself. She waved a hand at the crowd. "All of this disgusts me. Demons use humans for their own pleasure, and I don't want any part of the magical world."

"For a smart girl, you have awfully simple analyses of complex situations."

He wanted to distract her with his moral equivalence again. "Using humans comes easily to you, doesn't it? I saw how you treated Josiah. It's just in your nature. You were born to feed from humans for sustenance."

"And you were apparently born to make my life hell by recklessly invoking the wrath of every demon you encounter. Including me." He took a slow, steadying breath, clearly trying to control himself. "You need to stop talking. I'm going to help you calm down, not because I want to control you, but because it's the only way you'll get out of here without one of these demons murdering you." He whispered, and his aura wound around her skin before pulsing through her chest, relaxing her muscles.

Some of the panic ebbed, leaving behind a gnawing emptiness. The world as she'd thought she understood it was gone—the divisions between good and evil, the order of things, her place in it all. None of it had meaning anymore, so what was the point of her life?

Trying to ignore the hollowness in her chest, she rose.

Caine stood, taking her by the hand to lead her from the club. The lights flashed garish shades of red and orange, pulsing over gyrating dancers. The thumping bass rattled her bones, and she tried to push out all thoughts of the evil lurking in her body.

She caught a glimpse of Tammi and Aurora dancing, losing themselves in the music. How was she going to break this news to her friend?

The question didn't linger in her thoughts long because, in the next moment, the valkyrie stepped into Rosalind's path, her cold eyes scanning Rosalind's body. "You're not a real courtesan. You don't behave like one."

Dread rushed up Rosalind's spine, mixed with an odd sense of relief. Maybe this encounter would end it all.

"I'm a novice courtesan," she said, her voice hollow.

In a blur of white and copper, the valkyrie lunged, long fingers clamping tighter on Rosalind's throat. Mists's aura, cold and furious as storm clouds, flooded Rosalind's body.

As the aura filled Rosalind, she surged with icy rage, and a deep desire to hurt anyone around her. *Kill.* She slammed her arms through the valkyrie's grasp. She ducked to avoid a punch, then brought her fist up hard into the demon's ribs, hoping to snap something. Caine pulled her back, wrapping his arms around her.

With Caine's arms around her, her body began to calm again, her pulse slowing. What the fuck had Mist just done to her? The demon wasn't lunging again, but her gray eyes locked firmly on Rosalind, glowing with a stormy fury. From the growing crowd, Aurora and Tammi looked on, eyes wide.

"Get Tammi out of here," Caine shouted to them.

The valkyrie's steely stare had Rosalind rooted to the spot. "I knew you were a fighter." Her eyes flicked to Caine. "You brought a human warrior in here?"

Caine began whispering a spell. His aura swirled through Rosalind's chest, stroking her skin. Heat shot through her core, and she could think of nothing but his warm, strong body pressed up against hers. She had a sudden desire to spin around and kiss him hard. *What the hell?*

The valkyrie seemed to be thinking the same thing. As she approached Caine, cheeks flushed, her finger trailed down her chest. She licked her lips.

That was when Rosalind understood: Caine was using his incubus magic, and she'd been caught in the crossfire. Right now, she wanted nothing more than to run her hands all over his bare skin.

Mist stepped closer, a low moan escaping her lips—until her gaze landed on Rosalind again. A look of confusion crossed the valkyrie's beautiful face, and she clamped her eyes shut, shaking her head. "Don't use your magic on me, incubus." Her voice was a low growl, and when she opened her eyes again, savage rage contorted her features.

She ripped Rosalind from Caine's embrace before raising her clawed hands, transfixing the pair in place.

A pale blue light flowed from her hands, freezing Rosalind's body.

"Let's see which of you lovers is stronger," the demoness said.

As the light hit Rosalind's body, the valkyrie's aura slammed into her like a hurricane wind. A cold, deadly battle fury coursed through Rosalind, so powerful that her limbs trembled. Anger blinded her like a white light, and she clenched her fists, fingernails piercing her palms. She wanted to break through bone and gristle, to slice through necks with a sword.

I need to kill.

Her vision cleared, and before her stood the one person that she'd been waiting for. Pale gray eyes, tousled brown hair—his whole existence was a lie, a grotesque monster wrapped in a veneer of beauty. A devil sent to test her faith.

His gaze bored a hole in her. "I should have known how you'd turn out. You've always believed you were born better than others."

"I am better than beasts like you." Underneath it all, he was just like the other demons—a beast of prey, waiting for the right moment to rip her to shreds.

Her eyes lingered over his perfect form, stoking her anger further. *All beautiful things must die.* She wanted to crush his stunning body like a rose in her fist. She pulled the dust from her cleavage, ready to burn him.

When his eyes darkened to a deep black, and a ghost of wings rose behind him, dread whispered through her—but her fear only ignited her rage. Dark shadows curled around his muscled body.

Rosalind stared into the face of wrath itself, ancient and venomous —the face of floods and storms, trembling earth and mountains of fire. Something in the primal part of her brain shrieked at her to run, but her body would no longer obey. She needed to kill.

She was no longer Rosalind. She was a great queen of war.

With a lightning-fast gesture, she uncorked the dust, flinging it at the incubus. Primordial ferocity coiled through her, ready to strike its prey. She belonged to Rage now.

Caine growled—a deep animal sound that rumbled through her gut, chilling her blood. But she wasn't running away until she'd stopped his heart.

She'd snuffed out his magic in the most painful way possible.

He snarled, "Good. Now you know that when I win, it will have been a fair fight."

"I'll remind you of that when I'm ripping your ribs from your back," she said in a deep voice, one not quite her own. "I'll give you real wings, and maybe you can fly to hell with Lilu."

She slipped the thin hawthorn stake from her hair, just as the incubus lunged. He gripped her hands, forcing them down to her sides so she couldn't stab him. Her body pulsed with fury, and she head-butted him, listening to the delicious *crack* as she broke his nose. He dropped her hands.

A smile curled her lips. As she lifted her stake again, his hands flew out a second time, clamping down on both her wrists in a crushing grip. He was going to break her bones, but the anger dulled her pain.

Caine leaned in close, whispering into her ear, "Give up, little girl. You're outmatched."

Asshole. Rage burned through her, and she tried to kick him in the groin, but he pinned her arms to her sides with impossible strength. She strained against him, kicking at his shins, desperate to crack his bones. But instead of doing any damage, she struggled helplessly as he lifted her body in the air, as easily as if she were weightless. Her breath caught in her throat as he hurled her across the room.

She slammed against the dance floor, toppling out of her ridiculous shoes. The fall knocked the wind out of her. She gasped for air, fighting to catch her breath as Caine closed in. As soon as he closed the distance between them, she swung her legs in a wide arc, taking him down.

With a shrill battle cry, she leapt on top of him, raising the stake. His hands flew out, clamping onto her wrists, and he flipped her over, pinning her arms over her head. He pressed himself on top of her, and a low growl escaped his throat.

His eyes trailed down her chest. Something else was overcoming him—not battle fury, but another type of need. His distraction was a vulnerability. He lowered his warm mouth to her neck.

She arched her back, marshaling her strength to fling him off her. He slammed against the ground, and then she hooked her leg around him, straddling him.

His hands still gripped her wrists, but a sense of victory bubbled through her. *I am in control.* She leaned closer, momentarily distracted by his earthy scent, then bit into his neck as hard as she could. Her prey instinctively released his grip on her wrists. She lifted her arms high, and plunged the stake into his heart.

CHAPTER 20

*T*he rush of fury flowed from Rosalind's body, like the wind over the ocean. She stared down at her blood-soaked hands gripping the hawthorn stake. Caine's shocked eyes had returned to gray, and he glanced down at his chest.

Panic clenched her heart, and she ripped the stake from his chest. Her mind spun with horror, and she pressed down on his heart, as if she could staunch the flow. *What have I done?* Blood seeped through her fingers. Caine took a shuddering breath.

Lilu fluttered overhead, squawking, before flying for an open window.

If Caine were fully human, he'd be dead by now. But even so— she'd staked him with iron and hawthorn. *Seven hells, what have I done?* Both could be lethal to a night demon. Pressing on his chest, her hands shook uncontrollably. "Caine. I'm so sorry."

Heels clacked over the floor, and she looked up to find Mist, standing over her arms folded. The valkyrie appraised Rosalind with a clinical stare. "I see you're the stronger fighter. I guess that answers my question. Now get out of here before I slaughter you, too. Take his body with you."

Rosalind heaved a sob, and tried to lift Caine from the ground, her body shaking. At the sound of his pained gasps, tears stung her eyes. As she wrapped his arm around her neck, Aurora burst through the door, Lilu trailing behind her. *Thank the gods, the raven went for help.* It only took an instant for Aurora to hurtle through the crowd and snatch up the incubus. Carrying Caine, Aurora rushed for the door in a blur, and slammed it open to the night air. Rosalind ran after, her breath ragged.

By the time Rosalind got outside, Aurora had laid Caine out below a maple. The vamp frantically cleared the dust off Caine's skin while Tammi looked on.

Caine rested against the trunk, blood pouring through his fingers, and grief pierced Rosalind.

Tammi's hand flew to her mouth as she took in her friend. "Rosalind, are you okay? You're covered in blood."

"It's not her blood." Aurora flashed her fangs. "It's Caine's. What the bloody hell happened in there? Why is he covered in your dust, and why isn't he healing?"

Rosalind's hands shook, and she couldn't seem to make her voice obey.

She glanced at Caine, whose eyes were fixed on hers. He was still conscious, at least, though his skin had paled.

He took a deep breath. "We had a fight. She won."

Aurora snarled, "You did this, human?"

"The valkyrie," Caine said. "She imbued us with battle rage. It wasn't Rosalind's fault."

"A hawthorn stake," Rosalind managed.

Aurora's eyes widened. "This human girl *won?* You must've been holding back."

"I got distracted," he said, his voice choked. "She looks pretty when she's twisted by bloodlust."

Aurora turned her furious gaze on Rosalind. "Fix it, then. He needs a human female."

"What do you mean?" Rosalind knelt by Caine's side, holding her hand over his heart, as if her fingers could heal a shredded artery. Her hands shook wildly. *She'd* done this to him. "I don't know how to fix this. I don't know how to stop—"

"He's an incubus," Aurora cut in. "He heals through sexual contact."

Rosalind's mind raced. "You want me to have sex with him?"

"It doesn't have to be the full thing, but at least kiss him. It's not that complicated. Just hurry up."

Tammi raised a hand. "I'll do it."

Rosalind met Caine's eyes, her chest flushing as she thought of his warm, protective arms around her in the club, and his aura pulsing through her body. "No, I'll do it."

"Good," Aurora said. "We'll look out for that valkyrie arsehole, or Bileth, or anyone else whose wrath you managed to incur in the past few hours." She pulled Tammi away, leaving Rosalind alone with Caine.

Rosalind glanced at the blood pouring from his wound. "Does it hurt?"

"What do you think?"

"Sorry."

"Do you want to heal me? Tammi seemed willing."

She glanced at the blood on her own hands, her heart fluttering. "Yes, of course. I'm so sorry."

"Not your fault. You do understand how this works, don't you?"

"Yes. And I understand it's purely practical. It's how you heal. It doesn't mean anything." She wasn't sure why she needed to say that, but it was a reminder to herself more than anything.

Moving closer to him, she slid into his lap. As she slipped her arms around his shoulders, he gazed into her eyes, pupils dilating. Her heart hammered against her ribs. *Don't forget what he is, Rosalind. Deep down, he's a predator, and he can't be trusted.*

But even if he wasn't human, his proximity alone heated her body.

His breath quickened, and he slid a hand around the back of her neck, his touch sending a jolt of energy through her. At that moment, she almost forgot he was a demon. She only knew she wanted to run her hands over his smooth skin.

His eyes darkened to a deep abyss of midnight black. As his aura strengthened, it fluttered over her skin in a thrilling rush. He slipped his fingers into her hair, and in the next moment his warm, soft lips were against hers. His magic rolled through her body, making her tremble with need. When his tongue brushed hers, heat shot through her belly.

He kissed her hungrily. One hand gripped her hair, the other tightened around her waist. All panicked thoughts flew from her mind, and there was nothing left but Caine.

As she curved into him, his kiss grew more sensual. He lightly traced down her spine with his fingertips, and she gasped.

He folded his arms around her and lifted her from the ground. As he pushed her against the tree, she wrapped her legs around him. She threaded her fingers into his hair, pulling him in for another kiss. Instead, he teased her—nipping her lower lip before brushing kisses down her neck. Her body burned, and she wanted more. She wanted all of him.

"Rosalind!" Tammi shouted.

Caine's face turned away from her. She could have killed Tammi right then, but thank the gods it didn't go too far.

"We were just finishing the healing," Rosalind said, her legs still wrapped around Caine. His aura caressed her skin, and she needed to get the hell away from him before this got really embarrassing.

Something about the stricken look on Tammi's face pulled her attention from Caine, but it was the person standing behind Tammi who sent a jolt of panic through Rosalind.

Josiah stood with his hands at his weapon belt, his eyes blazing with pure loathing.

CHAPTER 21

With her dress hitched up around her waist and Caine's body pressed against her, it took a few moments to register what was happening.

Josiah gripped a can of iron dust, and before anyone could stop him, he unleashed a spray.

With Rosalind wrapped around him, Caine's muscles tensed. The dust burned the aura off his skin. It must be excruciating pain. His heart beat against her, strong and rhythmic—at least she'd healed him.

Rage contorted Josiah's face. "You're not going to control my mind again, incubus. I look forward to watching you burn."

Rosalind unlocked her legs from Caine as he lowered her to the ground, and she tugged down the hem of her dress. "Josiah. You found us." She tried to steady her voice.

"Rosalind. I came back to tell you about my progress. I've been on the phone all night, begging General Loring to consider your case, and I think he was starting to listen." His voice cracked. "And then I track you again, and I find you with your legs wrapped around a demon, letting him use you as his plaything. There I was, like an idiot, telling General Loring that you were pure. That you were going to get an exorcism."

All at once, her encounter with the sybil came flooding back to her. Caine's kiss had been a distraction, but it didn't erase the fact that she'd just learned her life was over. There was no way to get the exorcism she so desperately needed.

"Josiah—" she began.

"I told you to stay away from him. I should've seen what the other Hunters told me. You're nothing but a whore."

The disgust in his voice sent a flash of anger through her. This wasn't just about Hunters and demons, about good and evil, about fighting for what was right. Caine, for all of his arrogance and obnoxiousness, had been on to something: Josiah wanted control over her body.

She crossed her arms. "The incubus needed healing."

"He's a predator, you idiot," Josiah said. "He's using you."

"He's helping me, and I stabbed him in the chest. Anyway, why do I need to explain myself to you? For one thing, you broke up with me, and for another, you were supposed to be acting as my Guardian—not my stalker."

"He's an animal." Josiah took a step closer, flecks of spittle flying from his lips. "You should never have been anywhere near him, but you couldn't resist throwing yourself at him."

"I've been stuck with the demons out of necessity." Fury ignited in her heart. "That's what happens when the Brotherhood wants to throw you in one of their interrogation rooms. You end up fighting for your life and joining forces with the demons." *Seven hells.* She'd just officially declared herself on the side of the demons, to a high-ranking representative of the Brotherhood. Was this really happening? She was still hoping to wake from the world's longest nightmare.

Josiah stepped closer. "I should have known your softness was something other than compassion. It was merely your repulsive, corrupted soul, drawn to the other abominations like a bitch in heat."

She wasn't scared of him. Right now, loathing overwhelmed her. "I should have never let you convince me to do what we did, Josiah. If my soul has been corrupted, it was because of your influence."

"What we did saved lives," he spat. "*Human* lives. Thousands of them—though I can see you don't actually care about those."

"I need you to tell me if it's true." She searched his face. "Are the Brotherhood burning people?"

Josiah's eyes bulged, and he enunciated each of his words like he was talking to a particularly dim child. "They're. Not. People. The animals deserve to burn, and so do their accomplices."

Horror burst through her mind, and her knees nearly gave way. The realization that she'd been fighting on the side of sadists hit her like a punch to the gut.

And now, they were coming for her and Tammi.

Caine stepped in front of her, blocking her with his arm. "She's heard everything she needed to hear. Get out of here before I relieve you of your heart."

Red tinged Josiah's face, and he jabbed a finger at Rosalind. "You think this freak is going to look after you? That he's not just using you like a disposable toy?"

She had no idea what Caine really thought, but that wasn't the point. She belonged to no one—not to the demons or the Brotherhood. As anger roiled in her chest, she pushed past Caine. "I don't need people looking after me. And just so you know, I'm stuck with this witch's soul. I'm corrupted, just like Mason always said, and I'm going to stay that way. So the Brotherhood will have to hunt me down, but when you run back to the General Loring like a loyal little dog, you tell him he better stay the hell away from Tammi."

Rosalind wished desperately that Caine hadn't been covered in dust, or he'd be able to use his magic to make this all go away. He could have hypnotized Josiah into forgetting all about Tammi.

What had Caine called her? *A staggering hypocrite.* She was beginning to see his point.

Josiah's hand twitched by his weapon belt. "You want me to deliver a message to Randolph Loring from the demon's whore."

She cocked a hip. "Call me whatever you want, but you can tell Randolph I have the power of a psychotic mage in my body, and I'm not afraid to use it." At least, part of that was true.

She was declaring war on Randolph Loring, and her mind buzzed with an intoxicating mixture of thrill and terror.

Josiah's mouth tightened with barely controlled rage. "You think your evil possession is enough? It didn't work out so well for Miranda."

Caine stepped forward again, and she tensed with irritation. She could fight her own battles. She knew how the Brotherhood worked better than he did, but Caine's body was suddenly alert.

"The Brotherhood found Miranda?" Caine asked, his voice a growl.

Rosalind shook her head, trying to keep up. "Wait. Who the hell is Miranda?"

Josiah's eyes bored into her. "Interesting. Apparently your new lover didn't want to mention her."

Caine's voice was glacial. "I suggest you get out of here before I tear your spine out through your throat."

Josiah's nostrils flared. "You can threaten me all you want, but none of you will last long. The Brotherhood have been slaughtering demons like you for millennia, and we're stronger than ever. The angels will glory in your demise when the smoke from your body reaches the heavens." He glared at Rosalind, and the vein throbbed in his forehead. "I look forward to getting my hands on you in the inter-rogation room, and when Miranda burns, I hope to light the match."

In a fraction of a second, Caine's hands clamped around her Guardian's neck, and Josiah's eyes bulged.

"You will stay away from Rosalind and Miranda, or I'll make you wish for death." The wrath in Caine's voice chilled Rosalind to the core. "Perhaps I should grant you that now."

With a hammering heart, she watched as Caine tightened his grip around Josiah's throat. *Caine is going to murder him.* For a moment, she almost wanted to watch the life seep out of her former Guardian. After all, Josiah would report all this information to the Brotherhood, feeding them her location, and Tammi's too. It would bring the Broth-erhood down on them like a plague of locusts.

But she couldn't stand by and watch him die. She'd cared for him once, and he'd cared for her, too.

A horrible, garbled sound escaped his throat.

"Caine." She grabbed his arm. "Please stop."

Caine's eyes met hers, and he loosened his grip. Josiah gasped for breath, stumbling back—right into Aurora. The vampire lifted him by his collar, baring her teeth before she yanked his cell phone from his pocket. She crushed it in her fist. "Run along, and we'll let you live, for now. You're a soldier, aren't you? You should know when to retreat." Growling, she hurled him out of the park, and he landed on the pavement with a loud thud.

Josiah slowly pushed himself up from the ground, shuffling over the pavement without sparing a glance. Even he knew there was no way to take on an incubus, a vamp, and an angry-ex girlfriend at the same time. As he slunk away, his shoulders slumped. She almost felt bad for him. At least, until she remembered what he'd said about looking forward to interrogating her and burning people.

Tammi's face had gone pale. "So I guess a reconciliation with the Brotherhood is out of the question."

Rosalind's chest tightened. "Honestly, we're screwed. I'm so sorry I got you into this, Tammi."

"You're not screwed," Caine said. "As long as you're willing to work with Ambrose, you'll have his protection."

Tears pricked Rosalind's eyes. She'd just declared herself on the side of the demons. "I don't know that I can do... whatever it is that he wants me to do. And what about Tammi?"

"I'll tell Ambrose she's your assistant. She'll get a salary." Moonlight skimmed over Caine's skin. "We'll work out the details later, but right now we need to hide the both of you before Josiah alerts the Brotherhood. I would use magic to get us home faster, but that twat glitter-bombed me."

"Let me handle the teleportation." With a determined look on her face, Aurora stepped out of the park—and directly in front of a car. A blue Toyota screeched to a halt, and Aurora flashed her fangs, smacking a hand on the hood. "We need a ride." She glanced at Caine, jerking her head at the car. "Get in."

Caine rushed over to the car, with Rosalind and Tammi close behind. As Tammi hopped into the back seat, Caine pulled open the door, beckoning Rosalind inside. An empty car-seat took up the middle, and she had to squeeze in on his lap.

The woman in the driver's seat turned to them, her dark eyebrows furrowed. "Um, are you all vampires?"

Aurora slid into the front seat, slamming the door shut. "Just me. Take us to the end of Hardy Street."

"Please take us there, Ma'am," added Rosalind from the back seat. Her bare feet rested on a collection of discarded sippy cups.

The woman frowned. "Call me Marisa. Now, I don't mind working with vampires. In fact, I run a demon-human ally group to improve inter-species community relations. But I will not drive if you're not wearing a seatbelt."

Caine's arms folded around her. "She'll be fine. Trust me."

"Seatbelt," she repeated, her voice stern.

"Yes Ma'am." Caine reached around, pulling the seatbelt to strap the two of them in.

"Marisa," the woman corrected.

As the car took off, Rosalind leaned into Caine. She could feel his heartbeat through his clothes, and his warm breath against her neck. She resisted the urge to nuzzle his throat. She had no idea if that kiss had actually meant anything, but she was probably stupid to even consider the possibility. He *was* an incubus, after all, and he was obviously deeply untrustworthy.

Tammi let out a long breath. "I'm going to need to process everything that just happened. I don't suppose I can call my Thorndike counselor about this. I'm just a little confused about what the fuck is happening with my life."

"You and me both," Rosalind said. Her mind still reeled from that awful encounter with Josiah. While Caine's warm body was a welcome distraction, she couldn't stop her thoughts from running wild. For one thing, she'd just learned that the Brotherhood were as bad as the demons. And then there was the valkyrie fight, the kiss, the threats from Josiah…

Exhausted, she rested her head against Caine's shoulder. "Imagine if my parents had never done this to us. We'd been living happily in Maremount still."

"You would have been living happily. I would not."

"Why not?"

"That's a long story. Some time I will tell you all about Maremount."

"Now that I'm apparently on the side of the demons—" Her voice broke. "I should probably learn about my homeland."

Caine took a deep breath, and she sensed something was roiling through his mind. "If you're on the side of the demons, do you still think we're evil?"

She gazed into his pale eyes. Did he actually care what she thought? "I guess the idea of good and evil isn't as clear cut as I once thought it was. I'm sorry I called you an abomination. That's what Mason used to call me, and it just popped into my head. I don't know why. He's a complete asshole, and you're not an abomination."

He let out a sigh, his breath warm against her skin. "I wouldn't go that far," he said, his voice barely audible.

Whatever he meant by that, now wasn't the time to get into it. "Also I'm sorry about the stabbing thing."

"If it gets your legs wrapped around me again, I might risk another stake to the heart."

She almost smiled, but something else whispered through the back of her mind. *Miranda.* Both Josiah and Caine seemed to know who she was, and Caine actually seemed to care about her.

Unable stop herself, she touched his chest, feeling his body's heat through his shirt. "Caine. Who is Miranda, and why did Josiah say he wanted to watch her burn?"

His muscles tensed. "It's complicated. I don't want to get into that now."

His constant evasions irked her. "Will you at least tell me what Ambrose wants with me?"

"Yes. We're pulling up to my house."

"Hardy Street!" Marisa said. She pulled over by the empty green field.

After thanking Marisa, Rosalind stepped out of the car, her thoughts whirling. Whoever Miranda was, both Caine and Josiah seemed to find her important, and they weren't letting Rosalind in on their secret.

CHAPTER 22

Still barefoot, Rosalind paced the warped wooden floor inside Caine's house.

It only took a few seconds for Tammi to find his whiskey decanter. She poured herself a glass. "I was an art history student. Less than three semesters till graduation."

"I know," Rosalind said. "Everything is a disaster."

Tammi took a sip, then wiped the back of her hand across her mouth. "Maybe we need to move to France or Vietnam or something."

Aurora leaned on a granite counter in the open-plan kitchen. "You both are starting to spin out. Do you need a snack or something?"

Rosalind *was* starving. But it wasn't just her hunger—her mind was a raging storm, and she could hardly concentrate on one thought at a time. "What I need is for the Brotherhood to drop my case and to leave Tammi alone."

Tammi knocked back her drink. "I don't blame you. I blame that stupid cult. Your ex-boyfriend is an *asshole*."

Aurora rifled around in the cabinets. "The two humans are losing it. I'm making them a snack of food."

Rosalind's fingernails pierced her palms. "We need a plan. Caine, what exactly is Ambrose's grand plan?"

He leaned back, stretching out his arms on the sofa's back. "Ambrose's plan is for us to take on the Brotherhood. With the combined auras of two powerful mages, we can find a way to get past their security systems."

Dread whispered through Rosalind. He wanted her to *take on* the Brotherhood?

Aurora sliced through the top of a tin can with a knife, spilling juice all over the counter. "Have some faith in Caine. He's a brilliant military strategist. Ambrose made him a Duke."

Tammi ran her fingers fretfully through her hair. "Is there another plan? Like, one that doesn't involve provoking the wrath of an ancient society of lunatics?"

Rosalind stared at Caine in disbelief. "Just the two of us are supposed to topple their security systems."

Aurora dumped a pile of mandarin slices onto a plate. "You're more powerful than you know."

Caine ran a finger over his lower lip, studying her. "We break into the building, and then we free the captives, so the sadists you once worked for don't burn them to death. Aurora can tell you all about their torture techniques."

Seven hells, the torture. She couldn't let this happen to more people, not after what she'd done with Josiah. Maybe this was her chance to atone. She knew what it felt like to burn now, and couldn't subject others to the same fate—not if there was something she could do about it. "I'll do it. I'll help you free them."

Caine let out a long breath. "Good. And now I have to teach you magic. We haven't got much time."

Rosalind stopped pacing, folding her arms. "Before what? Is there a specific deadline?"

"I have a good friend in there," Caine said. "Two, actually. And I don't want them to die."

"I don't really want Rosalind to die," Tammi said. "Do I get a vote in this?"

"No," Aurora said, spearing mandarin slices with toothpicks.

Two friends. At least one of them had to be Miranda, but she didn't need to ask about that now. And the other—she could only hope the other was not an incubus too. *Oh gods, what if the demon I interrogated was Caine's friend?*

All at once, a wave of guilt slammed into her. She'd been trying to keep the memories at bay, but she couldn't hold them back anymore. *I've done terrible things.* She slid her hands over her face, and her chest heaved with a sob. *Such a simple set-up for an interrogation. A chair, cinderblocks, cloth, and water.* She suppressed the urge to be sick. *It could have been Caine.*

Caine clenched his jaw. "There's no need to cry. You're supposed to be a warrior, and I'll make sure you don't die."

Josiah had looked her straight in the eye and told her she needed to hurt the incubus. He'd sworn the demons were planning a massacre to rival the Boston Slaughter, and that the only way to stop it was to break the monster's will. Josiah had said it was her duty to force the incubus to confess everything he knew until the Brotherhood could stop the carnage. It was the life of one monster sacrificed for the lives of thousands of innocent people. Simple math.

But half the stuff Josiah had told her was a lie. She wanted to smash his smug face in.

She lifted her eyes. "That's not why I'm upset. You don't understand. I'm not a good person."

Confusion flitted across his features. "What are you talking about?"

She was half tempted to confess everything. "I thought demons and mages were all evil. I never would have agreed to the things I did if I'd known the truth. Maybe some demons deserve to die, but it's not like we took the time to find out." Every second they stood here was another moment wasted. "Why are we wasting time? We need to get in there now before anyone else gets hurt."

Tammi raised her hands in the air. "You've officially lost your mind."

Aurora handed Rosalind a plate of mandarin slices and raisins, each speared with a toothpick. "You can't just go in there now. You sound like a nutter. Have a sodding snack and a nap, or you'll be no good to anyone."

Caine caught her eye. "The whole building is rigged with iron dust. That means I can't use my magic until we disable the sensors. There are scanners to block our exit, and machines rigged with stakes."

He was right. With all the defense systems at the entrances and the ID scanners, no supernatural creature could gain access to the building.

At Aurora's insistence, Rosalind forced herself to eat a raisin. "And how do we disable all that?"

"We have a plan," Aurora said. "I learned about the building's design during my escape, and I'm guessing you can fill us in on what we don't know."

Caine shrugged. "Basically, I want to blow up half their building and disable their dust."

"Why do you need magic for that?" Tammi gripped her plate of speared fruit. "Why not just use explosives?"

"Too messy," Aurora said. "We might kill the people we're trying to free. We want to save all the captives we can."

Rosalind swallowed a mandarin. "How do we make sure no one from the Brotherhood gets killed?"

Caine furrowed his brow as though this question was absurd. "We don't."

Rosalind closed her eyes. "I don't want to kill people. That's the whole point."

Caine eyed her. "Am I wrong in thinking that just yesterday, you were trying to kill a vampire?"

"Yes, but not everyone in the Chambers deserves to die." She shot an uncertain glance at Aurora. "I know you were tortured, and you have every right to want to hurt the people who did that to you, but most of the novices don't know about that. Most of them just thought we were stopping demons from massacring humans."

The vamp glared at her. "Caine can hypnotize the novices to leave the building. Then the two of you need to blow up the front entrance, the great hall, and the offices. All of this means you need to take off your stupid ring and start learning Angelic, like you should have started yesterday."

Rosalind froze, the full implications rolling through her mind. On the side of the demons, she'd have to abandon the only thing keeping her remotely sane—though, given her whirling emotions, maybe it wasn't doing its job so well anymore.

She closed her eyes, trying to lock her terror into her mind's vault. Her atonement would depend on her ability to master her fear. No longer hungry, she set the plate on the table. "Let's get started now."

CHAPTER 23

*A*s they stood in Salem Woods, the wind rushed between birch and ash leaves, and Lilu circled overhead.

Caine stood across from her in the grove. Before they'd left, he'd created a new outfit for her—black jeans and a long-sleeved shirt. Of course, because he was Caine, they fit her like a second layer of skin. But at least if the spirit wanted to jump his bones again, Rosalind wouldn't end up with a skirt around her waist.

Caine looked down at her. "When you take off the ring, I want you to imagine the mage's aura inside your mind. Concentrate on trying to condense it smaller, so it no longer takes over your whole body. I want you to imagine it as a ball of light, right here." He touched her sternum, and her skin sparked at his touch.

"Is that how you stay sane?"

"Eventually I figured it out," he said. "Are you ready to start?"

"I thought we would learn some spells first."

He shook his head. "The mage already knows the spells. I'm going to prompt her to think of them, and then you need to draw on her knowledge."

"What if she tries to assault you again?"

"I don't mind."

"I don't want it to happen." Sure, Caine was beautiful, but it wouldn't be *Rosalind* kissing him. It would be the mage. On top of that, she knew better than to get involved with an incubus. "What happened outside Elysium was just strategic so you could heal. And anyway, we're here to learn magic so we can save the captives, not to get distracted by having fun."

"Fine. If you're worried about what the mage will do, I can tie your arms and legs."

Just like Mason used to do when he beat the crap out of me. "No way."

"It would help keep you safe. If she wants to do something against—"

"—I said no. The whole idea of it makes me want to stab you with another hawthorn stake."

He glanced at her shaking hands. "Gods below. What's wrong with you?"

Shit. Why was this coming up now? She didn't need to dredge up her screwed up childhood with Caine. "It doesn't matter. I'm just overtired. Let's get on with what we need to do."

"Fine. I'll keep control of the spirit. And when we get home, you need to eat and sleep, because you seem like a mess."

"It's been a rough night." *Understatement of the year, right there.*

"You're a warrior. Your enemy has made a move, and its time for you to fight back. Muster your mental strength and take off the ring." He closed his eyes, marshaling his patience. "Please take off the ring when you choose to."

She twisted the ring around her finger, trying to work up the nerve. "If I seem like I'm burning, will you touch my shoulder or something? It seemed like your aura helped stop the pain."

"Of course."

After closing her eyes, she yanked the ring from her finger, shivering at the tumultuous presence of the aura. It swirled through her body, skimming over her skin with a tingling and buzzing. Tendrils of green unfurled in her mind like spectral ferns.

Rosalind tried to curl them up again, forcing them together into a small sphere, but the aura wouldn't obey. In the heavy spring air, her body vibrated with exertion.

The spirit was winning, forcing her to move, making her open her eyes. She stared up at the stunning incubus. Pearly moonlight filtered through the oaks, dancing on his smooth skin, glinting in his pale eyes.

The spirit wanted Rosalind to run her hands over his strong, tattooed arms, his perfectly muscled chest. But it wasn't just how he looked. Something in his aura drew her closer, like a gravitational pull. The spirit *knew* his aura.

She took two steps, slipping her arms around his neck, reveling in the warmth coming off his body. She thrilled at his sharp intake of breath when the spirit pushed Rosalind's body against his.

She studied his face, and the ethereal silver aura spiraling skin. Another soul lay inside the incubus, one the spirit knew well. "Richard."

His muscles tensed, a hint of confusion in his beautiful eyes. "Cleo." He gripped her forearms. "Rosalind. You need to control the aura."

His touch sent thrills through her body, but the spirit looking out through her eyes didn't like the name *Rosalind*.

"That's not my name," she warned, her voice laced with venom, no longer her own.

His grip tightened. "Rosalind. I need you to gain control. Close up her aura."

The aura surged through her body, and her voice came out low, strangely accented. Her arms tightened around the incubus. His body was rigid against hers, and she tried to pull his head down for a kiss, but his perfect lips were out of her reach.

He swallowed hard, closing his eyes, and took a steadying breath. "Rosalind. Crush the aura."

The spirit forced her to stand on her tiptoes, but she couldn't reach his mouth. "Richard. I missed your touch, but I like your new body better."

Caine pulled her arms from his neck, gently pushing her back. "Rosalind. Get control of the aura."

The green tendrils spiraled through her in whirlwinds, and she tried to get control of them, but the spirit was stronger. It began speaking in Angelic, and Rosalind's body hummed with the growing aura, a thrilling rush of power.

At her words, the incubus's eyes widened, and he spun her around, wrapping his strong arms around her. He clamped a hand over her mouth to silence her.

She didn't like being pinned. Rage burned through her nerves, and she bit into his fingers, drawing blood. He released her, and she broke into a run through the forest, the damp air whispering over her skin. This was Cleo's true home, her world before the evil ones snatched it away from her.. *How would you like the flames, Rosalind?*

The spirit forced her to stop and hold out her arms. Somewhere inside, Rosalind screamed, trying to regain control. The scent of burning flesh filled the air, and in the next instant, searing pain ripped her apart. Flames blazed from her limbs, and she loosed an agonized scream.

It must have been only a few moments before a pair of masculine arms surrounded her again, cooling the flames.

In the next instant, Caine slipped the iron ring on her finger, and Rosalind let out a long, shuddering breath. Her body trembled. She'd only been on fire for a few moments, but the ghost of her torment still whispered through her nerve-endings, reverberating in her skull.

"Fire," she whispered.

"I'm sorry." His voice was so quiet she hardly heard him.

Her breath rasped, and he held her from behind, his skin smooth over muscled arms.

Exhausted, she melted into him. "She called you Richard."

"I never knew my spirit's name before," said Caine. "But as soon as she said it, I recognized it."

"You said the name Cleo."

He took a deep breath. "Richard knew her. There was some connection between them. I'm guessing they were lovers."

"She was starting to chant a spell. What did it mean? Why did you stop her?"

His arms loosened. "An aphrodisiac," he said, his voice husky. "If she'd finished it, I wouldn't have been able to control what happened next."

"She has a one track mind."

"Can you blame her? It's probably been hundreds of years since she inhabited a human body. She obviously wants to make the most of it."

She stepped out of his arms, turning to look at him. "That was a total disaster. She *wanted* me to burn. She was vengeful, and I had no control over her. I don't think I've ever failed at anything so shockingly. I'd rather fight the Brotherhood with weapons."

"That won't work."

"*This* won't work." Her nerves were frayed, the memory of pain still whispering through her. "I can't control her. She's too powerful."

"It was only your second try. Aurora was right. You need to rest and eat. You won't be able to gain control of anything when your body is falling apart."

She dug her palms into her eyes, trying not to think of what might be happening to the captive incubus. "We need another plan."

CHAPTER 24

$\mathcal{B}$y the time they reached Caine's house, the rising sun stained the sky a pale coral, streaked with steel. Caine opened his front door into a quiet house.

In his living room, someone had drawn the curtains closed, and only a faint glow filtered in through the edges, dimly lighting the living room and kitchen.

In the darkness, Rosalind could just make out that Aurora had fallen asleep on the sofa, while Tammi dozed in an armchair, wrapped up in a blanket.

Caine trod quietly into the kitchen, motioning to one of the chairs that stood by the marble island. "Have a seat. I'm going to make you some food."

He lit a candle, and it cast a wavering light over the countertop.

Her stomach grumbled, and she wasn't going to argue with that declaration. "You said you didn't know how to cook."

"I lied." He pulled a bowl of eggs and another of ricotta from the refrigerator.

At the sight of actual human food, her stomach rumbled. "What are you making?"

He cracked an egg into a bowl. "Something you may remember from Maremount. Or not, in all likelihood."

She straightened, suddenly alert. "I don't remember the food. The one thing I remember clearly is your eyes."

He paused for a moment, his hand hovering in the air, clutching an egg. "You remember me? Are you sure?"

"I remember a boy with eyes your color. They're quite memorable." Her gaze roamed over his muscular arms, and an uncomfortable thought twisted in her gut. "You promise you weren't my stepbrother?"

He worked the eggs and ricotta into a batter. "Would it bother you if I was your stepbrother?"

He loves making me uncomfortable. "You know it would be weird. I mean, after I healed you."

He opened a metal canister, scooping out a measure of corn flour into the batter. "You can calm your fluttering heart. I'm not your stepbrother. The few remaining incubi are enslaved in Maremount. All the succubi have been killed. In fact, the entire city is built around the Lilitu fountain, where the last remaining succubus was killed. Her petrified head spews the town's drinking water. A few incubi were kept around for the pleasure we provide. You and I were not of equal standing in the Atherton household."

"Atherton." It struck her suddenly that she hadn't ever known her own birth name. "Rosalind Atherton."

"*Lady* Rosalind Atherton. It has a nice, noble ring to it."

"And you were some kind of *slave?* I don't remember a boy in chains." That didn't suit his imperious nature at all, though neither did the fact he was cooking her breakfast. She watched as he pulled out a steel skillet, turning on the burner to melt a hefty dollop of butter. "How could they keep you enslaved?" He was far stronger than any human.

He shot her a perplexed look. "Magic. I wore an iron collar, charmed by a powerful sorcerer. Your father." He salted the batter before pouring a thin layer into the hot pan.

Her stomach turned. Every new tidbit she learned about her

parents only made her dislike them more, but she was still desperate for more information. This was the first conversation with Caine where he was actually willing to divulge information. Still, she knew if she pushed too far, he'd shut down. "If you're half-incubus, does that mean your father was a full incubus? Did you know him?" she asked. *Shit.* That was probably too personal.

The look he shot her iced her veins. "Just because I'm making you food and teaching you magic doesn't make us friends. You need to keep up your strength so we can achieve our objectives. That's all."

"I didn't say we were friends," she shot back, too exhausted to come up with a better retort. His rebuke stung, though she had no idea why. He'd already warned her not to trust him, and he'd offered nothing more than an uneasy alliance. That was all. "I get it. You're very mysterious and you don't like personal questions. So tell me about my own parents. Why were they so eager to experiment on us?"

He flipped her cakes onto a plate and slid them across the table. "They wanted you to be the most powerful mage Maremount had ever known. It was a time of turmoil for the city, and they wanted to take advantage of it."

"Lovely people," she said drily. She picked up a fritter, biting into it, her mouth exploding with the rich, buttery tastes. "Mmmmm."

Thunder cracked outside, and the room darkened further. She glanced at Caine, his skin warmed to a deep gold by the candlelight. "Tell me, is Maremount still in turmoil?"

He leaned on the countertop, holding a fritter. "No. A war broke out a few years ago. Eventually, the monarchy was overthrown."

"Were you involved in the fighting?"

A muscle worked in his jaw. "Is there a reason you need to know that?"

She swallowed a mouthful of her breakfast. "Right. No personal questions. But do you know what happened to my parents?"

He paused for a long time, and she almost wondered if he hadn't heard her. "We didn't stay in touch."

Considering they'd ruined her life in the quest for power, she wasn't sure she even wanted to see them. Still, she felt an overwhelming urge to ask Caine what had gone so horribly wrong that her parents had shipped her off to the Brotherhood. But the last time she'd tried to pose that question, his eyes had turned black, and he'd nearly murdered her. She took a large bite of the corn cakes, and her mouth rejoiced. "This is the most delicious thing I've ever eaten. I think I could die happy after this."

His face changed, and he flashed a brilliant smile. She'd never seen him smile so genuinely before, and his beauty nearly took her breath away.

Rosalind swallowed. "Was I nice to you and the other servants?"

He quirked an eyebrow. "You used to dump things on the floor just to have the servants clean them, and you only referred to them as *Servant*, never by name. But you were only four, so it was hard to take you seriously. Especially since you couldn't pronounce anything properly, so it sounded like you were calling them *swabents*."

She shielded her eyes with her hands. *Oh, gods. I was a nightmare.* "Please tell me you're joking."

Something struck her about the way he'd phrased that. He'd referred to the servants in the third person. Was he not among them?

He swallowed a bite of his fritter. "Truthfully, you were a horrible, spoiled brat."

"I'm so sorry."

"It doesn't matter to me. You were only four."

Imagining herself ordering around servants, even as a little girl, made her cringe. "Maybe it's a good thing my parents had me sent out of Maremount so I didn't turn into a full-blown asshole." She finished her breakfast in silence, and glanced down at her crumb-littered plate. "I'll clean up."

"No need," he said. He whispered a spell, and crumbs disappeared off the dishes.

Thunder cracked outside, and a hard rain battered the house's old wooden exterior.

Rosalind rose, stretching her arms over her head. "Where should I sleep?"

He beckoned her to a stairwell. "My room is upstairs. Since I'm feeling generous, I'll let you take my bed." As they climbed the stairs, he shot her a sly look. "Don't worry. I'll sleep in the study."

It was such a big house, she was surprised there was only one bedroom. "Are you sure?"

"You need proper rest if you're going to learn magic."

Right. It was all part of meeting their objectives.

At the top of the stairs, he led her into a hallway. Dark wood arched above, and sharply peaked windows overlooked sailboats bobbing in the stormy harbor. Lightning speared the water, followed by a loud crack of thunder. The sky was black as smoke.

She shivered. "There's only one bed in the house?"

"No one else has ever been here. There was never a need for more than one bed. I do all my entertaining in my other apartments."

"I guess with all those vampire women trying to kill you, you'd need a secret hideout." She almost felt a pang of jealousy, but that was stupid. He was an incubus, and there was nothing real between them —not even friendship.

"Precisely."

She followed him past several closed doors to the end of the hall. "What about human lovers? Isn't that where you draw your energy from?"

"They want to kill me too. Only, human women aren't much of a threat." He stopped to open a large oak door, glancing back at her. "Though you did put up a good effort with the hawthorn stake. I've never had a woman come that close before."

He held open the door, and she stepped into a tidy room. A four-poster mahogany bed took up most of the hardwood floor. The soft gray blankets and pillows looked inviting, and she wanted to sink into them. Black curtains framed tall windows. Rain hammered the glass panes.

Lanterns hung from the ceiling, carved with stars and moons. Bookshelves covered one wall, crammed with faded tomes. A painting of an imposing stone castle hung on the other.

Rosalind pointed to the picture. "That doesn't look like the castle in Lilinor. What is it?" She was stalling. For some strange reason, she didn't want him to leave. In fact, she really wanted to slide her arms around his neck again and find out exactly what he did to drive all those women so crazy.

"You don't recognize it? It's the Throcknell Fortress in Maremount. It dominates the city."

"Have you ever been inside?"

He stared at the painting. "No."

So much for that conversation. It obviously had some meaning to him, but—of course—he wasn't up for sharing.

"Okay," she said. "I don't suppose you have an extra toothbrush?"

He walked over to a small table by the window, set with a pewter cup and pitcher. "Another thing you don't remember from Maremount." He poured a pale green liquid into the cup, handing it to her. "Charmed sage water. All you need to do is drink it."

She took a sip, rolling the clean taste around on her tongue. He pulled the cup from her, sipping from it before setting it down. "Don't worry about our attack on the Brotherhood. I'm not going to let anything happen to you."

"What if you can't control it?"

"Don't say that. It's not a good idea to dwell on your worst fears right before you sleep."

"That's not my worst fear. I don't want to to die, but my worst fear—"

He stepped closer, touching a finger to her lips. "Not before you sleep. You'll have bad dreams. I'm a priest of the night god. I know these things." He lowered his hand, studying her. "And anyway—if you solidify your worst fears in your mind, they can be used against you. Some demons are just as awful as the Brotherhood have said."

She took in his smooth skin, and the lean, muscular physique molded by years of leading Ambrose's army. It was no wonder women lost their minds over him. Part of her wanted the release he could give her—the quieting of her raging thoughts, a short respite from her most disturbing memories. She wanted to feel his calming aura flood her body, and more than that, she wanted to feel his perfect mouth on her skin.

But getting involved with an incubus was a terrible idea, and he'd just said it himself: he wasn't her friend. He was only working with her because it was what Ambrose wanted, and because it served Nyxobas's goals. If she started to think of him in any other way, she'd only turn into another one of his jealous maniacs.

And more than that, she could never forget the darkness lurking inside him. Even if she'd changed her mind about the sharp divisions between good and evil, demons were fundamentally *different* from humans. A part of any demon's mind would always see humans as toys to manipulate and use.

"Get some sleep." As he walked to the door, he whispered a spell, and the curtains closed, shrouding the room in darkness. He gently closed the door behind him.

She crossed to the bed, pulling off her boots. She still wanted to know who Miranda was. *Caine's girlfriend, probably.*

She slipped out of her pants, leaving them in a crumpled pile on his floor. *No point mulling it over now.* She was a warrior, and had a job to do.

She slid into his bedsheets, pulling the duvet tight around her shoulders.

She closed her eyes, and the pounding rain lulled her into sleep. Her mind offered up an image of Bileth, stalking through Salem's winding streets on a pale, white horse, hooves clopping against the pavement. As he approached, a drumbeat sounded, slow and deep, rumbling through her gut.

Rosalind stood with Caine, holding his hand in the cool moonlight, while Bileth walked closer, his eyes burning red. When he grinned, Rosalind felt horns grow from her head, her teeth lengthen. A knife appeared in her hand. Bileth howled, and forced Rosalind to jam the knife into Caine's neck, plunging in and out until blood soaked her body.

Her eyes snapped open, and she gasped, her heart pounding. Caine had warned her about dwelling on her worst fears before sleep.

What if Caine knew the incubus she'd hurt? Her pulse raced. She'd have to tell him. A part of her wanted to tear through the hallway and confess everything, but she was terrified of what he'd say.

Taking a deep breath, she closed her eyes again. This time, she imagined Caine's strong arms around her, his aura caressing her skin, soothing her muscles. His bed smelled like him—the heady scent of fresh earth after a rainstorm. She shouldn't let herself think of him like that, but she was too exhausted to fight it. The sensation of his presence was so vivid that it almost seemed real, like his perfect body was pressing against hers in a warm embrace, and she melted into the illusion.

She drifted off to the sound of the rain battering the windows and steep-peaked roof. She dreamt of a hawthorn grove, with a ground blanketed by falling petals.

CHAPTER 25

a banging noise jolted her from her sleep, and she sat up.

"Rosalind." Caine shouted through the dark, his voice urgent.

She threw the covers off, suddenly alert, and jumped out of bed. "What's going on? What time is it?"

He sparked the candles, and for a moment, his eyes trailed over her bare legs. "Bileth is near, and you need to leave before he finds you."

Her pulse raced. "Where is he?"

"He's a few streets away. The house is invisible to him, but he's scented us somehow."

"What time is it?"

"Nearly ten at night. You slept for fourteen hours." He was dressed for battle—sleek, black clothes, dark armor over his chest, and a sword slung over his back. Smaller blades glinted from holsters strapped to his legs and arms.

She crossed to the window, pulling aside the curtain. Moonlight glinted off the harbor.

"Can he get in here?" she asked.

"No, but if he figures out where the house is, he can draw us out with fire. I'm going out to speak to him, but I want you to get out of here with the other girls."

Something about his phrasing irked her. *Get out of here with the girls.* "I'm a trained fighter, you know. I don't need to run away from demons."

He stared at her in disbelief. "You're the one he's hunting. If he gets anywhere near you, he'll torture you to death. I need to keep him as far away from you as possible. He'll forget about you eventually, but right now he wants to impale you. Repeatedly."

Even though her vision of stabbing Caine had only been a nightmare, guilt still weighed heavily on her, crushing her chest like a load of rocks. On top of that, she was starting to feel strangely protective of the incubus. "I'll hang in the shadows or in the house, but I'm not leaving you alone. You were too closely matched last time for me to feel good about it. I'll only step in if I think you're about to die."

He inhaled deeply before handing her a knife. "Fine, but you must promise to stay inside. I'm still hoping to fix this with diplomacy." He eyed her carefully. "What, exactly, do you know about high demons?"

Hardly anything. When encountering a high demon, novices were just supposed to run. "I know they're immortal. Speaking of which, can I have more blades? I don't feel like one is enough."

He pulled two more daggers from his holsters, and a thin stiletto. "There are ways of killing them, but the weapons need to be charmed. To deliver a death blow, you need to be a powerful mage. I fit the criteria, but let's hope it doesn't come down to that. If we killed Bileth, we'd have far worse problems than the Brotherhood."

"You mean we might have eighty legions of demons hunting us."

"Precisely." His eyes trailed up her legs again, lingering on her tiny black underwear. "As much as it pains me to say it, you should probably put on some clothes."

"Oh." She hurried over to her pile of clothes, slipping into her pants and boots. She slid two of the blades into her boots, and the stiletto into her belt. "Where are Tammi and Aurora going?"

"They're taking a boat to Great Misery Island. I know a sorceress there who is quite fond of me. She should be able to keep them hidden for now."

Footsteps pounded up the stairs, and within seconds, Tammi's flushed face was in the door. "Rosalind. Let's go. We're taking a sailboat from the dock."

She shook her head. "I'm staying here. Caine might need me."

Tammi's face blanched. "Are you high? I haven't heard such a terrible idea come out of your mouth since you decided to dress as a slutty sheep for Halloween."

Rosalind scowled. "You already know I hunt demons. Why is this surprising?"

Tammi stared, her voice incredulous. "You hunted pixies who screwed up the plumbing."

"Is that true?" Caine arched an eyebrow. "And the slutty sheep outfit, too?"

Rosalind looked between them, her resolve growing. She projected her voice, imbuing it with as much authority as she could. "I'm not going to argue with you two. I'm staying. I'm the one who caused this situation, and I'm not letting Caine take the fall for it by himself. And then I'm going to help tackle the Brotherhood. Got it?"

Caine glanced at Tammi. "We'll meet you on the island. Aurora knows the way."

Tammi pointed at him, scowling. "You make sure Little Ho Peep comes back in one piece." She turned and hurried down the hall.

Caine approached Rosalind, standing so close she could feel the heat coming off his skin. He brushed his knuckles against her cheek, studying her face. "You're brave for a noble-born girl, but please stay in the house. You have a tendency to screw everything up by making stupid decisions. I'm even firmer in that belief now that I've heard about the slutty sheep costume."

She tightened her fist around the knife hilt. "You need to stop talking or I'll stab you with one of your own weapons."

"Wouldn't be the first time. Would you heal me again?"

A deep, rumbling noise resonated through the house, shaking the walls and rattling the windowpanes.

"He's outside," Caine said. "I'm going. Please stay in here." He wrapped his fingers around her knife-holding hand. "If he gets past me somehow, use this."

He turned, stalking down the hall, moving silently as the wind through the trees.

She closed her eyes, taking a deep breath and trying not to think of her nightmares. *I can't dwell on my worst fears.*

She stepped into the hall and peered out the window, staring at the moonlit street outside Caine's house. Mounted on an ivory horse—just like in her dream—Bileth strode into a streetlight. Tendrils of his red aura curled off his skin like smoke. His steed's eyes blazed red, hooves clopping slowly over the pavement. He carried a scythe slung over his enormous, bare back. Curling tattoos covered his pale, muscular body, and horns swooped back from his forehead. She almost thought she heard the low rumble of a drum…

At the sight of him, fear stole her breath.

Caine pushed open the front door and strode toward the high demon. Bileth halted and dismounted, nostrils flaring. When the demon's feet landed on the pavement, the ground trembled, and shock waves shuddered through the earth.

Caine held up his hands, as if trying to placate Bileth, but the high demon pulled his scythe from his back before charging. Bileth swung, but Caine lifted his forearm, blocking the attack. In a blur of move-ment— so fast Rosalind's eyes could barely track it—Caine maneu-vered behind Bileth, pinning the demon's arm behind his back. As Caine pushed Bileth's neck down, forcing him lower, the high demon lost his grip on the scythe. Caine leaned into him, whispering in his ear, no doubt trying to placate him with promises of submissive courtesans.

But Rosalind knew what the high demon really wanted. He wanted *her.*

Bileth's body vibrated with fury, skin blazing bright red with his aura. When he flung out his arms, he threw Caine back in a blast of magic. The incubus landed hard on the pavement; in the next instant, he was on his feet again, his silvery aura whirling around him.

What the hell is he supposed to do? He was clearly the stronger fighter, but he couldn't kill Bileth, which meant he was at a severe disadvantage. Diplomacy clearly was not on the table, and neither was an all-out battle with Nyxobas's crony.

Bileth snatched his scythe from the ground, and Caine slid his sword from his scabbard, blocking another swing. The two demons whirled and parried in an intense blur of movement, their blows ringing out into the air. Metal sparked in the night air.

Bileth's aura burned hot around him, and he intoned a spell. His voice rang through the air like the knell of a hundred discordant church bells. As he spoke, Caine's spine arched, and his body lifted into the air, suspended in apparent agony. Caine dropped his sword, and a look of intense pain contorted his beautiful features. His eyes turned black as pitch while his primal instincts took over.

Bileth was torturing him. Caine's fingers curled, his body shaking.

Horror spread through her. This was her fault, and she needed to help him. Clutching the iron blade, she sprinted through the hallway, thundering down the stairs. She had no plan beyond ripping Bileth's attention away from Caine, and her seething fury leant her courage. She slammed through the front door, heart pounding.

Bileth whirled, locking his red eyes on her.

"Bileth," she said. "I think you were looking for me. What the fuck do you want?"

His lips curled in something like a smile, and he beckoned her closer with a long, taloned finger. She gritted her teeth, but his noxious red aura seeped into her body, infecting her limbs. She clamped her eyes shut, imagining a clear sphere that forced out the red tendrils. Her pulse raced with the effort. When she'd pushed his magic out, she threw the knife.

The blade pierced Bileth's shoulder. He roared, and the sound slid through her bones. In the next instant, his hands were around her throat, pressing hard on her airway. In about six seconds, her neck would be crushed. "You filthy, human animal. You were born to serve," he whispered.

Panicking, she strained her foot up until she could yank a knife from her boot. She slammed it hard into his arm, and he lurched back, roaring. She reached for the other knife, ripping it from her boot.

A burst of powerful magic from Bileth surged through her veins, overtaking her. It seeped into her limbs, claiming territory in her muscles too fast for her to block it out. Her stomach churned as Bileth compelled her to stalk over to Caine.

Caine's large eyes landed on her, black as smoke from a funeral pyre. Her heart squeezed in her chest. Bileth would force her to stab Caine.

This is my nightmare come true. I'm going to murder him.

Her arm reared back, ready to plunge the knife into Caine's neck, and dread ripped her apart.

Caine's silver aura exploded from his body, and in the next second his hand darted out to grab her arm, lightning fast. He tightened his fingers around her wrist until she dropped the knife, and pulled her closer, slipping the iron ring from her finger.

Power bloomed in her body as her mage took over. Caine chanted an ancient spell, and something in her mind recognized the words: a spell for traveling. Instantly, she joined in, the familiar Angelic words tumbling from her lips. As they spoke, their bodies glowed with a protective light—a thick, vernal aura that rushed over her skin, whirling around the pair like a storm wind.

At the spell's completion, mist surrounded them, and Caine slipped the ring onto her finger again. His arms encircled her protectively, his heart pounding hard against her chest.

Where were they? She didn't want to utter a word in case Bileth still lurked nearby, but when the air thinned, she found herself looking at a thick grove of firs. This wasn't Salem.

Rosalind let out a long, slow breath as relief flooded her. "Where are we?" she whispered. Caine's body was a beacon of warmth in the cool forest, but she forced herself to step out of his embrace.

He smiled. "Great Misery Island. You do realize we just performed a powerful spell together? Our auras mingled beautifully."

Her head throbbed. "You mean, your aura mingled with Cleo's perfectly."

"Either way, I couldn't have done it without you," he said.

In the chilly sea air, she hugged herself. "I didn't feel the flames. The mage seemed more focused."

"I was with you the whole time. And Cleo must have known it was life or death. Maybe she hates you, but she doesn't want her host's body to die. Especially not before she got a chance to get her hands on me."

Rosalind studied him. "Were you pinioned by Bileth's magic the whole time? It seems awfully convenient that you only broke free at the last second when I was about to stab you."

"I let Bileth torture me," Caine said. "He wanted revenge, so I let him have some. And I wanted to see what you would do. I would have stepped in if it seemed like you were about to die."

"Seven hells, Caine. He practically murdered me."

"I did tell you to stay in the house. If you were a foot soldier in the army I commanded, I'd have to punish you."

She forced *that* image out of her mind. "You're not my commanding officer, and I don't foresee that happening. We've already established I can take you in a fight. But maybe you should find some courtesans for Bileth so he'll leave us alone. Perhaps you could glamour yourself to look like a beautiful, submissive woman and tend to his needs. I hear you're an expert in the seductive arts."

He grimaced. "Ugh. That sort of comment would get you a severe punishment if you were my foot soldier."

"Stop with the punishment thing. You like that idea a little too much."

"Right." He turned, trudging through the thick undergrowth. "We need to keep going. We must find Tammi and Aurora. Omerelle lives somewhere nearby, and they may arrive soon."

She followed him, snapping over twigs. "Omerelle? Who is this woman?"

"She's a mage. She's quite lonely out here. Her husband died a few years ago, and I keep her company sometimes. She'll probably be thrilled at the visit."

Rosalind didn't want to think about what sort of "company" he provided.

Lilu circled over their heads, fluttering through oak leaves. Streams of cold moonlight pierced the canopy, and a cool breeze kissed her skin. A heavy scent of brine, moss, and oak leaves hung in the damp air. She could envision herself living out here in the wilderness, lulled to sleep every night by the gentle sounds of the waves against the shore, and the wind rustling the trees.

"Rosalind," Caine said. "There's something I have to ask you."

His grave tone had her full attention. "Yes?"

"You said you remember my eyes from your childhood. Do you remember anyone else?"

"No. Just you, and glimmers of the sea and of flowers. And—weirdly—I remember seeing my own face a lot. When I told Tammi that, she thought I must be a narcissist."

Caine paused, lightly touching her arm. "That wasn't your face."

His words made her stomach swoop. "What do you mean?"

He inhaled sharply. "That was Miranda."

She gasped. "Who is she?"

"Your twin."

The ground seemed to tilt beneath her feet as this news hit her. "I have a *twin?*"

"Miranda, yes."

"And the Brotherhood have captured her?"

"According to Josiah."

"Why didn't you tell me about this before?"

"You've only just given up your allegiance to the Brotherhood, and I had no idea if you were trustworthy. And moreover, you're impulsive and overly emotional. I didn't think you'd approach it strategically. You've been very worked up this whole time."

Everything about what he was saying made her blood boil. "You can't trust me because I'm impulsive?"

"You followed me through a portal into another world, with no thought for your own safety. You decided to defy the orders of the Vampire Lord." He held up his fingers, counting out her offenses. "You threw a fit in Elysium that drew attention to us. Oh, and you stabbed an ancient high demon—three times—in a direct contradiction of my orders. You're not trustworthy."

"Well when you list it all out—" She stopped herself. She didn't want to get sidetracked by an argument. "Forget about all that. I need to know more details. Where has Miranda been this whole time? In Maremount?"

He started walking again, and she followed. "Miranda has been living in Maine. Your parents sent her to live with another member of the Brotherhood, but he didn't treat her well. She ran away at some point."

"Where did she go?"

"I have no idea. She must have been sleeping in the streets like a peasant."

A flood of guilt and anger rushed through Rosalind. "I wish I'd known."

"I wish I'd known too," Caine said. "I assumed you were both living safely in the pedestrian world, until Ambrose told me otherwise. I was supposed to bring you both to safety, but the Brotherhood came for you first."

"And she's possessed, like me?"

"Yes. And that's why Ambrose is interested in the both of you," Caine said. "He wants all three of us together for a triumvirate of power."

Stunned, Rosalind tried to picture her twin. "I think I remember her braiding my hair."

"She was the sweet one. She used to give the servants food when they were hungry."

The servants. There was that third person again. "And I used to torment them. Are you telling me that I'm the evil twin?"

"If you forced me to choose between good and evil, that would be my best guess."

"What else can you tell me about her?"

"I haven't seen her since she was four or five. But I know she completes our circle. Three mages, each aligned with one of the shadow gods. Together, our power would be unparalleled. He has a few old scores he'd like to settle, including one against the Brotherhood."

Rosalind's knees felt weak. "Three shadow gods."

"Right. The night god, the forest god, and—"

"The sea god." Her mouth went dry. She'd felt the sea mage on Thorndike's campus.

She'd sent the Brotherhood after her own sister.

She stumbled over a tree root, her mind a whirlwind of revulsion and guilt. "Caine. What if I've done something terrible?"

"What have you done?"

Her heart pounded in her rib cage. She had to tell him about Miranda, and the temptation to confess about the incubus was overwhelming.

She closed her eyes, an image flashing in her mind of Josiah, handing her the knife. "If you don't do this, humans will die," he'd said.

Rosalind's body shook like a leaf in the wind. "I did terrible things for the Brotherhood. And I think I'm responsible for—"

"Shhh," he lifted a finger to his lips. "Something's happening."

She listened to the wind whispering through the trees. Distant screams floated along the breeze, and her chest tightened.

"We need to go." Caine broke into a run.

She sprinted with him, snapping through twigs and branches. The screams grew louder as they ran. As orange flames came into view, Rosalind's heart constricted. Was this their destination —burning?

She pushed on faster, her breath ragged in her throat, until they reached the clearing. A young woman stumbled in front of a blazing gothic mansion. Blood streaked her beautiful face, and a tiara hung limply from wild, blonde tangles. A black cat stood before her, its back arched.

"I fought them," the woman said, her eyes frantic. "I fought them with magic, but they'll be back for me. They found me here."

Caine rushed to her, grabbing her hands. "What happened?"

"It was the mage Hunters. I used a protection spell, but it won't last. They wanted to burn me. They burned my house."

"How did they know you were here?" Caine's voice was urgent.

She wiped a shaking hand across her forehead, smearing the blood. "I never thought they'd come for me. I didn't have the shields up."

Caine gently wrapped his fingers around her arms, staring into her face. "Omerelle. Tell me what they said."

"They didn't say anything, but I read inside their minds." Her sorrowful, brown eyes glistened. "The witch-Hunters had been spying on two women—a vampire and a pedestrian. The Brotherhood heard them saying they were coming to Great Misery Island. The girls are friends of yours. The witch-Hunters are accusing me of aiding the fugitives."

At Omerelle's words, a crushing panic began to take root. "Do you know what happened to the two women?" Rosalind asked.

Omerelle stared at her, and the woman's willowy body trembled. "The witch-Hunters had already taken them by the time they got to me. They're in the Chambers."

Bile rose in Rosalind's throat, and she covered her face with her hands. Not only did the Brotherhood have her twin sister, but they had Tammi and Aurora, too.

Anger crackled through her body. She wanted to storm the Chambers and punch a hole through Josiah's face. As Caine tried to calm Omerelle, Rosalind took a deep, shuddering breath, trying to steady her nerves.

Omerelle picked up her cat. "I'm not staying here. Alu and I are going to hide from them." She closed her eyes and chanted a spell; her body shimmered away.

Caine's shot a worried look to Rosalind. "We need to get out of here now. Do you think you can do the teleportation spell again?"

She glanced down at the ring. "I think so. If you stay near—"

A hail of bullets cut through her thought, and pain speared her body. She crumpled to the ground, gripping her ribs. Caine rushed for Rosalind, his eyes black. He touched her chest, chanting the beginnings of a spell. Rosalind could feel the wound start to heal, until a spray of iron dust blasted Caine's skin, snuffing out his aura. Another hail of bullets blasted Caine onto the ground. She looked up, catching a glimpse of a tall, thin man walking closer. *Longshanks.*

She gasped for breath.

Before she could sit up, pain exploded through her skull, and her world went dark.

CHAPTER 26

Icy water ran down Rosalind's face, and she gasped. Her eyes snapped open, but she could see only white light filtering through dark canvas. Panic coursed through her, nearly drowning out the screaming pain in her lungs. Something covered her head—a hood, probably, and a rough piece of fabric gagged her mouth, compressing her tongue. She coughed, nearly choking on the cloth. Its oily taste was suffocating.

She needed to get out of there, but she couldn't move. Coarse rope bound her wrists behind her back at an awkward angle. She tried to tear her wrists free, and her skin chafed against the rope. Terror exploded through her skull. Her arms had been fastened tightly behind the back of a chair. When she tried to move her legs, she found they were trapped by rope, too. She was completely helpless, unable to do anything except exist.

She took a deep breath, the air burning her lungs. *Gasoline.* She was in one of the interrogation rooms.

By the deep ache in her chest and the sharp whistling sound, she could tell a bullet had collapsed one of her lungs, even if Caine had partially healed it.

Heels echoed on a concrete floor, and someone yanked the hood from her head. Her captor strode in front of her, peering into her bleary eyes.

Rosalind stared into the pale, freckled face of Randolph Loring. She glanced to the right and caught a glimpse of Caine, his body bound to a chair with thick, iron chains—chains that would leach all the power out of an incubus. Black duct-tape covered his mouth, and blood soaked his chest from gunshot wounds to his shoulders.

She gazed around at the iron-walled room. It was nearly bare. A bright light shone overhead, and a metal watering can stood on the floor by two cement blocks. There was a video camera mounted on a wall. She'd seen this setup before, and the sight turned her blood to ice.

Caine's blackened eyes burned into General Loring with an ancient, primal hatred.

Loring leaned down, examining Rosalind's eyes. His cold fingers slid over her cheeks, and she shuddered.

In desperation, she wanted to tell him how much she hated being tied up, but the cloth still gagged her. Raw panic gripped her lungs like a vise.

"Mmm. I can see you'd like to speak," he said tonelessly. He pulled a knife from his belt, cutting through the cloth.

She gasped, looking up at him. "Please untie me."

"I don't think so, Rosalind. You look so much like your sister." He shook his head. "Do you know, Rosalind, that I'd wanted to promote you? We were alike, or so I thought. Not everyone understands that we must take extraordinary measures to fight evil, or that there are strict lines separating the pure from the corrupted. Not everyone has a visceral revulsion to magic like I do. Not everyone understands that the demons won't respect us if we're weak and refuse to fight back. I thought you and I were the same."

"Magic still repulses me," she said. Apart from Caine's magic, but she wasn't going to bring that up now.

"It is a poison. A toxin that corrupts a human body. You seemed to understand that. I'd been watching you from afar. I'd hoped you'd work on our security team. I'd heard about you, and your clever skills. I thought perhaps you'd make a nice wife for one of my officers, or even me. I didn't know we had a traitor in our midst. We'll have to be more careful in the future."

They were in one of the cells deep below the ground in the Chambers. A thick metal door blocked their exit. There was no way in or out of this room without a retinal scan. Even if she could get out of this chair, her own retinas wouldn't make the "approved" list. She was thoroughly screwed. In a frenzy, she tugged at her wrists, the chair rattling on the floorboards. "General Loring. I didn't realize you knew so much about me. It is nice to finally meet you."

Randolph folded his hands behind his back, pacing. "I think Josiah was in love with you. It must have broken his heart to learn you're corrupted with filth. I've promised he could interrogate you. I think it will make him feel better. He asked if Caine could watch, and I granted him his wish."

Her mouth was dry, and she tried to focus on his words as she tugged at the ropes. "Watch what?"

Randolph tilted his head. "Watch what he does to you. It's an acceptable strategy. The demon may choose to confess everything to save you. But of course, demons have no compassion at all, nor do you, I suppose. You're not human anymore. It's fascinating, really. You do look human. Beautiful, even. Though when Josiah is finished with his interrogation that may not be the case."

Cold dread snaked up her spine. "I want a trial."

Randolph crinkled his brow. "What for? We know you're guilty. We're no longer required to waste time with paperwork and legal nonsense. We're at war. Moreover, the sixth amendment only applies to humans. Same for the eighth amendment."

"The prohibition against cruel and unusual punishment."

"Exactly. They don't apply to your species." He stared at the floor as he paced, his eyes never meeting hers.

"I'm human."

"We've changed our thinking about that. Once a person uses magic and creates an aura, they are no longer considered human. A person who provides protection for a witch is no longer human, either."

She struggled frantically against the ropes, sweat beading on her forehead. This was insane. "You can't just make up your own definitions."

"Of course we can. It is people like me who create reality. It is people like me who define our terms. This is the way it's always been. The Brotherhood is an empire, and Blodrial has called on me to lead it." His cheeks reddened, his pace increasing. "Weak-minded scholars might huddle in libraries, arguing over semantics and ethics. Fine. With their noses stuck in books, they're out of my way while I create reality. Meanwhile, I'm going to act, molding the world into the way it should be according to divine principles."

She gasped for breath, her lungs burning. "If you torture people, what makes you any better than the demons?"

"We don't call it torture, so it isn't." His heels clacked faster over the floorboards. "Anyway, that you would even question me in that way shows how far you've fallen."

She wanted to distract him—if only because she knew what was coming next. "Your lack of introspection is breathtaking."

He paused his pacing, cocking his head but refusing to meet her eyes. "I do often request that our interrogators refrain from leaving marks, because they can make for unfortunate pictures in the wrong hands, but I can't promise Josiah will heed that request." He turned with a tight smile. "Well, it was interesting to meet you in person. I'll let Josiah know you're ready for him. You already know how this works, Rosalind. You've been in here before."

Terror vibrated in her skull, and she tried to rip her arms from their ties as Loring strode from the room.

Tammi. Where was Tammi right now? Rosalind's pulse raced. She needed to get out of here and search the other interrogation rooms— but even if she could get out of here, there was no way to unlock the secure rooms without the retina scan.

As she tugged the ropes, her chair legs banged against the floor.

Caine remained still, his black eyes cold as glaciers, devoid of humanity. He must have flipped some kind of switch.

"Caine," she said. "I need to find a way—"

The door opened, and Josiah stepped into the light, his brown eyes boring into Rosalind.

"Hello, my darling," he said, voice seething with anger.

"Josiah. You don't want to do this."

He crossed the room, reaching out to stroke her hair, eyes glistening. "That's where you're wrong. I've been so looking forward to this."

"Why? You know what happened to me. I was turned into a witch against my will."

His nostrils flared. "Fine, but then you opened your legs for the incubus and declared war on humanity."

"I haven't declared war on anyone."

"You're either with us or against us. You know that." He straightened, staring down at her. "When I was five, I hid in a closet and watched as demons ripped into my parents' necks, drank them dry. They did things to my mother that no child should have known about. Your lover here not only lives among them, but he acts as their leader." Josiah's eyes burned with fervid intensity. "To see you lusting after this beast set a fire blazing inside me that can never be extinguished. I want you to feel my pain. I want this monster to feel my pain when he watches me hurt you."

Caine's growl reverberated through the room, his demonic eyes dark as voids.

"Tammi didn't do anything wrong," Rosalind said, in desperation.

Instead of responding, Josiah shoved her shoulders so hard that the chair tipped back. As it slammed against the floor, she gasped in pain. The full weight of her body landed on her hands, bound behind her back. She struggled to catch her breath.

"Did that hurt? I see you're injured." He knelt down, pulling a knife from his pants, before cutting through the front of her shirt.

Revulsion spread through her. She couldn't believe she'd ever cared for this maniac. She should have let Caine kill him when they had the chance. "What are you doing?"

"Looking at the damage to your corrupted body." He studied her gunshot wound before pressing down on it with one of his thumbs.

Agony lanced her ribs. Caine had sealed up some of the wound, but fragments of her broken ribs still pierced her lungs.

"That must hurt a lot," Josiah said. "Your demon lover didn't get to finish healing it. He won't be able to heal your broken corpse when I'm done with it, either."

"You're a monster," she choked out. Her thoughts raced, and she tried to slow them, to think tactically.

What did the Brotherhood teach her? *Use the tools from your surroundings.* But what the hell was she supposed to use here? She was tied to a chair, and…

The stiletto knife. She still had the small blade in the back of her pants, she could feel the hilt jabbing into her spine. She pinched it between her fingers.

"You're going to torture me because you're mad about our breakup. Do you realize what kind of psychotic, bunny-boiling asshole that makes you?" Slowly, she inched the knife from her belt, but she couldn't get much leverage with her hands crushed beneath her.

"I'm not saying it won't hurt, but we don't call it torture, Rosalind. We've talked about this. It's an interrogation." He glanced at a small camera in the corner of the room. He crossed to it, covering the lens with a small cloth. "It may get a bit unconventional, so I don't want any of this recorded. But it will be an interrogation, nonetheless. I do hope you'll be as willing to share with me as you once were. Did you know that your information led to Miranda's capture?" He raised the legs of the chair on to a cinderblock, so they were now higher than her head. As much as she dreaded what was coming next, this position made it easier for her to move the knife, since her hands were no longer pinioned.

"The sea-witch I told you about," she said through labored breaths. Slowly, she inched the knife up and down against the knots.

Josiah picked up the watering can. "She looks so much like you. I enjoyed breaking her. Though, I'm not sure she was sane to begin with."

Rage flowed through Rosalind like molten lava. She wanted to crush him.

She cut a glance to Caine, who remained still as a statue, watching. In a room rigged with iron dust, his magic was useless here.

As she rubbed the knife's blade against the rope, Josiah pulled a dark hood over her face, and her heart rate sped up. She knew how this worked. It made it easier to torture people when you couldn't see their faces. Right now, the spotlight still penetrated the cloth, but that wouldn't last long. Next, Josiah would wrap her head with a towel, shrouding her vision in darkness.

She'd watched him do it to the incubus. She didn't want to think of the demon's name, but as Josiah blotted out the light with the second cloth, it came to her anyway: Malphas. Fair-haired, but with gray eyes just like Caine's. Josiah had staked him earlier that night. The hawthorn wood had still protruded from his shoulder when Josiah brought Rosalind into the cell. His pale eyes had looked so tormented, and she'd wanted to yank it out, but Josiah had stayed her hand.

I can't think about that now. She needed to focus on getting the hell out of there. Josiah was drawing this out, enjoying her panic. When she'd said humans didn't enjoy torture, that they only acted tactically, she'd been lying to herself completely.

Still, the longer Josiah drew this out, the better chance she had to get herself out of here.

Her heart galloped in her chest, and she slid the knife against the knots.

Maybe she deserved this, after what she'd done to Malphas. Josiah had told her that the incubus had brutally raped and murdered three women just days before. He'd said that the demon had left their naked, broken bodies in a Walden Woods. There were the pictures of three brutalized corpses, shown to Rosalind in the cell as she stood just inches from the incubus.

As she'd stared at them in horror, Malphas had eyed her evenly, his breath rasping. He hadn't said a word.

Josiah had done all the talking: "That's what an incubus will do if you ever get near one. This monster would tear you to pieces if we let him free."

The pictures of the broken corpses had twisted her gut with disgust.

After Josiah had wrapped the demon's head with the towel, he'd told Rosalind to pour the water over his face. All part of her training. She was too soft, apparently, since she made the fatal mistake of viewing demons as humans instead of as cold, sadistic predators. In a fight for survival, there was no room for gray areas.

She scraped the knife against the rope.

It was too late by the time she realized Josiah had a bad habit of passing on shitty information. There was every chance that Malphas had never been anywhere near those girls.

The watering can scraped across the floor as Josiah shifted it, and fear rushed through her body. She'd gotten nowhere with the ropes. You couldn't seriously cut through a thick rope by slowly rubbing a blade against it—

Her mind froze as the cloth dampened. It started with the slow flow of water trickling into her nostrils. She held her breath, still rubbing at the rope with the knife, trying to rip through the fibers. She held her breath for what seemed like an eternity, one agonizing second after another, and pain exploded through her lungs. When she couldn't hold it anymore, her body forced a breath out.

She knew not to breathe in, but her lungs burst with agony, and she couldn't control it anymore. Involuntarily, she breathed in, sucking the wet cloth against her face. *No air.* Panic burst through her mind. *There is no air. I'm going to die.* Her body shook, rebelling against the suffocation. Her vision burst with images of Malphas, his body convulsing as she poured the water on to the towel, the stake still protruding from his chest.

I'm going to die. All rational thought flew from her mind. She'd beg Josiah for mercy, do whatever he wanted to get out of this.

I poured the water. I'm the monster. Sheer terror and agony warped her mind.

After ten lifetimes, she felt the chair tilt up again. *Please.*

Josiah pulled the towels off her face before yanking off the hood. She gasped for breath, sucking in air. Her wet hair plastered to her face. Icy water soaked her shoulders.

Josiah looked into her eyes. "This is the part where I ask you questions."

What had her plan been? *The knife—gods help me.* She'd dropped the knife.

CHAPTER 27

She glanced at Caine, but he wasn't moving. He just stared at her, his eyes empty.

"He can't save you, Rosalind."

Josiah touched her cheek, and she flinched. *He's going to drown me again. He's going to kill me. I'm going to die at the hands of a sadist.*

She clamped her eyes shut, trying to get a grip. She needed to master her fear, to keep her wits intact so she could figure out how to get the hell out of here.

"Tell me about the Vampire Lord," Josiah said.

Shit. She'd already divulged too much. "The Vampire Lord?" she repeated, stalling. Frigid water dripped down her chest. Her teeth chattered; her body shook.

Josiah gripped her sodden hair, yanking her head backward. "Start with his name."

"I don't know," she stammered. She wasn't telling this asshole anything until her mind broke completely. "I just heard everyone call him the Vampire Lord."

"Where does he live?"

She gasped for breath, and her throat burned. "No one told me."

Josiah slammed his fist into her face. Pain burst through her cheek, searing her skull.

She glanced at Caine, who watched her impassively. In fact, he seemed completely unperturbed by this whole thing. *What the fuck, Caine?*

The incubus obviously had no plan to help, and couldn't get out of the chains, anyway.

Use what's around you, Rosalind, her mind screamed. But she couldn't get her hands on a single weapon. The only thing she could manipulate in the room, was—

Josiah.

Whatever it was he wanted, she could use it against him.

He yanked her hair tighter, nearly ripping it out by the roots. "Does the Vampire Lord have an army?"

"He didn't tell me," she said, staring in to his blazing eyes. She wasn't about to tell him that the General of Ambrose's army sat just a few feet away, staring at the two of them.

Josiah's breath was hot on her cheeks. "I know he has an army. And I want to know everything about it. How many are there? What are their plans? You will tell me every single thing you know," he said through gritted teeth.

"It's hard to think when you're hurting me," she said—stalling, again.

He tightened his other hand around her waist. "I want you to know that I will never let you out of my sight again. You're mine, Rosalind."

Fuck this guy. What he wanted was glaringly obvious: he wanted complete control over her, and he wanted to hurt her in the most brutal ways possible.

But what else did she know about him? He had an intense curiosity for all things demonic. He tended to underestimate her strength and her ability to look after herself. On top of that, he had a serious rage problem. These were all things she could use against him.

"I don't know. Josiah, please," she let out a sob. "None of this is my fault. I don't want this spirit in me. When the ring comes off, I burn with excruciating pain. It's like my whole body is on fire."

"You've told me this already." He slipped a large hand up her body, tightening it around her throat. "Tell me about the Vampire Lord, or I'll put the hood on you again for more water."

"It's a curse, Josiah," she said. "I don't want that magic. I never want to feel that pain again. You can't imagine the agony."

He looked into her eyes, licking his lips. "Oh really?"

She'd laid the bait. It was working.

"I never wanted this curse, Josiah. It's the worst pain I've ever felt."

He yanked a knife from his weapons belt, and slipped behind her back, cutting through the knot that bound her hands. He gripped her wrists hard, pulling her hand in front of her face so she could stare at the iron ring. "You still wear Blodrial's ring. He is your saving grace, and you betray him."

If she acted as fragile as possible, he'd let down his guard even further. "Josiah. You're hurting me," she whimpered.

"Good." He tightened his grip on her wrists. "Tell me what you know about the Vampire Lord, or I'll take the ring off and let you burn until you beg for mercy."

Manipulating Josiah was easier than she'd thought. In fact, a kernel of an idea began to bloom in her mind—a way to free every captive in the building—if she could manage to get out of there alive.

She lifted her eyes to his, letting them glisten. "I don't know anything about an army. But please, Josiah—"

With a tight smile, he stared at her ring. "I've wanted to see what would happen when the spirit takes over you." He dropped her other hand to slip off the ring, but he didn't get that far. As soon as he let her hand out of his grip, her hand flew to his throat. Within moments, she had both hands around his neck. She dug her thumbs into his Adam's apple. His eyes bulged, but she wouldn't be strong enough to choke him out like this. She just needed more of his rage to break her out of this chair.

"The truth is, Josiah, you could never satisfy me like an incubus could."

His face contorted with rage, and his fingers dug into her wrists before he ripped her hands from his throat. Snarling, he kicked her hard in the chest with one of his boots. The chair flew, slamming against the wall. The blow knocked the wind out of her, but it also had the desired effect. The crash splintered the chair into dozens of pieces.

She was free.

With an exultant smile, she grabbed a fragmented chair leg. When Josiah rushed for her, she jammed the splintered end into his thigh. It wasn't enough to kill him, but he wouldn't put up much of a fight after that.

Stunned, Josiah stared at her and staggered back—right into Caine, whose muscular arm tightened around Josiah's neck.

Where the hell did Caine come from?

"Caine?" she shouted. Wood splinters pierced her back, and at this point, she was sure half her ribs were broken. "How did you get out of the chains?"

His black eyes were fixed on Josiah. Instead of answering, he tightened his grip. *Shit.* She was quickly formulating a plan, but it was one that required Josiah to be alive.

"Caine!" She shouted. "We need him to live."

Caine's midnight eyes, as dark and empty as the opening of a cave, met hers. She wasn't getting through to him.

"Caine!" Panicking, she rushed forward and slapped him across the face.

He dropped Josiah, whose body landed on the ground with a thud. Rosalind knelt next to the Hunter and felt for a pulse. Blood still pumped through his veins. He was alive, but unconscious. Assuming someone found him before he bled out from the stab wound, he'd pull through.

Caine looked down at her. "You'd better have a very good reason for asking me to leave him alive. If this is sentimentality again, I'm going to kill him."

Pain wracked her body as she rose. "I know how we can use him to save the others, but we need to get out of here first. We won't be able to free them from their cells until I can get to a computer."

"What are you talking about?"

"I need you to trust me."

"Fine. Josiah was an idiot to underestimate you, and I won't make the same mistake." He eyed her torn shirt. "Hang on."

He stripped off his blood-stained shirt, tossing it to her. She tried not to stare at his muscular chest. *Focus, Rosalind.* They needed to get the hell out of there.

A voice crackled over Josiah's walkie-talkie. *"Agent Endicott. Please tell us the captives' status."*

Rosalind slipped into Caine's shirt, and it nearly hung to her knees. "Thanks."

"What's the best way out of here?" Caine asked.

She closed her eyes, trying to visualize the building. "Right now, we're underground. There are no secret tunnels, and there's no way to get out discretely. We're going to have to blend in. We'll need better outfits."

"Since you didn't let me kill Josiah, I'm feeling a bit unsatisfied. I'll be happy to divest some guards of their clothing."

Josiah moaned, and Caine kicked him in the head.

The walkie-talkie crackled. *"Agent Endicott. Please report immediately."*

"Let's go," Caine said.

Rosalind eyed him. "I still don't understand. How did you get out of the iron chains? I didn't even hear you escaping. The iron should have sapped your power."

"No. That's succubi. We're different creatures. Like I said, the Brotherhood gave you a lot of misinformation. We don't have time to get into that now. Let's go assault some guards."

Her pulse raced. "The chains didn't weaken your strength?"

"No. They did nothing, really. Not that I want the Brotherhood to know that. The less they know, the better."

Her pulse raced. "So—that whole time I was being tortured, you could have stopped it?"

His eyes remained black as pitch, cold and bestial. "Yes, but it would have been a tactical error."

Whatever he meant by that, one fact burned through her mind: Caine had sat there and watched Josiah beat the shit out of her. He'd let her think she was about to die. He could have stopped it, but he'd sat there impassively, watching it like a spectator. The betrayal burned. She rushed at Caine, shoving him hard in the chest.

"You watched me get tortured when you could have stopped it?" she shouted. "What the fuck is wrong with you? Did you not see him drowning me? I thought I was going to die."

Caine's voice was low and controlled, and he grabbed her wrists. "Stop shouting, if you want to get out of here alive. You're supposed to be a soldier. That's what you signed up for when you joined the Brotherhood, even if you joined the wrong side."

Seething, she ripped her wrists from his grasp, just barely restraining herself from snatching another wooden fragment from the ground and ramming it into Caine's neck. "Half my ribs are broken. Josiah ripped my shirt off like a sex offender. He punched me in the face, kicked me into a wall, prodded my bullet wound, and practically drowned me. You're just lucky I didn't give up any real information to him."

"I was planning on killing him, so that wouldn't have mattered."

"I see. But apparently the state of my broken bones wasn't enough to move you off your ass. How much would you have let me endure?"

"Did no one ever tell you that war could be a bit uncomfortable? General Loring seemed to think you were familiar with the interrogation room, so I can't imagine that its unpleasantness is news to you."

"*Agent Endicott. I'm ordering you to report your status immediately. Your video monitor has been disabled.*"

His words stung, and tears pricked her eyes. He'd *wanted* her to get hurt. "I get it. So that was revenge."

The black in Caine's eyes faded. "No, that's not it at all. The point was—"

An alarm sounded, and Caine's eyes flicked to the door. "We need to go."

She pointed to the circular scanner. "We can't get out without a retina scan."

"What about Josiah's eyes?" Caine asked. "I'd be perfectly happy to cut one out and aim it at the thing."

She shook her head, grabbing two shards of wood from the ground. "The scanners sense small movements. They won't work for an unconscious eye. We need to wait until the guards come in here. We'll kick the shit out of them and steal their clothes."

"Fine." Caine walked over the spotlight hanging from the ceiling. He reached up, crushing the light with his hand, and darkness fell on the room. "They're coming," he whispered. "Stand against the wall."

A buzzer sounded at the door, and a guard kicked it open. Four guards rushed in, guns ready. Rosalind threw one of the stakes for the door, jamming it open slightly. Pain screamed through her chest. She was in no condition to fight.

"Agent Endico—" A guard's words were cut off by the crunch of bone and the sound of a gun hitting the floor. Only a faint stream of light illuminated the room, and she struggled to see in the dark. Bodies whirled around her, and the room filled with the sound of fists slamming against flesh. Someone unleashed a hail of bullets, but a cracking sound cut the assault short. The sound of a bone snapping, maybe. After a few moments, silence descended.

"Rosalind?" Caine said. "I've disabled them." He handed her a bundle of fabric. "Put these on."

Her breathing came sharp and fast as she pulled off her boots to change her clothes. It was a small mercy she could get out of her piss-soaked pants. "Did you kill them?" she whispered.

"Of course."

She slipped out of her clothes. She was now an accessory to the murder of four humans—people who had once been her colleagues. "You couldn't have just knocked them unconscious?"

"They signed their death warrants when they volunteered to work in torture chambers," he said.

She'd worked in one of these rooms by Josiah's side, an instrument of misery.

The walkie-talkie crackled again. *"Agent Endicott, we sent reinforcements. Please let us know your status."*

She buttoned the new uniform as Caine began speaking into the walkie-talkie. "This is Agent Endicott." It was an exact replication of Josiah's voice. "The reinforcements have arrived, but you didn't need to send them. I have everything under control. The interrogation continues. *Lux in tenebris lucet.*" He dropped the walkie-talkie.

"Please report to the head offices, Agent Endicott."

"Are you ready, Rosalind?" Caine asked.

She pulled on the guard's hat before crouching down, groping around for a discarded gun. "I'm ready. Just keep your eyes down." A fragment of wood still propped the door open, and she pushed it.

The alarm continued to blare, and red lights flashed from the ceiling, pulsing over iron walls that stretched far into the distance. This corridor covered nearly half a mile beneath Cambridge's streets—a dizzyingly long line of cells, each filled with a monster—or, so she'd once thought. Now, she knew ordinary people like Tammi were locked in here, too.

"You're walking like you're injured," whispered Caine.

"I am injured, no thanks to you."

She had to mask her pain, or the guards would see it in her limping walk and rasping breath. Josiah had promised to break her body, and he wasn't far off. She felt as if she was breathing through a tiny straw, and pain ripped through her limbs.

She was out of the cell, but not ready to celebrate just yet. She was fairly certain several of her ribs were broken. She had a bruised tailbone, a wrist fracture, and she remained stuck in the bowels of an institution that wanted to torture her to death.

She swallowed hard, trying to block out the pain as they drew closer to the corridor's end. What hellish torments had the Brotherhood unleashed behind those doors in the name of humanity?

Miranda, Tammi, and Aurora were just a few feet away from them right now, but there was nothing she could do about it. It wasn't like she could break through six inches of metal door without getting caught; even Caine couldn't do that.

At last, they reached the end of the hall. Two guards flanked another set of metal doors, and Rosalind slowed, letting Caine take the lead. She couldn't let the guards see her face. Even if they didn't recognize her features, the raw pain written in her eyes would spook them.

A tall, dark-haired man nodded at Caine. "What's going on with the traitor?"

"Interrogation got messy." Caine kept his eyes down and mimicked Josiah's voice. "It's still going on, but the others are handling it. *Lux in tenebris lucet.*"

The blond guard pushed a button, opening the metal doors. "You get your hands on that bitch? I want a turn on her when they're—"

Fury rushed through Rosalind, and before she could stop herself, her leg swung up, and her boot connected with the man's face. His neck snapped back, hitting the wall, and a fraction of a second later Caine slammed his elbow into the other guard's skull. The two men slumped to the ground.

"Unconscious," Caine said. "At your request."

"Thanks." She gripped her ribs, suppressing a moan.

The door had swung open into the older part of the chambers—a brick hall that opened into a stairwell leading to the ground floor.

"We're almost out," she said through labored breaths, climbing the stairs. She tried to catch her breath, her lungs still burning. She held on to the rails, gasping for air. What she really needed was a goddamn hospital. Caine glanced at her before slipping an arm around her waist.

"Are you okay?" he asked quietly.

"I'm alive."

At the top of the stairs stood another set of doors. While these doors required scans to get in, there was nothing to stop them from leaving. Rosalind pushed open the door, trying to project an air of confidence as she strode past the guards into the central hall. A sigh slid from her. They were now clear of the maximum security part of the Chambers, and they just had to make it through the lobby and onto Oxford Street. She cast a quick glance around at the lobby's towering ivory columns, the busts of famous Hunters, and the crimson walls lined with portraits of the Brotherhood's most illustrious members: King James I, Cotton Mather, and England's witchfinder General. This had felt like her home once.

Was it only a week ago that she'd strode through here, certain that her future was secure in this building, that she'd one day lecture to a crowd of students in the Chambers' old Mather hall?

Her heels clacked over the marble floor as they crossed the lobby, striding past the wooden security desk to the glass doors, illuminated by streetlights outside. So close to freedom, her heart pounded harder.

Still, guilt tightened her throat. She was leaving Tammi and the others at the hands of the psychopaths.

With a final glance at Caine, she pushed on a glass door, but it didn't budge. *What the hell?*

Caine pushed another door, with the same result.

Locked.

The security guard's voice broke the silence. "You gotta use the scanner. When the alarms are going off, no one can leave without scanning."

CHAPTER 28

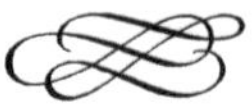

"Of course." Caine kept his voice even when he spoke to the guard. "The scanners."

Any minute now, they'd be found out. She couldn't let herself imagine the torture they'd endure after an escape attempt that left a trail of bodies.

"Get ready to run," she whispered to Caine.

She took a few steps back before pulling the gun, aiming it at the glass doors. If she couldn't scan her way out, she'd have to shoot her way out. She squeezed the trigger and broke into a sprint. Glass shattered all around them. Shards blasted against her skin as she bolted to the pavement outside. They cleared the door's entrance just as the guard unleashed a round of bullets. Caine pulled her out of the crossfire, taking shelter behind the building's brick facade.

He folded her in an embrace and pulled off her ring. In the shadows, he began chanting in Angelic. The mage joined in as their mingling auras whirled through her body. Panicked shouts echoed from within the building, but the magic was already rippling over her skin, and a thick, protective mist enshrouded them.

Caine slipped the ring back on her finger, and the mist thinned. Rosalind let out a long, slow breath. They stood in Mount Auburn

Cemetery, dwarfed by Abduxiel Mansion. Blood streaked Caine's neck.

Pain splintered her shoulder. She pressed her fingers to her collar-bone, wincing. "I've been shot three times in two days. This is not how I imagined my life turning out."

Caine slipped his arm around her waist. "Let me get you inside. I'll heal you."

As they approached the tall oak door, it swung open, revealing a cavernous hall. Moonlight shone through a stained glass window—an image of an angel. Twinkling lights hung suspended in the air like stars, flickering over an empty marble floor. If she weren't half-dead, she might actually enjoy this place.

Orcus rushed from a darkened archway. "I tried to keep her here. She wouldn't listen," he hissed. "Are you injured, Master? And what is happening with Bileth?"

"I'm fine, but she's badly hurt."

Orcus pulled off his hood, revealing black eyes and a pale, bald head the color of bone. "Take her into the celestial room. Try not to get blood everywhere. I've just cleaned up. I'll draw a bath in the adjacent washing room."

She leaned into Caine, and agony burned through her shoulder. He led her through an archway, pushing open a door into a candlelit room. Midnight-blue wallpaper, marked with silver stars, surrounded them. A silky, blue bed stood in the center of the room, and a twinkling chandelier hung from the ceiling.

"Lie down," instructed Caine. "You're walking like you're in agony."

She pulled off her boots, wincing as she bent over. *Nice of him to notice.* She lay on the soft bed, barely able to restrain the tears welling in her eyes. "I *am* in agony. And what about you? You're covered in blood."

"I was shot in the neck, and the rest is from the glass."

Her stomach clenched. "Shot in the neck? Why aren't you dead?"

"I can't be killed that easily, not unless it's a hawthorn stake."

A hawthorn stake—so that was why Malphas had been weakened. Her sense of relief at their escape was crushed by the weight of guilt—

not just because of Malphas, but the friends she'd left behind. "What about the others? What if Josiah and Randolph punish them for what we did? We need to get back there." Miranda probably looked exactly like her, and Josiah would be sadistic enough to act out his most depraved revenge fantasies on her.

Caine eyed her with concern. "You need to calm your breathing. You won't heal as well if you're panicking. We'll save them, but I need to heal you first. And then you can tell me about your plan. Open your shirt, please."

She unbuttoned the front of her shirt, grimacing at the pain when she moved her arms.

Caine brushed his hands over her sternum, chanting in Angelic. His aura seeped into her skin, soothing away the pain. He trailed his fingers lower, lingering lightly over her broken ribs and lung, before they moved to her neck and face, lanced with shards of glass. With each stroke of his fingers, the pain began to ebb, leaving behind only a dull ache in her muscles.

"Is there anything else?" he asked, his eyes roaming over her body.

"That's it. Just soreness."

His gaze met hers. "I didn't realize how bad it was. You had five broken ribs."

"You let him torture me." She sat up. "Why didn't you stop it?" She wasn't quite sure she wanted to know the answer.

"There were two reasons." He spoke quietly, gently picking up her hand. "One—the Brotherhood believed that iron chains were enough to bind an incubus. I didn't want to dispel that myth. If they believe iron alone can hold us, it works to our advantage. That meant I had to wait until it looked like you were the one to break us out—until you very ingeniously found a way out of that chair. And the other was simply that Josiah's interrogation gave me valuable information. I now know what's important to him and to the Brotherhood. I know what he knows about us, and what he doesn't."

"Sounds very practical." She pulled her hand from his grasp and drew her knees up to her chest, hugging them. "Is there anything he could have done that would have spurred you to action, or would you have sat there and watched him murder me as long as you got the information you wanted?" She wasn't sure why she felt so betrayed. He'd never promised her anything more than an uneasy alliance. Like he'd said. They weren't friends.

"Don't be absurd. I wouldn't have let it go that far." He looked down at his hands. "I didn't realize the damage he was doing. I forget sometimes how fragile human bodies are. But you need to get over it. You're alive. And if it makes you feel better, I plan to kill him in the most excruciating way possible."

"I'm not sure that makes me feel better. And that's another thing— how are we any better than the Brotherhood if we kill everyone just like they do?"

He shrugged. "We aren't any better."

She'd been expecting some kind of argument, and had no idea what to do with that response. "But I hate them and what they do. I don't want to be the same as them, or I'd have to hate myself. I used to think it was okay to kill people as long as they weren't human, but I've changed my mind. It's immoral to kill people unless it's pure self-defense. Like, if you're about to die."

"We're at war, Rosalind."

"Only because everyone keeps *saying* we're at war." Loring was right about that much—words had power.

"Mmm." He apparently couldn't stop his eyes from roaming over her bare skin now that it had been healed. "Well, let me know when your semantic argument convinces the Brotherhood to stop hunting demons, and I'll let things lie." Blood still poured from the bullet hole in his neck, and he winced.

"Can you heal yourself?" she asked. Even if he was a demon, a bullet to the neck had to hurt.

"No. It doesn't work that way."

"You can only be healed by human women."

"And Orcus. He's not quite as enjoyable, but I don't imagine you're going to volunteer."

"Orcus it is." She heaved a sigh of relief. It wasn't that she didn't want to kiss him again. She wanted it a little *too* much. His touch could distract her from what they needed to do. Maybe some moral quandaries were murky, but spending the night in the arms of an incubus while your best friend and sister were being tortured went into *full blown sociopath* territory.

The door creaked open, and Orcus poked his head in.

At the sight of his shining skull, Rosalind pulled her shirt closed. It was one thing for Caine to see her half-naked, but the grim reaper was another matter.

Orcus cleared his throat. "The bath is drawn for the lady. I left you both a change of clothes in the washing room. But could you please tell me what I'm supposed to do about Bileth? He has been here three times looking for you, and I'm fairly certain he intends to send you into the shadow hell in a most unpleasant fashion."

Caine rubbed the center of his forehead. "Arrange for ten courtesans to visit him. And find ones that look like Rosalind. Tell him they're a gift from me, and that I've already punished her severely."

"Of course, Master."

Caine glanced at her. "You should go soak your muscles. The bath he's drawn will heal the ache in your bones."

She clenched her fists. "We need to talk about breaking into the Brotherhood. I want to get in there now."

"I'll join you in a moment, and we'll talk." He eyed her thoughtfully. "I'll keep my gaze on the floor, if you want."

"Good."

Orcus's heels clacked over the flagstones. "Master, I must heal your neck."

Rosalind rose, holding her ripped shirt closed, and strode across the cold flagstones in her bare feet. She pushed open the door into a stone washroom. A silver, clawfoot bath stood in the center, filled with bubbles and herbs, and candles guttered in spidery sconces. A silver-framed mirror hung over a sink.

She draped the blanket over a chair before slipping out of her underwear and padding over to the tub. She climbed in, lowering herself into the warm water scented with rose petals and foxglove.

She leaned back, resting her neck on the tub's edge. If she weren't battered by worry, this would be heaven.

As the water melted the ache from her body, she mentally ran through her plan. Magic was useless in the Brotherhood's chambers, and technology controlled the whole building: retina scanners, key cards to get in and out, auto-locking doors, sensors that detected magical auras, the sprinklers of iron dust… If she controlled the technology, she controlled the Chambers.

She dipped lower in the bath, inhaling the steam. It all started with a laptop. What were the chances that Orcus had a laptop lying around —that he spent his nights gaming or watching online porn?

Behind her, the door creaked open, and she turned her head to find Caine, his eyes downcast. "I'm going to be exercising a lot of restraint for this conversation."

"I need a laptop."

"A *what?*"

"A computer. You know—a digital device? Zeros and ones? Do you have any idea what I'm talking about?"

"I've heard the word before, but Maremount technology is about four hundred years behind yours."

She turned to look at him. "Well, magic is no use to us in the Chambers, so we've got to use what's available. I don't suppose you have a spell that creates a laptop?"

"No. Most of our spells are medieval. I could blight someone's cabbage crop without a problem." He pulled off his shirt, and she caught a glimpse of the red streaking his perfect chest. Facing the mirror, he grabbed a cloth, scrubbing at some of the blood. "What, exactly are the details of this plan?"

"If I can hack into the Brotherhood's computer systems, I can control the building. We can get in; the prisoners can get out." Suddenly excited, she sat up, and the suds dripped down her skin. "I can turn off the dust, shut down the scanners, unlock the doors. I can control it all."

His eyes met hers in the reflection, and he paused, his cloth hovering mid-air. He swallowed hard. "I forgot what we were talking about."

"We were talking about you looking in another direction."

"Right." He finished cleaning off the blood and pulled off his pants.

For a moment, his strong, athletic form distracted her. *Focus, Rosalind.* She was turning into that full blown sociopath she'd imagined before. "So how do we get a laptop?"

He stepped into a pair of freshly-laundered black pants. "I could just take one from someone."

"Half of Cambridge will have one," she said, pushing aside any moral quibbles about theft. "We're not far from Harvard. The students will be walking around with them."

He slid his shirt over his broad shoulders. "Give me ten minutes."

CHAPTER 29

*A*fter Caine left, Rosalind stepped out of the bath, drying herself off with a towel.

She slipped into the clothes that Orcus had laid out—a pair of black leggings, a T-shirt, and a leather jacket. He'd even included a pair of bright red underwear, exactly her size. Either one of Caine's conquests had left these items behind, or Orcus had created them through magic, perfectly gauging her size. She wasn't sure which possibility was weirder.

Either way, she had more pressing matters on her mind. She pulled on her boots, zipping them over her pants. She was desperate for a computer.

She racked her brain for everything she could remember about assembly languages from her class last semester. Right now, lives depended on her ability to recall Professor Carroll's murderously dull lectures about compiling.

She pushed through the door into the celestial room, sitting on the edge of the bed, her nails digging into the blanket. An image burned in her mind—Miranda tied to a chair, her limbs beaten bloody by Josiah. Rosalind shook her head, trying to force the picture from her mind.

This wasn't the time to lose it. *Think of something calming: the water running over my toes at the beach, a hawthorn grove.*

It was strange. Lingering around the edges of her most cherished childhood memories were Miranda and Caine, ephemeral figures in the hollows of her mind. Caine's eyes were her only solid memory. Gray irises and sun kissed skin— such a beautiful combination of warm and cool, like when sunlight pierced the storm clouds. It was so much like Malphus...

She shuddered. She couldn't think of Malphus now.

She couldn't let herself picture the pained look in his eyes as Josiah had twisted the stake in his heart. Did the other incubus live still in those dungeons, or had she unknowingly participated in his brutal murder?

She stood, pacing the room. She'd have to tell Caine—maybe she should have told him already. An ache welled in her chest. She tried to force out the images flitting through her mind: Josiah beating Miranda, Tammi trembling in the corner of an empty cell room, Rosalind's own face as she poured the water over Malphus...

She forced back tears, gripping her hair by the roots. She had to keep it together. Tammi and the others *needed* her to stay sane, and if Malphus was still in the Chambers, this was her chance to make up for what she'd done, by saving him.

The door creaked open, and she glanced up to see Caine holding a laptop bag. He slid the bag onto the desk. "I got the thing you wanted. I hope this works." He eyed her. "Are you okay? You look a little... upset." He approached her, gently touching her shoulder.

"That's what happens when you get tied to a chair and tortured."

He folded her in an embrace, his strong arms encircling her, and she melted into him, listening to his heart beat. He ran a hand down her hair. "You're okay now."

"Maybe I deserved it."

"What are you talking about?"

Her heart thudded in her chest. "You said that you knew someone else in the Chambers."

He pulled away, studying her. "Yes."

"Was he an incubus like you?"

His eyes narrowed. "Yes. Did you see him?"

She nodded, hugging herself. "I saw him. Malphus. But he couldn't get out of the chains. He'd been staked in the heart."

Caine backed away, his eyes darkening. "Is he dead?"

She shook her head. "I don't know. I never saw him after that day. Josiah told me he was a murderer and a rapist. He even showed me the pictures."

"Josiah lies." His eyes flashed like storm clouds.

She tried to force back the tears. "Josiah said if we didn't interrogate Malphus, it would lead to hundreds or thousands of human deaths. We hurt one to save many. A demon for many humans. It was simple math."

"Math," he repeated, his voice glacial. "That's an interesting way of putting it."

"You know him." A hollow opened up in the pit of her stomach. "Who is he?"

"It's none of your concern."

Caine glared at her, his eyes cold, black pools.

The judgment on his face stoked her ire. "What are you on your high horse about? You seemed perfectly fine with torture a half hour ago when it was *me* in the chair."

"When Josiah was interrogating you, you didn't have a hawthorn stake jutting from your ribs."

"Humans don't need a hawthorn stake to feel the blows," she shot back.

"And I would have stopped it before he did any serious damage. I would have got you out of there. Can you tell me the same for Malphus?" His voice sent a chill through her. "Is he even alive?"

"I have no idea, but I guess you could say when I interrogated Malphus, I was acting tactically. It is a war, after all. Isn't that what you said?"

"Well, then." Venom laced his voice. "If you plan to be strategic, you'd best get to work on your brilliant plan. And I really do hope it's brilliant."

CHAPTER 30

Over an hour later, and after three cups of coffee, she'd managed to piece together what she could remember of assembly languages. She was fairly certain her plan *was* brilliant.

Now, she needed to shove all the panic into her mental vault so she could focus—just like she was attempting to block out the open hostility radiating from Caine, who'd been pacing back and forth across the room like a caged animal for the entire hour.

She sat at the edge of the bed, laptop open. Before emailing Josiah, she glanced at the clock: 3:14 a.m. She'd set up the email to come from a burner account, *Cleo.X@sanguinebrotherhood.ca*. In the subject heading, she typed "Info about Rosalind." She clicked the paperclip, attaching a document called "Rosalind_location.docx."

Only a lunatic would open a random file from a suspicious account, but Josiah probably fit that description. Her entire plan hinged on his fanatical need for control outstripping his judgment. The man was so desperate for revenge that he might not be able to restrain himself.

Once he opened the attachment, the worm she'd created would infect the system, allowing her to explore the network.

Her body buzzed with excitement—or possibly caffeine overload. If she'd gauged this right, she had the potential to gain control over the entire security system. Finally, all the time she'd spent listening to Professor Carroll's monologues would actually pay off with a stunning takeover of the Chambers.

Caine paced over the floor, clearly riled by the inaction. "You realize that we can only rescue Aurora before the sun comes up, right? I think we should revisit Tammi's suggestion to use explosives."

"Explosions would risk killing the people we're trying to save."

"I want to kill people. And you want me to wait while you tap away with your fingers."

"There's a point to this. I've created a computer worm." She took another sip of Orcus's weird, herbal coffee. Ignoring Caine's fierce glare, she opened Terminal and typed *tail -F access.log.*

"You've created a *worm*," he repeated in a tone that said she'd lost her mind.

"The US government used something like this to hack into Iran's nuclear centrifuges. The worm will install itself, giving me access beyond the firewall. Through the server, I'll be able to command the system. I can survey the network to see what's there. I'll be able to figure out how to control the building."

Caine rested his palms on the table, staring down at her. "You're not talking about a literal wall of fire, are you? That was the only thing I could picture from what you just said."

She let out a sigh. "Let me put it this way: If this works, we can shut down the Chamber's retina and ID scanners. Anyone will be able to get in the building. All the prisoners will be free to escape their rooms. And I can disable the sprinklers that spray iron dust, so anyone with magic can fight back."

He straightened, suddenly interested. "If we went in, I could use my magic in the Chambers?"

"Assuming you can do it without destroying the place."

"Destroying the place would be the whole point."

She kept her eyes locked on the dark screen, waiting for an update.

Everything—her chance to redeem herself, her friends lives—it all depended on one line of code. *Come on, Josiah, you psychotic asshole. Open the email.*

Her heart skipped a beat as a line of code updated in terminal—the Brotherhood's server had made a request. She loosed a long breath. "It's working. Josiah opened the attachment. Dumb fuck."

"What's happening?" Caine asked, leaning over her.

Her pulse raced, and she typed a command telling the Chamber's server to download mapping software. It would allow her to scan the network. "I'm looking for vulnerabilities."

"Exploit vulnerabilities," he said, a hint of admiration seeping into his tone. "Like you so cleverly did with Josiah."

"Same idea."

"Good. I look forward to finding out if your colleagues murdered Malphus."

She flinched, trying to scan through computer names in Nmap. "You're not helping me focus, Caine."

retinascan.brotherhood.agency.gov. And those would be the retina scanners. They weren't exactly very well hidden. The computers controlling the badge scanners had a similarly obvious name.

Probing further, she picked out the name *dust.brotherhood. agency.gov*—the iron dust.

If they'd promoted her to Guardian and put her in charge of their security systems, she would have renamed their computers, but they'd screwed that right up.

She inhaled deeply, picking up the gun she'd stolen earlier. "Are you ready to transport us? Once I make these changes, all hell will break loose in the Chambers. I want to make sure Tammi doesn't get lost. Or eaten by a starving demon."

"I've been ready for over an hour."

One by one, she picked through the computers—the ones that simulated sunlight to burn the vamps, those that blasted hawthorn stakes at incubi. She rewrote the code until *none* of them were functioning, and in a final masterstroke, she shut out the lights.

Chaos would rule the Chambers tonight.

After she disabled the last computer, she stood, facing Caine. Her body trembled with anticipation. "Let's go."

He wrapped his arms around her, anchoring her with his aura. This time, she pulled off her own ring.

<h1 style="text-align:center">CHAPTER 31</h1>

*A*s the mist cleared, Caine slid her ring back on her finger—
only to yank her forcefully behind a tree. They stood a
hundred feet from the Chambers, shielded by an oak. On the other
side of grassy courtyard, a line of armed guards stood before the old
brick Chambers.

Red lights flashed from the roof, glinting off the shattered glass
that littered the ground from their earlier escape. In the quiet night,
the guards' feet crunched over the shards.

From inside the building, gunshots rang out, and her stomach
turned. She hadn't even *thought* about the guns. She'd been so focused
on fighting with magic, that she hadn't thought about ordinary fire-
power—which, incidentally, could kill ordinary humans.

From the streets of Harvard Square, sirens blared. Reinforcements
were already on their way.

Caine whispered in her ear, "I'm going to build a shield around the
building. We'll be able to get out, but no one can enter. And I'll get rid
of the guards. Stay a few paces behind me, and you'll be protected."

He stepped out from the oak, holding out his arms to either side.
Rosalind followed behind, walking through the shadows over the soft
grass. Caine chanted in Angelic, and as he spoke, his silvery aura

whirled around his body, curling through the air across the courtyard. The guards stood frozen. After a few moments, they dropped their guns, stumbling away.

Something didn't seem right, and dread whispered over her skin. Why weren't the prisoners fleeing the building? She clutched the gun tightly. She wasn't trained to use it, but she'd managed to shoot through the glass earlier.

Her breath came faster as they approached the shattered doors, footsteps crunching over the glass. The flashing red lights cast a garish hue over the abandoned security desk. Behind Caine, Rosalind tentatively stepped through the lobby, her gun raised.

A rhythmic sound, metal against wood, grew louder in the stairwell, and the door swung open, releasing noxious black smoke.

A bearded man stood in the doorway, his chest bare. Copper boots encased his feet, and he wore a red hat, dripping with gore. Blood ran down his chin. Fear coursed through her mind. *A redcap.*

The man's pale eyes landed on Rosalind. "I'm still hungry, and you look delicious," he growled.

When Caine stepped closer to the demon, his body crackled with magic. "Get out of here while you still can, redcap."

Behind the demon, two large, black dogs bounded through the doors, their eyes glowing yellow. *Hellhounds.* At least some prisoners were making it out.

The redcap glowered, baring his long, yellowed teeth. "I'll eat elsewhere." A moment later, he sprinted from the building, metal boots clanking over the ground.

From the prisons below, screams pierced the walls, and the sound curdled Rosalind's stomach. *Gods, what is happening down there?*

The building smelled of burning wood and fumes, and Rosalind covered her mouth with her shirt. *Tammi must be terrified right now.*

Caine pulled open the door to the stairwell, glancing at her as smoke billowed past. "Please be careful down there."

She stepped into the stairwell, her heart squeezing in her chest as she glimpsed two guards' bodies lying crumpled at the bottom of the stairs, their throats ripped out. Blood pooled around them—no doubt the red cap's most recent meal.

As he descended the stairs, Caine chanted a spell, and tendrils of magic curled around him. Through the security doors, the prison corridor glowed orange, but as Caine chanted, the air grew damp. Thunder rumbled through the walls.

At the bottom of the stairs, he pushed open the doors, just as heavy rain began falling from the ceiling. Red lights flashed over the halls, and the acrid smoke burned Rosalind's eyes. Something felt *wrong.* Where was Josiah?

Rosalind followed after Caine, and the deluge he'd created soaked through her clothes. The air hissed with dampened fires, and she rushed to the first open cell.

A thin, ginger woman stood shivering in the center of the room, her green eyes large. Her feet were bare, and she wore a ragged white dress, the fabric now singed. Around her, the rain doused a circle of fire, and tiny licks of flames still lingered over the scorched floorboards.

A sharp ache pierced Rosalind's chest. Apparently, this was the Brotherhood's primitive back up system in case technology failed. This explained the gasoline stench that always pervaded these rooms. It only required a simple mechanism—something to drop a lit flame from the ceiling when the electricity cut out, trapping the prisoners with fire.

"Go!" Rosalind yelled to the woman. "Get out of here."

The woman flinched.

"The doors are open!" Caine's voice boomed through the corridor. "You're free to go!"

The woman scuttled past Rosalind.

When Rosalind turned back to the corridor, she gasped at the slew of prisoners pouring from their cells. Some sobbed, others growled. By their auras, she could see that some were witches and demons, but many were simply pedestrians.

Rosalind lowered her gun, tucking it into the back of her belt. *We've won.* She just needed to find Tammi. And why couldn't she shake the feeling that something was *wrong?*

Ignoring the pit in her stomach, she followed Caine against the stream of fleeing prisoners.

Through the crowd, Aurora hurried toward them, her dress torn and bloodied. "Caine!" She threw her arms around him. "I knew you'd come for me."

In the next moment, Tammi's voice cut through the crowd. "Rosalind! Those fuckers tried to light me on fire!"

Rosalind's throat tightened as she caught a glimpse of Tammi, her lips swollen and cheeks bruised. One of her eyes had swelled shut.

Rosalind gently ran her fingers over her friend's face. "Oh my gods, Tammi. What did they do to you?"

"Your fuckstick of an ex-boyfriend paid me a visit."

Hot rage burned through Rosalind's blood, and she had an overwhelming desire to hunt Josiah down and stake him again. "Do you know where he is now?"

Tammi shook her head. "I'd like to think one of the demons ate him, but I have no idea."

In the corridor, the crowd was thinning out, and Caine turned to them. "I have to find Miranda and Malphus. I can handle this on my own. The three of you should get out of the building. Wait for Miranda out there if I need to send her to you."

Rosalind shook her head, marshaling her resolve. She was the whole reason Miranda was in here, and she planned to get her sister out. "I'm staying with you."

"Who the hell is Miranda?" Tammi asked.

"My twin—" Rosalind stopped herself. There wasn't any time to get into this now. "Just go outside, and if you see someone who looks like me, that's Miranda."

"I'm taking Tammi to safety," Aurora said, grabbing Tammi by the arm. "With a bit of my blood, she'll be right as rain."

Apart from a few other stragglers, who limped on injured legs, the corridor was nearly empty. At least Tammi and Aurora were safe, but Miranda's absence was a bad sign.

Rosalind raised her gun as they walked quickly through the hall, checking one empty cell after another. If Miranda was a high security risk, maybe she wasn't even in here anymore.

As she looked into a dimly lit cell, she heard Caine's footsteps pause.

"Rosalind."

His tone made her stomach drop, and she turned, tentatively approaching across the corridor. Inside a cell, a man lay chained to a post. A hawthorn stake protruded from his shoulder, and his blond hair hung in his face. Deep bruises and gashes covered his body. *Malphas.*

At the sight of him, Rosalind's body began to shake. Josiah had completely brutalized him.

Caine ripped an iron chain from Malphus.

"Is he alive?" her voice cracked.

"Barely."

"Can you use your magic to heal him?"

"No. It only works on humans."

"What can I do?" she asked in desperation. "Can I heal him?"

"Not as long as he's unconscious. I think you should get out of here and leave me to sort this out on my own. Go find Miranda if you can, bring her to safety, and get out of the building."

Tears stung her eyes, and she turned to walk out of the room, crossing her arms. She'd been a part of that, and the guilt ate at her.

She walked further down the corridor, peering in each room for signs of Miranda. An eerie silence had descended—the only sound filling the hall was the distant rattle of Malphus's chains as Caine pulled them off, and the steady dripping of water. All of a sudden, her own breath sounded deafening.

She was about to meet Miranda, her own twin. The fact that Miranda hadn't run from her cell like everyone else was already making her stomach lurch. In the best case scenario, Miranda was unhurt, but in all likelihood she hated Rosalind. Why wouldn't she? Rosalind had sent her here.

Rosalind peered into a cell, expecting another empty room, but what she saw stopped her heart. Miranda—her mirror image—sat bound to a chair with an iron chain. She wore a ragged green dress, and faint bruises covered her skin. She looked exactly like Rosalind, except a network of ridged scars ran over her arms. This wasn't how a reunion of long-lost sisters was supposed to be. Still, at least she was alive.

Miranda blinked, staring at Rosalind. "You came for me." Her voice sounded small.

Rosalind rushed over to her, bending over to give her sister a hug. "I'm so sorry, Miranda. I didn't know it was you."

"Didn't know *what* was me?"

"I told the Brotherhood about the sea witch. I didn't know it was you. I was an idiot. I didn't know anything. I get it now. I'm not with the Brotherhood anymore." Her words tumbled out in a panicked rush, like she was some kind of maniac.

"Oh. I was looking for you." Miranda shifted in her chains. "Can you get the key, please? They left it on the floor where I could see it. But I can't reach it."

"Of course." Like an asshole, Rosalind had been blubbering to her sister instead of freeing her. She snatched a metal key from the ground, rushing around to slide it into the lock. She turned it, and it clicked open, releasing the chains. They fell to the floor in a heap.

Miranda sighed with relief, rubbing her arms.

"Do you need help walking?" Rosalind offered her arm.

Miranda took it, groaning slightly as she stood, and Rosalind led her into the corridor.

Rosalind eyed her sister's scars, and the collarbone that protruded from her chest. It looked like it had broken and healed over not long before. "Did Josiah do this to you?"

"Do what?" Miranda asked distractedly, wincing at the flashing lights.

"The scars and the beatings. Someone hurt you. I'm guessing it was Josiah."

Miranda glanced at her arms, as if seeing the damage for the first time. "Oh. That. Mostly Josiah, and Randolph. They were in my room a lot."

Rosalind felt sick. Where the fuck was Josiah anyway? She wanted to punch his face through the back of his head. "I didn't know what Josiah was like." She had a sudden desire to confess everything to Miranda, to try to explain herself. "I didn't know that he was a psycho."

Miranda squeezed her arm. "People aren't always what they seem."

They drew closer to Malphus's cell, and Rosalind peered into the room. Cain kneeled over the other incubus, and at her approach he glanced up.

His face brightened when he caught sight of Miranda. "Thank the gods. You're okay."

"Rosalind came for me." She pointed to Malphus. "Is he dead?" she asked sweetly.

Rosalind was starting to get the impression that Josiah had beaten some of the "normal human behavior" out of her sister, but Miranda would get better with time. She just needed to get out of this hellhole to recuperate.

"He's alive," Caine said. "I'm setting some of his broken bones before I move him. Go outside and wait for me. I'll bring him upstairs in a few minutes."

Rosalind gently pulled Miranda's arm, and they continued down the corridor, passing one empty cell after another.

"One thing confuses me," Rosalind said. "I still don't understand how the Brotherhood got to me so fast. I told them where you were, but they were already waiting for me by the time I got back to my room. How did they know about us?"

Miranda shrugged, her large eyes gleaming. "Malphus told them, of course. After Randolph Loring hurt him."

Rosalind's blood roared in her ears. "You know him? Who is he?"

They reached the stairwell, and began climbing the stairs.

"It's funny you don't remember him from Maremount. He was Caine's brother. I remember everything. I remember you. I braided your hair. And Malphus was the one who gave us bluebells and dandelions when our parents forgot our birthday. Malphus was the one who patched up your skinned knee with tree moss and barbery root. He was always good to us. I never knew he was a demon."

Rosalind's mouth went dry. The yellow and blue flowers, the person tending to her knee—it had been *Malphus*. She could hardly find her voice. "You remember much more than I do."

At the top of the stairs, Miranda pushed open the door. "I remember too much. Sometimes I can't quiet the voices in my mind."

None of this would have happened if Rosalind had never followed Josiah into the interrogation room. Revulsion climbed up Rosalind's throat. She'd been an instrument in her own downfall, and of the very people she should have protected. She'd told the Brotherhood where to find Miranda, and she was the reason they'd arrested Tammi and Aurora. On top of that, she'd tortured Malphus. When his spirit broke, her name must have rolled right off his tongue.

"I didn't know who he was. I didn't recognize him," Rosalind mumbled.

In the lobby, Miranda tugged on her arm. "It's okay. Come with me. There's something you need to see."

Rosalind shook her head, distracted. Flashing lights blared outside the protective shield that Caine had created around the building, and someone with a booming voice barked orders into a loudspeaker.

Rosalind glanced at Miranda. "What are you talking about? What do you need to show me?"

"It's in the Great Hall."

"What do you mean? How do you even know about the Great Hall?" Her skin prickled with apprehension.

Miranda tugged her hand, pulling Rosalind toward the great oak door. "My magic helps me see things. And I want you to see, too. You wear the iron ring. You're wedded to Blodrial. But I can show you something you've never seen before." She pushed through the door.

Rosalind didn't know what was happening, but she wasn't about to argue with the sister she'd sent to a torture chamber. Hugging her sodden clothes, she stepped into the Great Hall, and the door slammed behind her.

"Why are we in here, Miranda?"

Miranda walked to the circular stage. Through the darkness, Rosalind could now see an iron stake that stood in the center of the room, its base surrounded by a pile of wood. High above, moonlight streamed through the oculus, which someone had opened to the air, almost as if someone had prepared the room for... Her stomach hollowed out. "Miranda. Let's go. We shouldn't be in here."

Miranda backed away. Light sparked off metal on her finger—an iron ring. "I didn't have a choice. He makes me do things. He says he'll protect me from the pain."

"*Who* says he'll protect you?"

Miranda slipped into the shadows. "Josiah."

CHAPTER 32

a fist slammed into the side of Rosalind's head, and her world spun. She tottered. Through her blurred vision, she caught a glimpse of Josiah's enormous form. *What the fuck, Miranda?*

She hadn't even begun the fight, and was already at a disadvantage. Stumbling, she reached for the gun in the back of her pants, but Josiah gripped her arm hard. He grabbed the gun and pointed it at Rosalind's head.

"You betrayed me." His voice cracked.

Rosalind's head throbbed, and she stared into the barrel. She choked down a thousand angry retorts. This wasn't the time to argue.

"I was supposed to protect you. I planned to find a way to marry you. You were mine." The gun shook in his hands. "And then I saw you wrapping your legs around that monster."

Rosalind seethed with rage. She'd just risked her life trying to save people from Josiah's torture, and he was going on about a kiss that hurt his feelings. "It was tactical," she ventured, trying on one of Caine's lines. "I was doing what I thought I had to do to get back to you. You've always been the one I wanted." The words tasted like poison in her mouth.

"I can't have a woman who lusts after demons. What about the other incubus? Did you screw him, too?" He favored his left leg—the one she hadn't stabbed with wood.

"No. I had no idea who Malphus was." She still needed answers. "How did you find him in the first place?"

"It was my job to watch over you. I followed you some nights after we broke up. I waited outside your window, looking inside. And one night, I saw someone else following you. It made me so angry. I started hitting him, but he was stronger than a human. That's when I knew. I had to stake him. That's why I had to make you interrogate him. I needed to see what you'd do. You were willing to hurt him. So I let you go. I had faith in you." His voice broke. "I was wrong."

A cold sweat beaded on her forehead. Malphus had been searching for her—just like Miranda had. And Josiah had attacked him not as a noble soldier in the fight against evil, but as a psychotically jealous ex-boyfriend.

As the truth of the situation dawned on her, the rage in her chest burned hotter, flooding her body like a hot magma. Josiah hadn't been her Guardian. He'd been her stalker.

Her foot flew to his gun, and she kicked it hard out of his hand. It spun over the marble floor.

Josiah glared at her, rolling his shoulders. "I don't need a gun."

He uncorked a right hook to Rosalind's head, but she ducked, and his swing failed to connect. He threw another punch, and his fist grazed her head. *Gods damn it.* His arms were much longer than hers. This was not a fair fight. What had Aurora told her? That she was awfully preoccupied with fairness, and sometimes bad things happen to good people.

She just needed to keep her distance until the right moment. She backed away, weaving away from his blows until he started to overextend his reach. When he pitched his body forward too far, she slammed her foot into his gut with a front kick, and he doubled over. She used that moment to ram an elbow into his lower back, bringing down the full force of the blow right into his kidney. Josiah grunted, trying to right himself. She threw a right cross, connecting hard with his temple, and he staggered.

Adrenaline coursed through her veins. "Screw you, Josiah."

As Josiah stumbled back, she scanned the floor for the gun. This was the moment she needed to end this, or get out of there fast. She heard the sound of a gun cocking, and turned to find Miranda pointing the barrel in her face.

Tears streamed down Miranda's face. "I don't want to do this. But I know it's what Josiah wants. And he's the only one who can keep me safe."

Horror coiled through Rosalind. "Miranda. You don't have to do this anymore. You're free. You can use your magic now."

Josiah straightened, pulling the gun from Miranda's hands. "She knows what's good for her. She's going to chain you to the stake." Josiah pulled out a small metal spray can and soaked Rosalind with liquid. The sharp smell of gasoline burned her nostrils. "You broke one of my teeth," he said evenly. "And you stabbed me."

A pale, pink light glowed through the oculus. The sun was beginning to rise, and for the first time Rosalind realized there was someone else in the room. A stream of rosy light fell on Randolph Loring, who sat on one of the benches, watching.

"Are you here to watch the show?" Rosalind asked him, her legs trembling.

Randolph leaned forward, resting his elbows on his knees. "The flames will purify you. They illuminate the truth." He lifted a hand to the sunlight. "*Lux in tenebris lucet*: light shines in the darkness."

"Stand in front of the stake," Josiah said, still pointing the gun. "Miranda will bind you."

She glared at him. Maybe she could get close enough to kick him right in that injured leg. "No fucking way."

Josiah pulled the trigger, and pain exploded through her thigh. She moaned, and he unleashed another shot. Agony ripped through her stomach, and she clutched the bleeding wound. *I'm going to die here.* She staggered back, stumbling over the wood that surrounded the stake.

Josiah drew closer over the marble floor, and her mind blazed with pure panic. *Run, Rosalind.*

"Stand by the stake," he said through gritted teeth. "That's how it's supposed to happen."

Another gunshot ripped through her ankle, and she whimpered, nearly collapsing. *Stand up, Rosalind. Show him you won't bow to him.* Blood seeped from her stomach.

Randolph rose. "This is your chance to atone, Rosalind. This is the only way you will keep your soul. Better that you burn now than suffer an eternal torment in one of the shadow hells."

The door slammed open. Caine stood in the entrance. His black eyes glinted with ancient, primordial rage.

His sterling aura radiated around him, filling the large space. His magic enveloped Josiah's body, making him tremble. Josiah still held the gun, but his body stood immobilized. Clutching her stomach, Rosalind shuffled over the floor. She threw a punch to his temple, as hard as she could, though pain screamed through her gut.

Wrath burned through her blood. "You're a monster, Josiah." A part of her wanted to bash his skull into the floor, but she didn't have the strength, plus she'd lose the moral high ground. Still, she could get in one more punch. With a grunt, she slammed her fist into his throat, and he emitted a choking sound.

"Stop it!" Miranda screamed, pulling at her hair. "He promised to protect me!"

Rosalind stumbled back, and the pain she'd been ignoring flooded her body. She clutched her bleeding stomach, ready to collapse.

She watched with awestruck fascination as Caine's magic forced Josiah's arm to bend. Grunting, Josiah pressed the barrel against his own head.

"Stop!" Miranda shrieked.

Josiah's face reddened, sweat streaking his temples. He cocked the gun and pulled the trigger. The gunshot echoed off the high stone ceiling, followed by Miranda's anguished screams—almost as if she *cared* about her torturer. Sobbing, Miranda ran from the room, slamming through the oak door.

Rosalind glanced away, unwilling to look at the carnage. When she forced herself to glance back, she shuddered at the sight of Josiah's crumpled body and the gore pooling across the floor in a crimson puddle.

Caine glanced at her, and concern glinted in his eyes as she struggled to stand. He stepped over Josiah's corpse. Something moved in the shadows behind him, and her gaze darted to Randolph. She'd forgotten about him. There was something in his hand—

"Caine!" She shouted.

Randolph hurled a stake right for Caine's chest. Rosalind's hand flew to her mouth, and her world stopped as she watched Caine's tall frame crash to the floor by Josiah's. Caine's silver aura snapped into his body.

"Caine!" With pain fragmenting her leg, she tried to hobble to him, but Randolph blocked her path.

Stepping over Josiah's corpse, the Brotherhood's leader aimed a flamethrower right at Rosalind's gasoline-soaked clothes. "Your demon lover murdered one of my finest Guardians. It's okay. Josiah wasn't a true believer. He didn't belong with us. But I did want to watch you burn—not for my own pleasure, of course. But because it is Blodrial's will."

Fear tightened around Rosalind's heart like a honeysuckle vine, crushing the life out of her. With the flamethrower pointed right at her chest, Randolph was about to set her ablaze. She'd felt the flames before—when Cleo had taken over her body—but this time, her skin would blister for real.

Cleo. The mage was her one hope.

Rosalind pulled off her ring and hurled it at Randolph. The moment it was off her finger, Cleo's aura exploded from her body, and Rosalind's mouth began to form ancient, Angelic words.

Randolph's eyes bulged, and his flamethrower clanked against the marble floor.

He held up his hands, screaming in Latin, *"Exorcizamus te, omnis immunde spiritus, omnis incursio infernalis adversarii."* His words seemed to shield him from the tendrils of Cleo's vernal magic that curled around him. His body glowed with a golden light, and he backed over Josiah's body, chanting. *"In nomini et virtute Domini nostri Blodrial!"*

Cleo's temper flared. She would protect this body from the evil ones. Cleo chanted in Angelic, and her magic lashed out at him. She wanted to hurt him, to force his guts out of his throat, but those words he spoke shielded him.

They made Rosalind's body shake, as though he was forcing the aura out of her. Hot agony coursed through her. Still, he continued to retreat, his face reddening with the effort, and Cleo felt a thrill of raw power as he scuttled from the room like a bug.

When the door slammed shut with finality, Cleo turned her attention to the beautiful incubus on the ground, his breathing labored. Richard was in there somewhere, but the incubus's body was dying.

Trapped somewhere within Cleo's powerful vernal magic, Rosalind's mind screamed *save him.*

She walked closer. Ignoring the pain that wracked her body, she knelt down, her blood pooling on the floor and mingling with Josiah's.

Cleo pulled the stake from his chest. Caine gasped, his back arching with the pain. *Still conscious.* She lay next to him, stroking her hand over his chest, and pressed her mouth to his. His perfect lips parted, warm and soft, and he kissed her deeply. Hungrily, he drank in her energy, and his arm tightened around her back. At his intensifying touch, heat shot through her body.

The incubus's aura strengthened deliciously, swirling through her belly, caressing her skin. He pulled her on top of him, the kiss energizing him.

She had no idea who she was, or where she was, only that she wanted more of him.

She nearly gasped when he pulled away, looking into her eyes, searching.

"You're Cleo, aren't you?"

Cleo needed his mouth on hers, and moved closer to kiss him again, but he held her at bay, staring at the blood streaming from her shoulder. "You're hurt. I need to get you out of here. Say the spell with me, Cleo. Rosalind will die if I don't heal her."

He reached out, snatching the iron ring from the floor before he returned to her. Wrapping his arms around her, he chanted a spell for teleportation, and she joined in, their auras mingling together with an intense, euphoric power.

CHAPTER 33

$\mathcal{I}$n the celestial room, Caine carried Rosalind across the room. Thick, starry curtains blocked out all the sunlight, and candlelight danced over the room.

Caine gently lowered Rosalind to the bed, propping her up on the pillows. With the iron ring back on her finger, she gripped her shoulder, no longer able to block out the agony.

Excruciating pain blazed through her stomach and collarbone, and blood poured from her wounds.

She heaved a sigh of relief as she heard Aurora and Tammi's conversation pierce the walls from the next room. *Thank the gods— they're safe.*

Caine pulled off her jacket, and the pain took her breath away as she moved. "I need to heal you—now. You're losing a lot of blood." He ripped the front of her shirt open, unable to hide the fear flickering across his features when he saw her stomach.

"Miranda ran off," Rosalind said, her mind twisting with confusion. The blood loss made her dizzy, almost as if she could feel her heart rate growing fainter. "She thought Josiah was her protection."

"Don't worry about that now." Caine traced his fingertips around the wound, then closed his eyes, chanting in Angelic. His aura whispered over her skin. It pulsed through her body, slowly drawing the pain out of the wound.

She took a slow, shuddering breath. "What happened to Malphus?"

"I handed him over to Aurora before I went looking for you. I was nearly too late." He scanned her body. "You need to take off your pants."

She leaned back on the bed, unbuttoning the top of her pants as he pulled off her boots. Grimacing, she slid her pants down past her thighs, and Caine tugged them off the rest of the way. Blood streaked her legs, and Caine winced as he looked at her ankle. It was obviously in rough shape.

"You killed Josiah," she said.

"I can't imagine you'd object at this point." He ran his fingers over her ankle, and his aura assuaged the pain. She watched with fascination as the skin healed over, the wound shrinking.

"Not even a little."

His fingers traced higher up her leg, his touch tingling over her thigh, and the pain from the last gunshot drifted away at his warm, soothing touch. As he finished healing her, she took a deep breath, her body still throbbing with a faint ache.

"That should do it," he said, his gaze trailing over her body.

"I just want to clean the blood off before I find Tammi. She tends to freak out about blood."

"Give me a moment." His fingers still lingered on her leg, and as he chanted, his aura whispered over her skin, sweeping away the blood and gasoline. Her body thrilled at his touch. When he finished, she was suddenly very aware that she wore nothing but the red underwear, and that Caine's hand rested on her thigh. Her heart pounded harder, and her breath sped up as she looked into his perfect face. His soft, smooth lips had just been on hers, and—

The door slammed open, and Aurora stood in the entrance. "Seven hells. I heard someone's heart pumping hard, and I thought you might be injured, but no. We just barely got away from an evil cult with our lives intact and you two are stripping off to get it on with each other."

Caine turned, pulling his hand away from Rosalind's leg.

"I was healing her."

Aurora narrowed her eyes. "Is it just me, or are you two awfully fond of 'healing' each other? You know, you could just shag like normal people and not subject yourself to broken bones first."

Rosalind pulled her ripped shirt closed. "Josiah shot me."

"Josiah's a twat." Aurora cocked her head. "You know Caine doesn't actually need to touch you to perform magic, right?"

Caine rose, frowning. "It works better that way, actually."

With her body now healed and clean of blood, Rosalind slipped back into her pants. She tied the remnants of her shirt in a knot in front of her bra. "Is everyone okay?"

"Fine, yes," Aurora said. "Though I nearly burned to death in the sunlight on the way home. Next time you're planning on rescuing me from the death cult, please do it closer to midnight. And Tammi's not quite ready for this level of excitement. I had to give her two cocktails to stop her from babbling."

Tammi strolled in, her face now fully healed and slightly flushed. "There you are! What the hell happened to you? You were supposed to meet us outside the Chambers."

"Josiah," Rosalind managed. It was all she could get out right then. If she divulged the full details, she'd break into hysterical sobs—and she wanted to do that when she was alone.

Tammi frowned, approaching across the stone floor. "Caine said you found your twin. Where is she?"

Rosalind shook her head. "I found her, but she wasn't right. Mentally. I think Josiah warped her mind. The Brotherhood has a way of doing that to people."

"So what happened to her?" Aurora asked. "Ambrose will want to know."

Rosalind blinked, fatigue overtaking her. "She ran off. She seemed to think Josiah was her savior. My guess is that she's wandering around Cambridge, ranting about her protector."

"That's some serious Stockholm Syndrome shit," Aurora said.

Right now, Rosalind couldn't handle the guilt—the crushing weight of having sent her sister to the torture chambers.

Then again, maybe Rosalind was just as much a victim of the Brotherhood as Miranda had been—after all, the Brotherhood had a way of warping a person's mind.

"Is Malphus all right?" Caine asked.

"Orcus is tending to him," Aurora said. "What's our plan now? How long are we staying?"

Caine rubbed his sternum where he'd been stabbed. "Rosalind and Tammi should stay here for now. You and I will return to Lilinor with Malphus when night falls. We've just provoked an all-out war with the Brotherhood, and we need to report to Ambrose."

Aurora put her hands on her hips. "He won't be happy that we lost Miranda."

Caine glanced at Rosalind. "We'll find Miranda again. I promise. But right now I'm going to check on my brother. You should all get some rest."

Without a backward glance, he stepped out of the celestial room, and the girls followed behind him. Tammi closed the door, leaving Rosalind on her own.

Alone at last, she threw herself on the bed, her body burning with exhaustion. Caine was an amazing healer, but even he couldn't fix everything.

She pulled down the covers, climbing into the bed before blowing out the candles.

She closed her eyes, and the dreams that flickered through her sleep were of a girl whose face looked just like her own, of dandelions and bluebell flowers, and sea foam running over her toes.

When she woke in the darkness hours later, she was almost certain someone had brushed a soft kiss across her cheek.

CHAPTER 34

Rosalind heated the silver kettle in the cavernous stone fireplace, breathing in the strong, herbal aroma of Orcus's coffee. Since she'd met the night demons, her schedule had become completely screwed up. Strong coffee at seven p.m.—in a vast, stony living room—seemed a perfectly reasonable idea.

Tammi sat cross-legged in a mahogany chair, stretching her arms over her head. "I've never in my life slept as well as I have here. I don't know if Orcus is lacing our tea with opiates or if I'm just suited to sleeping during the day, but I feel amazing. What did Orcus say this place was called, again? I want to take up residence."

Rosalind sat across from her. "Abduxiel mansion. And, apparently, we're welcome here as long as we're in good standing with the night demons. It's kind of like a sanctuary for Nyxobas's allies."

Tammi sipped her coffee. "I wouldn't mind if a gorgeous vamp or two came in. I've read through half the library by now, and it's full of epic poems about hellhounds and angels of death. Not really my thing."

"I'll ask Orcus if he can find us some billionaire romances."

Tammi crossed her legs. "Speaking of romances—what's the deal with you and Caine?"

"The deal is that he's an incubus who flirts with everyone. Oh, and I nearly tortured his brother to death. We're not really well-suited."

"After Josiah, I'm not sure you can be trusted to choose your own boyfriends."

Rosalind flinched. "You have a point."

Josiah, for all his idiocy, had managed to lure her into trusting him. And what he'd done to Miranda had been even worse.

Though Orcus had forbidden it, Rosalind had been sneaking out during the day to search Cambridge's streets for her sister. She'd been desperate to feel that briny aura tingling over her skin, but she hadn't sensed the slightest glimmer. Then again, if Miranda was still wearing the iron ring, Rosalind wouldn't be able to sense her at all.

Footsteps echoed through the room, and Rosalind turned to see Orcus, his head covered by a hood. "Rosalind. There is someone here to see you."

Her pulse began to race, and she stood. *Miranda?*

Rosalind rushed through the door into the main hall, hurried over the marble floor, and pulled open the oak entrance. A tall figure lingered in the doorway, and the rosy sunset cast him in silhouette. *Caine.* Her breathing quickened.

"Rosalind. I just wanted to make sure you're okay."

"I'm fine."

He took her hand, his touch sending shivers over her skin, and led her out into the fresh spring air. The sunset hung hot in the sky like a ripe peach, bathing his skin in a tawny light. Around the gravestones, violet bluebells and broken acorns blanketed the grass.

Caine stopped by a towering oak, turning to look at her. "Ambrose has sent his men out to search for Miranda. Nothing to report so far."

"I've been looking for her too," Rosalind said.

"You're supposed to stay here. The Brotherhood want to murder you."

"You can't stop me from looking for her, just like I could never stop you from going after Malphus."

"Except that I *could* stop you." A muscle worked in his jaw. "Fine. I see your point."

"Why didn't you tell me you had a brother in there?"

He peered down at her, and the ruddy light stained his gray eyes a coral color. "If Josiah had known Malphus was my brother, Malphus wouldn't be alive right now. I'm not going to give up my secrets without a very good reason."

The lack of trust stung, but she couldn't blame him. After all, she had helped Josiah break him. "Miranda told me Malphus used to give me flowers. Is that true?"

"He did. I wasn't as nice."

"I want to meet him. If he doesn't hate me now."

"You'll meet him. Ambrose still has big plans for us."

"Plans that involve finding Miranda?"

"That's the first step. The Brotherhood will no longer be stupid enough to rely on technology the way they did. They'll be amassing an army of their own, and Ambrose wants to crush them with magic."

A shiver ran up her spine. "When Cleo was hammering Randolph with a spell, he protected himself with… magic. It was a different sort of magic. He was speaking in Latin, and his body glowed a golden color."

Caine nodded. "They don't use Angelic. But they have their own sort of magic. They give it another name. That's all."

Rosalind let her eyes trail over Caine's muscled frame, clad in a form-fitting black shirt. "Do Ambrose's plans involve me reporting to you as my commanding officer?"

A smile flickered over his lips. "Mmm. Yes. You'll be required to follow all of my orders."

"Good luck with that."

"Fair warning. There are a lot of female vamps in the army who will be competing for my attention. Can you blame them, honestly?"

She cocked a hip. "It must be quite a hardship for you to live in a vampire city. No mirrors."

"Nyxobas gives me the strength to endure. Speaking of Lilinor, I need to return before sundown, but I'll come back as soon as I hear anything." He nodded at the mansion. "You're safe here, but stay in Abduxiel Mansion."

Giving orders again. She crossed her arms, shooting him an irritated glare as he turned to leave.

He walked a few steps before pausing to turn back to her. "Stay here if you want, I mean. Your choice."

As he walked off to the crypt portal, a small smile curled her lips. For the first time in a while, something unclenched in her chest.

She now lived with a grim reaper in a cemetery, and her twin sister was missing. Yet after all the tumult of the past few days, she felt a strange sense of normalcy.

If nothing else, they were all alive—and somewhere deep within Rosalind, a sense of belonging was budding.

WITCH HUNTER - BOOK TWO

SUMMARY

A web of secrets. Bloodthirsty demons. A new nightmare.

Humans are going missing all over the city. Bloodthirsty shadow demons are attacking, and the Brotherhood wants to return to the old ways to control the chaos.

Digging deeper into these sinister new threats, Rosalind once again joins forces with Caine. But the sexy incubus has been keeping some major secrets from her—secrets that hold clues to her own history. And as Rosalind uncovers the truth about herself, she realizes she has to risk her sanity if she wants to save humanity.

CHAPTER 1

For a prison, it was very pretty. Long grass and wildflowers tickled Rosalind's bare ankles, and the sun setting over the cemetery lawns streaked the steel-blue sky with marigold and pumpkin.

But it was still a damn prison—she had Caine to thank for that.

Rosalind looked down at the skull in her hands. White fungus webbed the bony surface, and her *Rouge Dior* fingernails stood out against it like fat drops of blood. Gilded by the dying light, it all looked strangely beautiful.

Even from her prison, at least she got to watch the sunset every night. So what if she'd never envisioned her life turning out this way —trapped in a cemetery, clutching part of a human skeleton? At least the golden light made her feel like a normal human again—for fifteen or twenty minutes.

Her fingers trembled, and she tightened her grip on the skull.

Okay, she *nearly* felt normal. The eight cups of coffee she'd been drinking daily had her a little jazzed up.

But she needed that caffeine rush, like birds needed wings. The fact was, she couldn't deal with her nightmares anymore. She'd do anything to stay awake as long as she could. Two hours of sleep a night meant only two hours of seeing Caine lying half-dead on the Chambers floor, two hours of witnessing her insane twin sister trying to burn her to death in the Chambers.

The down side, of course, was that she was just about on the wrong side of sane right now. And sometimes, her dreams broke through her waking hours in terrifying flashes.

So she had to find ways to fill her waking hours, too. While Orcus slept all day, she worked through the little tasks the reaper left out for her: rearranging spellbooks, crushing herbs, selling poultices and bones to mages outside the mansion.

She tried not to think about Caine, tried not to let herself stew in resentment. But when she saw him again they were going to have a little talk about the magical wards he'd put up.

She let out a long sigh, crossing the grass. Two days after she'd arrived at Abduxiel Mansion, she'd awoken to find Orcus hunched over a yellowed piece of paper. Turned out it was a note from Caine, reporting two things: one, he'd taken Tammi to another safe house, for reasons he didn't bother explaining; and two, he'd sealed Rosalind in to Abduxiel Mansion for her own good. He'd thrown a warding spell around the place and swanned off into the night. Apparently, Rosalind was "impulsive" and "couldn't be trusted."

So here she was, hawking skull fungus and doing anything she could to avoid her dreams.

She leaned against one of the tombs—an enormous sphinx statue, its surface stippled with sage-green moss. Sighing, she slid down the cool marble. Spring's rich scent hung in the air, and the breeze caressed her skin.

She let her eyelids drift close. Immediately, another image flickered behind them: Malphas, hanging half-dead in one of the Brotherhood's prisons.

Her eyes snapped open again. *Nope. Don't think you can ever relax again, Rosalind. Rookie mistake.*

The sound of footfalls caught her attention and she rose, peering around the sphinx's side. The sun had dipped behind the oak trees, the sky darkening to a slate gray. A man was walking toward her, silhouetted by the setting sun—tall, broad shoulders, strong arms. Her heart skipped a beat. *Caine?* That incubus was her ticket out of this magical prison.

Barefoot, she crossed the grass, a cool wind ruffling her hair. But as the figure stalked closer, her stomach sank. The man didn't move with Caine's preternatural grace, and his hair was a dusty blond. By the faint magic flickering around him, she could tell he was a mage, but not quite as powerful as Caine.

He paused just a few feet from her and narrowed his brown eyes. "I was expecting Orcus."

"Orcus is sleeping." She ran her painted nails over the skull's surface. "You're here for this, I take it?"

He smelled like a mountain wind—granite, snow, and pine. "Complete with the night god's fungus, unless Orcus is trying to cheat me."

She forced a smile. "Of course it has fungus. Everyone needs skull fungus." She hadn't been expecting someone so young and cute, with a strong jaw and an athletic body. All the other mages who'd come to buy herbs had been withered crones.

But when her gaze flicked to his strong arms, her Hunter training kicked in. *Would I be able to take him in a fight if it came down to it?* Against most humans, her training gave her pretty good odds, but he had muscle and heft on his side. Part of her actually *wanted* to see how those odds would turn out—to feel the thrill of a fight again, to feel alive. If he attacked, she could grab him by the hair and bash his head against—

"Something wrong?" he asked, his voice tinged with concern.

She sucked in a sharp breath. *Definitely too much caffeine. And that's how screwed up I've become. I meet a cute guy, and within thirty seconds, I'm envisioning smashing his skull against a gravestone.* "Nothing wrong. Sorry. It's just—I've been trapped here, and my nerves are a little frazzled. Way too much coffee. And honestly, two weeks in a cemetery with only a reaper for company makes a person restless, you know?"

"Did you say you're trapped here?"

"Pretty much. There's a warding spell around us. Luckily for you, it's only designed to trap me."

"Ah. I thought I noticed the rush of an aura."

"You're a mage, I take it?"

"Yes, I'm a philosopher." He pulled out a silver coin, ready to exchange it for the skull. "Which is why I need that skull."

She cocked her head, her curiosity piqued. "A *philosopher?*"

"It's what we call mages where I'm from—Maremount."

Her stomach swooped at the reference to her homeland, and she tightened her grip on the skull. She wasn't letting him leave without answering a few questions first. Not only did she want to know what was going on in Boston, but this could be her chance to learn a bit about Maremount. This guy's visit was the most interesting thing to happen for weeks. "Maremount," she repeated.

"Right." He held out a hand expectantly. "And I'll be using that skull fungus for a powerful protection spell. There are dangerous forces out there now. I'm not sure what they are, but something sinister is floating on the wind."

She inhaled deeply. "Before I give you the skull, what can you tell me about what's going on in Cambridge and Boston? Any news with the Brotherhood, or any rogue mages?"

Sighing, he rolled the silver coin between his fingers, the movements rhythmic, almost hypnotic. "You'll have to be more specific."

What she really wanted to know was what the hell had happened to Miranda. "Okay. Have you heard anything about a crazy mage running around the streets of Cambridge? A girl who looks exactly like me?"

"A crazy mage who looks just like you?" He cocked his head. "Are you talking about yourself, by any chance? Can I just buy the skull? I have—"

Irritation flared, and she grabbed his arm, nearly dropping the skull. "No. I'm not crazy. I have a twin sister, but she ran off with the Brotherhood." *Calm down, Rosalind. You're going to freak him out.* She loosened her grip on his arm. If she was hoping to dispel his impression that she was nuts, clutching his arm like a maniac wouldn't help.

He frowned. "Why on earth would a mage run away with the Brotherhood?"

Good question. "I don't know. I guess… She was in one of their prisons, which was my fault, and then it seemed like they'd converted her or something. Like they'd tortured all the sanity out of her."

She caught his subtle shift away from her. "What do you mean, it was *your* fault she was imprisoned?"

Seven hells. We're going to delve into all my dysfunction here. At least it was good to have another human to talk to for once. "I used to be a Hunter with the Brotherhood. I used to hunt mages like you, but then it turned out I have magical abilities, and now the Brotherhood want to light me on fire." If there was a better way to phrase that, her brain was too fried to think of it right now. "I didn't know she was my sister when I turned her in to the Brotherhood. I just sensed her aura—the salty taste, the blue color. And then a couple of weeks ago, I think I sensed her aura around here, but I couldn't get to her. Not with the ward up."

He shook his head apologetically. "I haven't heard anything about your sister. I'm sorry. I'll come back to let you know if the Brotherhood announce anything. There's so much chaos going on out there. It's hard to figure out what's going on."

Her throat tightened. *I'm so out of the loop.* "What do you mean?"

"Humans have been going missing all over Boston and Cambridge. People are panicking."

"I hadn't heard that. No one knows what's happening to them?"

"Total mystery." He studied her closely. "Has someone trapped you here as punishment for your time as a Hunter?"

She flicked a stray strand of hair from her eyes. "According to a demon I know, I'm locked up for my own good. Apparently, I'm impulsive and likely run to my own death." She bit her lip. "I don't suppose you know how to unlock wards, do you?"

He glanced away, scratching his cheek. "Well… I'm not sure…"

Okay, he clearly doesn't trust me. Why would he? She'd just confessed to being an ex-Hunter with impulse control problems, one who'd thrown her own sister in jail. *Let's back up a little bit.* She held out a hand. "I'm sorry. Maybe I should introduce myself properly. I'm Rosalind."

He shook her hand, his grip firm. "My name is Drew. And I'm relieved you're no longer likely to hunt me to my death. I'm not sure I'd want to take you in a fight."

Her smile this time was genuine.

He nodded at the skull. "Isn't your friend going to introduce himself?"

"He's bone-weary." She nearly groaned at her own terrible pun, but her smile widened. "This is the first normal conversation I've had in weeks."

"Is this what passes for normal in your world?" He crinkled his nose. "That's a little bit sad."

Finally, she held out the skull to Drew. "At least you're human. And alive. That automatically makes you quality company in my book."

He took the skull from her, handing her the large silver coin in return. "Human and alive. Those are two of my finest qualities." His smile faded. "And, in regards to your question about destroying the ward, as much as I'd like to help free you, I don't want to anger a reaper like Orcus."

Her throat bobbed with disappointment. "All right. I guess I understand."

Pity softened his eyes. "I'm not sure how much you know about demons, but you don't want to provoke their wrath. I've got a coven to look after. We're involved in something big right now, and I can't risk it. I'll trade with a demon, but they're dangerous to have as friends. You understand, right? They may seem human at times, but their basic nature is to view us as prey."

She tensed. It was the same thing Josiah had told her, and he'd turned out to be a lying asshole. *Don't trust anyone, Rosalind.* "Some demons are different, surely."

"I suppose. But they don't value honesty the way we do, and it's in their nature to try to enslave us."

Her brow crinkled. Caine had made it sound like it was the other way around. "My friend said demons were enslaved in Maremount. Incubi especially."

He shook his head. "Not anymore. The city's leading philosophers found ways to keep us separated from demons. Before we gained control of the city, a monstrous demon nearly destroyed us. He viciously slaughtered the king and queen, tried to take over the city. His memory still haunts the kingdom. Parents scare their children with stories of the Ravener to keep them in line."

"The Ravener..." Goosebumps rose on her skin. "He sounds terrifying, but Orcus doesn't seem so bad."

"A Hunter living among the demons." He cocked an eyebrow. "Seems very strange."

"*Ex*-Hunter."

"And what are you now, if you're no longer a Hunter?"

She twisted her iron ring around her finger, shivering in the chilly breeze. "For now, I'm simply hepped up on too much coffee."

A smile ghosted across his lips. "I don't think there's anything simple about you, Rosalind." He held up the skull. "But, intriguing as you are, I need to get my new friend home. There are dark forces at work around us, and the winds are thick with menace."

The hair rose on the back of Rosalind's neck, but she couldn't let him go just yet. He was from *Maremount,* after all. "Before you leave— can you tell me if you knew the Atherton family?"

She heard his sharp intake of breath. "Why do you ask about them?"

"They're my family. Or so I'm told. I don't remember them. I left Maremount when I was little, and I can't remember a thing that happened there."

The corner of his mouth twitched, and Rosalind almost thought she felt a sudden shift in the air, a thickening of the shadows. But Drew only shook his head. "I didn't really know them. Only the name. Sorry. I can't help you."

"If you come back, can you help me learn about magic? I don't need a lot of help..." She trailed off. *How do I explain this?* "I already have all the knowledge inside me. I just need to access it. I need someone to help me not go crazy while I learn."

"Of course. I'll come back." A few of his blond curls danced in the wind, and he turned to leave before gazing back at her. "Rosalind.

Here's your first magical lesson: To create a ward, you must use a sigil. It's a type of symbol, something in a circle that your jailer would have marked somewhere. Perhaps a piece of paper... Once you destroy that, you'll be free."

She smiled. "Thank you, Drew."

He looked around him furtively. "Be careful. Demons don't belong with humans. Not even magical humans like you." He turned, walking off into the darkening cemetery.

CHAPTER 2

At the wooden table in the mansion's kitchen, Orcus hunched over a bowl of bacon bits, scooping them into his mouth. Only a dim, guttering candle lit the room. Shadow demons weren't fond of bright lights.

Rosalind sipped her coffee, frowning at his breakfast. "I don't think you're supposed to eat bacon bits that way."

"I'm four hundred eighty-seven years old. I can eat them however I like."

Four hundred eighty-seven? She sipped the strong coffee, studying him—his shiny bald dome and hairless face. Large, black eyes and thin lips. Come to think of it, she didn't actually know what a grim reaper was, or how long they lived. "I had no idea you were so old. Are you immortal?"

"No. I was human, once. And now I collect souls for Nyxobas."

"And what do you get out of that deal?"

"Once I've collected all the souls in my ledger, I'm free from my bargain."

"What did you bargain your soul for?" she asked.

"For the love of the most beautiful woman who ever lived. Now if I collect enough souls for Nyxobas, I can escape the shadow hell."

She beamed. "For love. That's awfully romantic. Where is she now?"

"Dead." *Crunch.*

"Oh." She'd learned about mortal demons when she was in the Brotherhood—they could live on for centuries, unless they were killed with the right combination of iron and hawthorn wood. The Brotherhood, of course, had those weapons stockpiled.

Orcus took another bite, his crunching echoing off the high, stone ceiling. "Did you sell the skull?"

"I did." *And now I'd like to find where Caine hid the damn sigil.*

Orcus held out his hand, and she pulled the silver coin from her jeans pocket, dropping it into his palm. "The mage told me humans have been going missing from all over Cambridge and Boston."

Orcus grunted, completely uninterested.

"Did you know your client was from Maremount?" she asked.

"Is that so?" *Crunch.*

"He said that in my homeland, demons and humans are kept separate. He said something went wrong in the early days of Maremount. The demons got out of control, and the city's philosophers had to put protections in place."

Orcus's looked up from his breakfast. "Seems awfully one-sided."

She cocked her head. "I'm totally confused. How did Caine end up with my parents as a little boy if the city was protected from demons?"

"Never mind that." His eyes darted back to his breakfast. "I have some dried bloodroot I need you to make into a paste."

"Bloodroot. Right." She dropped her empty coffee cup on the table, crossing her arms. "Do you know anything about my family?"

"I know you shouldn't be interrogating my clients." Orcus snatched the bowl of sugar from the center of the wooden table and poured out a mountain of granules. His long, pointed tongue darted out to lick his finger, which he dabbed in the sugar before sucking it clean.

Rosalind grimaced, her stomach turning. Nausea welled in her gut, and Orcus's eating habits weren't helping the situation. "What are you afraid I might learn if I speak to your clients?"

"A bunch of horseshit to nourish the soil of your nightmares. You should be sleeping soundly. And you should eat. You're getting too thin." He licked his finger again, jabbing it into his sugar pile. "I'm going to make you a soporific potion. You've become unhinged."

She'd been getting sick of Orcus telling her she looked tired, so she'd slapped on extra makeup from Tammi's stash today—a dewy blush, deep raspberry lipstick, concealer under her eyes. But apparently reapers couldn't be fooled with makeup. "I haven't been feeling well." Her leg bounced up and down. "And I feel out of the loop. It's strange to me that Caine took Tammi."

"I'm sure he has his reasons."

"You're sure Tammi is in a safe place? I just find the whole thing odd—Caine taking her while we slept, with no explanation."

"I told you. He put up the wards, and took her to a safe house. It's in the letter he wrote for me, marked with his seal."

She shook her head. "I thought *this* was a safe house."

Orcus's large, dark eyes surveyed her, and he leaned forward. "Listen, girl. I've been a warrior far longer than you have. But my orders are to keep you here. I don't like it any better than you do. I should be out there, collecting souls for Nyxobas, slaughtering hellhounds in the night. It delights me to hear their death cries, and I'm denied this simple pleasure by your stifling presence. And yet I do it, because it's my duty. I serve the god of night in whichever ways he requires."

Time for another tactic. She didn't give a flying fuck about Nyxobas, but maybe duty was the best way to appeal to Orcus. "What if I can serve the god of night by helping Caine? What if he needs me?"

Another lick off his finger. "For what?"

"I can help get him out of danger."

Orcus paused, mid-lick. "He can kill people with his mind. I don't think he needs the help of a human girl."

She crossed her arms. "When we were together, he needed my mage powers to transport us from one place to another during emergencies."

The reaper's pale face broke into an unnerving, toothy smile, lending him the appearance of a death's head. "Did he now? And how do you suppose he survived such a long time without you?"

"What do you mean, 'such a long time'?"

His eyes bulged and he stood, picking up his bowl. "I'm not here to engage in idle gossip. Get the bloodroot. It needs crushing."

Rosalind wasn't letting it go that easily. "I don't get it," she pressed. "If he didn't need me to chant the spell with him, why would he pretend that he did?"

Orcus blinked. "A spell like that requires a great expenditure of energy, I suppose. He'd burn himself out using it all the time on his own. And I suppose he was probably trying to get you using your magic. Impending death has a way of motivating people, I find. And you needed motivating, with all of your neuroses."

Seriously? As Orcus walked away, Rosalind's fingers tightened into fists. She was trapped here by Caine, who apparently had a tendency to lie about crucial information.

Definitely time to re-evaluate my lack of magical skills. She'd just have to deal with the fact that she lost her mind a bit whenever she took off the ring.

She crossed to the coffee pot, pouring herself another cup and letting the rich aroma fill her nostrils. As she took a sip, she caught a glimpse of herself in a cracked mirror hanging from the stone wall. Orcus was right—she was starting to look like a skeleton, with cheeks the color of bone and dark circles hanging below her brown eyes.

I need to get away from this prison. She downed the coffee, and its heat burned her throat. *First, I need to find the sigil.*

She had no idea where to look for it, or even what it might look like, but at least she had her first clue. And perhaps she could investigate the creepy old library for information about sigils.

Dropping her mug onto the counter, she crossed the kitchen to the hall. As she walked, she trailed her fingers over the cool stone walls, and her footsteps echoed off the flagstones as she passed into the cavernous library.

The room was amazing. Below a starry, vaulted ceiling, leather tomes stood crammed into oak bookshelves. Ladders reached up to towering upper stories of books. Across from an enormous, multi-paned window, a fire burned in a stone fireplace, casting dancing light over a well-worn embroidered rug.

Rosalind inhaled deeply, the scent of burning cedar filling her nose. *If I can't find the sigil, maybe I could just hole up here night and day, learning about magic until I can break myself free.*

She crossed to the shelves, tracing her finger along a row of book spines, scanning the titles. She half-hoped something obvious would pop out—like "Where to Find Sigils"—but that probably wasn't how arcane texts worked. Anyway, most of the titles were written in Angelic or Latin, neither of which she could read. The few in English had twee names like *Comptesse Amauberge's Love Remedies* or *Early Percy's Encyclopedia of Famine Curses.*

She sighed, crossing into an alcove, and her gaze landed on some-thing that sent her pulse racing. On a faded black spine, copper lettering spelled out the word *Maremount.*

Okay, so it wouldn't tell her how to find a sigil. But now her curiosity was beyond piqued. She had the strangest feeling that Drew had known more than he was letting on, and Caine was certainly hiding things from her.

Maremount was her homeland, and yet she hardly knew a thing about it.

She pulled it from the shelf, cracking it open. The first heading read *1692.* As she read the text, it gave an account of the Salem Witch Trials, which had led to widespread panic among the "philosophers." In order to escape the Hunter's purges in Salem, they'd created Mare-mount using a powerful spell.

She paged ahead, her heart speeding up at the word *demon.*

In 1693, a bestial demon known as the Ravener slipped through the city gates, his mind twisted by hatred of humankind. With the most evil inten-tions, he infiltrated the Throcknell Fortress, then slaughtered fair and noble Queen Sapphira, tossing her out a tower window. The Ravener ripped apart the castle, intent on regicide, until he found King Malchior and tore his heart from his chest. His terrible deed committed, the Ravener slipped from the city gates—

A hand yanked the book from her grasp, and she stared up into Orcus's cold, dark eyes.

Her cheeks burned with irritation. "I was reading that."

He turned, hurrying to the fireplace, and she gaped as he tossed the book into the flames. "*That,* little girl, will only feed your nightmares."

"I can decide what will give me nightmares." She glared at him. He was awfully preoccupied with her nightmares. "What don't you want me to read? Drew already told me about the Ravener."

Orcus furrowed his brow, pulling up his black hood over his head. "You don't know much, and that's the way it should be."

Anger simmered. *Don't trust anyone, Rosalind.* "Why is everyone so intent on hiding things from me?"

Orcus shook his head. "You're paranoid, Rosalind. You're not thinking right. You look like a crazy woman. Get some sleep before the nightmares fill your waking life."

Dark, acrid smoke swirled from the flames, and the room slowly filled with the scent of burning paper.

"I'm not paranoid." She cocked a hip. "You just burned a book to stop me from reading. I think my suspicions are justified."

"Let me make you a tonic to help—"

"I don't want a sleep tonic." Her pulse raced, and sweat beaded on her brow. "I want to search the streets for my sister. I swear I've felt her aura, and I can feel all kinds of powerful magic around us. And I want to hunt down Randolph Loring, beat him until he screams for mercy, and chain him to the walls of one of his prisons. I want to find out what Drew meant when he said the air was thick with menace." She could feel it, too—and it was starting to make her sick. She leaned over and retched.

"What's the matter with you? Never mind. I'll tell you what's the matter—all that coffee rotted your gut."

She retched again, clutching her stomach. This wasn't just nausea. There was something *familiar* about this sensation. The last time she'd felt this sick was when she'd first visited Lilinor. That feeling had been the magic at the boundaries—shadow magic and light magic magnetically attracted to each other.

"Hang on a sec, Orcus." She blinked, letting her eyes focus in the dim light as a shudder wracked her body. Thick tendrils of magic stained the air—pale shimmering copper, deep sea-green, dark silver. A whole rainbow of light and dark colors. *Why didn't I notice it before?* It was almost as if shadow magic and light magic were warring with each other, trying to cancel each other out, and she couldn't see them unless she concentrated.

Orcus tutted. "Are you going to stand there all night making those gagging noises?"

"Orcus. There's magic all around us—light and dark forces together. It's astoundingly powerful."

He sniffed. "What on earth are you talking about?"

"There's silver night magic, like Caine's, moving over my skin like a warm wind. Miranda's sea magic—salty and wet on my skin. But it's not just light magic. There's gold, copper, and pale gray."

"Light demons." A wicked glee tinged his voice.

She shook her head, trying to understand. "Why would light magic merge with shadow magic? I thought there was some kind of ancient war going on between those two."

"There is. And perhaps they're waging a battle now. I have no idea." He scowled, pacing across the floor. "If the reapers are fighting a battle with hellhounds, I should be there. They will need me to fight with them."

"We should both go."

"Don't be ridiculous," he scoffed.

"You can't leave me here unguarded. The Brotherhood could come in and kidnap me, and then Caine will be furious."

His nostrils flared. "Why would you *want* to go? You're no match for true demons."

"I can sense Miranda's aura. I don't know if she's in trouble, or if she's working with the Brotherhood—but either way, I need to find her."

Orcus straightened. "Fine. But you must stay near me. Caine will murder me if you get hurt."

Relief washed over Rosalind. "I'll stay near you. I promise."

Orcus cast a critical eye over her clothing. "You're going to wear *that?*"

She glanced down at herself, at her faded black T-shirt and coffee-stained jeans. She hadn't exactly been thinking about things like fashion lately, nor did she care to start now. "You're wearing a hooded cloak. I don't think you're in a position to judge."

"I suppose we'll be invisible anyway." He narrowed his dark eyes. "Another reason for you to stay close to me. The invisibility spell wears off after a while." His long teeth glinted in the firelight. "And if we come across any light demons, let me do the killing."

"I won't get in your way." She frowned. "But you don't have any idea what we're getting into?"

"No." He stepped closer, thrusting a bony finger in her face. "But I'll tell you this. You don't need to read the books about the Ravener and his murders four centuries ago. There are plenty of monsters around us now to fill your nightmares for a hundred years. And you'll see some of them tonight. That's why little girls like you get locked up for safety. Are you sure you want to go out there?"

Despite the fire, a shiver ran over her skin. "Miranda's out there. She's not exactly sane anymore, and she's in over her head."

"I thought she tried to kill you. What do you care?"

"It's the Brotherhood's fault she's crazy. Like you said, there are monsters all around us. Even the human ones."

Wordlessly, Orcus pulled a scroll from his cloak and unrolled it. Rosalind caught a glimpse of a circle, with a six pointed figure in the center. *The sigil?*

She frowned, trying to see it better, but Orcus blew on it, and it disappeared in a puff of black ash. "What was that symbol?" she asked.

"The symbol of Azazeyl. Why Caine used that, I have no idea."

"Who is Azazeyl?"

"A false god. He does not exist."

And yet, the magic worked. A sharp tendril of dread wound through her. There was something very strange going on.

What she didn't say to Orcus was that she had another reason for wanting to leave the cemetery: she wanted to know what the hell had happened to Tammi, too, because she wasn't buying this safe house story.

And right now, Rosalind didn't trust anyone.

The night air was thick with the sweet scent of blooming linden trees and the overgrown honeysuckle that climbed the sides of Brattle Street's Victorian homes.

In front of the moon, shadow magic and light magic swirled in large curls. The magic was all around, rippling over Rosalind's skin, disorienting her—silver, green, gold, copper, blue... too many colors and senses for her to keep track of. Dizzy, she rubbed her forehead.

Orcus trudged along a few paces in front of her. With the invisibility spell in effect, she couldn't see his body—only the curls of midnight blue magic emanating from his cloak. If she concentrated, she could follow his anise-scented magical aura. And if that wasn't enough, the sound of his wooden-soled shoes on the bricks was easy enough to follow.

Someone should tell that guy to purchase a pair of Keds if he really wants to go incognito.

She studied each pedestrian they passed, looking for signs of panic, but she could read nothing amiss on their faces. If there was a demonic war raging nearby, none of them seemed to know about it. A car rolled slowly by, blaring bass-heavy music, with the sharp scent of marijuana wafting from the windows. *Business as usual here, no signs of impending doom.* But none of these people could see the magic that whipped the air around them.

As Rosalind drew closer to Harvard Square, her entire body buzzed with apprehension. A wave of sickness climbed up her throat, and she turned to retch. The closer they got to the Brotherhood's home base, the worse she felt.

"Is that you making that noise again?" Orcus grumbled.

"I'm fine," she managed, her gaze landing on a tendril of blue magic. It undulated in the air like a sea-anemone, washing over her skin. "I think Miranda is near, but there are so many auras around. I can't figure out what's going on." She wiped the back of her hand against her mouth.

Her body buzzed, and she looked down. There was a reason she was feeling so sick—the magical auras were no longer just curling around her—some of them were rushing into her body in waves. She clamped her eyes shut, trying to force them out of her. As the magic thrummed over her skin, dipping into her bones, she felt an over-whelming desire to turn back.

I need to get control of this. She wouldn't be very effective at pulling Miranda away from the Brotherhood if she was too busy puking in the bushes.

Slowing her breathing, she concentrated on forcing the magic into smaller whorls, compressing it down as best she could.

"Are you coming, or do you want to run home?" Orcus snapped, tapping his foot on the ground. "If you're going back to the cemetery, you should know that you won't be able to get into the mansion. You'll have to wait outside in the bushes."

If she hadn't felt so sick, she would have had a witty retort at the tip of her tongue—but instead all she managed was, "Stop haranguing me. I'm not running back to the cemet—"

She was interrupted by the sound of metal slamming against metal, followed by shattering glass. From Harvard Square, screams pierced the air—distinctly human.

It's starting.

At the sound of human terror, Rosalind pushed all her reservations aside. "Let's go." She broke into a run, Orcus's footsteps keeping pace beside her.

Her heart pounded in her chest like a war drum. *If things get really messy, I'll have to rely on the magic of my extra soul.* Granted, the Brotherhood had taught her to fight without magic—to use the environment around her as her tools instead of spells and auras—but she was quickly coming to understand that rocks and broken bottles were poor weapons in a demon war.

If things got really messy, she might need the nuclear option: Cleo.

Pumping her arms, she picked up her pace. She had no clue what she was heading toward, but she was nearly certain Miranda was part of it. *I just have no idea what role she's playing in this battle.* If she had to guess, her twin sister had become a pawn of the Brotherhood.

Her feet hammered the pavement, and she gasped as a wave of cold, nocturnal power slammed into her—silver, just like Caine's. *He's nearby.*

Her breath was ragged in her lungs as they rounded the corner and came into Harvard Square.

The scene before her was chaos. The first thing she saw was the car accident. An SUV had plowed into a Porsche, and the sports car's driver lay slumped over the wheel, forehead bleeding. A few people ran into the road, eyes wide.

The next thing she noticed was the street performer dressed as a mime, standing still on a platform, his body trembling as he gripped two flaming sticks. He wasn't looking at the accident. He was staring up at the sky, eyes bulging.

He unleashed a horrified scream.

Rosalind followed his gaze, and a wave of cold fear washed over her.

A swarm of demons flew above, with eyes the color of starlight and flowing white hair to match. They wore ragged black dresses that fluttered in the wind as they wove and darted like birds of prey. Panic tightened around her heart. It looked like something from an apocalyptic painting, and a demon horde like this meant only one thing: a lot of people were about to die.

A driver leaned on his horn, desperate to flee the intersection, but the accident blocked his path. All around, pedestrians were running, screams piercing the air.

A middle-aged woman stepped from the damaged SUV, her eyes wide. "What are those things?" she shrieked.

As Rosalind looked up again at the black-winged creatures circling the air above them, the air left her lungs. So many different shades of magic whirled around them, a type of power she'd never seen before. They beat their wings, weaving through the sky, crowded so thick and vast they blocked the moonlight.

By their starlit eyes and white hair, she was pretty sure she knew what they were, even before Orcus spoke. *Night demons.*

"Keres," Orcus said, as if hearing her thoughts. "Nyxobas's creatures. What are they doing here, by the Chambers? We're only a hundred feet from the Brotherhood's headquarters. Keres don't normally venture out of their caves unless cloaked in shadows."

She swallowed hard. "It's probably an attack on the Brotherhood."

Swooping lower, a female ker smiled, her long teeth glinting in the moonlight. Rosalind's mouth went dry. Despite her beautiful face, her skin the color of pearls, the ker oozed pure menace—and she looked hungry.

Rosalind stepped closer to Orcus. "I don't understand what's happening. There's so much magic around the keres. There's coppery mountain magic, Miranda's sea magic… all kinds of auras."

"Someone must be fighting them. It's not working very well. They must have some sort of shield around them."

She narrowed her eyes, looking for signs of weakness. A few keres seemed to shudder, their wings drooping and heads lolling, and they fell from the skies. Someone was fighting them, but the counterattack wasn't having much of an effect on the swarm as a whole.

Her gaze darted to a black bird flying among the keres—a raven, darting between the demons. *Caine's familiar.* Her chest tightened. "Caine is definitely here. And I want to find him."

"I thought he was in Lilinor," Orcus growled. "You're sure it's him?"

Gleaming silver magic curled all around her and she breathed deeply, inhaling a fresh scent like damp earth after a rainstorm. "It's definitely him. I just have no idea where he is, or what he's doing." She glanced at the sky again, watching as some of the keres burst into flames, their wings burning bright against the night sky.

But for each falling ker, there was another to take its place.

Her pulse raced as she scanned the chaotic scene. Police sirens wailed in the distance, and streams of people scrambled across Harvard Square, trying to get away from the cloud of keres. The air was *definitely* thick with menace, just as Drew had said. And in this case, "menace" meant terrifying, sharp-toothed demonesses.

A shiver crawled over Rosalind's skin. She could tell by the keres' snarling faces that they had their gazes set on distinctly human meals. And human fear only excited their bloodlust. The only reason the creatures weren't leering hungrily at her was that they couldn't see her.

But where was Miranda in all this? Rosalind could only hope that Tammi was truly safe, just as Orcus and Caine had said. Rosalind had a nuclear option—but Tammi had nothing.

Around her, the magical auras intensified, streaming into people's bodies. Tendrils of magic curled into Rosalind, vibrating through her ribs. Her stomach churned, and her muscles seized up one by one as her body petrified. The keres' magic transfixed her. If she wanted to rip her ring off now to unleash her own magic, she'd waited too long.

We're trapped like prey.

Locked in place, she stared in mute horror as a ker winged lower. The demon plunged toward a beautiful blond girl in a floral dress, whose entire body shook. The girl was trying to call for help, but her mouth was frozen, and she could only unleash a garbled scream. She looked like the picture of innocence, a hunted rabbit about to be slaughtered.

The ker dove lower, and the girl's blue eyes went wide as the ker sank its teeth into her neck. Blood streamed from her veins.

Rosalind's throat tightened. *They're going to kill us all.*

CHAPTER 4

As she watched the ker tear into the blonde girl's neck, rage flashed in the hollows of Rosalind's mind—a cold anger, furious as storm clouds. *I'm not going down without a fight.*

When Caine had taken her into the woods to train with her, she'd gained a fraction of control in forcing the magic from her body. He'd told her to condense the aura into a ball, something she could manipulate.

She clamped her eyes shut, letting herself focus on the whorls of magic in her body. *I just need to concentrate.* Her ability to sense magic was her greatest asset—if she could see it, she could mold it. As her pulse raced, she tried not to listen to the agonized screams around her.

She cleared her mind of all distracting thoughts, imagining the streams of shadow magic and light magic condensing into tighter rings, like a solar system whirling into a black hole. As the magic grew tighter, her dizziness began to subside. When she'd pushed the auras into a tiny point deep within her chest, she tried moving her hand. With effort, she felt her fingers tighten and relax.

A man's scream nearly ripped her attention away; for a second the tendrils expanded again in her mind. *Focus, Rosalind. Condense the magic, just like Caine said.*

Slowly, she envisioned the colorful wisps swirling tighter, and when she'd tightened them into a tiny marble of light, she wiggled her fingers.

Free.

She opened her eyes, and horror washed over her. The blond girl lay sprawled on the ground, her throat ripped open by the ker. A pool of blood stained her curls, and her blue eyes gaped lifelessly at the demon-filled sky. Around the girl, three more half-eaten humans lay discarded on the pavement.

Rosalind's heart thrummed. She couldn't break her focus. *I need to keep control if I'm going to get out of here alive.* Any minute now, the invisibility spell would wear off.

Another ker descended, winging for a middle-aged man. The demon slammed into her victim, gripping his arm and sinking her teeth into it. Ignoring the man's agonized screams, the ker pushed him to the ground, taking a bite of his cheek.

Rosalind's legs began to shake; her knees threatened to give way. The demoness wasn't going to kill her prey fast—she was going to slowly eat him alive.

I can't watch this.

Maybe now was a good time for the nuclear option—except that Orcus said they were shielded.

Her pulse racing, Rosalind scanned her surroundings, desperate for a weapon, until her gaze landed on the juggler's discarded sticks. They still blazed. *Pretty sure you can kill a shadow demon with fire.*

"Orcus," she shouted. "I have to do something."

He spoke from her right. "I don't understand what's happening. I'm trying to use my magic, but it's not working..." His voice trailed off.

She ran for the flaming sticks, snatching one from the ground. She turned, her gaze fixed on the ker, who was tearing the flesh from the man's calf.

Rosalind closed the distance between them, and touched her

flaming stick to the demoness's white tresses. The creature's hair ignited, and she roared—a deafening, inhuman scream—and dropped her victim. Flames spread over the ker's body, and her head swiveled around as she searched for her attacker. She staggered back from her victim, screeching wildly.

Rosalind's pulse raced uncontrollably, but the demon didn't seem to see her. *Still invisible, then. But that won't last forever.*

She looked around, trying to get a glimpse of Orcus's aura again. But before she could, another ker plunged down to the earth, claws outstretched as she dove straight for a young man. The creature grabbed her prey by the shirt collar. Rosalind ran to them, but before she could get there the demon carried him off the ground, black wings beating the air.

Rosalind's mouth went dry. *What are they doing now?*

When the ker had dragged him high over Harvard Square's rooftops, so high that the ker's could be mistaken for a raven, the demoness simply let go. Rosalind stared in open-mouthed horror as the young man plummeted down.

At the man's screams, Rosalind's stomach tightened.

He hit the ground with a sickening thud.

Don't look at his body. She had enough fuel for her nightmares already.

More keres followed suit, diving down to snatch humans from the earth.

Horror crawled over Rosalind's skin. *Please, gods, don't let Miranda be involved in this slaughter.*

She couldn't fight the nausea anymore. She hunched over and vomited up the coffee she'd been drinking all day. She wiped a shaking hand across the back of her mouth. *I need to get out of here before I lose my mind.*

In the distance, helicopter rotors thrummed. *The Brotherhood. Am I actually happy Hunters are coming this way?*

"Rosalind!" Orcus bellowed.

She turned to look at him as his body shimmered into view. She glanced down at her own translucent body, her heart racing wildly.

"We're becoming visible again," she shouted. "The keres will be able to see us. And the Hunters are coming. We should get out of their line of vision. I have no idea where Miranda is." She couldn't feel her sister's magic anymore. The helicopter blades beat louder; white searchlights danced over the swarm of attacking keres. "We need to get out of here."

The reaper's dark eyes glistened and he scanned the air, forehead crinkled in confusion. "I don't understand why the keres are attacking here. And I don't understand why my magic had no effect on them." He held out his long, spindly fingers, and a long black scythe appeared in his grasp. "Something very strange is going on."

"Okay, but we need to take shelter before the Brotherhood start shooting." Another body slammed to the ground next to her. Her chest clenched. This was horrifying.

"What would block my magic against other shadow demons?" Orcus asked, still staring at the sky.

Rosalind's blood roared in her ears, and she gripped the reaper's arm. They had two threats now: the keres *and* the Brotherhood's Hunters. If she knew anything about the Brotherhood, they were about to unleash a storm of gunfire at any minute.

She pointed to the SUV. "We're going to hide under the car. If we don't, we're going to die."

Orcus continued to gape at the sky. "What color did you say their auras were?"

"Orcus!" she yelled, frantically tugging on his arm. "We need to get out of the way. The Brotherhood's weapons are designed to kill mortal de—"

Bullets whizzed past, and she dove under the SUV. Bullets shattered its windows, and shards of glass rained around her. She covered her head with her arms.

When she lifted her eyes again, her gaze landed on the grim reaper, and horror turned her stomach. Two bullets had pierced his forehead, and dark blood oozed from the wounds. Those would be the iron-lined hawthorn bullets, designed precisely to kill demons like Orcus.

Ice slid over her skin. He'd be in the shadow hell now.

Why didn't he listen to me?

Her breath came in short, sharp bursts, and from under the SUV she heard the whirr of motors. This was not a good time for a notorious "witch"—an enemy of the state—to be hanging around here.

Heart thumping, she crawled closer to the edge of the SUV, catching a glimpse of armored vehicles rolling into Harvard Square. Adrenaline flooded her veins. Any minute now, armed soldiers would be pouring from those cars, ready to kill anything that looked magical.

Another volley of bullets ripped through the air, and she watched as a few ker bodies slammed to the ground, screeching.

She swallowed hard. *Where do I run to?* A month ago, her safe haven would have been the Chambers. Not anymore. Now the Hunters in the Chambers would burn her on sight.

She could run back to Abduxiel Mansion, but Orcus had said she'd be locked out. Still, she had to get out of here, fast. Maybe she could hide in the shadows by the mansion until she found Caine.

She could hear the helicopters moving further into Harvard Square, taking their gunfire with them. *Now or never.*

She shuffled forward, inching out from under the SUV. With shaking legs, she pushed herself up. Searchlights danced around her, and the sky still swarmed with keres. From here, the heavens seemed to convulse like a living thing.

She cast one last glance at Orcus's body, then launched into a sprint down Brattle Street.

As her feet pounded the bricks, she put as much distance as she could between herself and Harvard Square. She'd just managed to get out of range of the ker swarm when the sound of a motor caught her attention. It sounded like one of the Brotherhood's armored vehicles, but she didn't want to turn her head. She kept her eyes forward, hoping to go unnoticed, and sprinted onward.

"Rosalind!" a deep voice called out. "Stop or I'll shoot!"

She whirled, her gaze landing on a Brotherhood soldier. Her blood roared in her ears. A bright white light from an armored vehicle glared, and it took a second for her eyes to adjust.

When they did, she nearly turned and ran again.

She knew this Hunter by his shaved head and ruddy cheeks. It was Dave, a novice asshole from her training year. And he had a Glock trained right on her.

She froze, raising her hands and glaring at him. Out of everyone she knew in the Brotherhood, he was the last person she'd want to arrest her—well, second to last, after Randolph Loring. Dave's handsy wrestling techniques when he trained with the women had led Rosalind to dub him Sweaty-Hands Dave. But it hadn't been a joke to him. When he'd lost to her in round after round, she hadn't failed to notice the rage burning in his eyes.

"Well, well," he said. "I've been hoping to find you." He stalked closer, gripping his gun. "Put your hands behind your head, and lie on the ground."

"Dave. How nice to see you." *There's no way I'm lying on the ground for this pervert.* Wind from the helicopters beating overhead rushed over her skin.

He paced closer, gripping his gun harder. "You're quite the target, witch. Randolph Loring is very eager to get you back in his cells. And I'm going to bring you there." His nostrils flared; his cheeks reddened. His disgust was palpable, and she knew exactly what a guy like him wanted: pure dominance.

CHAPTER 5

Rosalind stared at Dave. With Josiah, she'd been able to use his rage against him, to cloud his judgment. She had a feeling Sweaty-Hands was no different.

And I think I know exactly how to push his buttons. "Hiding behind a gun? I'm just a little concerned it might slip out of your sweaty hands, and you could injure yourself. Think about how sad the world's women would be if you accidentally shot your dick off."

"I said lie on the ground!" he shouted, stepping closer.

He wanted to get up close and personal, probably kneel on her back and force the gun up against her head. He was one of *those* guys.

Her heart raced as he took another step.

"Why don't you come over here," she said, "and show me what you want me to do."

He took another step.

When his Glock was less than a foot from her head, she slammed it out of the way with her left hand, punching him hard in the jaw with her right. As he took the blow, she kneed him in the groin.

He doubled over, loosening his grip, and she ripped the gun from his grasp, turning it on him.

Rubbing his jaw, he gaped at her. "You used your magic…"

"I didn't use any magic. You're just terrible at everything." Her eyes flicked to the sky. No helicopters.

She cocked the gun. She didn't want to kill the guy, but if she didn't disable him, he'd just come after her.

Her gut clenching, she pointed her gun at one of his feet. "Sorry about this." She pulled the trigger, and blood burst from his foot.

His screams pierced the night sky, and she wasn't waiting around any longer. She tucked the gun into the back of her pants and broke into a sprint along Brattle Street.

Rotors beat the sky overhead, whipping her hair around her face, and another searchlight swerved over the road. She could only hope that there was enough chaos going on that no one would notice Sweaty-Hands Dave and his shattered foot.

Her breath grew ragged in her throat as she tore over the sidewalk. A stream of magic whirled around her, growing stronger as she ran, and she tried to analyze the tendrils, to focus on one at a time. She sucked in a breath, and the scent hit her—a mountain wind, pine and granite, rough on her skin. *Drew. He's around here somewhere.*

Hadn't he said his coven had been planning something to protect against the attack? She ground to a halt, leaning over with her hands on her knees to catch her breath. She needed to hunt his mountain magic down. As she gasped for breath she caught a glimmer of the copper tendrils, leading her further down Brattle Street.

She glanced behind her, catching sight of an armored vehicle coming her way. *They're coming for me.*

Her breath ragged, she stormed down Brattle Street, following the trail of copper magic, watching as it curled to the front of an enormous yellow mansion.

Breaking into another sprint, she tore down the street to the mansion, leaping over its white picket fence. But as she neared the door, she slammed face-first into an invisible wall. The wind rushed out of her lungs. *A ward.*

Frantically, she glanced around. The armored vehicle was coming closer. From a speaker on the vehicle, someone projected, "Approach the vehicle with your hands above your head."

"Drew!" she screamed. *It has to be his house.* "Drew! It's Rosalind. I need your help!"

When no one responded, she looked down at her iron ring. *Maybe now is the time for the nuclear option.* She had no idea what Cleo would do when she took over her body, and there was no one around to get the ring back on her finger. But the mage's spirit had a tendency to save her life.

As her fingers tightened on the ring, the door to the house swung open. Drew stood gaping in the door. "Rosalind. Where the hell did you come from?"

Frantic, she pointed to the armored vehicle. "They're about to open fire. I need to come inside."

"Seven hells." He chanted a quick spell, and she could feel a shift in the air around her, a lessening of the magnetic charge. The ward released; she bolted up the stairs.

The Brotherhood opened fire again. As Rosalind reached the top of the steps, pain ripped up her thigh. She collapsed into the hall, and Drew dragged her the rest of the way in, slamming the door.

Agony sank into her thigh bone, and she leaned against the wall.

She clamped her eyes shut, listening to Drew frantically chant a spell, then exhale a shaky breath. "The wards are up again. That should hold against the bullets, I think."

Somehow, the air was full of several auras now—not just Drew's but shimmering hot gold, and salty blue magic that rushed over her skin like cold seawater. *Miranda.* "There's magic all around us," she breathed.

White-faced, Drew crouched down. "Gods below, Rosalind. Don't try to talk. They nearly killed you. Were you out there when the keres came?" He leaned down, examining her thigh.

"I was there," she said, glancing at the deep red bullet hole. Blood pooled onto Drew's floor, and the pain stole her breath. "Can you heal this?"

"I'm good with potions. Give me a minute." He rose, disappearing into another room.

Her blood pumped hard. Gripping her thigh to staunch the blood, she looked around at the hall, trying to calm herself. Compared to the chaos outside, there was something very soothing about this place. A stairwell swooped upward, and lantern light flickered over orderly rows of oil paintings. A soft, bronze rug lay in the center of a hardwood hall. It felt *safe* in here. Almost instantly, her ragged nerves began to soothe, even if she was bleeding on his floor.

It's only too bad Orcus didn't make it this far...

Drew returned a minute later carrying a glass flask filled with dark green liquid, and a pair of copper tweezers. He handed her the vial. "Drink this, and don't watch what I'm doing."

"I take it this will hurt."

"The potion will help."

She pulled out the small cork stopper, pausing to look at Drew. She wasn't sure that she could trust a mage she'd just met—but she didn't have a ton of options right now. He was certainly a better bet than the Hunters trying to shoot her outside, or the keres eating humans alive.

She put the vial to her lips and took a long sip. It tasted of juniper berries, and it instantly began to soothe her pain.

"Look at that portrait of the woman in the copper crown," he said.

While Drew crouched beside her, Rosalind stared at one of the paintings on the wall, a beautiful woman with platinum hair and red lips.

She winced as Drew pulled the bullet from her thigh, but the potion certainly helped dull the pain. Pinching the bloody bullet between the tweezer's pincers, he dropped it into a copper bowl on a small table. "That wasn't so bad, was it?"

She glanced down at her thigh, where the skin was already healing. "Thank you, Drew. You'd think I'd be used to getting shot by now."

He stood. "Come into the parlor with me. I need a drink."

She nodded at the painting. "Who is that?"

He held out his hand, helping her up. "A queen, from a long time ago."

"I'll take one of those drinks you mentioned." She wiped a shaking hand across her brow. "Do you have any idea what the hell happened out there with the keres? It was a bloodbath."

He led her into a room lit by a chandelier, its light dancing over the room's lush fabrics in warm honey and apricot hues. A copper disc carved with an eagle hung above the marble fireplace; below the bird was the motto *Loyalty Binds Me.*

With a flick of his wrist, Drew ignited a fire in the fireplace.

Rosalind breathed in the rich scent of burning spruce. Her legs burned, and she sat on an antique gold sofa. She couldn't rid her thoughts of the image of that beautiful blond girl, being eaten alive by a ker. What really terrified her was the idea that Miranda could have caused that horror. It wasn't so hard to believe—not after Miranda had tried to kill her.

Drew crossed to a wooden table crammed with crystal decanters, and poured two measures of amber liquid into tumblers.

Thank the gods, Rosalind thought. *I'll need that.* If the violent images in her head hadn't been bad enough before, now she'd never be clear of her nightmares.

Drew crossed the room, handing her the drink. She noticed his hands shaking slightly. As he sat on the opposite sofa, she sniffed the tumbler. Rum.

"I saw him tonight." Drew's eyes had taken on a glazed look. "He was controlling the keres."

Him. At least that put Miranda in the clear. "Who was controlling the keres?"

The flames danced in his brown eyes. "The Ravener."

A chill washed over her skin. "He's still alive?"

Drew narrowed his eyes. "What do you know about him?"

"Only that he killed the king and queen in Maremount over three centuries ago. I just read it in a book. What was he doing in Cambridge?"

"He thrives on human blood." His Adam's apple bobbed.

A deep sense of dread began to bloom in Rosalind's mind. "What sort of demon is he?"

"He's an incubus. Son of the great demon Abrax, prince of the shadow hell."

She took a long sip of rum, and it burned her throat. "What else do you know about him?"

"You wouldn't know he was evil by his beauty. But I saw him there, controlling the keres. One of the philosophers in my coven can see magic. He felt the Ravener's magic all around us. We knew something was brewing, and tonight it exploded. We ran to a meeting point in Harvard Yard." He shook his head. "We tried to stop it, but the Ravener was stronger."

"The coven's magic—that must've been all those auras I saw around the keres," she said. "But I don't understand. What was the Ravener trying to achieve? Why did he suddenly appear out of nowhere?"

"I think he was after vengeance," he said. "He hates full-blooded humans. Always has, since long before he first slaughtered our king and queen. A powerful demon like him, forged in the shadow void— he was born to hate humans. And after what the Brotherhood did to his brother, he wanted to teach them a lesson. So he attacked with the keres."

Rosalind felt a glacial shiver run over her skin. *What the Brotherhood did to his brother.* The Brotherhood—Rosalind—had tortured Caine's brother. But the Ravener couldn't possibly be the same incubus.

She cleared her throat, afraid to ask the next question. Her knuckles went white as she clutched her glass tighter. "What's the Ravener's real name?"

Drew looked at her as if snapping out of a trance. "He goes by Caine." He took a swig of his drink. "Caine Mountfort."

CHAPTER 6

Ice closed around her heart. "It can't be him. I know him."

Drew's jaw dropped, horror etched all over his face. "You *what?*" He rose. "Let me guess. He's the one who imprisoned you against your will."

She could feel the blood draining from her head. "Yes, but he's never tried to hurt me."

"Only because he wants to use you for something. Has he told you what he wants you for?"

She opened her mouth, then closed it again. She actually didn't know why Caine and Ambrose needed her and Miranda so badly. "Caine has some idea for me, but..." She shook her head.

Before she could continue, a rapid chilling of the air stopped her sentence. The flames in the hearth burned lower. She shivered as a dark and powerful aura filled the room—a silver aura, one that smelled of fresh earth after a thunderstorm. It rushed over her skin like a night wind.

The hair on the back of her neck stood up, and she turned. Caine—the shadow mage—stood in Drew's parlor, his powerful magic whirling off him in menacing silver tendrils. His gray eyes drilled into Drew.

He looked just as he had when she'd first met him: intensely beautiful, but terrifying at the same time. He wore all black, with sharp, claw-like tattoos visible on his neck and eyes cold as glaciers. His raven sat perched on his shoulder, black eyes glittering.

Drew dropped his tumbler to the ground. "He's here," he whispered. "My wards. They didn't stop—"

Rosalind held up a hand, determined to get to the bottom of things before these two guys started murdering each other. "Everyone calm down. I think there's been a misunderstanding." She shot a perplexed look to Caine. "He thinks you're someone called the Ravener."

Caine's cold eyes slid to her. "I *am* someone called the Ravener."

Her breath caught in her throat. Her grip was so tight on her tumbler she was about to crush it. *What the actual fuck?* "You threw a queen out a window four hundred years ago?"

"Closer to three hundred years ago."

"How old are you? *Who* are you?" Her body was rigid with tension. "I don't understand."

His face red with fury, Drew began frantically chanting a spell. Coppery magic unfurled around him. It smelled like pines, and felt rough against her skin, like a brush of granite—and more powerful than Rosalind would have imagined.

Was it her imagination, or did it shimmer with other colors—periwinkle, gold, and gray?

As Drew's aura swirled around, Caine chanted a spell of his own, his silver aura lashing at the air.

A choking noise turned Rosalind's attention back to Drew, and panic coiled around her heart. Falling to his knees, Drew grabbed his neck. His eyes bulged, his face turned purple.

Caine—*the Ravener*—was choking him to death.

"Stop it, Caine!"

The shadow mage continued chanting, attacking Drew with his magic. But she'd seen enough death for one night. She pulled her gun from the back of her pants, pointing it at the incubus. "Stop being an asshole. He just saved my life."

Caine's eyes narrowed, and his lips stopped moving. Behind her, she heard Drew's body fall to the floor—probably dead.

She stared at Caine, lowering the gun. "He thought you were responsible for that slaughter. Something about revenge—" She paused, her fingers still tight around the grip of the Glock. "You *weren't* responsible, were you?"

"It's fascinating that you'd ask me that." Venom tinged his voice. "All along, you've been eager to believe that I'm a monster. I see you've found yourself a new, more human friend."

"Can you just give a straight answer? I told him it wasn't you, but the whole 'Ravener' thing is news to me. You never told me that you were a billion years old and have a history of queen-slaughter."

"This new friend of yours told you all about me, didn't he? It seems you've become awfully close with him in the past two weeks, while I've been hunting for your sister."

"You *locked* me in the mansion! Anyway, that's not the point. The point is—" What *was* the point? She had so many questions to ask him, she didn't know where to begin. "Did you find Miranda?"

"No. I can't sense magic like you can. That's why I need your help."

I could have helped you if you hadn't locked me up. She glanced at Drew, who lay in a heap, his eyes bulging. "Is he dead?"

As soon as she took her eyes off Caine, she felt a cold stream of magic sing at the nape of her neck. She raised the gun. Caine now stood less than a foot from her—but she'd felt his magic, and she'd been ready for him. At the sound of the gun's hammer cocking, he raised his hands, just inches from the barrel. "Your reflexes are getting faster."

"Were you trying to disarm me?" She frowned. "You don't trust me with a gun?"

"You seem a little unhinged."

"That's exactly what Orcus said." She took a deep breath, sadness tightening her chest. "You should know that Hunter bullets killed him during the ker attack. I'd tried to pull him away, but he wasn't listening to me."

Caine sucked in a long breath, something dark flickering across his features. "He's in the shadow hell now."

"I'm sorry." She tucked the gun into the back of her pants again, then pointed to Drew. "He did save my life."

"He's still breathing, but only because you stopped me with that gun of yours."

She exhaled. "So what happened at the keres attack? I know you were there. I felt Miranda there, too."

"I was hunting around the Chambers for your sister when a powerful aura drew me in, and I felt the demons drawing closer. You can't possibly believe that I was behind the attack." His voice dripped with disdain.

She studied his stunning face. Firelight bathed his skin in gold, sparking off his gray eyes, and the flickering light danced over the beautiful planes of his face. In the V of his black T-shirt, she could see smooth, unblemished skin, marked only by his tattoos. His seductive, loamy scent drew her in. "No, of course I don't believe that. Drew was just confused. And I'm a little on edge. I haven't been sleeping."

"You were hurt? Why did he need to save your life?"

"I was shot by a Hunter." Outside, helicopters beat overhead, and she could hear someone speaking into a megaphone, but she ignored it. "I just don't understand. How can you be so old? I thought Malphas was your brother, and I remember him as a little boy." *Half-brothers, perhaps.*

"It's not important right now." He paused, listening to the rotors. "But you know what is important? There are armed helicopters flying overhead. And you're wondering why I can't knock them off course like I did before. That's because they're laden with bombs—small ones, granted, but large enough to destroy a house like the one we're in. So we can let them bomb this house while we're in it, or we could teleport out first. Those are our options."

Shit shit shit. Adrenaline blared through her veins. From above, the projected voice blared something about evacuating the area.

"Okay, let's go to Lilinor." She nodded at Drew's unconscious body. "But I don't want to leave him to die in a fire. Can we take him?"

"You must be joking."

"This isn't the sort of time I'd choose to joke."

"You do realize he tried to kill me? He wasn't good at it, mind you, but that was his intention. I'm not protecting him in Lilinor."

"It was a misunderstanding. You have a bad reputation, apparently."

"He's an idiot, and he should burn in a fire, though really he deserves to be conscious for that." A muscle tightened in his jaw. "Fine. If it will get you out of here." He glared at her before leaning down and picking up Drew's limp body. In a blur of silver and black, he flung open the glass doors and carried Drew outside. Within a few seconds, he was back, wiping off his hands.

"Thank you."

He held out his hand, and she crossed to him.

He pulled her closer, sliding a hand around her back. "Will you chant the spell with me?" She felt his muscled chest through his shirt, and breathed in his alluring, earthy scent. "As I get to the end of the spell, you should hold your breath."

She pulled off her ring, handing it to Caine. A green aura danced in her skull, scented of hawthorn groves and moss.

As they chanted together, Caine's strong arms enveloped her, his thrilling magic mingling with Cleo's—hungry vines intertwining with shadows. She held her breath, and in the next moment icy water pulled her under.

CHAPTER 7

Caine's strong arms held her close, but the shock of icy water froze her completely. Deep beneath the frigid water, she was dimly aware of Caine slipping the ring back on her finger. Instinctively, she pushed her way out of Caine's grasp and kicked her way to the surface. As she got to the top, she gasped. Her lungs felt frozen; her entire body shook with the cold.

She grasped for the fountain's edge, glancing around at Lilinor's dark esplanade. The sharp spires of Ninlil Castle towered over the empty town square, and its obsidian walls gleamed in the moonlight. The last time she'd come here, she'd been completely alone and with no idea what she was getting into. At least she was a little better informed now.

She hoisted herself over the fountain's edge, leaping into the rain-slicked cobblestone street. Caine followed—along with his raven, who cawed and flapped into the air.

Rosalind shivered, her drenched clothes clinging to her body.

Caine pushed his wet hair off his face, his black clothes melding to his muscled body like a second skin.

Rosalind's teeth chattered. "Orcus said you didn't need me to transport between worlds."

"I don't *need* you. But it requires an awful lot of energy without you."

She squeezed some of the water from her shirt. "What about Tammi?"

"Oh—her. I'll send someone for her when we get inside."

"Good." Shivering, she crossed her arms, walking alongside him. "I have some questions for you."

"Of course you do. You're a trained interrogator."

"I just want to know why you locked me in the cemetery. Like you said, I'm the one who can sense Miranda's magic. And she was just outside the ward you put up around me. I could have found her myself."

He shot her an irritated look. "What are you talking about? I never locked you anywhere."

She shook her head, still dizzy from the portal. "You locked me in the cemetery, with the ward."

He narrowed his eyes, looking at her like she was insane.

He really doesn't know what I'm talking about, does he? "One evening when Orcus and I awoke, a warding spell had been put up. I couldn't get much further than the sphinx outside the mansion. Orcus said there was a note from you, with your seal and everything. And there was a sigil that had trapped me in."

He stopped walking, fixing his glacial gaze on her. "And what did the note say?"

"It said you'd locked me in there for my own safety. Orcus wasn't allowed to tamper with the spell."

"You *should* probably be locked up for your own safety, but I didn't do it. I need you to help me, and I'm pretty sure I'd never hear the end of your complaints about being imprisoned."

"But the note said that you took Tammi—" *Oh, gods. If he didn't take Tammi...* "You didn't take Tammi to a safe house, did you?"

"Abduxiel Mansion *was* the safe house."

"Shit." Panic sank into her chest. "She hasn't been there in weeks." *If anyone hurts her I will hunt them down and make them suffer.*

"Who would bother abducting an ordinary, pedestrian human?"

"The Brotherhood would. They want her dead for escaping one of their prisons. And they want me dead. They could use her to lure me in."

"That's a fair point. They'll use your loyalty against you. It's an unfortunate vulnerability."

She shot him a sharp look. "They probably want to stage a big PR coup and lure me into the light. But their entire reason for being is to stamp out the existence of magic. And whoever took Tammi put up a magical ward to keep me in the house. So basically, I have no idea who took her."

"What about your little boyfriend Drew? I don't trust him."

"It could be…" She shook her head. "But he's the one who gave me a clue to getting free from the ward. Find a sigil, he said. Is that right?"

"I suppose."

"A lot of mages came to Abduxiel Mansion while I was there. Not just Drew. Orcus had me selling mushrooms, herbs, and potions the whole time." Tammi had been kidnapped, and Rosalind felt like she wanted to throw up. "And I'm certain Miranda was there briefly. I felt her watery aura wash over my skin, tasted the salt of her magic. I have no idea what she was doing around the mansion. Her mind has been warped, as far as I can tell. She might have taken Tammi." She took a long breath. "You didn't have any luck finding my sister?"

"I've been searching for her, using scrying spells. But the images are clouded."

Rosalind's forehead wrinkled. "Like she's shielded herself?"

"Either that, or she's flitting between dimensions."

Dread snaked up Rosalind's spine. "Do you think she took Tammi to another dimension? Like Maremount?"

"Perhaps. But I'm not going back into that city unless it's absolutely necessary, and I know exactly where I'm going." Steel underscored his voice.

"Right. You've got a bit of a history there, with all the regicide."

They approached the towering, arched portcullis, its silver bars gleaming like metal teeth. Menacing stone gargoyles leered above, and Rosalind was almost certain she saw one of them blink. No guards stood before the gates. A fortress this forbidding hardly needed extra fortification.

Tammi... Her throat tightened. If Miranda had taken her friend, there was no telling what she might do. *Hard to predict the actions of a complete lunatic.*

At the fortress's entrance, Caine whispered a spell, and his magic rushed over her skin. As the gate rose, it revealed a steep-peaked, blood-red hall. Bileth's enormous painted image hung at one end. The high demon had tried to kill her more than once, and his image only reminded her that this was enemy territory.

Caine's gaze slid to her. "Why, exactly, was Drew so certain I was behind the attacks?"

"He saw you there, and he thinks you're a monster." She hugged herself. Maybe Drew *did* have something to do with all this. She wasn't ruling anything out, nor was she taking anything at face value anymore.

Caine's footsteps echoed from the flagstones. "And who, exactly, is Drew?"

"Just a mage from Maremount, as far as I know." She shot a glance at Caine's perfect profile—his straight nose, strong jaw, icy eyes, and sharp black eyebrows. He certainly didn't look like a monster. He looked too beautiful to be real.

In Drew's opinion, Caine was only keeping Rosalind alive because he wanted to use her for something. But she just didn't believe that. He had the ability to control her mind, and he'd never used it. *That has to mean something, right?*

As they neared the end of the hall, an imposing set of black doors opened. In a stream of silvery light, a woman stepped forward, descending down the stairs as the doors closed behind her.

Caine's hand shot out, as if to block Rosalind. *Obviously, this chick is bad news.* Rosalind's muscles tensed, fingers reaching for the gun in her pants—but it was gone. It must have been sucked out in her portal trip.

A lump rose in her throat as she stared at the overwhelmingly beautiful woman before her. She stood nearly six feet tall, her skin the color of desert sand. Powerful, ancient magic swirled from her—a dark, shimmering silver, just like Caine's.

The woman's midnight hair tumbled over a delicate pearly gown cut in a deep V down to her belly. Only her eyes were wrong. There was something about her deep, amber eyes that seemed unfocused, hungry—almost like she'd been drugged. And was it Rosalind's imagination, or were there hints of other colors playing about the edges of her aura?

The woman flashed a brilliant, cold smile. "Welcome, Rosalind. My husband, Lord Ambrose, has sent me to greet you. I am Queen Erish."

Demons are hierarchical. Play along, Rosalind. She bowed deeply. "Thank you for welcoming me here."

"I'll have a servant show you to your room."

"I'm taking her to her room," Caine cut in.

The queen's nails dug into her own forearms, and her eyes flashed. "You're the son of the shadow prince and the leader of an army. Showing a human girl to her room is a servant's job," she hissed.

"I said I'm taking her to her room," he growled.

Rosalind frowned. *What is going on with these two?*

The queen prowled closer, heels clacking over the stones, and began to circle Rosalind, like she was inspecting a farm animal. The woman's hair began to snake from her head, undulating in the air, and Rosalind's blood turned to ice.

"*This* is her?" Erish said, her voice dripping with disdain. "One of the two girls who are supposed to defend Lilinor? I'd expected someone a little more... epic. She looks like a drowned rabbit who hasn't eaten in weeks."

Rosalind opened her mouth to speak, but Caine cut her off with a flick of his hand. *Oh right. The hierarchical thing.*

"She's been imprisoned in a cemetery and attacked by shadow demons," Caine growled. "Speaking of which, you wouldn't happen to know about an army of keres attacking Cambridge, would you?"

Erish's eyes widened. "Honestly, Caine. As if I don't have better things to do than meddle with keres. They are grotesque and traitorous creatures." She turned, climbing the stairs, and the large black doors opened just wide enough to let her through. She cast a final glance back at Rosalind before disappearing. "I'm sure you'll want to bathe, girl. You have that human stench."

After watching humans being eaten by demons tonight, a little insult about bathing was hardly going to rile her up. Plus, the queen seemed slightly mad.

"Follow me," Caine said. Instead of climbing the steps after Erish, he led Rosalind to a smaller oak door to the left and pushed it open to reveal a narrow, curving stairwell.

Rosalind's mind churned with visions of Tammi bound to a chair in a dungeon, and she tried to push the images under the surface. She'd need to keep a level head if she wanted to figure everything out.

Dim candles lit the dark stairwell, and she traced her fingers over the damp stones as they climbed. "What did you see at the keres massacre? You were there before me. I felt your magic as I approached."

"You could feel my magic before you even got there?"

"You're extremely powerful."

He turned, arching an eyebrow as if she'd said something filthy. "Am I now?"

She ignored him. "And I felt Miranda's, too."

Caine's footsteps echoed around the hall. "I knew Miranda was there. It was the first time a scrying spell had worked, and I caught a glimpse of her in Harvard Square. But when I got there, the atmosphere rippled with magic. I can't see it like you can, but I can feel the auras. I transformed and flew above the city. I saw the keres, and I was fairly certain Nyxobas hadn't sent them." Irritation laced his voice. "They shouldn't have been there."

"Orcus seemed perplexed, too." She frowned. "But what made you certain Nyxobas hadn't sent them?"

"He's the god of shadows. He doesn't like to draw attention to himself."

"I see." Her muscles burned as she climbed the steps. She rubbed her arms, her damp clothes chilling her to the bone.

At last, he stopped at a door, pushing it open into a long hall that seemed to stretch on forever. She crossed into the high-ceilinged hall. Moonlight shone through tall windows.

"I've secured this wing for you," Caine said, walking quickly. "No vampires are allowed in, so you'll be perfectly safe from all the monsters." He arched an eyebrow. "Apart from me."

"Thank you, Caine." Her teeth chattered. That fountain had been pure ice, and the vamps weren't big on heating in here. "Do you think Miranda would have given Tammi over to the Brotherhood? My sister seemed completely brainwashed. Although if she was working for the Brotherhood they wouldn't have let her put up the ward. You know how they are about magic. All I know is, the Brotherhood have the motivation."

"It's true—they would use her to draw you out of the shadows." Moonlight washed over his golden skin. "Tomorrow, when you're rested, we'll search for both of them with a powerful spell. But we must stay focused on our objective. Our first priority is retrieving your sister." Caine's silver magic whirled from him. "And, in the future, you'd be wise to limit your emotional attachments. The Brotherhood will prey on them. It gives them an advantage."

"Right. Loyalty is a weakness."

"It can be," he said, looking straight ahead.

Drew's family motto was *Loyalty binds me.* Apparently he was at odds with Caine on this issue, too.

Caine approached an oak door, stopping to turn the knob. He opened it into an enormous, dark-walled room. "This is where you'll be staying."

The room was beautiful, but strangely forbidding—not unlike Caine himself. A tapestry hung on one wall, depicting a beautiful vernal scene: a grove of trees and plants blooming. A canopied bed stood against a wall, opposite an expansive bay window draped with sage green curtains. A fire burned in the fireplace, and a stone table stood by its side, set with drinks and food. Across from the fireplace stood a tall, oak armoire.

Caine turned, letting his gaze slide over her. "You need to eat, and sleep. I need you at full strength." He pointed to another door by the armoire. "There's a warm bath already made up for you, and you'll find clothes in the armoire. You should have everything you need. I'll be back after you've rested."

"And we can't search for Tammi or Miranda until then?"

"The spell we need to use to search between dimensions will require a tremendous amount of energy from both of us. And you can't perform any powerful magic until you've rested. I'll admit, I kind of like the tired and drenched look on you. Your soaked clothes leave nothing to the imagination right now, and your eyes look like I've kept you up all night. On the other hand, they also tell me you won't be particularly helpful when it comes to magic."

She sucked in a sharp breath. He had a way of distracting her, but her mind resisted the idea of sleep. It would be even harder to turn off her brain now that she knew Tammi was in danger. "I'm not sure that I can sleep."

"It's about time you did something useful for once, and you need strength for that. Bathe. Eat. And sleep. In that order."

She leaned against the wall, crossing her arms. "You're quite bossy in Lilinor."

He took a step closer, his pale eyes rooting her in place. He moved with that strange, preternatural grace that always caught her off guard —the same way she was caught off guard when he seemed to stare at her without blinking, or when he sometimes fell completely still, forgetting to wear his mask of humanity. "It's in my nature to order people around, and it's in my history. I've been leading an army here for centuries." He shifted closer, and she could feel the heat coming off his body, warming her through her clothes. "You're alive now because you serve a purpose to that army."

"Is that the only reason I'm alive?"

He closed the distance between them, resting his hands on the wall, boxing her in. He smelled amazing, and Rosalind's eyes lingered over his perfect skin. "Are you asking if I could find another use for you?" He let his gaze roam over her body, leaving her with the distinct impression that he could see right through the pink lacy bra she was wearing under her T-shirt. "Because I can think of at least one." His words were cold, but his tone was pure velvet.

Suddenly, her clothes felt much too restrictive, and she wanted to pull them off. *Is he distracting me with his seductive spell?* She stared into his glacial eyes, reflexively running her tongue over her raspberry lip gloss.

He watched her lick her lips, his chest rising slowly in a deep breath, and his aura whispered over her skin like a breeze. He inched closer, his lips hovering just inches from hers. His leg slid between her thighs, and his eyes blazed with intensity.

She wanted to run her hands all over his perfect body, but she swallowed hard, forcing herself to focus. "I want to know the answer. Why do you and Ambrose want me here? How are Miranda and I supposed to protect the city?"

He pulled away from her slightly, staring at her for so long she thought he wasn't going to answer. At last, he said, "Daywalkers. You, Miranda, and I are going to turn Ambrose's army into vampires who can walk in the light."

"And that's how you plan to fight the Brotherhood." She shook her head. *There it is. The purpose I serve to him.* "Is that even possible?"

"It's been done once before, or so Ambrose tells me. King Cranaus of Athens, with three powerful mages. Just like us."

His aura slid over her skin, distracting her. She was still fighting the urge to pull him close, to feel his body against hers. "If you didn't need me for this daywalker spell, would you have come for me after the ker massacre?" *Would you have pulled me from the house before it was bombed?*

The air around them cooled. "I'm not going to engage in pointless hypothetical questions."

Her fingers tightened. *Who exactly are you, Caine Mountfort?* "How about a factual question? What did Erish mean when she said you were the son of the shadow prince?"

He backed away, taking his delicious aura with him. "Unless you need help bathing, I'm going to be on my way."

She exhaled slowly, watching him walk away. "I'll manage fine, I think."

Standing in the doorframe, he turned. "I'm sure I don't need to explain to you what could happen if you leave this corridor."

"Death by vampires." She nodded. "I know."

He closed the door behind him, and she pulled off her boots, then walked over to the fireplace. Thick, thorny hawthorn boughs hung over the hearth, blossoming with red berries and white flowers. She ran her fingers along the petals. *Hawthorn blossoms. He must have told the servants I love them.*

Her muscles burned, and she wanted out of these frigid clothes. Shivering, she tried not to think about what Tammi might be enduring.

She *did* need sleep, and she wouldn't get that by dwelling on her worst fears.

She lifted up her soaked shirt, pulling it off while she crossed to the bathroom—an octagonal room with a silver clawfoot tub in the center. Thin curls of steam rose from the water. Sharp-peaked windows overlooked a stony courtyard, and candles guttered in sconces. She let her shirt fall to the stone floor.

Maybe *Miranda* was drawing her into a trap, for her own deranged reasons. She pulled off her soaked pants, which stuck to her legs as she rolled them down her calves. She'd sensed Miranda in two places —near Abduxiel Mansion before the ward went up, and at the massacre tonight.

She unhooked her bra, letting it fall to the floor. Goosebumps rose over her skin as she pulled off her underwear. *Is my own twin a complete monster?*

She dipped her foot into the hot water, letting it turn her skin pink. The bath smelled of lavender and mint.

The water warmed her legs as she stepped into the bath, soothing her muscles. Her thigh still burned slightly where she'd been shot, even if Drew's juniper potion had almost completely healed it. His magic had left behind only a faint, white scar.

She inhaled the steam. When was the last time she'd actually bathed? She wasn't sure she had at Abduxiel Mansion. She'd been too creeped out by Orcus to spend much time naked.

Orcus. An image of his body flashed in her mind, and her muscles tensed. She sat up, pushing herself out of the bath. It didn't feel right luxuriating here after she'd just watched an entire city street slaughtered. She just wanted to go to sleep, so she could get enough rest to try the damn scrying spell as soon as possible.

She stood, letting the water drip from her body, then stepped from the bath. After toweling off, she stepped back into the bedroom.

And when she did, fear slid through her bones.

Three women stood in the center of the room. Three pairs of shining white eyes burned into her.

Keres.

The ker in the center wore a shimmering white gown, and a crown of pearls threaded into her pale hair. She opened her mouth to smile, revealing long, sharp teeth designed for tearing human flesh. Two other gaunt-featured keres flanked her, dressed for battle and built of pure, lean muscle. Sharp blades glinted at their belts.

And Rosalind stood before them, wearing nothing at all.

CHAPTER 8

*H*er pulse sped up. *So much for the safety of this corridor.*

The keres looked just like the ones in Harvard Square, only these didn't have wings.

And as she stared at them, she realized that wasn't the only difference. Their auras were different. Magic curled off them in black plumes that smelled of charcoal and felt rough on her skin.

I really wish I'd kept that gun on me.

Staring at them, she tried to steady her voice. "Who are you?"

The crowned ker cocked her head. "Come now. Is that any way to greet the queen of the keres?"

Rosalind's leg muscles tightened, ready for battle. "What were all the keres doing in Cambridge tonight?"

One of the shorter ker scowled. "She said she's queen. You're supposed to bow to Queen Antu."

"There are an awful lot of queens in Ninlil Castle." Rosalind narrowed her eyes. "And I don't really know how they're normally greeted, but I'd expect it to involve clothes. I don't suppose you could give me the chance to dress myself before we meet formally?"

Queen Antu's eyes roamed over Rosalind's body. "But I like you the way you are."

Rosalind folded her arms in front of her chest. "I thought Caine protected this hall."

The ker queen shrugged. "Perhaps he doesn't really care if you die. He has been with many women."

Irritation flared. "Are you here for a purpose? I just saw a city full of humans attacked by keres exactly like you." She cocked her head. "Except they had wings. What happened to yours?"

Antu flashed her long teeth. "That is none of your concern, human slave. You should be more concerned with your *own* impending mutilation."

Fear bit into her ribs. *Okay. Time to scan the room for weapons.* Rosalind backed away, her gaze landing on the table laden with crystal decanters and glasses. A fireplace poker stood by the hearth—just like one she'd used successfully on Bileth.

"Thinking of ways to kill me?" The queen arched an eyebrow. "I believe that's treason."

"I'm not your subject." Rosalind forced a smile. "And I'm just seeing if I can offer my queen anything to eat." She held out a hand. "You'll find food and drink over there." What she needed was a stake…

Her pulse sped up. *The boughs.* They weren't merely decorative. Of course they weren't—Caine didn't do sentimentality. They served a purpose. *Now what are the chances I can get to them?*

She took a step forward, and two of the keres pulled out knives, silver blades glinting in the firelight. *That answers my question. The chances are not good at all.*

The queen licked her lips. "We're not supposed to kill you. We're going to take you with us. And before we do, we're supposed to make your pretty face a little uglier."

A chill rushed over Rosalind's skin. *Holy hells. They're going to carve up my face.* Her pulse sped up, and she frantically searched the room for an escape. Could she make to the door? And even if she did, was it wise for a human to run naked through a vampire castle? *No, it is not.*

Before Rosalind could make a move for the boughs, one of the keres lunged, knife extended. Rosalind's hand flew out, grabbing the creature's wrist. The demon was fast, but lightweight, and Rosalind controlled the ker's arm, swiftly driving it toward the other, oncoming ker. The blade plunged between the second demon's ribs, and the creature staggered back, clutching her bleeding chest.

Rosalind elbowed the first in the face, and the ker snarled, leaping on top of Rosalind to bite her neck. Pain seared Rosalind's throat, and she fell to the floor, head cracking against the stone.

She raised her hips, throwing the ker off balance, then yanked her off by her hair. She threw the creature down, straddling her, then punched her hard in the face, one hit after another. Black blood poured from the ker's nose and mouth. The creature's eyelids fluttered.

Rosalind had seen what these monsters had done to the humans in Harvard Square, and she didn't want to stop—

A sharp tug on her hair wrenched Rosalind off the ker, and another hand clamped around her neck. Queen Antu was gripping her by the throat, and slammed her against the wall. Rosalind's feet hung suspended in the air, and her ravaged throat screamed with pain. The queen was much, much stronger than the other two, and Rosalind's heart thumped hard.

Antu narrowed her pearly eyes. "I want you to know a few things. One, humans are vermin, a plague on this earth. Two, you cannot defeat your demon superiors." Antu's fingers tightened on Rosalind's neck.

Rosalind couldn't breathe, and merely grunted.

The queen leaned in closer. "And, three, we haven't been sent to kill you, but to bring you to your new master—"

Rosalind kicked Antu hard in the gut, and the queen dropped her. Long, sharp claws sprang from the demon's fingertips.

Shit. Maybe I can drown this monster in the bathtub. Rosalind turned to run for the bathroom, but Antu grabbed her by the hair again, yanking her back. *I need to get out of here.*

Antu slipped her arm around Rosalind's neck, pinning her in a chokehold. "Let's start by getting rid of this pretty human hair of yours. Then I'll carve off some of your face."

Rosalind gripped Antu's arm, then thrust her hips back sharply, leaning forward. Grunting, she pulled the queen over her head, throwing her to the ground.

Gasping for breath, she watched half her hair fall to the stones along with the queen. She pressed her foot into Antu's neck, pushing down.

The ker grabbed her leg, twisting it so Rosalind spun to the ground. She smacked down hard on her back on the stone. Pain splintered her skull and ribs.

Antu would eat the flesh off her face. *Get up, Rosalind.*

She pushed herself up, panic gripping her heart. She could hear the other keres moaning nearby, and knew that she needed to end this fight before one of them found it within themselves to join the fray again.

As Rosalind struggled to stand, Antu slashed for her face with her claws. Rosalind darted out of the way, rolling over the cold flagstones.

She sprang up again, right in front of the bay window. *Maybe Caine won't be the only one around with the honor of defenestrating a queen.*

She'd seen Antu's reaction when she'd mentioned the wings—the queen had said something about worrying about her own mutilation. Strong word, and obviously a sore point. *I just need to throw her off guard.*

"I once saw a pigeon with broken wings," she said. "Just stuck in a parking spot."

"What?" Antu snapped.

"It couldn't fly, and just had to sit there in its own filth, waiting for death. I'd never seen anything so sad in my life, and I had to break the creature's neck to end its misery. I think it's time someone did the same for you. Because what's the point of a filthy little bird with no wings?"

Antu's black aura burst from her body like volcanic ash, and she charged for Rosalind. At the last second, Rosalind grabbed the queen's hand, using her inertia to swing her straight through the bay window. Glass shattered around her, and Rosalind peered down, watching the queen's white dress flutter in the wind as she plunged, screaming all the way down. Rosalind's blood roared in her ears as she watched

Antu smack against the stony ground nine stories below. Blood soaked her white dress.

Shit shit shit. That solved the immediate problem, the one about having her face cut off and becoming enslaved to a new master. But throwing a ker queen out the window *probably* brought a host of larger problems along with it. Not to mention that someone was trying to abduct her.

Her body trembled from a combination of adrenaline and fatigue. From the shattered window, freezing wind whipping into the room, rippling over her naked body.

She stared at the two injured demonesses on the ground. The one she'd stabbed clutched her ribs, moaning, while the other began to stir, black blood still pouring from her nose.

Rosalind considered knocking the ker out again—but maybe she could use her. She rushed over to the two demons, pulling all the weapons from their bodies and gathering them into her arms.

She crossed to the armoire and pulled it open, dropping the knives inside. Shivering, she surveyed the clothes. The entire thing was hung with long, flimsy dresses—most of them sheer, with plunging necklines. *Obviously chosen by Caine.*

She searched lower, and her lips curled into a smile as her gaze landed on sleek, black leather pants and shirt—not unlike the clothes the keres had worn. A pair of thigh-high black boots stood in the corner. *Jackpot.*

She yanked the clothes from the wardrobe, and when she did, she found a small arsenal of blades beneath them—even finer than the ones the keres had carried. Caine had thought of everything—too bad she hadn't found it all *before* Antu had paid her a visit. Running her fingertips over the leather fabric, she could feel its strength. It was fortified with some sort of thin metal—steel perhaps.

This wasn't just clothing. It was armor.

She cast a quick glance back at the two injured keres. They still lay prone on the floor, but one of them was trying to sit up. *I need to hurry.*

Crouching down, she pulled open an armoire drawer, revealing an array of lacy underwear. Unlike the leather clothes, these were the opposite of practical; each piece was skimpier than the next.

She slipped into a lacy lavender pair of panties with a matching bra before pulling on the pants and shirt. The clothing hugged her body perfectly. She grabbed the boots from the armoire, pulling them up over her pants. *Now I'm beginning to feel like myself.*

Conveniently, the pants came equipped with sheaths for the knives, and she grabbed several blades, sliding them in. She kept one in her hand as she crossed to the mirror in the bathroom.

With a gasp, she surveyed herself in the mirror. Blood poured from ragged puncture holes in her neck, and now she had meth-head hair to match her tired eyes and face—half of it was cut off jaggedly at her chin, while the other half hung, partially frayed, over her shoulders.

She gripped the knife, inspecting the blade. *Sharp enough.* With one hand, she pulled the long pieces into a ponytail, slicing off her tresses. *I'm not the same girl I used to be. There's no reason I should look like I am.*

Chunks of her glossy brown hair fell to the floor, and she stared at herself in the mirror. She looked like something from an apocalyptic nightmare.

A grim smile curled her lips. *But I also look like a warrior, and that's what I need to be if I want to get Tammi back.*

Something rustled in the next room, and she ran in, her knife ready in her hand.

One of the keres—the one she'd punched—sat up. The demoness hunched over, puking a stomach-full of crimson blood onto the stone floor. It occurred to Rosalind that at least some of that was her own blood, which made her stomach turn.

She grimaced. She'd only been in the room about fifteen minutes, and already the place was covered in blood, vomit, and human hair. *No one should ever invite me over as a houseguest.*

The ker wiped her mouth off on the back of her hand before looking around frantically. "Where are my blades?"

"I took them." *Time for a little questioning.* Rosalind knelt down, grabbing the demon by her throat and held the blade's sharp edge to her jugular. The creature's silver eyes looked glazed. Even if she'd had her weapons, she'd have been in no condition for a fight.

"Tell me your name," Rosalind commanded.

The ker's already pale face had gone completely white. "Bianca."

"Bianca. I need you to tell me what you know about at the massacre in Harvard Square tonight."

Bianca blinked. "I don't know anything about it."

Rosalind's fingers tightened on the hilt. "I don't want to hurt you, Bianca. But I will if I have to. And since you did try to kill me, I won't feel awful about it."

Bianca tried to inch away, but Rosalind gripped her hair tighter.

"I don't know about a massacre," the ker stammered. "She keeps us in the dark. The literal dark."

"How many of you are there?"

"Hundreds."

"What does she want with you?"

"I don't know?"

Rosalind bit her lip, searching the demon's eyes. She would do anything to protect people from another massacre—anything, perhaps, except torture. She'd tortured one demon before—Malphas —and he hadn't even turned out to be the bad guy. That was enough guilt for a lifetime, not to mention the fact that a desperate person was likely to say anything to stop the pain.

Still, even if she wasn't going to torture Bianca, she needed the demon to fear her. She pushed the blade harder against the ker's neck, the point just slightly piercing the skin. "Who sent you to kill me?" She corrected herself. "I mean, to abduct me?"

"Erish."

"Why?"

"She plans to take you to your new master. Erish has lost her mind, I think."

"Who is the new master?"

"I have no idea." The corner of the ker's mouth twitched as she answered, and Rosalind had the distinct impression she was lying.

She'd come back to that one later. "How did Erish recruit you?"

"You don't understand what she'll do to me if I tell you things. She's changed," Bianca hissed.

Seven hells. Rosalind bared her teeth. "Maybe you should be afraid of what *I'm* going to do to you."

"She promised to give us our wings back if we obey."

Rosalind shook her head. "She's not going to give your wings back."

"Why?"

"Because she's an asshole."

Bianca's eyes glistened, but she merely stared at Rosalind.

Rosalind glanced at the door. At any minute, someone was going to realize there was a dead ker queen on the esplanade, and she'd come from Rosalind's window.

She gripped Bianca's hair. "Okay, Bianca. I'm going to tie you up and come back for you. There's still a lot more I need you to tell me, and I know you're lying. But right now, I need you to tell me where Caine is. I'm going to find him. And as long as I make it there alive—if you've given me good information—I'll let you live."

Bianca's eyes scanned the room. "What happened to the queen?"

"She jumped out a window. She was upset about her wings."

Bianca's eyes widened. "You killed our queen."

"I realize that's probably a breach of protocol," Rosalind shot back, "but she *was* trying to cut off my face."

"Fair enough." Bianca eyed her warily. "You might as well kill me, too."

"Tell me where to find Caine," Rosalind commanded.

"Fine. It's simple. Walk to the end of the hall—the same way you came in. Take the stairs just one floor up. His room is near the painting of Lord Byron. But you'll need to do something about the smell of your blood, or the vampires will slaughter you in seconds."

A memory sparked in Rosalind's mind—the last time she'd been to Caine's room. It *had* been right next to a painting of Lord Byron in a turban. *She's telling the truth.*

Rosalind surveyed the demon for just a few seconds. The keres were gaunt as hell—someone had been starving them. "Thank you for your help. I'll make sure you're taken care of when I return. And that you get fed, once I get to Caine's room safely. What do I do about the blood?"

Bianca nodded at the other ker, who was bleeding out on the floor. "Use her blood. Rub it on your neck. It will mask your human smell."

"I'll have more questions for you later. Right now, I'm going to bind you in the hawthorn boughs so you can't escape. And when—"

"You really think Erish won't return my wings?" The ker's eyes were frantic.

Nope. "Why would she, if she can continue using you forever?"

The ker stared into Rosalind's eyes, then snatched at her hands, driving the blade into her own throat. Blood gurgled up through the wound, and her eyes bulged.

Rosalind stood, jumping away from the ker. Her heart hammered, and she wiped the blood off her hands onto her pants. What the hell had that been about? The wings, apparently.

I guess there is no point being a ker without wings.

She glanced at the other ker, whose black dress glistened with blood. The ker's chest was still. *Dead.* That wound shouldn't have killed her so fast, but the keres looked like they'd been starved. Black dirt was encrusted under their fingernails, and their pale skin looked sickly.

Rosalind crouched down, smearing her fingers into the ker's blood, then rubbing it onto her own gashes. She winced as the pain seared her neck. She rose, dizzy from her own loss of blood, and ripped a few large thorns from the hawthorn bough to add to her arsenal.

And now I'll find Caine, before I pass out and find myself a vampire's dinner.

CHAPTER 9

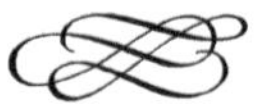

*R*osalind stalked the hall, her heart pumping the blood from her neck. Hopefully her own blood wasn't washing away the ker's. Moonlight cast long, silver shadows across the black flagstones. The sound of her boots echoed off the high ceiling; the only other sound was her own ragged breathing.

Just a month ago, she and Tammi would have been hanging out in her dorm room, listening to the Pixies or Beyoncé and trading clothes. Apart from the odd scuffle with a boggart as part of her demon-hunting gig, things never got much crazier than crashing frat parties or drinking Tammi's disgusting peppermint schnapps.

That part of her life was over, but she wasn't going to let anything stand in the way of getting her friend back. She'd find Tammi, and when she did they'd toast Tammi's return with champagne flutes full of peppermint schnapps. Somehow, Tammi made her feel *normal* again, like everything was okay. Even during the two days they'd been trapped in Abduxiel Mansion together, Tammi had instilled a sense of normalcy. Before the ward went up, she'd managed to sneak out to procure a whole bunch of makeup, and a bottle of *Rouge Dior* nail polish. She'd given them both manicures while they watched *The Bachelorette*. Normal stuff.

Right now, things definitely did not feel normal. Rosalind clutched her neck tighter, trying to staunch the bleeding. Maybe this wasn't the time to get lost in nostalgia.

At the end of the hall, she paused before pushing through the doors into the stairwell. Here, she was no longer protected by Caine's spells—not that they'd been helpful against the keres anyway.

Her muscles burned, both from tiredness and the fight, and she dragged herself up the flight of stairs. And the next landing, she paused. With so much blood pouring from her neck, she couldn't be sure if the smell of the ker's blood was enough to mask her own human scent.

If not, she had a collection of knives and makeshift stakes.

She took a long, deep breath, her hand hovering at the door leading into the hall; finally, clutching her neck, she pushed it open. Red candles in thorny silver sconces lit the corridor, and crimson curtains framed the arched windows. Apart from the dancing light, nothing moved on the dark stone.

She frowned. *What do vampires* do *with their time?*

She took a tentative step, her breath coming in short, sharp bursts, and waited to see if an army of vamps would bust through the doors.

No one's here. Just me.

She took another step, then quickened her pace, her hand clamped on her bleeding neck. *I'd be surprised if the vamps couldn't hear my heart thumping through the stone walls.*

Just a few doors away, Lord Byron's painted image stared mournfully out the window. *Made it.* Relief washed over Rosalind—until a door behind her creaked open, and she whirled.

A flaxen-haired vamp poked her head out of the doorway, licking her ruby-red lips. She stepped into the hall, running a hand down her white gown. "How delicious. I thought I heard a beating heart."

So close.

Fangs bared, the vamp prowled forward. Rosalind didn't wait for her to get any closer—she hurled one of the long hawthorns right at the vamp's chest. It struck her between her ribs and she stumbled back, clutching the thorn, eyes wide. Dark blood trickled between her fingers.

Another door creaked open, and Rosalind whirled, ready to hurl another stake.

Caine stood in the doorway, his arms folded. "Making friends, I see. How did you develop such a charming way with people?"

"I need to talk to you."

His gaze landed on her bleeding neck wound. "Get in here. Now."

"That was the plan." She stepped into his room, surveying the space. It was more of a hall than a bedroom, and made of pure luxury. An enormous four-poster bed stood against a wall, a blue and silver embroidered canopy hanging around it. Starry lanterns blazed from stone walls. The remains of a feast were laid out on an oak dining table.

Caine's raven familiar perched on an armchair, and a floral breeze blew in from a window. The room was beautiful; she wanted to lock herself in and sleep for days.

He pointed to the bed. "Sit down. What happened now?"

Gripping her neck, she crossed the room and sat on his blue-blanketed bed. "Someone tried to eat my neck. And my face, but that part is intact."

He frowned, gently pulling her hand away. "Why did you leave the corridor? I specifically told you not to, or you'd be savaged by vamps." He leaned down, inspecting her wound. "Of course you don't listen to me, since you think you know—"

"I didn't leave," she cut him off. "And it wasn't vamps who did this."

He stood over her, peering down. "Who was it?"

"Keres. Three of them. They were sent to take me to some sort of master, but the ker committed suicide before I could get the full story."

"Seven hells." His jaw tightened. "What are keres doing here?"

"I think Erish uses them as some sort of slaves."

"Gods below. I need to check the dungeons. And we need to speak to Ambrose." He gently pulled down her collar, growling as he examined her neck. "I see you managed to disguise your human scent. You reek of ker blood."

Dizzy, she could feel the blood draining from her head. "Bianca helped me before she offed herself."

"Stop talking for a second." He lightly traced his thumb around her ragged puncture wounds, chanting a spell—a melodious one she recognized from the other times he'd healed her. His cool, silvery aura curled around her body, caressing her skin, soothing her muscles. His magic whispered over her throat like a gentle kiss, and she sighed as the last of the pain left her body. She half wanted to throw herself back and curl up to sleep in his soft, blue blankets, wrapped in his calming, breezy aura.

"That should do it." He narrowed his eyes, studying her. "What the hell happened to your hair?"

"Queen Antu chopped it off with her claws."

He frowned. "The queen of the keres came into your room to cut your hair. I'm a little baffled by this turn of events."

"She wanted to cut off my face as well." She held up a hand. "Apparently, Erish sent them to abduct me—and look, before this conversation goes any further, I should probably tell you that I threw Antu out the window. Queen Erish had cut off her wings, so she didn't survive the fall."

Caine went completely still. "Start from the beginning."

"Three keres showed up—a queen and her two lackeys. Queen Antu said she wanted to take me to my new master. We all fought. When Antu attacked, I stole one of your moves and threw a queen from a window. I won the battle, but my hair lost." She crossed her legs. "On a scale of parking ticket to apocalypse, how bad is this situation?"

"I don't know yet." Candlelight glinted in his icy, gray eyes. "Queen Erish doesn't normally stop until she's gotten what she wants. We've got to contain the keres in case she has plans for them, but after that I'm not letting you out of my sight. We already lost track of Miranda. I'm not losing track of you, too."

"Or Tammi."

"Right." He crossed to his dining table. "Even if she serves no tactical purpose," he muttered, pouring himself some wine.

Irritation sparked. "Well that's the difference between you and me. I don't think of people just in terms of their utility. I actually *like* people, and since I like them, I tell them relevant things about myself, like 'Hey, by the way, I'm a million centuries old, and my father is something called a *shadow prince*, and in Maremount I'm considered a monster.' Oh no, wait, those are facts about you. Mine are normal things."

Shadows gathered in his pale eyes. "Do you know why I don't tell you things? Because sheltered, spoiled girls like you love to make judgments about good versus evil."

Her cheeks burned. "Is that right?"

"It's so nice to have a neat and tidy little world. You're drawn to clean-cut, utterly pedestrian humans like Drew, with his light magic, and his pretty little potions. Then you've got the bad guys, the demons and dark magic, the incubi and the succubi, and let's not forget the Ravener, son of the shadow prince. Everything is in its place, isn't it? How nice for you to never have to make tough decisions about morality or think for yourself—so you can save all that mental energy for wallowing in guilt."

"And at what point in your calculations do you mull over these complex moral judgments?" she shot back. "Before or after you decide someone's tactical value to your goals?"

He ignored her, crossing to a trunk on the floor. He unlatched it, revealing a set of silver-hilted swords.

Drumming her fingers on the bed, she studied him. She'd never seen him quite this worked up. "Is it my imagination, or are you jealous of Drew? You seem a little hung up on him."

"Don't be ridiculous." He strapped a sword to his back and rose. "Do you have any idea how easy it would have been for me to kill him?"

"Right. That doesn't sound jealous at all." She straightened, eyeing his sword. "Are you going to check the dungeons? The keres looked starved. And there was dirt under their nails."

"Yes. And then I want to bring you to speak to Ambrose." He touched a lock of Rosalind's butchered hair. "I am impressed you managed to defeat two armed keres and a succubus. The armor and weapons I left you must have come in handy."

She shook her head. "I didn't find any of that until after the fight. Antu surprised me. I was completely naked and weaponless for the whole encounter. I really appreciated the hawthorn—"

"Hang on. You're skimming over crucial information. You were completely naked?"

"I was about to take a bath when they showed up."

"I can't believe I missed that. Naked brawling. Another reason not to let you out of my sight." This time, his gaze slid over her more slowly. "I'm going to see what I can find out about the keres. I'll spell the room—properly, this time. No one will be able to get in except me. I'm sure you know not to leave for any reason." He left the room in blur of silver and black, the door slamming behind him.

Rosalind stood, pulling the knives from her holsters. She crossed to a small table that stood by his bed and laid out the blades, then lay back on the bed, spreading out her arms. She was exhausted. Fatigue burned her muscles. This wasn't the time for rest, and yet it called to her like a siren.

As she tucked her hands behind her head, she inhaled deeply. Caine's room smelled of jasmine, and the fabric below her was the softest she'd ever touched.

Her eyelids drifted shut.

She braced herself for the onslaught of gore that welcomed her every time she drifted off. But this time, a sunny image burned in her mind: a grassy field by a pond that smelled of brackish water, its gentle waves glittering in the sunlight. Dandelions and bluebells dappled the grasses along the shore. Someone came up behind her— the blue-eyed boy, handing her a tiny, curled seashell. She took it from his hand, then turned in a circle, letting the sea air rush over her skin.

But when she opened her eyes, a wave of horror slammed into her. The sky shimmered with waves of copper, silver, blue, and green... Four stakes stood by the shore, ready to burn four heretics.

Her pulse raced as shadows whirled around her, and in the next moment Caine stood before one of the stakes, gripping a woman by her collar. The woman's brown eyes were open wide. Fear tightened its claws around Rosalind's heart. The woman looked a lot like her, only older. Caine grabbed the screaming woman by her throat, pinning her to a stake.

And he drove a thick, iron nail right into the center of her heart.

* * *

THE SOUND of the door creaking snapped her out of her dream. She sat up, catching her breath. *Seven hells. I never want to sleep again.* Sweat dampened her brow.

Caine stood in the door, holding a delicate, shimmering gown in his hands. "What happened?"

She swallowed hard, staring at him, all her muscles tense. Maybe he was right, and she was still terrified of demons deep down. "Just a bad dream. It doesn't mean anything."

But her entire body had gone cold. Something deeply disturbed her about that image of Caine murdering a woman who looked so much like her. It was almost as though she'd seen her own death.

Caine narrowed his eyes. "I want you to tell me about it later. But right now, we need to speak to Ambrose and find out what he knows. I saw nothing in the dungeons, but I suspect the guards were lying to me. I could smell it on them."

"They're protecting Erish?"

"She has a way of convincing people to be loyal to her. I've sent ten trusted soldiers to scour the castle for her and to bring her to Ambrose in chains. If she truly keeps her own secret army, even if they're half-dead keres, she has committed treason."

Rosalind stood, stretching her arms over her head. "What the hell does she want? She's already queen."

Caine grabbed a small blue cloth from the dining table, and soaked it with water from a pitcher. "She's furious at Ambrose because he doesn't sufficiently worship her anymore. Plus, she's singularly obsessed with only one thing right now."

"What?"

He crossed to Rosalind, tilting up her chin. "Me, of course." Gently, he began cleaning the blood from her neck.

"I guess you and she have that in common."

"When we go to see Ambrose, I want you to tell him exactly what you told me about the keres. And then I'm taking you out of Lilinor. We don't know how many soldiers are loyal to Erish."

"Where are you taking me?"

"Another one of my homes." He ran his fingers over her throat, examining it. His face was truly stunning—with smooth, tan skin and eyes so pale they shined like starlight.

Why did I have that horrible dream about him?

He traced his fingers over her skin, his touch leaving a trail of tingles over her throat. "It healed well. You should be fine to travel." He lowered his hand, stepping away, and cast a critical eye over her outfit. "Take off your clothes."

"What?"

"I don't want anyone to recognize you. Her guards may be all over this castle. And anyway, you can't meet the high lord dressed like an assassin. You're a Hunter."

"Ex-Hunter."

"Regardless, no one here trusts you." He grabbed the dress from his bed and thrust it at her.

"Not even you?"

"I don't need to trust you. I could kill you before your fingers even touched your weapon belt."

"Whatever." *How I missed that classic Caine cockiness.* "Turn around. I'm not stripping in front of you."

He made sure she witnessed his eye roll before he turned his back, as if being shy about stripping in front of an incubus was the most ridiculous notion in the world. She pulled off her bloodstained leather shirt, then unzipped her pants, slipping out of them. "I do hope we're coming back for the weapons. I was growing attached to them."

"Of course. Someday, you won't be so dependent on them."

She lifted the dress in front of her, eying the stunning, dark fabric —a midnight blue that sparkled with tiny white gems like a spray of stars. The top was virtually sheer, apart from a few strategically placed embroidered leaves. She unhooked her bra. *I guess this has to go, too.* Visible bright blue bra straps were probably not the right look for a meeting with the king.

She pulled the dress over her head, and the thin fabric slid down her legs until it reached the floor. Layers of stunningly thin tulle formed the skirt, parting slightly above one of her thighs. "I don't think I've ever worn anything so beautiful."

He turned, inhaling sharply. "I think you need to do it more often."

She flashed a smile. "Let's go see the king."

"Not quite yet." He circled around to her back, zipped up the dress, and leaned in to whisper in her ear. "You look perfect." His proximity to her alone was disarming.

"Fit for a king, I hope."

His fingertips brushed over her shoulder, sending a thrill through her. "I want you to be cautious. Ambrose is just about to learn that his wife of five hundred years seems to be staging a coup. She's the one who made him. I honestly have no idea how he will react."

CHAPTER 10

They stalked over an impossibly long walkway, lined on either side by three guards. At one end of the walkway, a tower speared the night sky, its pale stone walls gleaming in the moonlight. "The White Tower," according to Caine, from which Ambrose ruled his empire—at least, when he wasn't seducing human women.

Despite Caine's declaration that she looked "perfect," he'd still called Aurora in to paint Rosalind with makeup and fix her disastrous hair, pulling it up on her head with a thorny crown of tiny white pearls. No one would mistake her for a Hunter now, in this wildly impractical ensemble.

Still, she'd strapped a knife to her thigh where no one could see it. Who knew how many of these guards might be working for Erish?

Warily, she eyed one of the vampire soldiers, armed with a silver pike. His eyes followed her every step along the way, and the hair on the back of her neck stood on end.

A cool night breeze chilled her skin, and she shivered, then paused to peer over the battlements. From here, she could see the entire kingdom of Lilinor stretching out below. The castle stood at the highest point of the city, giving them a view of the kingdom's twinkling white lights, which mirrored the starry sky. Thin alleys wound around the city in byzantine patterns, and sleek black buildings towered above. Glowing orbs lit the streets, burning like starlight, and sharp-spired towers pierced the air below them.

A flock of ravens flew overhead, cawing into the night sky, and her gaze lifted. The full moon hung in the sky like a fat dewdrop, and the constellations shone bright in a purple-hued sky. *Certainly beautiful, if not relaxing.*

She turned back to the walkway, hurrying to catch up to Caine. They were drawing closer to a tall, black door inset into the side of the White Tower. Two enormous vampire guards stood before the door, gripping spears, their pale eyes locked on her. They had long, tangled brown hair and beards—half vampire and half barbarian, then.

As Rosalind and Caine approached, she heard the low growl rise from one of their throats.

"Step aside," Caine barked.

The guard to her right narrowed his eyes at Rosalind. "Who's the human female? Ambrose has already chosen his courtesans for the night."

A chilly wind soared over the battlements, raising Rosalind's skin into goosebumps. *Please don't make this difficult for us.* There was already enough danger without a guard creating a scene.

As big as the guards were, Caine matched them in size. A fight between them would rock the entire castle. It shouldn't come down to that—Caine commanded the kingdom's vampire soldiers. But a queen had supremacy over a general, and who knew what sort of discord Erish had sown before leaving.

"She's with me, and I don't answer to you." Caine's voice tightened her stomach. Not a tone she'd want to argue with. "Step aside, soldier."

The guard's pale gaze bored into Rosalind. "Sir, Queen Erish told us to be on the lookout for a human girl. A traitor and a Hunter—" The guard's eyes bulged, and a choking noise rose from his throat. Caine's angry, silver magic whirled around him.

Her pulse racing, Rosalind watched as the guard climbed up the battlement. He swayed on the edge, the wind whipping his hair and beard, and jumped.

Rosalind let out a sharp breath, peering over the edge. About five stories below, the guard lay impaled on a sharp silver spire. He moaned, writhing and still very much alive despite the thick spike protruding through his gut.

Caine met her eyes and gave a slight shrug. "He'll live." He shot a sharp look to the other guard. "Do you have any questions of your own, soldier?"

The guard had paled; he shook his head, pulling open the black door to reveal a stairwell.

Rosalind peered up the stairs. A white marble staircase wound upward. Thin rays of moonlight streamed through windows, and tiny white spheres hung in the air. Rosalind lifted her hem, following after Caine as they climbed the stairs. *Just about ten stories left. My thigh muscles will rebel tomorrow.*

Caine turned to look her over. "I guess the outfit didn't work as much of a disguise. Though I'm still glad you're wearing it."

"Where do you think Erish went?" Rosalind asked.

"No one has yet reported finding her. I suspect she's fled the city."

"Any idea who the 'master' is?"

"Probably her. And she's probably jealous of you."

Rosalind frowned. "Why?"

"I told you. She's obsessed with me."

Rosalind arched an eyebrow. "Why would that have anything to do with me?"

"It doesn't," he said quickly. "She's paranoid and delusional. She's been acting increasingly insane in the past month."

Rosalind frowned. "Seems odd that a hundred-thousand-year-old demon would suddenly develop a mental illness."

As they climbed the stairs, Rosalind peered out the narrow windows, gazing out at the breathtaking city.

At last, they arrived at the top of the tower, and the stairwell opened into a short hallway lined by high, arched windows. A set of enormous black doors stood at the other end of the hall, with a line of guards before them.

Caine marched across the black marble floor, and Rosalind hurried to keep pace with his long strides.

The guards readied their spears. "Sir," one of them called out. "Queen Erish has instructed that—"

Caine flicked his wrist, and the crunch of bone echoed off the high ceiling. The guards' necks twisted to the side at unnatural angles, and they fell to the ground, grimacing.

Stepping over their bodies, Caine whispered another spell to open the doors.

They swung slowly open, revealing a hall with no ceiling; apart from thin, bony arches, the roof was open to the stars. Ivory columns rose from the walls, vaulting over them in a sort of peaked cage. Between the vaults, they had a perfect view of the moon.

Rosalind surveyed the rest of the space. Around them, enormous windows gave views of the city.

Ambrose sat in a silver throne by one of the windows, literally draped in a collection of half-naked human women. A white marble fountain lay inset into the center of the room. Apart from that, the room was nearly as bare as the women.

Looking at Ambrose's breathtaking features, Rosalind could understand why the courtesans would volunteer for this job. With his sharp contrasts, he was as beautiful as Caine: pale skin and black clothes, blond hair and dark eyebrows, sharp cheekbones and soft lips.

As Rosalind and Caine strode across the room, Ambrose casually stroked one of the topless women on his lap—just above her hipbone. Rosalind wasn't quite sure where to look. She only knew the girls were apparently a bit cold.

She glanced down at herself. *As am I.*

"Caine," Ambrose said, "you'd better have a very good reason for breaking my guards' necks, and for interrupting my evening."

Caine waved a dismissive hand at the courtesans. "What I have to say to you is not for them to hear. Nor any guards."

"I would suggest that the guards escort them back to the safe rooms, but you've rather inconveniently snapped their spines."

"There's one conscious guard at the bottom of the tower," Caine said, before touching his chin thoughtfully. "Well, two, but one of them is impaled on a spire."

Wide-eyed, the girls rose, walking as far as they could around Caine on their way out the door. After they left, he turned and flicked his hand. The doors creaked closed.

Ambrose's gaze slid to Rosalind for the first time, and she shivered under his scrutiny. "You brought me Rosalind. That tempers some of my anger, I suppose." He rose, his footsteps echoing off the floor as he walked closer, his movements fluid. His pale blond hair ruffled slightly in the wind. Closing the gap between them, he lifted a hand to her cheek, stroking it lightly with his thumb. He smelled of cloves. "Tell me Rosalind. If I took off your ring, would you still burn for me?"

"The queen has an army of keres," Caine cut in abruptly.

Ambrose dropped his hand, his features darkening. "She *what?*"

"Rosalind will tell you," Caine said.

"As soon as I arrived in Lilinor," Rosalind said, "three keres showed up in my room—Queen Antu and two lackeys. They wanted to abduct me, to take me to some sort of Master. Caine thinks that's Erish herself. And they screwed up my hair...but that's beside the point. The point is, I threw Queen Antu out the window, and I roughed up the other two until they gave me a little information. But they died, so I didn't get all the information."

"I would like to see you fight, Rosalind," Ambrose cut in. "I have a feeling it would be breathtaking."

Caine cleared his throat—an irritated sound—but he didn't say anything.

Rosalind continued. "One of the keres, Bianca, said Erish has been keeping them in the dark. It looked like she's been starving them, and she's cut off their wings. Hence, Queen Antu couldn't fly when I threw her out the window. And they had dirt under their nails."

"I didn't find them in the dungeons," Caine added. "But someone down there is bound to know something. Unfortunately, I believe some of our soldiers may be loyal to Erish. You must hunt them out."

The vampire lord went completely still. Rosalind thought he wasn't having much of a reaction to the news that his wife had been amassing an army, until she noticed the black shadows curling from his body in thorny spikes.

"I take it you knew nothing about this," Caine said.

Ambrose's fists had tightened, his knuckles white. "No." A silence fell over the room. "Tell our best soldiers to hunt her down, and bring her to me in chains."

"Already done," Caine said. "Any idea what she has planned?"

"My spies have been watching her for months. She's been coming and going out of the city, acting strangely. She's been paranoid. I suspected she was planning on taking Lilinor for herself." Ambrose stared directly at Rosalind, unblinking. "Keres once served the succubi, but they haven't done so in thousands of years. The succubi were once revered, and now they're reviled as monstrous whores. I think she's a little bitter about the whole thing."

Rosalind bit her lip. "Why cut off the keres' wings if she wants them to serve her?"

"Punishment." Shadows curled around Ambrose, slow and sharp. "For their disloyalty."

"Speaking of keres, there's something else you need to know," Caine said. "An army of keres—winged keres—attacked Cambridge tonight. I don't know where they came from or what they were doing there, but the Brotherhood will want to frame us. They're going to use this as an opportunity to expand their powers."

"Quite the coincidence," said Ambrose. "Two ker attacks in one night."

"But they were a different kind of keres," she said.

Caine shot her a perplexed look. "What?"

Her mind sparked with this idea. "When the three keres came to my room, their magic looked like smoke and smelled of charcoal. The air should have been thick with black auras in Harvard Square. But there was none of it in Cambridge. It was… there were all kinds of auras around them, but nothing that looked like charcoal."

Caine sucked in a breath. "Now that *is* fascinating."

"What do you think it means?" she pressed. "Why would the auras look different?"

Caine crossed his arms. "They wouldn't have ker auras if they weren't really keres."

"What else could they be?" Rosalind asked.

Ambrose's eyes were locked on her. "Now *that* is something I'd like you to find out."

"We still haven't located Miranda," Caine said. "If you want to create your daywalkers, she must be our priority."

"She is," Ambrose said curtly. "Find her. Then figure out what the fuck is going on with the keres."

Ambrose didn't seem in the mood for questions, but something had been nagging the back of Rosalind's mind. She swallowed hard. "You seem protected here in Lilinor. Why are you so concerned with the Brotherhood?"

Ambrose surveyed her for so long, his shadowy aura snaking around him, that she wondered if he was about to lash out at her. Her chest clenched. At last he said, "The Brotherhood are learning to adapt. They don't understand magic now. But I've lived long enough to know that things change."

"I see," Rosalind said. Perhaps he knew more than she did about the Brotherhood.

"I want to take Rosalind out of Lilinor," Caine said. "If Queen Erish has soldiers loyal to her, Rosalind could be in danger."

"Yes," Ambrose said. "Take her to your tower. But before you do, I want you to find where Erish is keeping the keres." His brow furrowed. "Kill them, if you must." He glanced at Rosalind again, running a finger over her delicate, pearly crown before his gaze slid lower. "You look like a queen."

"Not a queen," Rosalind said, suddenly unsure if a crown was a breach of protocol. "More of a soldier."

"Maybe, someday," Ambrose said.

She wasn't sure if he meant queen or soldier, but she didn't want to ask.

Caine shot her a sharp look. "This soldier and I have work to do. I'll report to you what we find down below the dungeons. And then we leave."

CHAPTER 11

Caine led Rosalind down a narrow, straight stone stairwell at the very bottom of the fortress. In almost total darkness, she ran her fingers along the walls to steady herself. She quickly jerked them away when they ran over something slimy.

"Fond of Ambrose, were you?" Caine asked.

"What?"

"He seems taken with you."

"Okay." The air down here was damp and musty, full of dirt particles. "Can you do one of those light spells? It's dark as hell down here."

"You have no idea just how dark hell is," he muttered, then whispered a spell, sparking a sphere that hovered just above their heads in the cramped space. It illuminated glistening stone walls, and a wooden door at the bottom of a long flight of stairs.

Caine was obviously in a weird mood, and she didn't respond as they trudged down the stairs. Quiet fell upon them, interrupted only by a rhythmic dripping noise.

At the bottom of the stairs, Caine chanted another spell, and the deadbolts on the door unlocked with a creak. The heavy door groaned open, revealing an arched stone corridor lit by torches. About fifty feet away, two armed vampire guards stood shoulder to shoulder.

Caine shot her a quick look. "There will be a lot of iron down here. If we need to use magic, it won't be very powerful. So let's hope it doesn't come to that."

"I would rely on my weapons and armor, but you had me dress in transparent tulle so I could look pretty for the king."

"If I remember correctly, you're perfectly adept at fighting naked."

As they walked, shrieks echoed from further down the hall. They drew closer to the guards, who looked like inverted images of each other: one with tan skin and a shock of white hair, the other raven-haired and pale as moonlight. Only their stony expressions matched.

Rosalind narrowed her eyes at the pair. After what she'd seen upstairs, she wanted to warn them to do whatever Caine asked if they knew what was good for them.

Caine stalked closer to them, staring down at one of the guards. "I don't suppose you've seen Queen Erish down here recently."

The white-haired guard didn't meet Caine's gaze. "No, sir."

Caine tilted his head. "Why do I get the feeling that you're lying?"

The vampire's hands began to tremble. "The queen protects all shadow demons, sir."

"The queen protects herself," Caine said. "Tell me what you know about the keres."

Nervously, the guard met Caine's gaze. "Queen Erish said she was protecting our city. She said the Brotherhood are coming—"

"Who has protected you in the past?" Caine cut in.

"You, sir. And the High Lord." The guard took a deep breath, holding Caine's gaze. "In the southwest corner—"

In a lightning-fast gesture, the other guard plunged a stake right through his back. A bloodied wooden tip protruded from the white-haired guard's chest, and he crumpled to the ground.

Rosalind took a step back, ready to grab for her knife, but Caine already had the killer by his neck. He lifted him into the air, then punched through the vamp's ribs into his chest.

Rosalind's blood drained from her head. Caine was gripping the vamp's heart. "What did she promise you?" he snarled.

A thin stream of blood ran from the corner of the vamp's mouth, and choking noises echoed off the ceiling.

"Tell me." Caine's voice was low and soothing. "And it will all be over."

"Daywalking—" the vamp choked out.

Caine's mouth twisted in a dark smile. "You thought *Erish* would help you become a daywalker?"

The vamp managed a nod before Caine pulled his heart from his chest, blood dripping down his arm. As the vamp crumpled to the floor, Caine slid his sword from his back. He sliced through the vamp's neck, severing his spine, before glancing at Rosalind again. "I guess we've got to find the keres on our own. How many vampires do you think she made these promises to? I'd wager she's manipulated all the prison guards, maybe more."

"If a lot of soldiers knew about this, surely someone would have told you or Ambrose."

"There has been a lot of discord among the soldiers. They're not happy with us."

"Why?" she asked.

"Ambrose promised to make them daywalkers. And it hasn't happened. I'm sure by now some of them think Queen Erish could do a better job of it."

Rosalind nodded at the white-haired guard. "He said something about the southwest corner."

"So we'll check that part of the dungeon." Caine sheathed his sword, then began striding down the hallway. "There may be some sort of hidden entrance in the ground. There's nowhere else in the city that they would have gone unnoticed."

His footsteps echoed off the ceiling. The narrow hall was barely large enough for the two of them to walk abreast, and her arm brushed his. As they walked, the distant shrieks grew louder—frantic, animalistic noises, half human and half beast.

The narrow hall opened to a wider corridor with a packed-dirt floor, lined on either side by iron cells. Gray, emaciated arms clawed between the cell bars, scratching and grasping at the air. They seemed to be reaching right for Rosalind, and with a twist of her gut she realized why they'd been screaming. They'd been starved down here, and they could smell her blood.

Caine turned to look at her. "I suppose I don't need to tell a former hunter to be careful around starved vampires."

"I gathered that."

The vampires' shrieks sent a cold shiver up her spine, and she stepped into the corridor, walking as fast as she could. Her heart thumped wildly. Frantic hands reached for her, but she wouldn't meet the vamps' eyes. She didn't want to see the desperation in them.

She crossed her arms as she walked, her gaze on the dirt floor, until a frantic banging noise interrupted the silence. Finally, she gave in, glancing to her right. A gaunt female vamp with wild brown ringlets was throwing herself against the iron bars, howling. Her fangs were bared, and her eyes burned with a bestial ferocity.

Rosalind swallowed hard and walked on, quickening her pace.

At last, the corridor opened into a central atrium. Five guards stood in the center, forming a circle, with each of them facing outward and surveying a corridor. Cell-lined hallways branched off from the atrium like spokes on a wheel.

The guards gripped silver pikes, and their shoulders straightened as Caine approached.

"Sir—" one of them began.

But Caine merely whispered a spell, flicking his wrist. The vampires fell to the ground. Caine never broke his pace.

"Are they dead?" Rosalind asked, stepping over a guard.

"No." He led her to another corridor of cells. "But they probably should be. This could never have happened without their knowledge. I'll let Ambrose decide their fates."

As they entered another long corridor of iron cells, the prisoners' arms began their frantic, desperate grasping again, and Rosalind tried to block them out. Still, their screams—full of hunger—cut to the bone.

As they approached the end of the corridor, Rosalind fixed her gaze on the ground, but even without lifting her head she knew they were getting closer to their target. A faint smell of charcoal wafted past her, a darkening of the dust particles that floated around them, a faint feeling of thin wires brushing over her skin. *Ker auras.*

"There's nothing here," Caine said. "Can you sense anything?"

"Yes. Give me a minute." Rosalind tried to block out a banging noise from her left. She stared at the air around her hands, swirling with faint wisps of black that brushed over her skin. She raised her fingers into the air, studying them closely, and the wisps grew thinner. *Bang. Bang. Bang.*

"It's coming from below," she whispered. She crouched down, watching the darkening of the air around her fingers, smelling the air thickening with charcoal. She shifted onto her hands and knees.

"I'm quite admiring the view," Caine said.

"It's coming from the ground." She brushed the earth back and forth. When she'd cleared away half an inch of earth, she caught a glimpse of wood.

Caine knelt beside her, helping her to clear it off. "And this is why I need you around."

Rosalind brushed and scraped away the dirt with her hands, keeping her eyes on the ground, still trying to ignore the slamming noise to her left—a sound like metal slamming against metal, accompanied by agonized screams. *Bang, bang, bang.* This place was awful. *Bang. Bang.*

Together, they cleared the wooden surface, and Caine dug his fingers down, pulling up a square of wood. He let it slam onto the ground next to them, a cloud of dirt puffing into the air. Coughing in the dust, he peered down into a narrow, earthen hole.

Bang. Bang.

"It's about a twelve-foot drop," Caine said. "I'm going to jump in first and make sure it's safe. Then you can follow."

Bang. Bang. Bang.

Caine sat at the edge of the hole, then jumped. She peered down at him as he landed, still trying to block out that cacophony behind her. *Bang. Bang.* She was about to lose her mind. Unable to control her curiosity anymore, she glanced at the source of the noise. A male vamp—middle-aged, with frizzy gray hair—slammed his forehead against the bars, his face streaming with blood. His cracked skull was visible through his forehead.

"Fucking hell," she muttered. *I want to get the hell out of here. Now.* "Caine?"

Uttering a spell, Caine sparked another glowing sphere, which cast pale light on an earthen space. He looked up at her. "I don't see any immediate threats. Jump."

She sat at the edge of the hole, dangling her legs over, and then let herself drop. Caine caught her around the waist. Her body slid against his as he lowered her; her pulse raced as her bare skin brushed against his thin shirt. His strong fingers lingered on her waist a little longer than they needed to, and an electric rush tingled over her skin. She met his gaze, and for a second she nearly forgot what they were doing.

"The keres," he muttered, as if reading her mind.

She nodded, stepping away. "Right." She surveyed this new space: a narrow, earthen tunnel, lit only by Caine's sphere of light. The air down here was stale—full and heavy with mold—and she had the uncomfortable feeling that the ceiling might collapse at any moment, burying them under the earth. Which, incidentally, was pretty much Rosalind's worst nightmare—particularly when that earth contained starved vampires. *Keep your cool, Rosalind. Soldiers aren't afraid of a little dirt.*

Caine sucked in a sharp breath. "How the hell did Erish manage to create all this? Who dug this for her?"

They pressed on through the narrow tunnel, and Rosalind tried to steady her breathing, willing herself to stay calm. The passageway curved around, back in the direction of the atrium. Hugging herself, Rosalind took deep breaths, trying to ignore the feeling that she was sucking in dirt instead of air.

As they walked, the sound of female voices floated on the air, and thin tendrils of charcoal auras wafted toward them. *The keres.*

Rosalind could only hope they were kept in cells like the vamps upstairs, but she really had no idea. Whatever the case, she didn't imagine they'd be fond of their queen's killer.

The sphere of light flew forward as they approached, and the keres' talking subsided. As she and Caine drew closer, Rosalind could see the light glinting off metal. *Good. They're locked up.*

The narrow tunnel opened into a wider earthen hall, and as Rosalind stepped into it she got a good view of the keres. On one side of the hall, the demons were kept in iron cells like the ones upstairs, but with packed-dirt walls instead of stone.

As Caine and Rosalind stepped into the hall, hundreds of silver eyes landed directly on them. Caine strode over to one of the cells, running his finger along the cell bars. "A ker prison in Ambrose's dungeons. This is certainly unexpected."

The pale, starry eyes gazed back at him. None of the keres responded.

"I don't suppose anyone wants to tell me what you're doing here?" he asked.

A heavy silence was broken by a call from one of the far corners of the hall. "We want our wings back!" someone croaked.

Caine crossed to one of the cells and reached inside, grabbing a ker by her ragged black dress and pulling her against the bars. "What is Queen Erish planning?"

The ker trembled. "She didn't tell us," she stuttered. "But if we do what she says, we get our wings back."

"And what does she want you to do?"

Frantic, the keres began shrieking, jumping up and down on the earthen floor. Through the din, Rosalind could make out shrieks of "Don't tell them! Don't tell them!"

Rosalind peered further down the hall, and through the black auras she caught a glimpse of something that didn't belong at all: swirls of copper, silver, blue, green, gray, and gold auras, curling into the air. *What the hell?*

While the keres continued their frantic jabbering, she stepped closer to the rainbow colors. Up ahead, there seemed to be a gap in the cells, and it was from that space that the colored aura rose.

As she walked closer, the hair on the back of her neck stood on end. Finally, at the gap's edge, she peered around the corner. A window had been carved in the dirt—and through it, a giant set of eyes stared at her from an enormous, humanlike head.

CHAPTER 12

*H*er mind whirled, trying to process what she was looking at. *A giant? I guess that's who dug the tunnels.* But giants had gone extinct thousands of years ago. Nevertheless, he looked distinctly enormous, and was staring right at her.

His eyes were a deep brown, glaring at her from below thick, wiry blond brows, and he smelled like a grave. His skin was rough and ruddy, with enormous pores, and she could see her own reflection in his enormous black pupils.

And I look scared as shit.

"Caine?" she shouted.

"What?" he barked, interrupting his interrogation of the terrified ker.

"There's a giant," she blurted.

"*What?*" he snapped again, in a tone implying that she'd lost her mind.

"There's a fucking giant!" she shouted, stepping away from the creature.

In a fraction of a second, Caine had dropped the ker and was at her side.

The giant's large brown eyes fixed on the incubus, and as soon as they did, a low rumble filled the hall. The ground trembled, and dirt fell from the ceiling. *Oh shit.*

From somewhere below, a deep, pounding noise reverberated through the earth, and chunks of the ceiling rained down onto her bare skin. The keres' screeching intensified, and the demons jumped wildly in their cages.

In the next moment, Caine was whispering a spell, his aura lashing at the giant's face The creature roared, tilting back his head, and the sound rumbled through Rosalind's gut, sparking the voice in the back of her mind that always told her when to run. *Buried alive,* her mind screamed. Instinctively, she reached for the knife strapped to her thigh—her only weapon. *Fat lot of good it will do against a giant.*

Clumps of dirt rained from the ceiling, and she grabbed Caine's arm. "We need to run."

But just as they turned to flee, an avalanche of dirt rained down, forming a wall where the tunnel should be. And with it, Rosalind caught a glimpse of gaunt limbs and faces, tumbling down.

Her knees went weak. The vampire prisoners had been freed. Nothing separated her from them now but a pile of dirt.

In the next moment, a giant fist punched through the earthen wall, then clamped around her waist. The behemoth clutched her hard in his meaty fingers, and panic clamped around her heart.

Her heart thrumming, Rosalind jammed her knife into the giant's finger. At the same time Caine ran for his fist, sword raised. He sliced into the giant's flesh, cutting straight to the bone. The giant only clutched tighter, crushing her ribs and pulling her toward his stubby, bloodstained teeth. *His eyes... go for his eyes.*

Panic lit up her nerves, and she ripped the knife from the giant's finger, then hurled it at his eye. It sank into his pupil, piercing her reflection. The giant shrieked, dropping her into the tunnel again. His wail was deafening.

Rosalind ran back to Caine, but they were trapped. Great chunks of dirt rained down on her shoulders and hair. A starved vampire with hair the color of sand broke free from one of the piles of dirt, running right for Rosalind.

Caine slid an arm around her waist, pulling her close and chanting a spell. His silver magic curled around them, forming a shield. Rosalind pressed in close to Caine, and the hungry vamp slammed into his shield, her eyes burning blood red. She slammed herself against the invisible shield, her forehead splitting.

All around the silvery bubble, earth and mud rained down around them.

She closed her eyes, slowing her breathing. Caine leaned in, whispering, "I won't be able to hold this shield forever. There's too much iron around here."

What will kill us first—the vamps, or the crumbling ceiling? They were about two minutes away from suffocating under the earth. She could already feel herself running out of breath. She tightened her fingers around Caine's arm, her breath coming in short bursts. "We have to get out of here."

"Stay calm." He brushed her hair off her face. "We've got limited air in here."

"That's supposed to help me calm down?" She closed her eyes, concentrating on slowly exhaling before she had a panic attack and sucked all the air right out of Caine's lungs. Her heart was beating fast as a hummingbird's. "Can we teleport?"

"I don't think it will work with all the iron, but we can try. I'll definitely need you to chant with me. Are you ready?"

"Yes."

Caine held her hand and slid the iron ring off her finger. Cleo's aura roiled in her mind, leaching away some of her fear.

Before she knew what was happening, she was chanting along with Caine, her lips effortlessly forming the words for the teleportation spell. Their silver and green auras mingled together in a thrilling rush. She felt the power lighting up her body.

In the next moment, she was breathing clear air, standing in the center of Caine's room. He slid the ring back on her finger.

She still gripped his arm around her waist. "It worked," she breathed.

"You've got better control now." Slowly, he released her, taking his warmth with him as he stepped away.

Her body burned from the exertion of the spell, and she flopped back on Caine's bed, only half-aware that she was coating his sheets with mud and dirt. *I'm alive. Thank the gods. I'm not buried under vamp-infested earth.* She pushed herself up on her elbows, staring at Caine. "I thought giants were extinct."

"So did I. And right about now, I need to figure out what the hell is going on. We seem to be under a ker attack, and I have no idea where the fucking giant came from." The fortress walls shook from a violent pounding noise, and a muscle clenched in Caine's jaw. "I need to get the army together, at least what's left of it after Erish recruited half of them."

A knock at the door interrupted them, and Caine quickly crossed to pull it open. In the doorframe stood a curly-haired female vamp, dressed for battle in tight-fitting black clothes, a sword slung over her back. She stared at Caine, squaring her shoulders. "Sir. There's a horde of keres swarming out from the traitor's gate. Someone or something blasted a giant hole in one of the dungeon walls."

The pounding continued, the fortress's walls rattling.

The temperature in the room chilled, and a whisper of black wings drew up behind Caine. "Get everyone to the esplanade. We fight them there." He turned to Rosalind. "Stay here. The room is spelled to keep you safe."

"I can help you."

"I don't have time to save you if anything happens to you," he said. "And you're as likely to get killed by a vamp as you are by a ker. You're staying here."

He has a point. "Fine."

Caine left, slamming the door behind him, and Rosalind crossed to the window. The breeze smelled different now—no longer just floral, but tinged with the scent of blood and charcoal. Rosalind peered out at the esplanade; it swarmed with snarling keres, their muddy skin glistening in the moonlight. At least thirty vampire soldiers stood among them, armed with pikes—the vamps loyal to Queen Erish.

Even from ten stories up, she could still see Antu's broken body on the stone. A few keres swarmed around her, lifting her broken body over their shoulders and ferrying it away.

A great thundering boom rocked the castle, and Rosalind gripped the windowsill to steady herself. The room tilted, and glasses slid off the shelves, shattering on the floor.

The earth rumbled with loud *booms*, and the giant appeared, crushing part of a stone wall as he climbed on to the walkway leading up to the esplanade. One of his eyes was clamped shut, and thick streams of blood dripped from his mangled fingers. He clenched his fists, screaming into the night.

The portcullis creaked open, and vampire soldiers began streaming into the open esplanade, their silver armor catching the moonlight.

Caine stood at the front of the charge, nearly a head taller than most of the vamps. Shadowy magic curled around him. He wore no armor, but two swords were strapped across his back and an entire arsenal of blades glinted from his boots and pants.

The giant took a step closer to the castle. He was going to crush the vamps and rip right through the fortress walls. But as soon as his gnarled, bare foot hit the ground, some of the vampires rushed forward, scuttling up his body like bugs, biting at his flesh, gnawing through his tendons and gristle. Moaning, the giant tottered, staggering back.

Caine pulled his sword from his back then launched into a sprint, fast as the night wind, and within moments he'd launched himself into the air. His sword found its mark right in the giant's heart.

Rosalind's breath caught in her throat. *Holy shit. He can fly?*

Groaning, the behemoth tilted backward, arms windmilling in large arcs. When he landed on the ground, the earth shook. Caine fell with him, still gripping his sword.

The brightly colored aura around the giant drifted away and disappeared into the night sky.

Screaming, the throng of keres swarmed around the giant's body, trying to flee from Caine and his army. They moved fast—but the vamps were faster. Caine's soldiers leapt onto the stone walls surrounding the street, swarming around the keres to flank them.

The demonesses were completely surrounded, wingless, trapped between the giant and the vamps. Their white hair gleamed in the moonlight.

Caine leapt down from the giant, gripping his sword. The vampires around him pulled their weapons from their sheaths.

A high pitched shrieking rent the air—the keres' piercing battle cries.

The mob of keres charged for Caine, and he swung, moonlight gleaming off his sword. He towered over the keres, slicing into the first one that ran at him. The demonesses were gunning for him, and he fought in a stunning whirl of silver and black, hacking into ker bodies. The keres moved with inhuman speed, but they were armed only with knives—probably iron ones that could injure vamps, but not very effective against the sword. It seemed like they were up for a suicide mission, if it meant they had a chance of getting their wings back.

Caine could probably have ended it all quickly, using his magic alone. But as she watched his elegant swings, saw his body glowing with a pale silver light, Rosalind had the distinct impression that he enjoyed every second of this.

Then, with one graceful movement, he sheathed his sword. He was going to fight bare-handed. With his magic whipping around his body, he gripped a ker by the head, then twisted it to the side until she fell, her neck broken.

Horrifying—but Rosalind felt a strange thrill at watching his savage grace.

As Caine snapped necks, Rosalind's gaze darted to the base of the fortress, and her mouth went dry. Three armed keres were scaling the wall, coming right for her. They scuttled up with a startling speed.

With a hammering heart, Rosalind slammed the window shut and locked it. She rushed to the table by Caine's bed, grabbing for the weapons. With her eyes on the window, she gripped two, long knives. Her blood pumped hard, warming her limbs.

Just outside the window, a shrill battle cry pierced the air. *They're here.*

Their faces only appeared in the glass for a moment before the window shattered, shards of glass spraying around the room. In an explosion of glass, the three ker women leapt into Caine's bedroom.

A large, muscular ker at the front growled. "Queen-killer."

Rosalind gripped her knives. *Oh, shit.*

The ker's sharp teeth flashed. "Let's see how you like being thrown from a window. You don't have wings. Can you fly, little human?"

Nope. Rosalind raised her knives.

The largest ker lunged, and the other two scuttled forward.

They're surrounding me. Well, I just have to take them out one at a time.

The keres would be expecting an attack with the knife, so maybe it was best to start with something else. When the muscular ker lunged, Rosalind pivoted, kicking the demoness hard in the chest. The crack of ribs echoed off the walls, and the ker flew back, slamming against the wall.

In the next moment, another stood in front of her, pressing a blade against her throat. "I want to see you jump. That, or I cut the skin off your body."

Rosalind's blood roared. *I need to get out of this.*

With a quick movement, she leaned away from the knife, then punched the ker in the face. The ker's head snapped back, her position faltering. Grabbing the ker's shoulder, Rosalind slammed her knee into the demon's stomach. As the ker doubled over, Rosalind kicked her hard in the face. The ker's knife clanged against the ground.

A violent tug on Rosalind's hair yanked her back; she slammed against the ground, her skull cracking.

A swift kick to her ribs knocked the wind out of her, and another to her head sent sharp pain through her skull. She tried to roll over, to stand up and fight. *They're going to throw me out the window, and a crowd of angry keres will gnaw into my guts.*

With shaking arms, she struggled onto her hands and knees, but a hard kick to her back knocked the wind out of her. She fell forward again, her face smacking against the stone floor. The rough stone bit into her skin. Two more kicks to her ribs, and agony blazed.

Just throw me out the fucking window. Her vision dimmed, and she tried rolling over again—but rough hands grasped her, lifting her up, claws digging into her skin. Thrashing, she struggled against them, but they forced her up, her back scratching over the jagged shards of glass on the windowsill.

"You can join our queen," a ker growled.

Rosalind's world tilted, and she felt the night wind whip against her skin. "Wait—"

The ker shoved her broken body over the broken shards of window, and Rosalind plummeted down.

CHAPTER 13

The cold wind whipped at her hair, and her life flashed before her eyes—Malphas as a little boy, giving her wildflowers. Miranda's young face by the seashore. Tammi, painting Rosalind's nails a lurid shade of red.

I'm not ready to die yet.

She raced toward the earth, finally landing hard. With the force of the fall, pain pierced her core. But she wasn't on the earth—someone was holding her.

She blinked, looking up into Aurora's face.

The vampire scowled. "Bloody hell, Rosalind. Who did you manage to piss off now?"

"I threw the ker queen out the window."

"Of course you did." Aurora put her down, but Rosalind still leaned against her, surveying the scene. Besides the giant, the esplanade was littered with ker bodies, some still twitching but most still. Some of the vampires picked over the corpses, plundering iron knives.

Caine stood in the center, his body soaked with dark blood. His pale eyes landed on Rosalind, and he stalked over to her, frowning. "I told you not to come out here."

"Tell that to the keres who threw me out the window," Rosalind shot back. Her body was on fire, her bones seared with pain.

"This one's disaster prone," Aurora said. "I caught her."

Caine stepped closer to Rosalind, his eyes roaming over her body. "Injured again."

"It was three against one," Rosalind said. She pulled away from Aurora, straightening, and agony pierced her chest.

Aurora exhaled. "Do you two need to get naked for this or can you just heal her?"

Ignoring Aurora, Caine traced his fingers over Rosalind's broken ribs and whispered his healing spell. His magic caressed her skin, soothing her pain. He brushed his fingertips over her back, and his aura thrummed through her body, filling her with euphoria. He let his fingers linger over the sheer fabric, his eyes scanning all the tears and rips on her tattered dress. "Better?"

With his hands brushing against her, she felt amazing. "Better."

"Caine," Aurora said. "Your soldiers are watching."

Abruptly, Caine yanked his hand away as if he was being burned. He turned to the esplanade, squaring his shoulders and stepping away from her. The armed vampires had begun gathering around.

"My soldiers!" Caine shouted, his voice booming off the fortress's stone walls. "We've easily defeated the keres, but they are not our true enemy. Your king and I ask you to continue this fight for him. Hunt down the traitor Erish, and bring her back to Lilinor in chains. You will have the freedom to move in and out of the city. Fill your bellies with the blood of any Hunters you can find. But whatever you do—find the queen. Find out how and where she got the giant. And know this—" He turned to Rosalind. "Rosalind and I will find her sister. And we will turn you into a legion of daywalkers, the most powerful vampire army since the days of King Cranaus. Erish is not your savior."

The vampires erupted into loud cheers, and Caine turned to her. "I'm taking you out of here. Aurora will join us later, but we can't stay. Erish is bound to have some loyal to her who will try to abduct you."

"Quite confident in your speech, there."

"Demigods don't lack for confidence."

She frowned. "What happened to the giant?"

"Suffocated." He grabbed her hand pulling her closer. As he slid his arm around her waist, his warm, strong body pressed against hers. She slipped her arms around his neck, relishing the warmth. She'd nearly forgotten all about the terrible dream she'd had about him.

He tucked his head down, whispering his transportation spell. She joined in, their auras tingling over her skin, vibrating through her healed ribs. Silver and green light flashed, and she closed her eyes.

When she opened them again, they stood in a forest, dwarfed by oak trees. Pearly streams of light danced between the leaves. She pulled her arms away from Caine.

Caine turned, walking over the deadfall. "It's not far from here. While we're walking, I want you to tell me about that nightmare you had."

Thorns caught on the hem of her dress, and she tugged on the fabric, ripping it some more. "That hardly seems important now."

The forest path wound through overgrown juniper and chokeberry shrubs. "Some nightmares don't mean anything. But if someone is after you, you'd be wise to pay attention to your dreams. Demons and mages can manipulate them. And they can tell you of things to come."

A shiver rippled over her skin. *Gods below. Does that mean he's going to crucify me some day?* "There were some stakes, set up for some sort of executions."

She felt a change in the air—a chilling of the wind, a subtle shift in the shadows—and the hair on her arms stood on end.

"Have you seen them before?" he asked.

She shook her head. "Nope. Only in my dream."

"What else did you see?"

The breeze blew her shortened hair into her face, and she brushed it away. This nightmare was the last thing she wanted to talk about with Caine—it would only confirm what he'd said about her tendency to divide the world up into good and evil, with him on the wrong side of the divide. "I've had lots of bad dreams. I've been having night-mares all week."

"What type of dreams?"

She shook her head. "They were mostly memories—things that have already happened. Tammi in the Chambers' prison. Me, torturing Malphas. You lying on the floor, bleeding. Do you think it means something?"

"It could be chronomancy. Stealing from the timeline of your life—visions of your past or future. The chronomancer feeds these snippets into your dreams." He inhaled deeply. "Did you see any auras in the dream?"

She thought back, envisioning the color of the sky over the four stakes. "Yes. But it wasn't just one color. It was a whole array. Copper, like Drew's. Silver, like yours."

"Like mine?"

"Or Erish's. You have the same aura."

Caine stopped walking, his silver aura snaking from his body. "We *what?*"

"Must be an incubus thing. Anyway, what does it mean if there were auras in my dream?"

"It means a coven of mages are interfering with your dreams. And apparently, shadow mages and light mages are working together, for some absurd reason." Caine turned and began walking again. "And perhaps they're the same people who created the pseudo-keres."

Please, gods—that nightmare of the stakes can't be my future. "What if the visions aren't real? What if the coven is sending me images they've manipulated?"

"It doesn't work that way. The reason it's called chronomancy is that the practitioner manipulates time in your dreams. They're mining your soul for glimpses of images on the timeline of your life. And these are stakes you're sure you've never seen before, so that can mean only one thing: they lie in your future."

A salty breeze rustled the leaves, chilling her skin. *So why the fuck did I see a vision of you driving a nail through my heart?* She swallowed hard, her mind churning. *And is this coven trying to threaten me—or to warn me to stay the hell away from Caine?* Her chest clenched. She had to believe it wasn't true, or she'd lose her mind. Perhaps Caine didn't know everything about magic.

"I want you to remember one thing," Caine said. "Erish, the Brotherhood, this new master of yours—all these people want to hurt you. And they'll use your weaknesses against you. When we learn where Tammi and Miranda are, you can't go rushing off half-cocked, trying to save them. Your enemies will use your emotional attachments against you. That's the most important warning you need."

"I see. This is part of your whole 'loyalty is a weakness' theory." Her footsteps crunched over the deadfall. She frowned, her mind reeling over the image of her crucifixion. "You can't be certain this vision will come to pass."

He cut her a sharp look. "Why are you so worried? All you saw was a bunch of stakes."

Whoops. "Well, wooden stakes are rarely good news."

"I told you. It's your fate. Anything a chronomancer shows you will certainly happen, unless it already has. But you didn't see anyone die, so don't throw yourself off a cliff just yet."

Dread wrapped its fingers around her heart. *No one died in my dreams except me—at your hands.* Either Caine was just using her, and would murder her when he was done with her—or perhaps she'd become insane like Miranda, and have to be put down like a rabid dog?

A spark lit in the back of her brain. Perhaps it *wasn't* her who was murdered by Caine. It could just as easily be Miranda. And who knew if Miranda would deserve it? Her twin had already tried to murder her once, and she probably worked for the Brotherhood now.

Her fists tightened. Whatever the case, there was no point in trying to change the outcome. She'd read enough of those Greek tragedies to know that you couldn't escape destiny. And this wasn't the most pressing problem right now. She still had to find out what had happened to Tammi, before her best friend ended up dead.

Caine held up a hand, stopping her march. "We're here." He chanted a low, melodious spell. His aura reverberated through the oak leaves. As he finished, the trees thinned out, revealing a large field that bloomed with yellow primrose and white moonflowers. A stone tower stood in the center of the clearing, reaching up to the starry sky. To the right of the tower, a serene pond reflected the moon, a milky crone's eye staring back at itself.

"It's beautiful," she murmured.

Caine marched through the flowered grasses, and she followed. "You won't need to worry about the keres here," he said. "This field is glamoured. No one can see it but us and the servants inside." He arched an eyebrow. "Though if keres did manage to find us, I wouldn't mind witnessing another naked fight between you and them."

Her cheeks warmed, and she pushed the image out of her mind. *So easy to be distracted by Caine.* "When can we try out this scrying spell to find Tammi?"

"I said you need to sleep first." His gaze raked over her body. "And you haven't been eating. You're no good to me when you're falling apart."

She opened her mouth, ready to protest, but it was completely true. "I haven't been feeling myself lately."

"I can see that. Is this some strange sort of Hunter penance? I'd love to know what it is that you're atoning for."

She tutted. "Oh, whatever."

"Maybe you feel bad that you watched your ex-boyfriend die, or maybe that you tortured Malphas. It could be that you lost track of Miranda." A faint smile crossed his lips. "But my money is on your uncontrollable lust for a demigod-like incubus known as the Ravener. It fills you with all sorts of internal conflict, lust warring with self-hatred."

"Wow. I forgot how much you love yourself."

"I quite like to watch you fight with yourself. There is something terribly seductive about self-hatred."

The tower loomed above them as they drew closer, and she could see its arched black door come into view.

"People don't really say the same for self-adoration," she said.

"Something for you to think about, if you ever want to evaluate your personality."

"Why on earth would I do that?" He folded his arms behind his head, and his black shirt sleeves slid up, giving her the best possible view of his muscled arms, covered in lethal-looking alchemical symbols. Somehow, as they walked in the woods, he'd completely cleared himself of all the blood and dirt covering his body. He smelled amazing.

"Speaking of demigods..." She swallowed hard. "What's the deal with the shadow prince—your father? Erish said *the* shadow prince. As in—there's only one. And if Nyxobas is the king of the shadow realm..."

"So you've worked it out," Caine said. "My father is prince of the shadow realm. Nyxobas's son. And now you know why I look like a demigod." Caine gestured for her to enter the tower's door, and she stepped into a stairwell lit by tiny, glowing white orbs. "I am one."

Seven hells. Caine was close kin to the god of night. No wonder his power was so overwhelming. Malphas must be his half-brother, fathered by the immortal shadow prince, but with a different mother.

"My father is a prince of night," he said. "And if you sleep near me, I'll keep the nightmares out of your head."

Rosalind began climbing the stairs, her stomach clenching. *But what if you're the scariest thing in them?*

CHAPTER 14

As she pushed her way up the stairs, her thighs burned with fatigue. But despite her exhaustion, her mind whirred as she tried to pick apart all the clues to Tammi's disappearance. The facts seemed ephemeral. She felt like she was stumbling in a darkened theater, trying to make sense of grainy old film images flickering on the screen. The keres, the giant, the strange auras, her nightmare about Caine… none of it pieced together in a sensible way. And meanwhile, Tammi could be in serious trouble.

Tammi had no past among the demons or Brotherhood, apart from her connection to Rosalind. Rosalind, meanwhile, had made a million powerful enemies. Erish, Bileth, her own twin sister, the Brotherhood…

If the Brotherhood weren't so dead set against using magic, she'd have been certain of their involvement. They'd love to stage some sort of PR coup, parading her and Tammi on TV as captured terrorists. A wonderful resolution to the whole ker massacre situation.

At least when they performed the scrying spell, they'd get something more tangible.

Rosalind's legs felt as if they were about to give way. *Too bad that teleportation spell uses up so much energy.*

At last, an oak door came into view, ending their climb.

Caine brushed against her as he stepped up to the door, pressing his fingers to the oak. The wood glowed with silver, and swung open to reveal a stunning, circular hall.

A glass dome arched above them, twinkling with constellations that seemed to burn brighter inside. On the gray walls, someone had painted a spray of inky black ravens that seemed to climb for the heavens. Pushed up against a wall, a table held a vast array of alchemist's equipment: flasks, beakers, and metal tools.

A mahogany dining table stood in the center of the room, and a breeze filtered in from a tall window. A round, stone bathtub nestled into the corner just under the window.

She glanced at Caine's bed, its purple blankets embroidered with thin silver vines. She was desperate to throw herself down on it, but she was still covered in mud and filth.

"Wow." She inhaled deeply, catching the scent of wildflowers in the air. "You stay here by yourself?"

"Just me and the servants. I have a very good cook."

A knock at the door interrupted them, and Caine crossed to pull it open. A stunning vamp stood in the door, twirling her platinum hair around her fingertips. She wore a black dress, cut in a deep V to her belly, and with equally dramatic slits up to her hips. A sparkling silver belt wrapped around her waist, and a crimson bag hung from her shoulder.

Caine leaned against the wall, clearly letting his gaze wander all over her. "Hello, beautiful."

She ran her finger down the front of Caine's body. "We haven't seen each other in a while. I was beginning to feel lonely."

Rosalind did everything in her power to resist rolling her eyes, but she failed.

The dreamy look fell from the girl's face as her gaze darted to Rosalind. "I saw you come in with a female. You walked up here very slowly."

"She's human. She moves slothfully."

"I'm right here," snapped Rosalind.

The girl frowned. "The human's clothes are torn and filthy. I brought some better ones. I don't like the thought of you with beggar women. Perhaps she should bathe."

Rosalind raised a hand. "Still here."

"You did beautifully, Kaila," Caine said. "I won't forget it."

Kaila narrowed her eyes. "Is she the Hunter I've heard about? Are you safe?"

Caine glanced at Rosalind. "I think I'll be able to handle her."

Rosalind crossed her arms. "I hate the Hunters more than anyone now."

Caine turned back to Kaila. "Please send someone up with a dinner. She gets cranky when she's hungry."

Kaila stepped out of the room, and Rosalind's stomach rumbled. "I actually am starving. Thank you for dinner, and thank you for taking me here." She stretched her arms over her head. "How long do I need to sleep before we can try the powerful scrying spell?"

"You'll sleep as long as you need. If you perform powerful magic while you're weak, you'll lose your mind, and you may not get it back." His raven fluttered into the window, perching on the edge of the bath. The bird cocked her head. Caine flicked his wrist, and the starry constellations above brightened, illuminating the space with a pearly glow. Was he controlling the stars, or was that just an illusion?

Caine leaned against his dining room table, studying her. "You're covered in several different kinds of filth. Demon blood, your blood, and a thick layer of dirt."

She glanced down at herself, at the mud encrusting her gown. Caine, on the other hand, was completely pristine.

"Don't you have a spell to clean it off?" she asked.

He ran his thumb over his lower lip thoughtfully. "Is a refusal to bathe part of your atonement, too? It might help you release some of that tension you're carrying in your shoulders, you know. And it will help you get some real sleep."

Her muscles screamed, and a bath sounded amazing. "Fine. A bath, food, sleep, and then the scrying spell. And then we rescue Tammi."

"Primarily Miranda, and perhaps Tammi." He crossed to the bath, turning on a faucet. It began to fill, and steam rose from the stone tub, curling into the air like ghostly magic.

Rosalind plopped down in a chair, pulled up her hem to unzip her boots, and slid them off. Caine sat at the edge of the tub, watching her. Under the starry midnight dome, his skin was a perfect pale gold against his dark hair, his eyes an arctic blue. He wore a black cotton T-shirt, so thin she could just make out his muscled form below the fabric, and she had the strongest temptation to cross the room and brush her fingers along his upper arms. *I really need some sleep before I lose the final remnants of my impulse control.*

Caine turned off the faucet. "It's ready."

"Right." She stood, folding her arms. "Um, you're not going to watch me. Humans aren't normally naked in front of each other."

His cheekbones looked razor-sharp in the glowing light. "I'm not human."

"But I am."

He sighed, standing. "I'll turn the other way if it makes you happy, though it's frankly a shame to let a beautiful body go unseen." He crossed the room to pour himself a glass of whiskey.

While Caine carried his drink to a deep blue armchair, facing away from her, she inhaled the steamy air and breathed in the mint and lavender scent. She leaned down, pulling off her filthy dress, and let it fall to the stone floor, then stood shivering in the night breeze.

Caine's raven fluttered to the back of his armchair, watching as she pulled off her underwear. Being naked in a room with Caine felt very different than being naked alone, even if he wasn't watching, and she felt acutely aware of every inch of her exposed skin, and the cool breeze that whispered over it, raising goosebumps.

She untangled the pearly crown from her hair, setting it down on the bath's edge.

"The lavender and mint will help with your nightmares," Caine said.

She walked up the stone steps to the bath's edge, eying Lilu. The raven seemed awfully intent on watching her bathe. "A bath can help with my nightmares?"

"I'm kin to the god of sleep. I know about these things."

As she dipped her leg into the hot water, her muscles began to relax a little. Instantly, it soothed her burning calf. She stepped further in, letting the steaming water envelop her skin up to her neck.

Tammi was missing, but at least she had a plan now—a chink of light in the darkness. She and Caine would find out where her friend had been taken.

Rosalind lay back against the smooth stone surface, looking up at the night sky through the dome. The stars seemed to burn brighter here, away from all the streetlights. "I love it here," she said. The thought was a surprise to her, but as soon as the words were out of her mouth she knew they were true.

"In my bedroom?"

"It's an extraordinary bedroom."

"In that case, I'll have to find a way for you to spend more time in it." He stretched his arms over his head. "Let me know if you need any help in the bath."

"Let me guess. Bathing is among your many talents."

"My hands are very skilled."

"Of course. Being a demigod and all. But I think I'll manage just fine, even with my slothful human ways." She dunked her head under the water, coming up again to reach for the soap. She worked it into a lather over her skin, washing the dried blood and dirt from her neck and chest.

After she rested, she'd have to use some serious magical power if she wanted to rescue Tammi. Erish had said she'd been expecting someone epic, and that Rosalind didn't fit the bill. Maybe she was right about that—Rosalind wasn't legendary.

Yet. She scrubbed the mud off her neck. *But I will be epic—even if it takes me to my death.*

She splashed water over her throat, washing off the suds. "Caine, I want to learn how to use my magic properly. Not just the scrying spell, but everything that Cleo knows how to do."

"This is an interesting change of heart. I thought you were scared of losing your mind?"

She lathered the jasmine-scented soap over her legs. "I am scared. But I can't let fear rule me. I'm not immortal like you. I've only got one human life, and I want it to count for something. If someone is coming for me and my friends, I want to be strong enough to destroy them. And I think I can handle the magic better now. When we were together in the woods weeks ago, you told me to condense Cleo's aura down to a tiny sphere. I think I know how to do it, now. It's how I got through the keres' attack in Cambridge, when all those auras were flooding my mind." She sat up, warming to this idea. "The forces that we're up against are too powerful for me to fight with conventional weapons. I want to take on whoever stole Tammi, and whoever caused the keres massacre. I want to be able to defend myself against demons like Erish. And I need to fix what I did to Miranda."

"What *you* did?"

"I mean, what the Brotherhood did. They tortured her into being a total maniac."

"I have a feeling she lost her mind long ago," Caine said.

She rubbed the soap under her armpits. "What makes you say that?"

"It's the curse your parents gave us. A human body was never meant to hold two souls."

And perhaps that's why you'll have to kill me or Miranda someday. "Then why have you been so eager for me to take the ring off and use magic, if I'm just going to turn insane?"

"I'm here to help you. I can tell you, for example, not to use a powerful spell when your body is tired. Miranda was just a girl, and she had no one. She wouldn't have known what was happening to her. She would have had no idea how to control it."

Rosalind rinsed the suds off her skin. "So who helped you control it?"

"No one."

"You don't seem insane."

"Not anymore," he said darkly.

"Are you ever going to tell me what happened?" Soapy water swirled around her. "You said that after my parents saw what happened to you, they sent Miranda and me away. You've just never told me what happened."

A cold silence enshrouded the room, and the night breeze rushed in, slamming the window shut. Something seemed to shift in the shadows, darkening. "That's not exactly how it happened," Caine said. "It's a little more complicated than that, and this is not the time to discuss it. It has nothing to do with our task." He stood, but didn't face her as he drained the last of his drink. "Your dinner will be here soon."

She bristled. It was hard to make decisions when she only had glimmers of the facts. Why did Caine get to decide what was relevant? "At least tell me about my parents. Drew seemed really weird about them when I asked." She frowned. "I feel like everyone is hiding something from me."

The light in the room dimmed for a few moments, as if the very stars in the sky were flickering, and Rosalind pushed up onto her knees, the warm water dripping down her skin.

"I thought you were focused on finding your friend?" Caine said in a low voice, snatching a bottle of wine and a corkscrew. "Dredging up old, irrelevant history will only take your mind off what we need to do."

Rosalind frowned. Despite what Caine said, she couldn't escape the feeling that whatever had happened in the past was somehow connected to the present.

A knock at the door interrupted the quiet.

Caine turned, and for just a moment his eyes flicked to her soapy breasts, then glanced away. "Why don't you get dressed before I open the door. If I remember correctly, humans don't like to appear naked in front of strangers for some absurd reason." He ran a hand through his hair. "Lilu, get her a towel and some clothes."

The bird flapped across the room, picked up a deep blue towel from a folded pile of linens on a shelf, then carried it over to Rosalind in her beak. Rosalind stood, the water dripping down her skin. She stepped out of the bath and dried herself off with the soft towel.

Caine faced the door, his shoulders completely rigid with tension as he uncorked the wine.

As Rosalind toweled off her hair, Lilu returned with a silver bra and underwear in her beak, followed by a thin blue gown that shimmered like a starry sky. Rosalind slipped into the underwear. How did demons always guess her exact bra size? It was unnerving.

She pulled the gown over her head, and the dress's smooth silk caressed her thighs as she slipped into it. "I'm dressed."

Caine turned to her, his eyes slowly sliding down her body, taking in the skin exposed by her low neckline. "It suits you."

He poured the wine into two glasses on the dining room table.

Another knock sounded at the door, and Caine crossed to open it. A blond male vampire stood in the door, wearing jogging pants and sandals. Apparently, not all vampires were glamorous. He lifted a domed silver tray. "Your dinner."

Caine took it from him. "Thank you, Andre."

Rosalind's stomach sank as she remembered what vampire food tasted like.

Andre slipped out of the room, closing the door, and Caine slid the tray across the table while Rosalind took a seat. The last time she'd eaten something prepared by a vamp, it had involved candy hearts glued to meatloaf with stale grape jelly.

Caine sat across from her, watching her over his drink. "For the love of Nyxobas, eat something. I need you at full strength. Plus, it would be a shame if you turned into a skeleton."

"If I recall correctly, vampires can't cook."

He quirked a smile. "You didn't enjoy your frozen waffle with meatloaf?"

"It was like there was a party in my mouth, and everyone was being arrested for war crimes."

"I have a Fae chef. It's a complete different eating experience."

She pulled the silver dome off the tray, and her mouth instantly began watering. Laid out before her was a leg of lamb seasoned with rosemary and mint jelly, and cherry relish on the side. She stared at a heap of roasted potatoes, and a bowl of steaming bread pudding. Her stomach rumbled, and she rubbed her belly. "Wow. The Fae seriously know how to cook."

"They are deeply hedonistic. It's why I get along with them."

She cut into the lamb, cooked rare, and took a bite. The meat practically melted in her mouth. In an instant, she was hit with the full force of her appetite, as if it had been suppressed until her first bite of delicious food. Her stomach growling, she alternated bites of lamb with potatoes, then demolished the bread pudding, scraping the last remnants of rich custard from the side of the bowl. She licked the spoon, wishing there was more.

Leaning back in her chair, she exhaled. Caine was staring at her.

"Sorry," she asked. "Did you want some?"

"No. I just forgot how you eat. It's somehow sexy and deeply disturbing at the same time."

"Sexy *and* disturbing. Like a clown doing a strip tease."

"That's basically what I envision when I think of you."

She leaned back in the chair, her belly full. For the first time in weeks, she was starting to feel more like herself again. She was ready to sleep for days. She glanced at his bed. Her eyes were practically drifting closed, and never had a piece of furniture seemed more appealing. She would have sold her soul to Nyxobas to sleep in that bed.

Assuming she wasn't going to dream about being crucified again.

"Go to sleep," Caine said, stretching his arms over his head. "When you wake, at full strength, we do the scrying spell, and all will be well again."

"Where will you sleep?"

"In my bed, the same as you."

"Is that your famous incubus seduction technique?"

"If I wanted to seduce you, you'd be out of that dress and lying across the table right now, begging me to touch you."

She could feel her chest flush. She wasn't sure she'd even be able to fall asleep next to him with that image in her mind. "Maybe you should wait until I'm asleep before you join me."

"I will. And when you sleep, I'll make sure to keep the nightmares away."

She swallowed hard. *Too bad you're the worst part of them.*

She crossed to his bed, then crawled in pulling back the covers, slipping between his silky sheets. Caine flicked his wrist, and the movement seemed to dim the twinkling stars above them until only the pearly moonlight lit the room. As she pulled the sheets up around her, she looked at Caine. He pulled a spellbook from a shelf across the room, then crossed to his armchair, settling in with a small sphere of light to illuminate his book.

Rosalind closed her eyes. Caine's sheets smelled of him, like thunderstorms and a hint of jasmine. A soft rain began to patter the domed roof, and her eyes drifted shut, her breathing slowing. As she drifted off into a deep sleep, images rose in her mind—a field of juniper trees, and eating cherries under a starry sky, the juices staining her lips and fingers red.

Her fingers dripped with bright red—not berries anymore—thick blood, pouring from her chest. *Is that me on the stake?* Her body shook as she watched the scene unfold. She was in the field again, beneath the colored sky, watching as Caine slammed her against a stake—it *was* her, only older. Caine's face was contorted with rage—pure beast, more demon than human—and he drove a nail through her heart, pinning her to the stake like an entomologist's specimen. Her crimson blood flowed down his arm, and he growled like a wild animal.

She gasped, and a pale silver light, like starlight, burned away the gruesome image. She was in the jasmine-scented bed, dimly aware of a body next to hers—strong, smooth arms that folded her against masculine contours, and enveloped her in a warm embrace.

CHAPTER 15

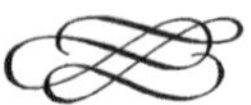

When she awoke, the sky was a dusky blue. *Dawn?* She stretched her arms over her head, turning to find that the bed next to her was empty. She had no idea how long she'd been asleep, but she felt amazing for the first time in weeks.

She pulled off the blankets and rose, crossing to the dining table. Someone had left out more food for her—cheese, fruit, and bread—and hunger gnawed at her stomach. She picked up a knife and spread some of the creamy cheese on a piece of bread, taking a bite. Within only a few minutes, she had worked her way through most of the bread and fruit.

Lilu perched on the edge of the bathtub, watching her.

"Lilu," said Rosalind. "Any idea where Caine is?" She wanted to get started on the scrying spell as soon as possible.

The bird cocked her head, and Rosalind frowned. *Stupid, talking to a bird, really.*

Just as she was considering searching the tower for Caine, the door opened. Caine stood in the doorway, a newspaper tucked under his arm. "I've got some bad news."

"What?"

He handed her the paper. "While you slept—for a day and a half, I

358

might add—the Brotherhood has been spinning a very interesting story."

Frowning, she picked up the paper. Caine's beautiful face stared coldly out from the front page, and the headline read *The Ravener Attacks Cambridge.*

"They're blaming the keres' attack on you," she said.

"Not just me. Turn the page."

A chill spread over her skin, and she flipped the page. There—just as large as Caine's photo—was Tammi, standing in Harvard Square, looking up at the night sky.

Rosalind's blood chilled. "What the hell is going on?"

"According to the Brotherhood, I called up a swarm of keres to attack humankind. And Tammi was there to help me."

Rosalind examined the picture, her blood pumping hard. Tammi was holding a small bag from *Painted Lady,* the makeup store. Rosalind pointed at the photo. "This was the night she snuck out, before the wards went up. She was just buying us makeup." Rosalind pointed at her own toes. "*Rouge Dior,* some raspberry lip gloss. This wasn't the night of the ker attack. But someone was *watching* her all the same."

She shook her head. This was bad news. The Brotherhood could be torturing Tammi to within an inch of her life. "The Brotherhood were watching her, apparently. How could they have put up the wards if they don't use magic?"

"You know how they operate. What do you think they're doing?"

She took a deep breath, scanning the article. Randolph Loring, the Brotherhood's leader, was already calling for more extreme measures. They needed to suspend the normal laws so the government could protect its citizens. Otherwise, the demons and witches would win. She'd heard all this before, but now they had the entire country listening. They were proposing an Act of Congress called the Liberty Act, which would expand their ability to imprison and punish humans without trials.

Rosalind bit her lip, anger surging. *This is working out so well for them, isn't it?*

She took a deep breath. "Josiah lectured us about leadership. He said that wars are fought with PR, and that if a populace doesn't believe in the work we were doing, it could limit the Brotherhood's effectiveness. They believe public perception and civil liberties can tie their hands with red tape and legal requirements." She slammed the paper shut. "This is why they like scapegoats. If people are scared enough of you, the Brotherhood can do whatever they want. There will be no limits to their power. They need the country to be horrified by magic. And whoever invoked the keres..." Her voice rose. "They handed the Brotherhood a major victory. People *are* terrified. The Brotherhood can take us back to the dark ages now. They can light people on fire in the town common if they want."

"Why, exactly, do they want this?"

She shivered. "I only ever wanted to fight demons. I saw what the demons had done in Boston, and I thought it was us against them—that we needed to protect ourselves from people like Bileth or Erish. But the people who run the Brotherhood are true believers. They worship Blodrial, and they want heretics to be punished. They want to claim souls for Blodrial, to purify the country in his blood. They want to bring back the golden age of witch hunting, and completely rid the earth of the Angelic language. They believe in racial purity—humans shouldn't mix with demons. And whoever created the keres massacre played right into their hands."

Caine arched an eyebrow. "They've simply scapegoated the only mages they knew of, and Tammi, who has nothing to do with anything. They're biding their time—hoping that you'll try to save her. If I had to guess, you're their real target." He reached out to touch her hand, gently tugging her closer. "You slept for a very long time. Night is falling again, and we have work to do. We're going out in the fields."

"What's out there?"

"Phobetor Pond. It works as a scrying glass. Plus, I don't like to perform powerful magic in here."

"Why not?"

He traced a finger down her arm. "Things can light on fire. Especially with that burning thing you do."

"That's very reassuring."

* * *

THEY STOOD at the bank of the serene pond by the tower. Crickets chirped nearby, and the water's surface reflected the pregnant moon that hung in the darkening sky. All around the water's edge, yellow primrose bloomed in silvery light, dappled with moonflowers and bluebells.

Caine pulled away from her, and the breeze caressed her skin. "This is a powerful spell—one that will allow us to peer between worlds. Your magic will double my power."

She took a deep breath. "I'm ready. Whatever we need to do, I'll do it."

"Your second soul—Cleo—will remember the spell. Let her tell you the words." He held out his hand. "Let me hold the iron ring. If you lose your mind and start incinerating everything or trying to tear my clothes off, I'll get it back on you."

Rosalind took a deep breath, and slipped off her magic-dampening ring.

The green, vernal magic welled in her body, snaking around the inside of her skull. Her skin began to heat, her eyes drifting left.

A beautiful man stood before her, his pale skin stunning against his dark hair. Soft, supple lips, stark cheekbones, and eyes the color of winter. Heat rushed through her core, and she wrapped her arms around his neck. *This* man was pure power, and she wanted some of it.

"Rosalind," he said.

Her lip curled in a snarl. She didn't like that name—she was Cleo. But she knew how to get men to stop talking. Smiling, she slid her fingers up his shirt, feeling the hard muscle underneath. She traced her fingers lower, reveling in his intake of breath. If she could just run her tongue—

"Rosalind!" he barked through clenched teeth. "Miranda needs you. So does Tammi."

Those words sparked something in her—recognition. There was something she was supposed to be doing. Her thoughts whirled with confusion. *Miranda. A girl who looks like me.* She pressed closer to the beautiful man, running her foot up the back of his leg. She knew what his kiss felt like, and she wanted more. But another voice screamed in her skull. *Tammi... she's in trouble. You need to help.*

With a slight tightening of his jaw, the man pulled her arms from his neck. "Rosalind. Tammi and Miranda will die if you don't get control."

The words hit her like a slap to the face, and an image flashed in her mind—someone chaining Tammi to a stake.

She shook her head, trying to wrench control from Cleo, focusing on the tendrils of unfurling green magic. If she concentrated hard enough, she could tighten them into a sphere, just as she had before. She straightened, pulling her arms from Caine's neck, but grabbing hold of his hand. His touch helped to anchor her, helped her keep control of Cleo's magic.

He gazed into her eyes. "Are you with me, Rosalind?"

She nodded. "I'm here."

"I'm going to chant the spell to locate Miranda. After you hear me say it once, you'll be able to join in. Are you ready?"

"Yes."

Caine began chanting in Angelic. This time—for the first time—she noticed she could understand the words. Caine was speaking of a scrying glass, asking men named Morpheus and Phantasos to bless him with a vision of Miranda. His delicious aura tingled over her body, and she gazed into the pond, chanting with him.

They repeated the spell over and over, until the full moon in the water began to ripple and swirl, transforming into Miranda's body.

At the sight of her twin sister, Rosalind's stomach swooped. Miranda wore a shimmering white gown, and her brown eyes stared vacantly. She stood in a gray room, its walls covered with alchemical symbols that moved and twisted. Thick, dusty bookshelves stood on one side of the room. The vision in the scrying pond sharpened, and Rosalind could read the books' spines: Angelic texts to control the weather, cure ailments, and summon demons.

The image swirled again, changing this time to a rocky fortress with gleaming marble walls rising from a bluish mountainside. A creature perched on one of the palace turrets—a woman with bare breasts and caramel-colored wings, long bronze hair tumbling down her back. Instead of feet, she had long, sharp talons.

The water swirled once more, and in the next moment Rosalind was staring at the moon reflected on the glassy surface again.

"Where the hell was that?" Rosalind asked, still forcing Cleo's magic into a tight sphere in her mind.

"I don't know yet." Caine's voice was low, strained.

She tightened her grasp on his hand. "What about Tammi?"

He blinked, as if trying to clear his thoughts. "Are you ready to try again?"

"Yes."

Caine began speaking again in Angelic, and she joined in, asking Morpheus and Phantasos to show him Tammi.

The water rippled, and as the moon disappeared in the light-dappled water, Tammi's image emerged. She was dressed in rags that hung from her thin frame, and sat with her wrists shackled in iron, chained above her head to a dank stone wall. She looked like she'd lost twenty pounds. Someone crawled in front of her—another half-starved human, then another. Rosalind's stomach clenched. Whoever had captured Tammi had crammed her into a mass cell. Bile rose in Rosalind's throat. Was this in one of the Brotherhood prisons?

Once again, the water shimmered, and the image sparkled away until another picture replaced it. Ice washed over Rosalind. It was the *same* building—the mountain palace—where Miranda was swanning about in a white gown.

Rosalind's heart thundered in her ribs. *What the actual fuck?* Miranda wasn't in chains. Had she imprisoned Tammi? It was entirely possible, given what Miranda had done in the Chambers. She was a lunatic, and she had a huge amount of magical power at her fingertips.

Miranda—her own twin—was involved in Tammi's disappearance. Miranda's mind was completely shattered, so what did that mean for Rosalind's ability to cope with this power?

She pulled away from Caine, her emotions whirling. *Let me back in,* said a voice in her mind. *Cleo will take away your pain.*

The tendrils of green magic curled around her mind, pushing the worries out of her head.

She turned to the beautiful man again. Grabbing him by his black shirt, she pulled him closer, feeling his body's heat against hers. She wanted out of this little blue dress, and began tugging down the shoulder. Caine stiffened, then whirled her around, pinning her arms to her side. She struggled against him, but in the next moment he'd slid the iron ring onto her finger. Still, he held her to him, breathing hard.

Rosalind's mind cleared of the magic, replaced instead by cold, gnawing dread. *Tammi is being starved and tortured, possibly by my sister.* Her breath came in short, sharp bursts, and fatigue burned her muscles. Her legs trembled; the blood drained from her head. *Caine wasn't kidding when he said the spell would take up my reserves of energy.* She could sleep for another two days right now.

Caine loosened his hold on her, and she stepped away, then turned to look at him. "You don't know where the mountain palace is?"

He shook his head. "No. It was hard to break through to where they were, and I didn't recognize it. Somewhere with harpies."

"What god are harpies allied with?"

"The mountain goddess."

Rosalind took a deep breath. "All of the gods have associated metals, right?"

"Yes. Nyxobas is silver, as you might have guessed."

"Which metal belongs to the mountain goddess?"

"Copper."

She bit her lip. "Drew has a copper aura." She twisted the ring on her finger. "He's from Maremount. Could it be there?"

"There are no mountain fortresses in Maremount." He frowned, moonlight glinting in his pale eyes. "Possibly outside of the city. But like I said, I'm not going to Maremount unless I'm absolutely certain."

"Right. After the Great Regicide Debacle of 1693." Sweat beaded her brow, and she wiped the back of her hand against her forehead.

"Anyway, you're right. We don't want to go on a wild goose chase into the wrong dimension." She glanced at the lake, now placid as a mirror. "At least we know the Brotherhood doesn't have Tammi yet. They might be evil assholes, but they're evil assholes who hate magic, and have no idea how to travel between worlds."

A flicker of movement in the corner of Rosalind's eye caught her attention, and she stared up at the night sky, now tinged with golden light.

Three shining, bronze-skinned women fluttered beneath the stars, fiery hair trailing behind them. In their wake, they left streaks of light—crimson, pumpkin, and lilac—and they flew in shimmering coral gowns with wings the color of honey.

"What are those?" Rosalind asked.

"Sometimes, the aura created by powerful magic attracts other magical creatures. These are Hesperides—spirits of dusk. Beautiful, and completely harmless."

The warm light of the Hesperides danced over Caine's golden skin. Hard to imagine this gorgeous, soothing man driving a nail into anyone's heart—though she'd seen him fight before, and he was ruthless.

Coral light glinted off his gray eyes. "I take it Drew is no longer your golden boy?"

She shook her head. "He never was. I'm not trusting anyone. His whole argument was that you wanted revenge for what the Hunters had done to your brother. I'm the one who tortured him, and yet you've done nothing but keep me alive. Drew seemed very eager to lay the blame on you. That automatically makes him suspicious."

"Good. I hope you remember that, whatever happens next."

She ran a hand through her chopped hair. "What *does* happen next? How do we find this place?"

"If I can find something that belongs to Miranda, it will help me complete a tracking spell. A piece of her clothing, a strand of her hair. You said that you sensed her around Abduxiel Mansion. Maybe I can find something small she left behind."

The three Hesperides drifted in front of the moon, staining the sky amber.

"And while we do that," she said, "we need to stay out of the Brotherhood's line of vision." Doubt welled in her chest. He *had* kept her alive all this time—but she couldn't rule out the possibility that he only wanted her alive as long as she served a purpose. He needed her to create the daywalkers, and he'd never disguised the importance he placed on a person's *tactical value*. "Caine, what will you do if we find Miranda and she has no interest whatsoever in helping Ambrose create his army of daywalkers? Because I don't think she has the same goals as you. She's either insane, or she's actively working against us."

"I don't know. I'm hoping to heal her mind."

"And if it doesn't work?"

He traced his finger down Rosalind's bare arm, and his seductive magic caressed her skin with a trail of tingles. "What are you worried about, specifically?"

She started to speak, but stopped herself. What she wanted to ask was *Will you still want me alive when I no longer serve a purpose?* But she wasn't sure she wanted to hear his answer.

Rosalind's footsteps echoed off the high ceiling in Abduxiel Mansion's drafty stone parlor. Small stone gargoyles leered from the walls, and the light from the TV flickered over the room—an odd mix of gothic and modern.

As Rosalind and Aurora waited for Caine to scour the grounds outside for a stray strand of hair, Rosalind was practically wearing a groove into the floor with her pacing. She was back in her fighting gear—the leather clothes Caine had got for her, and had enough blades to open a knife shop—but there was no one to fight. *Yet.*

She glanced at Aurora. The vampire had kicked off her heels, and sat curled up in a velvet armchair. As Aurora watched Orcus's old TV, she sipped some kind of combination of whiskey and gin, two olives bobbing in her toxic cocktail. She wore a vibrant blue dress, striking against her dark skin. Silver hoop earrings dangled from her ears, glinting in the warm light.

She frowned at Rosalind. "Stop walking in front of the telly."

"Sorry."

"This show's getting good. Someone's about to get eaten."

Rosalind gazed at the TV. In tall grass, a lion hunted a gazelle. The creature reared back on its haunches before leaping, pulling the gazelle down with her claws and sinking her teeth into her prey's neck.

At the sight of blood spraying from the gazelle's neck, Aurora raised her hands above her head, spilling her drink. "Yes! Now *that* was an amazing kill." Exhaling, she leaned back in her chair, shaking her head. "Nature's bloody amazing."

"I think I might need some of what you're drinking."

"I call it the Embalmer," Aurora said. "Not sure it's suitable for living types to be honest."

Rosalind crossed the bar, uncorking an old bottle of scotch. She poured two fingers into a tall glass before turning back to Aurora.

Aurora crinkled her nose. "What happened to you, anyway? You don't look the same."

"It's the hair."

Aurora twirled her drink between her fingers, nodding. "Yeah. It's all choppy. Not a good look for you, really."

"It wasn't done on purpose," Rosalind said.

"Looks like you sawed it off with a breadknife during a psychotic episode."

"That's basically what happened, only the psychotic episode belonged to someone else."

"The ker queen?" Aurora cocked her head. "I don't know what Queen Erish wants with all of them keres anyway. Filthy creatures. What's she after?"

"No idea. She disappeared from Lilinor. In Caine's view, everything she does is motivated by her obsessive lust for him." She bit her lip. "Although, according to Caine, everyone has the hots for him. In reality, that probably has nothing to do with anything."

Aurora arched an eyebrow, pointing a long, manicured nail. "Don't act like you don't have the hots for him."

Rosalind's forehead wrinkled. "Whatever." *My future with the Ravener apparently involves crucifixion, so I won't get my hopes up for a happily ever after.* She glanced at the door. "Don't you think Caine needs our help, searching for stray hairs or whatever he's trying to find? It can't be easy looking for tiny specks of evidence in a dark graveyard."

"He can see in the dark better than I can, what with him being part Night God. And his eyes are certainly better than *your* useless human orbs." Aurora popped an olive in her mouth. "Frankly, I'm surprised he waited so long to tell you about the demigod thing. Nyxobas's offspring are quite keen on being worshipped, even if they won't admit it."

"Maybe he and Erish would be well-suited, then." Rosalind pivoted, pacing the room again. "Any theories on where Erish went?"

Aurora took a deep breath. "Let me see if I can keep this all straight. Tammi's been kidnapped, maybe by your twin sister, who's a total nutter. And those two are in a mountain palace in another dimension."

"That's right."

"Possibly unrelated," Aurora continued. "An army of keres ate a load of humans in Harvard Square."

Rosalind took a sip of her scotch, letting it burn her throat. "Pretty much."

"Meanwhile, Queen Erish can't fucking stand you because she thinks you might shag her fella, even though she looks like a goddess, and you've got shit hair—"

"She caused the shit hair," Rosalind interrupted.

"Right. And she keeps a bunch of mutilated keres below the dungeon." Aurora touched her finger to her lips. "Well, I don't know what the fuck is going on, but I'm pretty sure Erish was involved in the ker massacre. It's too much of a coincidence. How many people have armies of keres? That was rhetorical. The actual answer is *not many*."

"But the keres at the massacre weren't real keres. The auras were all wrong. They were glamoured."

"I still think it's Erish. She's obviously got a weird thing about keres." Aurora sipped her drink. "In fact, I think they used to serve succubi."

"That's what Ambrose said. It *does* make sense. Maybe Erish created the new keres with magic. Maybe she's the new master I'm supposed to serve. And if she wanted me, she probably has Miranda. I have no idea why. Must be our extra souls. I don't suppose you have an idea of what Erish's game plan might be?"

"I think old demons like her just get bored after several millennia on earth. And maybe she's hoping to get you out of the way so she and Caine can worship each other's bodies or whatever succubi do with incubi."

Rosalind folded her arms. "She can have Caine to herself. I'm not going to stand in her way."

The temperature in the room chilled, and a shadow loomed across the flagstones. Rosalind whirled to see Caine standing in the door-frame. His deep silvery aura curled around his body like the milky way.

A shiver crawled up her spine. "Do you know that you have a deeply unnerving way of entering rooms?"

Ignoring her, he stepped into the light, raising his hand. He held a long strand of hair pinched between his fingers.

"You found a hair," Rosalind said.

He looked almost affronted. "Of course I did. I don't fail at things. I just need you to tell me if this belongs to your sister. Can you sense any of her magic on it?"

Rosalind plucked it from his hand, wrapping it around her finger. She closed her eyes, trying to get a sense of an aura. After a few moments, a vibrant green flickered in her mind's eye, and her nostrils filled with the scent of cedar and hawthorn groves. "No. It's mine."

"Gods damn it," Caine said.

"Guys." Aurora stood, her gaze locked on the TV. The screen flashed with a red and blue graphic that said *Breaking News*. In the next second, the graphic was replaced with an image of Malphas, staring into the camera like a mug shot.

A newscaster's voice spoke over the picture. "We have a breaking news story. Two more of the Cambridge Coven members have been identified. The first is Malphas Mountfort. Authorities believe he and his brothers *are* planning another attack. Residents of Cambridge are asked to vacate the area."

Rosalind hugged herself. *Here we go.*

"We would like to emphasize," the newsreader continued. "The accused have magical capabilities, and they are very dangerous."

Rosalind touched Caine's arm. "He's safe in Lilinor—" She stopped her sentence as the image on the screen was replaced with a still photograph of Rosalind outside Abduxiel Mansion at dusk.

Dread tightened her chest. In the photo, she was holding a human skull and laughing, and the camera continued to zoom in on her grin. The image and the tightening close-up made her look like some kind of maniac.

Drew, on the other hand, had been cropped out of the picture.

The newscaster continued, "A fourth member has been identified as Rosalind Atherton, the twin sister of Miranda Atherton of Maremount. The government's demon-hunting task force has explained that these witches use human skulls to invoke demon plagues, and as part of a ritual of human sacrifice."

Her photo disappeared, replaced by a video feed of a woman standing in Harvard Square.

A news reporter thrust a microphone in her face. "What do you think the government should do to combat this growing evil?" the reporter asked.

The woman's eyes were red-rimmed, and the wind toyed with her wild blond hair. "We need to take extreme measures. If they're murdering innocent people, if we're all at risk... I'm all for human rights and all that, but if demons are going to slaughter everyone right here in the middle of a city, we need to do whatever it takes to stop them."

Rosalind's mouth went dry. *This is all working out perfectly for the Brotherhood.*

The reporter turned to the camera, speaking into the microphone. "Some citizens are asking for a return to public executions, even talking about using burning as a deterrent—"

Caine flicked his wrist, cutting off the sound.

"I was watching that," Rosalind said, her legs shaking.

"I think we got the idea," Caine said. "They want to burn us. It's not news." He arched an eyebrow. "They did get a wonderful picture of you cackling over a human skull, though. Is that something you do often?"

"Drew showed up here to buy that skull from me." She took a deep breath. "And someone just *happened* to be there, snapping a photo that perfectly incriminates me in the Brotherhood's scapegoating plan."

"I told you I should have killed him when I first met him," Caine said.

"Fine. You were right. Probably." Her chest tightened. "Drew was at the keres attack, and he worships the mountain goddess. And you know who else worships the mountain goddess?"

"I bet you're going to tell us," Aurora said.

"Whoever lives in that mountain fortress we saw in the scrying spell. The one with the harpies, where they've locked up Tammi." She tapped her finger against her lip. *Loyalty binds me, my ass*, she thought. "I'm going to pay Drew's Brattle Street home a little visit."

"You really think he'll be there?" Caine asked.

"I don't know, but while you're looking for stray hairs, it's worth a shot. And anyway, maybe I can find something of his to use as part of the tracking spell."

"When we left Drew's house," Caine said, "there were helicopters overhead, ready to bomb the whole block out of existence. If your little mage friend was truly working with the Brotherhood, then his house will still be standing."

Rosalind's mind whirled. *Working with the Brotherhood.* Would the ancient magic-fighting organization really use a mage to do their dirty work? Their whole purpose was to hunt demons and "witches" —their derogatory name for mages. Their reason for being was to rid the earth of Angelic, and to collect souls for the god of iron and blood.

On the other hand, they'd stop at nothing to get what they wanted. What if they'd use magic just long enough to achieve supreme power on earth? They'd be unstoppable.

Dread crawled up Rosalind's throat. For all she knew, Miranda was playing right into their hands. A lunatic witch, working for the witch-hunters.

Good thing I'm a trained witch-hunter, too.

"Sometimes the ends justify the means," Rosalind said.

"What are you on about?" Aurora said.

Rosalind gazed at the TV, which soundlessly replayed the image of her holding the human skull. "It's what Josiah used to say. The Brotherhood's sole purpose is to destroy magic, because that's what Blodrial wants. But perhaps they'd be willing to use magic to achieve their goals." She met Caine's gaze. "While you're looking for a way to track Miranda, Aurora and I are going to find out if Drew's house is still standing."

CHAPTER 17

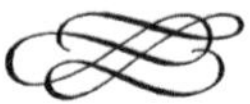

The heavy summer air on Brattle Street felt charged, as if a storm was coming, and a warm breeze rushed over Rosalind's skin. Aurora walked beside her, examining her long, silver nails.

Rosalind's whole body was tense. *Drew.* The bastard had been so eager to convince her that Caine was behind the keres slaughter—and for a second there, she'd nearly believed him. Who wouldn't be suspicious of a monster described in the history books as a *ravener?* A demon who'd murdered kings and queens?

And yet, she still had no clue why Drew would want to set her up, or why on earth Drew would hate Caine. What was his problem? She didn't even know Drew. Granted, there were one or two shadow demons who might want her dead, but a mage she'd never met? He had absolutely no reason to want her burned to death.

The huge yellow mansion came into view. Aurora pointed at it. "Is that Drew's place?"

"That's it," Rosalind said. "And there I was, certain that Drew had saved my life with his stupid potion. He was just setting me up all along."

Her stomach fluttered as they approached the white picket fence.

Aurora unlatched the gate, and Rosalind stalked up to the house. This time, no ward blocked their entrance, and Rosalind strode right up the steps to Drew's black door. She knocked twice and waited, biting her lip. *What am I gonna say to this guy?* If he was working with the Brotherhood, he would try to turn her in. She'd have to be on her guard, and rip the magic-dampening ring right off her finger if he tried anything.

"He's not home," Aurora said. "I don't smell anything human except you."

"Are you sure?" Rosalind asked.

"I smell something—not human. It stinks of caves and carrion."

Rosalind crinkled her nose. "I'm not sure I want to know what that is. But I want to get something from inside his house, so we can do a tracking spell." She tried the doorknob, and the door swung open into the darkened hall.

Rosalind stepped inside, her skin growing cold. She could still see traces of Drew's coppery magic, but there were other types of magic now, too: greens, blues, silvers, shimmering faintly.

She shivered. When she'd come here just a couple of days ago, it had seemed like such a warm sanctuary from the whirlwind of demonic forces. Now it seemed cold and empty.

She led Aurora down the hall into the living room, where Drew had tried to kill Caine. The room was dimly lit, with only pale moonlight glinting off the copper plates on the walls.

Rosalind glanced at Aurora. "Do you still smell the carrion thing?"

Aurora inhaled deeply and shook her head. "It's gone."

"That's… odd."

While Aurora began rifling through a liquor cabinet, Rosalind crossed to a desk in the corner. She cast a sharp look back at the vampire. "Do *not* drink anything here. The guy makes potions, and he's not trustworthy."

"Oh." Aurora returned a decanter to the table.

Rosalind turned to the desk, pulling it open to reveal an empty drawer. She pulled open another drawer, finding it similarly bare. "He doesn't have any stuff."

"Maybe he just moved in," Aurora said. "You said he was from Maremount."

Rosalind's eyed the copper plates on the wall. *Loyalty Binds Me.* With the eagle carvings, it looked like some sort of heraldic image—a family crest. She crossed to mantle, reaching up on her tiptoes to pull it off, and ran her fingers over the carved bird. "I'm going to try one of those tracking spells. If he's involved in all of this, like I think he is, we can use this to find him."

Aurora's brow crinkled. "You know a tracking spell?"

Rosalind shook her head. "No. but Cleo—my second soul—does." She touched her iron ring. "Any chance you know Angelic? From what I gather, the powerful spells need more than one person."

"I'm not great with Angelic, to be honest. I've mostly just listened to Caine."

"If I begin, can you repeat what I'm saying?"

"Probably."

"I'm going to take my ring off and hand it to you, so I can access her knowledge. If I seem like I'm getting out of control, I need you to tackle me to the ground and shove the ring back on my finger. Okay?"

"Am I allowed to bite you?"

"No."

"Outrageous."

"And if I seem like I'm losing focus, remind me about Tammi."

"Got it."

Rosalind tucked the copper plate under her arm, sucking in a deep breath. She pulled the ring from her finger, gasping at the sharp burst of vernal magic. Her nostrils filled with the smell of hawthorns and moss, and the magic brushed over her skin with a feeling of floral petals and dew-slicked leaves. She was dimly aware of someone pulling the ring from her hands. *Good riddance to that horrible thing.*

She scanned the room for that beautiful blue-eyed man, but he wasn't here—only a vampire with a sour expression.

"Rosalind," the vamp said.

Her lip curled. *Not that name again.* Her hands flew to the vamp's throat. *I will choke the life from this demon.*

But the creature grabbed her wrists, fangs lengthening. "Rosalind. You're making it very hard for me not to bite you. Remember Tammi. You're supposed to find Tammi."

Tammi... The girl with the nail polish and the outrageous cat obsession. The girl who'd brought Rosalind water when she drank too much at one of the frat parties, the girl whose hair smelled like vanilla shampoo. A dream of opening a cheese shop. Talking in her sleep about her grandmother's banana pudding. Homemade dresses. Parents who'd disowned her for not being a son.

Rosalind used these memories to claim space in her own brain, competing against the whorls of green magic. Gritting her teeth, she envisioned the aura growing smaller, tightening into a smaller and smaller ball, until it was only the size of a marble—a shining, green sphere in the center of her mind. She opened her eyes again, glancing at Aurora, who still gripped her wrists.

Aurora narrowed her eyes. "You better not try anything funny again."

"I'm okay, Aurora. It's me, Rosalind. I've got it under control."

Slowly, Aurora released her wrists, and Rosalind glanced at the ground—she'd dropped the copper plate. She stooped to pick it up, then traced her fingers over Drew's family's motto. "Now I just have to get Cleo to give me the spell."

She closed her eyes, unsure how this part was supposed to work. All the other times she'd accessed Cleo's knowledge, Caine had already begun the spell. She'd just joined in.

Maybe I should just ask her for help. She let herself envision the glowing green sphere. *Cleo, I need the tracking spell.*

A tendril of green lashed out. *Let me out,* Cleo's voice roared in her skull.

Rosalind's fingers tightened on the copper plate. *I need to stay in control. I'm fighting a battle, Cleo. And I need your help.*

The green glowed brighter. *Battle, little Hunter?* Cleo roared.

"I'm not a Hunter anymore," Rosalind said out loud. "I think I might be fighting them. They want to kill me."

The Witch Hunters are after you now? Curiosity tinged the voice in her mind. For the first time, Cleo didn't sound angry.

"Seems that way. They announced that I was behind the keres attack in Harvard Square. Which I wasn't," she added hastily.

The Brotherhood only pretends to care about guilt, Cleo whispered.

In the next moment, the spell's Angelic words appeared, emblazoned in Rosalind's mind like a shining beacon. Still gripping the plate, she began to chant them, one after another. She repeated them again and again, until Aurora joined in with her. Aurora's rosemary-scented aura mingled with Cleo's, whirling together outside of their bodies.

When Rosalind finished the spell, she opened her eyes. Projected on the wall was the shimmering image of a peninsula, roughly the shape of Boston. The perspective swooped lower, showing a glimpse of a stone city gate, part of its surface defaced. Something had been hanging from it once, but was gone now. Still, one word was still clear —*Maremount.*

The vision soared over the city gates, rushing over a wild wilderness of ash, pine, and fir trees that seemed to stretch on forever, crossing over along the side of a river, flying above the paths of hawks and crows, until at last it reached a verdant mountain. The picture tightened, closing in on a rocky mountain fortress, its towers guarded by a legion of harpies.

The image disappeared. "Drew is with Tammi and Miranda, just like I thought. They're in the wilderness outside the city of Maremount."

"Looked like south," Aurora said, holding out the ring. "Just follow the river there."

Cleo's aura roiled in her mind again, and Rosalind's body shook from the effort of trying to keep it in check. Grunting with effort, she slipped the ring back on to her finger, dropping onto the sofa. "Well, Caine's got that proof he wanted now. Maremount it is." Fatigue ate at her muscles, and she wanted to curl up on the cushions and sleep for days. It was a damn shame these spells took so much energy. "Just give me a second."

"That aura we created," Aurora said, dropping into a chair. "It was powerful. Let's hope it didn't attract anything."

"Right. Maybe we should get going." Still dizzy, Rosalind stood, but a scratching noise stopped her from walking out the door.

Aurora held up a hand, whispering. "Stop."

Something scraped against the floor in the hall, and Rosalind's chest clenched. A thick stench of carrion wafted through the air. Something tapped over the floor in the hall, coming closer, until the creature came into view.

She was nearly seven feet tall, with long, bronze hair that flowed over her naked back and bare breasts. Her eyes were the color of granite. Long, copper wings cascaded from her shoulders instead of arms, and she marched into the room on feathered legs that ended in sharp talons. Rosalind's mouth went dry. *A harpy.*

"Oh, fuck," Aurora said.

Rosalind took a step back. "What are you doing here?"

The creature's eyes twinkled. "Right now, I'm going to kill you."

"I don't think so," Aurora said, then whirled at a noise behind her. A second harpy perched in the tall, open window. Aurora hissed, fangs bared.

Shit.

Rosalind's heart squeezed in her chest. The first creature edged closer, a dusty bronze aura whirling from her body. Rosalind reached for one of the knives in her pants, but in the next second the harpy in the window lunged, slamming into her with the full force of a hurricane wind—right through a closed glass door.

Shards of glass lacerated Rosalind's skin, and before she had the chance to pull herself up off the ground she felt a sharp pair of talons rip into her flesh. Pain splintered her side, robbing her of rational thought as the harpy's claws bit into her shoulders. The harpy's copper wings beat the night air, and in the next moment, Rosalind was lifted off the ground. Rushing higher into the air, they soared over Cambridge's city streets, the streetlights waning to distant sparks of light.

The harpy began to speak, in her grating, otherworldly voice.

"Rosalind. It's your fault that Tammi has been captured. Do you know that? She never would have been dragged into a demonic war if it weren't for you and your stupid legacy as a Hunter."

A sharp agony pierced Rosalind's chest—something different to the pain of the talons. "How do you know that?" She managed between clenched teeth.

"You drove your sister mad. You drove your best friend into hell. And now, you'll get what's coming to you."

The harpy's words evoked something in her—a sharp pang of empty hunger, so intense she thought she'd never be able to fill the void in her gut. She just wanted it to end.

"You tortured Malphas," screeched the harpy. "He'd never showed you anything but kindness, and you drowned him. You let the Brotherhood brainwash you, because deep in your heart you're rotten to the core."

Emptiness gnawed at Rosalind, a painful, rapacious starvation. Pain and hunger mingled, until she couldn't remember her own name anymore. She was a ravening beast, desperate to fill the void.

"You destroyed Tammi's life," the harpy screeched.

Tammi. A flicker of familiarity sparked in her mind. She had a purpose. She was here to fight for Tammi, the girl who loved cats. *Fight, Rosalind.* The pain and hunger were dizzying, ripping her mind in two, but she needed to get control. Grimacing, she reached down and pulled off the iron ring. It fell from her fingers, moonlight sparking off it as it dropped to the earth.

Cleo's mossy aura burst into her mind, drowning out the pain. She couldn't remember now who she was, only that her body was in trouble. Deep, deep trouble.

"You've led Tammi to her death!" the harpy shrieked.

There was that name again. She squeezed her eyes shut. *I'm Rosalind.* She tried to claw out a corner of space in her own mind, forcing Cleo's magic into a smaller ball with all of her will.

Clenching her teeth, she crushed Cleo's magic into a tiny ball in her mind. *Cleo. I need strength.*

As the harpy's talons dug in deeper, Rosalind saw a spell burning in her mind; she called out the words, one by one. As she finished the final syllable, an immense power surged, numbing all her pain.

She drew her legs up until they were in reach, contorting her body, and pulled a knife from her pants, then reached back to slash for the harpy's leg. The demon shrieked, her voice rending the night air. As she unclenched her talons, Rosalind reached up to grab the creature's wing. The harpy shrieked again, her flight path careening wildly over the streets of Cambridge as Rosalind clung to her feathers.

Body surging with power, Rosalind hoisted herself up until she could get a grip on the harpy's feathered back. She hooked her leg over the demon's back, pulling her way up until she straddled the harpy's back.

The harpy screamed, "You caused all of this, Rosalind! No one has ever loved you until Tammi, and you drove your only friend into a prison. It's all your fault."

That painful, gnawing hunger welled in Rosalind's chest again, and Cleo's magic flared. Gritting her teeth, Rosalind forced the aura tighter again, then ripped another blade from her trousers, leaning down to press it against the harpy's neck. The demon growled, then fell silent.

Rosalind's breath came in ragged gasps, her body buzzing with this strange power that drowned out some of the hunger. "How do you know about Tammi?"

"I don't."

"You were talking to me about Tammi!" Rosalind screamed.

"I reflected the thoughts from your own mind."

Right. She'd forgotten that was what harpies did—they stole your own guilty thoughts and shouted them back at you. It didn't mean any of it was true. "What were you doing in Drew's house?"

"I'm one of his servants," she hissed. "And when he learns—"

Rosalind pressed the blade harder into the harpy's neck. "What do you do for Drew?"

"We protect his home."

She peered down at the city streets below. They were above Boston now, heading over a highway toward the airport. Cars rushed by below them. "Fly back to Brattle Street. I'm going to Abduxiel Mansion."

The harpy arced in the air, careening back toward Mount Auburn Cemetery.

Rosalind leaned down, gripping the harpy's hair. "Who else is Drew working with?"

"I don't know."

"I've got a lot of knives," she whispered into the harpy's ear, letting her voice drip with menace. "And I will cut your wings from your body, even if it kills us both. Who else is he working with?"

"Erish," she growled. "The succubus."

Anger ignited in her mind. *The first clue why Drew would want me dead—because Erish does.* "What about the Brotherhood?"

"Are you insane?" the harpy screeched. "Mages don't work with Hunters."

Maybe. Maybe not. The winds whipped Rosalind's hair. "Are Erish and Drew together in Maremount?"

The harpy merely growled, and Rosalind slid her knife a little deeper into the demon's skin.

"At Ekur Fortress," the harpy choked out.

As she flew, Rosalind caught a glimpse of Aurora, hurrying along Brattle street. She could feel the effects of the spell weakening, and fatigue pulsed through her muscles. Pain from the talon wounds bit at her gut and shoulders. She was running out of time.

"What are they doing with Tammi?"

A snarl erupted from the harpy. "You led her to her fate, Rosalind."

Hunger sank its claws into her gut, and she drew the knife along the harpy's shoulder blades, near her wing. "Answer my question."

The harpy tensed at the blade's touch, swooping lower over the cemetery in an erratic path.

Rosalind pressed hard against the shoulder blade. "Answer my question."

"She's going to die, Rosalind," screeched the harpy, veering for the earth. "And you'll stand over her starved corpse as her murderer. Your one accomplishment on this earth, ridding the world of another useless pedestrian."

A mixture of anger and a voracious hollowness flared in Rosalind. As the harpy screamed out her accusations, Rosalind slammed the back of her elbow into the harpy's head, gripping the demon's hair with the other. The harpy's head lolled, her wings drooping.

Cleo's aura began to whirl, spiraling vines of magic that furiously whipped around her brain, and she hit the harpy again as they careened for the cemetery grass.

Rosalind's eyes opened. Caine and Aurora stood above her, peering down under the moonlight sky. Caine knelt down, tracing his fingers over Rosalind's ravaged shoulder blade. "Gods below, Rosalind. Did you fly here on a harpy?"

"Looks like you battered the shit out of her," Aurora said.

"It was a fair fight." Pain tore apart Rosalind's gut. Each one of her muscles felt like it had been ripped from her body and run over with a truck. "Erish is working with Drew. They're at—"

"Quiet a minute," ordered Caine. Gently, he lifted up her shirt to look at her stomach. "Gods below, Rosalind."

"I can heal myself," she managed. "I'm not wearing the ring."

Caine's gaze met hers. "I'm glad you can heal yourself, but I'm doing this for you. Lie back."

Exhausted, she lay back on the grass. Caine chanted his soothing spell, his aura caressing her skin like a cool wind. The pain subsided from her body, leaving behind only a trace of that horrible, gnawing hunger, and an overwhelming sense of nausea.

Her eyes flicked to the harpy, who lay facedown on the grass. "Did I kill her?"

"Yes," Caine said.

Nausea climbed up her throat, and she rolled over onto all fours to heave up her breakfast.

"Are you going to get sick every time you kill someone?" Aurora said. "Can we get this girl some whiskey to wash away the sick?"

Rosalind wiped the back of her hand across her mouth, and Caine helped her stand, slipping his arm around her waist. Fatigue suffocated her body, and Cleo's aura began to whirl, jumbling her thoughts. She was too tired to control it.

"Iron," she said.

Caine glanced at Aurora. "Get us some iron from the cemetery gates."

The vamp nodded, rushing off in a bright blue blur. The beautiful man held her up, and she leaned into him, letting his soothing aura wash over her, drinking in his woodsy, earthy smell. She wanted him —if only her body weren't so sore.

They walked toward the mansion, its tall windows glowing gold.

In the next few moments, the vampire appeared, gripping a thin piece of iron. She handed it to the beautiful man, who held it up, whispering a blacksmithing spell. The iron glowed hot and red, then snaked into a thin ring shape, decorated with tiny sprouted leaves and branches. *Beautiful,* Cleo whispered. *But I don't want that iron near me. I'm in control now.*

She backed away from the beautiful man, but he grabbed her hand, his grasp firm. He slid the ring onto her finger.

Rosalind blinked, Cleo's aura now gone. She was completely exhausted, and still ravenous.

"Aurora told me you conducted a spell," Caine said. "You must be careful with the powerful spells. You're not ready for them yet, unless you've got me there."

"I think I did okay." She leaned in to him as they walked toward the mansion. "It was the harpy that nearly drove me mad."

"That's what harpies do." His arm slid around her waist. "What did you learn from the tracking spell?"

"They're in Maremount. South of the city—maybe ten or twelve miles."

Caine's grip on her waist tightened, and the shadows around them seemed to darken. "You're sure it's Maremount?"

"I saw the name on the city gates. The fortress is far outside it, beyond a wilderness of woods. The harpy called it Ekur Fortress."

"The fortress of the mountain goddess…" murmured Caine. "What in the seven hells would a succubus be doing in Borgerith's lair? Shadow demons are ancient enemies of the mountain goddess."

"No clue," Rosalind said. "But whatever her plans are, we're about to disrupt them, big time."

They stepped up to the mansion door, and Caine pulled it open. Inside, candles flickered in the chandeliers, and amber light danced over the cavernous stone hall.

"Go rest." Caine slid his hand from her waist. "You'll need to recover before we can go to Maremount."

First, Rosalind wanted a sip of that whiskey, then a little nap was in order if she was going to travel between worlds. She'd need some strength to battle Erish and Drew.

As she crossed to the living room, she gazed at the iron ring Caine had made for her. Oddly—for Caine—it wasn't purely utilitarian. A flourish of leaves was engraved on the exterior.

Aurora was already filling a glass with whiskey, and Rosalind sank onto the sofa, her muscles burning. The news was still flashing the pictures of Rosalind with the skull.

Aurora crossed to her, thrusting a glass of whiskey into her hand.

"Cheers," Rosalind said, lifting her glass. She took a sip, letting the rich, peaty taste roll over her tongue. "So now all we have to do is break into another dimension, travel through the wilderness to a mountain fortress, and defeat a legion of harpies, a succubus, and probably some other stuff."

"One thing at a time." Aurora plopped into an armchair. "That bloody spell ripped the life out of me. Or the afterlife. Whatever."

Rosalind's eyes drifted closed for a moment. She was going to travel to Maremount—back to where it had all begun. The city where the Ravener had once slaughtered a king and queen, where her family had given her an extra soul. Where her ancestors had lived and died.

Even with these thoughts churning in her mind, sleep beckoned to her. Her thoughts drifted to a deep and vast night sky, the stars blazing like gems—cold and beautiful, like Caine. She took a deep breath, her nostrils filling with the scent of seaweed and salty air.

Sea grasses tickled her bare feet, and ash trees lined a shoreline. Water lapped against rocks. She turned, her gaze landing on a stake, and horror slammed into her. *I know what's coming next.*

The sky darkened, black as a cauldron, and the clouds opened, unleashing the rain. Caine emerged from a blur of silver and shadow, gripping the woman. His angry aura lashed the air around him. Growling, he threw her against the stake. She looked so much like Rosalind.

Her deep brown eyes snapped wide open. The air was positively frigid as Caine slammed a nail through the center of her chest.

"Rosalind!"

Someone slapped her in the face, and she opened her eyes. Aurora stood over her. "You were having some sort of nightmare. And you spilled whiskey all over yourself."

"Just a bad dream," Rosalind said, looking down at her drenched clothes.

"Of what?"

Her gaze met Aurora's. "I think Caine is going to kill Miranda someday. I've dreamt of him nailing her to a stake."

The vampire's face relaxed. "Oh. I thought it was something bad."

"That *is* bad. Either that or he's going to kill me. We look alike."

Aurora sniffed. "He might nail you but I don't know about kill you."

"It feels like watching my own death," she said. "Like I'm in two places at once, and one of me is dead."

"You can get used to the idea of being dead," Aurora said.

Caine's electric silver aura entered the room before he did. As he crossed the threshold, he stared at Rosalind. "What are you two talking about?"

Rosalind straightened. "We're talking about how to get to Maremount."

"You and I will create a portal together. It will use up more of your energy, so we can't go until you've slept again."

"How does it work?" Rosalind asked. "Will we end up in another fountain?"

"Yes," Caine said. "I know of one in the center of the city. We'll arrive in Lilinor fountain, then travel into the wilderness. We need to limit our use of magic in the city."

Rosalind frowned. "Why?"

He sat beside her on the sofa. "There was a civil war in Maremount a few years ago—a rebellion. The monarchy was overthrown, and some of the poor took over. I don't know what this new government is like, but I can tell you this: the rulers of Maremount have always kept a tight rein on the use of magic. Any unsanctioned spells can be detected, and the outlaws hunted down by bone wardens that will tear your flesh from your bones."

Rosalind had never heard this before. "And my parents were loyal to the monarchy?" she asked. "Before the monarchy was overthrown?"

"They pretended they were, of course," he said. "It's the family motto: *Loyalty Binds Me.* Emblazoned on my jailer's lapels."

Loyalty Binds Me. Rosalind's heart stopped. "Do you know if I had other relatives? Besides my parents and Miranda?"

"I don't know. I was chained to a stone wall in your cellar. They didn't introduce me to the whole family."

She took a deep breath. "The badge the jailers wore—did it have an eagle on it?"

He quirked an eyebrow. "Yes. Why?"

Holy hells. She couldn't breathe. "Because that's Drew's family crest. It was hanging on his wall. It's how I tracked him—his heraldic emblem."

"Gods below," murmured Caine.

"Someone in your family kidnapped your sister and your best friend?" Aurora said. She stretched her arms over her head, crossing to the doorway. "Your family's well screwed up."

Caine knew more about her family's history than he was letting on, and it was beginning to piss Rosalind off. "You said my parents pretended to be loyal to the crown. What happened to them during the civil war?"

His eyes darkened with shadows, and the angles of his face seemed to sharpen. "They died."

The words hit her like a punch to her chest. "Why didn't you tell me this before?"

The ghost of black wings rose up behind him, and the lights flickered in the room. The sight of him screamed menace.

"Are you going to lecture me again, about how friends tell each other things?" he snarled. "We're not friends, Rosalind. We're on a mission to retrieve your sister. And the purpose of that mission is to strengthen the army I've been leading for three centuries. I'm going to destroy the Hunters who want to slaughter every demon and mage on the planet. That—and that alone—is my goal."

Anger burned in her veins and she rose, standing just inches from him. He towered over her, but she wasn't going to let this incubus scare her. "How did they die?" she demanded.

He stared down at her, their bodies nearly touching, and something electric crackled between them. For just a second, his features softened—then something caught his attention.

His head whipped around to stare at the TV. Rosalind followed his gaze.

Malphas's beautiful face filled the screen. He looked so much like Caine—beautiful, but with softer features. A hint of fear played around his gray eyes, nothing like Caine's cool, calculating stare.

As the camera angle zoomed out, Rosalind saw a phalanx of Hunters leading him up a wooden scaffold. It looked like Cambridge Common. Horror gripped her heart. "He's been arrested."

She stepped closer to the TV, pushing the buttons until the volume rose.

"And the Brotherhood have captured one of the primary coven members, a demon known as Malphas Mountfort. Authorities believe he comes from a demonic realm called Maremount, home to monsters known as Rawhed and the Ravener."

Malphas stood before a jeering crowd, camera lights flashing in his face. Iron chains hung round his neck. When the Brotherhood had captured Caine and Rosalind, they hadn't known the right type of magic to bind an incubus. The chains needed to be charmed—which, of course, the Brotherhood didn't know how to do.

But if they *were* working with Erish and Drew, they'd have all the information they needed.

Malphas looked exhausted, his face the color of bone. Dark circles hung beneath his eyes, and the sight of him cut Rosalind to the bone. Maybe it was her guilt for having hurt him, but she had the strongest urge to soothe the pain out of him.

She could feel the room fill with Caine's furious magic; it crackled through the air around her. He flicked his hand, cutting off the news story in a burst of shattered glass and sparks. Rosalind looked at him, at the black wings that grew from his back and his sharpened tendrils of magic. Her blood went cold.

Caine threw back his head, and his roar rattled the stones and glass around them.

CHAPTER 19

Cloaked by invisibility, Rosalind, Caine, and Aurora slunk along the tiny alley known as Appian Way, heading for Cambridge Common. Even from here, she could hear the crowd chanting.

"Whenever I get to a new city," Aurora said, "the first thing I want to know is where they executed people. London has Hyde Park, Tyburn, Spitalfields, Bow Church...a few others. Boston had the elm tree. And in Cambridge, they killed people on the Common. Did you know that they burned a woman here? A slave. Phillis, her name was."

"Can we talk about this later?" Rosalind whispered. She couldn't see Caine, but his vicious aura sliced the air around him. It looked like he was about to unleash his shadow magic over the entire city, leveling Cambridge in a storm of cold rage until no one but the immortals survived. *In fact, he might do just that.*

She hugged herself, her body still wracked by fatigue. With everything happening so quickly, she hadn't found time to recharge after the tracking spell.

"I'm just saying," Aurora said. "The horror and mob rage have been here all along, under the surface. The Brotherhood are just ripping off the mask."

Up ahead, an angry crowd bellowed. As they drew closer, Rosalind could hear what they were chanting: "Burn the witch! Burn the witch! Burn the witch!"

Rosalind's chest clenched. *Fucking hell.*

"I want us to be careful." Caine's voice, cold and controlled, belied the rage she could see whipping the air around him. "We're going to have to move fast—too fast for the Hunters to know what's happening. They'll have weapons trained on the platform, full of Hunter dust. They can easily destroy our magic the second they sense our presence."

"So what's the plan?" Aurora asked.

"The three of us slip up the scaffold, fast as the wind," Caine said. "Rosalind will need to take off the iron ring, and we'll invoke a spell for speed. We disable the Hunter guards. Before they even fall to the floor, we grab Malphas. Then we teleport out again."

"To where?" Rosalind asked.

"Phobetor Field," Caine replied.

Rosalind felt Caine's electrifying touch on her arm, and he pulled her in closer. "Make sure you keep control of Cleo. You can't let your emotions take over, and you definitely can't let *Cleo's* emotions take over. This has to be extremely fast and precise."

From Caine's reaction to Malphas's capture, Rosalind was starting to get the impression that she wasn't the only emotional one. She wanted to ask him if his whole *loyalty is a weakness* theory only applied to *other* people, because his obvious attachment to Malphas flew in the face of that theory. His brother had nothing to do with creating daywalkers, and yet here they were, saving him.

Still, she kept her mouth shut. If she provoked Caine right now, he was going to lose it completely.

"Let's go," he said.

The alley's mouth opened up to Garden Street, which lined the Common. The wide street was blocked off on either end by orange barriers, and no cars rolled through today.

On the grass, the crowd seethed like a storm cloud, bellowing their fury at Malphas. White lights blazed on his skin. With his hands bound behind his back, Malphas simply stared back, unmoving. His eerie, demonic stillness probably didn't endear him to anyone in the crowd.

Still, Rosalind's heart tightened at the sight of him. His gray shirt was torn and bloodied, and a trail of blood dripped from his lips. Deep gashes lined his pale, muscled arms. *He is not in good shape.*

Behind Malphas loomed a giant image of Randolph Loring's face. It seemed to glare down at Malphas in judgment. Meanwhile, the actual Randolph Loring stood at the front of the stage. He nodded solemnly as the crowd chanted "Burn the witch!"

As Rosalind crossed the empty street, Caine slipped his hand into hers, his breezy aura rippling over her skin. "Stay with me," he said.

They quickened their pace, approaching the crowd. From the platform, Randolph held out his arms to either side, and jumped. The crowd fell silent and parted as he walked into the mob like some kind of ginger-haired messiah, holding his palms open to the sky. A lapel microphone projected his voice. "The demonic attacks on our cities have threatened our lives, our sense of safety...our American way of life. Anyone who has seen a shadow demon or a witch tear apart an innocent human is asking, begging their leaders to end the horror."

The crowd roared, and Rosalind's mouth went dry. Cambridge Common was a tinderbox of fear and rage. They were ready to rip Malphas to pieces. With Caine and Aurora by her side, she stepped onto the grassy Common, heading for the platform through the crowd.

Randolph's voice boomed. "I alone have been granted the power to end the horror! We simply cannot stand by and let the demons take over our world because some people are too scared to take action, because we let elitists and appeasers make the decisions. Some people think we should make nice with the very demons who want to murder us. And do you know what those people are? They are traitors to our human heritage. And what do we do with traitors?"

The crowd roared, and Rosalind heard renewed chants for burning.

As they pushed closer, Rosalind surveyed the platform. Sweaty-

Hands Dave sat on the stage, his foot bandaged. On his chest, he wore an iron badge shaped like a chalice—a medal of honor for sustaining an injury during battle.

"Our country is in chaos!" Randolph shouted. "And despite what people say, The Brotherhood is not driven by hate! We are driven by love. Love for humanity. Love for order. Love for a deep, unwavering loyalty to the human race!"

The crowd roared, "Burn the witch!"

Rosalind's throat tightened. *So much for not being driven by hate...*

Besides Sweaty-Hands, twelve Hunters stood on the stage, forming a horse-shoe shape behind Malphas. Rosalind scanned them—all men, of course. The prestigious gigs like this one always went to the guys. She glanced up at the enormous image of Randolph, spying the tiny pistols trained on the platform just above his picture. She'd seen those before—they didn't contain bullets, but Hunter dust, designed to burn magic.

Thud. A glass beer bottle slammed into Malphas's head. Caine tightened his grip on Rosalind's hand and leaned in close. "I'll take the guards furthest from us, Aurora can take the ones in the center, and you take those closest. Tell Cleo not to kill any more than she needs to. That's four guards for each of us. We cut down the guards, grab Malphas, and we teleport together."

"What about Randolph?" she asked. She really wanted to hurt him.

"We're not here to kill Randolph," Caine said. "We have to get out of here fast, and we're going to need all the energy we have to teleport. We're here for one reason only, and that's to bring Malphas home. You or I will kill Randolph one day, but not today."

"I'll do my best to keep Cleo in check," Rosalind said. It wasn't going to be easy, though. Caine had said that the risk of losing her mind was higher if her body was tired, and she felt halfway in the grave right now.

"Give me the ring," he said.

"After I take off the ring," she said. "I need you to give me a moment to get control over Cleo. If I don't rein in her aura, it will be disaster."

"Of course," he said.

Taking a deep breath, she slid the ring off her finger, tucking it into her bra.

Cleo's green aura snapped into her skull, like a thousand ferns unfurling, and the scent of hawthorns and moss filled the air. She buzzed with delicious, ancient power, her eyes narrowing at the sight of the Hunters around her. *I will rip their throats out. I will call up the flames of Etna and slowly roast their bloated bodies. I will—*

"Rosalind." Someone squeezed her arm, hard, and a soothing aura tempered her rage. "Focus. We're here for Malphas."

Malphas. The word rang in her skull like a death knell. There was something she did to him, something that made her chest hurt... *Malphas.* She closed her eyes, forcing the magic into tighter and tighter coils, shrinking it down to a tiny, glittering gem of pure green.

I'm Rosalind. I'm here for one reason only. She opened her eyes again, gazing at Malphas on the scaffold, at his pale, chiseled cheeks. A rock thudded against his chest, then another. Fury simmered in Rosalind's chest, and her nails dug into Caine's arm. She leaned into his strong body, whispering. "I'm ready."

"Say the spell with me," he said. He began to chant, calling upon Nyxobas for the speed and fury of a celestial wind, asking the god of night to cloak him in shadows. His aura lashed out around him, and Rosalind joined in the spell. Their magic twined together, tendrils of silver and green rising into the air.

She could feel the spell overtaking her as Nyxobas's magic washed through her bones. Inky shadows slipped over her muscles—a gift from the god of night. Buzzing with energy, her muscles filled with a chilling surety, a dark power that smelled of earth and bone.

I am shadow and darkness, death incarnate. She grabbed two knives from their sheaths, one in each hand. *I am the great leveler, and I reap vengeance.*

"Now," she said.

With Caine and Aurora by her side, she leapt onto the scaffold, furious as a storm wind. In a fraction of a second, she sank her blade into a Hunter's back. *One.*

Pivoting, she slashed at another guard just as his fingers twitched for his gun, and her blade slid between his ribs. *Two.*

Shadow magic surged, and the Hunters didn't have a chance. She whirled again, cutting into a dark-haired Hunter, her blade finding its mark in his kidney. *Three.*

The night wind whipped through her hair, rushed over her skin as she pivoted. She plunged the blade into the final guard's abdomen. *Four.*

Around her, the guards began to stagger, and she rushed to Malphas, ready to teleport. She touched his shoulder, surging with protectiveness. *I must keep him safe.*

Cold, frozen rage slid through her veins as her gaze landed on Randolph Loring, and Cleo's aura roiled. Rosalind was dimly aware of Caine chanting the teleportation spell, but her attention was on the Brotherhood's leader.

Cleo wanted him dead.

Burn his flesh... Her mouth began to form the words for an inferno spell, but in the next second, she was standing in a forest. Moonlight streaming between the branches.

Gasping, her gaze landed on the beautiful, gray-eyed man—the one with fury in his blood.

She hadn't been finished with her work—there were Hunters to burn. "I was about to char the Hunters' flesh," she growled.

"Your ring." His eyes darted to her bra. "Do I have to take it out for you?"

Rosalind's mind began to clear a little, and she reached into her shirt, pulling out the ring. She slid it onto her finger.

Cleo's aura snapped out of her body, replaced by a grinding fatigue, searing her muscles. She faltered.

"You didn't chant with me," Caine said. "We're lucky we made it here at all."

"Cleo wanted Hunter blood," Rosalind said, looking around.

She was standing in the forest near Phobetor field, surrounded by ferns and oaks. She eyed Caine, whose athletic body was visible now.

Filtering through the trees, chinks of moonlight danced on his perfect skin and sparked white in his arctic eyes.

Aurora stood by his side, rolling her shoulders, her blue dress splattered with blood. "Nyxobas's spell has left me, but I still feel like death."

Rosalind glanced down at her own body, catching a glimpse of the streaks of blood glistening on her black clothes, and shuddered. She'd cut down four Hunters back there in less than a second.

With a jolt, she realized that Malphas was with them. *I have to face him.*

Slowly, she turned, and her gaze landed on Caine's brother. His arms were bound behind his back. Caine stepped behind him and tore the iron chains from his arms.

Malphas, meanwhile, stared right at her; Rosalind's chest ached.

The younger incubus was so much like Caine: the same straight nose, black eyebrows, and sharp cheekbones; same wintry eyes framed by black lashes; same beautiful, full mouth. But Malphas's expression was softer, and his skin was the color of porcelain instead of pale gold. He had large, poet's eyes, without Caine's calculating glint.

She swallowed hard. She hadn't thought about what she was going to say to him. *What do you say to a man you tortured? Sorry for the drowning?*

"Sorry about the..." she stammered. "Sorry about the drowning." *Shit.* She cleared her throat. "I'm sorry about everything."

Free from the chains, Malphas shook out his arms, rubbing his wrists. "You didn't remember me," he said. It seemed half a question, and half an accusation.

"I don't remember much from Maremount—mostly glimpses of Miranda." She reached out and touched his hand lightly, and he jerked it away. "But I do remember you. I remembered someone giving me flowers. I didn't know it was you, until after..." She bit her lip. "Until after the..."

"Until after she tortured you," Aurora cut in. "Gods below, you stammer a lot."

Wordlessly, Malphas turned, walking through the woods.

Aurora sighed, following after him. "That was awkward."

As she trudged through the woods, Rosalind's whole body was tense. *Switching sides in a war isn't exactly easy.*

Caine whispered a spell and the forest thinned before her eyes, replaced by the field of wildflowers and the stone building that towered over the pond.

She stepped into tall grasses, the air fragrant with the scent of wildflowers, and her thoughts whirled back to the scaffold. She was gaining in her ability to control Cleo's magic, but the aura had started to churn out of control when Cleo had laid eyes on Randolph Loring. Whatever her history was, the woman absolutely hated Hunters.

Maybe she'd prove to be a useful ally after all.

CHAPTER 20

*I*n Caine's bedroom, Rosalind sank into an armchair, her muscles screaming. Candles cast long shadows over the walls, shadows that twitched and danced like unquiet spirits.

Rosalind reached inside her shirt, running her fingers over the small divots in her flesh where the harpy had sunk her talons. *Malphas isn't the only one in rough shape.*

Still, the incubus wasn't meeting her gaze. Her chest ached; she wanted to help him, but to him she was basically a monster.

Caine nodded at his bed. "Sit down, Brother."

Grimacing, Malphas sat the edge of the bed.

Caine crossed his arms. "How did you end up with the Brotherhood a second time?"

"Erish poisoned me before she left Lilinor," Malphas said. "A legion of keres transported me, unconscious, to the Chambers."

Caine's gaze flicked to Rosalind. "So the Brotherhood *are* in league with the demons."

The concept burned into Rosalind's mind. For nearly a hundred thousand years, Hunters had been serving Blodrial, their sole purpose to rid the world of the Angelic language. Their whole reason for being was to destroy the demons that served other gods.

And now—for the first time—Randolph was changing the rules. With magic, the Brotherhood would be nearly invincible.

Their motivations were clear. Malphas, Rosalind, Tammi, Miranda, Caine—they were all scapegoats. They were the monsters— the raveners—who would haunt people's nightmares, the specters on whose bones the Brotherhood would build their empire.

But what the hell was Erish getting out of this? "I don't understand," Rosalind said. "Wouldn't a succubus hate Hunters?"

"She does," Malphas said, his pale eyes boring a hole into her. "With good reason."

"But she recognizes power when she sees it," Caine added. "And the more the demons attack, the greater the Brotherhood's power grows. Demons win. The Brotherhood wins. The only losers in the scenario are ordinary humans."

Rosalind shook her head, trying to puzzle it out. "The Brotherhood are creating a new empire, a new reality. They hate magic, but they can always change the definitions of things to suit their purposes —just like they redefined what it means to be human. You're not human if you consort with demons. And it's probably not magic, anymore. It's an *enhanced warfare tactic*, or something like that." She crossed her arms. "Angelic isn't the only language that can create reality."

Caine's fingers curled into fists. "This is going to make them much more formidable to target."

Malphas winced, rubbing his shoulder. "I'm going to need to heal." His gaze flicked to Rosalind—still angry, but there was something else there, too. Hunger?

"What did they do to you?" Caine asked. "Take off your shirt."

Grimacing, Malphas complied, pulling off his torn gray shirt. Rosalind gasped at the sight of his skin. Unlike Caine, no tattoos covered his muscled chest, but his perfect porcelain skin was marred by ragged scars and a few open wounds. Dark shards riddled his body, and it looked like fragments of iron.

Caine growled, his aura flaring around him. He shot a glance to Aurora. "I need you to go outside and find some yarrow. Now."

Aurora stood, rushing from the room.

Caine turned to Rosalind, watching her carefully as if considering something—probably something to do with the fact that she'd once put Malphas in a similar state.

Rosalind took a deep breath, her fingers curling. "Let me help."

Caine's face darkened. "Help how, exactly? I don't think you should go anywhere near him." He glanced at his brother again; Malphas's face had paled to the color of milk and he lay back on the bed, his breathing labored. "I'm going to find someone to heal you. Just give me one minute."

Caine rushed from the room, slamming the door behind him, and Malphas clutched his chest, closing his eyes.

Rosalind rose, her legs shaking from fatigue. "Well for fuck's sake. We could take the iron out in the meantime." If she could help him, maybe it would be the first step toward redeeming herself.

Malphas's eyes snapped open, darkening to black. "Don't come anywhere near me." The anger in his voice tightened her gut.

Despite the anger on his face, she took a step closer. She was already growing used to the demon-death-stare from Caine. "I'm good with a blade. We had to learn how to remove bullets in the Brotherhood. I'll get the iron out." She desperately wanted to take his pain away, to make up for what she'd done as a Hunter.

His breath was labored. "You want to jam a knife into my flesh again."

"I'm going to help heal you."

His black eyes locked on her, and his silver aura beckoned her closer. His magic slid over her skin like silk, scented of lilies.

He was definitely looking at her like she was his next meal. She swallowed hard, glancing at Caine's alchemist table. "I'm going to fix this," she said. She rushed to the table, her gaze roaming over Caine's collection of tools. She pulled out a long, thin blade with a silver hilt.

Malphas's black eyes were on her as she crossed the room to him, the blade in her hand.

She took a deep breath as she approached. *I'm good with a blade, but I've never done this on a real person before.*

"Lie back," she said, in what she hoped was a soothing and authoritative tone. No one wanted a hysterical lunatic standing over them with a knife.

"Try to resist cutting any deeper than you need to."

"I'm not a sadist," she said quietly. She sat at the edge of the bed, leaning down to examine his injuries. "I didn't enjoy hurting you."

She scanned his chest. She'd start with the one by his shoulder. It looked the worst, the skin around it swollen and purple—possibly necrotic.

A shiver ran up her spine. She was pretty sure the bastards had rammed iron into an old wound—the one he'd had when she'd tortured him in the prisons. *Might as well get that one out of the way.*

She swallowed hard, and realized that she needed to come at it from above. "This isn't the right angle," she said. "It will be easier if I'm on top of you."

"Fine," Malphas said, closing his eyes.

Rosalind hooked a leg over him, straddling his waist. From here, she could lean down and cut the thing right out. She leaned closer, inhaling. Despite his prison sentence, he had a clean smell—like soap and sage.

Rosalind looked at him. "Maybe Cleo knows a spell to numb the pain. This is going to hurt. A lot."

"I'm a demigod," he shot back. "I don't do painkillers. I have my pride."

Okay, then. Rosalind gripped the knife's hilt. "Are you ready?" When he nodded, she added, "Like I said. This will hurt." Carefully, she slid the blade into his wound, to the very bottom of the shard, and circled around slightly until she could scoop it out.

Malphas closed his eyes, grimacing as she forced the iron upward until it protruded enough that she could grab it between her fingers. He grunted as she pulled it from his flesh, and she threw the gore-streaked piece onto the floor.

They each let out a long, slow breath. Malphas opened his eyes, his lips tight. "Can you get the next one over with?"

Rosalind scanned his athletic chest. Three more small chunks of iron were lodged in his body, the skin around them red and swollen. Carefully, she worked one iron shard after another out, tossing the blood-drenched fragments on the floor.

When she'd finished, she ran her eyes over his skin. "Is that it?" Rosalind asked.

"That's all the iron," Malphas said, a hint of color returning to his cheeks. She could already feel his aura strengthening, slipping over her skin like silk. Something about the way he was looking at her transfixed her, and his hands roamed up to her waist.

Her pulse raced. Of course. This was how incubi healed—but she hadn't bargained for this part of his healing when she pulled the iron out.

The door slammed open, and Rosalind's head turned. Caine stood in the doorway, his eyes flashing with pure ice. The room chilled, the long shadows deepening across the walls. It took only an instant for Caine to cross the room and grab her off Malphas. He pushed her against the wall, his fingers tight on her shoulders. "What do you think you're doing?" His voice was a low snarl.

Her heart pattered fast, and she stared into his wrathful face. Obviously, he didn't trust her around his brother, not after what she'd done. She'd seen him angry before—but not like this.

Except in my dream.

Fear slid over her skin at the completely inhuman look on Caine's face. "I was just healing him."

"Healing him? And what happened in the torture room—was that some kind of fucked up foreplay to you?"

She shoved him away, glaring at him. "I was just taking the iron out. Don't get your panties in a twist."

Malphas was sitting up now, completely ignoring his brother and looking at her like she was completely naked.

Rosalind cleared her throat, the tension in the room so thick she could hardly breathe. She was getting the impression that coming between two incubi was a very dangerous idea. She folded her arms, shooting a sharp look at Caine. "Did you find another human for him?"

Breathless, Aurora ran into the room, clutching a fistful of yarrow. "I got the herbs. What's happening? Is Rosalind going to heal Malphas?"

"No." Caine was doing that eerie thing again where he didn't move, and only his aura whipped around him. "Not Rosalind. She's still in a weakened state from her ill-advised battle with the harpy, and I'm going to need her power when we go into Maremount." He turned to Malphas. "There's another human woman for you downstairs."

Malphas rose, his eyes still on Rosalind as he crossed the room. "I know my brother has good taste."

Caine nodded at Aurora. "Take him to the Orion room downstairs. There's a bath for him there, and you can staunch the bleeding with the yarrow. Lola will heal him. She's very good."

Who the fuck is Lola? Rosalind crossed her arms. *And why does it matter?*

As Malphas and Aurora left the room, Rosalind went back to the armchair and dropped into it. She desperately wanted to rest her burning limbs, but her muscles had gone completely tense. Caine's fit about going near his brother stung quite a lot. "What was that all about? You know I'm not going to hurt him now."

Caine crossed to a table below his window and uncorked a bottle of wine. He poured two glasses. "I just didn't want you near him. That's all." He moved to her, handing her one of the glasses.

She took a sip, trying to blink away her tears. Caine's angry outburst, combined with her complete exhaustion, had her feeling overwhelmed. The battle with the harpy, followed by the use of all that powerful magic, had completely sapped her energy. She took another sip of wine, her muscles finally relaxing.

Under the pale, glowing light of the starry dome, her eyelids drifted closed, and her breathing began to slow. She didn't want to dream, but she couldn't fight it anymore. Sleep enveloped her.

Her mind spun with silver, gold, copper, and green auras, and when they disappeared, she was staring at a stunning vault of stars. Frothy waves lapped at the rocky shore. A warm sea breeze whispered over her skin, soothing her, and it smelled just like Miranda. She started to turn slightly, but something tugged in her middle, keeping her from turning all the way. *I don't want to see what's going to happen.*

Pale blue wildflowers, like the ones Malphas had given her, dappled the seagrasses. She glanced down at her toes, sunk deep into the sand.

But a cold feeling of dread began to crawl over her skin. *I know what's coming. This is where I die.* She braced herself, forcing her head to turn. That familiar wave of horror slammed into her. Four stakes stood by the shore, their wood old and rotted in the sea air, like decayed piers.

As sure as death, Caine appeared in a vortex of menacing silver and shadow, moving like a storm wind. He gripped the woman and slammed her against the stake. Her brown eyes—Rosalind's eyes—snapped open with horror.

Rosalind opened her mouth to scream.

Instantly, a cool, soothing presence rushed over her skin, caressing her body. Muscled arms wrapped her in a masculine embrace. She was dimly aware of a strong body carrying her, chasing away her nightmare. Her eyes slid open, bleary with sleep, and she stared at the smooth skin on Caine's neck.

Bending down, Caine gently laid her on the bed. She stretched her arms over her head, staring as Caine carefully unzipped her boots, pulling them off. She'd felt it like it was her own death, but this couldn't be the man who would kill her.

His gaze met hers, and the way he looked at her made her pulse speed up. He leaned in closer, his eyes lingering over her clothes, still soaked in Hunter blood.

He traced his fingertips over her shoulder blades, whispering a spell. His light touch sent shivers over her skin, and the Hunter's blood lifted off her body.

"I was having a nightmare," she said.

He leaned in closer, stroking her cheek. "I know. You can tell me about it when you wake up. Don't think about it now."

He smelled amazing—that beautiful, loamy scent. It was hard not to stare at his exquisite beauty: his pale eyes and full lips, his eyebrows dark against his skin. She felt electrified under his gaze. A lock of his dark hair hung in his eyes, and she pushed it away, listening to his sharp intake of breath.

He let his eyes run up and down her body like he was memorizing it, and she had that feeling again, that he could see right through her black clothes and her lacy blue underwear to her bare skin, taking in every curve.

She stared at his beautiful mouth. Reflexively, she licked her lips, and he caught the movement, his eyes flashing hungrily. She wanted his lips on hers.

There were a million reasons she should turn away from him—not the least of which was his angry outburst just minutes ago—but right now she didn't care. She just wanted to feel his bare skin against hers. She was burning up in her clothes, and she wanted to strip them off.

Caine slid his hand under her shirt, then his fingers roamed just below her waistband, sending a hot thrill through her belly. "I want to explore every inch of your body." When his thumb grazed the hollow of her hip, just along her hipbone, her back arched. Her breath quickened. He leaned in closer, his breath warming her neck. "But tonight isn't my night." Another slow, lazy stroke of her hip, lighting her on fire with his touch. "Tonight, I need you to sleep."

He pulled his hand away, and she nearly groaned with frustration.

Staring into his pale eyes, she took a deep, shuddering breath. Her whole body was damp with a light sweat. *Gods below.* She was burning up.

She bit her lip, trying to marshal some control over herself. "Whatever you say, Caine. But in the meantime, I'm not sleeping in leather. It's far too hot." She unzipped her pants, sliding them off her sweat-dampened legs. They dropped to the floor.

Caine's eyes flashed with pale light, his gaze slowly tracing up her bare legs, lingering on the thin blue lace of her underwear. She pulled off her top, and heard his breath catch. His carnal gaze devoured her, and she could see him warring with himself for control.

Rosalind leaned back, letting him get a full view of her body before she slid under his covers. "Are you going to sleep next to me again?"

His eyes fixed on her, he exhaled slowly. He rose, pulling off his shirt.

She swallowed hard, gazing at his muscled torso—the tattoos of constellations, the moon's cycle, and the pointed alchemical symbols that covered his skin. For the first time, she noticed a tattoo on the inside of his arm that stood out from all the others. Not a magical symbol—more like a thin, sharp blade with a design at the top. *I'll ask him about that later, when I can remember how to talk again.*

He pulled off his pants and, clad only in his black boxer briefs, crawled in bed next to her.

With him so close to her, electricity still rippled across her skin. *I am never going to sleep with him next to me.*

"Sleep," he said quietly. He reached out to touch her forehead, and his aura caressed her skin, soothing her muscles like a gentle wind.

She felt her eyes drift closed—but when she did, an image slammed into her mind like a brick: Caine, bestial and enraged, driving an iron nail right into her heart.

She gasped, her eyes flying open.

Caine propped himself up on his elbow, dark hair hanging into his eyes. "What the hell was that?"

Swallowing hard, she stared at him, clutching the covers by her shoulders. *Maybe it's time to come clean.* Her heart banged against her ribs. "I've been having the same nightmare. Repeatedly. About you."

His entire body went rigid, and his aura sliced the air around him. "Tell me."

"It's not something from the past. So I guess it's from the future."

His eyes flashed. "Tell me."

She looked down at her shaking hands and took a deep breath. "There are four stakes on a shoreline. It's night, and there are waves lapping the rocks. The stakes are old and rotted, like an ancient pier. Then you show up. You're with a woman, and she looks like me. Only older." She shook her head, her pulse racing. "I thought it was me."

Caine had gone completely still, and shadows seemed to draw up behind him, cloaking his body. Only his wintry eyes shone.

Rosalind bit her lip, suddenly unsure of herself. "But I figured maybe it's not me. Maybe it's Miranda."

Not a single muscle seemed to move on Caine's body. His eyes were locked on her. He wasn't pressing for details anymore, and she had a strange sense that he might know what was about to happen.

"You take the woman—me or Miranda—and thrust her up against the stake." The words came out in a rush. "She's scared. And then you shove a nail into her heart. You nail her to the stake, so she's stuck there, dying."

Caine's eyes darkened. A chill fell, frosting the room. Goosebumps rose over Rosalind's skin, and she suddenly felt completely cold in nothing but her underwear.

"Go to sleep, Rosalind," he said softly.

She frowned, disbelieving. *That's it?* "What do you think it means?"

"It means you need sleep if you want to fight whoever is tormenting you."

Now that she'd finally got this out in the open, he just wanted her to shut up about it? "I thought dreams meant something. Do you think you're going to kill Miranda? I feel like this deserves a theory, at least."

The gray returned to his eyes, and he lay down, folding his arms behind his head. "I'm going to kill you if you don't stop talking. When day breaks, we have to transport into another dimension and fight our way through the wilderness, probably plagued by bone wardens and all manner of lethal creatures, and then defeat an unknown enemy to rescue your sister. We're not going to stay up all night discussing dreams that probably don't mean anything."

"Right. If it didn't mean anything, why did you go all weird and shadowy?" Her whole body was tense. "This is feeling a lot like when Orcus pulled the book out of my hands and threw it in the fire because he didn't want me to know things."

"I really liked you better when you were just sitting there in your lacy blue underwear and looking at me lustily. With your mouth shut."

Anger flared, and she glared at him. *Dickhead.* She rolled over, her chest tight. *No way am I going to sleep now.*

She could feel Caine shifting in the bed. He wrapped an arm

around her. She had half a mind to elbow him away, but he folded her into the curve of his body so gently, his smooth skin pressing against hers. Her hair stuck to her damp cheek, and he brushed it off her face.

"Sleep, Rosalind," he whispered.

Despite herself, his soothing aura whispered over her skin, sending her into a deep sleep.

She dreamed of a starlit field of wildflowers, completely devoid of stakes.

CHAPTER 21

Rosalind woke, tangled in Caine's bedsheets. Sitting up, she rubbed her eyes and surveyed the room. The first rosy blush of dawn glowed through the dome, washing away the darkness —and with it, the strangeness of the night before.

Caine was nowhere to be found, but someone had left a silver tray on his dining room table.

Rosalind stood, letting the sheets fall, and crossed the floor. She pulled off the top of the tray to find a pot of herbal tea on the silver platter next to fresh bread, butter, and jam. Her stomach rumbled, and she sat in the chair, slathering a pat of butter over the bread. She ate her way through three chunks of bread, washing them down with the tea. Hunger and fatigue wouldn't slow her down today.

When her belly was full, she stood, crossing to Caine's silver-framed mirror. At least she looked strong and rested now, but she still had ragged hair.

I'm not going to turn up to fight my estranged family looking like I've clawed my way out of the grave.

She grabbed a towel, a fresh bra, and a pair of underwear from the bag of clothes—red this time, the color of war—then crossed to the bath. Leaning down, she turned on the faucet, then stripped off her underwear. She let them drop to the floor and stepped into the bath as it filled.

She leaned back, breathing in the steamy air. She had no idea what lay ahead for her in Maremount—only that she would have to confront her own family. Her parents were dead. But how many other Athertons would she find in Ekur Fortress?

She grabbed the lavender soap, lathering up her legs and under her arms. The shallow bath water filled with pale lilac bubbles. She scooped up a handful of water, splashing it over her skin to rinse off. All the aches and pains of yesterday had subsided. For the first time in a while, her body felt amazing.

Stretching her arms above her head, she rose, and the soapy water slid off her skin.

Stepping from the tub, she snatched the towel from the floor. She dried herself off, folded the towel over the tub's edge, then picked up the pair of bright red underwear and slipped into them. Just as she bent over for the bra, Caine pushed open the door and Lilu swooped into the room.

Instantly, Caine glanced away—an unexpected move from an incubus. She hooked the bra behind her back.

Caine's shoulders looked rigid, and he was already dressed for battle, a sword slung over his back. Under one arm, he held a small arsenal of weapons: a belt, a sword, and several sheathed blades. "Will you be half-naked around me all the time from now on?"

"Since when did you get shy?" She frowned, picking up her pants. "I'm just getting dressed."

"It's hot as Emerazel's inferno out there. Dress accordingly."

"Fine." Rosalind crossed to the red bag Kaila had brought days ago, which still lay on the floor.

"We're leaving soon. Malphas will be up here in five minutes."

"I'll be ready." She rifled through the bag and pulled out a thin black dress. Lifting it above her head, she slid into the silky fabric, pulling it down to her mid-thighs.

Once she'd covered herself, Caine looked at her again, his body relaxing. "Any idea how to use a sword?"

She pulled on her boots. "I've trained with wooden sticks. And I watched you fight."

"Hmm. There's a battle fury spell you can use if you need it." He slid a sword and scabbard across the table.

Her body began to buzz with nervous energy. Who, exactly, would she be fighting today? Her sister? Her own brother?

Her hands began to shake a little, and she strapped the scabbard over her back. Within the next few minutes, she'd slipped a weapon belt around her waist, then crammed it with blades.

Caine began pacing. "What's taking Malphas so long?"

Rosalind peered at herself in the mirror again. *Perhaps it's time for some war paint.* She crossed to Caine's alchemical table, surveying the small pots of colored powder—the gold dust and colored pastes. "Is any of this dangerous?"

"Not really, no. Metals and berries mostly." He frowned. "What are you planning to do with it?"

She rubbed her finger into a pot of berry-colored paste, then dabbed it onto her lips. "Getting ready for battle." She smudged a bit of pink on her cheeks, then dusted a gold powder for highlights. She stared at her reflection. *Perfect.*

When she turned, Caine was staring at her.

"How do I look?" she asked.

"Beautiful. As you did before you rubbed ox-blood paste on your lips."

She frowned. "I don't suppose you can fix my hair situation?"

"Are you joking?" he asked. "I rip people's hearts out of their chests for fun. I singlehandedly killed an entire legion of hellhounds in Prussia. I don't fix hair."

"Fine." She glanced down at the iron ring he'd made for her. "Let me get a little magical practice in with one simple spell." She pulled off the ring, letting Cleo's aura wash over her in a rush of mossy green magic. Gritting her teeth, she seized control of it, forcing the magic into a ball. When she'd pressed it down into a marble-sized sphere, she touched the ends of her hair.

"Cleo," she said out loud. "Give me a spell for my hair, please."

Why on earth would I do that? Cleo snarled in her skull.

"I'll give you something you want in return."

Take me back to Lilinor, Cleo whispered. *Keep that damned ring off your finger, and let me live again.*

Rosalind nodded. She could promise Lilinor. *Why not? I just need to get through this day first.*

She almost heard a faint peal of laughter, and in the next moment she was whispering the words to a spell about a goddess named *Sif.*

Silky locks slid over her shoulders. With a tug of rebellion from Cleo, she slid the ring back on her finger and opened her eyes. "See? I can do things on my own."

"Good," Caine said. "I don't give a fuck about the hair, but you're getting better control over Cleo."

"I had to promise something to her in return. She wants me to take her to Lilinor."

He frowned. "Lilinor? Why?"

"I have no idea. But I think she likes me better than she used to. At least, that's what I gather from the fact that she's no longer setting my skin on fire."

He arched an eyebrow. "You are quite good at interpreting subtle nuances, I see."

She ran her fingertips over her weapon belt. "Well, I'm ready to go. But maybe you should give me an idea of what to expect when we get to Maremount."

"We'll arrive at the Lilitu fountain in Lullaby Square. The sun is only just rising. Most people will still be wrapped up in their bedsheets, or steeping their breakfast tea. We'll go unnoticed."

"Do you know the area well, then?"

His face darkened, and he glanced at the door. Something about the question seemed to agitate him. "Where the hell is Malphas?"

"Stick with me for a second, Caine. So once we get to this fountain, then what? We teleport to the fortress?"

"No." Caine shook his head. "One, we can't use magic in the city.

And two, you can't teleport somewhere unless you've been there before. We'll need to get out of the city, and then fly as fast as we can to the fortress. Not literally fly, unfortunately, since you can't."

Shit. That was way more time than she wanted to take getting there. "It's got to be at least ten miles."

"Can you run ten miles?"

The door slammed open and Malphas strode in, scowling. He held a newspaper, which he threw down on Caine's dining room table.

Rosalind stepped closer to the table, glancing at it. On the front page, four stakes stood on Cambridge Common. The headline read: *Justice for Cambridge.*

"What is this?" *Four stakes.* Her mouth went dry. "Did you read it?"

"They're not going to wait to find us," Malphas said. "They deeply regret they must take these measures, but it's time to start protecting ordinary, human citizens from the demonic threat. They must bring back the old ways as a deterrent against witchcraft. That's the gist of it."

Caine snatched it from the table. "What, specifically do they have planned?"

"They're going to burn someone named Tammi," Malphas said. "I take it she's a friend of yours. They plan to kill her today, in about four hours. And this time they're assuring everyone that the area will be completely secure from mages and demons. Apparently, I'm next. They just have to find me first."

Caine's eyes flashed. "It's a bluff. They're trying to get Rosalind to panic. They're preying on her sense of loyalty to draw her in. They're setting a trap for us there."

"What if it's not a bluff?" Rosalind said.

Caine stared at her. "Why would they care about burning Tammi? *She's* an ordinary human. A pedestrian, the people they say they're protecting."

Rosalind began pacing. "You could be right. She's not their real target. I am. In the Brotherhood, there's no greater sin than betrayal." Her mind whirled with gruesome images. In the Sanguine Hell, the traitors of Blodrial supposedly faced the worst punishments. After traitors crossed the Bridge of Dread, Blodrial froze them in blood and pierced their flesh with thorns. *I have no idea if any of that is true, but I sure as shit hope not.* "But it could be that they just want to light her on fire for show. I realize now they don't really care who's guilty and who isn't. They want more power, and you get power from that intoxicating combination of terror and scapegoating. We're the scapegoats, of course. And the people want our blood."

"Seven hells," murmured Malphas.

Rosalind's heart hammered hard against her ribs. "How do we know Tammi is still in Maremount?"

"I've already performed a scrying spell," Malphas replied. "She doesn't seem to be in this world. But they could shift her back here at any moment. I don't know what sort of magic Drew possesses."

Caine's gaze met Rosalind's. "If Drew and Erish wanted to hand her over to the Brotherhood, where would the Hunters keep her?"

"In the Chambers, probably. Most of the building was damaged when we freed the prisoners, but not all of it. And it's near where they set up the stakes." She pivoted, pacing again. "But I don't know for sure."

"I'll stay near Cambridge," Malphas said. "I'll use a scrying tool to keep an eye on the stakes and the Chambers. If I see this little blond girl, I'll find a way to summon you both."

Rosalind studied Malphas. "Why are you helping me? I know you want Miranda back to make your daywalkers. But why would you help Tammi? She serves no tactical purpose to you."

Malphas crossed his arms. "Anything I can do to disrupt the Hunters' plans is well worth my time."

Caine put his hand on his brother's shoulder. "If anyone can free another person from chains, it's you."

It seemed an odd comment. There was obviously some deeper meaning there, but this wasn't the time to ask.

Rosalind took a step closer to Caine. "Let's go. We've got a lot of territory to cover."

Caine pulled her in close, and she slid her arms around his neck.

"Remember to hold your breath," he said. "And get ready to fight. We don't know what awaits us when we arrive in the Lilitu Fountain."

"As soon as the first demon comes for us, my hand will be on the sword's hilt." She pulled off her ring, letting Cleo's vernal aura fill her mind, feeling the dew-slicked leaves brush over her skin. Caine began chanting the portal spell, and their auras curled together, strengthening. Closing her eyes, she sucked in a long breath.

In the next moment, freezing water enveloped her skin. She freed herself from Caine's grasp, kicking her way up to the source of amber light streaming into the water. As her head breached the surface, she gasped for air. She kicked her way to the fountain's edge, draping her arms over the side, then slid the ring back on her finger.

Catching her breath, she stared up at the fountain. A giant cube of stone stood in its center. From the top of the cube, a verdant yew spread out above them. Sunlight streamed between its boughs, dappling the ground around them in dancing flecks of nectarine.

From the fountain's side, a beautiful stone head spewed clear water. Something about that carving unnerved her—the features were a little too real, the stone eyes full of silent dread.

Teeth chattering, she pulling herself out. She hauled herself over the side, jumping a few feet to the ground.

Caine followed, his black clothes drenched.

Rosalind surveyed the square, her mind tingling with a strange sense of familiarity. She inhaled, breathing in the salty, slightly fetid scent of nearby water. A spark of recognition lit in the back of her mind. *Maremount. My home.*

She surveyed the square. Steep-peaked, timber frame houses lined one side, the aged wood painted in shades of chestnut and marigold. Boards covered one set of windows—a shop with a sign reading *theurgeon* and a snake insignia. Apart from that, everything else looked in good shape.

Opposite the shops, a stone fortress towered over the square. It looked as if statues had once decorated the facade, though nothing was left except their bases. Caine stared at the fortress, seemingly transfixed. For a moment, his eyes darkened to a midnight black.

Something had happened here that he wanted to remember, but clearly it wasn't a happy memory. She'd seen the painting of the fortress hanging on his bedroom wall in Salem. Maybe it was something to do with that king and queen he'd killed.

Shivering, she hugged herself, casting one last glance back at the fountain again—at that disturbingly lifelike stone head.

Caine stood by her shoulder, and water dripped off him to the flagstones. He nodded at the fountain's head. "Does she look familiar?"

Rosalind frowned. She *did* look familiar—that straight nose, those beautifully full lips. "It looks like Erish."

"That's her sister, the last succubus killed in Maremount."

"And then they turned her into a fountain?" Rosalind shuddered. "I'm starting to get an idea of why Erish hates humans so much. I get a bad feeling just standing here."

"There's a reason you don't like it here. The tree is new. This is where they executed people—hanged them, cut their guts out, chopped off their heads." His gaze met hers. "And, unless we want to meet our own deaths, I suggest we move along." He turned, crossing the square.

She followed, hurrying to catch up with him. "Do they still execute people? You said they have new leaders now."

"I have no idea. But if we get separated or..." He frowned. "If something happens to me, find your way back here. I'm leaving the portal open."

"Should I say the spell again?"

"No. It's a portal, and anyone can fall into it. Let's hope no one from Maremount decides to bathe in the fountain anytime soon."

"Where does it go?"

"To the pond in Phobetor Field."

They crossed the square to a narrow alley; the name carved into the wall marked it as Loblolly Row.

The sun had only just risen, and the heat was already bringing out beads of sweat on her upper lip. Her hair stuck to the back of her neck, and her dress molded to her skin. As they passed between the stone walls, she turned to Caine. "Where was my family's home?"

"This city is laid out just like Boston was three hundred years ago. The Atherton mansion is in the Northwest, near Maremount Common—opposite the north end, and safely secure from the filthy Tatter villages."

"And you've never heard of this mountain fortress?"

"Never. But I spent as little time as possible in Maremount."

The alley opened up to a canal. Stone walkways lined the murky water, and on either side stood rickety homes that towered up to the skies at crooked angles.

As Rosalind and Caine strode down the walkway, people began shuffling out of their homes—women hanging laundry, a man packing up a wooden cart to bring into town. All of the women wore long dresses that reached their ankles, and a few cast a critical eye at Rosalind's bare legs.

Her mind whirred. *If we manage to rescue Tammi, what are we going to do with Drew?* She couldn't understand any of it—why was Drew coming after Rosalind, but protecting Miranda? It was almost like they'd started a civil war within the family, and no one had bothered to fill her in on the details. Maybe they could just lock Drew in this creepy city and forget about him.

She twisted the iron ring around her finger. *Whatever happens today, I'm going to use all the power I have at my fingertips. Assuming I can keep control of Cleo.*

Up ahead, the canal flowed under a tall stone gate that arched high over the water and the walkways—one of the entrances to the city. As they approached, she could see more clearly that the gate's surface was covered in carvings of fish and sea creatures. A broken stump of stone jutted from the top—no doubt another relic of Maremount's former glory.

They crossed under the arch, and the canal opened up into a bay. Outside the gate, the city's buildings ended abruptly. To the right, river birch and maple trees lined a rocky shore, and to the left, the bay narrowed again into a tree-lined river.

Morning light bathed Caine's skin in amber. "According to your vision, which way do we need to go?" he asked.

"Hang on." She closed her eyes, bringing up the memory of what she'd seen during the tracking spell—the vision rushing over the river and forest to the mountain fortress. If this city was oriented just like Boston, they now faced the southwest. "We need to cross to the other side of the canal. We follow along the river, heading south. About ten miles, maybe."

"We can get there in a couple of hours, as long as you don't walk like a normal, slothful human."

"I can run most of that." She frowned. "There's got to be a spell for flight."

"There is, especially for Druloch's followers. You can tear a sapling from the ground to fly with. But unless you've practiced, you're likely to break your pretty little neck." He turned and dove into the canal water.

She followed, plunging below the water's murky surface and kicking her way across. On the other side, Caine extended a hand and helped her out.

She stood, her soaked dress hugging her body, and wrung out her hair. *Good thing it's 80 degrees out.*

"Talk to Cleo," Caine said. "There's a spell for speed you can use. If I have to travel at your pace, I'll die from boredom on the way." He folded his arms. "As long as you think you can keep her under control when things get stressful. When we were in Cambridge, Cleo nearly went on a rampage."

"I'll do my best, but I haven't had training yet."

"I'll help you now. I'll be your anchor until you get her under control." He stepped closer, looking down at her. "Take off the ring."

"Okay." She pulled off the ring, shoving it in her bra. She gave in to the now-familiar feeling of Cleo's leafy magic flooding her mind.

Caine's fingertips brushed over her temples. "Compress her aura."

Closing her eyes, she tightened the whorls of green into smaller coils, just as she'd done before.

"Where do you see her aura?" Caine asked.

"It's in my head… in the center of my skull."

He began tracing his fingertips down the sides of her face. "I want you to bring the magic lower. Let it follow my fingers."

The sphere moved down into the base of her skull, following the path of his fingertips. It shifted down the front of her throat, her skin tingling all the way. He traced a single finger down her sternum, stopping just between her breasts. "Where is the magic now?"

"Where my heart is." She breathed deeply, trying not to focus on where his finger was.

"Good." He pulled his hand away. "Cleo will be easier to control when the magic isn't in your head."

In Rosalind's mind, Cleo screamed. *You trap me in your ribs, in a coffin of bone? You want to bury me under the earth, feed me to the worms?*

"I need to stay in control right now," Rosalind said out loud. "I'll let you out to play some other time."

When I come out to play, I'm going to find Ambrose, and then watch the world burn.

Rosalind tightened the magical coils down, tighter in her chest. *Ambrose?* What the hell did Cleo want with Ambrose? Whatever it was, she didn't have time to get into her second soul's drama now. She needed to get to Tammi—fast.

I need a spell for speed, Rosalind thought. *If we make it out of here alive, I'll take you to Ambrose or whatever other hot guy you fancy. As long as you help me.*

Rosalind wasn't going to let the world burn, but she could take the crazy mage to the vampire lord if that was what the spirit really wanted.

Ambrose, Cleo's aura breathed in her chest.

Rosalind's body buzzed with the mossy aura, and an image arose before her—the Angelic spell, engraved in light. Rosalind chanted the words, and a thrilling power invigorated her muscles. She opened her eyes, a smile curling her lips. "Let's go."

She launched into a sprint. Briny air rushed over her skin as she whipped past the river birch trees, crunching over deadfall and flying over rocks.

By Caine's side, she ran like a storm wind.

She ran—until a familiar sight slammed the wind from her lungs. She ground to a halt, and her heart hammered like a war drum.

Before the forest line, four stakes stood along the rocky shoreline, their wood old and rotted. Dread tightened its grip on her heart.

This is where it happens. This is where I die.

CHAPTER 22

She stared at the wooden posts, her legs trembling. Something sharp and desperate slammed at the walls of her mind, a ravenous image trying to free itself.

"What?" Caine asked. "Why have you stopped?"

She wanted to keep the thought locked away, but it hurled itself against its prison, demanding to be seen.

Rain sliding down her skin, Miranda's scream piercing the air. Miranda's scream...

"What?" Caine asked again.

Shaking, she pointed, and Caine turned his head to look at the stakes. His body went still.

My feet sank into the dirt. Miranda screamed. He made us watch...

The air around her chilled. When he looked back at her, his eyes were pure ice. His aura snapped around him.

A shudder ran up her spine. "Have you seen them before?"

"You've seen them before, too," he said, his voice distant, as though it were coming from a chasm.

Her world tilted. The memory in the back of her brain was screaming at her, coming for her blood. "Where did I see it—in my dream? Will you please tell me what the fuck is going on for once?"

The hair on her arms stood on end. She could feel Caine all around her, darkening the shadows and whispering over the back of her neck.

Far beyond the river, charcoal storm clouds rolled in, and distant thunder rumbled across the horizon. *Just like it did the other time.*

Her fists clenched, and she shook her head. *What other time?*

Caine's icy gaze bored into her. "I thought you wanted to save your friend. I thought we were here on a rescue mission. If it was important for you to know right now, I'd tell you."

The thing in her mind clawed and bit at the edges of her consciousness, stoking her anger. *Why do you have to be such an enigmatic bastard?*

Anger smoldered, and Cleo's aura fanned the flames. "We *are* on a rescue mission. But I want to know what the stakes mean. What did you mean I've already seen them?"

He's lying to you, Cleo whispered. *Never trust a beautiful shadow demon.*

Lightning cracked the sky, and the gathering clouds began to unleash a torrent of cold rain. *Just like it did the other time.*

Caine merely stared at her, unmoving.

Anger hammered at Rosalind's skull, and she lunged, grabbing him by his shirt collar, now wet with rain. "Tell me," she seethed.

He cupped her face—an oddly gentle gesture, given the circumstances. "Or what? You'll torture it out of me? Anything to get your hands on me." It was his usual cocky comment, but this time no humor sparked in his eyes.

She tightened her grasp on his shirt, and Cleo's aura flared, breaking free from its box.

Hurt the shadow demon. You know what he did. It's the same—he's the same.

"Rosalind," Caine whispered. "We're here to stop Tammi burning to death. We don't have time for this."

She closed her eyes, coiling Cleo's aura tighter under her sternum. The bastard had a point—the clock was ticking on Tammi's life. If she didn't get to her friend in time, Tammi would end up an ashy pile at the bottom of a Brotherhood stake.

Through clenched teeth, she said, "Cleo wants me to hurt you. I'd like to hurt you. I'd like you to know I'm exercising a significant amount of restraint. We'll keep going. I'll torture the answers out of you later if I need to."

She unclenched her fingers from his collar and turned, breaking into a sprint again. Her feet moved swiftly over the riverbank, spattering mud on her thighs. There was something wild in her now that wanted to get out—but if she gave in, she'd never find Tammi. The thing would eat her alive.

As the rain fell, her boots pounded the muddy shoreline. *He doesn't kill Miranda. Miranda was screaming on the shore.*

Her mind spun. But as they ran, the sound of beating wings turned her head, and she lifted her eyes to the sky. Ice flooded her veins, and she ground to a halt. Streams of brightly colored auras roiled in the skies, just below the storm clouds.

Caine stopped running, his fists clenching. "What do you see?"

"Some sort of demons are coming right for us. I can't tell what kind yet, but I can see the auras." Her heart sped up, smashing against her ribs. "How the hell did they know we were here?"

"What do the auras look like?"

"All different kinds, like the keres in Harvard Square."

Caine sucked in a sharp breath. "I see them now. I see their black wings. Definitely keres. But if they're the same kind who attacked in Cambridge, my magic hardly did a thing against them."

"It's their auras. There are so many types of magic to protect them. I've never seen anything like it."

Shadows gathered in Caine's eyes, but his voice was low and controlled. "Ask Cleo for a war spell. Now."

She reached for her sword, pulling it from its sheath, and closed her eyes. *Cleo. Help me fight the Brotherhood's monsters. I need a spell for war. And like I said—if we get out of here alive, I'll take you to Ambrose. Whatever you want.*

Green light flashed from her chest, then a spell dedicated to Nyxobas rose in her mind. She chanted the words out loud, and the air filled with the scent of hawthorns and moss.

As she chanted the spell, something ancient and angry simmered in the back of her brain. A preternatural surety ignited her limbs. *The battle is coming. I'm ready.* Smoldering rage lit her up. *Kill.*

She glanced at the sky again, her cheeks burning with her pumping blood, limbs shaking with anticipation. The air was dense with the keres' beating wings—whirling with copper, black, silver, green, and blue auras.

Battle fury ignited her nerve endings, and she felt a growl rise in her throat. She wanted to see the spray of blood, hear the crunch of crushed skulls.

Her teeth chattered.

The keres drew closer in a writhing cloud—and she wanted to sink her sword into all of them. Their black wings pounded the cool air, and the breeze whipped Rosalind's hair around her head. Her senses were piqued, and as they drew closer, she took in every feather, every bead of sweat on the creatures. They had swords of their own—iron swords—but she didn't feel fear at the sight.

A growl tore from her throat. *What the hell kind of demon carries iron? What are these things?*

Caine's gaze slid to hers. "I can feel your bloodlust from here—and I like it, but I want you to understand that they're harder to kill than you'd think."

Fury simmered in her chest. "So let's start killing them now."

A smile flickered across his lips, and he held out his hands to the side, chanting a spell. His aura burst from his body in a thrilling flash of power that pulsed through her bones. Electrified, Rosalind joined in. Her aura intertwined with his; spirals of green and silver wound together, dancing toward the heavens.

Tendrils of his magic snapped around the keres' bodies. A few of them burst into flame, plunging from the sky, wings burning like torches. Black plumes of smoke spiraled from their falling bodies, and the sight of it filled her with a dark thrill.

Still, even through the red mist of battle fury, a chill washed over her skin. *There are so many of them...*

Ignoring the fallen, the rest of the horde pressed on. Caine shot her a look—was that a flicker of concern in his eyes? He raised his fingers to the heavens, switching to another spell—one about the winds of Nyxobas. As he spoke, an icy breeze rushed over her skin. Rosalind joined in with him, and their auras clawed higher into the sky, buffeting the keres in hurricane winds.

A few keres veered off, straying from the swarm—but most stayed on course. She'd seen Caine knock helicopters from the sky in the same way, but the keres' strange, powerful magic kept them on course.

She chanted louder, and her green aura brightened against the dark sky, curling around the oncoming horde.

But there were just so many, flying lower now, heading straight for Rosalind and Caine. She gripped the sword's hilt. The closest were only a few hundred feet away now, their eyes flashing with cold, pale light. She lifted the sword, her body singing for blood and broken bones.

A hundred feet away.

Caine gripped his weapon, changing spells once more. He called on Druloch for a great shield of tree branches.

Fifty feet.

Rosalind chanted with him, and Cleo's vernal aura strengthened the spell's power.

Thirty feet.

Green and silver boughs shot through the air around them, knitting together in a branchy dome. As the last of the branches knitted together, enclosing them in darkness, the oncoming keres slammed into the shield. They thudded against the bark like birds hitting a window.

In the dark of the arboreal vault, Rosalind let out a long, slow breath, her body surging with a strange combination of fear and frenzy. *I want to cut them to the bone, I want to burn them to the marrow.* The keres stood between her and Tammi, and if she didn't destroy them soon, her friend would be dead. She growled, fingers tightening on the hilt in a death grip. *Nyxobas demands blood.*

Caine sparked a sphere of light, and it cast an amber glow around them. He cast a critical eye at her. "The downside of that shielding spell is that I'm now trapped in a tree with a full blown berserker." He narrowed his eyes. "Don't even think about trying to disembowel me. It will not end w—"

A great crack rent the air, and Rosalind's head snapped up at the sound. Light pierced the dome where the keres had smashed a hole. Rosalind raised her sword, ready to slice into flesh.

Caine began whispering another spell. Before he could finish, a horde of snarling keres poured into the gap.

CHAPTER 23

osalind unleashed a fierce battle cry. A ker flew at her, and she sliced into the creature's neck. Guided by Nyxobas's spell, her sword carved vicious arcs, keeping the keres at bay.

Battle frenzy electrified her body, lending her an otherworldly speed. She whirled as the keres closed in, her sword clashing against their iron. From the corner of her eye, she caught a glimpse of Caine, a ferocious blur of silver and black.

Surging with strength, she sliced through another ker neck. Blood sprayed in a wide arc above her. The old Rosalind, a dull voice buried under red fog, recoiled at the carnage. The old Rosalind wanted to teleport back to the city.

But the old Rosalind wasn't in control anymore.

Nyxobas's spell drove her on. Time seemed to have slowed down, allowing her to slash into each target. *Swing. Stab. Bathe your sword in their blood.* But this battle couldn't last forever—not when there were so many of them. Even drunk on bloodlust, she had a faint sense of being hopelessly outnumbered.

A battle shriek turned her head, and she swung her blade at another ker, tearing into the demon's gut.

The keres were pressing in closer. *So many of them.* They didn't seem to care for their own lives. *What the hell is wrong with them?*

A sharp pain pierced her skull, and she staggered, dropping her sword. At the sound of it clanging to the ground, some of her battle fury ebbed. *This is not good.*

Dizzy, she felt the ground sway below her, and fell forward into the mud.

A horrible realization hit her like a fist. *They're going to eat me alive.*

Pain splintered her head, and she began pushing herself up, but a ker boot slammed into her back, smashing her down. Sulfurous dirt filled her mouth, and sharp-clawed ker hands pinned her to the ground. Grunting, she struggled against them, trying to free her limbs.

They're going to eat me alive.

Frantic, she tried ripping her arms free, but their grip on her was iron-clad, fingernails piercing her flesh. They yanked her arms behind her back, nearly ripping them from their sockets, as a boot pressed her back into the mud.

One of the demons snapped iron handcuffs on her wrists. As soon as the iron touched her skin, the magical aura rushed from her body, leaving her muscles with a burning fatigue, her limbs trembling and weak.

Oh fuck. Oh fuck.

That was it. She had no power left. She was just... Rosalind.

A ker punched her in the back of the head, slamming her face into the mud. She spat out a mouthful of dirt. Nausea climbed up her throat, and her teeth chattered uncontrollably. Sorrow extinguished her fire.

A ker bit into one of her shoulders, and she screamed. She bucked, managing to flip herself over again, knocking the ker off her—but a mob of keres still stood over her, hissing.

Caine's roar rumbled over the dome, and she watched as a burst of his silver magic flared into the air.

The keres around her seemed to falter, their eyes bulging for just a moment—but the spell hadn't worked, and the keres turned their cold gazes on Rosalind again. *Caine's magic doesn't work on them. And I'm going to die here, lying in the mud in this wretched place.*

A ker boot slammed her hard in the gut. As she coughed and spluttered, trying to catch her breath, rough hands grabbed her body, hoisting her up. With claws digging into her flesh, the keres began to beat their wings. The pain from her bite mark ripped her shoulder apart, and she gasped, frantically searching for Caine. But the keres were everywhere, lifting her off the ground, gripping tight to her shoulders and waist.

As they took flight for the opening, a phalanx of flying demons surrounded her, their black wings pulsing in the air. Fear sank its talons into her mind, and she glanced down at Caine. A whirlpool of keres surrounded him. For just a moment, his arctic eyes locked on hers, and his lips moved in a spell. But as his magic burst around him, the keres closed in, dragging him to the ground, trampling him into the mud.

"Caine!" she screamed. One of the keres yanked her head back by the hair, hissing. One final burst of Caine's aura flashed as they lifted into the sky. His silvery magic curled around the keres. One of the demons at Rosalind's shoulders moaned, her eyes rolling back in her head. Her grasp on Rosalind weakened, her head lolling. Her fingers slipped away. She dropped from the sky, her black dress whipping in the wind. Still, the other two keres tightened their sharp grasps.

Rosalind turned her head to glance down over her shoulder, hoping to see a raven taking flight—Caine coming to save her. Instead, she saw only a writhing mass of white-haired demons on the ground, smothering Caine. The sight cut her to the bone. *I need to get back to him.*

Maybe his demigod status could get him through a legion of iron-wielding demons—but it was a long shot. She'd seen what happened when she drove a single iron stake into his heart in Salem. Was that what it had been—her nightmares, her visions? Simply guilt, for what she'd done to him?

Her chest ached, and she stifled a sob. High in the stormy sky, rain battered her body. She had a gnawing certainty that she was being dragged to her own death. Around her, cauldron-dark clouds seethed, and lightning cracked.

The keres' black wings rhythmically beat the air, their pale eyes glowing with an empty light. Something about them seemed *different* from the keres she'd encountered in Lilinor—their expressions were blank, their features a little more human. Beautiful, but vacant. If she didn't have handcuffs on, she could do some damage with that battle fury spell—maybe crawl on one of their backs like she had with the harpy. *Please, Nyxobas, don't let Caine die.*

She flexed her wrists. Bound by the damn iron shackles, she wasn't going to get her frenzy going. Her gaze flicked to the keres. Not only did they wield iron weapons—they wore iron necklaces. *What the fuck?* How was their magic still working? Iron was supposed to destroy magic. It certainly did in her case.

Strong storm winds whipped over her body, freezing her skin, and her teeth chattered. She glanced down at herself, at the ker blood soaking her clothing. *This is a complete disaster.* They were supposed to sneak up on the mountain fortress, undetected—that was the whole advantage to keeping their group small.

How did the keres manage to find them in all this wilderness—to home right in on them like a beacon? The demons had known exactly where they were. A tracking spell, perhaps? But somehow Drew had known exactly when he'd needed to search for them, had known that they were coming into his city. How?

And why were they dragging her off to the fortress, and leaving Caine behind? Surely a demigod was a greater prize than her. She swallowed hard. She couldn't leave him there to die. Maybe there was some way out of her cuffs. If she could get her hands on a thin enough blade in her weapon belt, she might be able to slide it into a lock. The misericorde, maybe.

She glanced at the keres to see if they were paying attention. Their expressions were blank and stony as they carried her along the river's southward bend.

She strained her arms, trying to reach for one of the blades, but the keres were gripping her too tightly for her to maneuver.

In the driving rain, she could see the mountain fortress coming into view, just like the one from her vision. Nestled into a blue-hued hill stood a dark granite castle, with copper statues of goddesses gleaming from its turrets. Harpies circled the air above it like birds of prey.

A shiver wracked her body. *Is this horrible place my ancestral home?*

The keres were heading for a rocky outcrop in front of the fortress's portcullis. Swooping lower, they dove straight for the ground at an alarming speed. The fortress loomed larger as they hurtled for the ground.

Rosalind braced herself for a rough landing. Just outside the portcullis, they let her drop a few feet from the ground. She rolled on the rocky ledge, grimacing with pain.

And this is how my family summons me.

Grunting, she pushed onto her knees, and the keres yanked her the rest of the way up. Her gut clenched with dread as she stared up at the pale stone fortress. *I have no idea what awaits me here, but I don't have a good feeling about it.*

The copper portcullis creaked open with the sound of turning gears. When it gaped fully open, the keres pushed her in. Her heart skipped a beat. Two literal giants guarded a set of doors at the other end of the hall. They must have been twenty feet tall, their half-naked bodies formed from pure corded muscle. Their eyes gleamed a pale granite, strong jaws set tight. Each one gripped a spear in enormous, meaty hands.

She swallowed hard. *Where the hell is everyone getting these giants?*

The keres shoved her forward, and she started walking slowly. As they crossed the marble floor, her boots echoed off the high ceiling. She eyed the alcoves filled with copper statues, and a sigil marking the pale marble floor. A shiver ran up her spine. It was the same one she'd seen at Abduxiel Mansion: Azazeyl's sigil. The god who might not be real.

Altogether, the palace held a faint hint of familiarity. She'd been here before—she was fairly certain of that. She closed her eyes, trying not to think of Caine—that poisonous dream of the stakes, the dream that wanted to eat her alive. And she couldn't let herself think of what was happening to him now—being overwhelmed by writhing ker bodies, his flesh pierced over and over by iron…

Stop it, Rosalind. She needed to keep her head together if she wanted to get out of this alive. And then she'd go back for him—or what was left of him. And together, they'd get Tammi.

Rosalind's knees shook as they approached the second set of doors. The two giants stared straight ahead. Like the keres, their auras formed from a wide bouquet of colors and smells—gold and silver tingling over her skin, soft mossy green and a wet, briny blue. She didn't even want to think about what kind of damage those bastards could do. Whatever her escape plan entailed, she'd need to stay the hell away from the giants.

As they walked up the stairs to the next set of doors, the doors swung open, revealing a second hall. A deep bronze rug led right up to a dark granite throne.

And on the throne sat Drew, lazily tracing a finger over the rim of a chalice. A copper crown, inset with emeralds, gleamed on his head.

The corner of his mouth twitched. "Rosalind."

"Drew. My loving… what are you? Brother? Cousin?"

A raised eyebrow registered a hint of surprise. "Ah. You've worked it out, at last."

"Is it true?"

He shook his head slowly, his eyes locked on hers. "Not your brother. Cousin, yes—*and* your future husband. Did you finally remember your family?"

CHAPTER 24

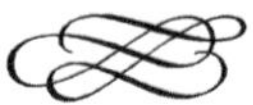

Her mind churned. "Caine told me about our family crest. And I saw the same motto hanging on your wall. *Loyalty binds me.*"

"It doesn't bind you, though, does it?"

"Who are you?" Her voice echoed off the high ceiling.

"I loved your parents like they were my own. Worshipped them, practically." He frowned. "But sadly, they were not my own."

"What do you mean, future husband?"

"We've been engaged since you were born. As we should be. We needed to ensure we could keep the Atherton bloodline pure. We're not like other people, Rosalind."

She swallowed hard. She needed to buy just enough time to slide a blade out of her belt and wrench the cuffs open. "In what way are we not like other people? I mean, besides having a fortress with giants and harpies?" Pain seared the puncture wounds in her neck, and she grimaced as he spoke.

He narrowed his eyes, studying her neck. "You're injured. I'll send someone for a potion."

"I don't want any more potions." Her fingers curled. "What was in the last one you gave me?"

434

"It healed you didn't it? And it helped me keep track of you." He shrugged. "Otherwise, I might not have known you'd come for me."

Slowly, she reached for one of the blades in her belt. Her fingertips tightened on the knife's hilt, and she began inching it up. It was the misericorde—a long, needle-like knife intended to deliver a merciful death stroke. Perfect for picking the cuffs' lock.

She just needed enough time to make it work. She cleared her throat. "You were saying something about a pure bloodline? We're not like other people?"

Drew steepled his fingers, staring down at her. "I'm trying to re-establish the Atherton dynasty. We are descendants of the One Who Is All. We deserve to rule. We will create a new Atherton kingdom from here, just like the kingdom of old. Your parents had the same mission."

Slowly, she inched the hilt up higher. *This is not going to be easy.* "My parents wanted to create a new kingdom. And that's why they needed three ancient mage's souls—for all that power."

"It was part of their plan," Drew said.

Her wet fingers were slippery on the hilt. "Why are you working with the Brotherhood?"

He straightened, his face paling slightly. "You must understand that I had nothing—nothing but a common enemy with the Brother-hood. Mutual hatred tends to unite people."

She shimmied the knife up a little higher, trying not to let it slip. "What mutual enemy?"

"The Ravener."

Her pulse raced, and sweat mixed with the rain on her fingertips. It was hard to get a good grip on the hilt. "Why is he your enemy?"

"I wasn't happy to find you with him, Rosalind. Not very *loyal*. And you're too stupid to realize what he's doing. First, he ruined our family, and now he wants to make you into his whore, to further debase the Atherton name."

"That's not true." *Almost out, Rosalind.* "If he wants to make me into his whore, then why hasn't he used mind control? Or his incubus powers?"

"He likes a challenge. It excites him. Feeds his ego." Drew looked at his fingernails. "I almost gave you over to the Brotherhood to burn, but I changed my mind at the last minute. I loved your parents very much, and you seemed so helpless when I spoke to you at the mansion."

Just one more inch. Rosalind's chest tightened. "I don't even remember what Caine did. How did he destroy our family?"

Before Drew could respond, a ker smacked her in the back of the head, hissing. Rosalind dropped the blade, and it clanged against the ground. Her heart sank, her knees nearly giving way.

Drew tutted. "Rosalind. Were you trying to escape? I had a feeling I couldn't trust you yet." He released a long sigh. "I'll have to keep you and Miranda in iron until you can demonstrate your loyalty."

"Miranda hasn't shown herself loyal to you?"

"The woman is half-mad. Whatever your Hunter friends did to her has ripped her mind apart. I think she has a strange fondness for Caine, despite what he did. So I'll keep the chains on both of you for now." He bit his lip. "The Brotherhood were hoping for four of you, of course. Caine, Malphas, Tammi, and you. But they'll just have to settle for the two incubi alone. I'd still like you to be my wife." He shrugged. "The Brotherhood can always choose another scapegoat. I don't get the impression they're picky about guilt."

He's not going to give Tammi up. This was the first bit of good news she'd had. "So you won't give Tammi to the Brotherhood either. I'd heard she was going to burn today." She straightened. "I want to see her."

Drew rose, stepping down from the dais. "In time, Rosalind, you'll understand that the king is the one giving the commands." He crossed the marble floor, and slid his arms around her. "But there's plenty of time for you to learn that."

He whispered a spell, his aura crawling over her body. It was no longer just copper, but tendrils of green and blue, gold and silver, the smells and textures overwhelming—slippery and rough, cold and burning, salty and spicy.

The phrase *the One Who Is All* whispered in the back of her skull, and the auras rushed into her bones.

In the next moment, they stood on a high walkway overlooking an enormous courtyard. A horde of keres swarmed below, bodies slick with the rain water. Their skin had an odd, shiny sheen, and they wore ragged black gowns. *What the hell is going on here?*

On a raised stone dais in the courtyard, Erish stood above an altar, her hair wild. Her aura had changed—in fact, it looked just like Drew's. Wild tendrils of gold, copper, silver, and green whipped from her body. Her dark hair snaked around her head, and her eyes shone a deep black. Something looked definitely *wrong* with her.

"What's happened to her?" Rosalind asked.

"She drinks my blood, and that means she drinks from The One who is All. She's been gorging on Blodrial's blood as well. I'm not sure she's handling it well. Mentally. But her powers are breathtaking. It's been a long time since giants have roamed the earth, and she created the ones you've seen."

Rosalind's heart raced. "What are you talking about?"

His gaze slid to hers. "If you hadn't been wearing that iron ring when you were in the Brotherhood, you'd know exactly what I was talking about. When you drank the god's blood, you would have seen it for yourself. You and I descend directly from the One Who is All, he of the seven gods."

She scanned the crowd of keres, desperately searching for Tammi. Fire flooded her veins, and her pulse raced out of control. *Keep your composure, Rosalind.* "I don't have the first fucking clue what you're talking about. But where is Tammi?"

He drummed his fingertips on the stone ledge. "I imagined you'd have a hard time recognizing her. She isn't really Tammi anymore. It's why I can't give her to the Brotherhood. They wouldn't recognize her either."

Dread bloomed in Rosalind's chest, and she watched Erish stalk off, storming through a wooden door into one of the towers. "What do you mean she isn't Tammi anymore?" She knew where this was going, but she didn't want to believe it. She kept the thoughts locked behind bars, trapped below the surface with all the dreams she didn't want to remember.

He took a deep breath. "This probably makes me seem worse than I am. But let me explain. After the revolution in Maremount, I was in utter and complete exile for years—"

Her blood boiled. *Slam.* Something was hammering at the cage in her mind. "I said where is Tammi?"

"After years of living like a savage," he continued, his voice soft and controlled. "I made it into Boston, but there, the Brotherhood rule the city. Gods below, I was eating discarded food out of trash cans, sleeping in—"

Slam. Slam. Slam. She gritted her teeth. "Answer my question."

"So I made a deal. The Brotherhood allowed me to use my magic freely. All I had to do was turn in a few traitors—you and Caine among them—and they would help me re-establish my dynasty." His eyes took on a dreamy look. "It was a blessing in disguise—fate, really. They wanted me to drink the god's blood. They're a bit fanatical. But when I did, the most wondrous thing happened." He turned to her, eyes glistening. "The One Who Is All awoke in my blood, blessing me with all kinds of magic. And now, I can see it and feel it, like you can. And I can control it." He closed his eyes, tilting back his head to let the rain run down his face. "And that's when Erish found me. She helped me rebuild part of the Atherton legacy. This fortress was here centuries ago, and we've created it again."

Slam. Rosalind's face grew hot, and even without the spell she could feel the battle fury rising. "Get to the part about Tammi."

"I'm getting to it." He opened his eyes. "The Brotherhood won't supply us with the god's blood unless we do certain things for them. They wanted a demon massacre, so we gave them a demon massacre." He looked out at the crowd of keres. "First, Erish and I had to make the demons. She'd ruined her own ker army, and these ones are much more docile."

Slam. Fear slithered over her skin. "Where is Tammi?" her voice came out in a whisper.

"I'd only intended to create a few," he continued. "That's all we needed for a solid massacre, and I didn't know how to control the magic. I'm still learning. But Erish did. Really, she conducted the entire massacre. I think perhaps she's starting to lose her mind. She's been drinking me dry, sure. But she was never meant to drink from the iron god, and now she gorges herself on his blood. She's too strong for me to fight, even with my growing powers." He waved a hand. "And that's how we ended up with this mess. Tammi, unfortunately, was one of the casualties."

In horror, Rosalind turned to look at the crowd of keres. *Tammi is down there, dead-eyed and squatting in the courtyard. Tammi, who knew all the lyrics to every Beyoncé song. Tammi, who cut Rosalind's hair when she couldn't afford the salon, who came up with the most hilarious nicknames for all their professors, who dressed as a flapper every Halloween.*

Tammi—*that* Tammi—was crouching in the rain, demon-like and lobotomized.

Uncaged, white-hot fury surged. She wanted to kick the shit out of Drew, to unleash her battle frenzy like she had with the keres. But, bound in iron, she couldn't get to the magic she needed. Her heart hammered. "What did you do to Tammi? I want to hear you say it."

Erish slammed open the wooden door again, dragging a human woman by the throat.

Drew nodded at the courtyard. "You'll want to see this."

Erish threw the woman down on the stone slab, her red hair spread out behind her. She screamed, and kept screaming. The succubus snarled, fixing the woman's neck in an iron cuff that bound her to the stone.

Rosalind's stomach clenched. *This is what happened to Tammi.*

A guttural growl rose from Erish's throat as she chanted an Angelic spell, and colored swirls of magic exploded around them. Rosalind watched in horror as the woman's skin slowly blanched. She convulsed and shook on the stone. As she screeched to the stormy heavens, her eyes began to blaze like starlight, teeth lengthening into sharp spears. Her vibrant red hair paled to a gleaming white, and long, black claws lengthened from her fingertips.

Bile rose in Rosalind's throat. *All the missing people...* Her legs threatened to give way. Her mind whirled. She needed to find Caine again, and they could drag Tammi out of here and undo the spell.

Maybe the magic lay in the necklace itself. "How are you doing this?" she whispered.

"The One Who is All—the original fallen—gives us powers you've never dreamed of. I always thought it was a fairytale until I saw it for myself. Soon, you'll be a believer, too."

Her heart thrummed against her ribs. She wanted to call down the wrath of the gods on this place—but she needed to get out of the cuffs first. She scanned the skies, desperate for a sign of Caine flying in as a raven.

"Are you looking for the incubus?" Drew shook his head. "He won't be coming for you."

All the air left her lungs, like she'd been punched in the chest. "How do you know?"

"I watched him die through a scrying mirror. It was exactly as I'd always wanted to see him die—impaled on a stake and left there to rot. The light just went right out of his eyes."

His words slammed into Rosalind. He stepped closer, wrapping his arms around her once again, and whispered a spell, his overwhelming auras rushing over her skin. She tried to swallow her revulsion as he whispered the teleportation spell.

In the next instant, they stood in the hall again, not far from Drew's throne. The keres who had held her were now gone, and they were completely alone.

"You saw Caine die?" she said, her legs trembling. She pulled away from him.

"I'd been looking forward to that moment for years. I wanted so badly to kill him when he came into my house in Cambridge, but my magic wasn't as powerful then."

She didn't care anymore *why* Drew hated Caine; she just knew that cold, icy wrath flooded her body.

Maybe she couldn't access the battle frenzy spell, but she had fury of her own. The Brotherhood had taught her to fight without magic. Rage surged in her blood, and her teeth began to chatter, just as they'd done when she'd used the Morrigan's spell. Only this fury was her own, blazing through her nerve endings, igniting her body.

Fight. Rosalind pivoted, then kicked, slamming Drew in the face with her boot. His head snapped back, and she hammered him two more times in the nose. She heard a crack—the bone snapping—and the sound thrilled her. Blood poured from his face, and she slammed him again, wanting to break his skull in two.

He killed Caine. He destroyed Tammi.

Dazed, he staggered backward, trying to chant a spell, but his words slurred together and he fell on his ass.

Rosalind let herself drop to the ground too, contorting her body so she could pull her legs through her arms. Blazing with adrenalin, she rose, her cuffs now in front.

From the ground, Drew began chanting another spell—clearer this time—and she sprinted behind him. *He killed Caine,* her mind screamed. She hooked her cuffs around his throat, and pulled. Hard.

Bloodlust whispered around her heart, urging her to end his life. *He destroyed my friends.*

Drew's face reddened, his eyes bulging. As soon as his body went limp, she pulled the cuffs from his throat. He fell back, his head cracking against the marble floor. She stared at the angry red indentations on his neck. He was unconscious, not dead. His chest rose and fell slowly, his breath raspy.

At the sight of his helplessness, some of the rage in her chest subsided. She didn't need to kill an unconscious man, but she'd make damn sure he couldn't use his powers.

She just needed to get out of these cuffs.

She snatched her knife from the ground where the ker had dropped it—the thin stiletto blade was just narrow enough for what she needed. She slid the point in beside the teeth, sliding it deeper into the locking mechanism. Pushing on the cuff, she inched the knife in deeper, inching it slowly, until at last, she heard the lock click, unlatching.

She exhaled and glanced at Drew, who lay flat on his back, then she switched her focus to the other wrist.

When she'd pried her way out of that one, she grabbed the cuffs, crossing to Drew. She hauled him up, dragged him over to the throne's base, and cuffed his hands behind his back with the cuff's chain around one leg of the throne.

Free from the iron, she closed her eyes, letting Cleo's aura swirl in her chest. Hugging her exhausted body, she chanted the spell to teleport back to the four stakes.

Her body burst with green magic, and a vernal wind rushed over her skin. She landed in the mud on her hands and knees, next to the branchy dome. Rain still hammered down, and her dress stuck to her skin. After using the powerful spell, her body felt ripped apart with fatigue. She had to fight the urge to lie in the mud and sleep.

When she looked up at the stakes, the world seemed to fall out from under her.

CHAPTER 25

There, nailed to a stake, was Caine. His head drooped, and blood poured from his heart. An iron nail had been rammed right through his chest.

It was just like her dream, only it was all backward. Caine had been killed, not her. She rushed to him.

A thin stream of blood dripped from his perfect lips. His entire body had been slashed by iron swords, and his head lolled. She slid her hand over his neck. Faintly, so faintly that she could hardly feel it, a pulse beat beneath the surface of his skin.

Relief washed over her. Nearly dead—but not quite. *I guess a demigod doesn't die so easily. But there's only one way for an incubus to heal.* Whatever he'd done, whatever had happened at these stakes—she had to heal him now if she didn't want him to die.

She stared down at his chest again, at the nail's thick iron head. Digging her nails around it, she slowly eased it out. When she'd pulled it out a few inches, she swallowed hard. *If he's conscious for this, it will hurt. A lot.*

She gripped it hard in her fist, then yanked it out. Caine moaned, his pale eyes fluttering open. He stared at her, seemingly without recognition. His eyes had darkened to fathomless, inhuman voids.

He glared down at her, and fear ran up her spine. Near death, he'd reverted to a primal state, a low growl rumbling from his chest. His fingers clamped onto her waist, claiming her. She wasn't looking at Caine. She was looking at a shadow god, one full of primordial wrath, and every instinct in her body told her to run.

He only had one way to heal, and he wanted it. Now.

His fingers tightened around her waist in a vise-like grip. Possessive. Hungry. He pulled her closer, his heat seeping into her, his aura curling around her, brushing against her rain-soaked skin. She was his salvation, and he wasn't letting her get away from him.

Slowly, his dark gaze magnetized her, and she no longer wanted to run from him. He grabbed her by the hair, turning her head to expose the vulnerable skin of her throat.

She shivered. Caine was in complete control here. If she tried to pull away from him, she didn't think he'd let her get very far.

He leaned in, his teeth brushing her throat, sending a jolt of fire through her.

Wrapping her arms around his neck, she arched into him, tangling her fingers into his hair. His grasp on her hips tightened, and he nipped at her skin. His lips replaced his teeth, and he kissed her neck softly, disarmingly. Heat blazed through her core, and her breath caught in her throat. She leaned back, exposing more of her neck to him, wanting his hands all over her.

Without warning, Caine spun her around. In the next second, he was pinning her hard against the stake. The rough bark chafed her skin through her thin dress, but she didn't care. Caine, black-eyed, overwhelmed her. With a low snarl, he wrapped his strong arms around the backs of her thighs and lifted her from the ground. He pushed in closer, pressing her against the wood. Pulse racing, she wrapped her legs around him, pulling him in tight. Her dress hitched up to her waist, exposing her thighs. She reached up to touch his perfect face, and desire flooded her.

Hungrily, he pressed his mouth against hers, devouring her. She parted her lips for him, letting her tongue brush his. His kiss was hungry, desperate, electrifying. She arched her back, and his kiss lit her up.

Then his kiss softened, deepening, his tongue velvety smooth against hers. Gently, he brushed the rain-slicked hair from her face. He loosened his grip, his fingers tracing her inner thighs, electrifying her body with his touch. His fingertips moved higher, and her pulse raced. *I want him.*

He pulled away, meeting her gaze. His eyes had returned to a clear, icy blue. Caine—but he wore an expression she'd never seen before. Almost perplexed. "I didn't think I'd be able to find you."

She cupped his neck. "That's fine, because I found you."

He stroked her thighs, staring into her eyes. Rain poured down his pale gold skin in rivulets, his dark hair soaked against his skin. "I saw them carry you away. I couldn't get to you."

"That's because you were nailed to a stake."

Caine's breath quickened, his gaze moving past her, focusing on the rotting wood. As his eyes cleared, it almost seemed like he was waking from a dream. Suddenly, his body went rigid, a deep breath rushing into his lungs. He released his grip on her, letting her slide down his body. He pulled his arms from her neck and stepped away.

She pulled down her dress, feeling rejected. *Well, I guess that's over.* It was for the best though, really. They still had to get Tammi. She crossed her arms, trying to clear her mind. "We need to go back to the fortress. I've been there now, so we can teleport. Are you healed?"

"Beautifully." His gaze darted to the stake, as if it were still tormenting him. "There's something I have to tell you."

Dread filled her chest, and a memory slammed at the cage of her mind again. She had a sinking feeling that whatever he was going to tell her would change everything. But now wasn't the time for that. She'd come here for Tammi, and she was leaving with Tammi. "Not now, Caine. Tell me after we get Tammi and Miranda back."

His features relaxed almost imperceptibly. "Did you see them?"

Rosalind shook her head, hugging herself. "No, but I saw what they were doing—what Erish is doing. She's lost her mind. She's turning humans into keres, and I think Tammi was one of them. I don't think Miranda is."

Caine's jaw flexed. "How?"

"Something about The One Who Is All. Drew says we're descended from him. Erish drank Drew's blood; she drinks Blodrial's blood. It's all fucked up over there, but the bottom line is, I'm getting Tammi back. And Miranda, too."

His eyes narrowed. "The One Who Is All is just a legend. He's not real."

"Who was he?"

"Some say that the seven gods come from one: Azazeyl, the one who gave humans the Angelic language, the one who taught the Watchers to lay with the daughters of man. They say that for his transgressions, he was split into seven parts, then trapped in the earth. They say the seven gods don't remember. They only know they don't feel whole anymore, and they're desperate to return to one."

Rosalind hugged herself. "They can use magic from all the gods. I've seen Drew do it. And Erish, too."

Caine frowned. "What's the layout of the place, and what are their defenses?"

"The human keres are in the courtyard. There are harpies patrolling the skies, at least two giants—"

"More giants?"

"Apparently, Erish knows how to make them."

"Seven hells." Caine ran a finger over his jaw. "If they're somehow drawing on the power of seven gods, I've been using the wrong spells entirely. In fact, I don't know any spells for that kind of magic."

"So maybe we just go in covertly. We turn invisible, you find Miranda, and I look for Tammi. I don't know how I'll find her if she looks like a ker, but I'll figure something out."

"I'll find Miranda, and slaughter the succubus. What's the layout of the castle?"

She scanned her mind, trying to picture the aerial view. "There are at least three towers, maybe five, with some kind of halls between them. Then there are more towers in the interior, all different heights, like it was designed by a crazy person. There's a courtyard, and a lot of… rocks." Her description petered out.

He arched an eyebrow.

"Look, I'm not an expert in castle architecture. And I have no idea where Miranda is in all that. But I can tell you the keres and Erish are in the courtyard, and Erish was standing over an altar."

"Go to the courtyard. Find Tammi, and bring her as close to the altar as you can. When you see the signal, rush over to me, and the four of us will teleport out."

She frowned. "What's the signal?"

"Erish, impaled on an iron sword."

She swallowed hard. "Perfect."

His eyes raked over her body, taking in the puncture marks on her neck, the bruises. He lifted her arm, inspecting the claw marks. "Gods below," he muttered. "Did they break anything?"

She shook her head. "Not this time."

"You still need healing." For a brief instant, she had a brief pang of regret that humans didn't heal in the same way as incubi, but she pushed the thought to the back of her mind.

Running his fingertips over her ravaged skin, he lifted his gaze to meet hers. "I changed my mind about the signal."

"What will it be?"

"Erish exploding into a spray of flesh, blood, and bone."

"Lovely."

He chanted the spell for healing, and his touch sent shivers over her skin. He brushed his fingers over her neck, soothing her body and thrilling it at the same time. He traced down the back of her spine, his perfect lips just inches from hers, the air between them electrified.

"That should do it," he said softly. "I'm getting your sword for you. You might need it." He disappeared in a blur of silver and black, speeding into the dome, and in a few moments he'd returned with her weapon.

She took it from him, slipping it back into the sheath, and ran her eyes over his healed skin. All the gashes had disappeared. She swallowed hard, wanting so badly to close the distance between them.

"Are you sure you're healed enough for all this? You were nearly dead."

Instead of making another flippant remark about how she wanted to get her hands all over him, he just pulled her close, wrapping his arms around her and cupping the back of her head. His heart beat hard under his drenched clothes, not far from her ear. "I'm fine."

He whispered the spell for invisibility, and she watched as his strong chest shimmered away. He leaned down, his breath warming her neck. "Take us to the fortress."

CHAPTER 26

*R*osalind breathed in his earthy scent for a moment, then whispered the teleportation spell. Caine joined in, and their auras mingled together, whirling around their bodies. In the next moment, they stood before the portcullis. Rain still poured from the skies.

She leaned into his warmth. "The giants are within those doors. We'll need to find another way in."

Caine leaned in close. "Ask Cleo for Arachne's Blessing. Scale the walls."

Rosalind closed her eyes, focusing on the green sphere of magic in her chest. *Cleo. I need you to help me use Arachne's Blessing.*

Cleo whispered, *I need Ambrose.*

Whatever you want, Cleo.

Instantly, the spell's words flashed in her mind, and she repeated them out loud, the aura tingling over her skin.

An uncanny sureness filled her limbs, and in the next second, she was at the base of the castle. Her fingers touched the smooth marble wall, adhering to it, and she scuttled up the rain-slick surface. A peal of thunder cracked the air, and the stormy winds whipped her air as she climbed higher. *Don't look down, Rosalind.*

Fatigue pounded her body to the bone. She climbed higher, the wind howling.

At the top of the castle wall, she hoisted herself onto a wide marble walkway that stretched between two towers. She gazed out at the landscape—from this rocky outcrop at the mountain's summit, the fortress seemed a thousand feet high. Overhead, harpies whirled, oblivious to her presence.

She turned, surveying the fortress's center, trying to plan her route to the courtyard. Another square of towers stood in the center, connected by long buildings. Two circles of towers stood nearly twenty feet apart, but she had an almost certain feeling she could leap that distance with Arachne's Blessing.

She climbed to the top of the battlement, her muscles tensing as she concentrated. She crouched down, then leapt into the air, soaring over the marble flagstones far below. She came down in an arc and landed just shy of the walkway—but she managed to grip the edge, clinging on with her fingertips.

Her heart hammered as she hoisted herself up, gasping for breath. She crossed the second walkway to peer down into the courtyard. Ragged keres—once human—crouched in the driving rain, their bodies completely docile. Her stomach tightened. *What the fuck did they do to Tammi?*

If she couldn't get her friend back to her old self, she'd drive a nail right through Drew's heart.

The damn human-keres looked completely uniform, even down to the same iron necklace they all wore. Her jaw tightened. Erish had put one of them around the redhead's neck before turning her, like some kind of collar. Maybe there was some enchantment in them. Was it possible that if Rosalind took the necklace off Tammi, the spell would wear off?

Whatever the case, she really needed a plan before she headed in there.

Her pulse began to race. *I need to hurry.* If Erish exploded, and she was nowhere nearby, things would get messy fast. She just needed to know where she was going first, some help with finding Tammi.

She closed her eyes. "Give me a spell for vision, Cleo, and I'll give you what you want." The air filled with a mossy aura, and in the next moment words blazed in her mind, engraved in sunlight. She chanted a spell for Athena, and Cleo's leafy aura brushed over her skin.

When she opened her eyes, the sight before her was almost overwhelming. Each raindrop shone clearly as it fell—the air full of tiny, watery spheres. She could see each strand of gleaming white hair on the keres, each pore in their skin.

But where the fuck is Tammi?

They all looked exactly alike: the same straight noses and wide, white eyes framed with black lashes. Same gleaming white hair, same full breasts and narrow hips. Same long, black claws and sharp teeth. All had large black wings drooping from their backs. Rosalind searched for some distinguishing features in them, her stomach churning with a growing nausea.

Her fingernails pierced her palms when she noticed a distinct flash of color—a distinct flash of chipped *Rouge Dior* nail polish, in fact.

Tammi.

Rosalind stared at her friend's face, hoping for some flicker of recognition, something recognizable in her eyes, but saw only emptiness. Tammi—the ker—sat cross-legged on the ground, her shoulders slumped.

Sadness pierced Rosalind's chest. *Am I too late? Is this all that's left of her?*

Her pulse raced, and she leapt over the side of the wall, scaling the wet marble to the courtyard below. When she reached the ground, she whirled around, fixing her gaze again on the ker with the chipped red nail polish.

She stepped between the docile keres, brushing against them as she walked. A few turned to look at her, but their silvery eyes never focused. When she reached Tammi, she grabbed her by the arm, trying to hoist her up, but her friend's body was limp.

"Tammi," she whispered. "Get up."

A flicker of confusion whispered across Tammi's strange, pale features, but she didn't react to this disembodied voice.

Gods below. They've ice-picked her brain.

"Tammi," she whispered again, yanking her friend to her feet.

Tammi rose for a moment before slumping down again.

Lightning cracked the sky; thunder rumbled over the rocky terrain. Rosalind wiped the rain out of her eyes. She was about to collapse into the mud.

Cleo, I need a spell for strength.

The words of an Angelic spell burned into her mind, and she chanted each word. Her muscles blazed with power. She searched around for any sign of Drew, but saw nothing.

She leaned down and hoisted Tammi to her feet.

Tammi's brow furrowed with confusion, and she let out a low growl.

Rosalind gripped Tammi's waist, pulling her friend's arm around her shoulder.

At least, I hope this is my friend.

She glanced up at the altar. Erish had disappeared, no doubt to fetch another human. Rosalind's stomach flipped. *How many humans do they have trapped in this fortress?*

As she dragged Tammi closer to the altar, her gaze roved over the sad collection of human-keres littering the courtyard. What was the point of all this? She understood why the Brotherhood wanted them: more demonic attacks meant more power for them, and mob fear meant that they could take any measures they wanted, that they could purify the country in Blodrial's ambrosia.

And she supposed she understood why Erish hated humans with such a deep and relentless passion. Look at what humans had done to her sister. But Erish should have been happy in Lilinor, reigning as queen.

Maybe it was true what Caine had said, that Ambrose had fallen out of love with her. Maybe she was driven by an insatiable hunger, like the one the harpies had instilled in Rosalind—a void gnawing at her from the inside out—and only the devotion of a beautiful man could fill it. A biting, ravening hunger, one that could be filled with worship alone.

Maybe Caine wasn't the only ravener.

As she dragged Tammi to the altar, cold rain slid down Rosalind's skin, and she shivered. *The Ravener.* Part of her didn't want to know what he'd done. Part of her thought she already knew, but when her mind tried to put a name to it, tried to label the vision, an iron fist shoved the thoughts back into their cage.

As she approached the altar, she stilled her march. Erish had returned, dragging another human woman with her—a middle-aged woman with frizzy brown hair, wearing mom jeans and a floral T-shirt. She looked like she could be someone's mother, or third-grade teacher.

Terrified, the woman thrashed; Rosalind gritted her teeth. The plan was for her to simply drag Tammi's half-comatose body over near Erish, and then wait until Caine turned the succubus into aerosolized flesh. But Caine wasn't there yet, and in the meantime here was someone's mom screaming for her life while a succubus slammed an iron cuff around her throat, pinning her to the stone slab.

Caine had given her a whole spiel about not letting her emotions cloud her judgment, how loyalty could be a weakness. And she wasn't sure where her loyalties lay—humans or demons, Athertons or incubi —but she was pretty sure right now they lay with this woman in her floral top, with her cracked Coke-bottle glasses, shrieking up at the storm clouds.

The thought nearly shattered her mind—but what if it was already too late to turn Tammi human again?

It wasn't too late for this woman in front of them.

Rosalind edged closer to the succubus, who slammed a fist into the woman's face, then clamped the iron ring around her neck.

Maybe there was a chance to save her.

Rosalind closed her eyes. *Cleo... Help me get this woman out of here, and I'll let you out to play.*

The woman scratched at Erish's face until the succubus forced down her hands. But Cleo's green aura was already roiling in Rosalind's chest, and she chatted the Angelic words—a spell for iron and chains. Rosalind's eyes remained locked on the woman, whose entire body was wracked by sobs.

As Erish began a spell of her own, the woman's hair blanched and grew longer, her skin paling.

Rosalind finished the final words of the spell, and iron binding the woman's neck creaked and groaned, bending away from her body. Erish's eyes widened, and her surprise gave the woman just enough time to slug her. Erish staggered back, wiping the blood from her lip, her feral eyes on the woman as she jumped from the stone slab, trying to flee across the courtyard. She wouldn't make it far before the keres slaughtered her.

Rosalind changed spells, chanting a spell for invisibility that targeted the woman, and the woman's body shimmered out of view. Gods knew if she'd find her way out of the fortress, but at least she'd been given the chance.

Rosalind let out a long, slow breath, but when she looked back at the succubus, Erish's midnight gaze was right on her. Her body tensed, her grasp tightening on Tammi's waist. She stood only two feet from Erish, and she was supposed to be invisible. But at Erish's gaze, her blood went cold. It seemed Erish could see auras, too—a gift from The One Who Is All.

The succubus's roar rumbled off the castle walls, and she leapt over the altar. Rosalind released Tammi, reaching for her sword—but she didn't get to it in time. Erish grabbed for her neck, squeezing hard —so hard Rosalind thought her throat might collapse into her spine. *Fuck. She's going to kill me.*

Erish leaned in closer. "Is that you, Rosalind? Little Hunter? Are you here to try to kill me?"

Rosalind's windpipe was being crushed, and pain ripped apart her lungs.

"I belong to The One Who Is All now," Erish hissed. "Blodrial's veins give us true life."

Rosalind kicked Erish's shins. *She has lost her fucking mind, and I'm about to die.*

Cleo, give me strength. Rosalind slammed her hands down on Erish's wrists, pulling them away from her neck and smashing her boot into Erish's stomach. The succubus doubled over for a split second—just enough time for Rosalind to pull out her sword before the succubus sprang up again.

Rosalind swung for Erish, but the creature ducked with breathtaking speed, her colored aura whipping out of her body. Wrath blazed in her darkened eyes, and she slammed Rosalind in the face with her fist. Rosalind staggered back, dropping her sword.

"The One Who Is All claims you." She grabbed Rosalind by the shoulders, lifting her into the air and throwing her down on the rock.

Rosalind's head cracked against the granite, agony splintering her skull. She pushed herself up on her elbows, but Erish slammed her down again. As Erish clamped an iron cuff on her arm, she flexed her wrist, making it larger. This was the one legacy her abusive, adoptive father had given her—a serious skill at getting out of restraints. She *hated* being bound.

She gritted her teeth, trying to keep her cool and grasped with her free hand for a hawthorn stake in her belt. But she didn't get it out before Erish slammed her other wrist down. Rosalind thought her heart was going to break her ribs. *Holy hells.*

Erish's dark eyes seemed unfocused, frantic.

Rain poured over Rosalind's skin, and rage bubbled in her chest. *Stay focused, Rosalind.* "Why are you doing this?" she shouted.

Erish leaned in closer. "Do you know how many succubi once roamed the earth?"

"No."

"There were thousands of us. We were once revered as sacred, as goddesses. Now, only four remain. The world fears women with power. Remember that, after I turn you into a ker. I watched seven of my sisters—and our mother, Lilith—tortured to death. My sister Shamhat decorates Maremount's drinking fountain. It's not enough to crush us into submission in life. They must humiliate us in death, too. And yet the incubi still live. It's time for the tide to turn. I will have my own army now."

Rosalind relaxed her wrists, making her hands as narrow as possible, and began to shimmy them out. She needed to keep Erish talking, just long enough so she could fully pry her hands from the bindings.

In the stormy skies above, the harpies began to shriek and wail—screaming at her? At Caine? It was something about a murder, something about the true king and queen. Rosalind crushed her hands together. "Why do you need the army of keres?"

Erish leaned in closer, her breath sweet. Rainwater poured down her stunning, almond skin, and she threaded her fingers into Rosalind's hair. "To defend me. To help me rule."

"Why did you torture the keres in Lilinor? You cut off their wings." *Keep talking, you lunatic.*

"The keres once served succubi. But they're a disloyal race. They abandoned us when the world stopped revering us as goddesses. The keres have been punished."

The iron scraped Rosalind's skin as she tugged her hands out. If Erish kept leaning in close, she might not notice Rosalind's arms slowly shifting. "Surely Ambrose will protect you. He's powerful."

"I can't rely on him anymore." Rain slicked Erish's eyelashes into peaks and dripped from the ends; her midnight eyes took on a glazed look. "He's grown tired of me after five hundred years. His gaze turns to little human things like you." Her fingers slid around Rosalind's throat, and she leaned down. "So I've found a new protector. Drew, and my army of keres. He wants to marry you. But he won't once I turn you into a ker. Everyone likes the human girls."

Rosalind felt the base of her palm slip through the iron loop—though it felt as if her bones were being crushed and she was taking off a layer of skin. "Of course you need protection," she said, hoping to keep Erish focused on her. "It isn't fair for so much to be taken from you." She hoped her words sounded genuine—and deep down, part of her did feel sorry for the succubi.

Erish's gaze met hers. "The One Who Is All has given me new powers. I can see auras now, and smell them. I drink from Blodrial's veins, and I can create new demons, using the magic of the seven. And now no one will be able to hurt me. No one will be able to wipe the last of the succubi from the earth's surface."

She's really pouring her heart right out. The succubus seemed lonely as hell, like this was the first conversation she'd had in months.

"That sounds like a reasonable plan," Rosalind said, trying to force her knuckles through the gap.

Erish's eyes swiveled to hers, and Rosalind read in them a flash of madness. She was left with the distinct impression that Drew was right about Erish—the iron god's blood had twisted her mind. Demons were never meant to drink from his veins. "Drew wants you to be his wife," the succubus said plaintively.

Rosalind strained against the iron cuffs. Rainwater and sweat slicked her hands, and she nearly had them out.

Erish leaned in closer, rain spilling down her skin and onto Rosalind's body. She cupped Rosalind's face, almost lovingly. "I like you. You'll make a lovely ker in my legion. Together, we'll make a new world."

Erish began to chant her spell, her aura whipping around her body, and Rosalind felt it rush over her skin, climbing up her bare legs, hot and cold at the same time. Her heart hammered, and with one frantic, skin-ripping tug, she tore her hands free.

Erish screamed, trying to push her down again, but Rosalind was already chanting Cleo's battle fury spell, and raw power blazed. She pulled a hawthorn stake from her belt, ramming it into Erish's chest, up beneath her ribs, and right into her heart. Blood spurted from the queen's chest.

The succubus staggered back. She should have collapsed, half-dead, onto the ground; instead, she pulled the hawthorn stake from her chest. The auras whirled from her body—only the silver dimming.

Oh, shit. So this is why they were impervious to magic and the usual weapons. You could extinguish one type of magic, but the other gods still protected her. Rosalind had only snuffed out the shadow magic.

Rosalind reached behind her back, drawing her sword. She swung it in a rapid arc, slicing through Erish's neck, severing her spine. Crimson blood arced in the air. The queen's beautiful head thudded onto the stone, her body crumpling.

Rosalind swallowed hard, looking down at the body. Erish might look dead, but she wouldn't be until Rosalind carved her heart from her chest. But before she could plunge her blade into Erish's chest, the keres unleashed rumbling growls that trembled over the stone walls. At the sound of the keres springing to life, a shudder ran over Rosalind's skin.

She whirled, gripping her sword and staring at the snarling keres. They prowled forward, teeth bared, and ice inched up Rosalind's spine. She was about to meet the keres' wrath. Raising her sword, she gripped it tight. She needed a spell, but even with the Morrigan's battle fury spell she couldn't kill this many keres. Plus, she didn't want to slaughter Tammi in the melee. She could scuttle up the walls again, but the damned keres could fly.

A line of keres at the front of the horde beat their wings, rising into the air. They were blocking her in.

Rosalind's gaze slid to the wooden door that Erish had used. She pivoted, then broke into a sprint, her feet pounding through the mud. The keres screeched, and Rosalind ripped open the door, slamming it shut. She bolted the iron lock. The keres slammed against it, hacking into the old wood with their claws.

Frantically, Rosalind looked around. She stood in a long, marble corridor. To her right, a stairwell curved up.

Let's start here. She ran up the curving stairwell. She needed to get to the walkway—from there, she might be able to get a better view of whatever the hell Caine was doing, and she'd be able to tell exactly where Tammi was.

Hurrying, she sprinted up the stairs, adrenaline and the battle spell fueling her speed. Seven flights up, she could hear the keres footsteps echoing up the stairwell, pounding against the stone like a hundred battle drums.

She pulled open the wooden door at the top of the stairs, sprinting onto the walkway. A shadow loomed over her, and she glanced overhead. The keres' heavy, black wings whipped the stormy air. The iron gray sky was unleashing a torrent of rain, turning the courtyard into mud.

A loud slam turned her head. The keres had slammed through the wooden door, onto the walkway.

They're here. Rosalind climbed to the top of the battlement, her eyes scanning for Tammi.

A screeching ker swooped in the air above her, and Rosalind caught a glimpse of crimson nails.

With a thundering heart, she crouched down, and leapt.

She grasped Tammi around the waist, and her friend—or what was left of her—screeched, raining punches onto Rosalind's arms. Rosalind held on tight, chanting the teleportation spell, letting her vernal aura charge the air and curl around Tammi in waves of green. Rosalind's body hummed with the spell's power.

In the next moment, they were by the four stakes again.

Screaming, the ker—Tammi—careened for the ground. Just as they were about to make a hard landing, Rosalind reached up and ripped the iron chain from her friend's throat.

They slammed into the mud, tumbling. The impact knocked the wind out of Rosalind. Catching her breath, she pushed herself onto her hands and knees. The strength spell was wearing off, and her entire body was on fire. It took a moment for her to remember what was going on.

Tammi.

Still on her knees, she turned to look at her friend, certain she would see Tammi's familiar blond hair and blue eyes.

But it was a silver-eyed ker who stared back at her, and the only thing Rosalind recognized was the chipped *Rouge Dior* polish on her toes.

CHAPTER 27

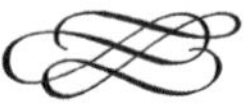

The ker—Tammi—stared at her, starlight beaming from her eyes. The multicolored aura still whirled from her body.

It took Rosalind a moment to remember that she was invisible, and she chanted a spell to bring her body back into view.

But Tammi wasn't looking at her. Tammi was looking down at her black claws, her fingers trembling. She still looked like a ker—yet something about her had changed. Her eyes had a new life to them, and her mouth was opened in distinctly humanlike horror.

Her body groaning, Rosalind stood. "Tammi?"

Tammi continued to stare at herself, turning to try to catch a glimpse of the black wings sprouting from her back. "What the fuck?" she demanded, her voice breaking.

"Tammi!" Relief flooded Rosalind. Her friend didn't look the same —but *that* was definitely Tammi. She ran over to Tammi and hugged her, trying to avoid the black wings.

Her friend's body was shaking uncontrollably. Rosalind stepped away, looking Tammi over. Gods, it was good to see her—even if she looked like a ker. "We can probably get you changed back," Rosalind said. "I'm sure there's a spell…" She trailed off.

Tammi looked down, her fingertips running just below her new breasts. "Are these real?" She stared at Rosalind. "What the *fuck*, though. Am I a monster?"

Rosalind shook her head. "No. You look different, that's all."

Tammi touched her long, pointed teeth. "These will have to go." She splayed her fingers. "And the nails."

"You actually look very beautiful," Rosalind said.

Tammi pulled open the top of her dress, peering down. "I mean, it's not the worst thing but..." She looked up, her features clearing. "What the fuck happened? The last thing I remember was being in a prison in that fortress. And then the succubus... I was really hoping you'd come for me, Rosalind."

Rosalind lifted her shoulders. "Well, I did. Just... not as soon as I should have. I didn't know where you were." Rosalind's legs were shaking, too. All the magic she'd been using was draining the life right out of her.

Tammi glanced at the stakes. "Where are we? Why are we here?"

Ankle-deep in mud, Rosalind began pacing. "We're still in Maremount. I need to go back for Caine and Miranda. I'm not sure what happened to them. Caine was supposed to grab Miranda and destroy Erish, but he never showed up in the courtyard."

Tammi rubbed her temples. "Hang on. I'm extremely disoriented. The last thing I remember was that succubus bitch—"

"—she's creating an army of keres," Rosalind completed her friend's thought. "Do you remember anything that will help me if I go back there? How the magic works, or where they were keeping Miranda?"

Tammi's brow furrowed. "Snippets. Flashes of things..." She shook her head. "I remember more from when I was human in the prison cells. They had us all crammed into cells below the fortress, built into the rock. It was damp down there. Pretty sure some people had trench foot." She hugged herself, shivering. "Anyway, an old woman said she'd overheard the guards talking. Miranda was in one of the towers, but not in a cell like ours. She was heavily protected. Giants, harpies, wraiths—Drew didn't want her getting out." Her silver gaze met Rosalind's. "Maybe Drew was expecting Caine to come for her. From what I heard, he's been building his power. He plays games with people. He lures people into traps."

Rosalind's body tensed. "And you think all this could be a trap? He really seems to hate Caine." She turned, pacing. "Do you have any idea what tower Miranda is in?"

Tammi shook her head. "I have no idea. She wasn't kept with the rest of us. But I know how to find the other prisoners." She took a step closer, her fingers twitching. "There was water flowing in the bottom of the caves. And if I stuck my head between the bars, I could see a tiny little point of light. There's a way in, I think, through the side of the mountain."

"But you said Miranda isn't in there."

"Right, but there are a ton of other people there. Humans who Erish wants to turn into keres. We need to get them out."

Rosalind glanced at the sky, searching for any oncoming keres. "You want us to free all the prisoners?" She shook her head. "That's not our goal. We're there to get Caine and Miranda."

"I saw people starve to death in there. Half of them have dysentery. There's a twelve-year-old girl with gangrene. We can't leave them."

Rosalind's fingers tightened. "We need to find Caine and Miranda first. They could be in trouble."

"The prisoners are definitely in trouble," Tammi said. "And there are more of them, so why wouldn't we help them first?"

"Because..." She couldn't think of a reason. *I don't know the other people* didn't seem like a great rationale. "Because Caine and I came here together, and we're going to leave together. And Miranda's my sister."

Tammi crossed her arms, frowning. "There's only two of them. There are hundreds in the prisons. And if anything happens to us while trying to find Caine and Miranda, those humans will never make it out. Freeing them is the right thing to do. This is two lives versus hundreds. It's simple math."

Rosalind's face flushed. In one of her psychology classes, they'd been asked to discuss a morality problem: if a train is heading for a group of five people on the track, and you can divert the train to a track with only one person on it, should you do it? You were supposed to say yes. It was supposed to be simple math.

But she always hated those kinds of problems, always had more questions that you weren't supposed to ask. What were they all doing there in the first place? What if some of them wanted to die? What if the group of five were a bunch of child murderers? What if she loved that one person and didn't want him to die alone?

Quantities alone weren't enough.

"It's not simple math," she shouted. "If anything happens to us while trying to free the prisoners, we'll never get to Caine and Miranda. There are more factors than just arithmetic that go into deciding whose life to save."

Tammi narrowed her silver eyes. "Factors like being a super-hot incubus who could blow your mind in bed? That kind of factor?"

"No." Flustered, she searched for the words. "Factors like..." *Loyalty.* She didn't know where Miranda's loyalty lay, but she and Caine were some kind of team now.

Still, his admonition rang in her head. *Loyalty is a weakness.* She didn't know what was the right thing to do—but right now, she knew they were wasting time.

"Oh, for fuck's sake, Tammi. Fine. We get the prisoners first. And if we die in the process, I'm going to be extremely pissed off at you in the afterworld."

In the distance, so faint she could barely hear it, a bell began to ring. Rosalind threaded her fingers into her hair, her pulse racing. *This is getting a little more complicated.* "I don't think we can take on an entire army of keres, Tammi. It's nearly impossible to hurt them, even with magic. And if what you said about Drew is true—that he's becoming crazy powerful—I don't think we stand a chance."

"I can see your aura now. Cleo's aura, I guess. It's green."

Rosalind scowled. "Can we stay on topic?"

"That *is* on topic." Tammi folded her arms. "I think that's part of what makes the keres resistant to magical spells."

"What do you mean?"

Tammi rubbed her forehead, closing her eyes as if she was

searching her memory. "We were flying in the sky." She turned, pointing to the clouds. "There. A mission or something... I don't remember what it was, but I remember silver and green swirls of magic coming for us. I could see the magic, and that meant I could control it. I could force it away from me."

"That makes sense." Rosalind bit her thumbnail. Maybe now wasn't the time to tell Tammi she'd been trying to light her on fire. "I've been learning about that myself. And if I can control it... maybe I can send it back where it came from."

Tammi touched her lips. "Want to try a trial run?"

"You know Angelic spells?"

"No," Tammi said, raising her hand. "But like we said, if you can see an aura, you can control it." She stared at her open hand, until a whorl of colored auras formed in her palm. She wound up her arm, and threw it like baseball.

It slammed into Rosalind's gut, and the auras surged over her body, like jolts of electricity. Rosalind staggered. *Gods I need sleep.*

Tammi clamped her hands on her hips. "Not good, Rosalind."

Rosalind shook out her arms and legs. "Okay. I wasn't ready that time. Let's try this again."

Tammi summoned another vortex of colored auras into her palm, and hurled it at Rosalind. This time Rosalind paused it in midair, and the sphere of magic hovered between them.

"Good," Tammi said. "Now send it back."

Rosalind concentrated hard, willing the aura to shift back. It slowly slid back to Tammi, gently bumping into her and spreading over her body.

Rosalind let out a long, slow breath. "That's good, but I don't think that skill is battle-ready yet. I think we need to sneak in as best we can and hope no one sees us. We can blow out the iron bars on the cells—"

A rhythmic noise beat the stormy air above them, and Rosalind's gaze flicked to the skies. Colorful auras swirled in the air around another horde of keres.

Rosalind's heart sped up. "Tammi, the bad news is that the keres are coming right for us. The good news is that the keres are no longer at the fortress."

"Maybe now's our time to go, then."

"I can transport us back to one of the walkways. Can you get us to the prison cells?"

"I think so."

Rosalind grabbed Tammi's hand, whispering the spell for invisibility. Cleo's green aura curled around their disappearing bodies, and Rosalind switched to the teleportation spell, her body shaking with exhaustion.

In the next instant, they flickered to the castle walkway. A sonorous bell—some sort of alarm—rang out.

Rain hammered down, and Rosalind peered over the battlement's edge into the courtyard. Queen Erish's headless body still lay on the ground, her blood mingling with the mud and rain.

Above, the harpies screeched, copper wings beating the air. Tammi grabbed her arm, pulling her up to the battlement. "I think we need to get going now. I think the harpies sense something. Grab hold of me. We're gonna fly."

Unlike the harpies, whose wings grew from their shoulders, Tammi's wings stemmed from her back. That meant Rosalind would have to hang below her as they flew.

Rosalind tightened her arms around her friend's neck, then locked her legs around Tammi's waist.

"Bet you're wishing I was Caine right about now," Tammi said.

"Oh, be quiet," Rosalind shot back.

She could feel the rush of air as Tammi's wings began to whip the air, and they launched off the battlement. Rosalind's stomach swooped as they flew, and she turned her head to see the fortress's pale walls zooming past.

She arched her neck, getting an upside-down view of the mountainous fortress. The slopes beneath the fortress walls were a steep, rocky drop.

The wind howled around them, and she had to shout over it. "Do you have any idea where you're going?"

"I'm looking for the entrance."

Rosalind craned her neck, but trying to survey the terrain from this angle was awkward.

"I see it," Tammi said.

Rosalind felt them dive lower, and the wind whipped hair into her face. Between strands of her own and Tammi's hair, she could see an opening in the side of the mountain, below the fortress. A stream of water poured from the cave to the river below. Rosalind watched the entrance grow larger in her vision as they approached.

"Hang on," Tammi said.

They flew straight into the darkened cave, splashing down in the running stream. In the hard landing, Rosalind let go of Tammi's neck, and the current began to drag her out until she grabbed hold of a jagged rock.

Tammi flapped her wings, straightening in the current.

Rosalind closed her eyes, mentally asking Cleo for the spell for light. The words blazed in her mind, and she chanted a quick spell for the sun spirit. A pale, glowing sphere appeared in the air, lighting up the dank cave.

"You think this is the right way?" Rosalind asked.

"It was the only entrance I saw," Tammi said.

Rosalind pressed forward against the current, her boots sloshing through the water.

Exhaustion was ripping her apart. Soon, she'd need to use another strength spell. But she'd wait until she really needed it. She didn't want to lose her mind by using too much magic when her body was weak.

Just as her teeth were beginning to chatter from the frigid mountain water, the tunnel opened up into large cavern. Here, carved from quartzite, were three chillingly lifelike statues of people dressed in ornate clothing.

Rosalind shivered, looking up at them. A dripping noise echoed off the cave walls. "What do you think all this is?"

"If I had to guess," Tammi said. "They're probably the ancestors of whoever owns this place."

Rosalind shuddered and peered up into the face of one of the statues—a woman with long hair falling over her shoulders in two braids. She had Rosalind's high cheekbones and straight nose, and wore a spiky crown. A long gown draped over her stony body, with a deep V neck and long, wide sleeves that reached the floor. The garments were clearly medieval—these ancestors went beyond the founding of Maremount.

She glanced at the other two: medieval knights with chainmail and swords. There was something eerily lifelike about these statues. Rosalind hugged herself. "I guess there's something I should mention about that."

"What?"

"Drew and I are cousins. This is my ancestral home, and he thinks I'm going to marry him."

"You've got to be fucking kidding."

"Nope. Apparently, Drew and I were supposed to be married." She trudged on. "Drew said my parents were trying to re-establish their dynasty. That they once ruled in another kingdom, a long time ago. Drew wants to pick up where they left off. I think he was homeless or something before he started working for the Brotherhood. And now he fancies himself a king."

"And I thought my family was screwed up," Tammi muttered.

"There's something going on between Drew and Caine that I don't understand."

"You're making it more complicated than it is. Men only ever fight about one thing when it comes down to it. They both want to have sex with you. End of story."

Rosalind shook her head, happy to put distance between herself and the statue. "No. It's more than that. There's more to the history between Caine and my family that he's been hiding it from me. He finally almost told me what it was, and I stopped him. I feel like it's something terrible, and it caused all the shit that's happening now."

"You didn't want to ruin your illusion of him." Tammi's footfalls splashed. "What if you're related?"

"Ew. We are not related."

"Forbidden fruit is the sweetest kind."

"Stop."

At last, the sound of murmuring drifted through the dank caves. Rosalind and Tammi fell silent, listening to faint voices echo off the rocky ceiling.

Their footsteps splashed as they walked into a larger cavern. The statues that had stood so proudly in the rest of the cavern were not to be found here. Instead, rocky ledges jutted out above them. Rosalind glanced up as they walked further into this new cavern; between the stalactites and iron bars, she caught glimpses of people, their hands grasping bars, faces peering down. The faint talking fell silent, and more faces appeared at the bars, staring.

"Here we are," Tammi whispered. "But they won't recognize me. Especially when I'm invisible."

"I can make you visible," Rosalind said. "Even if I can't make you human again.

She closed her eyes, finding the words for the spell, and chanted them out loud. When she opened her eyes again, she was looking right at Tammi. "How far down do you think that drop was to the river?

"A hundred, maybe a hundred fifty feet."

"They should be able to make the drop. I can try to turn them invisible, too. They'll have to make their way to Maremount from here, just following the river. In the center of the city, they need to jump into the fountain. It will take them to Phobetor Field." She grabbed Tammi's arm. "The river flows toward the city. Maybe they can ride the current with branches. I have no idea what the people of Maremount will think of they see a horde of starved humans jumping into their fountain, so they'll need to hurry. The invisibility spell doesn't last forever."

Tammi nodded. "I'm going to speak to them." She flapped her wings, rising into the air. Droplets of water fell from her wings.

Panicking, the people in the cages shifted away from the bars, whispering to each other. If any of these prisoners had seen a ker before, it would have been when they were eating people's necks in Harvard Square.

Tammi held out her hands, like she was taming a wild beast. "Everyone stay calm. We've come to get you out of here. I know I look like a demon, but I'm not. I mean, maybe I am now, but... I was in there with you. Some of you might remember me. Linda, I see you in there. And Steve. And Ben! You knew me as Tammi."

"Tammi?" a voice called out. "What did they do to you?"

"They're turning people into demons. And that's why we're going to get you out of here. You need to take the river—"

Panicked shouts echoed around the chambers, drowning out Tammi's instructions. Someone screamed that her friend was too sick to move, her legs infected.

"Tell them I'll heal them!" Rosalind shouted. "I'll strengthen them. We need to move quickly."

She bit her lip. *Shit.* How was she supposed to quickly conduct spells on hundreds of prisoners? *I need to move this along—fast. If I can see magic, I can control it.*

"Tammi!" Rosalind shouted. "Carry me up there. I can help heal them. Then they need to get the hell out of here before someone discovers us."

Tammi flew lower, and Rosalind wrapped her arms around her friend's neck. Tammi beat her wings, lifting Rosalind out of the water. Craning her neck, Rosalind glanced around at the people stuck in the rocky prison cells. The sphere of light dimly illuminated ragged clothes, gaunt faces, haunted eyes. They stared at her, gripping the bars.

Rosalind swallowed hard. All these people in here were now counting on her and Tammi to get them out of this. "I'm going to open your cells," she said. "I'm going to use magic."

"Witch!" someone shouted.

Oh, right. To everyone in here, magic was the ultimate enemy. Magic was what had led to their capture and imprisonment, to horrific massacres of innocent people. What she needed was some sort of rousing speech to help them understand the complexities of the situation—that it wasn't simply good versus evil, that sometimes things were nuanced.

"I'm a witch," she said, raising her voice. "But I'm a good witch. Like Glinda." *Or I could just reference Wizard of Oz.* "Listen," she continued. "We're going to get you out of here, and that's better than starving to death or rotting from gangrene under a mountain. So, witches or not, we're your best bet."

The prisoners fell quiet, and Rosalind closed her eyes, trying to focus on Cleo's green aura. For the magic she was about to conduct, she'd need a staggering amount of power.

Cleo's magic burned in her chest, a tiny green sphere of light blazing from her sternum. *Cleo, help me open the iron bars. Like we opened the iron for that woman before.*

Cleo whispered, *Ambrose.*

The spell shimmered into her mind, in words emblazoned with light. Rosalind spoke the words out loud, her body vibrating with Cleo's spell. This time, the aura surged like electricity, and she felt a thrilling rush at its power. She concentrated on moving the aura with her mind, branching it out so it curled around all the cell bars. The power flowing from her body felt immense. She was a conduit, letting it out.

She closed her eyes, letting her head fall back, and the aura bubbled up her chest, tingling and brushing over her skin.

As the raw, vernal power ignited, she caught a glimpse of something... A rowan grove, the leaves illuminated by pure, golden sunlight, berries bright as fresh drops of blood. After the shadows grew long like grasping fingers, and the sun dipped below the flowery knoll, he would come for her in darkness. She burned for him...

"Rosalind!" Tammi called out.

"What?" Rosalind's eyes snapped open. Her body ached to the bone. She glanced around at the prison cells. The bars gleamed with a green aura, and they'd been bent wide open in the center—leaving enough room for people to escape.

"You got lost there for a moment," Tammi said. "What the hell was that?"

Rosalind gasped for breath. "I think I was sucked into Cleo's life." Must have been the power of the spell that let Cleo take over.

"You need to keep going," Tammi said, clinging to her. "I think the spell might have alerted someone's attention. Can you heal them?"

The walls around them rumbled, and dust fell from the cavern's ceiling. *Damn right we need to get going.* She didn't want to get caught in another collapsing tunnel. But gods, that spell had sucked the life out of her, and she wanted to curl up in a ball. Nausea welled in her gut, and aches bit at her bones.

She closed her eyes, asking Cleo for help again—this time for a healing spell.

Ambrose, Cleo whispered, offering up a spell.

Rosalind began to chant. Once again, her body blazed with vibrant, leafy power. A stream of green aura poured from her body, and she concentrated on branching it out into each cell, letting it curl around the sick and injured prisoners like shimmering ferns.

No longer tired, she felt a giddy rush light up her body from within. Cleo was here, filling up her chest, sneaking up into her mind, urging her to close her eyes and see…

The night sky blazed over the rowan grove, graven with chinks of light. Cloaked in darkness, he was coming for her over the tall grasses, grasses thick with yarrow and cowslips.

"Rosalind!" Tammi pinched her. "Stay with us. I know this is hard. We just need one more spell."

The image vanished, and Rosalind blinked. Her chest ached with a strange longing at the loss of the vision. Now her muscles were on fire, and she wanted to go back to that cool, beautiful field under the night sky, to see the man who was coming for her.

She glanced around at the cavern—at the prisoners standing in their cells, some of them smiling, a few sniffling. Above, the cavern ceiling continued trembling, and small pieces of rock fell into the rushing water below them.

Just one more spell.

Rosalind closed her eyes, resting her head on Tammi's shoulder while her friend shouted out instructions: jump into the water, follow the river, and leap into the fountain.

As soon as Tammi had finished her instructions, Rosalind asked

Cleo for another spell to turn the prisoners invisible. Power flooded her body once more, and she watched the glimmering green aura unfurl before her. She concentrated on forcing it to curl out, like hundreds of vines unfurling, wrapping around the prisoners.

With the rush of energy, her eyes closed.

She stood with her back to a rowan tree, its leaves rustling in the breeze. Gracefully, he walked in shadows, coming for her. He would run his fingers over her skin, lighting her body on fire with his touch. *Ambrose.* His name filled her with—

A sharp pinch pulled her from the dream. Exhausted, she rested her head on Tammi's shoulder once again, watching as the cavern's water splashed with each invisible prisoner making their escape. *What the hell, Cleo? Leave me out of your weird sex life.* What the hell was this weird obsession with Ambrose?

"Rosalind," Tammi said. "I'm taking us out of here. Something's coming for us."

Tammi turned to fly from the cavern, when up ahead the sound of terrified screams echoed. Curls of multicolored magic streamed into the air. *Oh, shit.*

"I hope you're ready for a fight," Rosalind muttered to Tammi. Her body felt-half dead, and she wouldn't be much good in a fight now. She needed to use one last spell, but at some point, she'd run out of energy completely.

Closing her eyes, she chanted the spell for battle fury, letting her body charge with hot, angry fire. She let go of Tammi's neck, dropping into the water, then pulled the sword from her back and rushed toward the screams.

As she ran into the narrow cavern, her mouth dropped open.

The statues they'd passed were not statues at all. They were *alive* now; their skin and clothing were still the color of sand, but they moved—and two of them were armed.

"Prisoners!" Rosalind screamed. "Run!"

One of the knights ran for Rosalind, his sword drawn. She parried, and their blades clashed, echoing off the rock.

"We will protect the Atherton Dynasty," the knight growled, his voice like gravel. "Loyalty binds us."

"I am an Atherton," she shouted back, her sword clanging against his.

"Traitor," he snarled.

What did he know? She wanted to crush him into gravel, into dust. She wanted to melt him with her fury. But her bones ached already, and the knight began to close in. His blade pierced her arm; blood spurted. Her heart pattered like a hunted animal.

She lunged, driving her sword into the knight's chest before ripping it out again. His stony eyes bulged, and he staggered back, though it didn't look like the blow had killed him. She had no idea how to kill a statue.

Around the statues, the colored auras burned brighter. Her gaze darted to the female, who now chanted a spell, trying to target the fleeing prisoners. Rosalind wanted to grind them to dust...

If you can see the aura, you can control it.

Gritting her teeth, she focused on the woman's aura, freezing it in its path. The magic hung in the air around the woman. While Rosalind was concentrating, the second knight ran for her, slamming a fist into her head. Dazed, she stumbled and fell to her knees, and the knight forced her head under the freezing water. A stream of water ran down into her mouth, and for a second her throat convulsed.

Panicking, she struggled against him, gripping her sword below the rushing water. With all her effort, she forced herself up again until her mouth breached the surface. She gasped. Just before the knight could force her head under again, she swung her sword in a wide arc, cutting through his legs.

He fell into the water.

Rosalind rose, coughing up water, listening to the shouts of the escaping prisoners. She could feel some of them brushing against her as they ran.

And now it was time for her and Tammi to make their exit.

Tammi flew over, reaching out, and Rosalind wrapped her arms around Tammi's neck. Tammi beat her wings, carrying Rosalind above the fleeing prisoners who splashed through the water.

Rosalind's body felt torn between complete exhaustion and the remains of a power rush. Her limbs shook violently, and nausea welled in her gut. Had she really seen Ambrose in her vision? Where had *that* come from?

Rosalind chanted the spell for invisibility, as they approached the cave's mouth.

Tammi soared into the open mountain air, circling over the river. "That was amazing, Rosalind. You're one hell of a good witch."

"Thanks."

"I have no idea where to look for Caine, by the way."

Rosalind closed her eyes. She still had no way of knowing if she'd made the right decision or not. If Caine and Miranda had been killed while they were freeing the prisoners, it would gut her.

They swooped around the mountain, and Rosalind's hair whipped into her eyes, obscuring her vision.

"Rosalind." Tammi's voice held a hint of panic. "I can see Caine. And it doesn't look good."

CHAPTER 28

*R*osalind pulled her hair out of her eyes and craned her head, trying to get a glimpse, but all she saw was a steep rock wall, overgrown with some vegetation.

"What's happening?"

"I'm taking us to the summit, near one of the towers. Caine is there. With Drew. And Miranda."

Rosalind's chest tightened. *Fuck.*

Tammi dove lower, and the wind rushed over Rosalind's skin.

She arched her neck, catching a glimpse of a wide ledge, about thirty feet across. She could see Drew and Miranda; Miranda's arms were bound behind her back. "Where's Caine?"

"Chained to the cliffside, wrapped in iron."

Rosalind's stomach turned. "What the fuck?"

"I'm going to drop you off on the cliffside, by Drew. Maybe you can take his legs out with the sword, or whatever you need to do. I'll swoop down and try to free Caine."

"I can do this," Rosalind said. She just needed to take out one person, and she'd already beaten him once.

"Get ready for a hard landing," Tammi said. "I'm still not that good at this."

As they drew closer, Rosalind craned her neck again. For just a brief moment, as they approached the cliff, she caught a glimpse of Caine. He hung, bound to the cliffside, shirtless. *What the hell is going on?*

There wasn't time to mull it over. She braced herself, and in the next minute she felt herself tumbling onto a rocky ledge, tangled up in Tammi's limbs.

When she rolled onto her back, pulling herself out of Tammi's grasp, Drew was staring right at her. He chanted a spell, his colorful aura bursting from his hand. Instantly, Rosalind and Tammi were visible again. Just as she'd said she would, Tammi leapt off the cliff's edge. *Good. She's going to help Caine.*

Rosalind stared at Drew. He took a step over the rocky ledge, picking her up by the shoulders and slamming her up against the wall. Pain wracked her spine. The battle fury spell was wearing off faster this time, and Cleo's aura needed time to recharge.

Drew leaned into her, whispering into her ear. "I guess I underestimated your treachery. I've got your lover now. He will have a slow death. Just like Azazeyl, who didn't deserve it. I wanted Miranda to watch, too. I think she has a certain fondness for him, just like you."

Rosalind glanced to her right, hoping to see Tammi carrying Caine in her arms. Instead, she caught a glimpse of the harpies heading right for Caine.

Her legs felt weak. "I don't understand. Who is Azazeyl?"

Drew tightened his grip on her arms, his thumbs pressing into her wrists. This wasn't much of a fight so far, but the aura felt dull and weak in her body; her tendons ached. "You'll understand his power soon. I'll drive it into you."

She glanced to her right again, horror twisting in her gut as she watched a harpy dive right for Tammi. The harpy ripped Tammi from the cliffside, grasping onto her arms with her talons.

Okay. Time to get those spells going again. She mentally asked Cleo for the battle fury spell, and the words blazed in her mind. But as soon as she opened her mouth to speak, Drew clamped a hand over her mouth, pressing her hard against the rocky wall. "I think you need a reminder of Azazeyl." Drew whispered into her ear. "I think you need a reminder of a lot of things, Rosalind."

He began chanting, his spell tingling over her body, crawling over her skin; the skin on her stomach began to burn, and hot pain ripped her gut open. She screamed into his hand, then bit his fingers, hard.

He snatched his hand back, roaring. With all her remaining energy, she slammed him in the stomach with her foot. He staggered back, and she launched into the battle spell. As she finished, her strength surged like molten lava through her veins, burning away the pain where Drew had seared her skin. The battle fury raged, hotter than before, like a dying star.

I want blood.

The image of Ambrose in the rowan grove flickered into her mind, and she blinked it away. *Not now, Cleo.*

She pulled the sword from her sheath, but Drew held out a hand, enveloping the sword with his magic. It shook in Rosalind's hand, no longer in her control. Trembling, she concentrated on the magic, trying to force Drew's auras away from her sword.

But Drew could see magic, too, and he'd had more practice.

The sword flew from her hand, soaring over the cliff's edge, and her rage ignited. She needed to kill someone. Cleo's wild green aura ran wild, curling inside her skull.

Ambrose walks in darkness. He is coming for me...

"Not now, Cleo!" she shrieked.

Drew rolled his shoulders, ready to fight with his hands. "Careful, Rosalind. You're losing your mind. Just like Miranda and Caine."

The rowan trees were on fire... *He made me burn one night.*

Rosalind gritted her teeth, clearing her mind. "I don't need a weapon to fight you, Drew." Battle fury rattled her body, and she clenched her fists. She kicked him in the head, listening to the crunch of bone. He staggered back.

I was waiting for him one night, but it wasn't Ambrose who came for me.

"Shut up, Cleo!" she shouted, trying to push the dark grove from her mind.

When her vision was clear again, she was staring at Drew, who chanted a battle spell of his own. Rushing for her, he slammed her into the rock once again, with what seemed like enough force to shake the mountain. Her bones sang with pain. He punched her in the face, and it felt as if her skull splintered.

The stars burned like graven diamonds... What did I do to deserve this, Ambrose?

Drew gripped her by the shoulders, throwing her to the ground.

Already, she could feel the battle fury fading from her body, leaving behind the gnawing pain and an overwhelming sense of grief. Powerlessness. Before she had the chance to push herself up again, Drew was on top of her, crushing the breath out of her. He gripped her wrists, forcing them against the rocky ground.

"You don't know how to control that magic. It's driving you mad, you little fool. I can see it in your eyes."

Lightning cracked the cloudy skies above. Overhead, an eagle screeched, diving for the cliffside.

Grunting, she tried to get him off her, but Drew gripped her tight. His eyes blazed. "Perhaps it's time that you learn what your lover did before my eagle eats his guts from his body."

Panic slammed into her. "I don't care what he did," she choked out, staring at the eagle, diving for Caine.

"I tried sending you the images, but you refused to pay attention. You were there, Rosalind. You should have remembered."

Her heart beat hard in her chest, but all the fight was ebbing out of her. There was something about his words, the key to unlocking that caged memory.

Rosalind stood by the shore, staring at the four stakes. Caine grabbed her, forcing her up against the rotten wood. He plunged the iron nail through her heart. But he wasn't finished—there was a man there, too, screaming.

Her eyelids flickered, and the realization punched a hole through her heart. It wasn't her future. It was her past.

Drew's face reddened. "Caine killed the one true king and queen. Not the ones in the history books. Not the king and queen hundreds of years ago—though he slaughtered them, too. A demon like him can't stand for any human to be worshipped above him."

Drew's words pierced her to the bone, and she simply stared at him.

"Caine murdered the *true* king and queen. The Atherton line. He slaughtered your father and your mother before they had the chance to establish their rightful kingdom, blessed by Azazeyl. Caine drove iron nails right into their hearts while you watched, left them to bleed to death on the stakes. And I will build my kingdom on their bones."

Horror knocked the wind out of Rosalind, and she opened her mouth to speak, but no words came out.

"You were there, Rosalind!" he shouted. "I tried to remind you in your dreams, but you don't have a fucking clue, do you? Now he wants to make you his whore, to destroy the last of the Athertons—and you've played right into his plans. Your faulty memory is the only reason I haven't already slaughtered you for your disloyalty. You're an Atherton, Rosalind. Loyalty is supposed to bind you."

Sorrow choked her, and she closed her eyes. *My mother and father.* She couldn't remember them even now—apart from their deaths.

Her gut churned, and she glanced out at the stormy sky. Tammi was still out there—trapped on the losing side of an aerial wrestling match with a harpy. In fact, it looked like the harpy was choking the life out of her. Rosalind didn't know where the eagle had gone, but Drew had just ripped her heart out and thrown it into the chasm.

She could remember it all so clearly now—Caine stabbing her mother. She remembered every drop of blood spilling from her parent's chests. She just didn't know why.

Her gaze slid back to Drew. The fact was, she *knew* what he was up to. He'd been helping the Brotherhood slaughter humans. He'd allowed Erish to imprison hundreds of people, starving them and turning them into keres. He'd nearly destroyed Tammi completely.

As Rosalind looked out into the roiling skies over the chasm, she stared in horror as the harpy let Tammi drop, unconscious.

One last blast of frozen rage gave Rosalind strength, and she brought her knee up, hard, into Drew's groin. His eyes bulged, and she grabbed him by the back of the hair, thrusting up her hips and pulling him off—letting go right over the cliff's edge.

She rolled onto her hands and knees, her body wracked with pain. Swallowing hard, she peered over the cliff's edge, the blood rushing from her head. She caught a glimpse of a sheer cliff face—no Caine in sight.

Just before her vision blurred, she was in the rowan grove once more, waiting for Ambrose.

osalind's eyelids flickered open, and she rolled onto her back, trying to get her bearings. *I'm not in a gods damned rowan grove. I'm in Maremount.*

Her gaze landed on Miranda, who stood with her arms behind her back, still gagged. She wore one of those iron necklaces, and her eyes looked glassy.

Rosalind groaned. She felt as if she'd died and only come halfway back to life. A sharp pain pierced her head, and she swallowed her nausea. Cleo's starry night sky flickered in her mind, and she forced the image away, trying to remember what had just happened.

A jolt of fear tensed her muscles. *Tammi.* What had happened to her? She sat up, glancing out into the chasm. Her gaze landed on Drew—carried into the sky by one of his harpies.

But when she looked down, she saw him. *Caine.*

He'd grown enormous, black feathered wings—like a raven's—and he was flying up from the river. Tammi lay in his arms. Her head drooped, but her chest rose and fell. She was still alive.

Caine—the angel of death, the demon who'd murdered her parents. Dread coiled around her at the sight of him. She could remember him now, that day when the earth had shaken below her feet. She could remember the ferocity in his darkened eyes when he drove the nail through her mother's heart.

Miranda screamed and screamed.

That stake, the one where she'd been kissing him… bile rose in her throat, and she retched.

Never trust Nyxobas's demons, Cleo's voice whispered in her mind.

As Caine approached, she pushed herself away from the cliff's edge on her backside, too tired to stand. She wanted to put distance between herself and him.

He will betray you, Cleo whispered. *He's just like Ambrose. Run from him as fast as you can.*

Caine landed on the cliff's edge. Rain ran down his tattooed chest. "Your little boyfriend Drew laid a trap for me. I'm just glad you came back to stall him before that eagle made a dinner of me." He frowned, watching her carefully. "What's happened to you?"

She shook her head, unable to get any words out.

He gently laid Tammi down on the cliff's edge. "How much magic have you been using?"

"I remember now," she said at last.

His face seemed to pale, and his wings folded into his back, disappearing. He reached out, as if to stroke her face, then lowered his hand. "You remember."

"The four stakes. I was there. It wasn't me or Miranda. It was my mom that you killed. And my dad."

Something flickered in his eyes for a moment, then his face hardened. He stood, crossing to Miranda. He pulled the gag from her mouth.

When he ripped the necklace from her throat and chucked it over the cliff, she gasped.

"It was nothing they didn't deserve." Gritting his teeth, he pulled apart Miranda's iron chains.

Miranda blinked, staring at her sister. "Rosalind's mind is splitting in two."

"Why did they deserve to die?" Rosalind screamed.

Don't trust a shadow demon, Cleo urged. *They cloak the truth in darkness. You know this.*

Caine glanced into the stormy skies, and Rosalind followed his gaze. A cloud of keres was approaching, flaring with colored magic. The sight knocked a glimmer of clarity back into Rosalind's mind. "We need to go," she said. She couldn't stop the trembling in her hands.

Caine lifted Tammi from the ground again, nodding at Rosalind. "I'll come back for Erish. I'm going to bring her to Ambrose in chains, like he asked."

Ambrose... Rosalind tried to stand, forcing herself onto her feet.

Miranda crossed to her, crouching down. She slipped an arm around Rosalind's back, helping her up.

Rosalind leaned in, resting her head on Miranda's shoulder. Caine and Miranda chanted the teleportation spell. Miranda's briny scent filled Rosalind's nose, and Rosalind let her eyes close.

Her mind whirled with images of a rowan grove outside a sandstone manor house. *Ambrose knew I worshipped Druloch, the forest god, and he brought me a wreath of blackthorn and forget-me-nots.*

She was dimly aware of Miranda's arms around her, holding her as they plunged into icy water. It bit into the wounds on her stomach.

Ambrose told me he'd come for me, but it wasn't he who came for me over the fields...

Her head breached the water's surface, and she gasped, breathing in the floral air near Phobetor pond. A storm raged here, too, and dark clouds churned in the sky. Rain hammered down on them, pounding the lake. Rosalind kicked her legs, using what was left of her strength to swim to the shore. Her stomach felt like an open wound.

Caine carried Tammi in his arms, and laid her down in the tall grasses.

Rosalind crawled on her hands and knees, clutching her stomach. Whatever Drew had done to her, the pain was eating into her like acid. Kneeling on the rocky shore, she yanked up her dress, not caring who was watching.

She pulled the dress over her head, tossing it on the ground, and stared down at her stomach, at the sigil seared into her flesh by Drew's magic. It was the same sigil Drew had given to Orcus, the one that had bound her in the cemetery.

Her fingers trembled as she touched the edges of the burned skin. *What has he done to me?*

Caine rushed over to her, kneeling by her side. "The mark of Azazeyl," he said. His fingers gently traced over her waist.

Don't let the murderer touch you, Cleo whispered in her mind.

Rosalind recoiled from him, pulling away. He clenched his jaw, rising. "Let your sister heal you, then."

Miranda was at her side in the next moment. She chanted the healing spell, and her blue aura washed over Rosalind's skin like water. Slowly, the spell leached the pain from Rosalind's body, rejuvenating her muscles—but a deep, pounding fatigue still sapped her energy.

Her gaze landed on Caine, and a sharp crack of lightning lit up his face and his chiseled body. He stared down at her, eyes cold as winter. He was beautiful, the angel of death. He'd murdered her parents while she watched. He'd known all along what had happened to them, and he'd never said a thing.

Rosalind stood. *I have to get out of here. I have to get away from Caine—he's not Caine. He is Death.*

She walked over to Tammi, pulling her toward the water.

"Where are you going?" Miranda shouted.

Go to Ambrose, said Cleo's voice. *Find my lover.*

Rosalind grabbed Tammi under the shoulders, pulling her back to the water's edge.

"What are you doing?" Caine bellowed.

She ignored him, her gaze flicking to her sister instead. "I'm going to Lilinor. You can come with me if you like."

Miranda stood by the death spirit's side, shaking her head *no.*

Rosalind didn't need him to use the portal now. Cleo would take her there. *Take me to Ambrose, Cleo. Just like you wanted.*

Rosalind began chanting the spell to open the portal, and Cleo's aura whirled around her body, filling the air with the scents of the forest.

The pond swirled with black shadows, and Rosalind dragged Tammi into them, plunging into the darkness.

CHAPTER 30

A strong pair of arms lifted her from the fountain, setting her down on the floor.

Rosalind turned onto her front, coughing up water onto the black marble. When her lungs were clear, she turned to look at Tammi, at her friend's chest, which slowly rose and fell.

She pushed herself up onto her hands and knees, and craned her neck to look up at Ambrose.

That image flickered in her mind: Ambrose standing in the silvery light of the rowan grove.

He's here, Cleo whispered to her.

"You were supposed to come for me," she said, "but you sent the Hunters instead." Her legs shaking, she forced herself to stand. She wouldn't be on her knees before him. "You gave me a wreath of blackthorn."

Ambrose's eyes widened, his body going very still. He didn't say a word.

She stepped closer to him, grabbing him by his shirt. Her wet hands left dark imprints on his pale blue shirt. "I came back for you."

"Rosalind." His gaze lowered to her bra. "You need to put on your ring." He gripped her wrists. "You are Rosalind. You've dragged an unconscious ker into my room, and I'd like to know what the fuck is going on." Anger tinged his voice.

Right. An unconscious ker. Tammi. She closed her eyes, trying to force the wild aura tighter and tighter. She was no longer quite sure what she was doing here in Ambrose's room.

She reached into her bra, pulling out the iron ring Caine had made for her. For the first time, she noticed something engraved in the interior. An Angelic word, and with Cleo's help, she could translate it: *warrior.* She slid it onto her finger, and the wild green tendrils faded. "Sorry, Ambrose," she stared at the Vampire Lord, her legs shaking. "I needed a lot of magic to get out of Maremount. I wasn't thinking clearly."

"You're lucky you've been given permission to enter the White Tower, or you would have drowned in that portal."

She let out a long slow breath, her thoughts slowly clearing, and realized suddenly that she was still wearing only her bra and underwear. "Sorry for the interruption."

His cold gaze raked over her. "I don't like interruptions, but at least you're naked and unarmed."

Her body was trembling, and she felt like a complete lunatic. Still, even with the ring on, she could feel Cleo's presence roiling in her mind. It should be gone by now, but Cleo wanted Rosalind to reach out and touch Ambrose's black shirt.

"Now is the time for you tell me what's going on," Ambrose said.

"I used too much magic." She hugged herself, shivering. "We collected Miranda from Maremount. She was being held prisoner by Drew. She's with Caine now, but I think she'll join us here."

Ambrose's eyes roved down her body again. "Why is Azazeyl's symbol burned into your skin?"

"Drew did that to me. Something about The One Who Is All. We're allegedly descended from him."

Ambrose drew his finger across his lower lip. "He believes in that legend?"

"Apparently if I drink from Blodrial's veins, I could have his powers, too." Rosalind closed her eyes, rubbing her throbbing forehead. "There's more you need to know. I decapitated your wife, but didn't rip out her heart. Caine was going back for her. He'll bring her in chains."

The corner of his mouth twitched. "And why isn't Caine with you?"

"I left him by his tower." Right now, she wanted nothing more than dry clothes and a bed. "I found out that he—" She stopped herself. Ambrose didn't need to hear about what happened to her parents. "Never mind. The important thing is that Drew is still out there. I tried to kill him, but a harpy saved him."

"And you came to find me because Cleo brought you here."

She shook her head. "Not just that. I want to fight the Brotherhood. I want to fight Drew. If we allow them to join forces—Drew and the Hunters, military strength and this new type of magic—they'll enslave us all. We won't have a chance. I want to help make your army of daywalkers. I don't have a great history with vampires, but I prefer most of you to the Brotherhood these days."

Ambrose brushed a strand of hair from her face. "All I ask for is your loyalty."

* * *

SHE AWOKE in silky sheets the color of pewter, fighting her way out of dreams of Ambrose and wreaths of blackthorn. She rolled over, gazing at Tammi. Her friend slept by her side, snoring lightly, black wings folded peacefully behind her. Faint bruises shone on her neck, but apart from that—and her new, demonic appearance—she seemed to be fine. Healthy, even.

Something shifted in the room—silk rustling against velvet—and Rosalind sat up. Miranda lay curled in an ivory armchair, stirring in her sleep. Rosalind hadn't heard her come in. *Ambrose must have brought her here.* Like Rosalind, she wore a new, clean gown of ivory silk.

Rosalind blinked, trying to clear her mind. She'd been half-asleep when she arrived in this room, and had barely taken in her surroundings. The walls were a deep midnight blue, glimmering with flecks of white. A jasmine-scented breeze filtered in through arched windows, and stars burned bright in the midnight sky.

When she looked at Miranda again, her twin was watching her, her brown eyes burning with curiosity. Miranda rose, stretching her arms above her head, and crossed the room. "You're awake." She sat on the edge of the bed. "How are the voices in your head?"

Rosalind studied her sister. They were nearly identical, apart from the tiny mole on Miranda's right cheek. "Her name is Cleo. She hates shadow demons, but she wants to screw Ambrose. They have some kind of history."

Miranda frowned. "I don't know as much about mine. He's a man. And he hates Hunters."

"I guess you've been through all this before."

Miranda nodded. "The people I lived with tried to make me wear iron, but I didn't like how it made me feel, and my other soul didn't like it at all." Her brow crinkled. "My adoptive parents only spoke to me about Blodrial. They said he would purify my soul. But I wouldn't drink the blood."

"You were sent to live with the Brotherhood, too?"

Miranda nodded. "I ran away when I was fifteen. And I took off the iron ring."

"Where did you go?"

"Sometimes I lived in the woods. Sometimes I slept in the streets. I ate the food people left over, and I found ways to stay warm in the winter. I had a sleeping bag. Sometimes my second soul spoke so loud, I couldn't hear my own thoughts…" She let out a sigh. "I looked for you for years. I thought we could live together, like we used to. Like, maybe we could've built a house in the woods. I didn't know you were a Hunter."

"That's why you came to Thorndike University."

"I was so sure I was close to finding you." Miranda's features darkened. "And then the Brotherhood found me. I always hated Hunters. So did my second soul."

Guilt pierced Rosalind's chest. "That was my fault. I didn't know who you were. I just sensed an aura."

"The Hunters kept me chained to a chair, and sometimes they drowned me with cloths and water. They cut my skin, and wanted to watch as I healed myself. They wouldn't let me sleep. Josiah told me that I needed him. The other guard used to stick iron nails into my knees and calves, and Josiah said he'd make it stop. And he did, as long as I did what he wanted. I thought I needed him."

Pain tightened Rosalind's heart. "I'm so sorry."

Miranda's face cleared. "But after Josiah died, I cleared my mind again. I took the iron off. I was looking for you again when Drew found me. He took me to Maremount."

"Did he hurt you?"

Miranda shook her head. "No. He treated me well. I had food, and a soft bed. But he wasn't going to let me leave."

Rosalind swallowed hard. "Do you remember what happened with our parents, and with Caine?"

Miranda blinked, shrugging slightly. "He killed them."

"Why?"

Miranda's brow furrowed. "Don't you remember, when Caine was like a wild beast? But he was beautiful, and I used to bring him food. Him, and the other beautiful man. I never brought you down there with me. I wasn't allowed down there, and I thought you'd get scared. You always got scared easily. You had nightmares."

Rosalind's chest tightened. Miranda wasn't making sense. "What other man?"

"The other one. He was injured, with iron in his body. Just like when we saw Malphas in the Chambers. He didn't speak." She scratched her cheek. "Malphas wasn't in chains. He was only a boy. He liked you. I don't know why. You were never nice to the servants."

Rosalind frowned. "I've heard that before. I was a brat, I understand." The skin on her stomach still smarted, and she rubbed it gently. "I don't understand. Why did our parents have Caine and Malphas? And why did Caine kill them?"

Miranda shook her head. "He said he needed to stop them."

"From what?"

"They wanted to recreate the Atherton Dynasty. The One Who Is All ran through our veins—but then it was all over, after Caine killed our parents. That's when the king sent us out of the city. He was scared of our magic."

The only person who could really answer her question was Caine himself. "Where is Caine?"

"Here in Lilinor, in his own room."

He won't tell you the truth, whispered Cleo. *Shadow demons lie.*

Rosalind blinked to clear her mind of Cleo's voice, and traced her thumb over her iron ring. "Miranda. I'm wearing the iron now, but I can still hear Cleo's voice."

"You have two souls, now. You'll have to get used to it." Her twin pushed a lock of hair from her eyes. "And you should go back to sleep, or her voice will eat you alive."

Miranda rose, crossing back to curl up in her armchair. Rosalind lay down again in the soft pewter-colored sheets, her gaze on the open window.

She stared out at the night sky, graven with chinks of light—drawn to its vastness, its clean, cold silence.

You belong here, Cleo whispered to her, *cloaked in darkness, with me.*

Rosalind's fingers curled around the sheets. It didn't matter if she was in the dark because now, she was no longer alone.

BLOOD HUNTER - BOOK THREE

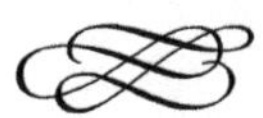

CHAPTER 1

Rosalind pushed through a tall oak door, leading to the Gelal Field just outside Lilinor's walls. The waxing moon hung in the sky like a god's eye, washing the shadowy landscape in silver. Even though she'd been in Lilinor for two full weeks now, she still hadn't become accustomed to the utter dominance of the moon over the kingdom.

A perfect home for creatures of the night.

But it was Caine's home. Not hers.

Her footsteps crunched over a dirt path. Lined with myrtle trees and sycamores, it meandered down a hill in gentle curves. The wind rustled through the leaves; nearby, a raven cawed.

In the crook of one arm she carried a wicker basket. She'd filled it to the brim with fresh-baked corn muffins, butter, and a jar of honey. Steam from the muffins warmed her arms as she walked, a small smile curling her lips. The idea of sneaking out of the castle thrilled her—plus tonight would nearly resemble a normal night. Food, wine, gossip. What more did she need?

At least she had her friends here in this city of darkness. She was supposed to meet Tammi and Miranda at the old Temple of Nyxobas. Aurora had said she might stop by, too.

Since arriving in Lilinor half-dead, Rosalind had hardly seen her friends—and that was probably because she hadn't wanted to leave her room over the past two weeks. For one thing, she'd been avoiding Caine. Whenever she thought of him, the first thing that sprung into her mind was his divine beauty. The softness of his kiss. The gentleness of his fingertips over her skin.

And the second thing to spring to mind was the image of him brutally slaughtering her parents while she watched.

The cognitive dissonance was a little too much for her to handle.

But it wasn't just Caine that kept her locked in her room. She also had to deal with the lunatic spirit in her head—Cleo, her batshit-crazy second soul. Since Rosalind had fought her cousin weeks ago, Cleo's voice had only grown louder. And the iron ring no longer kept her quiet.

Half the time, Cleo's thoughts drowned out Rosalind's own. Mostly, Cleo begged to see Ambrose, to touch the vampire lord. And when she didn't want to touch him, she wanted Rosalind to light him on fire.

And yet … out here, in the fresh air, her second soul had mostly muted. Maybe, when insomnia and Cleo's thoughts ripped her mind apart, she could creep out to nap among the bluebells and sycamores.

Rosalind inhaled the rich scent of jasmine and followed the curving path that wound down the hill. Her silky gown slid against her legs as she walked, and she pulled a black cashmere shawl tighter around her shoulders. At the bottom of the hill, she spotted the stone ruin—a forgotten temple—and her pace quickened. Somewhere in there, Miranda and Tammi waited for her.

As she neared the arched doorway, a murder of crows took flight from one of the crumbling towers. Shivering, she crossed into the temple—if it could still be called a temple. The ruin no longer had a roof, and moonlight washed over tall grasses and wildflowers.

"Rosalind!" Miranda and Tammi called out in unison.

Rosalind grinned. "Hello, my dears!"

Miranda and Tammi sat below an arched window, with a spread of food laid out before them: cheese, bread, grapes, a bottle of wine, and a few glasses. Around the blanket, bluebells and white poppies dappled the grass.

Rosalind joined them on the crimson blanket, folding her feet beneath her. "I'm starving. Sorry I'm late."

Tammi straightened, flicking her pale hair behind her shoulders. "Not to worry. I've been drinking all the wine."

From her seat on the grass, Rosalind surveyed the old hall. Only three walls remained, and six cracked columns formed a sort of aisle. Vines clung to the stone surfaces, as if trying to reclaim nature's territory.

Miranda leaned over to hug her, enveloping her in the scent of the ocean, and Rosalind smiled. *This is what it's like to have a sister.* "Have you been waiting long?" Rosalind asked.

"Only ten minutes," Miranda said.

Rosalind dropped her basket in the center of the blanket. "I brought some muffins."

Tammi shook her head, frowning. "I'm not hungry."

Miranda wore a wreath of wildflowers threaded with seashells. She picked up the bottle of wine, and filled a glass, handing it to Rosalind. "How's your extra soul? Is Cleo still messing with your thoughts?"

Rosalind groaned. "A little obsessed with Ambrose's dead body. The woman needs a cold shower."

"Or maybe she needs to get laid," Tammi said.

Rosalind frowned. "Not gonna happen here."

"Ambrose might be technically dead," Tammi said, filling her own glass, "but he *is* hot as hell. I wonder if he likes sharp teeth and creepy, empty eyes."

"Oh, stop," Rosalind said. She eyed Tammi's hair—the pale blue of starlight—and her glimmering eyes to match. "You're not creepy. You look beautiful, honestly."

Tammi's eyes lingered on Rosalind for just a little too long. Her friend's body went completely still, and she ran her tongue over her teeth.

Rosalind looked away quickly. *Okay, that look was a bit creepy.* Shaking it off, she turned to her twin. "What do you think of Lilinor?"

"It's beautiful." Miranda plucked a bluebell, and began threading it into a poppy's stem. "But I'm not sure we belong here. Apart from Aurora, most of the vampires can't look at us without thinking about our blood."

"I know," Rosalind said. "That's why I suggested we meet up outside. In the palace walls, there's always a vamp sniffing around."

Tammi emitted a low growl.

Okay. That was creepy, too.

Miranda pulled a seashell from her pocket, threading the poppy's stem through it. "All the vampires resent us."

"Us? Why?" Rosalind asked. "We're neither as glamorous nor as powerful as they are."

Miranda tied a pair of stems in a knot. "Haven't you noticed? Human women are here only as servants. As courtesans. Nothing more. Demons are supposed to use us. Not work with us like equals. And we have the ear of the king."

Tammi twirled her glass. "Honestly, the three of us don't belong anywhere. You're both an unholy combination of mage-spirits and gods-blood. I'm some kind of human-demon abomination created through your family's unholy magic. None of this was meant to be. Basically, we need our own world at this point."

It was true—they didn't really belong anywhere. Yet somehow, with Tammi and Miranda here, Rosalind felt like she *was* at home. Even here in the city of night, where everyone wanted to drink their blood.

"I feel like I belong with the two of you," Rosalind said. "Both of you are my family, and that's all I need to be happy. As long as we can avoid dying at the hands of vampires."

Miranda plucked another wildflower. "After we serve our purpose here, we'll just have to make our own tiny little kingdom, the three of us. We'll get a little house by the water, and we'll build a magical shield around it, and we can sit around reading books. I can paint land-scapes. You can…" She frowned at Rosalind. "What do you like to do?"

"I used to be into demon hunting. Guess I need a new hobby."

"I'll read romances and sew amazing dresses for us," Tammi said, brightening for a moment.

Miranda pointed at Rosalind. "Muffin-baking. That's your new hobby. You bake the muffins, Tammi reads to us by the fire, and I can paint portraits of us all. Caine can visit us if he wants. He's a demigod with an extra soul, so he's an abomination, too."

Tammi raised her glass. "We will call it Abominatonia! Only the godsforsaken may enter."

Rosalind bit into one of the muffins, relishing the buttery taste. "I don't bake muffins. Ambrose has instructed Caine's fae cook to send us these." Every day, an aggrieved vampire showed up at her door with a steaming basket of meat pies, bread, cheese, and pastries.

"This is from Caine's cook?" Tammi asked. "Another reason to invite him to Abominatonia."

"No," Rosalind said sharply.

"Why not?" Miranda asked. "He's just like us."

"Um, because he crucified our parents in front of us?"

"Oh, that." Miranda waved a dismissive hand. "Well, they did ruin his life. They chained him to a wall in the basement for a year."

Rosalind's heart clenched. "True."

"When our parents gave him the extra soul, he went insane." Miranda shook her head. "And our parents ruined *our* lives too. For years, anyway. We could have been together that whole time. We could have had a family. But they were mad for power. So maybe they got what they deserved."

Tammi sipped straight from the wine bottle, then wiped the back of her hand across her mouth. "And I thought my family was screwed up."

Miranda reached out, touching Rosalind's hand. "Well, we have each other now. Let's not dwell on the past."

Rosalind smiled faintly, her thoughts circling back to Caine. *Maybe he had a good reason to kill my parents.* They'd chosen to imprison a shadow demon—a demigod, in fact—and they'd nearly destroyed his mind. Of *course* a demigod would seek vengeance. That's what demigods did when they were wronged.

Still, it didn't change the fact that he had a disturbing habit of keeping the truth hidden. He'd known all along what had happened to her parents, and he'd never told her. And clearly, he was still keeping his darkest secrets buried deep. What terrible revelation was coming next?

From outside the temple walls, the faint tinkling of bells whispered on the wind. The sound sent a shiver up Rosalind's spine.

CHAPTER 2

ootfalls made her turn her head, and she saw Aurora crossing the grass with a silver flask in her hand. She wore a beautiful nectarine dress that hugged her slender figure. "There you are."

"Aurora!" Rosalind smiled. "I'm glad you could join us."

Aurora took a sip from her flask. "Sometimes I forget this place is here. No one worships in the temple anymore."

Rosalind pulled her shawl close, still listening to the tinkling bells. "What's that noise?"

"What noise?" Aurora asked.

"The bells." Rosalind held up a finger until she heard it again. "There. Did you hear it?"

"Oh." Aurora nodded at one of the half-collapsed walls. "The Garden of the Dead. I've *got* to give you a tour. It's right over here."

Rosalind stood. *The Garden of the Dead. Now this I need to see.*

Aurora led her to another tall window, open to the air.

As Rosalind approached, her gaze landed on a moonlit cemetery. She clutched the crumbling stone windowsill, gazing out at the small necropolis. Crooked, old statues of angels and dragons jutted from the ground. Scattered around the cemetery stood yew trees. Even from here, she could see flecks of color decorating their boughs.

"The garden of the dead," Aurora said in a hushed voice. "When you hear the bells, it's the spirits, speaking to us."

The hair rose on the back of Rosalind's neck. "Who is buried here?"

"Courtesans, mostly, but some vampires too," Aurora said. In a heartbeat, she was over the windowsill. "Let me show you."

Rosalind followed after—landing not quite as gracefully, dust clouding around her.

Aurora started down an old gravel path that meandered between the graves, and Rosalind hurried to catch up. As they walked, the sound of tinkling bells grew louder.

Aurora pointed to an ornately carved obelisk towering over most of the other stones. "That's Old Willard's grave. From what I gather, he was a sexy little minx in his prime. The personal concubine of Lady Albintheen."

"How did he die?" Rosalind asked.

"Of old age. Lady Albintheen kept him youthful by feeding him her blood. But there's only so long that can go on. Eventually, his heart finally gave out over his dinner of lamprey pie."

"Right."

Before Rosalind could ask another question, Aurora was already hurrying toward another cluster of graves, surrounded by a small iron fence.

"These are the Aspinwall Sisters." Aurora shook her head "Mind you, they weren't actually sisters. Everyone called them that because they dressed identically. Same hair. Same clothes. Same makeup. Same knickers. The vampire they served, Otto Aspinwall, had a bit of a thing for twins."

"Oh." Rosalind grimaced. "Is he still alive?"

"Nah. Quite tragic, really. Otto was obsessed with his twins. Loved their blood. Loved the weird role playing twincest shit they did. And one night, when they got him a little too excited, he totally lost control to the blood-hunger. Drained them both. He was inconsolable for weeks. Then, he just gave up and went through a portal to the sunlight."

Rosalind winced. "Charming. I didn't know vampires committed suicide."

"Not often."

Rosalind ran her fingers over a rough stone, webbed with moss. "So, are there funerals for the dead concubines?"

Aurora shrugged. "For the ones who were loved. They get funerals and gravestones, and the rest are... sort of jumbled together in unmarked graves."

"And what are the funerals like in Lilinor?"

"They're called feasts of the dead. The ceremony opens a gateway to the afterlife, so the dead don't end up trapped in the House of Shades." She turned to Rosalind. "Others give their souls to Nyxobas, and they get stuck in the shadow hell—especially those who die at the hands of a vampire. Bottom line: don't take a vamp as a lover. It tends to end in death."

"Surely death among the vampires isn't permanent?"

"It usually is. Ambrose doesn't permit the creation of new vampires without his permission. And Caine doesn't allow bone-conjuring or necromancy."

They neared a strangely enormous yew. Great boughs, large as tree trunks, curved over them in a canopy. Ribbons and streamers, now faded by the weather, hung from them like Spanish moss. Keepsakes decorated every branch: ribbons and jewelry, tiny framed pictures, notes and letters. Some of them hung intertwined with the ivy that snaked around the trunk. Tiny, silver bells hung from the branches.

A breeze puffed the branches, and the bells rang softly in the darkness. Rosalind shivered. *The dead may whisper to us, but we can't know what they're saying.*

Under the canopy, Aurora reached up to pull down a blue ribbon, tied to an old skeleton key. She unfurled it, and read out loud. "Samuel Stocktown."

"Another concubine?

"I have no idea. Most people buried in this cemetery get their name hung from a branch. Some are vampires, killed in battle or by the sun. And some are human, like you." Aurora pointed to a large mound. "But most humans are buried there, in the common grave. No one remembers their names. Humans die so easily."

Loneliness welled in Rosalind's chest, and a cold wind whipped over her skin. Under the tinkling bells, a faint scratching noise rose floated on the breeze. "What is that scratching?"

"Ah. Those are the vamps Ambrose buried alive." Aurora shot her a sharp look. "So don't go digging around the roots of the yew, unless you have a death wish. Though I kinda get the feeling that you do, sometimes."

Rosalind's mouth went dry. Suddenly, she had a strong urge to get away from the terrible noise. She turned back to the gravel path that lead to the Temple. "Let's go back to the muffins and wine. This place is giving me the creeps."

Miranda was right: humans could never be at home here in Lilinor. Maybe humans and vamps were equal in death, but not in life. As far as she could tell, humans were basically here as sex slaves. And every now and then, a vampire might lose control to his blood-hunger and suck one dry.

If she and her friends stayed in Lilinor too long, there'd be nothing left of them but a few ribbons and bells on a yew.

Ambrose... Cleo whispered. *Touch me again...*

"Shut up, you lunatic," Rosalind muttered.

"I didn't say anything," Aurora said. "You talking to the voices in your head again?"

"If only there was some way to get Cleo so drunk she would just fall asleep."

"Why don't you just give her what she wants?"

"Sleeping with Ambrose, you mean?"

"Sure. Why not? I'm sure he'd be game."

Rosalind's nose crinkled. Apart from the fact that Ambrose creeped her out, she was pretty sure that wouldn't be enough for Cleo. Cleo wanted her to slaughter him, too. *Best leave that part out.*

At the top of the hill, Rosalind climbed through the windowsill. As they crossed the grass to Tammi and Miranda, she hugged her shawl closer. The cemetery had totally unnerved her, like she'd seen a certain vision of her future.

Still, the sight of her sister gently threading a wildflower wreath calmed her nerves, and she pushed the memory of the graveyard to the back of her mind.

Aurora plopped down on the blanket. "I misjudged. I don't think Rosalind liked the Garden of the Dead."

Rosalind sat next to her, then snatched up her glass of wine. "As much as I enjoy visiting dead courtesans, the sounds of vampires scratching in their coffins was a little weird."

"You need to be careful," Miranda said, still working on a wreath. "Sometimes, what's buried doesn't stay underground."

Rosalind sipped her wine. "Maybe we should choose a new picnic spot next time. Not sure I like eating cheese next to a mass grave for prostitutes. Nothing against prostitutes. It's just a little sad. No one even remembers who they are, or what their lives were like."

"And where do they bury the abominations?" Tammi's red nails dug into the flesh of her arms. She was definitely not handling this demon thing well.

"Are you okay, Tammi?" Rosalind asked.

"I'm *fine*," Tammi said through clenched teeth.

Miranda threaded a final wildflower into a seashell, then lifted the wreath, handing it to Tammi. "This will ease your mind."

Visibly relaxing, Tammi ran her fingers over the petals. "It's pretty."

Miranda dropped the other wreath on Rosalind's head. "And this one's for you. I can make another for you, Aurora. The bluebells will bring peace to your heart and mind. The ivy is for Druloch, Rosalind's lord. The white poppies are for the god of night. Aurora and Tammi's god."

Maybe it was a placebo, but with the wreath on, Rosalind felt her muscles relax. She let out a slow sigh. "And what are the seashells for?"

"Those are for Dagon, my god. They tie you to me." Miranda

smiled. "You see? Drew wants you to be his queen. He wants a magical Stepford wife. But this is the only royal crown you need."

Rosalind shivered at the mention of her cousin. She could only hope she'd never see Drew again, or she'd end up his obedient little slave.

Tammi's hands tightened around her own wreath, her knuckles white. "Erish still haunts my dreams. Her face hovering over me as she turned me into a demon in Drew's castle. I hate Drew just as much. I really want to rip out his throat. I *need* to feel his hot blood run down my chin, down my throat." She breathed deeply, in and out through her nose. Her silver eyes drilled holes in Rosalind.

Aurora leaned back on her hands, staring at Tammi. "I think I know what you're feeling."

Tammi's vision seemed to clear, and a horrified look crossed her face. Clutching the wreath, she rose and sprinted off toward the castle without saying another word.

Rosalind stood. "What was that?" she asked, more to herself than to anyone else. Something told her not to run after her friend. Tammi needed to be alone.

"That," Aurora said, "was blood-hunger. Guess she really does have a demon body."

CHAPTER 3

*H*ugging herself, Rosalind padded down a dark hall as quietly as she could. Candlelight danced over the flagstones; every flicker of light and shadow seemed to make her jump.

In the rest of the world, daylight was the most powerful protector against vampires. But in Lilinor, a land of eternal night, the vamps had free reign in the shadows.

Granted, Ambrose had given the vampires strict orders: anyone who harmed the human mages would suffer a traitor's death. Rosalind wasn't clear *precisely* what a traitor's death involved, but it probably involved an initial round of medieval torture, followed by a living burial in the Garden of the Dead.

But shadow creatures had ways of committing their worst deeds under the cloak of darkness, when no one was watching, so Rosalind wasn't taking any chances. She'd hidden anti-vampire weapons all over her body: hawthorn stakes strapped to her thighs, iron knives in sheaths under her dress.

Miranda was right: the vampires *did* resent them. Rosalind had seen a few too many bared fangs and darkened eyes as she walked past. And it wasn't like a human could go unnoticed here. In fact, as she walked past each of these doors, the vamps inside would be perking up their ears at the sound of her beating heart. Their nostrils would hungrily sniff at the scent of her sweat, the blood pumping beneath her skin.

And just maybe—when she got to Tammi's room—her friend would be just as eager for her blood.

But Rosalind was going to stop by anyway. Tammi had no clue how to fight, so Rosalind wasn't too worried for her safety. And Tammi needed a friend now more than ever.

As she walked down a particularly dark hallway, a door to her right slammed open. Rosalind whirled. There, just inches from her, stood a platinum-blonde vampire. Blood dripped down her chin onto a white gown, and her eyes blazed red. "I thought I smelled something."

"Sorry, lady. I'm off limits. Ambrose's orders."

The vamp snarled. She didn't look like she wanted to back down. *Blood hunger.*

Rosalind's muscles tightened, and she turned to walk on. Before she could take another step, the vampire grabbed her by the hair, dragged her into the room, and threw her down hard on the stone floor. Rosalind's knees smacked onto the flagstones, and she fell forward onto her hands.

Rosalind reached for one of the stakes at her thigh. Just as she lifted the hem of her dress, the vampire picked her up again—this time by her throat—and slammed her against the wall. Powerful fingers pressed into Rosalind's neck, cutting off her air.

A dark-haired male vampire stood behind the blonde, his expression almost bored. "Whose courtesan is this?"

Rosalind kicked the female in her ribs, and the vamp dropped her. In the next second, Rosalind had a stake gripped firmly in her fingers. Slowly, she straightened. *I really don't want to fight two at once, but I will if I have to.*

"I'm no one's courtesan," she said through clenched teeth. "Like I said, I'm off limits."

The male vamp stepped closer, running a long finger over Rosalind's shoulder. "You're not dressed like one of the whores."

Rosalind stepped away from him, grimacing. "That's not why I'm here. I'm a mage. I work with Ambrose and Caine."

The female bared her fangs. "Ah. She's one of the humans Ambrose is forcing vampires to serve." She spat on the floor.

The male growled. "I'm a lieutenant in Ambrose's army. I'm one of his trusted advisors. I will not fetch your sandwiches, little girl."

Rosalind clutched her stake tighter. These two vamps seemed a little jacked-up on blood, or perhaps meth. "Okay, well, thanks for the chat. I'm going to be on my way."

The female took another step closer, boxing her in. "You must think you're pretty special, little human. Traipsing around with the king and our general like you're someone important. But deep down, I promise you, Caine and Ambrose don't think of you any differently than they do the other human whores. When they're done using you, you and your sister will be working in our harem, or buried under the ground. Just two more bodies for the whore pit."

The male grinned. "Esmerelda. You do get feisty after drinking." He nodded at a passed-out girl, propped up on a chair.

Rosalind's stomach tightened. "Thank you for your concern, but after I'm done with Ambrose, I'm out of here."

Neither of these vamps seemed particularly worried about the hawthorn stake in Rosalind's hand.

"Believe me," Esmerelda said, her eyes burning red. "Caine, Malphas, and Ambrose have been through many human females, and all of them thought they were special. None quite as arrogant as you, but that will make your downfall all the more delicious." She leaned in closer, stroking Rosalind's hair a little too forcefully. "I know Ambrose said I can't kill you, so I won't. But I want you to know that demigods like Caine and Malphas see you as nothing more than tits and ass."

The male frowned. "What else is there to human females? Besides the blood, I suppose."

Esmerelda patted Rosalind's head, like she was a dog, and smiled sweetly. "If I were you, I'd make sure your door is locked tight at night, or you might find yourself splattered across the cobblestones.

Just like you did to that ker queen." The smile faded from her lips. "Let's go, Darren."

Esmerelda turned, stalking out of the room, and Darren followed.

"Darren is a stupid name for a vampire!" Rosalind called out after them. *Okay, so I don't always come up with the best comebacks.* She leaned back against the wall, then slipped the stake back under her dress. *Best to give Esmerelda and Darren a few minutes to clear out before I cross into the hall.*

While she waited, she surveyed the enormous, octagonal room: the tangle of bloodstained bedsheets on the four-poster bed, the gargoyles in arched alcoves. Starry lanterns hung from the ceiling. Then her gaze returned to the pale form slumped in an armchair, and she jumped. *I forgot there's someone else in here.*

Rosalind took a step closer, eyeing the vampire—no, a human. A curvy brunette, dressed in cherry-red high heels, a black corselet. Blood dripped down her neck, and white powder dusted the tops of her breasts.

That would explain why the vamps were so jacked up.

Rosalind stepped closer. Was she even still alive?

Leaning down, she tapped the woman's shoulder, but she didn't move. "Hello?" She lifted the girl's chin. Slowly, sleepy green eyes opened. Rosalind held the girl's chin up, so she wouldn't pass out again. "Are you okay?"

Drowsily, the girl straightened. "Where are Esmerelda and Darren?"

"They left."

She pressed a hand to her throat. "Oh, thank god. They nearly drank me dry. They're supposed to replenish me with their blood after, but frankly I'm glad they left. They get a little out of control after a few lines."

Rosalind glanced at the white powder. "Right. They seemed a bit excitable."

The girl's eyes drifted closed again.

"Do you need medical help?" Rosalind asked.

The girl straightened, blinking her eyes. "Sorry. I'm kind of tired."

Rosalind frowned. "Seems like a dangerous line of work."

The girl shrugged. "You get used to it."

"Feeding the vampires?"

"Yeah. I'm just hoping the incubus takes a shine to me instead of the vamps." She blinked her eyes. "He doesn't require blood. I've never seen him, but I heard he's super hot. And he's, like, a demigod. Only thing is, everyone seems to fall in love with him, which is kind of sad."

Rosalind schooled her face into disinterest. "He's fond of courtesans?"

"Aren't all demons? They're bred to use our bodies. It's in their DNA—or whatever demons are made of."

"Right."

The girl held out a hand. "I'm Bridgette."

Rosalind took her hand, smiling. "Rosalind."

Bridgette arched an eyebrow, taking in Rosalind's silky gray dress and the plunging neckline. "They let you dress like that? In a fancy gown, like a vampire?" Her forehead crinkled. "How come I haven't seen you in the harem?"

"I'm not a courtesan."

Bridgette's eyes widened. "So what are you?"

"A mage. Sort of. But I don't think I'll be staying here forever." Rosalind cocked her head. "Where is the harem anyway?"

Bridgette sighed. "They keep us below ground, near the armory. That's how little they're threatened by us. They don't even lock up the weapons. Then they send for us when they need blood or sex. We're not allowed to roam freely." She hugged herself, shivering. "And I'm constantly freezing, since vamps don't understand heat—or that, like, sometimes it's nice to wear sweatshirts and pajamas. They always have us dressed in this crap." She snapped the top of a sheer thigh-high stocking.

"How long have you been here?"

Bridgette bit her lip. "Let's see, two years? Right after I graduated from college."

Rosalind's eyebrows rose. "So… how did you end up here? Was it your choice, or were you abducted?"

"My choice. I graduated from college with, like, over half a million dollars of student loan debt, and an art history degree that no one seemed to care about. I couldn't even get a job at Starbucks. And I felt like, I'm either gonna jump out a window or join the demons. Probably not the best decision I ever made." She hugged herself, her eyes glazing over. "Sometimes I see the courtesans leave the harem, and they just don't come back."

Rosalind had a pretty good idea why. *More bodies for the whore pit.* "Aren't you scared of the vamps?"

"They're not supposed to kill us, but only because they think of us as a limited resource. It's not like they have empathy. I guess most of them are no worse than a drunken frat boy, apart from the blood drinking." She rubbed her arms. "Ambrose is different than most. He terrifies me. He just walks into a room and I want to run the other way. There's something really dark about him."

Ambrose, Cleo whispered. Rosalind could feel her body responding to the name, her skin warming. "Can you change your mind? And return home?"

Shivering, Bridgette rubbed her arms. "Are you kidding? They're very secretive about Lilinor." Her eyes glistened in the dim candlelight. "I'm never getting out of here alive."

"Maybe there's a way around it."

Bridgette smiled sadly. "I like your optimism, but I think I'm stuck here. Still, you're a mage, right? If you ever figure out a spell to fix the weird alpha male shit going on in this place, I'll owe you big time." She bit her lip. "Not sure how I'd pay you back, except I make really good red velvet cake."

Rosalind smiled. "Don't underestimate the allure of red velvet cake." She pulled off her cloak, handing it to Bridgette. "Here. Keep yourself warm."

Bridgette's brow crinkled. "Are you sure?"

"Of course. I've got more, and you're freezing down there. Take it."

Bridgette smiled, wrapping the shawl around her. "Thank you. Come visit us some time, if you can."

Rosalind smiled, turning to the door. "I will."

She crossed to the door. As she pulled it open, a sigh slid from her. She was living among people who viewed humans as a sort of subspecies. A resource. Slaves, even, who should walk around in skimpy underwear and live in a freezing basement—and above all, keep their mouths shut.

How many courtesans had Caine entertained over the years? And did he really think of her the same way? As a toy to use and discard when he was done?

Her fingernails pierced her palms. *Why does it matter?* It wasn't like Caine was her boyfriend—far from it. Their shared history was dark and twisted.

Yet she felt herself drawn to him, like a magnetic pull that tugged at her core. In fact, as she walked farther down the hall, she glanced at the painting of Lord Byron. The route she'd taken to Tammi had led her right by Caine's room.

The hair rose on the back of her neck. Had that been an accident?

Or am I as enthralled by Caine as Cleo is by Ambrose?

CHAPTER 4

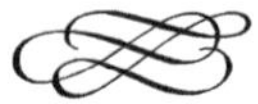

$\mathcal{A}$s she drew closer to Caine's room, the shadows seemed to thicken around her, climbing up the walls. The temperature dropped, and goosebumps rose on her skin. In the sconces, the candle's flames waned, nearly snuffing out.

He's here.

She considered turning to run, but something stopped her. That magnetic pull, she supposed. Pulse racing, she hugged herself and took a few steps back, pressing her back to the wall. The cold stone bit into her skin through her thin gown. *Maybe I can just hide in the shadows.*

A silver aura, scented of thunderstorms, twisted past her. She froze.

As Caine turned the corner, his icy eyes bored into her.

She swallowed hard. *So much for hiding in the shadows.*

A faint smile curled his perfect lips, and he slowed his gait. His soothing aura caressed her bare arms, warming her body. As he moved toward her, electricity seemed to charge the air between them.

This is what it feels like to be in the presence of a demigod. She'd been avoiding him for weeks, and seeing him so close felt like a punch to the chest.

Her breath caught in her throat as she took in his stunning contrasts: The dark lashes that framed his pale eyes. Sharp cheekbones above the gentle curves of his mouth. Soft skin over steely muscles.

Standing so close to Caine was an exquisite sort of pain, a sharp heat deep in her chest.

It would be so easy just to reach out from where she stood against the wall, and touch that beautiful face, to feel his skin, to press herself against his body.

So easy to kiss his perfect lips, to drag him into his bedroom and rip his clothes off, to feel his hot mouth against hers.

And that is probably what all those courtesans thought—the ones who fell in love with him. She tightened her fingers into fists to stop herself from reaching for him.

Her throat tightened. How many other women had thought they were special to him over the centuries? She'd be an idiot to ignore what Esmerelda had said. *I will not be just another body for the whore pit.*

You have interesting desires, Cleo whispered. *You want to bed the man who murdered your parents?*

Rosalind's heart skipped a beat, and she sucked in a breath, trying to gain control.

Caine studied her carefully. "Have you been waiting for me, just outside my room?"

She shook her head. Heat raced through her body, and she could hardly think straight.

He looked amused. "Your pulse is racing. Something wrong?"

She swallowed hard, willing her heart to slow down. Yes, she wanted him—but she didn't want him to realize how badly. It would give him too much control over her. She schooled her face to calm. "My pulse is always fast. It's a medical condition. Anyway, I was just walking past your room."

"So this little encounter is purely a coincidence." He arched a disbelieving eyebrow.

"I'm on my way to see Tammi."

"You've been avoiding me. Until now, when you've come to my room with your heart racing."

Rosalind's forehead crinkled. "Don't be ridiculous."

"You couldn't avoid me forever, whether you wanted to or not. Tomorrow, Ambrose wants us to work on the daywalker spell. You, Miranda, and me."

"Fine."

He cocked his head, owning her body with his gaze—up and down. "I see you're well-prepared for a fight."

She crossed her arms. *How does he know that?* "Can you see through my clothes?"

"I could if I concentrated—and it's a tempting thought—but I don't need to. I can see the outline of the weapons strapped to your thighs." He brushed his fingertips over the hilt of one of her knives.

She glanced down at his hand, her heart beating frantically. Had she never noticed before the strength in those large hands? She could imagine them tracing up the inside of her thigh…

She tightened her jaw; her cheeks warmed. *Get a grip, Rosalind.*

She was pretty sure Cleo was making this harder than it needed to be. "I need the weapons. Despite Ambrose's edict, the vampires aren't fond of me."

"Of course. You were a Hunter."

"That, and Ambrose has told them to bring me food, like they're my servants. I know how they think of humans—we're supposed to be slaves, dressed in lingerie. Some of the vamps apparently think we exist to fulfill every demon desire."

He narrowed his eyes. "Do you view any of them in particular as a threat?"

"I don't think so. They seem well-aware of Ambrose's edict. But they believe my place is in the harem, and they're particularly affronted about the muffins."

"Would you suggest that Ambrose stop sending you food? I do remember how lustfully you attack your meals. I can't imagine you turning them away."

"Let's not be drastic," she said. "Ambrose can keep the food coming, and I'll just keep the weapons strapped to my thighs."

Even as she struggled for control of herself, a new idea began to form in her mind. She wanted Caine. Badly. And maybe there was a way to use that desire to her advantage…

A seed of an idea began to germinate, taking root in her mind. Was it Cleo's thought, or her own?

A wicked smile curled Caine's lips. "Why do I feel like you have a second option in mind?"

Her chest heated. A vision bloomed: Caine's fingertips running up the inside of her thigh as she sat draped over his lap. She wore nothing but lacy, black underwear, and her back arched as he stroked her skin, his fingers moving higher and higher up her leg...

Her heartbeat thundered, so loud she was certain the entire hallway could hear it. And she was sure Caine could see the blush creeping into her cheeks.

Still, that one tempting idea began to bloom in her mind. Let the damn vampires think she was a courtesan—Caine's courtesan. After all, wasn't it an advantage to let your enemies underestimate you? Caine had taught her that.

She couldn't quite decide if it was genius, or if she was driven by Caine's overwhelming beauty. But the more she thought it over, the more it seemed to make sense.

She exhaled slowly, and tried to compose her thoughts. "The other option is that I let them think I'm a courtesan, I suppose. Just to stop them from deciding they need to kill me. Let them think I'm as harmless as any other courtesans—the ones who live by the arsenal of weapons no one bothers to lock up."

His eyes darkened, and heat radiated off his body. Just standing near him was turning her on. Her obvious arousal was embarrassing, and more than that—it was drawing out his incubus instincts.

Cleo's aura stroked her ribs. *Tell him what you want him to do to you —where you want him to touch you.*

Rosalind licked her lips, staring up at Caine. "Maybe they could think I was your courtesan. To play down my real power."

Boxing her in, he pressed his hands to the stone wall on either side of her head. He smelled amazing, and she had the strongest impulse to press her mouth against his neck.

"Is that really what you want?" he asked.

Excitement prickled over her skin, and she took a deep, steadying breath. His sweater was a thin, gray wool, and she wanted to stroke his muscled chest under the fabric. *Where do Cleo's thoughts end and mine begin?* Surely she hadn't been this crazy before Cleo had started taking up real estate in her mind.

She gazed up at his perfect face. What was the point in denying herself? "I think it's a good idea."

Her stomach fluttered. Could he see right through her?

Caine lowered his face to hers. "And what do you want me to do to you?" he whispered.

"You know," she said.

"I want you to say it out loud."

His powerful aura licked at her skin, and heat shot through her. Already, her back was arching. *Sweet heavenly gods, I'm in trouble.*

"Just kiss me, in front of the vampires." She swallowed hard, trying to think clearly. "It's only for their benefit, of course."

He leaned in closer, his breath warming the side of her face. "I see. We need the vampires."

His magic curled from his body, reaching down the corridor in silver tendrils. Within seconds, the hallway doors creaked open. Vampires began creeping into the hall, slipping through the shadows like ink through water.

Dozens of gleaming eyes locked onto Rosalind.

"We're not alone now," Caine whispered into her ear.

Her pulse was racing out of control, and she tried to slow her breathing. Her skin grew hot. She was getting dangerously turned on, and she had the mortifying feeling that Caine was enjoying his control over her.

He leaned in, skimming his teeth over her throat. At the contact, her thoughts became muddled. All she could process was that her legs seemed to be opening against her will. Slowly, he trailed kisses up her neck, until he stared into her eyes once more. There was a certain ferocity in his gaze, and she was sure he was holding back.

He ran his thumb over her lower lip. "Tell me. You want me to kiss you properly?"

Cleo's aura simmered. *Why are you denying yourself what you want? You'll be dead someday. Get it while you can.*

Oddly enough, the dead mage's words made a strange amount of sense. "Yes," she said simply.

His gaze slid over her body, as if he were mentally undressing her.

Then, he traced his fingertips down her arms and gripped her wrists. He raised them above her head, pinning them to the wall. Helplessly, she gazed up at his cold gray eyes, completely mesmerized. Her blood roared through her veins.

So this is what it feels like to be in the thrall of an incubus.

Caine leaned down, pressing his warm lips to hers. His kiss grew hungry, his lips parting, and a low growl rose from deep in his chest. As he kissed her, his grip tightened on her wrists, as if he was losing a little of that control.

His muscled body pressed against hers, and she opened her mouth to him. His tongue brushed against hers, and fire shot through her belly.

As his mouth claimed hers, she lost all sense of time and space, no longer sure where her body ended and his began, only that she wanted more of him.

Slowly, he ran his hands down her arms. His hands skimmed lower over her body, until he was grabbing her ass and pulling her closer into him.

She needed more of him, didn't even care that they were standing before a crowd of vampires.

Just when she thought she could no longer remember how to speak, he pulled away, with a nip at her lower lip. Her legs turned to liquid.

Caine took a deep breath, his eyes now black.

Rosalind wanted to strip off her dress right there and throw him to the floor. *Gods, I need him now.*

He stared into her eyes. Soft as a feather, his fingertips skimmed up her body again, sending shivers through her. The gentleness of his touch was pure torture. She'd seen him fight before—brutally, viciously—and she'd never have expected such a predatory creature to be capable of such a soft touch.

She gasped as he traced his hand higher, grazing her breast over her silk dress. Her breath hitched in her throat.

This was a strange sort of agony. She wanted him now, wanted to wrap her legs around his hips, and yet he moved so painfully slowly, like he had all the time in the world.

Gently, he trailed his thumb just over her hardened nipple. The silk strap of her dress slid down her shoulder, and he leaned in again, kissing her neck. A dizzying warmth surged in her as he grazed his teeth along her throat.

A low moan escaped her throat, and she felt his muscles tense in response, like he was struggling to keep control.

She needed the hardness of his body pressing against her. She was ready to beg him to run his tongue all over her body.

She wrapped her arms around his neck, opening her eyes. Over Caine's shoulder, her gaze landed on Esmerelda. The vampire eyed Rosalind with a satisfied smirk.

Suddenly, Rosalind's stomach tightened.

Another body for the whore pit.

The phrase rang in her mind, and Rosalind's cheeks burned. *Gods below.* At the sight of Esmerelda, her blood cooled instantly.

As Caine raised his face for another kiss, she forced herself to tilt her head away. She desperately wanted his mouth on hers again, but one more look at the redhead dampened her excitement.

She'd needed them to underestimate her, but she wasn't sure she wanted to subject herself to a full blown display of humiliation in front of Esmerelda.

"I should go," she managed.

A tendril of hair stuck to her damp cheek, and Caine brushed it away.

His breath warmed the shell of her ear. "If you don't want them to think you've got above your station, you need to let me end our encounter. Don't take this personally." He brushed his thumb over her collarbone again, then whispering, "Don't take this personally."

Casually, he released his grip on her, stepping away. With a completely composed expression, he sighed. "On second thought, I'm not in the mood."

Rosalind could feel herself turn red, and she pulled up her dress. The vampires stared at her, eyes wide. Surely her heart was beating loud enough to entice all of them. Suddenly, she had a deep desire to crawl back into the shadows and hide.

And there was Caine, cooly strutting away, completely unruffled. Like he did this all the time.

And, realistically? He probably did.

Esmerelda snickered behind her hand, and Rosalind crossed her arms in front of her chest. A large blond male leered at her hungrily, licking his lips.

Time to go, she thought.

Just as Rosalind took a step to leave, Caine pivoted, glaring at the vampires. "You do realize she belongs to me. I might not be using her now, but she is mine alone. Only I may touch her. Is that clear?"

Rosalind's head was spinning, and she could hardly string a coherent thought together.

As she hurried away from the vampires, she stared at the floor, ignoring Esmerelda's victorious smirk. *Nothing more than tits and ass,* she'd said. *I hope you can lay off now, Ginger Vamp.*

She shivered as she stalked down the hall, away from the hungry eyes of the vampires. *Well, that's not how I expected my night to go.*

Could she blame Cleo for that little episode? If she didn't find a way to get control of Cleo's influence, her second soul would drag her into a whole lot of trouble. The woman clearly had no boundaries.

CHAPTER 5

Outside Tammi's door, Rosalind took a deep breath, trying to forget the feel of Caine's fingertips skimming over her skin. When her pulse had slowed to a nearly-normal rate, she knocked on the door.

Her muscles tensed as she waited for a few moments. *How do you ask your best friend about her blood hunger?* This was definitely a situation she'd never had to handle before.

She knocked again, a little louder. After a few more moments, the door swung open. Tammi's eyes were wide, blazing like stars. Her long silver hair tumbled over a thin black dress. Her skin was milky white.

"What?" she asked irritably.

Nothing, just...do you want to drink my blood? Rosalind cleared her throat. "You ran off quickly at the picnic, so I just wanted to see how you were doing."

"I'm not in the mood to be around other people." Tammi crossed to a small dressing table, and sat on a stool in front of it. She narrowed her eyes at her own reflection, her entire body tense.

Rosalind stepped inside, glancing around the room. Steel-gray fabric draped over the bed, and candles flickered from a chandelier.

The dressing table stood against the stone wall, complete with a mirror. Tammi sat in front of it, gazing at her own reflection. She picked up a hairbrush and began brushing her tresses. "I'm not the same anymore," she said with a low growl.

Rosalind sat at the edge of Tammi's bed, her fingers curling around a blanket. "Not the same how?"

"Not the same," Tammi snarled. "Hungry."

Rosalind's mouth went dry. "Maybe I should go—"

Tammi's face contorted with rage, and she flung her hairbrush at the looking glass. She whirled, lunging for Rosalind. In the next moment, her teeth were on Rosalind's throat.

Without thinking, Rosalind flung her friend off, then punched her in the jaw.

Tammi stumbled back, a shocked look on her face. Rosalind stood, holding out her hands to the side. *Easy, girl.* Tentatively, she took a few steps back toward the door. She had plenty of sharp demon-hunting weapons, but she didn't want to use them on Tammi —nor did she particularly want her throat ripped out this evening. "I don't want to hurt you, Tammi. I'm just going to walk out of the room."

Apparently no longer capable of human speech, Tammi growled. Her sharp teeth glinted in the candlelight.

Rosalind took another step back. *Easy does it. Nearly at the door.* If she made any sudden movements, those pointed teeth would end up buried somewhere in her flesh.

Tammi snarled, and the sound rumbled through Rosalind's gut. *Not really Tammi anymore.* She took another step back, and spoke in her most soothing voice. "I'll just leave you to… brush your hair and stare in the mirror. Everything is fine."

She fumbled behind her for the doorknob until her fingers touched the silver. *Got it.* She turned the knob and yanked open the door. *Freedom!*

But just as she stepped into the hall, Tammi lunged again, knocking her to the stone floor.

"Stop it!" Rosalind lifted her hips, grabbing Tammi by the hair to pull her off. She rolled on top of her friend, pinning her arms to the floor. Tammi roared, baring her teeth.

"I said stop it!" Rosalind yelled. "Get a hold of yourself, woman!"

Tammi blinked, as if suddenly awaking. Slowly, her fingers unclenched from Rosalind's hair.

Footsteps echoed off the ceiling, and Rosalind looked up. Darren was walking toward her, flanked by two blond male vampires. The blonds looked distinctly like medieval Danes, with braided beards. They strode on either side of him, carrying spears.

"I thought I heard a kerfuffle." Darren's voice rang off the stone ceiling. "Is it just me, or was this human supposed to remain unharmed, under orders from Ambrose?"

"Not just you, sir," one of the Danes said. "She's one of the mages."

Rosalind released her friend's wrists, and Tammi rose slowly. Rosalind saw only fear on Tammi's pale features now.

"It's okay," Rosalind said. "Everything is under control." She stood, smoothing out her gray dress.

Darren stepped closer. "What's wrong with your ker friend? And what on earth is she doing here? I thought we killed all the keres."

Tammi crossed her arms. "I'm not a real ker. I was human, but some dickhead turned me into a ker. And now I want..." She ran her tongue over her teeth. "I have different cravings."

"Of course," Darren said. "Blood hunger?"

"Do keres drink blood?" Rosalind asked.

"Sometimes." Darren sniffed, wiping the back of his hand under his nose. "They don't require it. But this one isn't really a ker, is she? She's a new creature. A human given a new life as a demon."

Tammi's face fell. "Just like a vampire."

Darren looked at her. "If I'm not allowed to hurt the human whore, then you certainly aren't. What are we going to do with you?"

Rosalind glared at him. "She's new to this. She doesn't know how to handle it, but she'll get things under control."

Darren steepled his fingers, looking to the ceiling while he considered the situation. "Novice demons like Tammi are unpredictable and volatile. They must be trained. There's a place for them—the Abzu.

I'm sending her to speak to Ambrose, but I imagine he'll send her on to the Abzu."

Rosalind frowned. "How long would she have to stay there?"

"As long as it takes for her to gain control of her impulses. There's a cleansing ritual, some training. A novice must prove herself before she is released. Hard to know how long that will take." He sniffed again. The cocaine seemed to have irritated his nose. "Not everyone has the self restraint that I do."

Tammi crossed her arms. "Will I get blood there?"

"Yes."

She ran her fingertips down her chest, still eyeing Rosalind hungrily. "When do I go?"

Darren nodded at the two Danes. "Aldrich and Rodney will take her to Ambrose."

Without so much as a final glance goodbye, Tammi stalked down the hall, barefoot. Aldrich and Rodney hurried to flank her.

Darren's gaze turned to Rosalind, slowly taking in her body. He stepped closer, his gaze lingering on a tear in the shoulder of her gown. "I've heard that Caine has claimed you as his concubine, and no vampires may enjoy your womanly delights."

Rosalind's stomach turned. *Gross.*

She took a step to move around him, but he blocked her path. "I'm not finished speaking to you." He seemed transfixed by the torn dress, and he ran a long, pointed tongue over his lips. "Have you noticed that the most beautiful things are also the most fragile? How tempting it is to touch that which breaks easily."

Okay... "Right. I actually have to go somewhere else now."

Darren stared down at her. "Aren't you supposed to be working on a daywalking spell? I thought that was your whole purpose here."

"You're one of Ambrose's trusted advisors, aren't you? I'm sure he's filled you in."

Darren tapped a long finger against his mouth. "He's been promising us that spell for a while, and yet I haven't seen anything materialize."

"Maybe I don't like the idea of demons like you having more power than you already have."

She'd read about what could happen when humans meddled in nature. When wolves hunted caribou, they culled the weak. If humans tried to protect the caribou by shooting the wolves, it backfired. Diseases spread and took out entire herds. Any major changes to one species could mean devastation to another. Nature had its own balance.

"What are you talking about?" he scoffed. "We're *meant* to dominate humans. That is nature's way."

"Maybe vampires are meant to have limitations, to keep things in some sort of balance so they don't completely destroy humanity."

"Fine." Darren's pupils flashed with red. "But it won't be *all* vampires. Just those here."

Her thoughts whirled. She really *didn't* want to give vamps like Darren and Esmerelda more power over humans.

On the other hand— maybe daywalking vampires could act as a counterbalance to Drew's power. Without a powerful enemy of his own, Drew could turn half the human race into blood-drinking demons like Tammi. And the other half he'd probably sacrifice in the Brotherhood's fires, just to keep the Hunters happy.

The unholy alliance of witch and witch-hunter.

She shrugged. "Perhaps it's a *lesser of two evils* situation, but you're not doing the vampires a great PR service by blocking my path right now."

Darren cocked his head. "Lesser of two evils, hmm? And is that how you feel about Caine?"

Now he had her attention. "What are you talking about?"

"He's not the only powerful demon in Lilinor who wants your nubile flesh. I'm sure you can see Ambrose wants you, too. He sends you food; Caine does not. Yet you've chosen Caine. A hunter choosing an incubus. Is he merely the lesser of two evils, or have you been lured in with his incubus charms, like so many before you?"

Rosalind frowned. "Ambrose wants me?"

"Don't think you're special. Demons are drawn to humans like moths to a flame."

Ambrose... Cleo's words screamed in her skull. *I want him to burn, yet I remember the feel of his bare skin against mine.* An image burned in Rosalind's mind: Ambrose's hands cupping Cleo's pale breasts, leaning in and kissing her neck, his mouth hot on her skin. A wave of pleasure rushed through her body, and she nearly groaned.

"Not now, Cleo," she snapped.

Darren's eyes widened, as if Rosalind was suddenly the scary one. "Cleo?"

"Never mind."

"I suppose you've amused me for long enough. But if you're here to create daywalkers, do it fast. Whether or not Ambrose desires your flesh, he will only indulge you for so long." He turned, stalking off past her.

Cleo's aura roiled in her mind. *He brought me a wreath of blackthorn. He kissed my throat, his hands clutching my body—*

"Yeah, I get it, Cleo!" Rosalind's voice echoed off the ceiling.

Where was that wreath Miranda had made for her? That thing had actually subdued Cleo's ranting.

He brought me the sweetest wine—

Rosalind turned back to Tammi's room and pushed open the door. She snatched the wreath from the floor and frantically pulled it onto her head, sighing as Cleo's voice faded in her skull.

CHAPTER 6

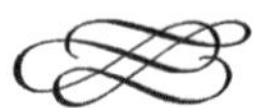

In the apple orchard, the sound of violins drifted on the evening wind. The air hung thick with blossoms. I pulled open my dress, letting the spring air kiss my bare skin, waiting for him to come to me...

But the air chilled, and a storm wind rushed over my body.

Now the air fills with the smell of gangrenous flesh and rotting wood. An intruder lurks in here.

Wake, Rosalind. Wake and see it.

Rosalind's eyes snapped open. Tangled in her sheets, she slept in her thin silk nightgown next to her sister. Milky daylight streamed through the edge of the closed curtain.

Something wasn't right. The room smelled terrible, and when her eyes adjusted her heart thundered against her ribs.

Daylight. There is daylight in Lilinor.

That alone was very wrong. The sun didn't shine in the City of Night. She sat upright, her panicked gaze landing on Miranda.

But Miranda wasn't alone.

Crouching on her sister's chest was a gaunt figure. White light gleamed off his bald head, the color of unbaked bread. The creature had no mouth or ears—just two slits for a nose, and gaping black eyeholes. He smelled like the bottom of a grave. Before she could reach for him, the creature wafted away like black smoke on the wind —so quickly that Rosalind had to wonder if it had just been the remnants of a dream.

She glanced down at her pillow. She'd been sleeping on her half-crumpled wildflower wreath, while Miranda's crown still rested on her head. Rosalind rubbed her eyes, trying to clear the fog of sleep from her mind. *What was that thing?*

Her gaze trailed over Miranda's throat; at the sight of an iron necklace, Rosalind's adrenalin surged. It looked like the charmed necklaces Drew used to control people. Around the metal chain, colored magic swirled into the air—gold, silver, blue...

Rosalind ripped the thing from Miranda's throat, examining it. The exact same type of thin iron chain the keres had been wearing in Maremount—a collar of sorts. And Drew's strange magic was all over the damn thing. He couldn't be in Lilinor, could he? Either way, he'd be able to control anyone wearing one of the chains.

Miranda's eyes opened, and she sat up. "What's going on?"

Rosalind shook her head, still gaping at the necklace. Had the creatures gone after anyone else, or just Miranda and Rosalind?

Whatever the hell was going on, there had clearly been some sort of breach of Lilinor's defenses. Maybe Drew's strange magic allowed him to open portals without permission.

"What's happening?" Miranda asked, still blinking.

"There's daylight in Lilinor." Rosalind threw off her bedcovers. "And Drew might have seized control. I need to warn people."

Rosalind rushed for the door. She flung it open, then raced through the corridor, her heart thrumming. Where *was* Ambrose? Sometimes he slept in the White Tower, but not always.

But she knew exactly where to find Caine—one floor up, next to the painting of Lord Byron.

She pushed through another door into the stairwell, her pulse racing. Her feet pounded the stairs as she raced up. This had to be Drew's doing. No one else could use that type of magic—apart from Erish, but she was locked safely in the dungeon. Wasn't she?

Rosalind pushed through the door at the top of the stairwell. The sunlight streaming through the windows looked so *wrong* here. How many chains had the demons distributed?

Rosalind opened a door to one of the rooms. There, sprawled over a bed, lay Esmerelda. An iron chain hung around her neck. She rushed to the next door, turning the knob. A muscular, blond vampire lay in the middle of the stone floor. Another iron chain.

Rosalind's throat went dry. The demons could have hit the whole city.

She turned, sprinting for Caine's room. Her bare feet pounded over the stone floor, and she screeched to a halt at the painting of Lord Byron. Frantically, she flung open the door to Caine's room.

In the center of a silver bed, Caine lay wrapped in his bedsheets, his chest bare. His thick black lashes rested against his cheeks. At the sight of his beauty, her heart skipped a beat. For just a moment, she forgot why she'd come, letting her eyes linger over the tattoos that snaked over his muscled chest. The moon and stars, the strange thin dagger on her forearm… Together, the symbols were like a map of his life—one she couldn't quite read.

She blinked to clear her mind, and her gaze moved up his body…to the iron necklace on his throat. Tendrils of magic—blue, gold, and silver—wafted off the iron.

Drew was here, and every demon in Lilinor might be mind-controlled by him.

She rushed to Caine's bed, then jumped up next to him to rip the necklace from his throat.

With a growl, Caine's eyes snapped open. The next thing she knew, he'd flipped her onto her back. The back of her head landed on his pillow, and he gripped her hair with one hand while the other pinned her own hands over her head.

How had he managed that so quickly, without hurting her?

Her pulse raced as his hard body pressed against hers. Through the thin silk of her nightgown, she could feel his warm skin, his powerful body. *So that's what happens when you wake up an incubus from a deep sleep.*

He inhaled deeply and laced his fingers with hers.. "Rosalind.

You're not wearing your ring. Isn't that dangerous if Cleo takes over your mind?" He leaned in close, his breath warming her neck. "But maybe now isn't the time for me to ask questions like that."

"I don't wear the ring anymore," she whispered. "It doesn't work."

His leg pressed between hers, and heat flooded her body. *Focus, Rosalind.* She swallowed hard, trying to clear her mind. "I came here to warn you. There's been a breach of Lilinor's defenses—some creatures that can disappear like smoke. They've clamped iron chains on everyone. I just ripped yours off. And the city is flooded with daylight."

He blinked hard, as if trying to clear his mind, and released his grip on her. He sat up, glancing at the window. "Daylight." He raked his hand through his hair. "Seven hells."

"Daylight, and mind-control." She held up the necklace. "These are the same chains Drew used on Tammi and Miranda in Maremount. They're charmed with his magic. He'll be able to control anyone wearing one."

Caine jumped from his bed in a blur of silver, suddenly completely alert. "We need to get to Ambrose."

"Where does he sleep?"

"That's anyone's guess. Sometimes in the Ishtaritu hall, sometimes in..." Caine's golden skin paled, and a look of complete horror crossed his face. "The White Tower."

Suddenly, Rosalind understood. *Ambrose's open-air lair.* Ambrose often slept there, beneath the stars. If the creatures had slapped a collar on him, he'd be burning to death in his bedsheets right now—a charred body in the blazing sun.

"Come with me." Caine held out his hand, and she stepped closer to him, folding into his embrace.

He began chanting the teleportation spell, and she joined in, feeling his electric aura rush over her skin.

When she opened her eyes, they stood in Ambrose's tower room. Sunlight blazed between the open vaults, but not a single smudge of ash stained Ambrose's sheets. Relief washed over her, and she heard a sigh slide from Caine.

"Thank the gods. He's not here. But I want to find him now. As lord, he'll be the primary target for the demons."

Rosalind grabbed his arm. "Maybe we can use magic."

"For what?"

"Hang on." She crossed to one of the tall, peaked windows, gazing out at Ninlil Castle. The cobblestone courtyard below was ringed with rickety stone towers; they pierced the blue skies, each crowned with a sharp spire. A fountain stood in the center of the courtyard.

From here, Caine and Rosalind had a view of all the living quarters, and she would be able to direct the spell into each of the rooms. "I used a spell in Maremount," she said, "to free the prisoners and take their necklaces off. We can do the same here—a spell for bending iron. We'll need to work together, to make it as strong as possible. It'll save us hunting around the whole fortress for Ambrose."

He shook his head. "No. Ambrose is the priority. If we use a spell—"

The opening of courtyard doors interrupted him, and Rosalind's heart skipped a beat. From each of the doors, vampires walked into the sunlight, moving as silently as wraiths. Smoke rose from their skin.

"The iron spell," Caine said. "Now!"

Her heart hammering, Rosalind began chanting the spell for warping iron. Caine joined in with her, their magic curling together in swirls of silver and green.

Is it too late? Before they could get to the end of the spell, flames sparked around the vampires' bodies. And yet they still moved steadily forward like blazing viking funeral boats.

Caine stopped chanting and raised his hands to the skies. His silver aura whipped from his body, streaming to the heavens.

What is he doing? Whatever it was, Rosalind needed to stay focused until she could get the damn necklaces off the vamps. Once freed, they could plunge into the fountain to douse the flames.

Her heart clenched as the smell of burning flesh reached her nose, yet she kept chanting.

Even as the vampires burned, an eerie silence enshrouded the courtyard. Not a single voice cut the quiet. The vampires simply walked onward into the light, pouring from the doors, skin blazing in the hot sun. Black plumes of smoke curled into the air.

Rosalind could feel Cleo's dark delight. She *liked* this.

Watch the little vermin burn... Cleo whispered.

Rosalind felt sick. *Crazy twat.*

If she wanted this to work, she'd have to block out the chaos on her mind, the warring emotions. With all the mental focus she could muster, she directed Cleo's vernal aura around the iron collars. At last, the metal necklaces twisted from the vamps necks, and fell to the cobblestones with a loud clang.

And that was when the screaming began.

Agonized shrieks ripped through the air, and the vampires staggered, limbs blazing. A few dove for the fountain, but most stumbled blindly, in too much pain to save themselves.

By her side, Caine's aura intensified, rippling over Rosalind's skin in a staggering burst of power. Rosalind glanced at the sky; somehow, Caine's magic was forcing the sun to set. The setting sun stained the sky a deep, blood red, but rays of sun still washed the city in gold.

I can help him. Rosalind closed her eyes. With Cleo's help, she launched into a spell for Mishett-Ash, the god of storms.

Her stomach flipped at the power of the magic whirling around her body. An icy aura froze her skin. With trembling legs, she chanted louder, calling on the god to bring his storm winds to Lilinor. Another aura rushed through the air, briny and wet.

Miranda. Somewhere in the fortress, Rosalind's twin was working her magic, too.

The sun sank lower, dipping just behind one of Ninlil's spires, and still, rays of sunlight streamed around it.

Rosalind closed her eyes, repeating the Angelic words to lure a storm into the skies. As she chanted, thunder rumbled over the horizon, and the hair on the back of her neck stood on end. Fat drops of rain fell on her skin, drenching her hair and clothes. The storm's power rolled through her body.

From the courtyard below, the screams quieted.

Softly, Caine touched Rosalind's arm, and she opened her eyes. All around her, Cleo's aura swirled in the air, mingling with Caine's.

Rosalind's entire body shook, and her eyes rose to the sky.

Not only had she called a storm over the city, but Caine had somehow turned the daylight to night. The sky over Lilinor was pure midnight black. Lightning cracked in the sky, casting pale light over the sodden piles of gray ash littering the stony courtyard.

Hundreds of vampires had wandered out to their deaths in just a few short minutes.

Across the fortress, shouts rang through the halls. At least they'd saved most of the city.

Still, with all the carnage below, Rosalind's knees had gone weak. She turned, leaning against the wall, and let herself slide down the cold stone.

From behind her, Caine spoke in a low growl. "You saw Drew's magic on the necklaces?"

"Yes. It's either him or Erish."

"I'm going to stab them to death with their own ribs."

"Did you see Ambrose out there?"

He shook his head. "No. He's safe for now. But I'm going to find him."

"How did the creatures get in here?" Rosalind asked. "And how did they get from room to room so fast?"

"Drew must have found our portal. And somehow, Nyxobas let him open it." He frowned. "What did the creatures look like?"

Rosalind shuddered. "The one I saw was missing a mouth and ears. Its flesh was gray, like a corpse. And it smelled like a grave."

"Alu demons," Caine muttered. "They belong to Nyxobas. They can travel on the wind, and disappear at will like smoke. They're extremely rare."

Rosalind's mouth went dry. "Maybe they're not demons. Maybe they were human until Drew turned them." She rose, unsteady on her feet. "And he's probably still in the city. Lurking in the shadows, planning his next move. We need to find him."

"Not you. You're too valuable, and I need your magic to keep the sun out of our city. If Drew made the sun rise once in Lilinor, I'm sure he can do it again." He glanced up at the dark sky. "I need you and your sister to draw on your magic to keep the sun down. Under the cover of darkness, the entire vampire army can operate swiftly and hunt for Drew."

"Fine." Dizzy, she leaned against the wall, trying to focus. "But I don't understand. I didn't hear you chant a spell for the night. You just raised your hands up and magic burst out of your body."

"It's a demigod privilege. Gods-magic. You won't be able to do the same. Ask Cleo for a spell."

Cleo's aura whipped around Rosalind's head, throwing her off balance. Rosalind rested her head in her hands. *He brought me a wreath of blackthorn...*

Caine gently grabbed her elbow. "You look like you're about to collapse. After we get Drew and his demons out of here, we need to heal your mind. With powerful magic like we're using, Cleo will take over."

Rosalind looked at his face, so close to hers, and Cleo whispered, *A beautiful man draws you into his spell like a moth to a flame.*

Rosalind stared into his eyes. "I know."

CHAPTER 7

With Cleo's whispers ringing in her skull, Rosalind sprinted through the halls, her bare feet pounding the cold flagstones. She thundered down the stairs, pushing through the door into her own hall.

Miranda stood outside the bedroom door, still in her nightgown. "Rosalind!" Her face had gone pale. "I tried to stop it! I tried to help you call a storm!"

"I know!" Rosalind hurried to her sister. "We need to work together. I need you to chant with me." She pushed open the door into their room and, as soon as Miranda was inside, bolted the door behind them.

It's not enough, Cleo whispered. *If Drew wants to kill you, he'll find a way.*

Rosalind's hands shook, and she gripped her hair to steady them.

No way to be safe, Cleo snarled.

"Rosalind!" Miranda shouted. "Focus! What spell do we need to do?"

Seal the door, Rosalind, Cleo whispered. *He'll come after you. He'll find you.*

Shaking, Rosalind turned to the door and raised her hands, and she let Cleo whisper a spell through her lips. *"Ezebu, utuk xul daltu."*

The green aura surged around the room, sealing the door, and Rosalind let out a slow breath.

Miranda touched her arm. "What spell do you need my help for?"

"We need to make sure the sun doesn't rise again," Rosalind said, crossing to the window. Total darkness still covered the city. "Our second souls will know the spell, according to Caine. And we have to appeal to Nyxobas."

Shouts pierced the air. Rosalind flattened her palms against the window, listening to the rain hammer the cobblestones below. Then silver, gold, and blue magic unfurled into the air, lighting up the courtyard.

Drew. He was still here, still weaving his sadistic spells.

Below, more vampires stumbled into the courtyard, necklaces glinting in the light of the magic.

Rosalind's heart thudded, and her gaze flicked to the sky. Through a break in the storm clouds, the sky had brightened to a deep indigo.

He's raising the sun once more.

Rosalind's breath caught in her throat. "The sun's coming back. Chant with me. Help me appeal to Nyxobas."

Miranda slid her hand into her twin's, and together they launched into a spell for night.

Margidda Nyxobas, ed Nanna...

Their green and blue auras curled through the window, spiraling up to the brightening sky. As they chanted, Miranda's watery aura washed over Rosalind's skin, soothing her muscles. Using magic with her own twin felt powerful, and strength coursed through her body.

Sisters. Together. Like we were meant to be.

Rosalind closed her eyes, entreating Nyxobas to hide the sun once more. As she chanted, an image rose in her mind: a man with a ivory skin, black hair and eyes like starlight.

Nyxobas.

His powerful aura surrounded her. She could almost lose herself in the darkness, if she let herself. She could almost fall into the abyss...

Her body trembled at the power of the magic's spell, and she forced her eyes open again. The sun had set once more, the sky darkening to a deep, midnight blue. She glanced at the courtyard again—at the vampires still stumbling through the doors, dazed—and felt as dazed as they looked. The powerful magic had completely drained her body, and her knees nearly gave way. She wasn't sure she'd be able to conduct another spell if she wanted to.

"Look." Miranda pointed out the window at a human man, clad in tight black clothes. "A Hunter."

Behind the man, more humans poured from the doors, weapons drawn. The vampires stood there—dazed, completely defenseless.

Rosalind swayed, her body shaking. Even through her fog of exhaustion, one thing rang clear in her mind. "They're going to slaughter them," she whispered.

As Rosalind stared, unsteady on her feet, a dark-haired Hunter stalked over to a female vamp wearing only a thin red nightgown, and grabbed hold of her long auburn hair.

"We need to do something," Miranda said.

Before Rosalind could launch into another spell, one of the courtyard doors exploded with silver magic. In a blur of silvered light, Caine sped over to the Hunter's side. His black eyes burned with an animal ferocity. The ghost of dark wings rose from his shoulders.

Rosalind's heart thudded at the sight of him. This was Caine, without the mask of humanity. And he was terrifying.

It took him less than a heartbeat to grip the Hunter's throat. Another beat for him to rip the human's head from his body, blood spraying in a crimson arc. Caine whirled, his hands finding their way to another Hunter's neck.

"Or maybe we don't," she murmured. Where Caine was, Ambrose was sure to follow. Caine wouldn't be here if he hadn't already saved the vampire lord.

"Caine against a few dozen Hunters," Miranda said. "My money is on the incubus."

Sure enough, Ambrose was next through the shattered door, black magic curling from his body.

Out in the courtyard, the vampire lord tilted back his head, and roared. The sound rumbled through Rosalind's bones, imbuing her with primordial terror and a desperate need to flee.

Still, she stayed rooted to the spot, watching the action unfold.

A female Hunter threw a stake at Ambrose, and he caught it deftly, hurling it back at her. It struck its mark right in the woman's chest, and she fell to the ground.

"And now we just watch the slaughter," Miranda said.

Rosalind watched, her jaw open, as Caine and Ambrose ripped through the Hunters, tearing out hearts, cutting off heads. Blurs of silver and black, breathtaking in their graceful savagery, leaving crumpled corpses in their wakes.

Ruthless predators, with the speed of gods, they seemed to have the courtyard entirely under control. Caine tore out the heart of the last remaining Hunter, tossing it on the ground.

Then—from nowhere—multi-colored magic burst around Ambrose. In the next moment, his body was gone.

Caine paused, still gripping the heart. Blood dripped down his arm, and he stared at the place where his king had stood.

Rosalind's heart skipped a beat. *Drew found a way to get to Ambrose after all.*

The shadows behind Caine's shoulders thickened into powerful, black-feathered wings. Caine tossed the heart to the ground, then beat the air with his wings, lifting into the sky.

Rosalind's heart jumped into her throat. "What the hell just happened?"

"Drew just stole our king," Miranda said through clenched teeth. "And Caine is going to find him."

As Caine took flight, Rosalind's gaze flicked back to the vamps. They were moving among the Hunters now, circling each other like feral creatures. Tendrils of blue, silver, and green magic curled from their necklaces.

Darren prowled around another vampire—a petite brunette, her fangs bared. With a loud roar, Darren pounced, leaping onto the woman and ripping into her neck.

Rosalind's stomach churned. "Drew is using the vampire army against itself."

Where is Aurora? Frantically, Rosalind scanned the courtyard, and caught a glimpse of her friend stumbling over the grass in a singed nectarine-colored dress.

Exhausted or not, if Rosalind didn't act now, Aurora could be killed by another vamp any moment. Her heart hammered. She'd have to use her last reserves of magic on another rendition of the iron spell. "We can use the iron-bending spell again," she told Miranda. "Will you help me?"

"Of course. Are you sure you're up for it? You look completely exhausted."

Rosalind gripped the window sill harder, steadying herself. "We don't have a choice."

"How are we supposed to help all of them?"

"I can direct the magic to the right places." She glanced at her sister. "Can you start the spell?"

Miranda launched into Angelic, her briny aura trickling over Rosalind's skin. Rosalind joined in, watching as their magic curled into the courtyard. The auras curled together in perfect whorls of blue and green, and she was struck once again by how *right* it felt to work together with her twin. Like being home.

She focused on channeling the magic around the vampire's necks, starting with Aurora. The metal around her friend's neck began to twist, and—

A thundering boom interrupted her thoughts, and she whirled.

Standing in her doorway, with magic bursting from his body, was Drew.

Her betrothed.

The world seemed to fall out from under her feet. In a rush of power, his aura rushed over her skin, disorienting her with a flood of sensations: soft moss and the smell of leaves, gravel, wind and water trickling over her body. With all this powerful magic at his fingertips, he'd be nearly impossible to fight.

Not to mention that she had nothing left in her system.

But I have to try.

He was here to slaughter her friends, and he wanted to own her like property—to use her for breeding his terrible, incestuous Atherton progeny. She'd do anything she could to keep him away from her.

"My dear betrothed," he cooed.

Rosalind's adrenalin surged, and she scanned the room for the nearest weapon. Her gaze landed on the silver pike resting near her bed. She hurtled across the floor to the weapon, snatching it from the ground. Heart pounding, she whirled.

Drew was right behind her. She swung for his head, hoping to bash in his skull.

Without breaking a sweat, he lifted a hand, catching the pike in his grip.

Her stomach flipped. *Not good. He has some kind of superhuman strength.*

With a placid expression, Drew twisted the pike, knocking her backward onto the bed. In the next heartbeat, he was on top of her, pressing his powerful fingers around her neck.

He squeezed. She kicked him in the groin, and he grunted. Still, his fingers tightened, crushing her throat.

She shot a panicked glance at Miranda, who threw a knife at Drew. The throw should have buried the blade in his skull, but Drew ducked in a blur of whirling auras. The knife plunged into the wall.

Rosalind kicked him in the stomach, and he grimaced, locking his gaze on her. His fingers clenched harder around her throat.

He stared at her, eyes flashing with licks of red, green, and silver fire. "You haven't even seen the real magic yet. Do you want to feel it? Inside you?"

"Get off of her!" Miranda threw a second knife, but Drew's free hand whipped into the air, snatching it. He pressed the blade to Rosalind's throat, then looked up. "If you take another step closer, Miranda, I'll slit your sister's throat. If you utter one syllable of Angelic, I'll slice through to her spine before you can draw another breath. It's a better punishment than you both deserve, after your betrayal."

Rosalind's breath left her lungs. "What do you want, Drew?" she choked out.

He stared down at her, arching an eyebrow. "You. Under my control. And now, I'll show you both the real magic. You'll be ever so impressed." Still pushing the blade against her throat, he slid his hand down the front of her chest, pressing it against her stomach. His fingers grew cold as ice, and a chill spread through her. Glacial cold filled her ribs, freezing her skin, icing the inside of her mind.

Dread tightened her heart. Her body was no longer her own.

Drew dragged the knife lower, pointing the tip just over her heart. "Stand," he said to Rosalind. His voice seemed to come from the inside of her own mind, and her skull filled with icy eddies of his magic.

Slowly, he backed away, still pointing the knife at her chest. Against her will, she felt herself stand. She stared right at him. Somewhere, deep under the icy chill of his magic, her mind churned with horror.

How is he doing this—a type of magic only possessed by demons?

He hadn't put a collar around her throat—yet he could control her.

"What are you doing?" Miranda shouted.

Drew stroked Rosalind's hair. "You keep quiet. or I'll force her to walk right into my knife." He leaned closer, whispering into Rosalind's ear. "Turn around."

His voice reverberated from the base of her brain. A part of her mind screamed in outrage, but her body followed his command, his frigid magic snaking around her skull.

Drew stepped closer, sliding his arm around her waist and pulling her in tighter against his body. His fingers traced up and down her side, running over her ribs. With his other hand, he pressed the blade against her throat, nicking her skin.

"You're probably hoping that monster you're fucking will come to save you," he purred. "He won't. I've sent the alu demons after Ambrose. Right now, your incubus is protecting his king. He's not here, protecting you. Now you know where his priorities lie. I told you before, and I'm telling you now: he's using you. You're his trophy. After he executed your parents like common criminals, defiling their daughter is the final nail in the coffin of Atherton's respectability. Surely even you can see that."

Miranda shouted again. "Let her go!"

"Keep your voice down, little girl," Drew snarled, "or we'll find out what a traitor looks like on the inside. Are you wondering how I've controlled her mind? After all, I'm not a demon. And she's not wearing a necklace."

Rosalind swallowed hard, finding that her mouth couldn't form words, but even if she wanted to, she couldn't for the life of her think of what she'd want to say. Her own thoughts were buried under the icy rush of his magic.

"Take the knife from me," Drew said. "Hold it against your own throat."

Tendrils of Drew's colored magic clouded inside her head like frozen mist. She couldn't remember what she was supposed to be doing, only that she wanted to take the knife from him.

I'm supposed to lift the knife. Trembling, her hand rose and grasped the hilt. Drew released the weapon, and she felt herself pressing the blade to her own jugular.

Still gripping her waist, Drew stroked the back of her neck. "It's that little scar I gave you," he murmured. "A reminder that you belong to Azazeyl, the One who is All. It lets me control you. And it will never leave your flesh, not as long as you live."

As soon as the words were out of his mouth, the scar on her stomach began to freeze her skin, arctic cold. Her body shook, and cold sweat beaded on her forehead.

Under the icy fog of Drew's magic, one thought thundered through her mind: *Something terrible is about to happen.*

She knew this feeling. She'd been here before.

"Let her go," Miranda whispered, her voice pleading.

Rosalind closed her eyes, trying to clear a space in her mind, free from Drew's aura. Her own thoughts were sluggish and frozen, but they still lurked deep in the hollows of her brain. She needed Caine here; he could manipulate magic without using Angelic. She'd seen him do it. There would be no warning before his aura exploded from his body, no need to move his mouth to launch into a spell. If only she... If only...

What was I thinking about?

All she knew was that she wanted to press herself into Drew, to rub her body against the body behind her. To keep herself warm in this frozen vacuum.

Drew leaned down, his mouth near her ear. "Did you really think you stood a chance, with that broken mind of yours? Half in our world, and half in Cleo's." His hand snaked up her neck, and he gripped her by the hair, pulling her head back. "I wanted to see you struggle. Wanted to watch the sheen of sweat on your throat. It wouldn't be any fun if you didn't put up a fight. And you know what? I'm ready for some real fun."

He kissed her neck, and icy dread spread through Rosalind's chest. *Get away from me.*

"Leave her alone!" Miranda shouted.

"I still intend for you to be my wife," he said. "Our children will be powerful, like us. We'll rewrite the world. I'll create a new empire, a new reality." He stroked her ribs just below her breasts. "But you'll need to obey me. And that means I need to teach you a lesson—one you'll never forget. Because you've done something awful, Rosalind. Don't you know that? You've been fucking the man who killed your parents."

"She hasn't," Miranda said. "Not that it's any of your—"

"Silence," he growled, his fingers pressing into Rosalind's ribs.

Involuntarily, Rosalind pushed the blade harder against her throat. Her teeth began to chatter.

He has complete control over me. Why can't I get the auras out?

There was a way—but she couldn't think clearly enough to remember how to do it.

"I know what I know!" Drew yelled, his fingers digging into her sides. "She thinks about Caine, and thinking is just as bad as doing. She wants to be his whore—him, our sworn enemy! But she belongs to me. That's the way it was always supposed to be. And with her at my side, I will rule the world. I just need to tame her first. And then I will control the rocks, the sea, the skies, the night…"

As he spoke, images rose in Rosalind's mind: her own fingertips, raising up mountains, sending storms raging with a flick of her wrist. A cold, raw power thrummed through her body, a glimpse of her future.

Drew pointed to the iron necklace that lay discarded on the bed between two crumpled wildflower wreaths. "Pick up the necklace, Miranda," he said. "Put it on. Or Rosalind cuts her own throat."

Deep under the ice of Drew's magic, Rosalind's mind screamed. *Don't do it, Miranda. Something terrible will happen.*

Miranda stood rigid, glaring at Drew. Her blue aura undulated around her body, like anemones deep underwater. Rosalind could feel it rushing over her skin, cool and wet, yet she couldn't use her magic. Not without getting through an entire Angelic spell first.

Don't do it, Miranda.

Drew flicked his wrist, and glaciers closed over Rosalind's heart. Rosalind slid the blade across her throat, cutting just into the skin, but deep enough to draw blood. Crimson streaked her white nightgown.

"Stop!" Miranda shouted, hurrying to the bed. Visibly shaking, she snatched the necklace from the sheets and fastened it around her neck. As soon as she'd secured it, her dark eyes glazed over and her jaw slackened.

Deep under the fog of Drew's aura, dread knelled in Rosalind's skull. Buried under the layers of his magic lurked the gnawing certainty of impending doom.

Something terrible is going to happen.

Drew stepped away from Rosalind. "Drop the knife, Rosalind. Then I want both of you to walk into the courtyard." His toneless voice echoed off the inside of her skull.

Drop the knife, Rosalind. Her fingers unclenched, and the knife clanged on the stone.

Walk to the courtyard. She felt her legs move, her feet pivoting over the cold floor. Beneath the frozen mists of Drew's magic, panic tore her mind apart. *He's taking us on a death march.*

But despite the protests in the darkest recesses of her mind, she pulled open the door and stepped into the hall.

In the corridor, Miranda walked by her side. Drew's heels clacked behind them, slow and rhythmic like a war drum. The name *Caine* whispered through her mind. Was he supposed to be here? She couldn't keep her thoughts straight.

Caine. He's someone important...

With Miranda by her side, she stalked through the corridor. Frozen to the bone, she stared at the shadows dancing over the floor. *This is the type of cold that seeps into your blood and never leaves. The type of cold that drags you down into the frozen earth, and never lets you out again.*

From behind her, Drew's footsteps echoed off the stones in the stairwell.

At the bottom of the stairs, Rosalind marched into the long hallway, Miranda by her side. *A cold that covers your body like a funeral shroud. The world is cold when it ends.*

In Ninlil's entrance hall, her bare feet padded over the crimson carpet.

This is where the world ends.

She couldn't remember what she was doing, only that she needed to keep walking. She had a vague sense that someone was driving her forward—someone who had completely lost his mind, who wanted to hurt her. But she couldn't grasp the ephemeral wisps of thought long enough to make sense of them.

Her body shook, and she pushed through the front doors into the still-dark esplanade.

"There's a wooden post in the northwest corner of the esplanade. March to it. Both of you."

Icy fear wound through her chest, but her leaden legs carried her forward across the rain-slicked stones.

It shouldn't be so empty here.

Her thoughts moved like glaciers. The heavy silence wasn't quite right. If someone was going to die, the air should be full of screaming, clashing swords, the beating of drums. The army was somewhere else, fighting another battle. But this was where the world would end.

Her fingers tightened. *And this is how the world ends—cold and quiet, thoughts trapped under ice and rock. No one to shout or cry, just a damp death rattle, then silence.*

"Miranda," Drew barked. "Stand with your back to the post. It's time you learned some respect for the One True King."

Rain poured over Rosalind's skin, soaking her thin nightgown. *This is how the world ends, in damp shadows.*

Rosalind stared as her sister, dull-eyed, backed up to the wooden post.

Drew lifted Rosalind's hand and pressed something into it—a thick iron nail. Horror stole her breath. And even beneath the icy fog of his magic, rage ripped her mind apart.

I've been here before. I watched this happen. I saw the monster. And now the monster is me.

Drew traced his fingertips over her wrist. "Do you remember what Caine did to the true king and queen, your parents?"

The image flashed in her mind—rain, just like this. Feet half-sunk in the mud. Miranda's scream. Caine pinning her mother against the stake, driving the nail right under her ribs into her heart. Blood dripping from her mother's pale lips, her brown eyes wide.

Rosalind nodded slowly. *I remember.*

"Good," Drew said. "I want you to drive the nail into Miranda's heart. Just like that."

Rosalind's hand tightened on the nail, and her hand shook violently. Miranda looked so skinny against the post, shivering in her thin nightgown, nearly sheer in the rain. She was going to freeze like that. Someone should get her inside, in the warmth.

But Rosalind had a job to do. First, she had to stick this nail into her sister's heart.

Under the ice of her mind, she had a vague sense that this was all wrong—that she needed to run from here and take Miranda with her—but she couldn't figure out how to do it. The scar on her stomach felt as if it was cutting into her flesh, controlling her thoughts.

Drew pushed her wet hair off her face, a strangely gentle gesture. "You've been disloyal, Rosalind. And you must pay the price. Say it."

Her mouth formed the words. "We've been disloyal. And now we must pay the price."

This is how the world ends.

"Do it, Rosalind," he said. "Pay the price. Kill your sister, just like Caine killed your parents."

Rosalind lifted the nail, taking a step closer to her sister. For just a moment, a flicker of life sparked in Miranda's eyes—a pleading look, her dark pupils glistening.

Deep in Rosalind's chest, a hot rage simmered, burning away some of the ice.

Drew thinks he owns us. We're his playthings.

Fury blazed in her mind, clearing just enough space that she could hear her own thoughts.

It was just like this. Driving rain, clothing drenched. Miranda's scream...

"Do it, Rosalind," Drew shouted.

Rosalind's scar froze her skin, and she gripped the nail tighter.

Blood dripping from Mother's pale lips, brown eyes wide.

She paused, forcing her hand down. *I won't let it happen again.*

Trapped under all the ice and rock, Cleo's voice whispered along with her own. *Turn, Rosalind. Turn and fight.*

She was stronger than this. With a grunt, she pivoted, forcing herself to face Drew. At the sight of him, nausea turned her gut.

Rain poured down his skin in tiny rivulets. Surprise flickered across his features—just enough of a shock to distract him from the twisted spell he wove. "What are you doing?" he demanded.

Gritting her teeth, she stepped closer to him. Her body still moved glacially slow, but it was her own now. She clutched the nail.

This belongs in your heart, Drew.

Before she could strike, Drew punched her in the jaw. Pain splintered her skull. Staggering back, she lifted the nail into the air. She was going to drive it right into his neck.

But before she could bring down the weapon, Drew caught her hand mid-air. He crushed her wrist in his fingers until she dropped the nail. It bounced off the stones.

Hot wrath flooded her body, and she slammed her forehead into his nose, cracking the bone. Blood poured from his nostrils, and she rammed her knee into his groin. *A wedding gift from your beloved wife.*

Grunting, he doubled over, and Rosalind smashed him hard in the kidneys with her elbow.

She reached down, snatching the nail from the ground. She'd kill him right here.

As she rose, Drew slammed a fist into the side of her skull, knocking her back. When she looked up at him again, his powerful aura filled the air around him.

She lunged.

His colored aura slammed into Rosalind's body. He snatched her wrist in his fingers, squeezing so hard she was sure her bones were turning to dust. She moaned, and he punched her in the throat, stealing her breath.

Fluidly, like a trained dancer, Drew whirled—and drove the nail into Miranda's heart, just below her ribs.

Miranda's eyes opened wide with the shock. Horror ripped Rosalind's mind apart.

It's too late.

Miranda didn't shout or cry; she just let out a damp sigh. A thick drop of blood dripped from her pale lips.

This is how the world ends.

CHAPTER 8

osalind couldn't lift her eyes to Miranda's face, didn't want to see the slackened jaw or the blood dripping from her sister's lips. She didn't want to see the half-closed eyelids, or the crimson streaking her twin's gown. She didn't want to think about the plans Miranda had made, or their house quiet, smelling of fresh-baked bread.

If she gave in to those thoughts right now, they'd bury her alive and she'd never claw her way out again.

Give in to the rage instead. The rage will save you.

Fury blazed through Rosalind's blood, igniting her veins. She grabbed Drew by the hair, pulling him back. She hooked her arm around his neck, squeezing hard. If he couldn't speak, he couldn't use Angelic, couldn't mold reality to his will with his lips.

Her chest tightened. *But I saw him use magic without speaking in Angelic.* He could tap into nature's power directly, just like Caine. Like a god, as if—

Before she could finish her thought, a staggering blast of magic knocked her off Drew. She slammed back against the rock, and pain splintered her skull.

He killed Miranda, her mind whispered. *It's too late.*

Drew whirled and pressed his foot over her throat. For just a moment, she thought about giving in, letting him press the air out of her. Letting him take her as his mute mountain queen.

But a sharp sound hammered in her head. It was the memory of Miranda's ribs cracking when Drew broke them with the nail. Replaying in her mind, over and over...

Rosalind grabbed his leg and twisted, knocking him down. *I'll hear the crack of his ribs...*

Her body burned with wrath, and she leapt onto Drew, straddling him. He gaped at her—afraid for just a moment—and she gripped his hair, slamming his head into the ground once, twice...

In the next instant, his body disappeared—transported away through his strange magic, smoke on the wind.

It's just me now.

A hollow chill crept under her ribs, eating her from the inside out. She kept her eyes locked on the ground, on the stones and tiny rivers of rain. If she looked up, the sight of her sister's body would devour her whole.

Her knees shook, so hard it seemed the earth itself was moving.

Dead.

Footsteps moved past her on the stones, but she couldn't lift her face.

The hero is supposed to come in before the world ends.

"Rosalind!" It was Caine's voice, but she wasn't looking up. *Look up, Rosalind. Face it.*

Slowly, she lifted her gaze, staring at the deep crimson staining Miranda's gown. Caine stood before her. Gently, he pulled the nail from her heart. Miranda's body collapsed into his arms, lifeless. He laid her on the cold stone ground, tracing his fingertips over her heart.

She's dead. Rosalind was certain of this down to her marrow. One more corpse to feed the soil of her nightmares. *I can't look at her face.*

Caine lifted his gaze to Rosalind.

He didn't get here in time.

Her thoughts and Cleo's scuttled around her mind like beetles, and she couldn't grasp any of them.

In the next moment, Caine was standing before her, his hands warming her arms. Was he just going to leave her sister there?

He lowered his face, staring into her eyes. His pale eyes glistened. "I need you to focus, Rosalind. What happened to Drew?"

She looked into his eyes. What difference did it make now? It was all over.

His fingers tightened on her arms. "What happened to Drew, Rosalind?"

Her teeth chattered; her body shook. "He disappeared. He can do magic like you can. Without Angelic. Not just shadow magic. All kinds, I think." She closed her eyes, feeling the auras washing over her skin—faint tendrils of leafy green and a burning gold.

He was still here.

"I can still feel him in Lilinor. He's not far. He still plans to take me as his wife. He wanted to teach me a lesson first."

"I need you to conduct a spell with me. I've driven most of the alu demons out, but I need you to help me track Drew. We can seal up this city after we rip his spine out of his body and bury him under the earth."

A deep pain gnawed at Rosalind's chest. "What about Miranda?"

"She's gone."

Her sister's voice played around the edges of her mind. There was something she'd said. *The things that are buried rise up again.*

Rosalind grabbed Caine's arms. "You can bring her back."

Caine's face hardened. "No. Listen to me, Rosalind. We need to find Drew."

Right. Aurora had said Caine didn't approve of necromancy.

Fine, then. She'd just have to do it without him. Her fingers curled into fists. *After, all, what's the point of being a powerful mage if I can't raise my sister from the dead?*

A tear slid down her cheek. "Why weren't you here? We needed you."

Caine's face changed, his brow furrowing in an expression she'd never seen on him before: vulnerability. "I was with Ambrose. I thought I was supposed to be with him. I thought he was the target."

Rosalind shook her head. "Drew is obsessed with punishing me."

"For what?"

"He thinks I chose you over him."

Caine brushed his knuckles over her cheek for just a moment, then his features hardened again. "We need to act now. I'm going to use gods-magic. I'll shield us. We'll travel on the wind. I need you to direct me, to help find Drew's aura. Are you ready for this?"

She shot a glance at her sister, whose blood mingled with the rainwater. She looked like she'd be frozen if she woke now...

How long would Rosalind have before Miranda's body was too far gone?

Still, it wasn't like she could ask Caine these questions. "I'm ready to go."

Caine wrapped a hand around her waist, pulling her in close, steadying her shaking body. He arched his neck, and black wings sprouted from his back. "Hold on to me tight," he said.

She wrapped her arms around his neck.

She felt a strange liquid darkness flow from his chest into her own, quelling some of her rage. His magic seemed to make her body weightless. *A taste of the void, gifted from Nyxobas.*

"Hold tighter," he said.

In the next moment, they were in the air below Lilinor's magic-darkened sky. Her dress slid up, and she wrapped her legs around Caine's waist, turning her head to look at the city. They rose high above Ninlil's sharp spires. Caine's powerful arms held her tight, his heart beating against hers.

Craning her neck, Rosalind scanned the city for the tendrils of Drew's magic. And there, she saw what she was looking for—curling from Ambrose's White Tower, whorls of copper, gold and blue.

Drew had a perfect view of the city he planned to conquer.

"There, in the White Tower," she whispered. "I see his magic."

They moved lower, closing in on the tower. Cold air rushed over

Rosalind's skin, but at least the spell had been broken. At least the cold no longer iced over her soul.

They landed on Ambrose's marble floor. Rosalind unclasped her arms from Caine's neck, and whirled to face Drew.

He'd hidden himself with magic, but she could see him all the same. He stood by one of the windows, magic curling around him—a broad silhouette in a maelstrom of colored auras.

As she stepped closer, she felt the heat coming off his body. Her fury ignited, and she lunged for him, grabbing him by the throat.

He killed Miranda.

She squeezed her fingers, tightening them around his neck, feeling his body twitch—but before she could finish ripping the life from his body, the air cracked with white heat. Drew's body burned with white light, and he disappeared.

Slippery fucker. How was she supposed to kill him if he wouldn't stay in one place?

Rosalind stepped away from the window, her eyes flicking to the sky. Red tinged the darkness again, and sunlight pierced the storm clouds. But she could no longer feel Drew's magic.

She shivered, glancing at Caine. "I failed."

"Do you think he's still in Lilinor?"

She stared out the window again. With that strange magic gone, she felt a shift in the air. It was like a white noise that you didn't notice until it turned off. "Pretty sure he's gone."

"I need to raise a shield so he doesn't come back for you. We're going to find him, Rosalind. And when we do, the next time... it will be on our terms."

"How did he get here in the first place?"

Caine scrubbed a hand over his mouth. "You said he used magic the way I do? Gods-magic?"

She nodded.

"Then he used Nyxobas's power to create a portal. Only Malphas and I are able to create them, between Lilinor and the rest of the world."

"What if I'm wrong and he's still in Lilinor?"

"I'll make sure he can get out. But he won't be able to get back in."

She felt tears rising to the surface, but she couldn't give in to her sorrow. Not now. She still had to find a way to save Miranda.

Rays of amber sunlight broke through the clouds, bathing Caine's face in gold. "I need to darken the skies. Then I'll work on the shield."

"I'll help with the spell."

He shook his head. "You need to stop using magic for now. It's affecting your mind."

Her nails pierced her palms, and Cleo whispered, *Don't listen to him, Rosalind. He fears your power. All men fear women's power. It's why they call us witches.*

Caine closed his eyes, and she stared as the shadows around him thickened, growing denser. Silvery vines of magic grew from his body, reaching to the reddening sky over Lilinor.

Wracked with fatigue, Rosalind crossed to Ambrose's bed. She threw herself down on the silky sheets, watching as Caine began to work his magic. Under the blood red sky, his strong body glowed like starlight.

If Caine can use the night to cloak a world, she thought, *I can bring life into Miranda's body.*

CHAPTER 9

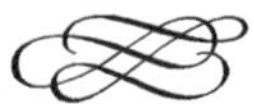

Rosalind pushed through the door to the Gelal Field, retracing her steps to the last place she'd seen her sister smile: the old temple of Nyxobas.

Everything was in its place again. The moon hanging in the sky, the stars twinkling from a blanket of black.

She'd slept just long enough so she could walk steadily again—enough time for Caine to fully shield the city from any more alu attacks, or from Drew's return—but her legs still quaked. And that sound… the breaking of Miranda's ribs… it replayed in her mind, hammering over and over like a war drum.

Her footsteps crunched over the dirt path. It hadn't been that long ago that she was walking down here to meet Miranda. But now the myrtle and sycamore trees didn't smell quite as sweet. In fact, their scent was overpowering, the sickly perfume of a funeral wreath.

It wouldn't be long before they'd want to bury Miranda's body. The wind rushed over her skin and rustled the leaves. Everything had begun to rot. Miranda was dead. Tammi was gone. Half of Lilinor had been slaughtered. And in the chaotic aftermath of the slaughter, Rosalind still didn't know what had happened to Aurora.

A sharp pain pierced her chest. *So this is what it feels like when your heart breaks.*

A tear rolled down her cheek, and she wiped it off with the back of her hand.

She was supposed to bury Miranda soon, by the old yew tree. She was supposed to tell stories of Miranda's life, to free Miranda's soul. But she hardly knew any.

She just needed some time alone, to think things over. To cleanse her mind of Cleo's thoughts.

The sound of tinkling bells floated on the wind, and Rosalind crossed through the door into the old ruin of a temple. She glanced at the spot where Miranda had woven the wildflower wreaths, then crossed to the tall window. From here, she had a perfect view of the giant yew.

She climbed through the window, landing in the dirt. Hugging herself, she trod the path that meandered down to the yew. Where would they want to bury Miranda? Would she get her own grave, or would they throw her in the whore pit?

Emptiness bloomed in Rosalind's chest. She had no idea what had happened to her parents' bodies. Out there in the wilderness, they'd probably been left on the stakes until they'd rotted off.

And that was what Drew had planned for Miranda—to leave her pinned to the post like an entomologist's specimen, after he'd forced Rosalind to kill her.

Bile rose in her throat, and she choked it down.

As she drew closer to the yew, the tinkling of bells floated on the wind. Aurora had said that was the dead speaking... Was Rosalind losing her mind, or could she hear Miranda's voice whispering on the wind?

Sometimes, what's buried doesn't stay underground...

Rosalind's pulse raced, and she hurried under the canopy of the yew boughs. Around her, mementos of the dead sparked in the moonlight—silvery ribbons and lockets. She traced her finger down a sheer streamer, to the tiny glass bottle at the bottom. The keepsakes here were beautiful and delicate—but forgotten. No one came here to remember the dead. How many years until Miranda was completely forgotten, until Rosalind had forgotten the sound of her voice and the briny smell of her magic?

She turned her back on the trunk, sliding down to the ground. A threadbare gold ribbon dangled near her head. She turned and saw the name *Julietta* written in old, faded ink. Who had Julietta been? No one remembered her now.

Another body for the whore pit.

Rosalind wasn't going to let her sister lie here. Miranda deserved a second chance.

Sometimes, what's buried doesn't stay underground...

Bone-conjuring. That's what Aurora had called it. And whether or not Caine approved, Rosalind was going to learn how to do it. She'd get her revenge on Drew. And when she did, her sister would be by her side.

A flicker of movement through the branches caught her eye. From the darkness, a raven fluttered to the ground before her. Rosalind stared, her pulse racing, as the raven began to grow larger. With the sound of a hundred bones cracking, and a low grunt, the raven transformed before her eyes.

In the next moment, Caine stood before her, silver magic curling off his body.

Rosalind's heart thumped. "What the hell was that?"

"What?" He took a step closer.

Her throat had gone dry, and she stood slowly. "Nothing. It's just that I've never seen you transform before." As she spoke she realized her cheeks were wet, and she wiped the tears off with the back of her hand. "How did you know I was here?"

"I could smell you."

She wrinkled her nose. "That's disturbing."

"I like your scent." Caine closed the distance between them. "I needed to find you."

"For what?"

Gently, he wiped a tear from her cheek. "I know what it's like."

She flinched at his touch. She wasn't ready for kindness right now.

Rage was the one thing keeping her from collapsing under a wave of grief. "What do you mean? You know what *what's* like?"

His expression darkened. "Never mind. Tell me what happened with Drew."

Not a question, she thought. Even when Caine was comforting someone, he gave orders.

"Is it important now?" she asked.

"I need to understand our enemy." His voice was low but insistent. "If he can truly use gods-magic, I need to know what he wants, how he operates. We need to understand his power."

"Right." She squeezed her eyes shut, trying not to picture the crimson stain on Miranda's gown, the blood pooling in the rainwater. She wrapped the bluebell stem around her finger. *Focus, Rosalind.* What was important here? "For one thing," she began, "Remember that scar that Drew gave me in Maremount?"

"On your stomach, yes."

"It serves a purpose. It wasn't purely sadism. He could control my body, like a demon can."

Caine growled. He, too, had the power to control her mind—but he'd never once used it.

"He uses gods-magic like you do," she continued. "But not just one. All the gods. I saw and felt all their auras."

The shadows around Caine grew heavy, so thick they almost seemed tangible. His magic crackled the air. "And what did he do to Miranda?"

His voice was low, laced with cold fury. She could feel the rage coming off him, darkening the very light from the stars. No matter how many times Caine saved her life, when he turned primal, the ancient part of her brain told her to run.

She took a small step away from him, backing up to the tree trunk. "Drew thinks you're his nemesis. He thinks my parents were the true king and queen, and that you killed them. He thinks I'm a traitor for sleeping with you."

Caine cocked his head, but didn't respond.

Maybe her grief had made her a little reckless with her words. "I told him it wasn't true," she added. "But he said it was just as bad if I thought about it. He's totally lost his mind."

The temperature dropped in the cemetery, and goosebumps rose on her skin. A cloud of steam rose from her mouth when she exhaled.

"What else did he say?" Caine pressed. "What did he do when he controlled your mind?"

"He put a collar on Miranda. He made us walk outside, into the rain. To the esplanade." She swallowed hard. The sound of Miranda's ribs cracking played again in her skull.

"What happened next?" he asked softly. The air chilled further, and frost spread over the yew leaves.

"He wanted to teach me a lesson. He told Miranda to stand against the stake. He told me to take the iron nail from his hand."

Caine's eyes had turned to pure black, and his body was completely still. When she glanced into his eyes, she felt as though she were looking into the void itself. She had the feeling that he kept his energy coiled tightly inside that lean, muscled body, and if he were ever pushed too far it could burst forth at any moment, leveling the whole city.

"A stake and an iron nail. Recreating your parents' death, what I did to them. He was punishing all three of us at the same time." Icy venom laced his voice. She could feel the shadows seeping off him, cold and empty. "He made you stab her."

Rosalind shook her head. "I was able to stop it; I'm not sure how. But I didn't stab her—Drew did. He's really rotten at his core. I don't know if he was always this way, or if the magic twisted his mind."

"I'm going to slaughter him in the most painful way possible," Caine seethed.

"I almost killed her." Her voice broke. "I really wanted to stab her. I nearly did it."

"But you didn't." A sharp tone undercut his words. "Count yourself lucky."

At his words, hot rage simmered. "Lucky? Are you serious?"

"You didn't kill her. Drew did. It was a lucky escape for you."

"Not so great with your people-skills, are you? Sometimes, it's like you have no humanity. When someone watches their sister murdered, you don't tell them three hours later that they're lucky."

He glared at her, his dark eyes completely demonic.

"Of course, you're not really human," she muttered.

"And I suppose your humanity makes you better than me, right?" Bitterness poisoned his words. In his black eyes, she couldn't find a hint of compassion. "You resisted. A demon would have given in to the lure of the slaughter."

"Yeah, probably," she snapped. "I guess I am lucky, then." *And I'm going to raise Miranda from the dead. Not a damn thing you can do about it.* "I just ask that you don't bury my sister in the whore pit with all the other humans you've discarded in Lilinor."

His silver aura sliced the air around him. "Where the hell did you hear that term?"

"Esmerelda. She quite helpfully pointed out that Miranda and I would end up in the whore-pit. Another body for the mass grave. And since you won't help raise her from the dead, I guess she'll stay there, right?"

"I'm going to murder Esmerelda."

"You can't solve every problem by murdering people, you know." She shook her head to clear her mind. "Do you need anything else from me, or are we done?"

"Ambrose is calling together a small council. Aurora, Malphas, me, and you. He wants a debriefing."

"Aurora and Malphas are okay?" This was the first good news she'd heard.

"They're fine." His eyes had returned to their usual pale gray. "Meet us in the armory as soon as you can."

He turned, walking away. And just as he took his third step away from her, his body darkened, condensing in a burst of silver magic. In his raven form, he took off into the air, leaving Rosalind alone with the faintly tinkling bells.

CHAPTER 10

*R*osalind stalked through a long stone tunnel, deep in the bowels of Ninlil Castle.

A dark, empty hole burned in her chest. Her whole body felt cold, like she'd died alongside her sister. She certainly didn't feel lucky.

She hugged herself, rubbing her arms. After the chaos of the massacre, at least she'd see a few more familiar faces. Aurora might be her only friend left in the city, since Tammi had been stuck in the Abzu.

And then there was Malphas, Caine's brother. She hadn't seen him since arriving here. The incubus had hardly left his room, from what she could tell.

Would Malphas help her raise Miranda from the dead? Not likely. He probably blindly followed the same rules as his older brother. He'd probably tell her she could count herself lucky since she hadn't delivered the final blow herself, and she should just get on with things without complaining.

That meant there was only one person who could help her: the demented witch who inhabited her body. "Cleo, I need you now. I need to know how to bring the dead back to life."

Cleo's aura washed over her skin. *That magic belongs to Nyxobas, and I belong to Druloch. Why don't you ask your lover?*

A lump rose in her throat. "He won't allow it. Neither will Ambrose."

So how else was she going to figure this out? Maybe Lilinor had a library or something. A collection of forbidden spell books.

And how would she find that? Maybe Aurora knew. Aurora, at least, had known the term *bone-conjuring*.

At the end of the hall, she pushed through the door into Ambrose's armory, a large black dome crammed with weapons. In the center of the room, Malphas leaned against an obsidian altar, its sides hung with ornate silver axes.

She didn't want to meet his pale gray eyes—she wasn't sure what she'd find there. After all, she'd tortured him. Maybe he thought she deserved what had happened today.

Either that, or he'd look at her with sympathy. She wasn't sure she could take that, either.

Instead of meeting his gaze, she surveyed the room, scanning the medieval armor hung from the walls. She crossed to one of the displays, running her fingers over a smooth, silver breastplate. The sharp-peaked silver helmets screamed menace, yet the armor drew her in. How would it feel to live shielded by impenetrable silver, immune to arrows and bullets, to iron nails?

What would it be like to stop feeling pain?

She shoved her hand into her pocket, curling a bluebell's stem around her fingertip, and her chest unclenched just a little. Miranda had been right: the wildflowers did bring peace to her mind.

"Rosalind," Malphas said. He spoke quietly, but his voice echoed off the high ceiling. She turned to look at him, and when she did, she recognized the sadness etched on his beautiful face. "I'm sorry for what happened to your sister."

Rosalind could only nod mutely. She couldn't tell him about her plans, that she'd find a way to bring Miranda back.

"She was always kind to me," he added, "when we were little. She gave me food when I was starving. She gave me a blanket to sleep in when I went to bed at night in the prison cells."

A lump rose in Rosalind's throat. This wasn't what she wanted to hear now. She was holding it together by shoving her grief and fury deep under the surface, like ravenous demons too dangerous to unleash. It would take just a light brush of kindness to unearth them, and who knew what destruction they'd wreak. "Yes," she said. "She was the sweet one."

His brow furrowed for just a moment, as if he was confused. "I loved you both."

A hot tear poured down her cheek, and she wiped it away. She hadn't expected to hear that at all. She blinked away the tears. "Where are the others?"

"Coming," he said.

At just that moment, the door creaked open and Caine stalked into the room. Like her, he was dressed for battle: black leather clothes, laden with silver blades. In contrast to his battle gear, his features were soft when his gaze met hers. As he crossed to her, his aura rolled off his skin in waves of thrilling power.

He stopped mere inches from her. "How are you?" The question sounded almost unnatural for him, like he'd never uttered those words in that sequence before.

"Still alive. I guess I'm lucky." Tears brimmed again, and she blinked hard. *Keep it together, Rosalind.* "But we're not here to talk about me. We're here to talk about what we're going to do next, right? Ambrose must have a plan."

Caine's arctic eyes were fixed on her. She had the uncomfortable feeling that he could read her thoughts, unearthing her darkest secrets. *He can't do that, can he?*

"Ambrose is planning a death feast for all the fallen," Malphas said. "In six hours, after the dead are buried. We will honor Miranda there."

Miranda wasn't going to stay underground, but Rosalind wasn't going to bring that up now. "What's a death feast?"

"It's a ceremony to honor the dead," Malphas said. "It's where people tell stories about someone's life and drape mementos on the yew branches. They offer bread to Nyxobas, and pour libations. It helps to open the gates to the afterworld, and frees the souls from the House of Shades. Miranda's spirit will have an easier time finding its way to the celestial realm."

"We have very little control over what the gods do," Caine said. "Death is their domain. We just do what we can to placate them."

"So it's mostly just for show."

"Not just for show," Caine said. "It helps people accept death." For just a moment, he shared a dark look with his brother, his gray eyes piercing in the low light.

"Something we all need to accept," Malphas said.

"Even those of us with very long lives," Caine said. "We must watch the ones we love grow old and sicken."

Rosalind's fingernails pierced her arms. *Maybe. Maybe not.* She nodded. "And what do I need to do at this death feast?"

"You only need to tell stories about her," Malphas said. "The things you'll remember the most."

She stared at the floor, her chest tight. "I hardly know any, apart from the ones you told me. And the past few weeks, I was only starting to get to know her." She straightened. "Anyway, we have more pressing concerns than symbolic gestures. First and foremost, we have to deal with the delusional maniac who nearly razed the city."

Candlelight wavered over Malphas's porcelain skin. "It's all related. We need your power, and your power is no good if your mind is fractured. The death feast will help you heal."

Cleo's aura roiled in her skull. *Don't listen to them. They want you to bury your twin in the whore pit.*

Rosalind heaved a sigh. "Miranda needs her own grave. I don't want her in the mass grave." She didn't want Miranda waking up surrounded by rotting corpses.

"Of course," Caine said. A lock of hair fell in Rosalind's eyes, and he pushed it away, studying her. "Have you been hearing Cleo's voice?"

She really couldn't keep anything from his gaze. "The iron ring doesn't work anymore. But Miranda told me bluebells would bring me peace, and they work better. I've got wildflowers in my pocket. She made me a wreath…"

"With magic as powerful as yours," Caine said, "you have to take care that it doesn't warp your mind. Especially with everything that Drew did today. He was trying to break you."

Her fingernails dug harder into her skin, and she shook her head. "I'm not broken."

"I know," Caine said. "But you can't use more powerful magic. Understood?"

At the far end of the hall, Aurora pushed through a silver-plated door into the circular room, her normally tidy hair flying around, unkempt. Her bright gold dress was torn and singed. For just a moment, her gaze flicked to Rosalind. "I'm sorry about Miranda." She stalked over to a high-backed chair and sat, her gaze lowered.

Rosalind swallowed hard. She wasn't the only person in here who'd lost someone today. Everyone in the room had watched their friends die at the hands of Drew. She turned to Caine, staring at his perfect profile—the thick eyelashes framing his pale eyes. "Did you lose anyone you cared about?" she asked. "Any friends?"

"Soldiers. Not friends."

She was nearly certain she caught a subtle eye roll from Malphas.

The silver door opened again, and Ambrose strode into the room, leveling his emerald gaze on her. His black aura curled from his body in thorny spikes, and an icy breeze whispered over her skin, scented of rowans and cloves.

At the scent of him, Cleo's aura roiled, a vibrant, leafy power. Even now, as Rosalind was dealing with the shockwaves from her sister's murder, Cleo wanted to jump on the vampire lord and rip the clothes off his perfect body.

Down, girl. This is not the time.

"Who can tell me what the fuck happened today?" Ambrose's voice was a low, animalistic growl that seemed to rumble in her gut.

Apparently, vampires weren't into offering condolences or sympathy. Maybe a side effect of watching one generation of humans after another die.

"What happened today," Caine began softly, "is that we lost half our army. And we lost our chance at creating daywalkers, when one of our mages was murdered. By a *human*."

Contempt filled his final word, and she couldn't help but think of what he'd said by the yew tree. *And I suppose your humanity makes you better than me, right?* By his tone, she'd known exactly how he felt about humans.

"How did this happen?" Ambrose asked, his words low and controlled.

"Drew can apparently control the sun. Rosalind says he uses gods-magic. He's protected by the Brotherhood in Boston, and he has the power to control Rosalind's mind."

"In other words," Aurora said, "we're fucked."

CHAPTER 11

"What happens to Miranda's second soul?" Ambrose's gaze slid to Rosalind, as if he was searching for a reaction.

She kept her expression impassive. *This isn't the end for Miranda. Sometimes the things that are buried will rise again.*

Caine crossed his arms. "My best guess is that her second soul is trapped in the house of shades. I can retrieve it."

"That's dangerous," Malphas said. "You know you could get lost there."

Caine shook his head. "I'll be fine. And once I find it, we'll need another human to take it on."

"Or a half-human," Malphas said. "Like you and me."

Caine's expression darkened. "Not you."

Malphas frowned. "Why not?"

"You *know* why not, Malphas," Caine snapped.

Ambrose stalked closer, his gaze fixed on Caine. The vampire lord was nearly as tall as Caine—at least six foot three. "He may be your brother, but this is my kingdom. If Malphas agrees to do it, then so be it. He understands what's at stake."

An electric tension crackled through the room, and goosebumps rose on Rosalind's skin. Dark magic curled off the two men.

Who would win in a fight between these two, if it came down to it? Caine had a broader, more muscled build, but Ambrose had a certain quiet ferocity to him that unnerved her. Caine might be the grandson of a shadow god, but a lethal darkness ran deep in Ambrose. If they ever came to blows, the carnage would be brutal.

Clearly, neither of these men were used to hearing the word *no*.

Ambrose was a king. But when it came down to it, he was just a vampire. Caine was a demigod. He'd been allowing Ambrose to rule the city for centuries, probably because he had no interest in being a king. Rosalind had the sense that Caine felt he owed Ambrose something, though she didn't know what. He seemed to have some deeply ingrained sense of loyalty—but after five centuries, that loyalty might have started to wear thin.

"Relax, brother," Malphas said. "We know the risks now, and we know how to avoid them. It won't be like last time."

The vampire lord narrowed his eyes, studying Caine. "We lost half the city today," he hissed. "Half our army. And we'll continue to lose them, as long as they're vulnerable to sunlight. Malphas is the only answer we have. He's the only human in Lilinor who isn't a courtesan."

"So use a courtesan," Caine snapped, his eyes blazing with a pale light. "The shield I created will hold. Drew, the alu, the hunters—they won't be able to get through."

"And then what?" Aurora asked. "We stay trapped in here until we starve to death? We won't be able to get a fresh supply of courtesans or other humans."

"I'll be able to get to and from the other world. I'll ensure that some of us can come back through the shield," Caine said quietly. Even he seemed to understand this wasn't a long-term solution.

Rosalind's gaze flicked to a row of silver axes lining the sides of the altar. *If the vampires are going to start starving here, maybe I need to upgrade my weapons.*

"Quite the impressive arsenal," she said. "I don't suppose I could get my hands on some of that, considering you all are gonna be pretty hungry within a few days."

Ambrose stared at her. "These weapons are six hundred years old. We captured tens of thousands of humans in Târgoviște. The vampires showed no mercy, and impaled each human on a stake. We created a forest of the dead that the world has never forgotten."

Rosalind's skin went cold, and she swallowed hard. *Not sure how to respond to that.*

His black aura cut the air around him. "I want to recreate the glory of that army. I can't always depend on night attacks, as I did back then. We need the power of daywalkers for true glory."

Rosalind winced. "A forest of dead humans isn't exactly my ideal vision of the world. Nature has its own balance, don't you think?"

Aurora leaned down, pulling an axe from the altar. "We need to be able to defend ourselves from Drew's new empire. Just like you need to defend yourself." She crossed the room, handing Rosalind the heavy silver weapon. "Drew not only has the power of the Brotherhood on his side, keeping him safe, but he can use gods-magic. It's an abomination. And if daywalking vampires are an abomination too, maybe that's what we need to be to fight back."

Rosalind gripped the ax. "What can you tell me about gods-magic?"

Caine raised his hand, and inky shadows curled from his fingers. "As a demigod, I have a direct line to shadow magic."

"Right. And Drew can use magic from all the gods," Rosalind said.

"But Drew wasn't sired by the seven gods," Ambrose said, "so what the fuck is going on?"

Rosalind cocked her head. "Actually, according to Drew, we're both sired by the seven gods. We're direct descendants of Azazeyl. The One Who Is All. The original fallen god. He fragmented into seven broken gods, who slowly went insane from the split."

"Seven tormented gods," Caine said, "desperate to be whole again."

"Ridiculous." Ambrose frowned. "Azazeyl never existed. He's a myth that only lunatics believe."

"Apparently not," Rosalind countered, "given what we've seen my cousin do. He says that the blood of Blodrial—the seventh god—awakened his powers. Now he drinks it regularly. I've had the ambrosia before, but I was wearing an iron ring, so nothing happened. Except it gave me the ability to see magic."

"It's real," Caine said, so quietly she almost didn't hear him. "When Rosalind's parents called the second souls into our bodies, they used the seal of Azazeyl."

Ambrose's dark aura curled from his body. His green eyes locked on Caine.

Rosalind's throat tightened. "I want to get more ambrosia. If Drew is right, I have the same powers he does. I'll need to leave here long enough to steal some blood from the Chambers. I can be just as strong as he is."

Caine's gaze slid to hers. "You said Drew lost his mind."

Her lip curled. "I'll only use it long enough to murder the bastard."

Aurora shook her head. "You want the power of seven gods at your fingertips? Why do I feel like this won't end well?"

Rosalind sighed. "I get it. Humans weren't meant to have this power. Drew seems far crazier than when I first met him. And given that a bluebell stem is the only thing keeping me from being controlled by the voice in my head, there's a serious risk I could end up completely mental. But like you pointed out, maybe we need to fight Drew with another abomination. You'll just have to help me get back to normal when it's all over."

Deep in her pocket, she wrapped the stem tighter around her fingertip, nearly cutting off the circulation. "Gods-magic is what we need to kill Drew. I'll drink the blood. You all can pay for my therapist when we're done."

"Don't do anything yet," Caine said. "I'm going back to Maremount first."

"Why?" Rosalind asked.

"I'm going to rip Drew's flesh from his bones," he said. "And I'm going to find the seal of Azazeyl while I'm there. If I can get into the House of Shades, I should be able to find Miranda's second soul. I'll trap it in the sigil."

Rosalind bristled. She wanted to be there to watch Drew die, but she couldn't leave Lilinor. She still had to raise Miranda from the grave.

"Good. Find the sigil," Ambrose said. "And how, exactly, do you get into the House of Shades?"

"That's for the gods to know," Caine said.

Rosalind's stomach tightened. What was going on with Caine? That was no way to address a king.

Ambrose tilted his head, his eyes darkening. "Fine." His controlled voice belied an icy rage. "But do not try to hunt down Drew on your own. We will have an army to do that, once you return with the sigil. We will create my daywalkers. That is our priority, and I'm not losing another one of my mages."

Caine's eyes had turned black as coal. "My priority is slaughtering Drew."

"You may be a demigod," Ambrose said, "but if Drew is what you say he is, he has the power of *seven* gods. And I need you to return alive. Do you understand me, incubus?"

Caine simply tilted his head, staring at Ambrose. The air between them seemed to crackle with tension.

Rosalind took a deep breath. "The legend is true. I've seen the magic with my own eyes. If I drink the blood, I could be used as a weapon against Drew."

"This should get interesting," Aurora muttered.

Caine touched her arm. "You don't need to figure this out now. You're still mourning your sister's death. Humans are not meant to wield gods-magic, just like you said."

Ambrose surveyed Caine coolly. "If these legends are as real as you say, she should drink the blood. Maybe we won't even need a third soul to create the daywalkers. Rosalind might be enough. I'll believe it when I see it, but it's worth a shot—unless you're worried that your little girlfriend could become more powerful than the great demigod?"

Caine glared at him. "Has it bothered you all these years, Ambrose, that I'm connected to your god more than you'll ever be?"

An oppressive silence enshrouded the room, and the candles flickered in their sconces.

"Let's stay focused," Malphas said, before his gaze slid to Rosalind. "My brother is right. You should mourn your sister before you make any big decisions."

"No." The word came out of her mouth too quickly, too insistently. But the fact was, she wasn't going to mourn her sister. She was going to bring her back. When she spoke again, she tried to soften her voice. "I mean, we have plenty of other things to worry about. Mourning won't kill Drew. And you know what will make me feel better? Killing Drew."

Burn him, Cleo whispered.

She shook her head, trying to clear her mind. Maybe her own sanity was no longer worth preserving at all costs. "The point is, I think Ambrose is right."

"Of course I am," he said. "If this works, I'll want to see how you fight. I'm not convinced the Brotherhood trained you properly."

Rosalind thought she heard a low growl rise from Caine's throat. The temperature in the room cooled again, and Caine's icy gaze bored into Ambrose. "You don't know how to use gods-magic."

"I want to see how she fights," Ambrose said. "Malphas can teach her the rest. Unless you're worried about another incubus getting his hands on her."

Caine's sharpened silver aura sliced the air around him. "Why does the idea of this turn my stomach?"

Aurora straightened. "Because Ambrose and Malphas are the only men on earth who look as good as you, and you're all thinking with your dicks."

Caine turned to Rosalind, and nodded at the ax in her hand. "I trust you know how to look after yourself."

She frowned. "What, exactly, are you worried about?"

"Just take care of yourself. And don't let anyone get in your head."

CHAPTER 12

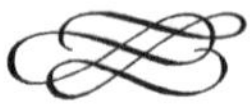

osalind stood in her bedroom, wrapped in blankets. She wore a black gown, and had her hair piled up on her head.

How long would it be before Miranda would rot beyond repair?

Through the open window, the sound of chanting floated on the wind. Beyond the Gelal Field, and past the temple of Nyxobas, the vampires were holding their funeral in the Garden of the Dead.

She'd lasted about thirty minutes at the death feast—just long enough to listen to some of the eulogies and to give her own half-hearted tribute under a yew tree. She'd felt entirely numb as she'd stood by Miranda's corpse, with the eyes of an entire vampire city on her.

She told the one story she knew: that Miranda had never stopped looking for her. It wasn't a brilliant tale, with a beginning and an end, but it was the one thing she knew for certain. As she'd spoken, Caine and Malphas had stood on either side of her. And when Caine leaned in to tell her she could go if she wanted—before they covered Miranda in dirt—she took off up the hill on her own.

Now, from her spot on her bed, she could still hear the mournful songs drifting through the city. She hadn't shed a single tear today—

but maybe there was no point in mourning a sister who wasn't going to stay dead.

A knock on her door interrupted her thoughts, and she rose from her bed. She wrapped the sheet tightly around her as she crossed the room to pull open the door.

Aurora stood in the hall, dressed in a long red gown, a red rose tucked behind her ear. All the vampires had been wearing red at the funeral—apparently it was Lilinor's color of death.

"Caine sent me to check on you," Aurora said. "He couldn't leave yet."

"I'm fine. I'm just taking the time alone to think a few things over."

Aurora studied her. "Why do I feel like you're planning something?"

"Maybe I am. Come in." Rosalind turned, stalking back to her bed.

Aurora stepped into the room. "Starting to get a bad feeling about this."

"Miranda's story wasn't finished. No one even knows what it was."

"I'm sorry." Aurora reached into her handbag, pulling out a small, silver flask. She handed it to Rosalind, and when she did, Rosalind noticed the tremor in the vampire's hands.

"Are you okay?" Rosalind asked.

Aurora plopped down on the bed. "I'm sick of watching vampires burn. A couple of months ago, the Brotherhood's Hunters took us to a field in Belmont. They opened the van in the broad daylight. Caine saved me, but I heard the screams as the other vamps died. I still hear them in my dreams. I can still smell their flesh burning. Today, it was worse."

Rosalind's chest ached. "I can see why you'd want the daywalker spell so badly. "

"All I know is, if we don't do something, all of Lilinor will burn. And now we've lost Miranda."

"What if we could get her back?" Rosalind asked.

"What are you going on about?"

"Caine will never let Malphas take on the extra soul. I don't know what happened to Caine after he gained his extra soul, but whatever it was, he won't talk about it. And he doesn't want the same thing to happen to his baby brother. Neither Caine nor Ambrose trust the courtesans enough to allow them to take on this power. Plus, they'd have to be trained to control magic, and we don't have time for that."

"Right. But Miranda's dead."

And if we don't act quickly, we won't be able to get her back. Rosalind's fingers tightened on the bedsheets. "But maybe she doesn't have to stay that way."

Aurora stared at her for a long moment. "I hope you're not talking about bone-conjuring."

"You said it's possible. Isn't there a book somewhere?" She took a deep breath. "The night before she died, she said something to me: 'Sometimes what's buried rises again.' I think it was some sort of message. I heard her voice again, whispering through the bells by the yew."

"No," Aurora said, frowning. "Caine won't allow it."

"Why?"

"Because it's a sacrilege to steal souls from the gods."

"I have no loyalty to the gods," Rosalind said. "Do you? Because they don't give a fuck about us."

"I'm not particularly religious, but Caine's a bit close to Nyxobas. And I'm loyal to Caine."

"You didn't want to see any more vampires burn. This is your way out. Bring Miranda back. We'll get the soul back in her."

"And how do you expect that to work, when we're relying on Caine to complete the spell?"

"He's forbidden people from conjuring the dead—but once it's done, it will be too late. I mean, he's not going to kill her. And surely Ambrose will back us up. He wants his daywalkers more than anyone, and Miranda is the best person to handle the task."

Aurora just stared at her.

Rosalind continued. "We'd have the three mages we needed, too. We could perform the daywalker spell, just like we planned. We'd have to wait for a courtesan to be trained, or wait to see if she lost her mind. Miranda knows how to control the magic already. With the three of us reunited, we could stop the Brotherhood from immolating you all again and again."

"It's tempting. Extremely tempting." Aurora took a deep breath. "But Caine will cast me out of the city if he finds out."

"I'll take full responsibility. I'll never let them know you were involved. I promise."

Aurora stared at Rosalind for so long that Rosalind couldn't quite hold her gaze.

At last, Aurora spoke. "Fine. I'm not promising anything." She took a long swig from her flask. "We can look for the spell. And then I'll decide. Don't tell a single person."

* * *

ROSALIND STOOD by Aurora's side on the third story of Ninlil's library, a balcony overlooking the pale stone floor.

Silver moonlight streamed through the tall, arched windows, sparking off glittering silver titles on the books' spines. A portrait of a beautiful dark-haired woman, her skin illuminated by pearly light, hung between the shelves. She held a scroll unraveled in her hand, inscribed with Angelic. Behind her, walls of scrolls burned. *Alexandria.*

Aurora turned, walking to another shelf; her heels clacked over the floor. She ran her fingers over the spines, scanning the titles. "These are the plague and pestilence grimoires."

A flicker of movement caught Rosalind's eye, and she glanced at the stone vaults that arched high above. Bats circled overhead. *Eerie place.*

"Here!" Aurora plucked a black grimoire from a shelf. A silver skull marked its spine. "Necromancy. Death spells. This is the one."

Rosalind's pulse raced. *We have what we need.*

Aurora cracked the book open, flipping through the yellowed pages. "It's here. The song of the Manzazuu." She narrowed her eyes. "We will need to make preparations. We'll need a fire pit under the stars, human blood, and a life to sacrifice to Nyxobas."

"Please don't tell me that has to be human, too."

"Animal is fine. We need to drink some wine and eat some black bread, whatever that is." She glanced at Rosalind. "You'll have to do the eating. I don't eat food."

"What's the purpose of that?"

"Nyxobas wants us to acknowledge death's power. Decay, decomposition, rotting flesh. All that good stuff. When you eat fermenting foods, you acknowledge that you're mortal, that the gods rule your death. You're stuck in a body that's slowly rotting until it gives out and you cease to exist. The gods are quite keen on that idea."

"Well, I feel better already."

"And you're acknowledging that when you bring Miranda back, it won't be forever. She'll be brought back to life, but in a mortal body, slowly dying, as all mortal bodies do."

"Right. Lovely."

"The gods are fucked up. Now you know why Caine has some personality issues." Aurora glanced down at the page. "We need a magic circle. Nyxobas's sigil. We put Miranda's corpse in the center, add in a few of her belongings, and we incant the spell. *Usella Mituti Ikkalu Baltuti.* And that's it. The spirit will be called back from the House of Shades, and will inhabit Miranda's body once more. From what I can tell, anyone can do it." She closed the book, meeting Rosalind's gaze. "But are you sure you *want* to?"

"I have to," Rosalind said. "Miranda went through hell to find me, to reunite us again. I feel certain that if the roles were reversed—if I'd died—she'd do whatever it took to bring me back." She took a deep breath. "But I want to make sure you don't get in trouble for this. Are you sure you want to do the spell with me?"

"You'll only screw it up if I leave you to your own devices. But you can't tell anyone." Aurora slammed the book shut. "I don't suppose you want to do this now?"

Tempting, but... Rosalind shook her head. "I won't be able to. Right after the Feast for the Dead, I'm supposed to meet Caine by the portal. He's going to open the shield for me before he leaves for Maremount. And then I get the gods-blood."

Aurora took a deep breath. "Once you've got gods-magic, you'll owe me one. I'm going to be asking for some favors."

"You trust me with gods-magic?"

Aurora arched an eyebrow. "Not even a little, but I don't get to call the shots here."

CHAPTER 13

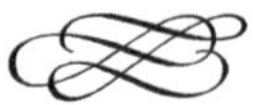

$\mathcal{R}$osalind climbed the pale marble stairs to the White Tower, where Caine and the portal waited for her. Thin rays of moonlight lit her path. She ran her fingers along the cold stone walls as she climbed the steps.

She had a pretty good idea what she'd be getting into when she got to the portal room. A plunge into freezing water before climbing into a cemetery crypt, just a mile from the Brotherhood's headquarters, the Chambers. Unless things had changed drastically in the past month, the Chambers' halls would be equipped to sense magic. Guards would patrol the halls, and the whole place would be rigged with electronic devices to attack intruders.

Still, she had a good idea how to get to the ambrosia she needed. She just needed to disable all their alarms. And if anyone got in her way, she'd have to do a bit of ass-kicking.

There had been a time when she would have found all this intimidating.

At the top of the stairs, she pushed through a set of doors into a marble hall. Her footsteps echoed off the high ceiling as she walked down the hall, her eye on the two guards standing before the door.

The guards pulled open the doors; Rosalind climbed the stairs and crossed the threshold.

Caine stood waiting for her by the placid pool. Moonlight bathed his broad form in frosty light. As she crossed the marble floor, his icy gaze pierced her through the darkness. "Rosalind. Are you ready for this?"

"Of course."

"I don't think this is a good idea."

"Why?"

"You told me that Drew is insane. You have enough mental demons to contend with."

She heaved a sigh. "I know. I haven't decided for certain yet, but I'm going to get the blood all the same. Then I'll make up my mind. There are bigger factors at play than just my own mental state—like that whole thing about how Drew and the Brotherhood want to enslave the human race."

"And you're the sacrificial lamb."

"You're taking a risk, too," she pointed out. "You're going into Maremount on your own." She ran her fingertips over the hilt of one of the knives in her belt.

"Fine." He nodded at the pool. "And you know what to do when you get there?"

"I know exactly where the ambrosia is kept. I know how the building operates. I'm going to cut the power before going in. The magic sensors will be disabled, and I'll use an invisibility spell to get around the building."

Plus, she probably had more weapons on her than the entire vampire army.

He studied her closely, the moonlight sparking in his eyes.

Cleo's vernal aura flared at the sight of his beauty. *It all started with him,* Cleo whispered. *He slaughtered your parents, and now you've paid the price with Miranda's death.*

He's a god. Rosalind's fingers tightened.

Cleo's voice rang in her skull. *Don't you know that gods are meant to be killed?*

"What's she saying to you?" Caine asked. "Your second soul? She's speaking to you, isn't she?"

Rosalind took a deep breath. Pain gnawed at her chest. "She thinks Miranda's death is your fault, since you killed my parents in the first place. She suggests that I should kill you."

Caine stood perfectly still, but for the wisps of his dark hair caught in the wind, and the silver aura snapping the air around him. "And what do you think?"

"It's Drew's fault." But she still had so many unanswered questions. "I just need to understand. Why did you kill my parents? Was it revenge?" She crossed her arms. "Why did you have to do it in front of us?"

He stared at her for so long that she thought he'd never answer the question. She considered just turning and jumping through the portal, but he finally spoke. "I wasn't fully in my right mind."

She turned to face him head on. "What happened when you lost your mind?"

He nodded at the pool of water. "It's time for you to go, Rosalind."

She took another step closer to him, so close she could feel his warmth. There were so many things he wasn't telling her. "Miranda said you were tortured in the town square—that it was a punishment. But that was before you killed my parents. So what were you punished *for*?" Even as the words were out of her mouth, she knew she was touching a raw nerve.

Shadows whorled around him, cloaking his body, and his eyes flashed with an eerie silver light. "It's buried history." The coldness in his voice slid through her bones. "And it's time for you to go."

"Right. I know. You've got to get back to Maremount."

"Yes." He nodded at the pool. "You can come back through this portal. Only you, Ambrose, and I will be able to get through the shield for now."

"Be careful in Maremount. I want to see you back here soon."

"You will." He leaned in closer. "And like I said, don't let anyone get inside your head. Understood?"

"You mean, apart from the dead witch who controls my thoughts?"

"Apart from her, yes."

"I'll do my best." She turned to the pool, momentarily entranced by the moonlight glinting off its surface. *Here I go.*

She jumped into the icy water, plunging deep under the surface. Frigid water enveloped her body, dragging her under. The silver weapons weighed her down.

As she sank deeper, her lungs burned. When she saw a faint sheen of greenish light streaming through the water, she kicked her legs, pushing her way toward the air. Gasping, she breached the surface, pulling her way to the side of the pool.

She'd emerged in one of the crypts in Mount Auburn cemetery. The air hung heavy with the smell of moss and mildew, and silvery light streamed in through latticework in the stone doors.

* * *

SHE GRUNTED, pulling herself out. Murky crypt water soaked her clothes and hair, and her teeth chattered. Her body still ached from the battle with Drew. She stood, wringing out her hair, then peered through the door into the old Victorian cemetery. No one lingered on the hawthorn- and maple-lined paths at this hour.

I'll need Cleo for this. She was getting a little tired of having to negotiate with her second soul for everything, but until she memorized an entire library's worth of spells, this was the best she could do. Shivering, she hugged herself. "Cleo," she whispered. "I need you to show me the spell for invisibility."

Cleo's leafy aura curled in Rosalind's mind, and she tried to envision forcing it lower, into her chest. Cleo was easier to control there.

And what will you do for me, pet?

Rosalind sighed. "I know what you want. We'll see Ambrose when I return to Lilinor."

And will you run your hands over his perfect porcelain skin? Will you kiss his neck, listen to his breath catch in his throat? He likes it when a woman strips completely—

"Seven hells, woman," Rosalind snapped. "No. I'll hold his hand or something."

The vernal aura churned in her chest. *I want you to kiss his neck.*

"Fine. I'll kiss his neck." She would do no such thing, but she'd have to deal with the fallout another time.

As soon as the words were out of Rosalind's mouth, Cleo offered up the spell, graven in white light. Rosalind read the words out loud and felt the magic whisper over her skin, hiding her body from the rest of the world.

The spell completed, she pushed through the cemetery door. Stone scraped against stone. Outside, the air was clear, heavy with magnolias. She broke into a fast sprint along the path, her feet pounding on the pavement of the winding cemetery paths. At the entrance, she scaled the wrought-iron cemetery gate and leapt over the top to the sidewalk below. She pumped her arms, running hard toward the Chambers by Harvard Yard.

As she ran, her eyes flicked to Drew's house, the yellow mansion on Brattle. She halted her sprint for a moment, sniffing the air for the scent of his aura, and held out her arms, waiting for the powerful tingle of his unmistakable magic. *Nothing.*

Of course. Even he wasn't stupid enough to come back here. It hadn't been long ago that she'd stood in his entryway, letting him heal her flesh with a potion of his own making. How stupid she'd been then, drinking from the devil.

Her stomach clenched at the thought of him.

She pushed her disgust to the back of her skull and broke into a run, heading once more toward the Chambers. Hardly anyone walked the streets, which meant it must be well after midnight. Without regular daylight in Lilinor, it had become impossible to keep track of the time.

As she sped through Harvard Square, her eyes trailed over the empty streets. *This is where the keres attacked, where they ripped into human flesh.* At the time, they'd seemed like pure monsters. She'd had no clue that they were actually humans under the alabaster flesh and black eyes—or something in between, at least. Just like Tammi.

Rosalind crossed into Harvard Yard, the night air rushing over her skin. As she sprinted closer to the Chambers, she pulled a long, silver blade from her pocket. Before she went in the building, she was going to make sure she'd disabled all the electronic weapons. The hawthorn stakes rigged to shoot from the ceiling. The aura-burning dust.

And now that she had the power of Cleo's magic at her fingertips, she didn't need to hack into their system.

Just outside the Chambers, she stopped, catching her breath below the yellow glow of a streetlamp. Through the Chambers' glass windows, she could see pale light illuminating the marble floors, and tiny red lights glowing from the network of alarms and weapons in the stone walls.

Most of that was familiar, yet the Chambers had changed. It hadn't been long since she and Caine had rampaged through the building, shooting through windows, lighting the walls on fire and freeing prisoners—yet the building now stood in a pristine state. What was more, an entire new wing had appeared near Oxford Street. The architecture there—a classical stone façade adorned with Greek columns— stood out in stark contrast to the Victorian brick.

Where the hell did that come from?

There was no way all this could have been built in a month. Not without the use of magic.

The Brotherhood—the ancient organization of soldiers who existed solely to rid the world of magic—had thrown themselves wholeheartedly into Drew's thrall. All it took to turn them, apparently, was for their favorite witch to drink blood from their god. But who was really in control—Drew, or the Brotherhood?

There's time to figure that out later. Now, she had to get some blood of her own. She closed her eyes, trying to ignore the fatigue burning through her body. "Cleo," she whispered. "I need a spell for..." She swallowed hard. It had only just occurred to her that a sixteenth century spirit would have no clue what she was talking about. "I don't suppose you know what an electromagnetic pulse is?"

Cleo's aura roiled. *Speak in English, girl.*

She folded her arms. Electricity wasn't discovered until the seventeenth century, but she could work with this. "You know lightning?"

Cleo's aura sparked green in her chest. *I'm not a complete fool.*

"I need to mix that power with magnetism. The technology that powers compasses, or that draws metal to rocks. I need to send out a shockwave of that power."

A vernal aura licked at her ribs. *For magic such as this, I'll need you to seduce Ambrose. Walk into his bedchamber, and take off your clothes so he can see your body. Then let me take over.*

Rosalind hoped Cleo didn't pick up on her eye roll. "Sure. I'll get naked." She was making all sorts of sordid Faustian bargains tonight. "Can you help me with the spell now?"

Magic simmered over her skin, and from the depths of her mind, a spell rose, blazing in white light. She spoke the words, and a powerful flare of hot, electric magic burst from her body, rippling over the horizon. A low rumble filled the air, and she opened her eyes. As the magic spread from her body, the street lamps flickered and snuffed out. In front of her, in the Chambers entry hall, the red lights dimmed to black. Pure, thick darkness enveloped the campus.

Nice work, Cleo.

Rosalind prowled to the front doors. At the glass doors, she peered inside. Nothing moved. She narrowed her eyes. All was quiet inside—but it didn't seem quite right. A faint hum of magic vibrated over her skin.

Magic. In the Chambers. Was Drew here?

She pulled open the front door, stepping into the hall. Part of her wanted to hunt through the Chambers for Drew, but she wasn't strong enough to fight him yet. When they came face to face, she'd be the one in control. She'd see the fear in his eyes as he trembled before his angel of death.

And for that, she'd need the ambrosia.

Luckily, she knew exactly where to find it. She tiptoed through a set of doors toward the Great Hall, straining her eyes to see in the dark. A shiver rippled over her skin as she took in the chalice carvings on the hall's oak door. This was where Miranda had nearly killed her;

in the dark hall beyond this door, she'd nearly burned to death. Both she and her sister had had their minds broken and twisted by Blodrial's followers.

She checked over her shoulder, making sure the hall was empty, then pulled open the door. As soon as she did, a deep crimson aura curled through the air—and with it, the sound of a blaring siren. So they were using magic now.

Heart racing, Rosalind closed her eyes. *Cleo. I need some help now, or your little vessel won't live long enough to seduce Ambrose.*

In an instant, shining Angelic words blazed in her mind; she incanted them, letting the magic ignite her body with power. As she chanted, the alarm faded.

Still, the damage had been done. A banging noise made her turn her head, and she glimpsed two men running down the hall—Hunters, gripping canisters of dust. A tall, wiry man and a stocky blond. She didn't recognize either of them.

Good. That'll make this easier.

Her pulse raced. *Kill or be killed.* She drew her knives. If she let them spray her with that dust, she'd be helpless here—visible, magic-free, and in extreme pain.

She threw the first knife, and it arced through the air, finding its mark in the wiry Hunter's heart. The blond's eyes widened, in too much shock to act quickly. She threw the second knife, and it buried in his chest—a few inches to the right of his heart.

Shit. She'd missed the mark.

He fell to the ground, dropping the canister and gasping. Her heart thundering against her ribs, she ran to him. As she stood over him, he stared into the air, unable to see his executioner. A gurgling rose from his throat. A drop of blood slid from his lip, and his eyes blazed with fear. He was going to die, and he knew it.

Rosalind's throat tightened. It was a lot easier to kill a guy from far away. Still, she had to act fast; more Hunters would follow. She pulled the misericord from her belt, crouching down. She plunged the thin blade into his ear, watching his eyelids flutter.

There wasn't time for guilt now. She stood, rushing for the door.

Adrenalin surged in her veins. *Where the hell is the magic coming from?* She pushed through the door. Moonlight streamed through the oculus, casting a circle of light on the floor. Just outside the pale sphere stood a stone lectern with an iron compartment, locked by an electronic keypad.

The Hunters were still using human technology, but it wouldn't be long before they evolved.

Luckily, she didn't need to know the code—not after Cleo's electromagnetic pulse. Her hands shook, and she hurried to the lectern, yanking opening the compartment. An iron flask stood in the center. She snatched it, shoving it into her belt.

But as she rose, a familiar aura seeped into her nostrils: moldering hemlock, the color of dried blood. Fetid magic crawled over her flesh like spider legs, erasing the cloaking spell. She glanced down at herself. She was completely visible now.

Slowly, Rosalind turned. Stepping into the light was a behemoth of a demon with bone-colored skin and cheekbones sharp as knives. Horns grew from his forehead, and sharp tattoos marked his bare chest. He glared at her with empty, ivory orbs.

Bileth.

CHAPTER 14

*R*osalind's heart climbed up her throat. "What are you doing here?"

"I was going to ask you the same, my little beauty." His voice rumbled through the hall. "And then I saw you take the ambrosia."

If there was ever a time to have a direct line into magic, it was now. She was trapped in a standoff—unable to chant an Angelic spell without Bileth snapping her neck with his mind.

He took a step closer, a grin curling his lips. "I do remember with fondness the time you impaled me with a silver spear. In fact, it fuels my most depraved fantasies. I trust the memory is fresh in your mind as well?"

Her throat went dry. She'd always wondered what had happened to Bileth—he'd been full of fury, desperate for revenge. And then he'd simply given up.

Still, she couldn't quite get her mind around what he was doing in the Chambers. Drew was one thing. Drew, at least drank Blodrial's ambrosia. But Bileth was pure, muscled shadow demon. An ancient acolyte of Nyxobas, forged in the shadow void.

"What are you doing with Randolph and the Hunters?" she asked in desperation. "Why have they allowed you in here?"

He clenched his meaty fingers and took another step closer. "The enemy of my enemy is my friend." His deep red aura curled off him, and he glided closer. "Accomplice. Close enough."

She didn't understand. "You mean me?"

A low growl rumbled through the room. "You really think you're that important, little girl? You think *you're* my enemy?"

She needed to get out of here. Any second, a phalanx of Hunters could appear. At least with Bileth, she could figure out a way to distract him long enough for her to launch into a teleportation spell.

"Okay, so I don't know who your enemy is." She took a step closer to him, and surprise flickered in his eyes. "But you still think fondly of the time I stabbed you. What do you mean it fuels your most depraved fantasies?"

If she could pull a knife from her belt, she could stab him a second time. It wouldn't kill him, but it would stun him just long enough that she could get out of here.

He glided another inch closer, and her fingers twitched at her belt. Before she could grip a knife's hilt, Bileth's powerful hand was around her throat. With one hand, he lifted her from the ground, crushing her neck. She kicked at him, but the demon simply reached down, ripping the blades from her weapon belt and flinging each one across the room. Her lungs burned as he squeezed her throat.

He pulled the flask from her belt, looking it over. "Poison," he snarled.

He dropped her, and she fell to the ground, gasping. She touched her bruised throat. *Shit. So much for the knife plan.*

"What do I mean about my depraved fantasies?" Bileth reached down, pulling her up by the hair. "When I think of your impertinence, your stunning human arrogance, it makes it all the more exciting when I think of all the ways I will punish you. You thought you'd escaped, didn't you? You thought I'd forget?"

His fetid aura slithered under her skin, and her heart hammered. He was going to try to control her mind.

And maybe she'd play along, just long enough to figure out how to get out of here.

She focused on forcing the maroon tendrils out of her body. *If I can see magic, I can control it.*

"Take off all your weapons," Bileth growled.

Rosalind widened her eyes, giving her best impression of a compliant little victim.

Bileth shifted closer, stroking his thumb up her cheek. The demon's touch was cold and damp, and she tried not to shudder. Still gripping her hair, he trailed his thumb over her lips, then shoved it in her mouth. His waxy skin tasted of stale milk, and she tried not to gag.

Her stomach turned. *Okay. I don't want to play along anymore.*

He released his grip on her hair. "Take off your clothes."

Rosalind's heart pounded. *Cleo, I want the spell now.*

Cleo's aura roiled. *Not yet, Rosalind. Wait until he can't see your mouth moving.*

Swallowing her disgust, Rosalind reached down, unbuttoning her shirt. Bileth let out a low growl, staring at her. He reached out, stroking her collarbone. Then he pinched her skin between his fingers, twisting it hard.

Her breath caught in her throat, and she tried not to shout. She needed to act compliant.

Bileth pulled his hand away. "The rest. Now."

She bent down, unzipping her boots and sliding them off. *Any time now, Cleo.* She slid her hands down to her pants, unbuttoning them. *Fucking hell. This was a bad idea. I should have kept the weapons on me.*

Revulsion twisted her gut as she slid out of her pants. *Cleo, I need to get out of here.*

No spell rose in her mind as she straightened, staring straight into his blazing ivory eyes.

The door slammed open, and from the corner of her eye she saw a line of Hunters burst into the room, guns drawn.

Her cheeks burned. *And here I am, standing in my sheer black underwear.*

Cleo's aura blazed. *It's your body, you fool. Don't be ashamed of it, and they have no power over you.*

Her mage friend had a point.

"Lie on the ground and put your hands behind your head," shouted one of the Hunters.

Bileth held up a hand. "She's mine right now. You can watch."

So they knew he was here, and they allowed it.

"But, you..." one of the Hunters stammered. "We need to arrest her."

You. Hunters addressed their officers as *Sir.* Rosalind had the sense that the Hunter didn't know how to address Bileth. He was stronger than they were, completely lethal, and to some degree the Brotherhood had opened the doors to him.

But they didn't accept him. He terrified and revolted them. *As he should.*

Bileth gripped the back of her hair again, pulling her head back. Her heart tightened.

I need two spells. One for the flask, and one to leave. Two spells, Cleo.

The Hunters looked on as Bileth slid his other hand around her waist. He pulled her closer.

Two spells, Cleo.

Bile climbed up her throat as the demon opened his mouth. Her stomach clenched as she waited for a slimy tongue or cold lips on her neck.

But Bileth had another idea. He opened his mouth and bit down hard on her shoulder, tearing at her flesh.

Pain ripped her apart, and she clenched her teeth, trying not to cry out. *Two spells, Cleo.* She tilted her face away from the Hunters just slightly. She didn't want them to see her grimace, to see her lips move.

Letters blazed in her mind, an angelic word for magnetic rock. Rosalind whispered it, holding out her left hand out of the Hunters' view. The iron flask flew into her grip.

Bileth bit deeper, and the pain nearly blinded her.

Cleo offered up the second spell, the one for teleportation, and Rosalind whispered the words, keeping her head slightly turned. The pain was excruciating, but after one last rip of Bileth's sharp teeth, she was free, her body teleporting away.

At the edge of the dank crypt, she fell to her knees, clutching the flask. "I'm free," she whispered to herself. She touched her ravaged shoulder, wincing at the deep wound. Her body trembled, and nausea flooded her.

She needed to get back to Lilinor *now.* Bileth knew how to find the portal to Lilinor. In fact, Bileth could probably come into Lilinor whenever he wanted—his ugly portrait hung over the damn entrance to the castle.

Shit shit shit.

Flask in hand, she stood and leapt into the pool of freezing water. The cold shocked the pain from her body, and she sank deep under the water. When her lungs burned, she glanced up, glimpsing the rays of moonlight streaming into the water. She kicked her legs, fighting her way up.

Her arms breached the surface, and she pulled her way out of the pool. The pain from her shoulder stole her breath, and she watched the blood pour from her wound, pooling in red rivulets on the tile.

It was only a moment before strong hands were lifting her up. Ambrose's green eyes widened, and he slid a hand around her waist. He pulled her closer, his touch like silk on her skin. Moonlight streamed in from the open ceiling, washing his skin in silver. He wasn't wearing a shirt.

In the next moment, his mouth hovered over her neck, his fingers clamping on her waist in a vice-like grip. He emitted a low groan.

Rosalind's heart pounded against her ribs. *Shit. I've just presented a bleeding neck to a vampire.* She slid her hands up his chest, hard as marble, and tried to push him away. "Ambrose. Stop."

He growled, gripping her tightly. A full head taller than her, he stared down. Fury blazed in his eyes. "Don't ever come to see me like this again—half naked and covered in blood."

Cleo's aura swirled off her body, stroking Ambrose's skin, and her voice rang in Rosalind's skull. *Why don't you give him what he wants?*

Rosalind ignored her, trying to gather her thoughts. Her body burned from the exertion of the teleportation spell, and it was hard to concentrate with Ambrose's iron grip around her. "Ambrose. I need you to listen to me. Can Bileth get through Caine's shield?"

Ambrose's entire body went rigid. "Why are you asking about Bileth?" he growled.

"He's the one who took my clothes and the chunk of flesh from my shoulder." A cool breeze whispered over her back.

Almost imperceptibly, Ambrose's fingers tightened on her waist. Dark rage crossed his features, nearly distracting her from the searing pain in her shoulder. "Bileth did this? How? Why?"

"He was in the Chambers. He seems to be working with the Brotherhood. He mentioned that old adage about 'the enemy of my enemy is my friend.' But I have no idea who he's talking about."

Ambrose loosened his grip on her, forcing himself to step away.

Her gaze flicked to the bed, where two nubile blonde courtesans pulled up sheets to cover their naked bodies. Blood dripped from their necks. Apparently, she'd interrupted a little vamp-on-human menage.

A drop of blood glistened on Ambrose's lip, and he licked it off. "Bileth can't get in here with the shield Caine put in place."

"What did he mean about his enemies? Why is he working with the demon hunters?"

"He's talking about me."

Pain still screamed through her shoulder, but his eyes transfixed her. Her pulse raced, and Cleo's voice rose in her mind. *You should feel his kiss.* "Why would Bileth consider you his enemy? I thought you worked together. His picture hangs in the castle."

He lowered his mouth to her neck. Without thinking, she tilted back her head, exposing her throat. *So that's how vampires control their victims.*

Before his fangs reached her throat, he abruptly dropped his grip on her. His body buzzed with dark magic. "I can't think straight around you." His gaze slid down her body, taking in her bare skin. "I need to heal your shoulder. Now."

Ambrose, Cleo whispered. *Come closer.*

He bit into his wrist, letting his own blood pool, and held it to her mouth. "Drink." Blood dripped from his wrist.

You'll like this, said Cleo.

"What will happen if I drink your blood?"

"You'll heal. Drink."

"If I drink your blood, won't it change my thoughts and make me one of your mindless followers?"

"Drink."

Her lip curled. "I like the way Caine heals me better."

Ambrose inched closer, and an impulse from the ancient recesses of her brain compelled her to tilt back her head again. He pressed his bleeding wrist to her mouth, and as soon as the first salty drop hit her tongue, she began to suck.

A dark heat flooded her body, a primal power. As she drank from Ambrose's wrist, the pain in her shoulder melted away. She drank deeper, letting it drip down the back of her throat. Deep in her core, a slow fire simmered.

Ambrose gripped her hair, pulling her mouth away from his wrist. "That's enough, Rosalind."

Raw power blazed through her veins, and she stared at the vampire lord. His pupils had turned blood red.

"You got the ambrosia," Ambrose said, slowly pulling his gaze away from her. He stared at the night sky, obviously trying to avoid eye contact. "Good work."

Cleo's aura lit her body on fire. *Now, Rosalind. It's time to make good on our bargain.* With Cleo's iron will urging her on, and the intoxicating rush of Ambrose's blood burning through her veins, she couldn't resist taking another step, running a hand up his chest...

A sly smile curled his lips, and his fingers found their way around her waist again. His gaze trailed over her neck. "I thought you belonged to Caine."

"I don't belong to anyone." *Except Cleo, apparently. Sweet earthly gods, I can't do this.* "Cleo demands things from me," she blurted. "Every time I want a spell from her, I have to strike a bargain."

He froze. "What sort of bargain?"

"I know you have a history with her. She *knows* you. And you know her, too, don't you?"

Ambrose's muscles tensed, and he pulled his hands away from her waist, grabbing her chin. "I could smell her on you the first time we met." He stared into Rosalind's eyes, and her pulse raced. Ambrose was every bit as unnerving as the first day she met him. "And I think I know what she wants from me." He dropped his hand.

Rosalind tightened her fists to keep herself from touching him. *She wants to bang you, and then murder you.*

"She wants my death," he said.

"That's part of it." Rosalind wiped her chin, glancing down at the smear of blood on the back of her hand. "Who is she? What happened between you?"

Ambrose stared down at her. "Here's the part you need to know. I want you to drink that gods-blood. Now. You need to tap into the gods-magic. You can't strike a bargain with Cleo every time you need to use a spell. You can't let her control you. You will use her only when it's time to make the daywalkers."

I just love how these vampires speak in commands. "I need a little more time."

"For what?" he barked.

"Just give me an hour to do a little research first." What she really wanted to do was to dig Miranda up from the earth and try the spell for Nyxobas, but Ambrose seemed to be pushing her along at a break-neck speed to develop the gods' powers.

"And how do you intend to do research?"

"I'm going down to the dungeons. I'm going to talk to your wife."

"Whatever you need to do, Rosalind, do it fast. We have work to do."

CHAPTER 15

*R*osalind stalked down the narrow stairwell, clutching a flask.

She tugged up the front of her dress—a delicate gown of sea-foam green, flecked with gold threads that curled down to the hem like vines. Not exactly standard dungeon-attire, but it would do the job for meeting with Erish. Ambrose had quite helpfully called for a servant to bring her a dress, so she wasn't forced to climb down to the dungeon half naked.

And on her way down she'd stopped by her room for a few crucial items—namely, the weapons she now had discreetly strapped to her thighs below the tulle.

Apart from her blades and stakes, she carried only one thing: a flask of ambrosia. The blood of a god, right at her fingertips—a potential bargaining chip for her meeting with Erish.

At the end of the stairwell, she pushed through a misshapen oak door into a dank, earthen hall. The old dungeons had been crushed by a giant, but Ambrose had ordered his men to work day and night to build a new one. It now held a single prisoner: Ambrose's wife.

From silver lanterns, warm light danced over the hall. It smelled like a grave down here.

A sharp pain pierced her chest. Was this what Miranda felt, buried under all that dirt? Suffocating under the earth, trapped in darkness? Her fingers curled into fists, and she shook her head. *No. Miranda doesn't feel anything.*

Tears stung her eyes, and she blinked them away. As soon as she was done with her little interview, she and Aurora would try to raise Miranda.

She ran her hand along the earthen walls as she walked toward the dungeons. A single lantern lit the space, casting wavering light on an iron-barred cell at the end of the hall. As she moved further into the hall, her chest tightened. Crumpled in a heap on the stone floor lay a bag of bones, dressed in rags.

Erish. The stunning succubus queen.

Rosalind swallowed hard, crossing to the iron cage. Erish's black hair, once lush, lay snarled over her emaciated arms. Iron chains bound her neck, wrists, and ankles.

Rosalind crept up to the cage.

Is she even alive?

"Erish?" she said softly.

The queen lay still. *Sweet earthly gods.* Erish was a traitor and a terrible person, but her husband could have at least given her some food and a blanket.

Standing just outside the cell bars, Rosalind crouched down. "Erish?"

In the next instant, the queen lunged, her hand flying for Rosalind's head. Rosalind dropped the flask, trying to dodge backward, but the queen had her by the hair. Erish snarled, and Rosalind caught a glimpse of a savage red scar on the queen's neck.

"Rosalind," Erish spat. "The special little human." Her eyes were wide, her grip on Rosalind iron-clad. "Did you think you could decapitate a succubus and live?"

Rosalind's heart raced. Gripping the bars, she kicked between them, her foot connecting with Erish's face—but quick as a flash, Erish grabbed her foot, twisting it. Rosalind slammed forehead-first onto the stone.

She yanked her foot out of Erish's grasp, recoiling. When she touched her forehead, her fingertips came away coated in blood. Thick red drops stained her green gown, now smudged with dirt.

"Great to see you, Erish," she said from the floor. "I'm so pleased captivity hasn't dampened your spirits."

Erish leaned back on her haunches, her snarl more animal than human. "You're the reason I'm here, filthy human wench. And now you've come to gloat, dressed like a queen. If I could, I'd eviscerate you slowly and drape your entrails over my shoulders like a shawl."

Shuddering, Rosalind brushed the dirt off her bodice. "I'm not here to gloat. I just came to ask you a question."

"Do you remember that time you cut my head off?" Erish pulled down the iron collar just an inch, exposing the angry red scar on her neck. "I'm not clear why you think I would help you."

Because I'm reasonably sure you're an addict. "I'll give you a taste of ambrosia."

Erish's eyes widened, and her body went completely still.

Now I have your attention. Rosalind would give her just a drop— enough to tempt her. Not enough to imbue her with fresh powers.

"What do you want to know?" Erish asked in a low voice.

"If I drink the ambrosia, what will happen to me? I've had it before, but only when wearing iron. I've never used the gods-magic the way Drew has."

Erish's lip curled. "What are you afraid of? Are you scared some little human tart will sever your head from your body, and you'll wake up in a dank sewer, chained with the rats? That your husband and king will bury you under the earth, that he'll let you starve? I can't imagine where you'd get that idea."

Rosalind crossed her arms. "Lay off the guilt trip, Erish. You were kidnapping humans to turn them into mindless, flesh-eating demons —including my best friend. You caused hundreds of deaths."

"I was revered as a goddess in the ancient world," Erish hissed. "I deserve an army to defend me. And now you find me sitting in my own filth. That is your fault."

"If you tell me what I want to know, I'll have a word with Ambrose about your living conditions. I'll make sure you're sent food, and something to wash with."

"And why would he listen to you?" Erish lunged forward, gripping the bars. "You think you'll be his new queen? You think your pretty face is enough for him?"

Rosalind frowned. She was growing impatient—she had a sister to raise from the dead, and Erish was stalling. "What? No. I'm not going to become his queen."

"That's right, you won't. You spend enough time with Ambrose, and he'll rip through that delicate human neck. And if somehow you managed to survive his rapacious blood hunger, he'd have to watch you growing old and wrinkled. Rotten with cancer. He'd be repulsed at your sagging skin, your creaking knees, your bladder giving out. That is your fate, after all. Another body for the whore pit."

Suddenly, Rosalind wanted to be anywhere but here. "I have no desire to become queen."

Erish's grip tightened on the bars. "Turning humans into demons —is it really so terrible? I gave them eternal life. Without me, they'd be cursed with corrupted, rotting bodies. Just like yours." Her mouth twisted in a bitter smile. "What a choice for a sanctimonious cunt like you—become a demon, or die. You do realize those are your only options?"

Rosalind shrugged. "I guess I could live forever and watch myself abandoned one by one by everyone who ever loved me, until there was nothing left but my narcissistic rage. But somehow, that doesn't seem appealing."

"Do you know what will happen when you die, Rosalind? Will you be trapped in a void, with nothing but your sad little memories?" Erish licked her lips. "You'd best figure it out fast. You're dying right now."

"And you're stalling. Why do I get the feeling you're trying to keep me here as long as possible? Getting a bit bored of hearing your own bitter thoughts? Even you're growing sick of yourself." Rosalind rose to her full height, brushing off the back of her dress. She was quickly losing control of this conversation. "I'm here to ask about the blood. The ambrosia. Did it drive Drew insane?"

Erish sneered. "Have you seen him lately?"

"Yes. He paid us a visit. I guess you missed all the excitement down here."

"Did he seem sane?"

"No."

Erish tilted her head. "You already know the answer. You're just not willing to admit it to yourself. You've already lost half your mind anyway. What difference does it make if you lose the rest?"

"You didn't lose your mind though, did you?"

"Like I said, I'm practically a goddess. Don't expect the same rules to apply to me." She frowned. "Do you ever wonder what your corpse will look like?"

Rosalind's stomach tightened. "I don't have to wonder anymore." Not since she'd seen her identical twin's graying corpse.

"Now that's intriguing."

"Will I become addicted to the ambrosia, like you are?" Rosalind asked. "I mean, I've had it before. But I've never used the gods-magic. Is that what's addictive?"

"I don't expect that you'll be any stronger than I am. You can hardly deal with your second soul. Honestly, you should just give up and let her take over." She licked her lips. "I can see her in your eyes now. Look at your reflection."

She knew that Erish was playing mind-games with her, but curiosity compelled Rosalind to lift the metal flask, gazing at her own face. Her breath froze in her lungs. She stared at a stranger: long, platinum hair, pale skin, and green eyes. She blinked hard, and her dark hair returned once more. *What the hell was that?*

She glared at Erish. "Did you create that illusion?"

The succubus lifted her chains. "I can't do any magic with this iron all over me. I can see Cleo—that's her name, isn't it?—taking over. She's really quite beautiful. I see why Ambrose would have given in to his carnal desires all those centuries ago."

Rosalind's fingers curled. "What happened between them?"

Erish arched an eyebrow. "Are you jealous of your second soul? Tell me, which demon do you want more: the incubus who killed your parents, or the vampire who wants to fuck you and kill you?"

"Neither," Rosalind grumbled. She unscrewed the cap on the flask, poured a few drops into the cap, then handed it over. "I have to go. Here's your payment."

To her surprise, Erish didn't complain about the tiny pour. She simply glared at Rosalind and sipped it, before handing Rosalind the cap and wiping the back of her hand across her mouth. "Maybe someday I'll tell you what Ambrose did to Cleo. Then we'll see how much you like him."

Rosalind screwed the top back on the flask. "I'll ask Ambrose to send down some food and blankets."

"Where is it you have to run off to so quickly, little tart?"

"I have to go visit my sister."

Erish only grunted as Rosalind turned, stalking through the dirt tunnel again.

Her stomach churned. Her worst fears could be true. Drew had probably been driven insane by using the gods-magic.

Maybe human bodies weren't meant for such power. And as much as she hated to admit it, Erish was right. She didn't have much of her mind left to lose. Not with Cleo taking over, one brain cell after another.

Rosalind rubbed a knot in her forehead. She didn't want to lose what was left of her sanity, but she was running out of options. And if they needed an abomination to fight Drew, maybe she'd have to fill the role. She pulled open the door and began climbing the stairwell.

Despite Erish's claims of addiction to ambrosia, she'd spent the entire conversation stalling, trying to prod at sensitive topics. She hadn't really *seemed* like an addict. Maybe Erish was desperate, but it wasn't blood she craved. She was starved for attention, desperate for conversation—even if it meant talking with her worst enemy. Maybe isolation was the worst punishment of all.

Do you know what will happen when you die Rosalind? Will you be trapped in a void, with nothing but your sad little memories?

At the top of the stairwell, Rosalind pulled open the misshapen door.

Suddenly, nothing seemed more important than raising her sister from the grave.

CHAPTER 16

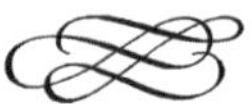

Rosalind pulled a shawl tight around her shoulders as she walked down the winding path to the yew. She could already see Aurora standing near a fire pit. By the tree, cedar smoke curled into the air, and the flames cast a glowing light over her sister's corpse. The sound of tinkling bells filled the air.

Thank the gods for Aurora. The vampire had volunteered to arrive early for the necromantic spell, so Rosalind wouldn't have to face digging her own sister out.

As Rosalind drew closer, she could see a thin layer of dirt covering Miranda's skin and her white gown. She took her place next to Aurora. "I can't tell you how much I appreciate this."

The vampire wore a long, black gown and held two silver cups. "Are you sure you're up for this?"

"We have to try," Rosalind said quietly.

Aurora handed her a silver cup. "Here. Wine."

"Is wine the first step?"

Aurora took a sip. "Wine is always the first step. Especially when you're standing over your sister's corpse."

"Good point." Rosalind sipped the fruity wine—the same wine she'd had at her picnic days ago.

But for this picnic, Aurora had brought a macabre feast: black bread, a necromancy book, goat blood, and a caged raven. Aurora bent down, snatched the spell book from a wicker basket, and flipped through the pages.

Against her will, Rosalind's gaze slid to her sister's body. Miranda's face had taken on a greenish tinge; her lips were a deep blue.

Rosalind couldn't breathe. She felt as if she was staring at her own corpse, glimpsing her own future. A hollow opened up in the pit of her stomach. *It's not me. It's Miranda.*

"Rosalind?" Aurora said. "Are you with me?"

She tore her gaze away. "Yes. I'm here."

Aurora held out a piece of black bread. "Eat this. Food doesn't agree with me. I had Caine's fae chef bake it for us."

Rosalind took it from her, and her stomach rumbled. *When was the last time I ate?* She took a bite, chewing into the black bread, delicately sweetened with molasses. "Now what?"

"Now you throw the bread into the fire."

Rosalind took one more bite and tossed the rest into the bonfire, to a burst of flame. Black smoke curled into the air.

Aurora stepped closer to the fire, opening a silver flask. She took a sip, then poured a thin stream of blood onto the fire; it hissed as the flask emptied. "Now all we have to do is drink more wine, and sacrifice the bird."

Rosalind took a sip of her drink. "Would Caine be upset about the raven? What if she's a friend of Lilu? His familiar?"

Aurora glared at her, picking up the birdcage. "I told you, Caine would be upset about all of this. Anyway, Nyxobas likes ravens."

Snatching the spellbook from the ground, Rosalind shivered. *Right. Well, good thing he's not here.*

The raven flapped its wings, squawking, and Aurora cooed gently, stroking its head. In a split second, she flung open the birdcage and with a soft crack, she snapped the creature's neck.

Brutal.

Aurora tossed the bird's limp body onto the fire and glanced at Rosalind. "And now, all we need is the spell."

Rosalind propped the book on her hip, holding it open with one hand. Hand-drawn skulls, ravens and waning moons decorated the spell's page. She scanned for the spell, then chanted: *"Usella Mituti Ikkalu Baltuti."*

Aurora joined in. Their voices mingled with the tinkling of the bells. The wind picked up, toying with Rosalind's hair.

Usella Mituti Ikkalu Baltuti.

Rosalind's veins flooded with a strange power, dark and ancient. She closed her eyes, her vision swirling glimmers of stars. And with the piercing glow of starlight in her mind, she thought of Caine's eyes. Caine was the closest thing she knew to the god of night. She tried to imagine how he conducted the magic—his body blazing with pale light, shadows moving around him, his movements predatory and precise.

A scent wafted past her, electric and earthy at the same time. The whorls of stars gave way to an earthly vision: a room with dark wood, dirty ivory sheets. Sunlight streaming through a warped window. A shapely woman dressed in a ragged nightgown, brushing her blond hair.

Where am I?

A wail pierced the air. She glanced down and saw that it was a baby crying in a basket on the floor. She reached down to pick the child up. It looked at her with gray eyes. Cradling the infant in her arms, she soothed the baby, and a protective warmth enveloped her.

She glanced up at the crooked bedside table. A hairpin lay on the surface—a sharp spike of silver, with a thorny design decorating the top.

Recognition hit her like a fist. *Caine.*

The night sky swirled again, enveloping her, and a sharp hollow rose in her chest, eating at her ribs. The image was replaced with a thick forest, gleaming with daylight. Pines towered over her, and she gripped a sword. She glanced down at her arm, taking in the thickly corded muscle and golden skin. *Caine.*

He slid his fingers into the V of his shirt, feeling the small divot over his heart. The scar that Rosalind had given him. The sunlight seemed to darken, and through Caine's eyes she looked up at the sky. A legion of shrieking valkyries were coming for him, and he tightened his grip on the sword.

White light burst in her vision, and she gasped, opening her eyes.

She stood before the yew, and the night breeze whispered over her skin. Her body shook from her visions. Had they been real, or some sort of hallucination?

Aurora touched her arm. "I think I felt the shadow magic."

All around them, deep, silvery magic whirled through the air—but when Rosalind glanced down at her sisters body, Miranda lay still. None of the magic had actually been directed *into* her body, and it was already disappearing like smoke.

Rosalind's stomach dropped. Maybe it had worked? Her legs shook, and she rushed to her sister's body. She traced her fingertips over Miranda's skin. *Cold.* She stared at her sister's chest, willing her lungs to swell with air.

Aurora, her brow furrowed, pressed a hand over Miranda's chest. "There's no heartbeat."

Rosalind lifted her fingers to her sister's throat, feeling for a pulse. She felt only cold, dead flesh. "Nothing." Sadness tightened its grip on her heart, and she pulled her hand away. "I felt the shadow magic. I think I even got some mental images from Caine. But the magic didn't go where it was supposed to."

"What mental images?"

Grief ate at Rosalind's chest, sharp and hollow. A tear streamed down her face, and she wiped it away. This had been the best plan she had.

"I think it was an image from Caine's life. That tattoo on his arm that looks like a knife? It's not; it's a woman's hairpin." Her chest tightened. "But that's not the concerning vision. I saw a legion of valkyries coming for him. It could be a vision of where he is now, because he already had the scar I gave him, but I sure as hell hope not. It wasn't looking good for him."

Aurora shook her head slowly. "Maybe it was just a hallucination. Just nonsense."

Rosalind rose on shaking legs. "Why do you think the spell didn't work the way it should have?"

"I have no idea. Apparently, Nyxobas doesn't want to give your sister back."

CHAPTER 17

*D*ressed in her battle gear, Rosalind stalked down the hall to the armory, choking down her bitter disappointment. She was supposed to meet Ambrose; he'd said he wanted to see how she handled herself in a fight.

She shuddered. It would be hard to focus on Ambrose when she could still feel the shadows of Nyxobas whispering through her blood, tempting her to the cold, clean void.

As she walked, her footsteps echoed off the ceiling. Nyxobas had dominion over the dead, and she'd toyed directly with his power. They'd tried the spell three more times, and each time she'd thought of Caine, and felt the power of the night god flowing through her. She'd seen the visions from his memories: the woman with blond hair, the child with gray eyes. She'd watched the valkyries attack Caine, closing in on him in the forest, had recoiled as he'd cut into their flesh.

But each time the visions cleared, the magic simply wafted uselessly in the air above her sister's corpse before disappearing into the night sky.

Why the hell didn't it work? Maybe we baked the bread wrong. Maybe the ancient alchemists weren't big on the specifics of spell mechanics.

And by the final try, the spell hadn't worked at all. No visions from

Caine, no rush of shadow magic. Nyxobas hadn't granted her permission, and Miranda still lay dead in her grave.

Almost as bad was the nagging worry that she might have seen a vision of Caine in some serious trouble, plagued by a horde of valkyries. She was pretty sure he'd been in a forest in Maremount.

Or maybe Aurora had been right, and it was nothing but a hallucination.

The cut on her forehead, from where Erish had knocked her into the floor, still stung. She reached up to touch it, and a smudge of blood came off on her finger. She hadn't had time to clean up properly—it had been a mad dash from Erish, to the yew tree, back to her room to change, and now down to the armory.

She approached the armory, wiped the blood off on her pants, then pulled open the door. As soon as she stepped into the room, her pulse sped up.

Ambrose stood in the center of the room, dressed in black. He stood rigid with that eerie, preternatural stillness that raised the hair on the back of her neck. Shadows licked the air around him.

"Close the door," he snarled.

His steely tone unnerved her, and she swallowed hard, pulling the door closed behind her. She was suddenly acutely aware that she was alone in a room with a predator. One who—right now—seemed more demon than human, who seemed to be staring at her from the depths of hell itself.

Silently, he cocked his head, the movement oddly reptilian.

She wanted to break the tension, to draw a spark of humanity from him. "I went to see Erish," she ventured. "To find out about the ambrosia. She confirmed it would make me lose my mind."

"A small sacrifice."

"She's very skinny, and cold. And she's filthy. I told her I would speak to you about—"

His eyes flashed with white light. "Lock the door."

So much for that. Her heart thudded, and she turned to the door, sliding the bolt to lock it. When she faced forward again, her heart leapt into her throat.

Ambrose had crossed the room in that fraction of a second, and was standing within inches of her. His hands shot out, and he gripped her wrists, pinning them to the wall. He stood a head taller than her, his body made of pure muscle. His eyes—two dark abysses—stared down at her, and her stomach flipped.

Why do I get the feeling that I screwed up, big time?

His sharp incisors glinted. "You've done three things wrong. Can you tell me what they are?"

Rosalind pressed herself flat against the wall, desperate to get away from that dark, penetrating stare.

She had a guess about one of those infractions. She hadn't been willing to leave Miranda, so she was probably a minute or so late. *Is he really that particular about lateness? Seven hells.*

Still, with her arms pinned to the door, this didn't seem like the time to argue. "Why don't you tell me?"

"One, you showed up late."

Okay. So he is a stickler for punctuality.

"You won't waste my time again." His lip curled in a sneer. "Two. You won't show mercy for our enemies. Not Erish. Not Drew. Not anyone who has tried to kill us. Mercy will be your death."

"Right now I feel like *you'll* be my death."

Lantern light contoured his sharp cheekbones, like a perfect marble sculpture. "That brings me to my third point. I told you not to come to me when you were bleeding." His gaze lowered to her neck.

Her pulse raced. He had her pinned in a vice-like grip, and there wasn't a damn thing she could do if he wanted to tear out her throat. Cleo's aura whorled through her belly, warming her body. *He's beautiful, isn't he? Now is the time. I told you to take off your clothes and show him your body. Kiss his neck.*

Part of her was deeply, seriously pissed off at this flagrant display of vamp testosterone, yet Cleo wanted her to give in to it. Wanted his mouth on her neck, his teeth in her throat.

Somehow, she no longer felt complete control over herself. She felt her head tilting back, exposing her throat to him. Heat warmed her chest. Her heartbeat pounded in her ears.

Ambrose let out a low growl—softer than she'd expected. The tips of his fangs grazed her skin.

But this wasn't why she'd come here. She hadn't come to give Ambrose her blood.

She was here to fight.

With Ambrose's spicy scent in her nostrils, Cleo's magic curled around her spine. *Touch his powerful body,* Cleo whispered.

"Shut up Cleo," Rosalind said through clenched teeth.

Immediately, Ambrose dropped her hands and jumped away from her, a horrified look on his face. "What did you say?"

She rubbed her wrists where he'd been gripping them. "Nothing. I was just telling Cleo to shut up."

"Cleo," he said. His skin had gone a shade paler than normal.

"Right." The name *Cleo* seemed to agitate him. She swallowed hard. "My extra soul."

For now, maybe best to leave out the part where she wants to bang him and then light him on fire.

A muscle worked in his jaw. "Sorry about the blood hunger. That's why you mustn't come here with blood on your body." He looked away from her, staring at the wall. "There's water for you on the altar. I know humans require it when you exert yourselves."

She crossed to the altar, picking up a small pitcher. "What, exactly, are we doing here?"

"I want to see how you fight."

"I can fight fine. But if I drink the ambrosia, I'll need magic training." She poured a few drops of water onto her hand to wash off the blood on her fingertips. "I'll need help controlling the gods' power. And I need Malphas for that."

"I didn't ask for your opinion." He ran his tongue over his sharpened incisors. "Apparently you don't know the true place of humans here in Lilinor."

A shiver ran up her spine. *What the hell is his problem?* "Oh, I've met one of your courtesans," she said, glaring at him. "but I'm not here as one of your human slaves. You need me—that's clear enough. Maybe you're forgetting *your* place."

She didn't know Ambrose well, but she didn't think Caine would let her stay here under the protection of a complete psychopath—and with that thought, a strange revelation bubbled in the back of her mind: *Apparently, I actually trust Caine.*

Ambrose took a step closer, letting his eyes rake over her body. "I'm going to enjoy punishing you."

Her anger simmered. "What is *wrong* with you?"

In the next moment, his hand was around her throat. "I've added a fourth rule to my list: Don't speak until I've asked you a question. And don't presume to look me in the eye."

A hundred retorts blared through her mind, like *Take your hands off my throat, you alpha dickhole.* But she choked down every one of them, because the fact was she couldn't take Ambrose in a fight. She knew better than to argue with a vampire lord in the thrall of blood-hunger.

But her anger simmered, and Cleo's rage was only adding fuel to the fire. In the darkest recesses of her mind, Cleo's melodic voice sang, *Fuck him to oblivion. Then kill him.* Cleo's song drowned out Rosalind's own thoughts, until she could think of nothing else. Angry heat warmed her cheeks, and her body began to shake. Her teeth chattered as molten anger flooded her veins. *I know what's coming next. I know what it feels like when battle fury claims my body.*

Surging with adrenalin, she slammed her forearms into Ambrose's wrists, kicking him in the groin at the same time. He dropped his grip, and she punched him hard in the carotid artery.

His eyes bulged, then his hands flew out, gripping her wrists again. With stunningly swift power, he pinned them to her side. He stared down at her again, his lip curling in a terrifying smile.

He thinks he owns you, Cleo whispered. *Punish him now. Kiss him later—when you've tamed him.*

Anger flooded her, and she headbutted him. His head whipped back, but he only held tighter to her wrists. She brought her knee up into his groin a second time; when it connected, his grip loosened just a little. She yanked one hand free, slipping it into his hair to pull back his head.

I have you in my thrall now.

Cleo's aura surged, claiming Rosalind's mind. She was no longer in the armory, but standing in the center of the rowan grove, in a silky dress that caressed her thighs. *Stars engrave the night sky. When Ambrose comes, he'll run his fingers over my hips, over my belly, gentle as a flower petal... He'll bed me in the wildflowers. He says he'll always keep me safe...*

Rosalind's vision cleared, and she was in the armory again—pressed between the altar and Ambrose's strong body. He pinned both wrists behind her back, gripping them tightly in one of his hands. Inky shadows curled from his cold body, and a low growl rose from his throat as he glared down at her.

Her stomach lurched. "What the hell are you doing, Ambrose?"

Cleo's aura caressed her ribs. *He's doing what's in his nature. Taking what he wants. Using you, like he did to me.*

Damn it, Cleo. That was the worst possible time to hit me with one of your visions.

What exactly was Ambrose doing here? Caine had told her not to let anyone mess with her mind, and she was pretty sure Ambrose was doing exactly that.

And there it was again: She actually trusted Caine.

Cleo's aura stroked her skin, raising goosebumps. *You have more than one way to disarm him, Rosalind.*

Rosalind tilted her head back, exposing her neck. Cleo purred in the back of her mind, and the filthy scent of blooming rowans enveloped her. *Now I remember how sweet you were, Ambrose. Don't you remember how sweet I could be, before you destroyed me?*

Rosalind pulled Ambrose closer, and his beautiful lips hovered just over hers. "You said you'd always keep me safe," she whispered, leaning in to kiss him.

Ambrose pulled away. "What did you say?"

Rosalind blinked, shaking her head. "That wasn't me. That was Cleo."

Ambrose's eyes widened. Hands shaking, he smoothed his shirt.

Rosalind frowned. "Can you explain to me what's going on? Or am I not allowed to speak unless I'm spoken to?"

He straightened. "Now you understand why you must never come to see me while you're bleeding. If I see your vulnerability, I won't be able to control myself. It's part of the curse of the vampire."

"Complete domination of anyone you perceive as weak."

"That is the heart of any demon. If you want to survive among the monsters, you must remember our nature."

This was the first time she'd heard a demon admit that. "Surely not all demons have the same nature."

"Some want blood; some are driven to rule your mind. We all want sex. And an incubus in particular… well, I'm sure you understand."

She knew how incubi were supposed to work. But Caine had never lost control around her, had never tried to control her mind or force her to do anything she didn't want. He'd been completely in control of himself, even when she'd stripped off in front of him. "I haven't seen that side of him."

Ambrose arched an eyebrow. "Apparently he has more restraint than I do."

She crossed her arms. "Honestly, he's always been a perfect gentleman around me."

Ambrose smirked. "Then I would assume he has no interest in you. He has been with many beautiful women before."

His words stung, and suddenly she wanted to change the subject. "Why am I here? What were we *supposed* to do before you went psycho-vamp?"

"I need to teach you to fight. *Real* fighting, not what you've learned among the humans. I know how you practice at the Brotherhood. You have rules—no gouging out eyes, no tearing out flesh with your teeth. You'll have to abandon those trappings of civility."

"I see. You're accusing me of being civilized."

"You fight more viciously than I would have expected. Was that you, or Cleo?"

"At least some of it was me," she said. "I'm no stranger to fighting after the past month, and I've been training in combat fighting. I just need to learn magic. Do I really need to learn how to gouge out eyes, or can we get on with figuring out how to take on Drew?"

Ambrose cocked his head. "If you let that sort of savagery out when you fight Drew and the Brotherhood, perhaps you don't need me. Maybe you need to let Cleo do the fighting."

Rosalind bit her lip. "What did she look like? Blonde hair, pale skin, hazel eyes?"

He narrowed his eyes. "How did you know?"

"I saw her reflection. Erish saw her too, a glimpse of her when she looked at me." She frowned. "What happened with you and Cleo?"

Ambrose's eyes darkened. "It's none of your concern. I need to know if you're going to drink the blood."

Rosalind stepped closer to Ambrose, grabbing him by the wrists. "This is how you like to have conversations, isn't it? And my answer is… I'll tell you when I'm ready."

CHAPTER 18

Rosalind strode down the dank, earthen hall, on her way to see Erish a second time. According to Ambrose, she wasn't supposed to show mercy to her enemies. But Ambrose had a little preoccupation for total domination that she didn't share. She could think for herself, and her own thoughts highlighted two things.

One—there was no benefit in making a captive suffer. Erish needed to be caged, sure, but they gained nothing by freezing and starving her.

And two—maybe Erish could be useful. Erish knew how to use gods-magic, and she knew how Drew operated. And she wasn't likely to give up her secrets when resentment boiled her blood.

Rosalind carried a basket full of fresh bread and cheese, some freshly cleaned and folded clothes, water and washing cloths. Tucked under her arm were a wool blanket and a small pillow.

Dim candlelight danced over Erish's barren cage, and the succubus sat rigid in her cell. She looked more skeleton than human. Only her dark eyes swiveled to Rosalind, glinting with anger. "Ah. You've come to gloat again."

"I told you I'd speak to Ambrose about your conditions." This wasn't the time to ask for a bargain. If she wanted to get Erish on her side, she'd have to be patient.

"And now you're sneaking down here on your own. Looks like he takes your opinion very seriously."

"He's got a bit of a god complex."

"So you've noticed."

Rosalind sat on the dirty floor, lowering herself to the same level as Erish. She handed Erish the bread and cheese. The succubus snatched them, ripping into the bread with stunning ferocity.

As she chewed, she fixed her eyes on Rosalind. "You're not gloating, are you?" she said between bites. "You're miserable." She swallowed hard. "What do you have to be so miserable about? Apart from the fact that you're dying, you have everything you need. Beauty. Food. The attentions of gorgeous men who want to fuck you."

"When we were in Maremount, you said that your sisters were killed."

"By humans," Erish snarled.

Rosalind had seen one of their heads—now petrified—adorning the city's drinking fountain. "Well, now we have something in common."

"Your twin?" Erish ripped off another hunk of bread. "What happened to her?"

"Drew killed her. Right in front of me."

Erish swallowed a bite of bread. "He is a bit twisted, isn't he?"

You don't know the half of it. As she sat across from the ancient demon, an idea sparked in her mind. "I don't suppose you know how to raise a body from the grave?"

"Is that why you've come here with this bread and those clothes?" Erish snarled. "I was wondering what you wanted."

Rosalind shook her head. "Never mind." She pushed the blankets and fresh clothes through the bars, glancing at Erish's chains. "Do you need help washing and changing your clothes?"

Erish stared at her. "I'll manage."

Rosalind stood, brushing off her pants. "I'll come back with more food tomorrow." She turned, but as she began to walk away, Erish's voice stopped her.

"Rosalind. Wait."

Rosalind stopped walking.

"Drink the ambrosia," Erish continued. "Use Nyxobas's shadow magic to raise your sister."

The ambrosia. Rosalind turned back to Erish.

"I wish I'd had the gods-magic when my sisters died," the succubus muttered softly.

"When I saw you in Maremount, after you drank the ambrosia—"

"I lost my wits." Erish cocked her head. "But they've returned. I can't promise the same will be true of a human. You must decide if it's worth the risk."

"I don't yet know how to use gods-magic. Malphas is supposed to teach me, after I drink the blood."

"It's shadow magic. Just think of your lover, and he'll find a way to help you."

"What lover?"

"Don't play coy. I've told you everything you need to know."

Rosalind nodded, gripping the empty basket. "Thank you."

She turned again, hurrying down the earthen hall. *Gods-magic.* She had a choice to make, but it wasn't much of a choice at all. She could abandon her sister to the afterworld. She could let Drew take over Boston and Cambridge, burn all the vampires, destroy Caine, and force her to be his mindless, brainwashed wife. A dead-eyed vessel for his progeny.

Or she could drink the ambrosia.

What did she have to lose? *Her mind.* And what good was that anyway, with a dead witch taking control?

Climbing the stairs, she pulled the flask from her pocket. *If Caine were here, he could tell me what gods-magic feels like. How to use it.*

How was he doing, anyway? She couldn't tell day from night here in Lilinor, but it must have been two days at least since Caine had left. Loneliness pressed on her like a hundred rocks.

At the top of the stairwell, she pushed through a tall oak door into a dark stone hall. Moonlight streamed through the windows, but shadows crept over the hall like long fingers. A chill rippled over her skin.

Maybe it was time to pay Miranda's grave a visit again. Maybe it was time to drink from Blodrial's veins.

Drink, child, said Cleo. *Let the gods-magic flow through your veins.*

Rosalind stalked through the dark halls, the candlelight dancing over the stone floor. As she walked, the hair rose on the back of her neck. She shivered. *Why do I have the feeling that I'm not alone?*

A scraping noise turned her head, and she caught a flicker of liquid movement in the shadows. She reached down to her waist, pulling a hawthorn stake from a holster. "Who's there?"

"Easy there, Hunter." Frowning, Tammi stepped from the shadows, dressed in white.

Rosalind heaved a sigh of relief. "Tammi? What are you doing in here? I thought you were supposed to be stuck in the Abzu."

Tammi crossed to Rosalind, wrapping her arms around her. "I knew something was wrong. No one would tell me what had happened." She squeezed Rosalind tight, and Rosalind hugged her back. "I just snuck out to find you."

Gods, it was a relief to have Tammi back. Rosalind sucked in a deep breath. "Something terrible happened."

"I knew it. What was it?"

"Miranda is dead." Rosalind's eyes filled with tears.

"*What?*"

"Drew found his way into our city, with an army of demons. He's turned into a complete psychopath. He burned dozens of vampires." A tear rolled down her cheek. "He stabbed Miranda. He tried to make me do it, but I didn't. So he killed her."

Tammi's jaw dropped, and her eyes filled with tears. "No."

"I'm going to try to bring her back."

Tammi wrapped her arms around her in a tight embrace. "And how do you plan to do that?" she asked, her voice muffled by Rosalind's neck.

"Ambrosia. The starved succubus in the basement tells me it will work."

Tammi pulled away. "You can't possibly trust her. Won't the ambrosia make you mental?"

"I'm already mental."

"You seem fine to me."

Rosalind shrugged. "Well, I guess I have practice wrestling with the voices in my head. So maybe I'll deal better with madness than Drew has."

Tammi narrowed her silver eyes. "I'm not sure about your reasoning."

Rosalind clutched the flask—her new salvation. "It's not just to raise my sister. We need it to stop Drew. He can wield a new kind of magic that's nearly impossible to fight. And since I'm from the same blood line, apparently I can too. I need to fight fire with fire. Otherwise I'll end up as his slave, and he'll turn half the country into mind-controlled demons."

"There's got to be another way."

Rosalind waved a dismissive hand. She didn't want anyone dissuading her, now that she'd made up her mind. "It'll be fine. How did you find me here, anyway?"

"I smelled you."

Rosalind wrinkled her nose. "Seriously?"

"Your blood smells amazing." Tammi took a step back. "I probably shouldn't hug you again."

"Right." She lifted her flask, whispering, "Speaking of blood, it's time for my medicine."

Tammi narrowed her frosty eyes. "You want to do this now?"

"Yes. We need to get Aurora, and then we're heading right for the Garden of the Dead. I don't know a lot about necromancy, but I'm pretty sure it can't be a good thing to let the body rot for weeks." She lifted the flask. "So are you going to help me, or are you going back to the Abzu?"

* * *

Flanked by Aurora and Tammi, Rosalind stood before the yew, covering her nose and mouth with her hands. Aurora had unearthed Miranda again, and this time the smell of death was overpowering. Her skin had turned even more greenish, and dark blood dripped from her nose and mouth.

"I'm not sure about this," Tammi said, coughing into her hands. "She seems a bit… putrified."

Rosalind swallowed hard, trying to steel her resolve. "There must be some healing process as part of Nyxobas's resurrection magic."

"There are two options," Aurora said. "Either you get Miranda back, or you get Zombie-Miranda back. If she's all rotten, we'll have to put her down. Then she'll be dead, which is no worse than she is now. So, two options: life or death. That's all there is."

"Right. We have nothing to lose by trying." Rosalind's fingers tightened into fists. "I'm ready."

She unscrewed her flask, taking a sniff. She hadn't tasted this since she'd been in the Brotherhood's chambers. Now, the smell turned her stomach. Would this really work? Or would it merely drive her mad?

Only one way to find out. Grimacing at the taste, she took a swig of the blood. She wiped a hand across the back of her mouth. Nothing but the cold trickle of salty blood down her throat. *Gods damn you, Drew.*

But just as she began screwing the cap on, a burst of power flooded her body, rushing over her skin and through her bones. Wet marine magic, rough coppery auras… electric silver and spicy gold. Her knees trembled at the rush, and she opened her eyes again. Whorls of colorful magic snaked around her body.

Tammi was staring at her wide-eyed. "Is it working?"

Rosalind nodded. "It's definitely working."

She closed her eyes, feeling the breeze rush over her skin, whipping her hair around her face. She'd watched Caine use this magic. He'd simply held out his hands, and let the gods-magic flow through him. But then—he was part god himself. It must come naturally to him. Right now, she felt such a stunning rush of power she hardly knew where to begin.

At last, the tendrils of magic rushed into her body—filling her bones and blood—almost as if they were becoming part of her. She rolled her neck.

"So what do you need to do?" Aurora asked.

"I need to figure out how to use shadow magic."

Think of your lover. Erish must have meant Caine—not exactly Rosalind's lover, but he *was* the last man she'd kissed. He was the closest thing she knew to Nyxobas, so close that when she'd used the power of the night god, he gave her a glimpse of the incubus's life. And while he wasn't her lover now, she was lying to herself if she didn't admit that she wanted him.

Caine was her closest connection to Nyxobas. She'd been there when he'd used his gods-magic. She knew how it felt when his electric power rushed over her skin, how the air looked as the silver tendrils whipped out of his body. She just needed to tap into those memories.

Closing her eyes, she called up an image of Caine in her mind. His golden skin. Those glacial eyes. Warm and cold, sun and ice. The shadows curling around his powerful body, the black tattoos marking his chest. She could almost feel him wrapping his strong arms around her, lighting her body on fire with his touch.

Not my lover... yet.

Dark magic coursed through her veins, and Caine's smell, loamy and electric, enveloped her. In the next moment, she found herself in that wooden room again. Sitting in a chair, facing a dark wood wall, a blonde woman brushed her hair. A baby's cry pierced the air, and Rosalind watched herself pick up the gray-eyed child, cradling him in her arms.

Shadows crept over her vision, and an empty ache rose in her chest. She wanted to see that child again, but darkness stole him from her. Her stomach lurched as she reached out, trying to grasp something tangible and finding only wisps of shadow.

Where am I?

Now, she walked through a dark stone hall, surrounding by whispering voices. Shadows climbed the walls like fingers. A deep voice rumbled from the emptiness. *What are you doing here?*

What *was* she doing here? She could hardly remember her name. Right now, she wasn't even sure she'd ever existed.

What are you doing here? the voice demanded again.

She had a purpose. She just needed to remember what it was. A sister, one with brown eyes who smelled of the sea.

"Miranda!" she screamed, suddenly finding her voice. "I want to fix her. To bring her back."

An electrifying power flooded her, rooting her feet on the earth once more. She opened her eyes, watching the silver magic flow from her fingertips. It rushed over Miranda's body, washing her in moonlight.

This time, the magic found its target.

Miranda's skin warmed, her cheeks reddening. At the sight of her sister's fluttering eyelids, Rosalind's breath caught in her throat. Miranda's back arched, and the blood disappeared from her face. Rosalind's pulse raced.

It's working. Nyxobas's will is my own.

Miranda gasped, sitting up straight, her eyes wide. Blood pounded in Rosalind's ears, and she lowered her hands, her body drained. Miranda looked up at her and screamed; the sound pierced the air, and Rosalind's knees nearly gave way.

Something is wrong.

Tammi rushed to Miranda, wrapping her arms around her. "Shh-hhh, girl. It's okay."

Rosalind stared wide-eyed at her sister, who pulled away from Tammi, crawling on her hands and knees. She vomited dark bile onto the grass.

"Are you okay?" Tammi asked.

Miranda sat back on her knees, wiping the back of her hand across her mouth. "What's going on?" she asked, her voice husky. "I don't feel so well."

Rosalind took a breath for the first time since Miranda had opened her eyes. She ran to her sister, hugging her.

Miranda's body felt warm through her thin dress, and she hugged Rosalind back.

And once again, she smelled like the sea.

625

CHAPTER 19

As she waited for Malphas, Rosalind stood at the shore of the
Astarte Sea. Waves gently lapped at the rocks, and moonlight
flecked the water with silver sparks.

She'd spent a long night, watching over Miranda as she'd slept. So
after just an hour of sleep, she'd rushed off to find Malphas. Today he
was supposed to teach her how to use Borgerith's magic—the
coppery, mountain aura that Drew had used the first day she'd
met him.

But that was just the beginning. Tonight, she'd also learn to
harness Dagon's power. Yet she wasn't sure she was up for meeting
the god of the depths. Tiredness had claimed her mind, and she
swayed on her feet.

When was the last time she'd slept for more than six hours? It was
nearly impossible to keep track of normal sleeping hours in a city
with no daylight.

Last night, after some tea and a warm bath, Miranda had seemed
almost normal again. Exhausted, but speaking in full sentences.
Except she didn't seem to remember having died, or anything about
Drew's invasion of Lilinor.

And how, exactly, did one broach that subject delicately?

"Remember that time you died? No? Well, you did. Want another muffin?"

Rosalind didn't want to break it to her just yet. Whatever death did to a body, it had to be a shock to the system. She saw no reason to add another shock just yet. What if Miranda's newly pumping heart just stopped again? So during the quiet hours when she'd normally have been sleeping, she'd watched over her newly-living sister, listening to her deep breaths. She'd watched the blood pump through the veins in Miranda's neck, and marveled at her own creation.

Now, on the Astarte shore, Rosalind blinked hard, fighting fatigue. A briny wind rushed off the waves, and she pulled her cashmere shawl tighter around her shoulders. She wouldn't be fighting today, and she'd worn a long dress, the color of sea-foam.

When she looked at the dome of stars above the sea, she could see a faint shimmering of Caine's silver magic. *The shield.* If she let her eyes go out of focus long enough, his magic became clearer—the stunning sterling gleam rippling over the sky.

Cold magic thrummed over Rosalind's skin, scented of lilies. *Malphas.* She turned.

He stalked toward her, the wind ruffling his brown hair. Moonlight washed his milky skin in silver, and he carried a faded maroon tome under his arm. The sight of him tightened her chest. Sharp cheekbones, porcelain skin, cold eyes and dark lashes. She couldn't help but think about her own hands, drowning that delicate beauty in the Brotherhood's dungeons.

Whenever she looked at him, the memories hit her like fist. The nail, driven into his chest. The chains. The water poured on his face, his legs kicking as he drowned. Hard to forget what she'd done, when it was staring her right in the face with those pale eyes.

And yet, she reminded herself, his fragility was an illusion. As an incubus, steely strength coursed through his muscles.

"Thanks for meeting me." She glanced at the dark sea. She wanted to ask about Caine and the valkyries, but that particular vision was hard to explain without delving into the whole necromancy subject. "Do you think Caine will be home soon?"

"That's the thing." Malphas's aura snapped the air around him. "He should have returned already."

A sharp tendril of dread coiled through her chest. "You think something happened to him?"

"I don't know. I haven't been able to see anything through scrying, because of the shield Caine created. That's why I want to make sure we get this right. We might need to get him back. Are you willing to do whatever it takes to win this war?"

No pressure. "Of course. I'll do whatever I need to."

Malphas closed the distance between them, and she could feel the warmth coming off his skin. In the V of his shirt collar, pearly light illuminated the top of his scarred chest—marks left by Rosalind. A chill crawled up her neck, and she tried not to stare at the slashes of raised skin.

"From what I've seen," he said, "you are the type of soldier who will do whatever it takes to get the job done. Even if it involves pain."

Her body went cold. *Okay. He's still thinking about the torture thing, too.* "What sort of pain are we talking about?"

He leaned down, smelling the air near her neck. So close to him, his aura crackled over her skin—a sharp, electric thrill that made her lean in closer.

"Oh, Rosalind," he said. "I know the smell of Nyxobas's magic. The smell of damp earth and the air after a rainstorm. So why would you smell like the gods-magic, if you haven't used it yet?"

Her stomach tightened. *Guess the secret is coming out anyway.* Maybe it was for the best. She was desperate to come clean about what she'd seen in her vision, and to ask Malphas what he thought.

"After I drank the ambrosia," she said, "I tried a little spell. I tried it several times before I drank the ambrosia, and something happened— almost like I was channeling Caine's magic—but I had no way to direct the power. It wasn't until I drank the blood that it worked effectively."

Malphas stared down at her, and the hair raised on the back of her neck. No matter how much time she spent around demons, their preternatural stillness and penetrating eyes still made her want to run far in the other direction. It was an intent focus, like a coiled snake about to strike.

Still, she held her ground. After all—she had gods-magic now, too. Maybe she didn't need to be scared of demons anymore.

Malphas's dark power thrummed over her skin. "What sort of spell?" he asked.

"Just a little one," she lied. "I snuffed out the candles and extinguished the flames in the fireplace, like Caine does when he's angry."

Shit. I hope incubi can't tell when you're lying.

"You're lying."

Of course they can. "Let me guess. You heard my heart rate speed up?"

"And your pupils dilated. Your skin warmed. A thin sheen of sweat rose on your forehead. Incubi are skilled at noticing these hallmarks of arousal. Either you're extremely turned on by talking about fireplaces, or your pulse is racing at the lies tumbling from your lips."

She frowned. "I don't suppose I can convince you I have a thing for fireplaces?"

He cocked his head, ivory light glinting in his pale eyes. "What kind of spell did you conduct, Rosalind?"

Rosalind waved a dismissive hand. "It's not important. The important part is…" She cleared her throat. *I can't talk about this.* She needed to change the subject. "I think it was connected to Caine's magic somehow. And I think I saw visions of his life. Maybe visions of him now."

A heavy wave crashed over the rocks, and briny spume misted the air.

"What did you see?" Malphas asked.

"I saw a woman with long blond hair. And a baby with grey eyes, the exact same color as yours. On a table by a bed lay a hairpin." She held out her arm, running her fingers from her wrist to the hollow of her elbow. "It was the same as that tattoo Caine has here."

Malphas seemed entranced by her fingertips. "You've stolen a glimpse into my brother's life."

Ocean spray dampened her skin, and she licked the salt off her lips. "But then I think I saw him in Maremount, surrounded by valkyries. They were closing in on him."

The air seemed to thin around Malphas. Had he blinked once this entire time she'd been speaking to him? She was sure he was searching her for signs of lying again. "And then what?"

"In the final vision, he was walking in a dark stone hall, surrounded by whispers and shadows."

Malphas's body glowed with a deep silver light. "It sounds like the House of Shades, where spirits go after death. Perhaps that's where Caine is now. Looking for Miranda's second soul."

"Is it dangerous?"

"Only if he stays too long, and gets lost among the dead."

She shivered.

Caine had once said to her, *You have no idea how dark hell is.*

<h1 style="text-align:center">CHAPTER 20</h1>

osalind frowned. "How did I end up with those visions?"

"I think you borrowed power from Caine, not Nyxobas. Caine must have allowed it. You wouldn't have been able to use his magic unless he'd granted you permission. It's good news. It means he's still alive."

"Would he know what sort of spell I'd conducted?"

Malphas arched an eyebrow. "What *exactly* did you do, Rosalind?"

"Would he know?" she repeated.

"No, only that you used it. And I do hope it was important. You might have weakened him, and he may need strength to free himself from the House of Shades."

A chill washed over her skin. *Please be okay, Caine.* "He'll come back soon. And if not, I'll find him with the gods-magic you're going to teach me." She rubbed her arms. "Where do we start?"

He opened the book, thumbing through the pages. "You're lucky I found this book in the library." He met her gaze. "Or perhaps unlucky. From what I read earlier, in order to use the gods-magic, you'll need to go into many hells. They will be painful, and agonizing, and you'll want to die. I've been to one only—the shadow void. But you'll go into all of them."

Her heart skipped a beat. "Was there not a better way you could have phrased that?"

"There's no point sugar-coating it. You'll learn soon enough." He narrowed his eyes. "You know, I remember quite vividly the feeling of iron nails driven into my chest, and the water you poured into my lungs. Perhaps that will help me put some of my sympathy aside so we can get on with things." He ran his fingers over the jagged scars on his chest. "But the real question, Rosalind, is do *you* have the stomach for it?"

"I'll do what I need to. We have to stop Drew somehow."

"Good. I know you can take orders—I saw you follow Josiah's. And now you have to be prepared to follow mine. You'll have to trust me."

She nodded. "I'm ready."

"You'll have to keep your second soul in check. It's easy to let someone else take over when your mind is ripped apart by terror and agony."

Rosalind's pulse raced, and Cleo's aura curled around her lungs. *Let me come out to play. I can take it,* the mage whispered. Rosalind schooled her face into calm. "Where do we begin?"

"Tonight, we begin where life began, on the sludgy rocks and in the sea. I'm glad you asked about Borgerith first. It's a good place to start."

"Why is that?"

"She will grant physical strength and help stabilize your magic. Ambrose tells me that when you fought in the armory, he was able to overpower you easily. The only reason he didn't rip your throat out was that some part of him exercised extreme restraint. So you've learned to fight, but you still need strength on your side."

"And when I have this power," she ventured, "I won't need to use a spell to conduct magic. Physical power will just flow through my body. Like yours."

"Exactly. Once you're finished visiting all the hells, you'll be able to defend yourself against anyone. Vampires. Demons. Even me, should we ever find ourselves on the opposite side of a war again."

"I hope we don't."

"But most importantly, you'll be able to fight Drew." He nodded at the ground. "Take off your shoes. I want to see what you can do before you experience Borgerith's hell."

She slipped off her thin flats, stepping onto the damp, jagged rocks. The marine wind kissed her skin through her dress.

"Close your eyes," he said. "Tell me what you feel."

She cleared her throat. "Wind. Seawater. Slimy rocks and sand. Jagged stones and pebbles."

Malphas stepped behind her, his aura tingling over her skin. Heat radiated from his body. "I want you to feel Borgerith's power through the rock. Bend her will to your own."

Rosalind arched her back, opening herself up to the power of the mountain goddess. A rough aura brushed over the skin of her ankles, and the smell of a craggy breeze surrounded her. When she opened her eyes, she caught a glimpse of a coppery magic, curling around her ankles and up into her dress. The magic snaked around her waist, and buzzed over her ribs.

"I feel it," she said.

Malphas ran his fingers down her arm, sending shivers over her skin. He let his fingertips rest at the end of hers. "Do you feel the power flowing through your arms, into your hands? Call the pebbles into your fists. Use a magnetic charge. Borgerith has the power of magnetism."

Rosalind looked down at her fingertips, which brushed lightly against Malphas's. A coppery aura played about their hands. *Right. I just need to lure the rocks to my hands, with the power of my mind.*

Borgerith's power flowed around her, along with Malphas's magic, a stunning vortex of silver and copper.

What would Caine do if he discovered she'd raised her sister? He wouldn't kill Miranda—would he?

Malphas leaned down, whispering in her ear, "You're not focusing."

She closed her eyes, imagining the pebbles on the ground. She tried to picture them flying through the air into her palms.

Malphas's fingertips continued to brush hers, but her palms

remained empty. He exhaled. "I was hoping to avoid the hells, but it's not working." He stepped in front of her, scrubbing a hand over his chin.

"So, now it's time for Borgerith's hell?"

"Yes. You'll need to lie back on the rocks."

Her pulse raced. "Of course."

Seawater misted the air as she lowered herself to the rocky ground. She lay back, her head resting on the cold, damp stone. Sharp rocks bit into her skin through her dress.

Malphas stood above her, the moon forming a silvery halo around his head. "Spread out your arms and legs. Press your fingers to the rocks." He spoke in a low, soothing voice. "Root yourself to the earth."

She flattened her palms against the damp, sandy rock, and spread out her legs. The wind flowed over her skin.

Malphas knelt down. "Let her power flow into your body through your skin. Feel her immense strength, rooting you to the ground."

She closed her eyes. A wave crashed on the shore, splashing over her feet. Rough magic brushed over her legs, faintly scented of pine.

His fingertips traced over her arms. There was no way around it. Incubi were extremely tactile.

"Let her magic flow into your body," he said. "You must let the ancient part of your brain take over."

Power thrummed over Rosalind's skin, and she breathed in the scent of mountain air. Another wave rushed over her, misting her dress with cool water.

"Feel the weight of Borgerith's strength," Malphas said.

As he spoke the words, Rosalind felt an immense pressure on her chest, crushing her ribs. She gasped, her eyes snapping open.

"Don't resist it," Malphas said. "Let her strength become part of you."

Gods, the weight was grinding her ribs into dust. She struggled for breath. "Malphas." She choked out the word. Agony crushed her like a boulder on her chest, stealing her breath. Any minute, her ribs would crack and pierce her lungs, her heart. She squeezed her eyes shut, trying to block out the pain.

"Take the power into your body," he said.

Another ton of rocks pressed her into the hard earth, ready to break her body. She opened her eyes, nearly ready to cry uncle, but a coffin of rock surrounded her.

She hated being trapped more than anything. Panic blazed through her mind.

I'm going to die here, ground into dust.

The weight of a mountain crushed the breath out of her, and pain tore through her body. Deep within her rocky coffin, an image began to play before her eyes: Smooth stone walls. Another buried room. Malphas, chained to a chair, his porcelain chest bleeding.

And there was Rosalind, standing before him, gripping a jagged iron shard in her fist.

Raw fear shone in his pale eyes.

But as Rosalind rammed the nail into his chest, a very different emotion glinted in her eyes: pleasure. A dark thrill. As the vision disappeared, the word *monster* roared in the back of her mind.

Monster. Monster. Monster.

And what happened to monsters? They needed to be locked up, to be buried deep within the earth's core.

Grinding pain cut her to the marrow. This was her punishment. The rocks would rip her body apart, would bury her under the earth.

I have to get out of here, before the weight of this destroys me.

CHAPTER 21

She looked down at the copper magic whirling over her chest. *Let it in.* Right. That was what Malphas had said, right? It was so hard to think straight when the pain was ripping her mind apart.

Even as her chest felt like it would cave below the weight, she concentrated on forcing the magic further into her own ribs. A scream tore from her throat as the aura plunged into her body, cracking her bones. Yet, as it flowed into her, power surged through her muscles. The weight on her chest lifted, and her back arched with a blazing power, healing her body.

A cool mountain wind rushed over her skin, and her coffin of stone thinned, giving way to a canopy of stars. She sucked in a deep breath. *I can breathe.*

Slowly, some of the agonizing pain left her body. A cool wave washed over her legs. She grabbed her ribs, her eyes flicking to Malphas, who knelt over her.

Malphas touched her cheek. "You made it." He let out a long breath. "I wasn't sure what would happen."

Magic ignited her nerve endings, but so did pain. Flinching, she rose, her limbs shaking. She couldn't stand straight. She was lucky her ribs hadn't punctured anything. "I think something's broken."

"Come here."

She stepped closer to him, suppressing a groan of pain.

Frowning, he brushed his fingertips over her ribs. "Broken in three places. After tonight, you won't break so easily." He closed his eyes, whispering a spell. His aura caressed her skin, soothing her body.

As the pain left her ribs, she sighed. She had to admit, incubus magic felt amazing.

He dropped his hand, eyeing her carefully. "What did you see?"

A wave lapped at her feet. "Me. And you. In the Brotherhood's prisons." She hugged herself. "I was hurting you."

"I see. And how did you feel when you were doing it?"

She let out a slow breath, her gaze trailing over the brutal scars on his chest. She couldn't exactly tell him she'd looked like she was having a great time. "What difference does it make?"

"Did you enjoy hurting me?"

"Of course not."

In a blur of silver movement, Malphas lunged closer to her, pinning her arms with one hand, and grabbing her throat with the other.

She struggled against him. "What are you doing?"

"You're lying to me."

Her heart raced, hammering against her ribs. "Malphas! Stop!"

"Do you know the natural instincts of a demon?" he snarled. "To take what's ours. To fuck and kill. To rip out the throats of our enemies and leave twitching carcasses in our wake. And when you stabbed me and left me for dead, you marked yourself as my natural enemy."

She stared up at his pale eyes—no longer sad, but full of icy rage. Still, he was Caine's brother. He wouldn't kill her. Would he? "Can we talk about this inside?"

His large fingers tightened around her neck.

Anger simmered in her chest, and she glared at him. "I thought we were moving beyond the past," she choked out.

"I was. I'm not sure that you did. And maybe the vampires are right. Maybe you need to be put in your place."

The raw power of Borgerith burned through her muscles, and fury ignited her veins. She'd have to fight back if she wanted to get out of this intact. Malphas's demonic instincts had been inflamed, which meant she was in some serious danger if she didn't break free.

She slammed her forehead into Malphas's nose. He dropped his grip, and she followed with a hard punch to his jaw. Malphas staggered, his head swiveling with the blow. When he turned back to her, blood dripped from his lip. His eyes had turned completely black. In a whirl of silver magic, he rushed to her, spinning her around and pinning her arms to her side.

He's lost his fucking mind. She struggled against him, but he'd been too fast, and his steely body pressed against hers, trapping her.

"What the hell, Malphas?" she shouted.

And yet, somewhere, deep in the hollows of her mind, Cleo was enjoying this. She relished the fighting, the adrenaline, the feel of Malphas's powerful body against her own.

Malphas leaned down, whispering into her ear. "It's okay, Rosalind. I needed to see if it worked."

"What?"

"I needed to know how you'd handle it when you had to fight for your life."

"You could have warned me." Raw power coursed through her muscles.

"Then you wouldn't have really fought."

She leaned back, turning her head to look at him. "If I'm so strong, why are you the one pinning me?"

"You don't have speed, and you haven't been trained. Yet." He loosened his grip and stepped away from her. "And when you have both speed and training on your side, you'll be terrifying. I've probably seen more of your vicious side than I need for an eternal lifetime."

Her body burned with a strange mixture of energy and fatigue. "One hell down, five more to go. That's right, isn't it?"

"Yes." He pulled the book from under his arm, flipping through. He landed on a page with a drawing of tentacled appendages gripping a galley ship. Muttering to himself, Malphas dragged his finger down the spidery text. "It says you must return to the place where life itself began."

The black sea churned, and marine air rushed over her skin. *Time to meet Miranda's god.* "What can I expect from this hell?"

"According to this text, the sea teems with life, but it's not always beautiful. It can be ancient, brutal and ravenous." He met her gaze. "If you want Dagon's power, you must keep swimming under the water until you find him. Don't come up for air until you feel the gods' arms around you, and he embraces you with his magic."

She shivered. "So I just swim into the sea?"

"Seems that way."

She stared at the churning black water, and the chilly moonlight glinting off the waves. "You think I'll make it through this?"

Malphas closed the book, his expression softening. "I know you'll face whatever challenge you must. I remember when you were a little girl. You led the way through the Tuckomock Forest when we explored. You were first into the dark caves. You were fearless."

"Sounds vaguely familiar."

"You were attacked by a wolf. The thing ripped right into your leg. And the next time we went into the woods, you were first in the cave again. Like you had no sense of self preservation. I don't think you'll come up for air until you meet Dagon." He stepped back into the shadows, leaving her alone on the shore.

A faint memory sparked in the back of her mind. *The boy with gray eyes, bandaging her bleeding leg.*

On the dark Astarte shore, cold wind rushed off the sea, chilling her body. As she walked over the rocks, icy water rushed across her toes.

The sea's dark, oily sheen warned her away, but she had to go through with this. It might be the only way to free herself from the One True King. She needed the pure, intense power of gods. She took a deep breath, her body buzzing with adrenaline. A waved rushed over her legs, cold as a grave.

Deep below the waves lurked one of the dark gods.

640

Rosalind stepped deeper into the water, her muscles bracing at the cold. Her teeth chattered as the water reached above her belly button.

A strange baptism, Cleo whispered. *Are you sure you can handle the gods-power without losing your mind, little blossom?*

Rosalind tried to block out Cleo's voice, focusing only on the feel of the icy water swarming around her ribs and the algae-slicked rocks below her feet. She really didn't need Cleo's doubts adding to her own apprehension.

A wave rushed over her skin, shocking her with cold.

Time to make the plunge.

With a deep breath, she dove under the chilly water, kicking her legs to take her deeper under the waves. With the power of Borgerith still pulsing through her limbs, she was moving at a fast clip, plunging deeper into the sea.

After what seemed an eternity, her lungs began to burn, and the waters grew darker.

Where the hell is this god?

She was desperate for air. Pain ripped through her lungs, and seaweed brushed over her legs. She turned her body, glancing up at the water's surface. Faint shards of moonlight streamed through the dark water.

Air. I need air now.

She kicked her feet, turning for the surface. But before she could get anywhere, a slick limb wrapped around her leg. Her heart thudded hard against her ribs, and a cold dread bloomed in her chest.

Dagon.

His presence alone filled her with a terror that pierced her to the bone.

A long, slimy appendage slipped up her dress, climbing up her leg and pulling her deeper under the water. Another curled around her waist. She kicked her limbs, flailing in the water.

I need air.

Dagon's limbs gripped her tight, pulling her deeper. Pain blazed through her lungs, and a vision rose in her mind. She was standing by the shore of Maremount's river, rain hammering her body. Miranda stood by her side. Four rotten stakes jutted from the ground, skeletal fingers clawing out of the earth. In a blur of silver, Caine dragged Rosalind's mother through the mud. Her mom kicked helplessly, eyes wide.

Caine's magic chilled the air as he slammed her mother against one of the stakes, pinning her arms.

Icy terror trickled into Rosalind's lungs. *I know how this ends, but I don't want to see it.* She wanted to tear her eyes away, but there was no escaping the vision.

It took only a fraction of a second for Caine to ram the nail through her mom's ribs. The crack of breaking bone sent a shudder up Rosalind's spine, and she gasped as her mom's eyes snapped open.

When Caine turned to look at Rosalind, his eyes had turned black as the void. Here he was, the angel of death, come to wreak his vengeance.

He disappeared in a blur of silver, but she knew he was coming back.

Why had her parents thought they could defeat a god? What kind of insane hubris had led them to that conclusion?

While Miranda screamed, Caine returned with their father, throwing him with brutal force against the second stake. Rosalind had forgotten what her own father looked like—those narrow hazel eyes, the full beard. A strange familiarity surged in her chest.

Her father tilted back his head, screaming, "I am the One True King! I am—"

The thrust of Caine's second nail cut him short. Her father's eyes bulged, and a low moan rose from his throat. Blood dripped from his lips, and his head slumped. The life left his eyes.

Miranda wouldn't stop screaming—or was that herself?

Caine turned to her again. Black wings rose from his back. His eyes were deep and dark as the opening of a cave. Her stomach curdled.

Here he was—her executioner. She took a step back, slipping over a rain-slicked rock and falling to her back. The fall knocked the wind out of her. When she pushed herself up again, Caine was gone.

Sobbing, Rosalind glanced at her twin. Her shoulders shaking, Miranda looked so small. Rosalind watched as her sister turned, running back for the city.

Her father's head lolled. The One True King, pinned to a rotting piece of wood like a butterfly specimen.

She stood on the river's shore, her clothing soaked. Completely alone. A bitter loneliness pierced her to the core. Rain poured down her skin, and emptiness welled in her chest. A gnawing, ravenous emptiness, like she was drowning here in the dark, under the waves. Dread trickled down her throat, filling her lungs.

Not dread. Water.

She was drowning—deep under the black sea, enveloped by the slimy limbs of a sea god.

Dagon, please.

Slick flesh wrapped around her head, covering her mouth. All the air had left her lungs, and death beckoned her closer. It would be so easy just to give in...

As Dagon tightened his grip, she bucked and flailed in his grasp. *I must get back. I must return to Miranda—to Caine.* Adrenalin surged, and she fought against his grasp. She couldn't die here below the waves, in the cold and the dark. *Sometimes the buried things claw their way out again.*

Her throat began to convulse. This was what Malphas had felt when she drowned him.

Let the magic in. Don't fight the gods.

As water poured into her lungs, she opened her eyes. A deep, blue magic undulated around them, like sea anemones caught in a current. She let her body go limp, imagining the blue magic filling her body. It flowed into her chest, mingling with the copper and vernal magic in a vortex of power.

Her lungs still burned, but as she let the magic in, the feel of Dagon's limbs around her changed; they were no longer slimy and alien. His monstrous body had been replaced by a man's. His smooth, strong arms embraced her for just a moment before releasing her into the water.

She turned to see him, but the god had disappeared. Around her, the ocean teemed with life, and shimmering moonlight poured through sapphire water. On the seafloor, amber and crimson urchins nestled among the undulating seagrasses. The sudden flash of beauty was so overwhelming she nearly forgot the water filling her lungs.

She kicked her way toward the moonlight, swimming between seahorses and colorful fish. Fatigue tore her body apart. This had been too much at once.

When her head breached the surface, she coughed and spluttered.

I'm not even sure I can make it to the shore.

As she pushed herself on, her mind churned. Deep in her chest, Cleo's aura was roiling.

Malphas nearly killed you, Cleo whispered. *Are you quite sure he's not after revenge? He was right about what he said. Demons are made for one thing—fucking and killing.*

Malphas had been right. With her mind ripped apart by terror and pain, it was hard to keep her second soul quiet. She gasped for air. *Shut up, Cleo.* She kicked her feet, fighting her way to shore.

He is using you, Cleo whispered. *The demons let Miranda die. And if you die, they'll only find another vessel for their dark desires. They use people, then discard them. Don't think you're special.*

As she swam, her body drained of energy, Cleo's aura began to rage like a tempest.

They'll let you die when you no longer serve their purpose. Ask Ambrose what he did to me.

Rosalind's muscles throbbed. Just when she thought she could no longer continue, her feet brushed against the seafloor, and she stood. She trudged through the waves, falling to her hands and knees in the shallow water. Sharp rocks bit into her palms, and she coughed, spitting up salt water onto the rocks.

This is how the demons want you, Cleo whispered. *On your knees. Knowing your place.*

"What happened?" Malphas asked.

Get up, Rosalind.

The rocks scraped her knees, but she couldn't make herself stand yet. She heaved another lungful of saltwater onto the rocks.

Malphas kneeled. "It doesn't look like it went well."

Another series of coughs racked her body.

Get up, Rosalind. It's humiliating to be on your hands and knees before the shadow demons.

She coughed up a final mouthful of seawater before pushing back to sit on her knees.

Cleo's aura roared through her. *He's trying to kill you.*

With shaking legs, she rose, trying to steady herself. She gripped Malphas's collar. "I nearly drowned before I succeeded. You're sending me to my death."

Were these her thoughts, or Cleo's?

Malphas's eyes darkened, his fingers tightening around hers on his collar. "Did you want sympathy for the water in your lungs? I'm fresh out."

Cleo's vivid memories whirled in Rosalind's mind: the night she'd met Ambrose, and the gold rings on his fingers. He'd worn an embroidered shirt, and he'd looked at her like he'd wanted to devour her.

"No man should be that beautiful," Rosalind said, the words

tumbling from her mouth. "I should have known he'd be my ruin." She blinked hard, trying to clear her mind. "Stop it, Cleo."

Malphas pulled Rosalind's hands from his shoulders, and looked into her eyes. "I can see that we went too far. Next time, we do one hell at a time. You need to rest in between."

"No," she said, shaking her head. Her mind still flashed with images of gold rings and piercing green eyes. "What if Caine needs us?"

"You won't be much good to him when you're hallucinating. Next time you're starting to lose control, tell me. Go home and sleep."

He turned, walking off into the night.

As Malphas stalked off into the shadows, Rosalind glanced at the sky. She could still see the faint shimmer of Caine's shadow magic rippling over the sky.

Was it just her imagination, or did it seem less powerful than it once had?

She shivered, suddenly feeling very alone.

CHAPTER 23

*D*renched with seawater, Rosalind pulled open the door to her cavernous room. Her body trembled from both cold and fatigue. A breeze filtered into the warmly lit room, toying with the silver curtains and nearly snuffing out the candles.

Miranda sat nestled into the corner of the bed, cloaked in shadow. She was so still that Rosalind nearly missed her. She'd wrapped a star-flecked blue sheet around herself, and her shoulders shook.

Rosalind's heart tightened. "Miranda?"

"Where am I?" Her teeth chattered. "What happened to me? I feel sick."

Rosalind crossed to the bed, crawling closer to her sister. She wrapped her arms around Miranda, pulling her close. Miranda's body felt warm—definitely alive. "How sick do you feel?"

"Not so sick you need to smother me with your damp arms. You're getting the bed all wet."

A smile curled Rosalind's lips. "You're awake."

Miranda pulled away from Rosalind, her teeth still chattering. "Yeah but… I'm confused. Where are we? The last thing I remember is being in Maremount. Drew had put a necklace on me, and… I think Caine was there. My mind is cloudy."

Rosalind's chest tightened. *She really has no idea what's going on.* She couldn't hide this from Miranda forever, but she wanted to wait until she seemed a bit stronger before she broke this news. "We're safe now. We're in Lilinor, protected by the vampire lord—sort of. No one knows you're here. I snuck you in, so you must stay in my room for now. You need rest. You had a... an accident, and now you're recovering."

Miranda frowned. "An accident? Like a head injury?" She touched her temples. "I feel really dizzy. I think I'm dehydrated."

Rosalind stood, crossing to an oak table that stood below the window. "I can get you some water." She paused. *She doesn't want blood, does she?* "You *do* want water, right?"

"I wouldn't say no to wine, but water's probably healthier." Miranda frowned. "I don't understand. How did the accident happen?"

Good. Seems normal. No requests for human flesh. "You don't remember anything?"

"Nothing since Maremount."

Rosalind filled a glass of water for her sister. "Drew came into the city. You fought, and he injured you."

"Injured how?"

Too early to tell her—but she'd have to do it soon. "We'll talk about it later. We both need food, and sleep." Someone had left a basket of fresh cranberry bread, curling with steam, on the table next to the water. At the sight of it, Rosalind's stomach rumbled. "Are you hungry?" she asked.

"Starving, now that you mention it. It smells delicious."

Rosalind grabbed the whole bread basket along with the glass of water, and brought them to her sister. "Ambrose still sends me fresh food every day. The other vampires resent it like you wouldn't believe. They feel like they've been made into my servants."

Miranda shrugged. "Sounds like Ambrose wants you."

"What? No, he doesn't." Rosalind sat on the bed, sliding the basket over to her sister. "He hardly knows me."

Miranda arched an eyebrow. "What does that have to do with

anything? He *is* gorgeous. Haven't you noticed? I suppose maybe you wouldn't have. You're more focused on Caine."

Rosalind bit her lip. *Maybe I should revisit that death-conversation idea.* "You know our history with Caine. It's all a bit twisted."

Miranda grabbed a piece of bread. "It was horrible when it happened. But maybe he did us a favor. I think Father was like Drew. And face it, most demigods would have killed *us*, along with our parents, for what they'd done to him." She drained the glass of water, then wiped the back of her hand across her mouth. "Is he in Lilinor?"

Rosalind shook her head. "He's on a mission. He's looking for Drew in Maremount." *And with any luck, he won't end up lost in the House of Shades.*

"I can see by your face that you're worried about him," Miranda said, "but I'm sure he'll be fine. Last I remember, we were on a cliff-side, and Caine was flying through the air like an angel."

"True. But Drew is powerful, too. He uses gods-magic."

"Right. Drew told me all about that in Maremount—Descendants of Azazeyl. So what's the plan to fight him? Am I involved?"

Rosalind grabbed a warm slice of cranberry bread and shook her head. "No. Like I said, no one knows you're here."

"I don't understand why."

"I'll fill you in later. You've just woken up."

Miranda flexed her neck. "I can't feel my magic." She frowned. "I can't feel Dagon. Or my second soul." She took a shuddering breath, her eyes glistening. "What *happened* to me?"

"The accident... It sort of knocked the extra soul out of you."

"What the hell does that mean? What aren't you telling me, Rosalind?"

"You're alive and healthy, and that's all you need to know for now. I'm sure we can get the soul back if you want it."

Miranda took a hungry bite of bread, eyeing Rosalind. "*You* smell like Dagon."

"I went for a swim. I'm training for a fight with Drew."

"Training how?"

Rosalind let the tangy bread melt in her mouth. For a moment, her eyes fluttered closed, and Cleo assaulted her with an image: powerful hands bedecked with golden rings, sliding up a golden silk gown. Rosalind forced her eyes to open again, shoving the unwelcome images to the back of her mind. It wasn't the time to let Cleo take over. She'd just gotten her sister back, and this was the chance to learn Miranda's stories.

She rubbed her eyes. "I want to know about our past. I still don't remember anything from Maremount, apart from the thing with Caine, and a few flickers of Malphas as a little boy. I want to remember the *good* things. I want to know about you."

"You look like you want to fall asleep. You look half-dead."

Rosalind's shoulders stiffened. *An awkward word choice, given one of us is literally half-dead.* "I'm fine. Just a little tired from my swim." She'd just gotten Miranda back. She didn't want to sleep just yet, not when she still had so much to learn. "Tell me something fun. I want happy memories. What games did we play?"

"You liked the water back then." Crumbs rained from Miranda's mouth as she ate. "Our parents should have given *you* Dagon's magic instead of me. You liked to build little ships out of wood, and then we'd go to Athanor Pond to sail them in the water."

The image licked at the corners of Rosalind's memory. "It sounds familiar."

"I had a pet bird. A meadowlark named Poppet. When she died, we had a Viking funeral for her. We put her tiny body on one of the boats and set it alight. We let it drift into the pond, and you made up Viking prayers."

Miranda's voice soothed Rosalind, and the rich cranberry bread filled her belly. She leaned back on the pillow, not caring that her sodden dress dampened the blankets, or that crumbs stuck to the sheets. It was so much nicer to be here with her sister than out in the cold, being crushed with rocks. She rested her head against the stacked pillows. "What else do you remember?"

Miranda lay next to her. "You and me and Malphas, we used to sneak out sometimes at night. We'd lay in the dandelion beds and watch shooting stars. You always wished for the same thing."

"What?"

"Indian pudding. You were simple that way. I always wished that we could live on our own, away from our parents. You, and me, and Malphas, in our own little house."

Rosalind smiled, her eyes drifting closed. "What would you wish for now?"

"The same thing. Or maybe we could stay here in Lilinor," Miranda mused. "Except we need daylight here. And the vampires would have to stop drinking blood."

"And we'd free the courtesans." Rosalind's eyes began to slowly drift closed. "I need more stories."

Miranda pulled a blanket over her. "When we were little, you loved the wildflowers. We both did. We threaded them into wreaths."

As sleep beckoned her closer, Rosalind could nearly see the stars graven in the sky, and feel the dandelions beneath her back. Her arms stretched out over the grasses.

Not Maremount, Cleo whispered in her skull. *Fife. Scotland. We wait here for Ambrose.*

Rosalind's eyes snapped open. *Damn you, Cleo. You're taking up all the space in my head.*

CHAPTER 24

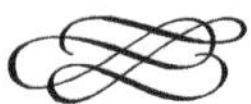

Rosalind sat in an armchair, taking a final bite of her cheese croissant. She didn't have long to linger over breakfast today—not with her next appointment with Malphas looming over her.

Sitting on the floor, Miranda chomped into a sugar cake, white powder dusting her lips. Warm candlelight danced over her pink cheeks, and she looked healthy as ever. Her appetite seemed particularly thriving. In fact, they'd only been awake for ten minutes, and Miranda had already chowed through three miniature sugar cakes.

"Ambrose is wonderful," Miranda said, "sending us all this food."

"It is honestly my favorite thing about him," Rosalind said. "And at some point I need to meet Caine's chef."

"When does Caine return? And what, exactly, is he doing?"

"He's supposed to find a seal of Azazeyl."

"For what?"

Rosalind swallowed her bite of sandwich. "So we can get your extra soul back to you." At least, that was Rosalind's part of the plan, even if Caine didn't know about it yet. "First, he has to find the soul in the House of Shades. And when you get the soul back, then we make the daywalkers."

"Right. Since the accident knocked my soul out of me." She frowned. "That doesn't make sense, you know."

Okay. I'm going to have to tell her soon. "I'm learning a new kind of magic with Malphas. And when I used it, I saw a glimpse of where Caine is—in the House of Shades, looking for the soul. Now we just have to hope he doesn't get lost there."

Miranda lowered the sugar cake from her mouth. "And you're training with Malphas to use this gods-magic?"

"I've drunk the ambrosia, like Drew has. Last night I was learning to use Dagon's magic, and Borgerith's."

Miranda frowned. "Why didn't you ask me for help with Dagon?"

"It's different from the magic you use. It doesn't require Angelic. I had to travel into Dagon's hell, and anyway, you can't leave the room."

"Shouldn't I have the ambrosia as well? If you can do gods-magic, I can too. We're both descended from Azazeyl."

Miranda had a point—and yet, death was just another unpredictable variable in this equation. Rosalind wasn't quite sure what would happen with this gods' blood in her system. "I need one of us to stay sane for now, plus you're still recovering from the accident. The power will drain your resources as you recover. And anyway, Malphas doesn't know you're here."

"I feel fine." Her forehead crinkled. "Explain to me again why no one is allowed to know I'm here?"

Rosalind swallowed hard. *Okay. It's time.* "The accident—"

"The one that knocked the soul out of my body."

"It wasn't really an accident."

"What do you mean?"

Rosalind bit her lip. "I thought you needed a night to recover; that's why I didn't tell you right away."

"Will you just spit it out?"

"Drew killed you. You were dead."

Miranda's jaw dropped. "I was *what?*"

"Drew murdered you. And then I used shadow magic to bring you back to life. It's just that no one knows I did that, except Tammi and Aurora, because it's against the law."

Miranda was staring at her own fingers in shock, as if searching for decay. "How?"

Rosalind touched Miranda's arm. She had a feeling that recounting the details would mean opening a mental wound she wasn't capable of closing. "The important part is, you seem fully recovered. The magic worked. I just had to commit a bit of sacrilege."

Miranda stared at her, her eyes brimming with tears. "Are you sure this was a good idea?"

"What else was I supposed to do? I wanted to get you back. It wasn't fair."

"I don't know." Her lip curled. "I just feel tainted. How long was I dead for?"

Rosalind shook her head. "A couple of days. It's hard to keep track of time here. But you're healed now. You're not tainted."

"Then why is it against the law?"

"Caine has prohibited necromancy. Aurora said it's considered a heresy to steal from Nyxobas. But I don't really give a crap about Nyxobas."

Miranda dropped the remains of her cake in the basket again. "I think I've lost my appetite."

"It'll just take some getting used to. And when Caine returns… I'm hoping we can convince him to give you the second soul back."

"So, I'm a serious abomination now."

Rosalind forced a smile. "I thought we established that we were already abominations. You, me, and Tammi. The land of Abominatonia. Might as well embrace it."

"You were never a corpse with putrefying organs."

Rosalind cocked her head. "No, but I've been drinking ambrosia, like Drew. I've been told by several demons that a human using a gods-power is an affront against nature with potentially monstrous consequences, and if I start to go power-mad, I need you to put me down."

"I'll do no such thing." Miranda raised a sugar-cake again, as if making a toast. "To the abominations, I guess."

Rosalind raised her water glass. "To us."

"And what do you plan to do with this gods-power?"

"First, I need to make sure the shield is functioning. Then, I'm gonna work on my ability to take down Drew in a fight."

She glanced at the old silver clock on the wall. 7:00. *Time to go.* She stood. As she crossed to the wardrobe, she stretched her arms over her head.

"Right," Miranda said. "So I'll just wait in here eating cake while you save the world. On balance, I guess I'm kind of okay with that."

"I don't think you'll be getting out of the fight that easily. You still need to help us make the daywalkers." Rosalind pulled off her night-gown, then bent down to pull a knife and holster from the wardrobe. "You know how to handle a second soul already. You're the best choice for the role. No point dragging Malphas into it."

She strapped the holster to her naked thigh. She wouldn't need weapons for training with Malphas, but she didn't like to walk the halls unprotected. She pulled a black cotton gown from the closet and slipped it over her head. Under a shawl, the long sleeves would keep her warm out in the fields of Enlil.

Rosalind pulled a silver shawl from the closet, wrapping it around herself. As she crossed to the door, she cast one last glance back at her sister. "Will you be okay?"

Miranda frowned. "I'm feeling quite violent toward him right now. Do you think that's a side effect of death?"

"No. I feel the same way. Completely normal." She flashed a faint smile. "I'll see you in a few hours—or however long it takes to master the power of Nyxobas."

"Sounds simple enough," Miranda said, her mouth full of croissant.

Rosalind pulled open the door, stepping into the hall. Her muscles ached and shook from the rush of magic the night before.

She walked through the stone corridor, half-entranced by the candlelight dancing over the stone floor. When she tried using shadow magic, would she get a glimpse of Caine's life again? It was hard not to think of him, getting lost in the House of Shades. It seemed such a dark and lonely place.

As she walked down the hall, she thought of that amazing kiss that had knocked the world out from under her feet. She could almost feel the soft brush of his lips against hers, or the electric touch of his fingertips down her arm…

She didn't really know what he'd thought of it. Maybe it hadn't meant anything to him, yet she was desperate to kiss him again.

She pushed through the door into the stairwell, lifting her skirt to hurry down the stairs. Her footfalls echoed off the ceiling as she walked.

At the end of the hall, she pushed through an oak door that led out of the fortress. The breeze caressed her skin. The waning moon loomed over the gently rolling fields. It bathed the fields of blue flax and calendula in silver light— the color of Caine's eyes.

She strained her eyes in the dim light, picking out a bare sycamore tree that stood in the field of Enlil. As she walked, a damp, floral breeze toyed with her hair. She pulled her hair high above her head, securing it with an elastic.

Last night, after visiting Dagon's hell, she'd nearly lost her mind— yet today she felt no more insane than usual. It seemed that some good sleep and good food went a long way.

At last, she stopped by the sycamore, pulling her shawl tighter. It felt painfully lonely out here on her own. When she glanced up at the sky, she could see the shield's silvery shimmer, thinning just by the moon. This time, she was certain: the shield was falling apart.

Footsteps made her turn her head, and she saw a dark form moving closer—tall, broad shoulders, just like Caine. If it weren't for his pale skin gleaming in the moonlight, she'd hardly be able to tell them apart.

"Rosalind," Malphas said.

"Thanks for meeting me here." She pointed at the sky. "We have a little problem."

As he drew, closer, he gazed up at the stars. "What?"

"The shield is thinning. I wasn't sure last night, but now I can see that it's disappeared in some places."

He arched an eyebrow. "You can see that?"

"Of course. One of my abomination powers. What will happen if the shield doesn't hold?"

"If it doesn't hold, Drew could create new portals into the city using his shadow magic." He stood by her side, the wind ruffling his hair. "Looks like it's a perfect time for you to test out your shadow magic."

"What if I used Caine's magic again?"

"Why?" he asked.

"Because then we'd get another glimpse of him. We'd know if he's made it out of the House of Shades."

Malphas cocked his head contemplatively. "You're quite concerned about him, aren't you?"

"I just want to know he's okay." She glanced at the sky, eyeing the shimmer that thinned just to the west.

His silver eyes blazed from the darkness like stars. "You're hoping to see glimpses of his life again."

She frowned. "Not to spy on him. It's just the only way we have to check on him."

"Why do I have the feeling that you're hiding something? Are you going to tell me what spell you did the last time?"

"Am I not allowed to keep secrets? Ambrose won't tell me what happened with him and Cleo. Caine has a million buried secrets: his tattoo, the blond woman and the baby, what happened when he lost his mind, why he killed the king and queen of Maremount centuries ago… And I don't know any of your secrets, but I know you help bury Caine's."

"The thing about secrets," Malphas said. "Is that they have a way of finding their way into the light."

"I guess we can both look forward to learning about each other when that happens." She tightened her fingers on the shawl. "So, what do you think of my plan?"

"It could weaken him, potentially."

Rosalind glanced at the sky, and the silver aura now seemed dangerously thin. "I think we need to act—"

Before she could finish her thought, a sharp crack sounded across the horizon.

"The shield," she whispered.

The ground began to rumble, and a geyser of water spurted from the ground of Enlil field.

"What's happening?" Rosalind asked.

"Drew is creating a portal," Malphas said. "I think his Hunters are about to enter Lilinor."

Malphas grabbed her arm. "Do the spell. Now. Use Caine's magic. And while you're sealing it, I'll fight whatever comes through."

Her heart galloped in her chest, and she closed her eyes, listening to sound of distant water gushing from the ground. With the adrenalin blazing through her nerves, it was hard to think straight, hard to think of Caine.

"Hurry up!" Malphas snapped.

"Fine." She closed her eyes, imagining the feel of Caine's lips on her neck. Instantly, she could picture him vividly, as if he stood before her in the hallway. She could imagine that sharp, hot pain of standing so close to him without touching him. His stunning contrasts of sun-kissed skin and icy eyes, the gentle curve of his full lips. She could imagine him moving closer to her, so close that the heat from his body warmed her skin.

He leaned down, his breath hot on her neck. *Are you looking for something from me?* He stroked his fingertips over her hips, sending heat racing through her body.

"Magic," she said.

His fingers slid around the small of her back. "What sort of magic?"

"The shield," she breathed. "I need to strengthen it. They're coming."

His powerful aura rushed over her body, thrumming up her legs and curling around her body. The vision changed, darkening and rippling before her eyes. Whorls of dark silver and black magic gave way to stone walls—powerful, masculine hands, grabbing a woman's throat. She wore a diamond tiara, crooked on her mussed blond hair —blue eyes wild with terror.

Fury exploded. *So easy to snap her little neck. But perhaps that's too easy.*

In a blur of silver magic, those powerful hands threw the queen through a closed window. Her white gown fluttered in the black night like a surrender flag. *Goodbye, queen.* She landed with a *crack* on the hard ground below Throcknell Fortress. *Maremount.*

The vision rippled—and Rosalind was no longer in the castle. She was outside, looking up at it. Rain poured, and lightning speared the dark sky. She'd seen this view before—in fact, she'd seen it in a portrait on Caine's wall.

As she stared up at the fortress, she became aware of a new sensation—pain, searing deep in her gut. She looked down at her body.

No, Caine's body.

A wave of horror slammed into her. Iron nails impaled him— pinning him to a wooden post. Now she felt his pain, and it ripped her mind apart. This was his punishment.

She felt Caine's lips move, and he uttered one word: *Stolas...*

In the next moment, the vision had shifted. Now he walked through Cambridge, but the city had changed. Where squat buildings had once stood around Harvard Square, now stood a labyrinth of towering stone temples and palaces.

A burst of Caine's silver magic flashed around her, and the vision cleared, but the agony still pierced her gut. She clutched her stomach, staring up at the sky over Lilinor. As the magic poured from her body, she lost track of time, lost in a vortex of magic. Some of the thrill of Caine's magic faded, and a cold void bloomed in her ribs.

Nyxobas's power.

The word *Stolas* haunted her mind like a curse.

Powerful shadow magic flowed from her body, spiraling up to the starry sky. It spread over the thinned gaps in a stunning web of silver magic. As the magic moved through her, some of the pain began to slowly ebb, healed by Caine's soothing magic.

At last, a sterling sheen covered the sky once more.

She whirled, searching for Malphas. There, in the distance, he fought a team of muddy Hunters. She lifted her dress, pulling a knife from her holster, then took off across the field. Malphas seemed to be holding his own—in fact, he'd snapped through two necks already. But there were still four of them and one of him.

As she ran, the wind rushed over her skin. A now-familiar ferocity spurred her on, and she felt a battle fury ignite her body. She wouldn't let these bastards get close to anyone she loved ever again, or find their way to Miranda's room. Not while she had breath in her body.

Burn them, Cleo whispered. *I want to hear their screams. It's what they deserve.*

Borgerith's power burned through Rosalind's muscles. Within an instant, she was standing behind a hunter, pulling the man's head back by his hair. She sliced her knife through his neck, slitting his throat. She heard a gun cock behind her, and she whirled, hurling her knife into the man's chest. But as she did, the Hunter unleashed a bullet into her gut. She fell back, hitting the ground.

Despite her wounds, magic coursed through her body, dulling the pain. From the ground, she kicked the legs out from under another. He slammed against the ground and reached for his gun. She kicked it out of his hands, and her next kick connected with his skull.

With the power of Borgerith's strength, her kick to his head completely shattered his skull, and his head lolled.

She glanced at Malphas, her body shaking.

He nodded. "I guess the magic is working out well for you." His eyes narrowed. "You're hurt."

She rested her hands on her knees, hunching over. As the rush of battle left her body, agony from her wound began to pierce her gut. The magic was flowing from her system again, leaving her shaking with pain. She suppressed the vomit threatening to crawl up her throat.

Malphas rushed to her. "Let me see."

Trembling, she straightened. As soon as Malphas touched her shoulder, his magic tingled over her skin, drawing the pain from her.

"This will hurt for a second," he said, examining the wound. "I'm going to get the bullet out."

She clamped her eyes shut and held her breath. For just a moment, pain pierced her gut. But within the next few moments, as his fingers traced the outside of the wound, his soothing aura washed over her. When she opened her eyes again, she looked to the sky, taking in the deep sterling gleam.

"How does the shield look?" he asked.

"Fixed. For now." She shot a glance at the portal, but it had been sealed over now with an oily mud. "But we'll need to keep an eye on it."

Malphas nodded. "Next time, you need to work your own magic. You can't keep borrowing from Caine."

For just a moment, the memory of Caine's torment burned fresh in her mind, and she pressed on her chest. What was it that he'd said? "Stolas," she whispered.

Malphas touched her arm. His pale eyes darkened. "What did you say?"

"What does *Stolas* mean?"

The air seemed to cool around them. "It means you should never use his magic again."

"Why?"

Black swirled in his eyes. "And more than that—never mention to Caine what you saw. Understood?"

Apparently, she'd stumbled upon another one of Caine's darkest memories.

"The thing about secrets," she said, running her finger over her new scar. "Is that they have a way of finding their way into the light."

CHAPTER 26

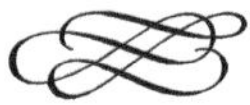

$\mathcal{M}$alphas stared at her. Nearby, the crickets started to chirp again, as if coming back to life. Six Hunter bodies littered the ground near their feet. Rosalind tried not to look at them.

"I suppose that's true about secrets," Malphas said, "but you'll need to develop shadow magic on your own anyway. You won't need Caine's."

He had a point. And, moreover, she wanted to try out her own shadow magic *now*. Yes, they'd just encountered an unexpected battle, and their bodies weren't yet cold. But she'd come out here to journey into the shadow hell, and already she needed to feel the rush of a new type of magic. She wanted to feel the power coursing through her veins.

"So let's do it," she said.

"Now?"

"That's why we're here, right?"

It felt delicious to kill, Cleo whispered. *Didn't it?*

Malphas frowned. "Are you sure you're up for it? You've just been shot."

"Yes!" she shouted, maybe a little too loud. "I'm fine. You healed me. And when I get back from the shadow void, you can teach me to move like the god of night—like Caine and you do. I want to feel that speed. I want to move like the night wind."

She'd seen Caine in battle, the blur of silver and shadow. If she could combine strength with that speed, she'd be a formidable force. Even among demigods.

"Fine." Malphas pointed to the moon. "This time, think about the jewel of Nyxobas, instead of my brother."

"Any tips for me to survive the shadow hell intact?"

"It's just like the mountain magic you used before. You'll need to let Nyxobas's power into your body without letting it overwhelm you."

"Of course." Her legs still shook from the magic she'd conducted earlier, and she needed to feel that raw thrill of gods-magic.

Malphas moved in closer and his aura curled around her body, whispering over her skin and sending shudders through her body. It smelled like moonflowers.

Caine's not around, Cleo whispered. *Why not take his brother for a ride instead? Believe me, when you're dead you'll regret wasting your time.*

"Shut it, Cleo," Rosalind snarled.

Malphas took a deep breath, and his eyes returned to their usual pale gray. "I'm not sure that you're ready for this power. I wouldn't have started with magic this intense if we'd had any choice. Flickering candles would have made more sense as a starting point."

"But like you said, we don't have a lot of time. So how does this work? Before, I lay on the rocks and then swam into the sea. But the night isn't a physical place."

"That's why it's a good thing you have me here, to lead you into the void."

She still sensed tension in his powerful body. Whatever *Stolas* meant, she'd touched a raw nerve. She stared up at the moon. "Lead away, Malphas."

As soon as the words left her mouth, silvery shadows thickened around them, enveloping Rosalind's body. Electric power crackled over her skin. Malphas's body seemed to fall away from hers, and his warmth disappeared.

And then there was nothing but the dark. No up, no down. No sound, nor comfort. Just a sharp emptiness that bloomed in her chest, and grew until it seemed like it would eat her from the inside out.

Dread took hold of her heart, and a loneliness so thorough she couldn't hear her own thoughts. All she knew was that she'd always been here. And she always would be. Rosalind had never existed at all...

The realization tore her mind apart, until she could no longer remember who she was, her name, or anything she loved at all. For what seemed an eternity, she drifted in the void, consumed by emptiness.

At last the darkness thinned, and she found herself on solid ground. She sat in an empty house—a room with glass windows that overlooked a dusty, gray landscape. When she glanced down at the chair in which she sat, she saw it was more of a throne, made of onyx. The cold marble chilled her skin. But at least she could feel again.

She took a deep breath.

I'm alive. I'm here.

Where, exactly, was she?

A cold room, built of white and black marble. Windows looming over a desolate landscape.

From the corner of her eye, she caught a flicker of movement. A figure loomed by one of the windows, but she didn't want to look. *I don't want to see...*

A deep voice, like thunder, rumbled over the horizon.

Look up, Rosalind. See your future.

Terror stole her breath.

I don't want to look.

And yet, she seemed to have no control over her body. She felt her head turn, her eyes swivel toward the window...

There, through the glass, her own face gaped, open-mouthed like a dying fish. Horror slammed into her. Somehow, she was in two places at once, and the world no longer made sense. And worst of all:

the Rosalind who stood on the other side of the window didn't look right. Her eyes were empty and lifeless, her skin gray, her body unmoving.

The Rosalind on the other side of the glass—the second Rosalind—was already dead.

See your future.

Bile climbed up her throat.

I need to get out of here.

With shaking legs, she stood. She ran for a black door, pushing through it into a gray, marbled hall. It seemed to stretch on for miles, and her footsteps echoed off the ceiling. She didn't know where she was running to, just that she was desperate to get away from her doppelgänger.

But as she ran, an aura filled the hall—tendrils of black, scented of the grave. From out of nowhere, a powerful hand gripped her by the hair, yanking her head back.

In the next second, someone was slamming her against the wall with a painful *crack.* Her heart thudded against her ribs, and she stared into the pale, waxy face of Bileth.

He was bare-chested, a sword slung around his waist. The stench of decay filled her nose, and a low growl rose from the demon's throat. He snarled, exposing his long teeth, and gripped her wrists hard; his nails pierced her skin. "My little Hunter. What has brought you here? To my home?"

This can't be happening.

Was she really here, or was this some sort of vision? It certainly didn't feel like a vision. Not from the nails digging into her skin, or his fetid aura crawling over her body.

"Is this the shadow hell, then?" she asked.

"No." He leaned in closer to her neck. "But you smell like you've come from there. I can smell the dread on you. And now you're here, in my manor. What have I done to deserve this pleasure?"

His hot tongue licked her neck, and disgust rose in her gut. As he touched her—without her permission—she could feel Borgerith's power flooding her body. It gave her a strange sense of certainty that she could fight him, an uncanny strength that blazed through her muscles.

And *speed.* Now, she had speed. Her power could match his. And he had no idea.

"Open your legs," he said.

"I have a better idea." She slammed her knee into his groin.

He grunted and dropped her wrists, his eyes widening with shock. Clearly, he hadn't expected her new power.

While he was dazed, she took the chance to punch him hard in the side of the head.

He staggered back, howling with pain. She followed up with a kick to his chin. His neck snapped back with the blow.

She had him where she wanted him. And yet... where the hell was she supposed to go? Somehow, she'd ended up in his manor. Where was this magic from Nyxobas she was supposed to let in?

She kicked him again, this time in the chest. The blow knocked him back into a window, shattering the glass. Broken shards rained over him, slicing into his skin. Then, in a blur of shadows, he pulled the sword from his sheath.

He swung for her, and she leapt back. But not fast enough. The blow cut into her gut, and she screamed. Bileth's dark magic whorled around her in a cyclone of shadows, wild wraiths that tore at her hair. As the world around her darkened, she found herself floating in the void once more. The painful emptiness gnawed at her.

But this time she was going to let it in.

She took a deep breath, letting the shadows fill her blood, until nothing remained but the dark. She fell to the ground—the wildflower and grass. She clutched her stomach, and in the next moment Malphas was leaning over her, gently touching her arm.

"Seven hells, Rosalind. What happened?"

Pain speared her gut. "I ended up at Bileth's house, I think."

Malphas shook his head. "That's not possible. You were here the whole time."

Blood soaked her fingers. "Then how do you explain what's going on with my stomach?"

"I'll explain in a minute. Right now, I need to heal you, okay?" Deftly, he ripped open the tear in her gown. His fingertips brushed over the skin around her wound, and she felt his magic thrum over her body for the second time, in waves of electrical power.

As his magic worked its way over her skin, the pain left her stomach, replaced instead by a soothing warmth.

She looked up into his silver eyes.

"What happened? he asked. "For fuck's sake. I just fixed the last one."

When she remembered that empty room—the sight of her own dead face—the agonizing emptiness still cut through her heart, so raw she could hardly remember how to speak.

"Rosalind?" Gently, he touched her forehead.

She swallowed hard, sitting up. "I definitely went to the void. Just at the start." She shook her head. "And then, somehow... I was in Bileth's mansion. We fought."

He nodded slowly. "You had a vision in the void."

"A vision?" She frowned. "Is that what it was? How does that explain the giant slash in my stomach, then?"

"Sometimes, your own mind has control over your body. If you believe it's real, then it's real."

Her body shook with fatigue. Images whirled in her mind: the dead Rosalind, staring at her through the window; the nails, piercing Caine's gut to the post; the fields of wildflowers, where Cleo waited for Ambrose...

The queen's murder. The hairpin on the wood table. The word *Stolas* falling from Caine's lips.

She shook her head, trying to think clearly. "No. I was in a lot of places. I was in Maremount, and Bileth's mansion. I've been with Ambrose, in the sycamore grove."

"Rosalind," Malphas said. "You're losing focus."

"I'm the collector of too many people's memories now—Caine's and Cleo's and my own, clamoring for attention in my skull. Trying to outdo each other."

"You need rest."

"I'm fine. I just…" She trailed off. She wanted more of that rush again. How would she convince this man to do what she needed him to do?

"You need rest, Rosalind. I'm not going to be responsible for your insanity."

"We need to keep going. I'm fine now." She clamped her eyes shut.

Think, Rosalind. Convince him.

She couldn't quite keep her thoughts from drifting away, couldn't remember how to speak clearly. But maybe Cleo could.

She let Cleo's aura bubble in her chest. "You know," she said, her voice clear as a bell. She sat up straight, smoothing out her hair. "I feel fine now. I just had some aftereffects from the shadow hell, but my mind is clear as day now."

Malphas narrowed his eyes. "What's the rush?"

"Caine seemed like he could be in trouble." She heard the words tumbling from her lips as Cleo took over. "And Drew could break through that shield at any moment. We don't have time to waste."

"You nearly died. Twice."

"I'm fine," she heard herself say, with a hint of growl. "Let's go. You said I needed to be prepared to go as far as it takes, and I am. Are you?"

There was no way around it. She was going to lose her mind. Might as well try to save the world while she was at it.

CHAPTER 27

They trudged into the Edin Woods, and Rosalind tried to ignore the gaping tear in her gown. Her mind was a whirlpool of images. Golden rings and bluebells. Blonde queens falling from towers, their gowns fluttering in the wind. Someone seemed to whisper the name *Stolas...*

Her head whipped at the sound, then she blinked her eyes. *Stay focused.* She was in a forest, and she had some more powerful magic to acquire.

The wind rustled through the ash trees towering above them, and faint streams of moonlight pierced the leafy canopy. In the distance, a nightingale trilled. The air smelled heavy here, like damp moss, like the undersides of rocks.

"Druloch is already your god," Malphas said. "You should be familiar with him."

"He's Cleo's god."

"Let Cleo lead you, then. Druloch's hell will be unpleasant, but I'm sure you can handle it."

"You think so?" She just needed to feel that raw thrill of magic once more. The godlike power. Already, her body was buzzing in anticipation.

He paused by a towering oak, and leveled his gaze on her. That silver, god-like gaze. "Back up. Against the tree."

She stepped back against the bark. "What will this sort of magic feel like?"

"Power over plants and the life of the forest. Power over death and decay. The power of a mob's fury, desperate to hang the latest scapegoat from the branches of an elm. The brutal strength of a primitive human mind, and the power to give in to divine, liberating frenzy."

"Plants?" She couldn't hide the disappointment in her voice. She'd been hoping for an earth-shattering power.

He shrugged. "Obviously you've never been in a famine, or near death from starvation."

Cleo's aura whirled, slamming Rosalind's mind with a vision of a dingy prison cell. She watched Cleo's emaciated hand, reaching for a half-dead rat.

"Oh, I've starved nearly to death," Rosalind said, with a ferocity that cut through the air. "I've eaten vermin from the filthy floor to stop myself from dying."

Malphas's eyes widened. "When you lived with the man who adopted you? I knew he was brutal to you. But I didn't realize how brutal."

Rosalind shook her head, dropping eye contact. It had been Cleo's memory, not her own. But she couldn't tell Malphas that. He wouldn't let her practice more magic if she was losing her mind, and she was already jonesing for more power. "Let's not talk about the past. What do I need to do for this magic?"

"You can start by feeling the trunk behind you."

She pressed her fingertips against the rough bark, and it scratched her skin through her dress.

Malphas took a step closer to her, and as he did, his eyes slid down to the tear in her gown.

Okay. Maybe he *had* noticed the rip.

She felt Cleo stir. The old witch seemed to like the way Malphas was looking at her.

"Close your eyes," he said, meeting her gaze again. The heat from his body warmed hers, and his silver magic curled around her protectively.

As if responding to Malphas's aura, Cleo's magic came alive, wrapping around her body in green tendrils. *Look at the beautiful incubus,* she whispered. *Until you finally make good on our bargain and throw yourself at Ambrose, I guess one of these demigods will have to do.*

Rosalind gritted her teeth, trying to marshal some control over her mind. She'd wanted Cleo to take over—but not so much that she was going to jump on any shadow demon in her path.

"You okay?" Malphas asked.

"I'm good," she said.

He nodded. "Cleo's aura should respond to Druloch's power. Do you feel it?"

She inhaled the deep scent of pines and oaks, feeling the leafy magic stroke her skin.

I feel Cleo.

"Close your eyes," Malphas whispered.

She did as instructed, letting her eyes drift closed, and her entire body buzzed with anticipation. As she lost herself in the vernal magic, vines slithered up her legs, wrapping around her thighs, pinning her arms to the tree. Her eyes snapped open at the sensation, and she stared at Malphas.

His eyes gleamed like icy beacons in the darkness, not a spark of humanity in them.

"What happens now?" she asked in a raspy voice.

"Now, you learn what it feels like to be on the wrong side of mob justice. Something you've only seen from the other side. You will learn what it feels like to be at the mercy of those who fear not only death, but life itself."

Her stomach dropped. "What?"

Shadows enveloped Malphas, and a low rumble filled the air. The vines tightened around her, pulling her back against the tree bark until she thought her ribs would crush. Slowly, the tree bark gave way, sucking Rosalind inside its soft wood.

The trunk molded around her, scented of decay. Bugs scuttled over her skin, up her legs.

So this was Druloch's hell.

From within her own mind, Cleo's voice answered, *No, Rosalind. Not even close.*

From within the tree, a chorus of voices began to chant:
We wait beneath corrupted frozen ground.
Unconsecrated, tangled roots enshroud
our crumpled necks and long-smothered embers,
where the hours fly, and death is remembered.

Her mind whirled. She didn't understand exactly what they were saying, but she thought she understood who they were. The voices of those killed unjustly—the witches, the outcasts, the scapegoats.

They'd come for a reckoning.

From the soft wood, hands clasped at her body, tearing at her skin. As the tree seemed to close in, bugs scuttled over her body—up her dress, into her mouth. She opened her mouth to scream, but a filthy hand clamped over her mouth.

A deep voice intoned in her ear: "The unlamented will claw back their fates from those who fanned the flames with pious breath."

Rosalind couldn't breathe. There was no air in here, and the tree was crushing her. Another bug scuttled into her mouth, climbing down her throat, and she gagged. The tree's walls pressed in closer, crushing the hands against her, and screams rose in her mind—the screams of the fallen, the unjustly slaughtered. The women whose feet danced over Salem's grass, and the men who dangled from elm branches.

The tree closed in, slowly crushing her bones for what seemed like an eternity.

Let the power in, Cleo whispered.

Rosalind closed her eyes, envisioning the vernal magic entering her body. Bony hands clawed into her flesh, ripping her open, letting the bugs in. She shrieked in agony, until at last, a vernal magic filled her.

The pain began to subside, and Druloch's power washed through her.

She opened her eyes once more. She stood beside the tree, looking into Malphas's deep, silver eyes. Her body trembled, and she looked down at herself. This time, she hadn't come back with a wound.

"It's okay, Rosalind. You're back now."

Her entire body shook, but ancient power now coursed through her veins. And it felt amazing. She wanted to sew a forest of yews, and bend the elms to her will. She wanted to wrap this shadow demon in vines, and keep him as a toy...

He touched her shoulder, moonlight dancing over his pale skin. "You've had enough for one day."

"No." Her legs were ready to give way. But she wasn't done yet-- two more gods to go. She trembled with the power at her fingertips, and Cleo's aura roiled in her chest. Images flashed in her mind: Cleo's emaciated hands picking up a rat; Ambrose's pale skin, glowing like a beacon in the night. Gold rings around his fingers.

"We keep going," she said.

He narrowed his eyes. "But how is your mind?"

Cleo purred. *Why not let me take over again, little thing? It's time for you to rest and let the real warrior take control.*

Rosalind plastered a smile on her face. "No worse than usual. Let's go on."

CHAPTER 28

Surrounded by towering elms, they walked through the forest. Here, the air felt damp and salty, and she could hear the distant crashing of waves.

Somewhere, under Cleo's visions, the mystery of Caine nagged at the back of Rosalind's mind. What did *Stolas* mean? And what had he been punished for so viciously in Maremount?

But she could hardly keep her thoughts straight with Cleo taking over.

She found herself staring at Malphas—and when she spoke, the words that came from her mouth were not her own. "You act kind. But surely it's an act. I believe that demons are driven to totally dominate anyone who is weak. For some it's through violence. For some, it's mind control. For incubi, sex. Am I wrong?"

"I suppose it's part of our nature."

Her lips formed Cleo's thoughts. "A demon can never truly love."

"Is that what you believe?"

She could feel Cleo's will urging her to say *yes*, but a little bit of her own remaining resolve stopped her mouth from moving.

Malphas took a deep breath. "We are driven by the instinct to dominate. If an incubus is injured, he will do anything he can to heal himself. If our lives are threatened, we'll do whatever it takes to survive. Incubi are born to seduce, I'll admit. But I know of only one incubus who takes women by force, and he's a deeply twisted soul."

The wind rustled the leaves, distracting her for a moment. Pale moonlight illuminated the leaves, and a sparrow fluttered from one tree to another. Had she never noticed before how truly *alive* the forest could be? "What were you saying?"

"I was talking about my father. And Caine's. Anyway, we're not just driven by lust and rage. We want to protect, too. To guard what's ours, what we love."

The certainty in his voice angered Cleo. If a demon could actually love, then why had Ambrose abandoned her?

Rosalind turned, clasping his arm. "Can demons love humans?"

His eyes widened. "Of course. But which demon in particular were you curious about?"

Cleo's magic snaked up her spine. *Take it from me, little girl. He's lying.*

"Never mind." She dropped the grip on his arm.

"Anyway, we're not that different from you. Demons are driven by lust and violence, fucking and killing. But so are humans." His eyes slid to hers. "Even you, Lady Rosalind."

A moth circled the air above her. "Don't be ridiculous."

"And now that you have become one with Druloch's magic, maybe you'll find out just how wild you can get in a divine frenzy. For a mortal like you, it lets you forget the greatest mortal curse."

For a moment, Cleo slammed Rosalind with an image of a charred body, tied to a stake. "Death," she said, her voice nearly a whisper.

He shook his head. "Your knowledge of your death—the anticipation. *That* is the real curse. A divine frenzy frees you, just for a while."

"And there we have the stories of witches dancing naked in the woods," she said bitterly. "And the Puritans afraid of life itself."

"Dancing naked in the woods. Is that something you're hoping to try today? I suppose I could accommodate."

Pale hands on my body, stroking my skin... "What?"

His eyes slid down her body, then slowly up again. "Frankly, I'm surprised my brother hasn't seduced you by now. You look amazing. And you smell amazing."

"I do?"

"Like Hawthorn wood, and lindens in full bloom."

Her footsteps crunched through the deadfall. Somewhere, under Cleo's thoughts, a painful thought nagged at the back of her mind. What was it she needed to remember now, while she was out here building her power?

Miranda. We'd lay together in the grasses, making wreaths of dandelions.

Rosalind fought to clear her mind from the webs of green magic. She'd been out here for a while, hoarding magical powers. But how was her sister doing right now?

This whole charade of pretending she didn't exist was getting ridiculous.

She blinked, trying to clear her mind. Recklessly, she asked, "What do you think Caine would say about raising Miranda from the grave, to get her soul back—"

He whirled, gripping her arm. His pale eyes burned into her. "Don't even think about it, Ros. Nyxobas doesn't do favors like that without a price."

A tendril of dread curled in her chest. "And what's the price?"

He turned, walking on again. "You must understand that death is the domain of the gods. It's not for you to toy with. And when we get Caine back, you must not speak to him about this. Don't even let him hear you contemplating it."

Cleo whispered, *If a demon could truly love, he'd entertain the idea. Caine can never love you, Rosalind.*

"Time to change the subject," she snapped.

Malphas shot her a sharp look.

She schooled her expression. "I mean, it's obviously a touchy subject, so we might as well move on." Power. She was here for the power. "What can I expect from the storm god?"

"I will tell you this much," he said. "You ever met a valkyrie?"

"Yes."

"Did she fill you with wrath?"

"Yes." *And you need to feel that thrill again.* "In fact, the last time a valkyrie touched me with her rage, I nearly murdered your brother."

He smirked, like this was a ridiculous concept. "Is that so?"

"I put a stake in his heart."

He arched an eyebrow. "If you got that close to his heart, I'm sure he allowed it."

"Why would he do that?"

"You know how incubi heal. Maybe his well had run dry."

She narrowed her eyes. "Maybe I'm a better fighter than you imagine."

At last, the woods thinned, opening to a rocky cliff that overlooked the star-flecked sea.

This is where I gain the power of the storm god.

Malphas opened his arms. "The realm of Mishett-Ash is in the skies. Stand at the edge of the cliff."

Deep in her chest, Cleo's aura stirred. *This power belongs to me. Give in to me, Rosalind.*

Rosalind trod over the jagged rock to the cliff's edge, and the sea wind whipped at her skin, biting her stomach through the tear in her dress. From here, she had a stunning view of the Astarte sea.

Malphas stood behind her, as he had on the sea shore. "Drop your shawl, and hold out your arms to the side."

Rosalind let her shawl drop to the rocks, and held out her hands to either side. Far below, waves crashed against the rocks. From behind her, Malphas's powerful body warmed her skin. Just being in the presence of an incubus filled her with a strange mixture of emotions—thrilled and soothed at the same time.

His silver aura, scented of lilies, curled around her body. His fingertips skimmed over her hips.

Incubi can't help themselves, Cleo whispered. *They just need to touch.*

Malphas leaned down, whispering into her ear. "Feel the wind skimming over your body."

Gusts of marine air raised goose bumps on her skin.

"Now," he continued. "Let the wind flow into your chest."

The wind howled around her, and she arched her back, opening herself to the sky. Nearby, thunder rumbled across the sea. Clouds gathered in the distance, rolling over the horizon.

As she stood on the cliff's edge, raw power flowed into her, spiraling inside her ribs.

This is what I need.

Another clap of thunder boomed. Rain began to hammer her skin, soaking her hair and dress. She could feel Malphas's warmth moving away from her.

Then, her shoulder blades cracked, and agony ripped through her back. With a sound like the tearing of tendons and bone, she felt wings sprout from her back. She arched her spine, reaching behind her. Her fingertips skimmed over feathers. Her wings felt as if they reached nearly to the ground.

Now the wind and driving rain sent a delicious chill over her body. As if driven by some ancient instinct, she walked to the very edge of the cliff, and lifted off the ground. She soared into the stormy air, the wind and rain whipping through her hair. Gray magic whirled around her, imbuing her muscles with strength. She soared higher into the storm clouds, above the churning sea, thrilling at the speed of her flight. Power surged through her veins.

This is what I need.

In the distance, she heard the cry of the valkyries. A white streak of lightning speared the sky.

She wasn't Rosalind anymore. She was an angel of death, and this didn't feel like hell at all. This felt glorious.

She circled slowly over the sea, but as she did a new feeling gripped her heart—a slowly building battle fury, so powerful her limbs began to tremble. As gray magic surged, her anger was nearly as blinding. She needed to rip into flesh, to tear through bone. She needed to slaughter, wanted to rip Drew's head off his neck. Her face grew hot, body shaking.

Why did she have the feeling that Drew was here, nearby?

She sniffed the air, scenting mountain air and pine. *He's nearby.* She knew he'd be here, that it was time to rip his ribs out of his back…

She turned, heading back for the cliff. Wind rushed over her skin as she dove lower. She'd find him.

There. He stood just before the forest's edge, his colored magic whirling around his body. His green eyes pierced the darkness, and one clear thought sang in her mind: *Kill.*

She swooped lower and picked up an intense speed, ready for battle.

I am the bringer of death, and I will crush your bones.

CHAPTER 29

She slammed into Drew with the force of a hurricane wind, knocking him back into the stones. His head cracked against a rock.

That should have knocked him out, but the man was practically immortal. He hurled her off of him, and she landed hard on a jagged rock. Fury surged, and she jumped up again.

She couldn't remember how to speak. She could only remember how to hurt.

Wrath consumed her, eating her up with a hunger she could never quench.

Drew stood, circling her. He wouldn't go down easily.

Let's try a little of Druloch's magic, shall we?

She didn't know if that was Cleo's voice or her own, only that fury commanded her.

She flicked her hand, and ropes of thorny plants spun from her fingers and coiled around Drew. With another flick of her wrist, she wrapped them tighter, watching his eyes bulge—but before she could split the bastard in two, he flexed his muscles, breaking through the vines.

Gods, he was strong.

"Rosalind!" he shouted.

"Don't you use my name," she snarled. "You murdered my sister."

Blood poured down Drew's skin where the thorns had stabbed him, and the beautiful red streaks entranced her. He stalked toward her, a wild animal ready to pounce.

Bring him down, Rosalind, Cleo whispered. *And this time, don't let him get out.*

Rosalind let Druloch's magic sing: blackbirds trilling, wind through the leaves.

The scent of death coiled around her.

"Rosalind," Drew strode closer, confident as a god.

The deep timbre of his voice made her falter. Was there a reason she shouldn't hurt him?

Kill him, Cleo chanted. *Kill him.*

As he closed in on her, she swung for him, landing a hard punch on his jaw. He returned the blow, and she staggered back, pain splintering her skull. His strength was otherworldly.

People must pay for their betrayals, Cleo sang.

With a roundhouse kick, Rosalind slammed her foot into Drew's head, reveling in the sharp crack of foot against bone. He grabbed his skull.

Time to finish your work, Cleo trilled.

Drew stumbled back, dazed. His vulnerability fully enraged her. Cold wrath erupted, and she charged for him, knocking him flat onto the rock. She straddled him, raining down one punch after another onto his face.

"You killed my sister, you sick fuck!"

Fury consumed her, and the more she hurt him, the more her anger sharpened, cutting her from the inside out like a living thing.

It's not enough. I will never be able to hurt you enough.

She grabbed a rock, ready to bash the bastard's skull in—but fast as a night wind, his hand shot out. He gripped her wrist so hard she thought he might crush it.

"Rosalind," he said, his voice quiet.

Not Drew's voice—Malphas's voice.

She caught her breath, staring down at eyes that slowly shifted from green to a pale gray, the color of starlight.

A silver aura curled around him, sliding over her skin like silk. He smelled of lilies.

She stared down at Malphas's bloodied face, and the fury rushed from her body like a mountain stream. Cuts lacerated Malphas's entire body, and blood spattered his forehead.

She gasped, dropping the rock. Her hand flew to her mouth. "Malphas."

He groaned. "I thought you said you were okay."

"What?"

He swallowed hard, as if trying to manage his pain. "You should have been able to control the rage better."

"I'm so sorry," she sputtered. "I thought you were Drew."

The black clouds were still unleashing a punishing torrent of rain.

His lip curled. "You've used too much magic. I asked you if you were losing your mind. Cleo's taking over, isn't she?"

Guilt pierced her chest. "She's been a bit loud, yes."

Malphas's still gripped her wrist—hard. As he stared at her, his eyes darkened, then trailed down her body, studying the tear in her gown.

Uh oh.

His other hand found its way to her waist, fingers trailing over her exposed skin, a touch so gentle she couldn't stop herself from arching into it.

"Malphas," she said. "What are you doing?"

His fingertips trailed lower, just over her hipbone.

Cleo's aura whirled around her, green and vernal.

Ambrose touched me like that once, a long time ago.

I told you I wanted you to kiss him. And you didn't listen.

Now, I take control.

Lightning flashed, and as it did an image slammed into Rosalind's mind.

She stood at the edge of a room. Candles cast wavering light over dark wood walls and tapestries. Guests sat around the table, dressed in fine slips the color of spring flowers.

A feast spread over the table: a roasted goose, a suckling pig, spiced wines, crisp biscuits, fresh baked bread, and steaming pies.

Her stomach rumbled. *So this is how the rich live.*

She didn't belong here. Alchemy didn't pay like it should, and she'd come in a gray, threadbare gown, with yellow cowslips threaded through her hair instead of jewels.

A hand touched her shoulder, and she turned to see him, her breath hitching in her throat. That beautiful, perfect skin. The high cheekbones and soft lips that she ached to feel.

Ambrose. The only reason she'd come, to see those beautiful green eyes—the color of her god.

He grabbed her hand, pulling her into a stairwell where they were completely alone. He moved so quickly, so fluidly, and in the next moment his arms were around her. His fingers gently gripped her hair, tugging her head back, and he pressed his mouth against hers.

His lips were soft and supple. Slowly, his tongue flicked against hers, sending shivers of pleasure through her. Hungrily, he tugged down the front of her dress, his fingers skimming her breasts…

Would he think her a harlot for giving in so easily? Surely she was supposed to play some sort of game—but she didn't want him. She only wanted Ambrose…

"Ambrose," she moaned.

"What?"

The vision faded, and once again, she felt the hard rain pounding her skin. Her lips hovered just inches above Malphas's.

His eyes widened. Suddenly, his fingers were tightening on her shoulders, holding her at arm's length. "Did you say *Ambrose?*"

Her mouth went dry, and she lurched away from him. *What the fuck am I doing?* She leapt to her feet. All at once, her body began to ache from fatigue. "Sorry. I was confused."

Still on the ground, he pushed up onto his elbows. He looked almost entirely healed. *Gods below.* How long had they been kissing for?

He knit his black brows. "I'm sorry. I'm still stuck on this. Did you say *Ambrose?*"

He looked deeply insulted. She couldn't imagine anyone had ever whispered the wrong name over his lips before.

Cleo's aura whirled through her mind. *The fun is just beginning.*

Rosalind pressed her fingertips to her temples. "Be quiet."

In a blur of silver, Malphas rose. "You're out of your mind."

She shook her head. "I thought you were Ambrose. It's fine. Things have... I just have too many memories." She could tell she was rambling, but couldn't quite stop herself. "Caine's and Cleo's, mine and Miranda's... But once I sleep... I need to sleep like the dead, under that heavy dirt where my sister lay."

Stop talking, Rosalind.

His silver aura whipped around his body. "You told me you were okay."

Icy rain poured down her skin in rivulets, and she wouldn't meet his eyes. "I just need some sleep."

He wiped the back of his hand across his mouth as if he was disgusted. "Is that so?"

Tomorrow, I take you to Ambrose, Cleo whispered. *You won't whisper the wrong name then.*

Rosalind squeezed her eyes shut. "I need some bluebells to mute the voice."

The air seemed to chill around Malphas, the shadows thickening. "We're going back to Ninlil. Don't even think of using any more magic until you're ready again. If the shield needs to be strengthened, I'll do it myself. Understood?"

Her body shook in the rain. "Yeah. I get it." She'd pushed things too far. She knew she had.

But they'd all known this was a risk. Humans weren't meant to have this power.

Malphas turned, walking into the forest. She hugged herself as she followed after him. Now that Cleo had achieved her little victory over Rosalind, her voice had gone a bit quieter.

And still, Rosalind craved the thrill of powerful magic.

Her teeth chattered in the cold. She'd left her shawl trampled into the mud back there, and the storm she'd created still lashed them with freezing rain.

As they walked back to the castle, Malphas didn't utter a word, quietly brooding. She couldn't tell if he was more disturbed by her lack of control, or if he was just pissed off that she'd said another man's name while kissing him.

She shook her head, suddenly mortified. What would Caine think if he knew that she'd kissed his brother?

Cleo's aura tingled over her skin as they trudged through the mud. Some of her memories still flickered through Rosalind's mind, but they'd grown duller now, like faded film.

As they approached Ninlil castle, she heard a sharp intake of breath from Malphas.

She glanced up at the castle walls. There, in front of one of the gatehouses, stood Caine, his silver aura glowing like a star.

CHAPTER 30

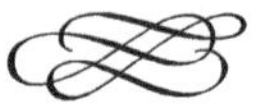

"He's here," she said.

It took only a few seconds for Malphas to get to Caine, moving in a blur of shadows.

Rosalind pulled up the hem of her dress, running to keep up. She still hadn't mastered the art of shadow running.

Still, she cleared the distance as fast as she could, rushing over the muddy earth to Caine.

"You're back!" she shouted, throwing her arms around him, breathing in the scent of thunderstorms and earth.

His hands found his way to her waist, but he was pushing her away. "What is going on here? What have you two been doing?"

Quickly, she stepped away, casting a nervous glance at Malphas.

Malphas frowned. "Come out with it. What happened? What went wrong?"

"Nothing went wrong. I had to fight an army of valkyries, but I found the sigil."

"And?" Malphas demanded.

Caine glared at his brother. "And why did Rosalind give me a panicked mental message about the shield if you were here to repair it?"

Rosalind cleared her throat. "We wanted to make sure you were okay. I thought you were supposed to come back as soon as you could. We couldn't see you through scrying, and using your magic was the only way to know you were making your way out of the House of Shades."

Caine's aura violently slashed the air, and his gaze slid to Rosalind. "You lied to me?"

Her stomach dropped. *Damn, he's scary as hell.* "No. The shield really was thinning. I just didn't mention the part about Malphas being here."

Shadows darkened his eyes. "And what of the first time I loaned you my shadow magic?"

She swallowed hard. "That was something different."

Malphas pushed his rain-soaked hair from his eyes. "Trust me. I've asked her a dozen times. Anyway—what happened to you, Brother? How long did it take you to find the sigil?"

"I found it after journeying through the Tuckomock Forest and fighting an army of valkyries. I spent a little too long in the House of Shades, but you should have had faith in me."

"You found the soul?" Malphas demanded.

"Of course I did." He pulled out a small disc, streaked with different colored metals—gold, silver, copper, tin. A six-pointed symbol had been carved on the front—the sigil of Azazeyl.

He slid it back into his pocket. "Miranda's second soul is trapped in here. Now, we just need a victim to take it on."

I guess Miranda is out of the question.

Rosalind's head throbbed. She felt like she needed to sleep for weeks. "Did you see Drew?"

"No. He wasn't in Maremount. Before you called me here, I was hunting for him in Boston, but he's protected by the Brotherhood army. And more than that, Boston and Cambridge have changed. Drastically. Drew has practically created an entirely new city with his magic."

Malphas's eyebrows rose. "You defied Ambrose? He told you not to hunt for Drew—that you were to return, and we'd create his army."

Caine shrugged. "His mind is clouded by his obsession with daywalking. I had to make my own decision."

And yours is clouded by your hatred for Drew, she thought.

Caine's icy gaze trailed up and down Rosalind's body. "You haven't told me what you two were doing out here in the rain."

Rosalind crossed her arms, her teeth chattering. Wisps of colored magic still curled from her body like smoke. "Learning gods-magic."

Cleo's voice tinkled in her mind like bells. *Aren't you going to tell him what you did with his brother?*

As if hearing Cleo's voice, Caine cocked his head. "And how loud is Cleo now? Is she drowning out your own thoughts?"

"I just need sleep," she said.

Caine stared at her. "Later, when you're not half-mad, I want you to tell me exactly what you saw when you stole glimpses of my life."

"Fine." She shivered. "I'm going to go inside now. I need to check on—" *Gods below.* She'd nearly said "Miranda." She really *was* losing her mind. "To check on Aurora. She was quite sad about all the funerals."

Caine nodded slowly. But of course the bastard could tell when she was lying.

As she turned to walk past him, he touched her arm, his gaze boring into her. The touch of his fingertips alone sent shivers through her body.

He leaned in, whispering, "And then, I want you to tell me why you smell like lilies."

* * *

Soaking wet, Rosalind walked down the candlelit hall to her room, each one of her muscles screaming in rebellion.

For the entire walk from the Gelal field to her room, Cleo had resumed shrieking in her head like a demented Banshee. *Find Ambrose. Seduce him, like I asked.*

Rosalind cringed. She'd kissed *both* brothers now. Would Caine understand that she'd been hallucinating the whole time, and that Cleo had taken over?

Or, more importantly—would Caine even care in the first place?

At least he was home. That was the important thing.

Half asleep, she stumbled to her door, then pushed it open. In the dancing candlelight, Miranda paced the floor, chewing on her fingernail. As Rosalind entered, her sister looked up at her, eyes wild.

"*There* you are!" Miranda said. "How long did you plan to keep me locked in here?"

"What?" Rosalind rubbed her eyes. "I thought you had everything you needed."

"I ran out of food ages ago. We need to ask Ambrose for more."

Rosalind sighed. "Fine. No problem."

"I'll go ask him," Miranda said. "I've been desperate to get out of here. I've worn the floor down with pacing."

"Absolutely not." Rosalind wasn't about to unleash her sister on the castle. Not with Caine roaming around. "I'll go. You need to stay in here."

Yes. Cleo cooed. *Go to Ambrose.*

Between her increasingly frenzied sister and the crazy voices in her head, Rosalind wasn't entirely sure she could keep control over anything at this point.

"No," Miranda said, shaking her head. "I don't want to be alone anymore." She pivoted, pacing again. "I'll be fine until morning."

"Are you sure?" Rosalind began peeling off her sodden gown.

"Yeah, it's just this hunger. I can't seem to fill myself. I want food and drink, and... I want to touch things. I want sunlight and grass and everything."

Rosalind dropped her torn gown over the back of a chair. "I guess you're making up for those days you spent dead. Getting all the life you can get."

Miranda raked a hand across her stomach. "This gnawing feeling..." she muttered.

Rosalind's chest tightened. *At least, I hope this is temporary.* She grabbed a towel from the wardrobe, drying herself off. "Well, I have some good news."

"Oh?" Miranda said.

"Caine is back. He has the extra soul."

Miranda's eyes widened. "He does? I want it back."

"I'm not sure Caine will give it to us. Malphas seemed pretty certain of that."

Miranda shook her head. "But I feel like something is missing. That must be it."

There were two people who would know exactly what this meant: Caine and Malphas. And Rosalind couldn't ask either of them.

Miranda looked up, blinking, as if waking from a dream. "But Caine is okay? He's not hurt?"

"He's fine."

Miranda crawled into the bed. "Good. Look, maybe I just need more sleep. And I'm sure you do, too."

"No argument here." Rosalind's muscles shrieked with exhaustion, and her bed called to her.

Go to Ambrose!

"Shut up, Cleo," Rosalind muttered. She crawled into her bed, her eyes already drifting closed.

Go to Ambrose, you faithless whore.

If only the lunatic in her brain would let her sleep.

Miranda peered over at her. "And now that Caine's back, what do you think the chances are that you can slaughter Drew?"

Rosalind swallowed hard. Based on what Caine had said, Drew had the power to create a new city in only a week.

And what had she done with her powers, so far? Some vines and rain. She had a *long* way to go before she could catch up.

Enjoy your life while you've still got it, Cleo purred.

CHAPTER 31

Rosalind woke tangled in her bedsheets. All night, she'd dreamt of Ambrose. She'd dreamt of returning to the stairwell with him, running her hands over his skin. Cleo had let her sleep, but had played scenes from her medieval life through Rosalind's dreams: Ambrose kissing her throat, touching her breasts, standing bare-chested under the starlight.

As the dreams cleared from her mind, Rosalind sat up in bed, letting the sheets fall from her. By her side, Miranda stirred, rubbing her eyes. The smell of freshly-baked bread wafted through the air.

Rosalind smiled. "Good morning, sunshine."

Miranda sniffed. "I smell food."

"Me too." Rosalind jumped out of bed, padding barefoot to the door. She pulled it open and found a basket of steaming baked goods, nestled amongst fruit and cheese.

Her mouth watered, and she lifted the basket. "Look what we have here." She dropped the basket onto a small wooden table by the bed. "And as soon as we're able to leave here, you can have all the food you want."

Smiling, Miranda grabbed a hot roll. "Good. I want to eat while sunbathing. I need daylight like you wouldn't believe." She ripped into her roll. "And I'd like a boyfriend, or at least a lover."

"I'm sure that can be arranged." Rosalind bit into a *pain au chocolate*, letting it melt on her tongue. "At some point."

Cleo's aura began to stir. *Go to Ambrose, you faithless whore!* she shrieked. *Seduce him just once, like you promised.*

Rosalind winced. Sleeping for hours hadn't helped to silence Cleo.

Go to him, Cleo commanded. *You owe me this.*

As if against her will, Rosalind felt herself rising from the bed. She crossed to the wardrobe and pulled it open. She stripped completely, then pulled out a pair of the smallest underwear she could find—sheer black with silver silk ribbons around the hips, and a bra to match.

"Where are you going?" Miranda asked. "In *that?*"

"I need to go somewhere," Rosalind muttered, as if in a daze.

"Where?"

"I need to see Ambrose—"

Cleo stopped her from telling the whole story. Miranda would only try to stop her.

Make up a lie.

"I'm going speak to Ambrose about giving us more food. Then I'll find out about the daywalkers, so we can get out of here."

"Oh. What time is it?"

Rosalind shook her head. "I'm not sure."

In a land of night, she had no clue how to keep track of the time. She pulled on a dress, a pale silver that slid over her legs, billowing slightly in the breeze. The neckline plunged. She snatched a long rope of black pearls from a jewelry box.

Perfect, Cleo purred. *But when you see Ambrose, I want you to look like me. I want him to see me.*

Numbly, she walked to the mirror. Her thoughts had become muddled, swirling with the name *Ambrose*.

Flashes of stars, a wren trilling...

She waited for him to arrive by the forest's edge. But the soldiers came for her instead. And then, the flames.

Through half-lidded eyes, she watched herself paint her lips a glossy red. She blinked twice in the mirror. The crimson shade looked nice with her dark hair. But of course, when she arrived in Ambrose's room, she'd no longer look like herself.

As she crossed to the door, she thought Miranda might have been speaking to her, but she ignored her sister's voice, listening instead to the haunting fragments of Cleo's memories.

They came for me through the shadows, in their tapered hats, with metal prickers in their pockets...

Rosalind pushed through the door into the hall.

Time to make good on your promise, Cleo purred.

She hadn't brought a weapon with her this time. It didn't matter. As she walked down the hall, the vamp's doors stayed shut. Probably still sleeping. She looked down at her long, brown hair, staring in a daze as it flickered to pale blonde.

I used to thread it with flowers...

Barefoot, she padded down the hall, the word *Ambrose* hammering in her skull. She twirled a strand of platinum hair around her fingertips. But somewhere, under the layers of green magic, her own mind began to stir.

What am I doing? I don't want Ambrose. I'm not going to screw him just to keep you happy. You cannot take over my body.

Yet her feet carried her onward. She felt as though she were walking underwater, her movements sluggish and dulled—until her gaze landed on the portrait of Lord Byron.

Caine's room. Even with Cleo trying to control her thoughts, she'd found a way to bring herself here.

Yes, Caine seemed to be able to calm her magic.

No, Cleo shrieked. *You made me a promise!*

Anger simmered, deep in her chest, and she stared down at the blond hair draping over her gray gown. *I'm not letting you take over completely. You had your life. This is mine.*

Rosalind focused on condensing that vernal magic as much as she could. She couldn't go into Caine's room with Cleo's face.

She envisioned the magic constricting into her body. Cleo's glamour slowly disappeared, leaving behind her own dark chestnut hair. She swallowed hard, straining to keep the magic in check. Caine would be able to quell Cleo's power. Whenever he touched her, it seemed to calm Cleo's shrill voice.

It took a few moments for Caine to pull the door open. He stood before her, wearing only a pair of black boxer briefs. Her jaw dropped at the sight of his perfect body—smooth skin over steely muscle. Warm candlelight danced over his tattoos. He leaned against the doorframe, his pale eyes framed by jet-black lashes.

Even Cleo stayed quiet.

"Did you come to tell me what spell you conducted with my magic?" he asked. "A midnight confession?"

Mutely, she shook her head. What *was* she doing here?

Mostly trying to avoid letting Cleo take over my life.

She swallowed hard. "I wanted to talk about the daywalker spell."

He stared at her. "I take it you haven't gotten used to Lilinor's schedule. Everyone is sleeping now."

She shrugged. "Are they? Someone left food outside my door, so I assumed it was morning."

His eyes slid slowly over her body, the thin gray dress that hugged her curves. "Is that really why you're here? To talk about our battle plans?"

She stared at his honeyed skin, the soft curve of his lips, his powerful arms. With him nearly naked, she could hardly remember how to string a sentence together. But she was acutely aware of his electric aura, caressing her skin.

Despite her body's intense reaction to the sight of him, his presence had calmed Cleo's aura. Rosalind no longer had to fight so hard to keep her under control. "And I wanted to know about Boston. You said the city looks completely different. I just need to know what we're up against."

"Admit it." He arched an eyebrow. "You wanted to see me naked. Any minute now, you're going to feign a chill and claim you need to curl up in my bed against the warmth of my body."

Her stomach fluttered, and she waved a dismissive hand. "Don't be ridiculous."

"You do have impeccable taste in men. I'll give you that much."

She rolled her eyes, and he opened his door wider, motioning for her to enter. She strode inside, trying to keep Cleo's aura as condensed as possible. Her gaze flicked to the round bath in the corner of his room. She'd bathed there once, enveloped by the floral scents of Lilinor, while Caine did his best not to look at her naked body.

"Have a seat," he said, gesturing at his bed. It stood against a wall, covered in rumpled silver blankets.

The room was nearly bare, apart from a wooden table with decanters and glasses, and the candles on the walls.

She crossed to his bed, settling down on his duvet. Caine stared at her and folded his arms in front of his chest. He seemed intent. "Before I tell you anything about Boston," he said, "I need to know three things. What spell did you do the first time I let you use my magic, and what, exactly, did you see?"

She swallowed hard. "I'm not telling you about the spell. You clearly don't tell me everything, so you're hardly in a position to demand the revelation of secrets. What's the third question?"

Suddenly, his mood shifted, and the air seemed to thin. The shadows darkened, and candles guttered in their sconces. "Why did you smell like lilies when I found you in the field with Malphas?"

She wasn't going to answer that either. "I'll answer one of those questions. I'll tell you what I saw in the visions. I witnessed you killing the queen. In another vision, I saw a baby with silver eyes like yours. There was a hairpin on a table, like the tattoo on your arm."

Shadows licked the air around him, and his gaze drilled into her. "And what else?"

"I saw your punishment in Maremount, when you were nailed to the stake in front of the fortress."

The rigid set of his shoulders told her not to bring up *Stolas*—that it would be too much for him.

"Is that it?"

"And I saw flashes of what you were doing at the time. The valkyries, the House of Shades. I saw you in Boston."

His aura sliced the air around him, and goosebumps rose on her skin. "Did you learn *why* I was nailed to that stake?" he asked.

"No." But whatever it was, it had to do with *Stolas.*

"I'd never have allowed you to use my magic if it weren't life and death."

Her fingers tightened on the edge of his bed, and she looked down at the floor. She'd already made up her mind that she trusted him, hadn't she? Despite how terrifying he could be, she'd already decided he wasn't going to hurt her. So what was she scared of?

If she truly trusted him—maybe she should just *ask* him about necromancy.

She took a deep breath. "And now I have a question for you." She gazed up at him from below her lashes. "Why have you prohibited bone conjuring?"

Silence filled the room, heavy as dirt. *Maybe this was a bad idea.*

Her muscles tensed, and she ventured, "I don't understand why we can't try to bring Miranda back."

"What do *you* know about it?" he asked.

She took a steadying breath. "Aurora told me you'd forbidden it. I just don't understand why. What's the price?"

"I knew you were leaving out part of the story." His eyes darkened, swirling with shadows and he took a step closer. He leaned down, his hands resting on either side of her hips, like he was searching her eyes for lies. "What else did you see in your visions of my life?"

"What?"

"There is a reason you're asking me about bone conjuring. What did you see?"

What, exactly, does he think I saw? "I didn't see anything from your life about bone conjuring. I wanted to understand why you don't want me to bring Miranda back. That's the reason I'm asking."

He straightened again. "I've prohibited it because death is the province of the gods. The original seven. Even I'm not meant to control it, as a demigod."

"Those are the only details you'll give me?"

Deep in her skull, Cleo began to grow restless again, and Rosalind found her gaze lingering over Caine's muscled body.

Still standing, his gaze pierced her. "Why don't you tell me what happened with you and Malphas?"

Deflect. She frowned. "Is it just me, or are you jealous?" She leaned back on his bed, and let the strap of her dress fall down. She didn't move to lift it again.

As if entranced, his gaze lingered on her bare shoulder and the curve of her breast.

Now, that is how you distract an incubus.

CHAPTER 32

s if lured in by a siren song, he sat next to her on the bed. His arm brushed against her shoulder. The feel of his skin against hers sent her heart racing, and they'd barely even made contact.

"Jealous?" he said. "Demigods don't get jealous."

She frowned. "Lie. I may not read pupil dilation like you and Malphas, but I know that's a lie."

He shrugged. "I just need to make sure you haven't been torturing my little brother again."

"Malphas trusts me, even if you don't."

He studied her. "Why did you come here?"

"When you were gone, I realized something about you."

"What?"

She took a deep breath, and straightened. "We might have a twisted history, and maybe you don't trust me. But you're always looking out for me." Her gaze slid over his powerful body—the rippling muscles and the vicious looking tattoos. She lingered on the hairpin on his forearm. "You've kept secrets from me. And I've kept them from you. And yet, I trust you anyway. I feel like you would keep me safe, even if Esmerelda says you'll dump me in the whore pit when you're through. So maybe you should trust me, too. Even if I don't tell you everything."

"You trust me, now, do you?" Slowly, he reached for her, then ran his thumb over her lower lip.

Her body stirred at his touch.

"I'm glad you're catching on, little Hunter," he said.

She had the strongest impulse to flick her tongue against his finger, but she resisted. "And I came here because you seem to have the power of quieting Cleo's voice."

He pulled his hand away. "I do?"

"Only when you touch me." Her pulse raced. Sitting this close to him, she wanted his beautiful lips on hers—all over her body. "And Cleo was being very loud, so I thought I'd pay you a visit."

He was looking at her so intently, like he wanted to devour her. Like he was holding on to his restraint by a thread. His grip tightened on the edge of his bed, knuckles whitening. She wet her lips, and his keen gaze caught the movement. His muscled chest seemed to rise and fall faster, and his aura curled around her, vibrating over her skin. Her body responded to the feel of his magic.

His gaze slowly raked over her breasts, then lower still. He looked so enraptured, she was sure his gaze went right through the silk to the black lace beneath her dress.

"Why do I feel like you're trying to distract me from the questions I'm asking?" he asked, as if in a daze.

"Is it working? Surely a demigod isn't so easily distracted."

His gaze met hers again. "I wonder, Rosalind. Perhaps there's another way to coax your secrets from you." Slowly, he unclenched his fingers from the blankets, and reached for her.

As he drew his fingertips over her ribs, his touch sent an electric thrill over her skin. Instantly, her back arched at his touch. He stroked her ribs, back and forth, and she swallowed hard.

Tracing lower over her abdomen, Caine leaned in closer. For someone who gave the impression of predatory lethality half the time, she was struck by the unexpected gentleness of his touch—just as when he'd kissed her before in the hall. And it was precisely that gentleness that was going to drive her nuts.

Her breathing shallowed.

As his breath warmed the side of her face, his eyes lost their shadows and returned to their starlit color, burning bright as a dying star. "Tell me about the spells you've woven, Rosalind," he whispered, sliding his fingers over her belly.

Through her gown, heat from his fingertips seemed to inflame her skin. *I'm not telling you a damn thing, but you better keep touching me that way.*

Her body warmed to his touch, heat swooping through her belly.

His fingers stroked lower, over the hollow of her hips. Her entire world narrowed to that thrilling touch. When he stroked just over the top of her panties, his touch painfully light, she had an overwhelming desire to tear off her gown. She was going to lose her mind if he didn't move any faster. She wanted his lips on hers, wanted his hands to grip her harder. He leaned in, but he kept his mouth just out of reach, hovering just an inch from hers.

"Tell me, my Hunter," he whispered.

Cleo's voice had gone completely silent. Rosalind heard only her own heated breaths—and her thudding heart—as Caine's aura caressed her skin.

Caine lowered his face into the curve of her neck, his breath warming her throat. She let her head tilt back, leaning further back on her hands. *Lower, Caine.*

"Tell me, Rosalind," he whispered, fingertips tracing over silk.

Her heart raced faster, heat surging through her core. Was he seducing her to get information from her? Right now, she wasn't sure that she cared. She couldn't even remember what his damn questions were. All she knew was that his fingers were *nearly* where she needed them, lighting her body on fire.

At last, the tips of his fingers slid lower down her silk dress, between her legs, and he drew small circles. Gasping, she let her legs open. She pressed harder against his hand, and a moan escaped her throat.

She couldn't wait for his kiss any longer. She reached up, cupping her hand behind his neck, and pulled him in. He pressed his mouth against hers, claiming her. At first, he kissed her fiercely, hungrily. Slowly, the kiss grew more sensual. Gently, his tongue slipped in, brushing against hers, and he groaned softly. In the next moment, he was gently tugging up her dress, the silk sliding along her legs.

Their kiss deepened, and her body blazed with heat. He slid one of his hands between her knees, fingers hot on her bare skin. Just when she thought she was about to lose her mind, he pulled away from the kiss, breathing hard.

Her lip curled. *How long is he going to draw this out for?*

Gods, she needed him now. She gripped his neck, trying to pull him closer, to press his body against hers. But he resisted, his touch achingly light on the inside of her thigh. "Hunter. You still haven't answered my question."

He was teasing her mercilessly, and her body trembled at his touch. He *liked* his control over her.

"Caine," she whispered, her heart racing. "I don't care about the question."

"But you care that I keep touching you, don't you?" His fingertips moved up the inside of her thigh—glacially slow. As they moved higher, her breath hitched in her throat. He paused—inches away from where she needed him, and he began tracing slow circles again on her thigh.

He was going to drive her insane. *Does he want me to beg?*

"Tell me what I want to know," he said, his voice rough. "Or I'll have to stop."

Her breath came fast, her body dampening with sweat. She didn't want to play his games, didn't even remember what he was asking for at this point. In fact, she wasn't sure she could speak right now, since the entirety of her world was now a few fingers on her thighs.

Maybe he needs some encouragement. She reached down to the hem of her gown, and pulled off her dress. She tossed it to the ground, then pushed the hair out of her eyes.

Caine's eyes slid to her peaked breasts, visible through her sheer bra. His fingers tightened on her thigh. He seemed to take in every inch of her skin, his attention completely rapt. Eyes blazing, his gaze raked lower, between her thighs.

She wasn't sure anyone had ever looked at her the way he was staring at her now, with such raw, animalistic lust. And she liked it. She lay back on his bed, propping up on her elbows. She'd wanted this since... well if she was honest, since she'd first seen him.

His aura whipped from his body in a flash of silver. Once more, he let his burning gaze roam over her body. A look of pure, carnal lust. He wasn't trying to get her to talk anymore. That game was over.

As he lay down next to her on the bed, he cupped the side of her face, kissing her desperately. Slowly, he slid his fingers just under the top of her panties. She groaned into his mouth, her fingers curling into his hair. His muscled body pressed against her, his skin warming hers. Slowly, she ran her fingers down his body, feeling every hard plane until she slipped her fingers inside the top of his boxers, delighting in his gasp.

With a low growl, he unhooked her bra, pulling it off. He kissed her throat, then his warm mouth slowly moved lower over her breasts. She wrapped her legs around his body. As his kisses trailed down to her hips, she arched into him. She tangled her fingers into his hair, her thighs brushing his sides.

With a smoldering glance at her, he ran his fingers over the silver ribbon at the top of her panties, sending shivers through her. He leaned down, kissing the skin just above it, his tongue hot against her skin. A hot thrill rippled through her. She needed him, now.

"Caine," she breathed.

As he hooked his fingers into the top of her panties, she lifted her hips, and he slid them off. Desperate for more of his mouth on hers, she pulled him toward her. He kissed her deeply, hungrily. And when his fingers slipped between her legs, she thought she was going to lose her mind. Her body writhed with pure pleasure, grinding against his hand. He dipped his fingers again and again. She moaned, moving against his hand, demanding more.

Pulling him closer, she kissed his neck. As he touched her, her hands explored his skin. She slipped her fingers into his boxers, pulling them off. At the sight of him, her breath caught in her throat.

He moved between her legs, his eyes burning an intense silver. *I need this now,* she pleaded with him mentally.

She reached up, caressing his face. Slowly—painfully so—he pressed inside her, his gaze locked on hers. *Pure rapture.*

Their hips rocked in movement, and every thrust brought her soaring to a wild peak. They moved together, increasingly frenzied.

With each stroke, she clawed her hands further down his back, pulling him into her, her back arching. Softly, he groaned her name into her neck, and the sound sent shivers through her body.

Their bodies moved in rhythm, a frenzied symphony of gasps and moans—faces dampening, bodies glowing with heat. Every inch of her glowed with pleasure as she felt herself merge with him, until her control began to slip.

A cry tore from her throat, and she shuddered against him with sweet release.

CHAPTER 33

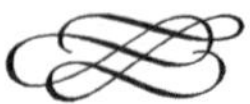

In the warm bath, Rosalind lay wrapped around Caine, listening to his beating heart. The smell of lavender filled the air. Caine's chest rose and fell with long, slow breaths, and his hand rested on her hair.

Gently, she traced her fingertips over the faint scars on his chest, the pale white markings. Now she wanted to know the story of each tattoo, each tiny line of scar tissue. She touched the one above his smooth belly, where he'd been impaled on the stake, then moved on to the constellation of scars over his ribs.

"I know there are things you don't want to tell me," she ventured. "Like, everything to do with your relationship with my parents." Or *Stolas*—she wouldn't even mention the name. "But surely there are other things you can tell me."

"Like what?"

"Like why you murdered the King and Queen of Maremount four hundred years ago."

"Ah." He sighed. "That."

Her fingers found the circular scar just below his heart. "Is that a story you can tell me?"

"That was the first time I was imprisoned in Maremount."

"What for?"

"You saw the succubus head on the fountain in front of the fortress —that was Erish's sister. Maremount purged the city of incubi and succubi. Except, the queen had a taste for incubi. So her husband procured one for her, to keep her happy."

Rosalind's throat tightened. "Ah. You said demons were enslaved in Maremount." She felt his heart beating beneath her fingertips. "But how could a human keep you as a slave? You're more powerful than they are."

"An iron collar, with spikes in my neck, chained to a bed. It drained most of my power." His hand covered hers. "And, truthfully, I could have found my way out—except that she threatened to slaughter someone I loved."

She felt her cheeks heat, and anger simmered on his behalf.

And underneath that anger, she couldn't help but wonder who he'd loved.

"No wonder you murdered her."

"I served her against my will for nearly a year, until I couldn't take it anymore. I killed her and the king so neither could make good on their promise."

"The promise to kill the person you loved." Since he was opening up to her, she didn't want to push him too far by asking *who* that person was, though she was desperate to know.

"Exactly."

"That must have been awful for you."

He stared into the distance. "Well. I ended it. I had to slaughter my way free from the city, through a horde of royal guards. And do you know what? That's when I learned I could get a thrill from something other than fucking."

"Killing?"

"I'm quite good at it, as I'm sure you've seen."

"Mmm. You're good at a lot of things." Her head rested on his damp shoulder. "Anyway, I'm glad you made it out safely."

He traced his fingers through the water by her hips. "I left Maremount, and escaped to Lilinor, where I met Ambrose. And I brought with me... the people I needed to keep safe."

"And that's how you became known as the Ravener, the legendary monster of Maremount."

"The children's stories fail to mention the part about me being chained up as a love slave."

Her fingers still covered the scar on his chest, and a twinge of guilt tightened her lungs. *That* scar had come from her. "Um, sorry about the time I stabbed you."

His lips curled in a smile. "I think you've made up for it by now."

Her brow furrowed. "Malphas insisted that the only way I could have stabbed you is if you'd let me. Because your incubus well had run dry, and you probably wanted to gain power through sex."

"Malphas doesn't know everything," he grumbled. "Speaking of Malphas—what happened between the two of you when I was gone?"

Okay. He's not letting this go. She straightened, looking him in the eyes. Droplets of water beaded over his golden skin.

"He was training me. I've worked my way through five of the hells. I have only one left—fire." She swallowed hard. "He was wary of pushing me too far, because of Cleo. So he kept asking if I was okay. He asked if I could hear her voice."

His body had gone tense. "And?"

"And I guess I was craving more power. I just needed to feel more of the gods-magic... We all knew there was a risk, that maybe humans weren't meant to have this power." She was babbling now, she realized. "I didn't let Malphas realize how much Cleo was taking over."

A muscle tightened in his jaw. "Let me guess. You lied to Malphas. Why do I feel like I know where this is going?" Abruptly, he rose from the bath, water dripping down his perfect body.

"Using the gods-magic warped my mind." She folded her arms over the tub's edge, watching as Caine toweled himself off. "I thought Malphas was Drew. I attacked him. And then I was in Cleo's world, getting visions of Ambrose getting frisky in a stairwell."

"According to Malphas, an incubus might put himself in harm's way if his well runs dry," Caine said. "Did Malphas's well run dry when he was training you, perhaps? And then, of course, he needed healing."

"I feel like you already know how this story goes."

Caine was already pulling on his clothes. Apparently, their post-coital moment was over.

"You let Cleo take over your mind," he said. "And Cleo has a thing for shadow demons. Whether it's Malphas or me, she's not too picky. Is that about right?"

"Wait a minute—"

"What *exactly* did you do with him?"

"*I* didn't do anything. Cleo kissed him."

"It must be nice to be able to divest responsibility so easily. You're not responsible; Cleo is. How convenient." Caine's gaze pierced right through her. "If I were able to divorce myself from the things I've done, what a different person I'd be. Except I don't think the way you do."

With Caine's fury chilling the room, she no longer felt comfortable sitting there naked. Shivering, she rose. "Well, maybe you shouldn't be so hard on yourself." *Or on me.* Maybe if she soothed his bruised ego... "Look, Cleo might have been the reason I kissed Malphas, but she wasn't the reason I came here."

He cocked his head, eyes narrowed, as he buttoned up his shirt. "Oh, really? So you weren't hearing her voice when you knocked on my door?"

She grabbed a towel from the side of the bath. "Well, yes, I was hearing her voice. But she wanted me to see Ambrose. I came here instead, because I wanted to see you."

"Are you quite sure? Do you even know which of your thoughts are yours and which are hers? Did she prompt you to put on that black lace underwear, or was that your idea?"

I thought demigods didn't get jealous. "Obviously you're pissed off."

"I'm not angry. I'm just unclear who I had sex with today—you or Cleo—and I'm not sure who I'll find you with tomorrow." He crossed to a table, pouring himself a whiskey. He didn't offer her any. "Not that it matters. I have plenty of courtesans to keep me busy."

Her cheeks burned as she dried herself off. "I'm sorry I kissed your brother."

"Was it you, now? I thought you said it was Cleo. Anyway, like I said, it doesn't matter." He leveled his steely gaze on her. "But you need to get control of that voice in your head. And in the future, try not to mislead people when they ask if you're losing control." He sipped his whiskey, leaning against his bedpost. "But then, misleading people comes easily to you, doesn't it? I do wonder what secrets I'll learn, when I find out about that spell you seem so keen to keep a secret from me."

As she dried off her body, irritation simmered. "You have more secrets than I have. You and Malphas keep referencing something that happened when you lost your mind. But neither of you will tell me what it is, or how you came into contact with my parents in the first place. And let's not forget that you neglected to mention that little detail about slaughtering my parents until I found it out on my own. I guess misleading people comes easily to *you*."

"Perhaps I have a good reason to keep things from you. Clearly, you can't be trusted."

"That's bullshit. Has it occurred to you that maybe you're projecting a little? You lost your mind, you did something terrible that I'm not allowed to know about, and now here I am to remind you of it all? Who are you really angry at, Caine? Me, or yourself?"

Shadows grew denser and heavier around the room, and the air chilled by ten degrees. Suddenly, the room was freezing, and goose bumps rose on her skin.

"Okay, Rosalind. Let me put this in a way you can't argue with. We can both agree that *Cleo* can't be trusted, and you share at least half of your mind with her."

Rosalind snatched her dress off the bed. The mood between them had been well and truly killed. "Right. I guess it's time for me to leave now."

He sighed, raking a hand through his hair. "Not just yet. We have things we need to talk about."

"Like what?"

"Like how we're going to defeat Drew. His power is immense. I've seen the new city he's built in Cambridge, using gods-magic. Obviously, The Brotherhood are letting him build his empire, working with him. If we're not careful, he'll break through the shields again. Do you have any idea what they might be planning?"

And just like that, he was ready to switch tacks and talk about military tactics. The shift of topic was disorienting.

"Okay." Her dress stuck to her damp body. She shivered, trying to gather her thoughts. "I suppose this is his new empire, for his brainwashed bride. I'm just not clear what the Brotherhood is planning."

"I suspect the Brotherhood may be the true architects of this new empire, with Drew acting as their artisan."

With a shudder, she said, "Tell me what it looks like."

"They're building temples to Blodrial, with great fire pits in the center. For publicly roasting demons, I presume. But I think it's beginning to backfire on them. As much as humans are terrified of monsters like us, they're growing even more scared of the new empire. After all, the Brotherhood are using magic now, and they want to kill heretics in horrific ways. The tide of public opinion is turning against them."

"The change of public opinion might sound like a good thing, but it's dangerous. The Brotherhood will do whatever it takes to turn that around. They're masters of propaganda. As soon as I get through the fire hell, I need to find Drew." She glanced at Caine. "And you'll need to allow Malphas to take on that soul. We can't kill them without an army."

Caine's face darkened. "We don't need to decide anything just yet. You're not going into Boston unprepared."

"You did. You were hunting Drew on your own before we called you back here."

"And I might do so again. But I've been fighting for five centuries. Gods-magic isn't everything. I have the advantage of centuries of warfare."

"Right."

"Malphas and I can keep the shield up, and you'll need to spend some time actually learning how to use the magic. It's not enough to just go through the hells. You have to practice. When it's time, we'll go into Boston together. I'll help protect you." His expression hardened. "Since you're a military asset, I mean. Ambrose wants you alive."

Dick. "And what happens to everyone in Massachusetts in the meantime?"

"In the meantime, The Brotherhood are terrifying everyone. Ordinary people are no longer on their side, and that's a good thing for us."

She shook her head. "They're dangerous when they get desperate."

"How? What are they likely to do next?

Her head throbbed, and she rubbed her temples. "If people are becoming fearful of them, they'll find a way to deflect the terror elsewhere."

"What do you mean?"

"They're going to create monsters worse than they are. Just like they did with the oneiroi. And then they'll execute them publicly, in a spectacle of violence. It serves two functions: keeps the rebels in line, and satiates the mob's fear-driven bloodlust at the same time." She thought of the pale white scars on his chest. "I think you know what it's like to be at the receiving end of that sort of justice."

His jaw tightened. "Right. Well, you'd best get back to your room. You'll need to sleep before you visit the fire hell, otherwise Cleo might have you seducing half the city while we should be fighting Drew."

"You're really irked at me and Malphas, aren't you?"

"Don't be absurd. I don't care what you do. Do you have any idea how many women I've been with? You came here, and removed your dress. I'm an incubus. How did you expect me to react?"

She flinched.

"And I only kissed you in the hall because you asked me to. Don't think it means anything more."

His words felt like a punch to the chest. "I get the point."

"I just want to make sure you stay focused long enough for us to kill Drew, and create the daywalkers. You need to remain sane for that. That is my one concern. Apart from that, I don't care whose room you strip off in."

Well, this went well.

Tears stung her eyes, and she wanted to get the hell away from him before he saw them. "Right. Time for sleep, then." She cast a quick glance around the room for her underwear, but decided to head for the door instead. She didn't want to spend another second in Caine's presence.

She pulled open the door into the drafty hall, and Ambrose's words whispered in her mind: *I would assume he has no interest in you. He has been with many beautiful women before.*

This was absolutely mortifying. A sharp pain pierced her chest, and she blinked away her tears.

CHAPTER 34

osalind managed to forget about Caine long enough to catch a few hours of sleep. As Caine had so nicely pointed out, if she didn't sleep before visiting the fire hell, she risked seducing half the city.

When she'd woken, Miranda had stirred. Within seconds, she'd literally begun tearing at her hair and ranting about *sunlight*. Rosalind had to run around, collecting an army of candles to recreate some semblance of daylight before meeting Malphas.

Then she'd snuck out through the fortress halls, and through one of the exits.

Now, by Malphas's side, she trod carefully through Edin Woods. He seemed to be leading her back to the rocky ledge overlooking the sea—the place where she'd jumped on top of him and kissed him.

She stared at the thick undergrowth as she walked. Moonlight filtered through the trees, dappling the moss and deadfall with flecks of silver.

If she let her mind go blank, maybe she could forget everything Caine had said to her earlier. That whole *don't think it meant anything* sentiment. Not only was she trying to clear her mind of Caine's words, but she also wanted to avoid thinking about what lay ahead of her in just a few minutes.

If she thought about the fire hell for too long, she'd flee back to the fortress in complete terror.

As they closed in on the cliff's edge, her mouth went dry, and all attempts to clear her mind failed completely. She dreaded this hell more than the others. She'd already felt the excruciating pain of the flames when Cleo had tormented her. As she walked, her legs began to shake, and her pulse raced at the memory of blistering, blackening skin.

When they reached the edge of the wood, she faltered, swaying. Swift as lightning, Malphas slipped an arm around her back to steady her.

He peered down at her. "Are you all right?"

"I'm not looking forward to burning."

"I know. Just try to remember that it's not real. It's your mind playing tricks on your body."

"But I came back from the shadow void with a giant gash in my stomach."

"True," he said. "The mind is a powerful thing. But if your body starts to burn, I'll stop it. You just need to trust me, okay?"

She swallowed hard. "Right."

"Look, you don't have to do this if you don't want. You've already been through five of the hells. Maybe you don't need fire magic if you've got five types of gods-magic already."

She shook her head. "Drew will have fire magic. And I think we need all the power we can get on our side. Don't you?"

"Probably, yes." He cocked his head. "On the plus side, flames won't hurt you after this. The Brotherhood can put you in one of their fires, but you won't burn."

"Really?" Now that was a serious plus.

"The fire goddess can't burn."

She took a deep breath. "Well, let's get this over with, then."

Malphas grabbed her by the hand, leading her to the cliff's edge.

He pulled a flask from his back pocket, unscrewing the top. "An important tool for fire spells." He took a sip before handing it to her.

She took a long swig of whiskey, letting it burn her throat, before handing it back to him.

"Good," he said. He was studying her closely, almost as if he was unsure if *he* wanted to go through with this. The sea wind picked up his dark hair, toying with it.

"What next?" she asked.

"I need to create a sigil around you. Just stay where you are." He began pouring the whiskey on the rock around her, encircling her with alcohol. When the circle had been created, he poured a triangular shape in the center, trailing over her skin. Cold rivulets of whiskey dripped down her legs and toes.

Concern flickered in his eyes, and he handed her the flask again. "You should take another sip. Or two." He cleared his throat. "Maybe finish the rest."

"I thought you had no compunctions about exposing me to pain, after I tortured you?"

"I may have changed my mind."

As she took the flask from him, her hand shook so hard she could hardly get the thing to her lips. Her throat burning, she drained the flask, then wiped the back of her hand across her mouth. She was about to learn exactly how it felt to burn to death, to let her body burn like a lonely bonfire on a dark cliff's edge.

I don't think I gave you enough of the flames before, Cleo whispered. *This will be good for you. Now you'll know how it truly feels.*

Rosalind swallowed hard. "Okay. I'm ready."

"It won't last long." Malphas pulled a lighter from his pocket; his hand shook nearly as bad as hers.

"Just do it," she said, her heart skipping a beat.

He flicked the lighter. She braced herself as he dropped the lighter to the ground.

Instantly, blazing hot sunlight burned the darkness from the sky, and a wall of flames erupted around her, searing her skin. She threw back her head and screamed.

Then she wasn't with Malphas anymore, but standing in a city square. Her arms had been tied behind her, fixed to a stake. Bundles of wood surrounded her, and smoke curled around her body. White-hot pain ripped her mind apart, and she unleashed another agonized scream. When her vision focused again, she stared through the dancing flames.

A braying mob surrounded her, their faces contorted with fury. A man with a black beard screamed *Witch! Witch! Witch!* Spittle flew from his mouth.

She looked down at her body. Black pitch covered her skin and clothes, and flames climbed up her legs. The smell of burning flesh filled her nose. Agony seared her nerves.

Her long hair caught in the flames—blonde hair. *Cleo's hair.*

This was where she'd die, surrounded by dark wrath.

Sobbing from the pain, she scanned the crowd, searching for another face, until her gaze landed on him. His hair a vibrant red, his eyes green. He was screaming for her, his arms pinned by three men.

Richard.

He would be next.

The flames reached her waist, scorching her skin, and another scream tore from her throat. She wanted to call for Richard, but her lips would form only one name: *Ambrose.* Ambrose the Betrayer.

In the next moment, her vision went dark. The flames disappeared. Instead, icy water enveloped her skin. Her eyes snapped open. Under the water, pale streams of moonlight illuminated Malphas's face, close to hers.

He gripped her around the waist, swimming with her in his arms.

When her head breached the surface, she gasped for air. Her legs had burned; the skin was raw. But it was all over.

It was night again here in Lilinor, where the stars gleamed in the sky like jewels. She'd never been so happy to see the night sky.

Dizzy, she wrapped her arms around Malphas's neck as she caught her breath. "What happened?"

"Your body was burning. It seemed like an intense vision. I couldn't stop it with my shadow magic."

They bobbed in the gentle waves. "So you jumped into the ocean, with me in your arms."

"Well, you're not burning anymore, are you?"

She unclasped her hands from his neck and began swimming for the rocks.

As they closed in on the shore, her feet touched the rocky ground. "Do you think the spell worked?"

"It looked like it worked to me. What was it like in the hell?"

She pulled herself up onto sludgy rocks, grimacing with pain. Her shoes had been burned, and her pants hung in threadbare tatters around her legs. Blisters covered her skin, and she winced as the salt stung her raw wounds.

Malphas hoisted himself up next to her.

"I saw Cleo," she said at last. "I *was* Cleo. I was in her body as she was burned in front of a mob. They were screaming about witchcraft. She was screaming for Ambrose. And Richard was there to watch it all."

Malphas grimaced at the sight of her legs. "Hold on, let me heal you."

He leaned closer, and she caught the scent of lilies. He traced his hand just above her legs, letting his silver magic soothe her skin. His aura enveloped her legs, caressing her skin. Instantly, the pain began to ebb away as her skin healed, and she heaved a sigh of relief.

When he finished, he met her gaze. "And who, exactly, is Richard?"

"Caine's second soul. Cleo has spoken of him before. I think the three souls might have been in a coven of sorts. I think Cleo and Richard were lovers, until she left him for Ambrose."

"I see." He nodded at her legs. "Does your skin feel better now?"

"Completely cured."

Her stomach still churned at the thought of what had happened to Cleo. No wonder the old witch had some emotional problems. That had been pure, unadulterated agony, and a terrible injustice.

Rosalind swallowed hard. "If we don't stop the Brotherhood, they're going to bring back the old ways. The screaming mobs, the women burning like torches in town squares."

Seawater dripped off Malphas's porcelain skin. "We'll get there, Rosalind. You've impressed me already, more than you know."

"If we manage to defeat the Hunters, I'm sure I won't be doing it alone. You, me, and Caine—we'll create the daywalkers together, and together we take on Drew. It's the only way this will work."

Malphas arched an eyebrow. "Richard and Cleo, reunited. Not sure I want to get involved in all Cleo and Richard's drama. Perhaps I'll avoid the soul Caine brought back."

"Do you think you could handle a second soul?"

He shrugged, looking out toward the sea. "Better than I could handle half a soul."

"What does that mean?"

He shook his head. "Never mind. Let's get you home. You still need to practice, and Caine and I need to bolster the shield in a few hours."

Half a soul. And there it was. Another tantalizing hint of the Mountfort secrets, with no explanation. She rose, hugging herself in the cool sea air. The waves lapped gently over the rocks.

As she walked with Malphas along the Astarte shoreline, an image burned in her mind: her blond hair catching in the flames, all those years ago. After Ambrose had betrayed her.

She blinked hard, trying to clear the image.

Not me, she reminded herself. *Cleo.*

CHAPTER 35

Standing in her room, Rosalind peeled off her soaked dress. Seawater pooled on the floor below her bare feet, and her sister stared at her.

Purple smudges darkened the skin below Miranda's eyes. "What were you doing outside?"

"Preparing to fight our cousin."

Miranda cocked her head. "Preparing how?"

Shivering, Rosalind pulled on a lilac gown—with long sleeves, to keep her warm. "Malphas has been helping me acquire gods-magic."

Miranda heaved a sigh. "Did you touch him?"

"What do you mean?"

"I haven't touched a man in far too long."

Rosalind crossed her arms. She'd never had this sort of conversation with her sister, and the eerie way Miranda was staring at her didn't make her want to start now. Still, she had to tell *someone* what had happened with Caine.

She crossed to the bed, sitting cross-legged at the edge. "Well, the thing is—Cleo has been confusing me. She's been sending me visions of Ambrose, demanding that I go see him. One of these nights, when I used powerful magic and Cleo started to take over, I ended up kissing Malphas."

Miranda bit her lip, her eyes wide. "What's it like to kiss a demigod?"

"I can't tell you what it's like to kiss Malphas. I was too busy hallucinating."

"Oh." Miranda ran her finger back and forth over her lips, as if she was thinking about Malphas's lips on hers. "That's disappointing. I want to know what it's like to be with a shadow demon."

Rosalind raised her eyebrows. "Well, after that, I went to Caine's room. And that time, I wasn't hallucinating."

Miranda lunged forward, a hungry look in her eyes. "What was *he* like?"

Rosalind thought of the light touch of his fingers over her body, his deep kiss, the way he looked in the warm candlelight.

And then, the positively frigid look in his eyes as he'd told her she didn't mean anything to him.

The memory still stung. Worst of all, she was pretty sure the experience had ruined her for life. How could she ever settle for a normal, human man after that?

"It was pretty much perfect, until it wasn't. He'd smelled Malphas on me, and wanted to know what had happened between us. I ended up telling him. And then he was like, 'well, I don't really care, because none of this meant anything, and I have tons of courtesans.' And he basically wanted me to leave the room and never speak to him again unless it was about military stuff."

For a moment, it almost looked as though shadows were swirling in Miranda's eyes. "Ah. Well. He's probably still upset about Stolas."

The word *Stolas* sent a jolt up Rosalind's spine. She was suddenly very alert. "What do you mean? Who is Stolas?"

Miranda blinked, as if awaking from a dream. "I don't know. I don't know why I said that."

Rosalind's fingers tightened "It's very important to Caine. Where did you hear the name?"

"I told you, I don't know!" Miranda shouted, her cheeks pink.

"Lower your voice!" Rosalind whispered.

"The word Stolas was just a stray thought, floating through my head like a feather on the wind." Miranda reached out, grabbing Rosalind's arm. "I need to get out of here. I want to find a shadow demon of my own."

"We don't need shadow demons. I thought we were just going to get out of here and get a house of our own in the woods or something. You, me, and Tammi. Abominatonia."

Miranda had that hungry look in her eyes again, and she clutched her chest. "It won't be enough. You know it won't be enough. You want Caine, even if he's hardened his heart to you. And I want…" Her fingers tightened on her dress. "I want *everything*. I need to feel alive again. Don't you understand? I need to feel the rain on my skin, and I need to feel the rush of a first kiss. I need to taste everything. And I belong with the shadow demons now."

Oh. Shit. Maybe this wouldn't go as smoothly as she'd hoped. She rubbed her temples. "It's just that Caine has some kind of prohibition against raising people from the grave."

"Well, you've got to figure something out. You've just found the best lover you could ever hope to find, and you can't lose him."

Her chest ached. "That's a dead end. He doesn't want to see me again anyway."

"Okay, fine. But I want to see the world again. You've taken me from one coffin and buried me in another."

She took a deep breath. She *really* didn't want to face Caine again after her last humiliating encounter. "I don't know, Miranda."

"Just tell him," Miranda said. "Then I can get the hell out of this grave of stone and actually see the world."

Rosalind bit her lip. "I suppose I could broach it gently, again. I tried before, but it didn't get very far."

Her temples throbbed, and Cleo mentally slapped her with an image. Not Ambrose's naked body this time, but Caine's golden skin, skimming against hers.

"Stop it, Cleo," she muttered.

Your sister is right, Cleo purred. *Broach it with Caine. See what happens. After all, you said you trusted him, didn't you? Are you changing your mind just because he doesn't love you?*

Rosalind stood. Maybe it was worth a shot, at least to feel out his reaction. "Fine. Both of you, settle down." She pointed at her sister. "But wait here, please, until I get back."

Miranda grunted, her lip curling. "Get me out of here."

Rosalind grabbed a knife in a holster, strapping it around her waist, then crossed to the door.

As she walked through the hall, her footsteps echoed off the ceiling, and her mind flashed with images of Cleo's death: the dancing flames, the horrified look in Richard's eyes.

When you're in love, you can't escape the fire.

Rosalind flinched. Maybe Richard had loved Cleo, but things were a little different between Rosalind and Caine. In fact, Caine didn't find her particularly special. He'd made that clear enough.

She pulled open the door to the stairwell. How *exactly* was she going to phrase this question to Caine?

She didn't imagine taking her dress off a second time would do the trick.

In the corridor, candlelight and shadows danced over the dark flagstones. She stopped at the door near the picture of Lord Byron. For a few moments, she steeled her resolve, then knocked on the dark wood.

After a moment, she heard his muffled voice through the door. "Who is it?"

"It's Rosalind."

A long pause. Then, "Is there a reason you're here?"

I don't have a good feeling about this. "I need to ask you something," she ventured.

The door unlatched, and swung open. Caine must have used his magic to open it, because he was on the other side of the room. He sat in a gray armchair by his window, sipping bourbon from a tumbler. His glacial eyes sent a chill through her blood. He didn't exactly look happy to see her.

She stepped over the threshold anyway, then took a seat on the edge of his bed.

"What do you want?" Ice tinged his voice.

Might as well dive in. "I need to know what you would do if I raised Miranda's body from the grave."

"I'd kill her."

His words cut her to the bone. "Why? Why would you do that?"

"Because the dead are supposed to stay dead." He took another sip from his tumbler. "Was that your only question? I'd prefer you didn't remove your dress again, because I have a dinner guest arriving soon."

Her heart constricted, and she scrambled to think of a response, but before she could get another word out, the door creaked open.

Esmerelda stepped into the room, her red hair cascading over a stunning crimson gown.

She shot a furious look at Rosalind. "What's the human doing here?"

"She's leaving." Caine glared at Rosalind. "Do you mind? I don't have much time with Esmerelda. I'll need to leave to work on the shield again."

His words felt like a punch to the gut, and Cleo whispered in her mind. *I told you, Rosalind. A shadow demon can't really love. Or at least, he'll never love a human.*

Tears stung her eyes, and Rosalind rose. "Right. I'll be on my way."

As she walked to the door, she tried to ignore Esmerelda's victorious smirk.

Maybe she'd been wrong to trust Caine. How much did she really know about him, anyway? How much did she really know about demons at all?

Kill them all, Cleo sang. *Dance in their blood.*

A part of Rosalind wanted to let Cleo take over, to see what destruction the old witch could wreak on the place, but she kept her grip on the spirit this time.

Still, as she walked down the halls, she caught her reflection in the silver sconces: stunning long blond hair, and green eyes. *Cleo's eyes.*

CHAPTER 36

osalind pushed through the door to the Gelal Fields, on her way to practice the gods-magic.

Her muscles burned. Over the past few days, while Caine and Malphas had kept the shield in place, she'd been practicing shadow running—moving from one place to another like a phantom wind. Thrilling, but exhausting. On top of that, she'd been trying her hand at the other types of gods-magic, like calling vines from the earth and shooting fire from her fingertips.

As if the magic weren't draining enough, there was the Miranda problem. With each day, her twin grew more desperate for freedom. Rosalind had snuck her out twice while the vampires slept, so Miranda could feel the sea air on her skin, and let the salt water run over her legs.

But it hadn't been enough. She seemed so *hungry,* like she couldn't get enough of the world.

Today, after practicing magic all morning, Rosalind had snatched a few hours of sleep while Miranda paced the room, gnawing through cakes.

Now, Rosalind glanced up at the cloudless sky, admiring the stars etched in the dark. She was definitely *not* going to think about how they reminded her of Caine's eyes. She hadn't seen him at all over the past few days, and she had an agonizing feeling he'd been spending time with Esmerelda, Rosalind's *least* favorite vampire.

Long grasses tickled Rosalind's legs as she walked, and a chorus of crickets chirped around her. *I'm not thinking about Caine. Or Ambrose. Or any other shadow demons. I'm just gonna focus on the storm I need to raise.*

As her eyes adjusted to the dark, she could see a pale silver glow of magic, just at the edge of the forest. *Caine?*

So much for her plan not to think about him.

She crossed her arms as she walked through the fields, and glanced at the sky again, at the faint shimmer of silver magic that protected the kingdom. Already, around the moon and the Big Dipper, the shadow magic had thinned again.

A shudder crawled up her spine. Drew was close to breaking through, and they were running out of time.

Her heart tightened. She still hadn't mastered most of the magic she was supposed to use. She couldn't quite get the rocks to obey her commands, couldn't call up a large enough flame to burn a twig. It hadn't exactly been easy to concentrate the past few days. While she'd been practicing all the new gods-magic at her fingertips, Cleo had been invading her mind with visions of torture and burnings, alternated with Ambrose-porn. Rosalind was pretty sure she could pick out Cleo's fondest memories: screwing in a castle, in a meadow, and up against a tree.

Not big on beds, those two.

As she drew closer to Caine, her heart began to speed up. Pathetic, really. She was going to turn into Cleo, obsessed with the memories of sex with a shadow demon—his exquisite kisses replaying on a loop in her mind for the rest of her life.

She should run the other way. And yes, despite herself, her pace quickened.

But when she'd come within twenty feet of him, she felt a flicker of disappointment.

Not Caine.

Malphas.

For the best, anyway. I have no idea what to say to Caine right now.

Pale magic curled from Malphas's body, snaking up to the sky like silver smoke.

She snapped a twig as she approached, and Malphas broke his focus, his pale eyes landing on her. The silver tendrils of magic snapped back into his body.

"Sorry to disturb you while you're working on the shield," she said. "How's it going?"

"Not well. I'm not sure how much longer I can hold it in place. Caine should be helping me, but I'm not sure where the hell he's gone."

"With Esmerelda, perhaps?"

"What?"

"Never mind. So what do you think Caine is doing, then?" she asked as casually as she could.

"Arguing with Ambrose again, I think. He won't produce the sigil we need. And he keeps threatening to go back into Boston on his own to slaughter Drew without us. He's certain he can solve this whole problem on his own." Malphas frowned. "He no longer seems keen to include you in his plans. Care to tell me why?"

"You'd have to ask him. But once I'm done practicing this storm spell, I'm going to have a word with him. Going to Boston on his own is the last thing he should do."

"Why?"

"They're looking for a scapegoat." Dread welled in her gut. "And Caine's the perfect specimen. He's powerful, demonic. The Brotherhood already hate him. He'd be a great coup for them. Granted, so would you and I. But we're going to have to look out for each other. No one is going alone."

"You think they could be waiting for him?"

"It wouldn't surprise me. Maybe they're trying to lure him out—first Caine, then me. Drew knows I'd go after Caine. He'd have everything he needed: his scapegoat, his revenge, and his mind-controlled wife to torture for the rest of her life."

Pale moonlight washed over Malphas's skin. "When do you think you'll be ready to fight him?"

A sigh slid from her. "I'm getting there. I just feel like I need a few more weeks. And I need Cleo to shut the hell up, so I can focus. She's quiet now, but when I'm using the magic her voice gets louder. She wants things that I can't give her."

"What does she want?"

Ambrose. "It doesn't matter."

As soon as the words had left her mouth, Cleo assaulted her with a vision of Ambrose kissing her naked hips. Rosalind nearly groaned at the image, and the hot flash of need that seared her body.

Her jaw tightened. "Not now, Cleo," she muttered.

Malphas stared at her. "That's not a good sign."

"I've got it under control," she snapped. "I don't have time to keep resting. Look, I've got to go practice the storm magic. And as soon as I get back, I'll have a word with Caine about his plan to go into Boston—"

A loud crack interrupted her sentence, and her gaze flicked to the sky. "The shield," she whispered.

Below their feet, the ground began to rumble. Once more, a geyser of water surged from the field by the castle wall.

"Help me fix the shield," Malphas shouted. "Now!"

She stared at the moon, letting the shadow magic spiral from her body. She could feel Drew's power just on the other side of the shield, the tendrils of colored magic snaking along the dome of shadow magic. When she closed her eyes, she saw a vortex of stars and night. On the other side of the portal, Drew's horde of Hunters waited to invade, ready to slaughter everyone she cared about.

Nyxobas's magic charged her body, and she let it flow from her, mingling with Malphas's. As the earth trembled below her, she lost herself in the surge of power, melding with the night sky and the jewel of Nyxobas.

I am the darkness. I am the eternal void.

When she opened her eyes again, three Hunters were crawling from a muddy portal. Filled with Nyxobas's power, Rosalind and

Malphas shadow-ran to them, flying on the wind in just a few seconds. Despite moving at an intense speed, she took in every detail of the Hunters' faces: a woman with freckles and a round face; a man with a trim black beard, no more than twenty-two; and a bald man with a square jaw.

They weren't monsters, but they'd chosen the wrong side of this war. All three would be dead within seconds.

The woman raised her gun, and Rosalind's fist connected with her jaw—once, twice, three times, her head snapped back. Fast as the night wind, Rosalind grabbed the gun from her, turning it on the woman.

She cocked the gun, and fired.

One for Miranda. Two for Cleo. Three for me.

Three Hunters fell to the ground, bullet holes in their chests.

Malphas stared at her. "I guess you're getting better at this."

She tucked the gun into her belt, still buzzing with night magic. "I guess I am." She looked up at the shield, examining the sterling sheen of magic. "I need one more practice session with my magic skills. But soon you, Caine, and I will just need to go into Boston. I could feel Drew's power on the other side of the shield, and he's desperate to break through."

CHAPTER 37

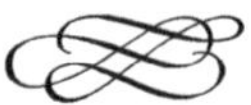

osalind stood on the cliff's edge, staring out at the Astarte sea. A damp breeze kissed her skin, and she licked the salt off her lips.

She swayed slightly on her feet. The sea wind toyed with her hair, and she drank in the briny scent of Dagon. She closed her eyes, trying to gather the energy she needed for a storm spell.

But as soon as her eyelids fluttered closed, Cleo greeted her with a vision of Ambrose kissing the tops of her breasts, her back flat against the wooden wall, dress hiked up around her waist. His firm hands gripping her waist.

Richard will be upset...

Rosalind shook her head to clear the vision. "Not now, Cleo. I need to practice."

Cleo slammed her with another vision—her legs around Ambrose's muscled waist, her back against the rough tree bark. He kissed her milky white neck, and her body writhed against his...

Rosalind's fingernails dug into her palms. *I don't need to be a voyeur into someone's sixteenth century sex life.* "Stop it. I get it. You liked fucking Ambrose. Can we move on?"

Her legs were shaking, and her gaze flicked to the starry sky. With the daywalker plans in complete disarray, they had few defenses against Drew. She'd have to master her abilities, or they'd all die when he invaded the city again.

She held out her arms to the side. Gusts of marine wind whipped at her hair. This time, she had no incubi to attack. It was just her and the vast skies. She arched her back, opening her body to Mishett-Ash, imagining a storm simmering on the horizon. An electric thrill surged through her limbs.

This is working.

Her eyes snapped open, and she stared up the stars, watching as dark clouds rolled in. An ancient, wrathful power vibrated through her body. Maybe she *was* mastering this magic after all. She narrowed her eyes at the sky, watching as the clouds covered the moon, blotting out the light. Far below, the sea began to seethe like a dying beast, slate gray and angry.

An electric thrill charged her muscles. She flicked her wrist, and lightning pierced the dark sky. *I can do this.*

A second flick, and the clouds opened, unleashing a torrent of rain.

Fat raindrops soaked her clothes, and the distant call of a valkyrie pierced the air. Filled with a soul-deep assuredness, Rosalind stepped off the edge of the cliff, and took flight into the air. Gray magic whorled around her body, and she soared over the frothing sea, dark as bitumen.

Thunder rumbled over the horizon.

Cleo whispered, *It feels good to wield the power of nature, Rosalind, doesn't it? Glorious. Until they punish you for it.*

Rosalind swooped lower, letting the ocean's spume wash over her, tasting the salt. Cold wind whipped at her skin, tearing at her dress and hair. Finally, she'd wielded the gods-magic successfully.

Too much power now. They'll burn you, too.

Her heart began to pound harder when she thought of Cleo burning in the funeral pyre, of Richard watching. But she couldn't think about that now—not with Drew eating at the shield, ready to invade the city and slaughter everyone.

Rosalind pushed the memories of Cleo to the back of her mind.

She swooped back over to the cliff's edge, landing with a hard roll on the jagged rock. She grunted, then righted herself, dusting off the gravel. Cold magic still rushed through her veins, dulling the pain from her landing's impact.

As she stood on the cliff's edge, another crack of lightning flashed in the sky. Reaching out toward the sea, she focused on the salty air, letting Dagon's magic curl from her fingers. Her mind flickered with an image of Dagon in his bestial form, his tentacles sliding over her skin…

She flicked her wrist, then watched as the ocean convulsed. Slowly, the tide retreated from the shore, leaving behind sludgy black rocks, hammered by the storm's onslaught. Dagon's phantom tentacles curled tighter around her body, encircling her waist as she used his power.

As watery magic surged through her blood, she flicked her wrist again, and the sea returned once more—this time, as a wall of black water, rushing for the cliffs. Rosalind stared, wide eyed, as a small tsunami rushed for the cliff's edge.

But before water met rock, Cleo seized her mind.

* * *

ROSALIND FALTERED, her vision going dark. Then, a shocking burst of green—Cleo's aura.

The green aura thinned, giving way to a sycamore grove. In the heavy spring night, she stood, dressed in her thinnest white dress—the one Ambrose liked, because he could see through the fabric when the sunlight hit it from behind.

Her blond hair tumbled over her shoulders—Ambrose and Richard were the only men who'd ever seen her with her hair down, threaded with flowers. Bluebells for peace of mind.

She sighed, leaning back against a trunk. She'd eaten dinner with Ambrose last night, at his manor. She shouldn't have gone to him like that, so recklessly—not with the witch hunters roaming Fife. But she couldn't resist his beauty, nor stay away from his touch.

She plucked a petal off a bluebell. Ambrose drew her to him like a moth to the flame. Some nights, she just stood outside his window, watching him. Trying to draw his attention to her, making sure his love wasn't false. She was sure he saw her, too.

But last night had been different. She'd stood in the garden just outside his manor. She'd needed to see him, needed to feel his hands all over her. But when she saw him with that other woman, the one with the raven hair, beautiful as a goddess—

Their quarrel had been terrible. She'd said things she regretted, and she was sure he'd never want to see her again. But then, he'd invited her to dine with him, just the two of them. Roasted quail, venison, strawberry pudding, and malmsey wine—enough to drown a man.

But they hadn't finished eating. Just as she'd finished her second glass of wine, Ambrose had pushed the food off the table, and he'd taken her right there. He'd laced his fingers through hers, and he'd given her the most amazing love of her life.

She hoped she'd see him again tonight. He knew he'd be able to find her here, and she was certain he'd want to see her again. Already, her body was warming—getting ready for his touch.

The sound of footsteps turned her head, and her heartbeat sped up. *He's coming.*

But as she stepped through the grove, looking for her love, the world seemed to tilt below her feet. It wasn't Ambrose coming for her.

How did they know I was here?

There were three of them, their black caps peaked, iron tools gleaming in the moonlight. It was the *Hunters.*

Her heart skipped a beat. *Ambrose and Richard are the only ones who know I come here...*

Her heart thudded, and she lifted her hand to begin a spell. But before her lips could finish the first Angelic word, an iron arrow struck her in the chest. She fell to the earth, pain screaming through her shoulder. Grief cut through her.

Ambrose turned me in to the Hunters.

A hunter kicked her hard in the gut, another slammed a boot into her ribs.

Ambrose is sending me to my death.

One of the Hunters—his face red as a devil's—tore the front of her dress, and she screamed.

Ambrose wouldn't come to save her.

Ambrose had sent them here.

* * *

AS THE STORM RAGED ABOVE, Rosalind clenched her fists tighter, until her fingernails pierced the skin. A hard wave slammed against the rocky cliffs. The black clouds seethed in the sky, dark as the smoke from a witch's pyre.

Cleo's wrath was hers now—and she had a score to settle.

Ambrose, you faithless prick.

She turned, rushing back toward the fortress.

Fury ripped through her nerves, colder than a valkyrie's rage. Ambrose had been Cleo's lover, and then he'd sent the Hunters for her. Instead of meeting her himself, he'd left her to be beaten and raped.

And then he'd let her burn.

Wrath shook her body.

Why had Ambrose done this to Cleo? Because she'd been too much trouble for him? Because he didn't know how to get rid of a lover he no longer wanted?

Shadow demons aren't capable of love.

No wonder Cleo hated the fucker. No wonder she wanted to light him on fire.

Rosalind's feet pounded through the forest. Her breath was ragged in her lungs. She ran, carried on the wind, and gusts of cold air billowed around her.

But Cleo had said something else. *Richard* had known where Cleo would be. He was a jilted lover. What if it had been him?

And what if Richard's angry soul had poisoned Caine's mind against Rosalind?

She lifted the hem of her dress, running faster through the Gelal Fields. She needed to get to the bottom of this, once and for all. She was sick of all the secrets.

But before she got to the fortress walls, a loud *crack* boomed over the horizon. Flicking her wrist, she flung open the entrance to the castle. She sprinted through a dark hall. As she ran through the candlelit corridors and up the stairs, her mind flashed with images of the fire.

Ambrose sent me to the flames, Cleo screamed.

He'd burned his lover. He'd left his wife to rot in a prison.

Demons can't really love, Cleo whispered. *They will use you, then kill you.*

Gasping for breath, Rosalind sprinted up the stairs to the White Tower. She knew where she'd find Ambrose: toying with another courtesan.

At the top of the stairs, she rushed through the long hall, her gaze on the two guards at the door. Two near-giants, large as vikings, wielding axes designed to separate intruder's necks from their bodies. But she didn't feel so intimidated anymore.

"Stop!" One of them shouted, readying his weapon.

She held out her hands, and two sharp bolts of lightning shot from her wrists, finding their marks in the guards' chests.

Good, Cleo purred. *Vengeance is glorious.*

Stalking past their unconscious bodies, Rosalind climbed the stairs. She flicked her wrist, flinging open the door. Blazing with power, she stepped into Ambrose's chamber. With the storm raging above, a glass dome covered the open ceiling, and rain hammered against the clear glass.

Ambrose stood, naked, by one of the windows.

Before she could even register surprise, he had her pinned against the wall, his hand around her throat.

CHAPTER 38

$\mathcal{H}$e pressed his muscled body against hers. Cleo seemed to thrill at his touch, wanted his hands all over her waist—but Rosalind heard nothing but the angry roar of blood in her ears.

Either you or Richard gave her up to the Hunters.

She slammed her fist into his cheek, knocking him away.

His head whipped to the side, and he touched his mouth, dabbing at the blood. He eyed her warily. "You've changed your tune."

"What did you do to Cleo?"

Rosalind felt her body shifting, lengthening. Her hips narrowed, and from the corner of her eye, she watched her dark hair lighten to a pale gold.

Ambrose's eyes widened. "Cleo," he whispered.

Rosalind's fingers twitched, fire magic sparking at the tips. "You better tell us now, vampire," she spoke, half in her own voice, and half in Cleo's. "Because we know what it feels like to burn. I'm not sure you do, but we can change that real fast."

His jaw dropped.

Despite her fury, Cleo's lust simmered, and Rosalind found her eyes scanning Ambrose's chiseled body. She could almost understand why Cleo had become obsessed with him.

Almost, but not quite.

"I won't speak to you in that form," he growled.

Now, Rosalind understood what Cleo wanted from Ambrose. It wasn't simply sex or vengeance.

She wanted a confession.

"Tell me the truth!" she shouted, her voice mingling with Cleo's.

In a fraction of a second, his hand was at her throat once more, squeezing ever so slightly. "I won't ask again."

Coolly, she surveyed him. Now she had the power to fight him—but she wasn't here for a slaughter. She was here for a confession. She let her body transform again, growing petite once more, her hair darkening. "If you don't give Cleo what she wants," Rosalind said. "I will turn into her once more and flay your skin from your bones. Are we clear?"

Slowly, he backed away. "I need to get dressed for this conversation." He crossed to his bed, pulling on a pair of black underwear. His clothing littered the silky sheets, and she had the distinct impression he'd been banging someone not long ago.

"Where'd your latest lover go?" she asked, taking another step closer. "Did you hire an army of thugs to burn her to death?"

As he stepped into his pants, Ambrose's gaze was positively glacial. "You really have completely lost your mind, haven't you, Rosalind?"

She shook her head. "I've just come to understand why Cleo hates you so much."

"You've lost your wits. You're no good to me if you're insane."

"Don't you get it?" Rosalind shouted. "She's not going to let my mind rest until you tell me the truth." She stepped closer to him, letting the flames spark from her fingertips. Smoke curled to the ceiling. "Confess what you did."

Still bare-chested, Ambrose gestured to the bed. "Sit."

She curled her lip. "I'm not sitting on sheets you just screwed on."

He took a step closer, his dark magic curling from his body. He was angry. Furious, even.

But he didn't scare her anymore. "Tell me what you did," she demanded.

He took a deep breath. "I met her in the 1590s. I had moved to Scotland nearly a hundred years before."

"Why?"

His eyes darkened. "You don't need to know that. You only need to know that it was the darkest period of my life—until I met Cleo."

Deep in Rosalind's chest, Cleo's aura sparked.

"She was different. A female philosopher. Smarter than any woman I'd ever met. She had a lover when I met her."

"Richard." Rosalind swallowed. "That's Caine's soul."

"Hmm. I guess that explains what happened earlier."

"What do you mean?"

He arched an eyebrow, jaw tensing. "You know what I mean. Anyway, I'd meet her in the sycamore grove, or among the wild-flowers at night. She was an amazing lover. Passionate beyond belief."

"Believe me, I've seen the mental video."

"But she always wanted more."

"So?"

His aura darkened the air around him. "You have to understand that in Scotland at this time, the whole country was overrun by prick-ers. Hunters, you'd call them. More powerful than at any other point in their history, except now. Anyone found guilty of witchcraft would be burned at the stake. I wasn't as powerful then as I am now. I hadn't taken over Lilinor yet."

Rosalind crossed her arms. She was losing patience. "And why did you give her over to the Hunters?"

"She'd become obsessed with me. She needed to see me every night. If I wasn't there for her, she'd send wisteria vines all over my manor, clinging to the brick. She'd practice magic in my garden. The people who lived nearby had begun to notice. There were rumors."

She swallowed hard. Cleo's magic roiled sharply in her gut. "So you turned her in?"

"Not until she spied on me one night. She caught me speaking to Erish in my home. It was before Erish and I had married, but Erish had… an interest in me. The jealousy ripped Cleo apart. She threatened, then and there, to turn me in to the Hunters. I tried to calm her. I invited her in for dinner. I thought I'd made her happy again. I thought I'd stopped it. But she was too unpredictable. She didn't forgive me. Because the next night the Hunters came for me. And there was only one way out of it. It was me, or her. They wanted a witch, and I gave them one."

Rosalind's fists tightened, fury still blazing through her blood. "She didn't turn you in."

His eyes had darkened to a pitch black. "She was trying to get me killed. And after what I'd already been through, I wasn't dying for a crazy woman."

"She didn't turn you in. Maybe they saw all the wisteria." Cleo's anger seethed, and Rosalind nearly punched him again. "They raped her, you know."

The room grew positively frigid.

"She didn't turn you in." She shook her head. "You said the Hunters were all over Scotland. Maybe they just came for you anyway. Or maybe they'd heard about the vines. Or, you know, the fact that you drink people's blood."

Ambrose seemed to pale, shadows thickening around him. "Are you certain she never sent the Hunters for me?"

"She thought you'd be coming for her in the sycamore grove. She was certain of it."

He dropped his gaze, staring at the floor. "When they burned her, I hid inside the nearby church, and I forced myself to watch the whole thing. She cried my name, over and over. And Richard screamed hers. He was the next to burn."

Bile crawled up her throat.

Cleo's voice had gone quiet.

"Those are the old ways that the Brotherhood wants to bring back," Rosalind said quietly.

"I'll never forget the sound of her screams."

Rosalind shook her head. "What did you mean about Richard's soul? How it explains what happened earlier?"

He glanced at her quizzically. "Caine's outburst, of course. His jealous rage."

A pit opened in the hollow of her stomach. "What outburst?"

"When he found you with me here earlier. You do realize that the only reason I didn't slaughter you for bursting in here is that you were the best shag I've had since… well, since Cleo. That, and the—"

Her mouth went dry. "I was here earlier?"

"You really don't remember?" He pinched the bridge of his nose. "I'm not sure if I should be insulted or concerned. I didn't know Cleo had taken over your mind that badly, or I never would have allowed you to seduce me."

Oh shit oh shit oh shit. Rosalind's breath caught in her throat. Cleo had compelled her to seduce Ambrose while she was in some sort of a haze. Maybe while she thought she was sleeping? She shook her head. "I don't remember anything about it. What happened? What did Caine do when he found me here?"

Dark magic whorled around Ambrose. "He knocked on the door, and you answered it. Naked. It seemed to upset him. He turned into the Ravener once more. It really doesn't ring a bell?"

She swallowed hard. "And what did he say?"

"That he should have known not to trust an Atherton."

Her stomach twisted in knots. She'd confirmed everything that Caine thought about her.

With adrenalin burning through her veins, she turned to flee from the room.

CHAPTER 39

Her feet pounded over the stone floor as she raced to Caine's room, heart thudding hard against her ribs. Her sodden clothes still clung to her legs, slowing her pace, and she lifted the hem. She didn't know what she was going to say when she found Caine, but she had a desperate need to talk to him. *Now.*

When she got to the painting of Lord Byron, her heart sped up. His door was *open.* Why would he leave his door open?

She rushed inside, but the place was empty. The storm winds rattled the window, and only a guttering candle lit the room.

What the hell was she going to tell him, anyway?

Panic gripped her chest, and she began pacing the room.

And as she paced, her mind stopped racing, and started actually working.

Maybe she'd gone to Ambrose's room and shagged him stupid while she was in a fugue state.

Or maybe she wasn't the only person walking around this place with her face on.

What if it hadn't been her? What if it had been Miranda? Ambrose had still been naked when she'd burst into the room, which meant it hadn't happened that long ago…

Miranda. Her stomach twisted in knots. It was worse than she thought. *Something is going very wrong with my sister.*

Maybe the spell had gone wrong, or living after death took some serious adjustment. Who the hell knew? This was completely uncharted territory, and the one person who could guide her hadn't told her a damn thing.

She needed to find her sister. Now.

Her pulse racing, she tore out of Caine's room and down the hall. With ragged breaths, she stormed down the stairwell. She pushed through the door into the darkened hall, where candlelight wavered over the flagstones. As she sprinted toward her room, a figure rounded the corner at the other end of the hall, silver magic curling from his body.

Her heart skipped a beat. *Caine?*

No. As her eyes focused in the dim light, she made out Malphas's features.

Shit. She wouldn't be able to go into her room with Malphas lingering around here. Miranda could be just on the other side of the door. She slowed her pace, trying to act calm. *Nothing to see here. No undead sisters, no postcoital drama with Caine and Ambrose.*

Malphas didn't slow his pace when he saw her. In fact, he sped up, moving toward her in a blur of shadows.

Her blood turned to ice. What the hell was happening now?

In the next moment, he was standing over her, silver eyes piercing in the dim light. "There you are," he said, his magic whipping around his body.

"What's happening?" *I mean, apart from the fact that your brother caught my undead sister screwing his boss?*

"Caine told me he was leaving Lilinor on his own, just to gather information. Maybe to find a human for us to use as a host for the mage's soul. He said he wasn't going after Drew." He narrowed his eyes. "But something seemed off with him. Like he wasn't telling me the whole truth. I tried to slow him down, but he went through the portal."

A growing sense of dread welled in her gut. "What do you mean, something seemed off with him?"

"He wouldn't look me in the eye. He seemed… angry."

Rosalind's gaze flicked to her door. She had a terrible feeling that, at any moment, her sister might burst from the door and try to bang another demon. Why stop at just one?

Malphas cocked his head. "What's distracting you?"

She swallowed hard. If Malphas spoke to Ambrose, he'd quickly learn what had happened. Might as well come clean with the truth now. Or at least, the fake truth.

She folded her arms, cheeks burning with humiliation. "He was upset when he found me in Ambrose's room."

Malphas took a deep breath. "And why was he upset?"

She cleared her throat, staring at the floor. "See… Caine and I had a moment—"

"A moment?"

"We slept together."

Malphas's eyes darkened, his icy aura whipping the air around him. "Ah. And then you had a moment with Ambrose?"

"I felt terrible when I realized what was happening, and when Caine found us. But Cleo is obsessed with Ambrose. I think she's settled down now, after she got what she wanted."

"Sex with Ambrose."

"A confession."

"Well that is unexpected." Malphas scrubbed a hand over his mouth. "You know that I can tell when you're lying. I'm just not entirely sure which part you were lying about. Probably the part about how you felt awful."

Well, now I definitely feel awful. Her gaze darted to the door again. What was Miranda up to?

Malphas crossed his arms, leaning against the wall. "Is this conversation keeping you from something important? It's just that I think my brother may have just run to his death. You know his theory about how emotional attachments are a liability? This is what he means."

"I don't know why he cares so much. He was with Esmerelda in his bedroom the last time I saw him. He pretty much kicked me out so they could have dinner."

"She works for him—she's a spy. I doubt it was romantic."

She took a deep breath. "Okay, well, we have to go after him. He's the perfect scapegoat for the Brotherhood. And if they're waiting for him outside Lilinor…" She let her sentence trail off. She couldn't even imagine what horrors Drew and the Brotherhood would have in store for Caine.

"We don't have daywalkers. We don't have an army. It's daylight in Boston. Our rescue force consists of two people: you and me."

She bit her lip. "And if anyone is waiting on the other side of the portal, they'll still be there."

Malphas nodded. "We'll lower the shields, just for a few minutes. Long enough to do some scrying. We'll ask about danger that awaits us on the other side. If it's clear, we can slip into the city quietly, using shadow magic. We'll drag his arse back here until we can make our army. Okay?"

She glanced at her door again. "I need a few minutes to change and get my weapons ready. I'll meet you by the portal."

"The one in Ambrose's room?"

She grimaced. She didn't want to face Ambrose again. "Gods, no. The one outside."

He glanced at her door, as if he knew she kept her darkest secrets locked behind it.

Her stomach clenched. "I'll meet you outside," she repeated.

He gave her a wary look before turning. Shadows thickened around him, and he disappeared like smoke on the wind.

She took a deep breath before opening the door to her room. Miranda sat on the floor, wrapped in a silky white bathrobe. Half-eaten cakes littered the ground around her, and custard and jam smeared her mouth. Her eyes looked wild, empty.

Rosalind's blood ran cold. *Something is definitely not right.*

"You've finally come back for me," Miranda said. "I thought you might have abandoned me."

"I told you I was coming back. I had to practice the magic I'm learning."

Miranda wiped a hand across the back of her mouth. "And how come I'm not allowed to have this power?"

Irritation simmered. "I told you why. No one is supposed to know you're alive. And you nearly ruined everything by running into Ambrose's room to shag him. Caine said he'd murder you if he found you. The only reason he didn't kill you was that he thought you were me. And now he's run off to Boston to get himself killed."

Tears glistened in Miranda's eyes, and she rose. Her body looked tense, her arms stiff. "And why is it that Caine has forbidden people from bone conjuring? Do you know?"

Dread crept around Rosalind's heart like wisteria, crushing the life out of her. "Aurora said he considered it a blasphemy."

Miranda inched closer, grabbing her robe just over her heart. "Or maybe it's because he understood what it would do to a person. There's a void in my chest that can never be filled, and if I don't get enough of the world it will consume me alive until there's nothing left but the darkness. You can't keep me in here, Rosalind—in this prison."

Rosalind's legs had begun to shake. "I won't keep you in here. But when Caine caught you with Ambrose, he rushed into Cambridge on his own. I'm worried Drew could have been waiting for him. I need to get him back."

"You always have something important to do. Don't you, Rosalind? While I wait here, in darkness. Ripped apart by loneliness."

Rosalind held out her hands, as if calming a wild beast. "I'm going to Cambridge, and when I get back we'll figure this out." Surely there must be another spell that could help heal Miranda's mind.

After all, what the hell was the point of magic if it couldn't solve your real problems? What use were grimoires and auras if they couldn't heal broken minds and dead bodies, if they couldn't overturn humanity's fundamental curse?

"We'll fix this," Rosalind said, more to reassure herself than anything. She pulled off her soaked dress, crossing to the wardrobe.

"We'll get our house. Abominatonia. We'll have our fireplace, our paintings. You'll have as much life as you want."

Miranda's lip curled. Her look was ferocious. "I want oak trees, and the smell of the ocean. I want to hear the call of a golden-crowned sparrow. I want sunlight, and the feel of water on my skin. I *need* these things."

"You'll have them." Rosalind pulled out her fighting gear: black leather pants and a tight top. "And you can sleep with as many vampires as you want."

"Oh really?" Miranda said tonelessly. "And when will this happen? After you save the world?"

Rosalind stepped into her clothes. "I'm trying the best I can, Miranda. We're in the middle of a goddamn war. You died. Drew killed you. I'm trying to fix that, but he's going to kill a lot of other people if I don't help to stop him."

Miranda sat on the edge of the bed, hugging herself. "I spent years wandering the streets, looking for you. I slept in train stations. I ate discarded food. I kept to myself," she muttered, seemingly lost in her own thoughts. "I just want a chance at the life I deserved."

Rosalind zippered up the front of her jacket. "I know. And you will. That's why I brought you back. Please just stay in here for a little while longer. We'll get out of Lilinor soon."

Staring at the floor, Miranda nodded wordlessly.

Why do I have the terrible feeling this isn't going to work out well? Grabbing her weapon belt, Rosalind pushed those worries to the back of her mind. Instead, she ran Miranda's mantra through her mind: *Sunlight, the smell of the ocean. Oak trees. Water on skin. The call of a golden-crowned sparrow.*

Mentally, she repeated these words as she strapped her weapons to her thigh.

They would have life again, once they left Lilinor.

She cast one last look back at Miranda as she reached for the door. "Please stay here. I'll be back for you. Get some sleep."

Miranda's gaze met hers for just a moment, and the pain in those dark eyes pierced Rosalind to the bone.

* * *

DRESSED FOR BATTLE, Rosalind walked toward the fountain in an abandoned square at the edge of Lilinor. Her heels clacked over the cobblestones, and the shadows around her seemed to creep and writhe like half-living creatures. The rain had stopped, but rivulets of cold water ran through the stones and dripped off the steep-peaked roofs.

As she approached the gently trickling fountain, she caught sight of two figures. Aurora stood by Malphas's side, dressed in an emerald-green gown, and dripping with silver jewels.

Rosalind took a shaky breath, her nerves burning. This was where it had all begun—where Rosalind had first entered Lilinor all those weeks ago, when she'd recklessly chased Caine through the portal. Now Caine was the reckless one. Apparently, emotions *were* a liability, though she had no real clue how he felt about her. His actions certainly didn't match his words.

As she approached, Malphas stared at her, his eyes blazing with cold light. "Are you ready for this, Ros?"

Aurora traced her finger in the pool's dark water. "When you're ready to lower the shield, I can help you both with the scrying. You two control the shield with shadow magic, and I'll chant the scrying spell. Got it?"

Rosalind nodded. "Thanks." She swallowed hard. "Before we start, Aurora, I want to talk to you for a minute." She glanced at Malphas. "In private."

Malphas scowled. "You really need to talk about your lovers' quarrel now?"

She glared at him, and Aurora raised a hand, dismissing him. "Give us a few minutes."

Malphas made sure they saw his eye roll before he turned, slipping into the shadows of a nearby alley.

Aurora cocked a hip. "What happened now?"

An ache spread through Rosalind's chest. She wasn't sure how to put her thoughts into words. "Caine told me that if I raised Miranda from the dead, he'd kill her."

Aurora crossed her arms. "Bloody hell. That's a bit much, isn't it?"

"Thing is, Miranda hasn't been acting right. She's talking about a void, and being lonely. She's desperate to get out of our room. And then, when I wasn't watching her…"

"What did she do?"

"She had sex with Ambrose. And Ambrose, Caine, and Malphas think it was me. Malphas thinks that's part of why Caine left the city."

Aurora's eyes widened. "Are you kidding me? Let me guess. You shagged Caine before all this went down."

"Sort of. Yes. And he was already mad because…" Her fingers tightened. *Maybe I should leave out the bit about Malphas.* "Anyway, he was already mad."

Aurora shook her head. "Woman, trouble's all over like moss on a grave."

"But I'm just wondering if there's more to Caine's prohibition than sacrilege. What if it's because… people don't come back quite right?"

"We knew that was a risk when we started. I told you—she was dead to start. If she came back wrong, she'd end up dead again. No worse than when she started."

Rosalind's chest tightened. "I'm not saying we should kill her. She deserves a chance."

Aurora nodded at the fountain. "We have time to figure it out after we find out what happened to Caine. Okay? I can't go with you into Boston—not with the daylight. But I'll be here when you get back." She turned to the alley. "Malphas! We're ready to go."

Malphas slipped from the shadows, crossing the rain-slicked cobbles to Aurora and Rosalind.

He shot a wary look to Rosalind. "We can only let the shield down for a few moments, just long enough to ask what danger awaits us on the other side. Any longer, and we risk letting Hunters in—or Drew and his army of godsforsaken demons."

"I've got it," Rosalind said. "Let's do it."

She leaned against the fountain, feeling its cool water over her fingertips. She closed her eyes, and Malphas's aura began to crackle the air around her. The smell of burnt air enveloped her, and electric shadow magic began creeping over her body. She arched her back as her own magical stores began to well within her. A hollow opened in her chest as a cold and ancient power ignited in her veins. She opened her eyes, staring at the shield's silvery sheen in the sky, just below the lingering storm clouds.

A deep, silver aura curled from her body, snaking up to the sky. Her magic curled around Malphas's, intertwining like lovers' bodies. Power flooded her muscles, and she watched as their magic ate gaps in the shield. As she stared up at the dark sky, a painful image flashed in her mind: sitting in an empty room, her own dead face pressed against the other side of the glass. She shuddered as the image cleared.

As the shield above her began to thin, she heard Aurora chanting in Angelic. A new magic rippled over her skin, smooth as silk. "Nyxobas, show us the danger that awaits these two as they travel into Cambridge," Aurora said.

Rosalind glanced down at the fountain's rippling surface, watching it swirl with silver and black magic.

Slowly, an image began to form—a face so beautiful it pained her. Golden skin, perfect lips—and eyes black as pitch. Caine's lips were curled back in a vicious snarl. The face of an angel, twisted with wrath. The bestial look in his eyes sent ice through her veins.

As the image clarified, her panic worsened. Bathed in milky white sunlight, black wings arched behind his back. He moved with a terrifying grace.

Rosalind's heart sped up. "What's going on?"

"We need to close the shield," Malphas said. "We can't leave it open."

Caine seemed to be stalking toward someone, like a beast of prey. The image clouded again.

"Rosalind," shouted Malphas. "We need to close the shield!"

Her pulse raced, and she looked up to the skies again, letting Nyxobas' power flow through her like a river of shadow. Magic surged to the skies, curling over the gaps in the shield.

What happened to Caine? He'd hardly even looked human. She had the unsettling feeling that she'd just seen his true face—and it was terrifying. She closed her eyes as the magic whirled from her body, and her head throbbed.

Caine was in trouble—deep trouble. How had everything become so royally fucked up?

Drew. It all came down to Drew, and the power-hungry maniacs like Randolph Loring. Had she really looked up to him once? When she found the bastards leading the Brotherhood, she wanted to burn them. A flame for Caine, a flame for Miranda. One for Cleo. She'd sow a garden of pyres across the city.

She could feel Cleo's purr of approval at the thought of burning Hunters. At least Cleo's voice had gone quieter—ever since Ambrose had made his confession. Maybe she wouldn't have to fuck him and burn him anymore.

Malphas touched her arm. "Rosalind. That's enough for now."

She glanced at him, her breath coming hard and fast. "We still don't know anything. We know Caine's in danger, but not what we're heading into. According to that scrying spell, the danger that awaits us is Caine."

Malphas's face had gone pale. "I can believe that Caine is the most dangerous thing on the other side of the portal."

"What do you mean?" Rosalind asked. "Why would he be dangerous to us?"

Malphas stared at her for a moment before nodding slowly. "I've seen him look that way before. Once, after your parents gave him the second soul."

"When he lost his mind." Her stomach sank. "You think it's happened again?"

"Maybe Drew is controlling him," Aurora said. "He can control his mind with that charmed iron."

Rosalind wanted to be sick. "He wasn't wearing a necklace. Maybe they've given him a scar, like mine."

Malphas shook his head, "Whatever the case, we've got to go after him before they decide to execute him."

"I'm ready," Rosalind said. Already, she was climbing to the fountain's edge. She dipped her feet into the icy water, and Malphas climbed up beside her.

Aurora touched Rosalind's arm. "Please bring him back in one piece."

Rosalind nodded. "I will. I promise."

Before she plunged into the icy water, a dark thought flickered through her mind. *Maybe I should stop making promises I don't know I can keep.*

She let go of the fountain's edge, letting herself sink beneath the water's frigid surface.

CHAPTER 40

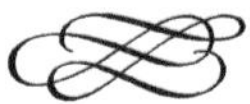

She plunged deeper through the portal, until her lungs burned.

But water couldn't hurt her anymore, not with Dagon's power flooding her veins. As she sunk lower, Dagon's phantom limbs snaked around her, caressing her skin. And when she let her chest unclench, it stopped hurting. Under the water, she no longer needed air. She could stay under the surface as long as she wanted.

Except she had a psychotic incubus to rescue. Her gaze flicked to Malphas, who swam beside her, his eyes beginning to bulge. *He* couldn't breathe down here.

A thin stream of light pierced the surface, and she grabbed Malphas's hand. Kicking her legs, she dragged him up to the light.

When her head breached the surface, she wrapped an arm around Malphas's chest, pulling him up with her. He clung to the ledge on either side of her, his body pressed against hers. Coughs racked his body.

"Thanks," he gasped.

"No problem." She scanned the crypt. Sunlight streamed through latticework over the crypt door. Lucky for them, no one seemed to be lying in wait here. "We should hide ourselves before we go out. We can use the invisibility spell. And as soon as we get out of here, let's move quickly, using shadow magic. I think this cemetery is dangerous. The Brotherhood might be watching it."

Water dripped down his face from his drenched hair. "Where are we going?"

"There's a hill in Huron Village, away from the Brotherhood's headquarters. Hold my hand, and I'll take you in the right direction. And then I'm gonna do a sweep of the city from the air so I can figure out where Caine is."

Malphas body still floated dangerously close to hers. Incubi just couldn't help getting close. "Sounds like you have a plan."

He blinked, as if waking from a dream, then began chanting the spell for invisibility. She felt his magic kiss her skin, and watched as his face shimmered away.

In the icy water, her teeth began to chatter. "Are you ready?" she asked.

"Let's go."

She hoisted herself out of the water, then reached down, feeling for Malphas's arm. She pulled him out, and water splashed to the floor. Grasping his hand, she said, "As soon as we're through this door, I'm taking us to the old Gallows Hill."

"What is it about that name that unsettles me?"

Ignoring the comment, she pushed through the door into the sun. For a moment, the sun blinded her and she blinked hard, trying to adjust. She hadn't seen proper light in weeks.

Then, clutching Malphas's hand, she let Nyxobas's power flow through her body. Shadows whispered through her bones. She focused on a point about twenty yards away, and let the magic carry her on the wind.

She knew that too much shadow running would burn the energy right out of her body, but it was a major rush. With Malphas's hand in her own, she shifted from one spot to another through the winding cemetery paths. As she moved, a warm, floral breeze rushed over her skin, toying with her hair.

Gods, it feels good to be in the light again. Even as she got power from the god of night, the sunlight felt glorious on her skin. With Malphas by her side, she rushed through the cemetery gates, down Mount Auburn Street to Brattle, and further up Avon Hill, whirring past the towering wood-frame houses.

At the top of the hill, her muscles burned, and fatigue pulsed through her body. They stopped by a dark wooden mansion, and Rosalind caught her breath.

By her side, Malphas's broad form began shimmering into view. "You're already becoming visible," he said.

"So are you."

"The invisibility spell won't hold long when you're burning through power like that."

Her pulse raced. "Well that's a real fucking liability. I can't be flashing into the Hunters' view while I'm expecting to be invisible."

"You have the power of seven gods now. Just like Drew. Maybe you don't need to be invisible."

True, but a thought nagged at the back of her mind. "I've seen how Caine operates. He stays focused on his objective, and he doesn't let the enemy know more about him than they need to. When we were imprisoned together in the Chambers, he took pains to make sure they had no idea what his powers were. He didn't want them to know his strength. We're here for one reason, and one reason only, right?"

"To drag Caine back to Lilinor."

"We're not here to defeat the Brotherhood and Drew. We'll do that when we have an army together. So I don't want to let Drew know I have this power."

"What exactly do you have planned?"

She felt a flicker of vernal magic stir in her chest. "I'm going to let Cleo fight this battle—or at least it will look that way." She let Cleo's magic snake over her body, curling over her skin and hair.

"Come out to play, Cleo." As the magic wound over her dark hair, she watched as it lengthened and turned blond. She felt her legs elongate, her hips narrow.

When she looked at Malphas, his eyes had gone wide.

"How do I look?" she asked.

"Like someone completely different. I had no idea you could do that."

"Cleo's been desperate to come out." She gazed down the hill, looking for any signs of chaos or destruction, but everything seemed normal on Mass Ave. Maybe she'd taken them too far from the Brotherhood's headquarters. She'd need a proper aerial view. "I'm going to find Caine. I'll signal to you with lightning, okay? When I find him, shadow run in the direction of the striking lightning."

"Do you really have that much control over your powers?"

"I created a damn fine storm not that long ago."

She glanced up at the cloudless sky, then closed her eyes. A cool wind rippled over her skin, and she held out her arms. Mentally, she called to the storm-god, and his ancient magic pooled in her body. Raw power ignited her veins, and she opened her eyes to find the sky churning with dark clouds.

A cold wind whipped at her pale hair. Or rather, Cleo's hair.

As she arched her back, the heavens opened, and a hard rain began to fall, soaking her clothes. She cast one last look back at Malphas, then let the wind rush through her body, lifting her with it. She swooped into the air, soaring over Cambridge's wooden houses and brick buildings, racing over Mass Ave. As she soared further along, a wave of horror washed over her. The city had changed completely closer to the square. Gone were the old wooden houses and squat buildings that lined the street; now it was all towering stone edifices, built to look like roman temples and colosseums.

And the closer she got to the Brotherhood's Chambers, the more a sense of unease began to crawl over her skin.

The good news was that no one was looking at her. The bad news was that they weren't looking at her because they seemed to be fleeing from Harvard square—not unlike the time that the keres had attacked.

Rain battered her skin, and she soared over Harvard, flying in the opposite direction of those fleeing. She was moving south, toward the Charles—the river that the Hunters had named after their witch-killing king. At least the river had a tactical advantage. If Nyxobas allowed it, she'd be able to use the water as a portal back to Lilinor.

But as she soared toward the river, her blood turned to ice. Wooden stakes jutted from one of the stone bridges that arced over the Charles, just waiting to burn the bodies of heretics. No wonder the people of Cambridge were terrified. And no wonder the Brotherhood needed a scapegoat to keep everyone in line.

As she swooped along the river, horror punched her in the gut again. There, on the road that gently curved round the river's side, she saw the pale silver glow of Caine's magic, curling from his body. He stalked down the center of Memorial Drive, black wings swooping from his back.

Around him, cars had smashed into each other. Black smoke curled from the wrecks, and shattered glass littered the pavement. And worse—broken and bloodied human bodies lay strewn on the ground in pools of blood. Had Caine done this?

She flicked her wrist at the clouds, letting Mishett-Ash's magic race through her fingertips into the sky. A sharp spear of lightning touched down on the river, illuminated the sky. Instantly, thunder cracked over the horizon.

She flicked her wrist once more, calling forth another sharp crack of lightning.

As the rain battered her body, she circled overhead, searching Caine's face for clues. His eyes were black as the void, his lip curled disdainfully. The way he prowled the street, muscles coiled, he looked like an angel of death.

And he wasn't wearing a necklace.

Had Drew managed to carve the mark of Azazeyl into his skin? Or had he lost his mind again—like he had in Maremount, all those years ago?

She circled again, watching with a growing sense of horror as he ripped off a car door. He pulled an injured man from the passenger's seat. The crash had crushed the man's legs, and he screamed in terror at the sight of Caine.

Okay. Time to stop this.

Rosalind swooped lower. Slowly, Caine's gaze slid to her, and he cocked his head. As he did, he snapped the man's neck, letting him fall to the ground.

She landed in front of him, her body buzzing with the icy fury of a valkyrie. Caine's aura blazed from his body, slicing the air around her. He took a step closer. A part of her felt terrified at his cold gaze. A part of her wanted to run—or fly—as fast as she could from his bone-chilling demonic rage.

But the valkyrie's strength coursed through her blood, cold and ancient as Caine's own power. She didn't want to fight him—but she could if she needed to.

"Caine," she said. "It's me. Rosalind."

A low growl escaped his throat. In a blur of shadow magic, he reached for her throat—but she was faster. She leapt out of his way, jumping back again and again—until she slammed into the back of a car.

Shit.

In the next second, Caine's hands were around her throat, ready to snap her neck. She raised her arms, slamming them into his forearms with the full force of Borgerith's strength. He dropped his grip on her, surprise alighting in his eyes, then moved toward her again.

Letting Nyxobas's magic whisper through her blood, she lunged for him, landing a punch at the speed of a hurricane gale. Her fist slammed into his jaw, knocking him off balance. He staggered back. She wanted a chance to see what she was up against—if he'd lost his mind, or if Drew had marked him.

Swift as the wind, she rushed at him again, ripping through the front of his shirt. She scanned his skin—just long enough to see his smooth abs, free from Azazeyl's mark—and in the next moment, his hands were around her throat again.

Okay, so he's lost his mind. Her heart thrummed.

And then she realized: Maybe he didn't know who she was.

Cleo, drop the glamour.

Instantly, she felt Cleo's aura flush from her blood. She felt her body shift, watching as her blond hair darkened in the corner of her eye. As it did, Caine's eyes widened, his fingers loosening on her throat.

"Caine," she said. If he *had* lost his mind, she actually had no idea how to cure it. She had neither the time nor the expertise to act as his psychotherapist right now. "It's me. It's Rosalind."

He leaned in closer, his body warming hers. It didn't seem like he wanted to rip her throat out anymore. But he definitely wanted *something*. He thrust his fingers into her hair, tugging back her head. He growled again, low and animal, and his teeth skimmed her throat. His fingers found her waist, gripping her tight. He had her pinned to the car, but at least he wasn't trying to kill her anymore.

"Caine," she said. "This isn't the time."

The wail of sirens pierced the air, and her heart began to race. They were coming for Caine.

She reached up, gripping his face, trying to get through to him. "Caine. What the hell is going on with you? I need to take you to a portal. I think we can use the river."

His eyes narrowed, but she wasn't convinced he understood a word she was saying.

Fuck it. She'd have to use her new brute strength. She cupped her hands around his neck, then slammed the top of her head into his face.

He staggered back again, dazed just for a moment. As she wound up again for a punch to his jaw, he caught her wrist, twisting it behind her back. He slammed her against the car, pressing against her.

Shit. Maybe she'd underestimated *his* brute strength.

"Caine!" she shouted. "You're acting like a psycho! Stop it or I will beat the shit out of you!"

Okay. So maybe that wasn't the most subtle of psychological techniques, but it was all she had time for. Caine leaned in again, growling, and his breath warmed the side of her face. He seemed to be enjoying this. In fact, from what she could feel pressing against her back, he was *definitely* enjoying this.

She raised her foot, smashing it down onto his. He grunted, but kept his grip on her.

The wailing of sirens drew closer, and she heard the screeching of brakes just behind her.

"Caine!" she shouted. Where the hell was Malphas?

In the next second, a hail of bullets ripped through the air, and Caine's body jerked against hers. Her world tilted, and the pure panic seizing her mind. *Iron bullets, probably.* They'd do some damage to Caine. She was damn lucky the bullets hadn't pierced through his flesh to hers, or they'd be stranded here without magic.

She turned to Caine, ready to shadow run with him to the river. But just as she wrapped her arms around his slumping body, a team of Hunters ripped him away.

And, in the next moment, Drew stepped from an armored vehicle, dressed in a black suit. He flicked his wrist, and Borgerith's magic shot from his fingertips. All the air left Rosalind's lungs, and she felt the weight of a ton of rocks pressing on her chest, pressing her in place. She stared, wide-eyed, as a team of black-clad Hunters dragged Caine toward the bridge.

As her ribs threatened to snap and pierce her lungs, one thought blazed in her mind like a torch in the night:

They're going to burn him.

CHAPTER 41

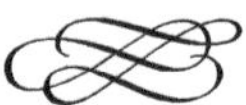

*D*rew clasped his arms tightly around her, still pressing the air from her lungs. She had magic now—the same as he did. But he'd had a lot more practice.

He dragged her to the bridge, her feet scraping over the pavement. As he did, she closed her eyes, focusing on pushing the tendrils of copper magic from her body—just enough that she could gasp for air. When she opened her eyes again, Drew gripped her chin, forcing her face to look in the direction of Caine.

The Hunters were chaining his slumped body to a stake. A crowd of onlookers had gathered at the Bridge's southern entrance.

I need to get us out of here.

She had no clue what was going on with Caine, but she wasn't going to let the Hunters burn him.

He didn't have a scar marking his skin, wasn't wearing any iron that had been specially treated with magic. And yet, he'd just slaughtered all those people. He'd attacked her, too. Sure, the man had secrets, but she just couldn't believe that this was really him.

She watched the Hunters pile wood on the pyre, and she strained to muster her magic as Drew crushed her lungs. If she could summon Borgerith's power like Drew could, maybe she could fight him back.

She struggled for another breath, trying to force the copper tendrils from her body.

But it was kind of hard to summon powerful magic when you couldn't breathe.

Her heart threatened to jump out of her chest. The rain had slowed to a dull trickle, not enough to douse the flames—especially not now, as the Hunters doused the wood just below Caine's feet with gasoline. Pure panic ripped through her mind.

Drew leaned in close, whispering into her ear, "Now you'll get what you deserve, my wife. You'll get to watch your lover die. Slowly, painfully, and without dignity. I want to watch the pain in your eyes as his skin blackens. Perhaps I'll make you light the flames to burn your lover."

She tried to suck in another breath, watching as Drew pulled a syringe filled with dark liquid from his coat pocket. A single thought struck her, like a bullet to the brain: *There's iron in blood.* Not a lot— not enough to extinguish magic. But maybe it was enough for Drew to control someone if the iron had been charmed.

Drew gripped her wrist, ready to inject.

Her pulse raced. She couldn't let him do this, or she'd have no chance of getting Caine out of here. *Maybe I'll have better luck with Druloch. Come on, Cleo.*

Green magic simmered over her skin.

As Drew lifted her sleeve, a rope of vines shot from her wrist, wrapping around Drew's neck. He clutched at his throat, and the magic crushing her chest lifted from her.

She glanced at Caine. To her horror, flames already curled around his feet.

A Hunter pointed a gun to her head. "Stop the spells!" he shouted.

Not a chance.

Her gaze flicked to the river, and she let Dagon's power ripple through her body, vibrating through her bones. The river churned, then roared as an enormous wave crested over the bridge, knocking the Hunters off balance. Black smoke curled into the air as water doused the flames.

So much for keeping my magic hidden.

She shadow ran to Caine. Using the strength of the mountain goddess, she tore the iron chains from his body. Already, the Hunters were mustering again, and Drew was breaking free from his chokehold.

She let vernal magic simmer in her body, then unleashed it on the bridge. In the next moment, vines sprouted from the bridge, weaving around the Hunters and Drew. A blur of shadow moved through them, and she heaved a sigh of relief. *Malphas.*

He stopped just before her, catching his breath.

"Use the river as a portal!" she shouted. "Take Caine to Ambrose, and tell Ambrose to drain his blood."

Malphas was already dragging Caine across the bridge. "You want him to *what?*"

"Just trust me! Drain his blood. He'll recover."

She watched as Malphas leapt over the side of the bridge, with Caine in his arms.

This was it: her chance to kill Drew, while he was completely within her control. She turned to her cousin, watching the tendrils of colored magic whirl from his body. She lifted her hand, and Emerazel's fire sparked from the tips of her fingers.

Deep in her chest, Cleo's aura thrilled at her power. *Roast these bastards alive.*

But just as the golden magic roared through her blood, Drew broke free from the plants' constraints. Moving on the wind, he leapt for her, punching her in the head with a loud *crack.*

Dizzy, she staggered to the edge of the bridge.

The portal is still open. It must be.

From behind, Drew gripped her hair, but she pulled away from him. As fast as she could, she climbed over the edge of the bridge, and leapt into the churning dark waters below.

As she plunged below the chilly surface, she felt a powerful hand grasp her leg, and her stomach sank.

CHAPTER 42

osalind swam below the water's surface, trying to free herself from Drew's iron grip. Shadow magic whirled around them.

The shield wouldn't let Drew into the city.

Unless—if Drew was clinging to her body, would the shield let him through?

She didn't want to find out.

Frantically, she tried kicking her way free of him, but he climbed higher up her body, wrapping his arms around hers. And even as she squirmed and writhed in his arms, she only kicked herself further toward the surface, until pale moonlight began to pierce the murky water.

It wasn't until they'd reached the air that she was able to gain enough leverage to wiggle one of her arms free—but by then, Drew had already breached the shield. She hammered his face hard with a volley of punches, until he dropped his grip on her.

I'm gonna have to fight him on land.

She grasped for a rocky ledge, pulling herself out into the cool night air, and launched over the fountain's edge—the same one they'd used to leave Lilinor. She landed hard on the cobblestones and yanked an iron knife from her belt, widening her stance.

I'm ready for you, cousin.

In the next moment, Drew burst from the fountain. Before his feet could even land on the pavement, she hurled the knife at his chest. His green eyes opened wide in shock, and he staggered back.

But it only took him a fraction of a second to rip the knife from his chest. He lunged for her, his movements too fast for an ordinary human to track. But with Nyxobas's power flooding her body, she saw him coming. She kicked him in the face, cracking his nose with her foot. Immediately, she dodged back. As he swung for her, she ducked, bringing up her fist into his groin.

She rose, letting the power of seven gods soar in her body.

I can take you, Cousin.

While he hunched over, in pain, she kicked him hard in the gut. He grunted, clutching his stomach.

But when he raised his green eyes to her, a chill rippled over her. There was no longer anything human in his gaze, just the senseless wrath of insane gods.

She pulled another knife from her belt, ready to throw. But with a tremendous roar, Drew leapt for her, knocking her back onto the pavement. The full weight of his body pressed on her, and he gripped her hair. Screaming like a wild beast, he smashed her head into the pavement—once, twice, three times.

Pain ripped through her skull, so sharp she thought she'd die. Dizziness surged over her, and she struggled to push him off.

Drew tightened his fingers around her throat, squeezing hard. Blood ran from his lip. Through gritted teeth, he said, "My wife. I know how to make you behave. I know how to make you serve me."

He pressed on her throat harder, threatening to crush her windpipe. How many seconds did she have before he crushed the life out of her? She needed to muster her magic—her strength. *Borgerith.* She envisioned the copper magic welling in her belly.

But just as she was starting to build her strength, Drew reached into his pocket. She stared in horror as he pulled out another syringe.

"I know you can be a sweet wife, when I tame you." He stabbed the needle into her chest. "I need to punish you, and break your will. Then you'll be my little toy."

He depressed the plunger, and panic ripped her mind apart.

But there's iron in blood.

And Borgerith controls magnetism…

As soon as Drew pulled the syringe from her skin, she focused on letting Borgerith's copper magic whirl around her chest, trying to draw the iron from her own blood, through that tiny hole in her skin. But even as she tried to focus, her thoughts began to move slowly, as ice seemed to encase her mind.

What *was* she trying to do?

Drew unclenched his grip on her neck, leaning down to stare into her face. Gently, Drew stroked the side of her face, then he leaned in closer to lick her cheek.

Somewhere, beneath the ice of her mind, she recoiled.

"Do you know," he purred, "I feel very close to you. I think I even understand some of your worst fears. I can see them in your dark eyes. We've got rid of Miranda, haven't we? But it wasn't enough. I have something even better in mind for you."

He gripped her hair, cracking her head against the stone once again.

* * *

SHE WOKE, flat on her back, in the bottom of a grave, staring up at the starry sky.

No—not quite the bottom of a grave. She couldn't quite clarify her thoughts, but she had a vague sense of lying on top of soft, rotten limbs. *A mass grave.*

The thought moved slowly under her mind's frozen surface, like an ice floe.

As a powerful stench registered, another thought simmered dimly under the ice: *I'm in the whore pit.*

Horror stole her breath, but she couldn't quite remember what she needed to do, or why she was here. She didn't seem to be able to control her own body.

A man leaned over the grave's edge. The moon formed a silver halo around his head. His green eyes pierced the dark, beautiful and intense. And yet, the sight of his face curdled her stomach.

"Comfortable, are you?" He frowned. "Is this what they call the whore pit? I'll wager they buried your sister here." He narrowed his eyes. "Now which rotten body is she? Do you suppose you're on top of her?"

The words sent a cold shiver up Rosalind's spine. There was something she needed to do—some way she could get out of this, but she couldn't formulate a clear thought. Not with all this ice encasing her mind.

The man shrugged. She thought his name might be Drew.

Suddenly, his face contorted with rage. "Fitting, isn't it, for my wife? The whore pit. After what you did with Caine." His face turned red, and panic gripped Rosalind's chest.

"When I break your mind," he continued, "you'll serve me eagerly, or I'll rip your bones from your body. Do you understand, little whore?" Spittle flew from his mouth.

Would anyone hear him yell?

She stared up at the night sky as Drew began flinging earth on top of her. Her chest tightened. Desperately, she tried to pick out clear thoughts, but they slid under the surface or her mind. Somewhere, under the glacier, she formed a thought about the bodies beneath her, slick and rotting. About the stench turning her stomach.

Thump. A clump of dirt hit her in the face, and she gasped.

Another thought bubbled to the surface. The one about how she wouldn't be able to breathe with all that dirt covering her. How she'd die down here in the whore pit. There was something she needed to do to break free...

Thump. The earth felt heavy from the recent rain—more mud than dirt.

She glanced to her right, vaguely registering a woman's half-rotten arm.

A long time ago, someone had told her it would end this way. *Buried in the whore pit.*

Thump. Particles of dirt slipped into her mouth, trickling down her throat. As the earth rained down, her body began to shake, that one phrase burning clearer under the ice. *Buried in the whore pit.*

Drew hurled another shovelful of dirt onto her face, and she gagged at the mud trickling down her throat.

This wasn't how it was supposed to end.

Sunlight, the smell of the ocean. Oak trees. Water on skin. The call of a golden-crowned sparrow.

She moved her head back, just an inch, and gasped for air. Within a few minutes, inches of dirt covered her body, until she couldn't see, could hardly breathe. And yet, under the dirt and the ice, rage began to simmer, burning away the ice.

Now, Miranda's words began to ring in her mind, clear as a bell. *Sometimes, what's buried doesn't stay underground.*

Before the glaciers had gripped her mind, she'd been trying to free herself. She'd had some kind of plan. *Get the iron out of your blood.*

Her body wasn't quite moving like it should, but her mind was clearing. Maybe Borgerith's magic *had* worked just enough to clear some of that charmed iron from her blood. Under a thickening layer of earth, she focused on the coppery magic in her body, letting it churn within her ribs. Then she imagined the copper magic drawing out that black liquid in her chest—a magnetic pull through that tiny hole in her skin.

Slowly, Borgerith's magic leached the iron from her blood, and she began to grow dizzy. Still, even as she grew lightheaded, she was able to move her muscles purposefully once more—curling her toes and fingers.

Sometimes, what's buried doesn't stay underground.

She let the magic flow through her muscles, charging her body with power and the speed of Nyxobas. A hot thrill rippled through her as the gods-magic began to blaze through her body. *I'm going to tear your bones from your body, Drew.*

In the next moment, she burst from the grave, dripping with fetid dirt. She leapt over the pit's edge, wind rushing over her skin.

And as her feet hit the ground, her gaze landed on Drew.

She was back from the dead, here to wreak a vengeance of her own.

This time she was moving with the speed of a god, her gaze locked on her prey. She must have looked like a true angel of death, because Drew backed away from her, his eyes wide.

But she wasn't letting him get away.

She rushed for him, slamming her fist into the side of his head, reveling in the crack of bone. She hit him again and again, and his head snapped back. Full of Nyxobas's icy power, she kicked him hard in the gut, and when he bent over, she hammered the back of his skull with her elbow.

He fell to the ground. Quick as a storm wind, she was on top of him, raining down blows onto his face, trying to smash his bones. In the distance, she heard the cry of a valkyrie, and the storm god's fury filled her body. *Go in for the kill.*

She gripped his throat tight, squeezing hard. It would only take a few seconds—

Water magic burst from Drew's body, and in the next second a small pond filled the space around them.

She tightened her grip on his throat. *Fine with me. I'll drown you in a ditch.*

But as the water began to rise higher, shadow magic whirled on its surface.

He's creating a portal.

The bottom seemed to drop out of the earth beneath her, and in a rush of murky water, she lost her grip on Drew.

Holding her breath, she swam for the surface, her fingertips finding purchase in a muddy ledge. She pulled herself out, her heart racing, and backed away from the portal.

She let out a roar. She'd been so damn close to killing him. But she couldn't go after him now. Not now, when she had no clue where that portal went—she'd made that mistake once before, and learned her lesson.

Still, she'd come for him soon enough.

Nausea gripped her gut, and she fell to her hands and knees in the mud, vomiting.

After another minute of catching her breath, she rose and stared at the small pond, still whirling with shadow magic. She wanted to make damn sure Drew wasn't coming back in anytime soon. With the last of her energy, she let shadow magic flow through her fingertips, sealing up the muddy gateway. When she'd finished, the ground had sealed over again—a slick of mud covered with a silver sheen.

She turned to walk back to the fortress, her entire body shaking.

As she walked along the path, a spray of purple-headed flowers caught her eye. Their long, thin petals pierced the air like fireworks, surrounded by green leaves. She reached for one, but as soon as she touched one of the leaves, the plant seemed to fold into itself, shrinking away from her.

Rosalind didn't know the name of this plant, but Cleo did.

Morivivi.

I died. I lived.

She plucked two blossoms from the plant—one for her, and one for Miranda.

These are for our new crowns—the ones we deserve.

CHAPTER 43

$\mathcal{W}$ith shaking legs, Rosalind stepped into the candlelit hall on Caine's floor. Filthy mud covered her body, and she looked like a swamp monster.

She crossed through the hall toward Caine's room. She didn't particularly want him to see her caked in mud and puke, but he had a bath in his room. Plus, she wanted to see how he was doing after Ambrose drained his blood.

Raw fatigue burned through her body as she walked the corridor, and each step felt like agony. It was a good thing she hadn't followed Drew through the portal, because she was pretty sure she didn't have a single drop of magic left in her body right now.

Drew had nearly killed her out there. Nearly suffocated her in the whore pit.

Mass grave, she mentally corrected herself. No need to insult the dead.

Her sodden feet left muddy tracks over the stones. At last, her gaze landed on the portrait of Lord Byron.

The door stood partially ajar—just the way she'd left it—and she pushed it open the rest of the way. *Empty.* No one lay on his silver sheets, and a single candle flickered in a sconce.

She dropped her two *morivivi* flowers on a wood table, then crossed to the bath.

Exhaling with relief, she turned on the hot water. As the steam rose from the bath, she pulled off her filthy clothes, dropping them onto Caine's floor. She'd clean all this up later, once she'd washed herself.

As she stepped into the bath, the warm water soothed her aching muscles. She submerged herself in the water up to her waist, and the caked dirt and blood lifted from her body, muddying the water. She pulled the soap from the edge of the tub, rubbing it over her skin, breathing in the soothing scent of lavender.

She still had to find a way to work things out with Caine. She couldn't tell him Miranda had slept with Ambrose.

Then again, maybe there was no point in correcting him. It wasn't as if anything could happen between her and Caine again. For one thing, he'd told her he didn't really care. And for another, he'd never be able to know about Miranda.

She rinsed her hair under the faucet, clearing the mud from it, watching it swirl into the water. She was basically bathing in mud at this point.

She uncorked the drain, letting the filthy water swirl down, then rinsed her limbs again under the faucet. She grabbed a cloth from the side of the bath, scrubbing at her skin until it looked raw.

Bending down once more, she rinsed her face again under the tap, scrubbing off all the muck with a ferocity that would wake the dead. As she washed her face, it occurred to her that she hadn't brought anything to change into, but she'd just have to borrow a long shirt from Caine.

With the last of the muck rinsed from her skin, she straightened, and her heart skipped a beat.

While she'd been washing herself, Miranda had crept into the room. She now stood by Caine's bed. As if on a ghostly breeze, her torn and blood-stained nightgown billowed around her. Her knuckles were bleeding, her fingernails chewed down to the bone.

The look in her sister's eyes unnerved Rosalind, and she shivered. "What are you doing here, Miranda?"

Miranda cocked her head. "Where did you go?"

Water dripped down Rosalind's skin, and she hugged herself, shivering. "I went after Caine in Boston. Drew seized control of his mind, then tried to burn him." She stepped from the bath.

"And he lived?" Miranda asked, her voice dull.

As Rosalind stepped from the bath, water splashed onto the floor. "Malphas dragged him back here through the portal. I'm guessing he's in Ambrose's White Tower. He should be able to make a fast recovery." She crossed the room to the wardrobe, trying to ignore the unsettling feeling of the hair raising on the back of her neck.

She should probably ask about the blood on her sister's hands, but she didn't want to.

I'll just pretend everything is normal.

"What's all the dirt from?" Miranda asked.

Rosalind pulled open Caine's wardrobe, and pulled out a towel. "Drew tried to bury me in the mass grave."

"You were luckier than I was, since you made it out alive."

Rosalind wrapped the towel around herself, trying to ignore the guilt nagging at her mind. "That's certainly true."

"Maybe you shouldn't have brought me back," Miranda said, her voice breaking.

"Why?"

"There's something wrong with me." A tear rolled down her cheek. "I'm empty inside, and I can't fill the void no matter what I do."

Rosalind shook her head. "We can fix this. There must be a spell to heal your mind."

Miranda's forehead crinkled, as if she was confused, and she pulled up the hem of her gown. Strapped to her thigh was a knife, which she pulled from its sheath.

Rosalind's heart thudded.

Miranda cocked her head, her eyes filling with tears. "But you can't fix me." She hurled the knife at Rosalind, striking her in the chest. Rosalind staggered back, dropping her towel. Pain ripped through her chest, and she stared down at the blade protruding from her body. Blood gushed from the wound.

"Miranda!" she shouted. "Why are you doing this?"

Panic stole her breath.

I need to pull it out.

She reached for the hilt, but Miranda was already kneeling before her, yanking the blade free. She reared back her arm to stab again, but as she did a blur of silvery shadow magic streamed into the room.

Rosalind stared in horror as Caine pulled Miranda off her—then, swift as a phantom wind, snapped her neck with a loud *crack.*

The one blunt sound ended Miranda's life for the final time.

The world seemed to fall from beneath Rosalind.

"Caine!" she shouted, tears stinging her eyes.

He leaned down, scooping Rosalind up in his powerful arms and carrying her to his bed. Brow furrowed, he said, "I told you not to bring her back."

Tears spilled down her cheek. "You killed her."

Gently, he laid her down on his bed. "I had to," he said softly. "I need to heal you."

She shot a glance at Miranda, whose body lay crumpled on the floor. "What was wrong with her?"

Caine's fingertips traced along the perimeter of the gash on the front of her shoulder, and magic curled from his fingertips. "I once raised someone from the dead. But I soon learned it was a mistake." His eyes glistened as his hand hovered above her chest. "I regret it, even now. When you raise a body from the dead, there is a price. And the price is that Nyxobas keeps some of their soul in the void."

"Why didn't you tell me this?"

His eyes clouded with unspoken grief. "I can't bring myself to talk about it."

Deep sorrow pierced Rosalind's chest. "So part of Miranda is still in the shadow void?" No wonder she'd felt empty.

Caine's gaze met hers. "Yes, but I can help. It took me years to learn how, but I can travel to the void and free her."

Caine's magic soothed her muscles, healing the tears and leaching away the pain. Faintly, Miranda's voice rang in the back of Rosalind's skull. *Sunlight, the smell of the ocean. Oak trees. Water on skin. The call of a golden-crowned sparrow.*

"When I traveled to the shadow void, I saw my own face there. Dead." A hot tear spilled down her cheek. "Maybe it wasn't me, after all. Maybe it was a vision of Miranda."

Caine wiped the tear from her cheek. "We're going to hold another death feast. You'll tell Miranda's story. And when you're finished, I'll claim her soul back from Nyxobas." He leaned in, touching his forehead against hers. Her heart had broken, but Caine's soothing aura dulled some of the pain. He pulled away from her, glancing at the mud spattering his room, his hand cupped around her neck. "What happened to you?"

"Drew followed me through the portal into Lilinor. He injected me with that iron. Like he did to you."

"He was waiting for me when I came through." Caine's eyes darkened, the candle dimming. "Is he still here?"

She shook her head. "No. He tried to bury me in the whore—in the mass grave. Flung dirt all over me. But I got the iron out."

Caine traced his thumb over her cheek. "So you did better than I did. I didn't make it out of there on my own."

She glanced at Miranda again, and raw grief washed over her.

Caine pulled away from her, covering her in his soft, silver blankets. "Close your eyes," he said. "I'm going to take Miranda away."

"I've left the remnants of a grave all over your room." She shivered, then a thought sparked in the back of her mind. "Caine? Why did you say I was lucky, after Miranda died? What was lucky about it?"

He touched her shoulder, and her mind began to calm again. "Get some rest, Rosalind. Tomorrow, you need to speak over your sister's grave, and then we'll free her soul."

She wasn't sure she'd ever sleep again—not after the horror of tonight. But after Caine carried Miranda's body from the room, fatigue claimed her mind, and she drifted into a deep sleep.

Rosalind stood, flanked by Caine, and Tammi. Moonlight streamed through the yew, dancing over the black casket deep in the earth. Behind them stood Ambrose, Malphas, and Aurora.

In one hand, Rosalind clutched a fistful of morivivi flowers—in the other, the dried wreath Miranda had woven from bluebells, ivy, and poppies. She turned from the grave, walking to the yew. Her finger shook as she tied the wreath with a shimmering blue ribbon marked with Miranda's name. Clutching the flowers, she turned back to the open grave.

Caine rested his hand on her back for reassurance, letting his aura wash over her.

She took a deep breath. "When she first died, I didn't remember our past. She died, and she lived again. And when she did, she told me the stories about us I didn't remember. How we built ships of wood, and we'd sail them in Athanor Pond. About her meadowlark named Poppet, and the little bird's viking funeral in a flaming boat."

As she spoke, the memory suddenly blazed in her mind: the tiny wooden boat, floating out in the dark waters of Athanor Pond; Miranda standing by her side, holding her hand.

"You told me we'd sneak out at night with Malphas, and we'd lay in the dandelion beds watching the shooting stars. For years, you wandered the cities, looking for me. Your own dream stayed constant as the North Star—our own little house, our own family."

Rosalind closed her eyes, breathing in the scent of muddy earth and the yew's boughs. She could nearly feel the bluebells in the grass beneath her, when she'd lay next to her sister. She plucked one of the morivivi flowers from the bunch, tossing it in the grave. *One for sunlight. One for the ocean.* She tossed them in, one by one. *One for the oak trees, and for water on skin. One for the call of the golden-crowned sparrow.*

She swallowed hard, turning from the grave. Grief pressed hard on her chest as she trod the path through the cemetery. Silently, Caine walked by her side.

She'd laid her sister in the cold earth for the final time, before Miranda had gotten the chance to really live. Drew—and her parents —had robbed Miranda of the life she deserved—a family and a home, where Miranda would paint portraits and thread her wildflower wreaths. Where she'd feel the rain on her skin, the warmth of the hearth. Where she could, at last, have lived among people who loved her.

Rosalind's chest ached.

As they walked up the path, Rosalind lost herself in visions of what might have been. The other life. The one that should have existed, but didn't...

Making tea. Talking about dates. Drinking too much on the weekends. They'd been so close to that reality that it almost seemed tangible, even now—as if somewhere out there, another Rosalind and Miranda sat on a sofa in a small house in the woods, laughing at each other's stupid jokes, bickering over who got to shower next.

As the others silently walked inside the fortress, Rosalind stood outside the castle walls, staring up at the night sky. It didn't seem quite right to leave Miranda in that cold field by herself. Caine remained quietly by her side—silent, but just close enough for the heat from his body to warm hers.

After a while, clouds began to gather on the horizon. Somewhere, below the sharp pang of grief, rage began to simmer.

"Caine?" she said at last.

"Yes?"

"I want to destroy the Brotherhood for what they've done to Miranda. And to Cleo, and all the countless others."

"You will," he said quietly. "And I'll be right by your side when you do."

DIVINE HUNTER -
BOOK FOUR

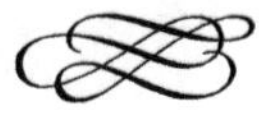

CHAPTER 1

osalind sat between Tammi and Aurora on a soft, silver blanket, listening to the bells tinkling over Miranda's grave. Shimmering ribbons intertwined with the yew branches, and with the baubles and trinkets left to remember the dead. On a long, opalescent ribbon, Caine had written the name *Miranda.*

With the picnic spread out before them, she couldn't help but think of their last picnic together—just like their last party, except one of them was dead.

It had been three weeks since they'd buried Miranda. For some reason, Rosalind felt the need to show up here every now and then for lunch or dinner to keep Miranda company, even though Miranda's soul had already moved on.

She took a sip of strong coffee from a silver thermos, the bitter brew sparking her mind with energy.

Tammi toyed with the ends of her silver-white hair. "If the bells are the spirits speaking to us, how are we supposed to know what they're saying?"

"I have no idea," Rosalind said. "I think they just like attention."

Aurora frowned. "Not sure I really believe the legend. Bells also chime when wind goes through them, and being as it is that we're outside, the air is moving a bit."

"You're the one who told me about the bells in the first place," Rosalind said.

"I talk a lot of shit."

"Someone's a bit cranky this morning," Tammi mumbled.

"I suppose," Aurora said. "I spent too long at Cerberus's last night. I didn't know it was still possible to get hangovers when you're dead, but apparently it is."

"Who is Cerberus?" Tammi asked.

Aurora took a sip of coffee. "He runs one of Lilinor's bars, not far from Ninlil Fortress. The one with the gargoyles. Blood, vodka, a bit of brawling, all the good stuff."

"And why haven't you taken us there?" Tammi asked.

Aurora scowled. "We are in the middle of a crisis here in Lilinor. Rosalind's cousin broke our defenses again."

"Please," Rosalind said. "Don't remind me that I'm related to him." After all, Drew was the reason Miranda was no longer here. And then, two weeks ago, he'd stolen Erish from Lilinor's prisons. The former queen of Lilinor was Drew's key to creating demons—his secret weapon.

Aurora straightened. "In light of these disturbing events—and our possible impending demise—it seemed more appropriate to go to the bar on my own. Less cheerful, you know? I could hunch over the bar, brood about things, have my bloody Marys that way. More respectful."

"Fair enough," Tammi said. "Any ideas about how we're getting out of this crisis so we can hit the bars together?"

Rosalind heaved a sigh. "Sure, I have an idea. We just have to break into the Brotherhood's magically-protected headquarters and retrieve an ancient succubus from an insane god-man. Then kill his entire empire of fanatics. Simple."

Tammi narrowed her eyes. "There's something you're not telling me."

Perceptive as usual, but Rosalind was saying no more. "It's as simple as that."

Tammi pointed at her. "And you don't have a particular plan that you're hiding from me?"

"I'm still working on something, but if you have any ideas, let me know."

Tammi couldn't know the truth, or she'd never let Rosalind leave.

Aurora refilled her cup with steaming coffee. "Any idea what Drew is up to with the succubus?"

"Creating his legion of demons, I imagine, so he can invade Lilinor, kill everyone, and impregnate me with his hell-spawn." She bit her lip. "I think I might need to hit up Cerberus's for a brooding drink after this discussion."

Tammi winced. "What are Ambrose and Caine planning to do to stop that from happening?"

"Just that we get Erish back from Drew before we find ourselves completely outnumbered. I'm sure Caine will come up with a plan."

A flicker of movement under the stars caught Rosalind's attention. A raven circled overhead, her wings silvered in the moonlight.

Lilu—Caine's raven.

"I guess lunch is over," Rosalind said. "I think that's my signal that I'm due for training again."

Standing, she surveyed the Gelal Fields. Even from here, she could see Caine's powerful, sterling aura curling into the air, gleaming against the night sky. His magic called to her like a siren song.

"More fighting?" Tammi asked.

"He's more keen on teaching me to land punches than for me to use the gods-magic that would actually destroy the Brotherhood."

Aurora narrowed her eyes. "Unlike Caine, I have full confidence in your destructive abilities. Now if you could manage to fuck up the enemy instead of causing chaos on our own side, we'll be getting somewhere."

"Thanks, Aurora," Rosalind said dryly. "Honestly. You kill one demon queen, and no one ever forgets it."

Tammi gave her a thumbs-up. "Go save the world and stuff."

The air felt warm and heavy, full of Lilinor's intoxicating scent of lavender and jasmine. As Rosalind crossed the field, she ran her fingertips over her weapons. She'd dressed in her fighting leather, laden with knives and stakes, and a black corset, her hair pulled into a ponytail.

As she walked toward Caine's aura, she searched the sky for cracks in the shield. The silver barrier—wrought with shadow magic—shimmered faintly, but it had thinned in some places. Drew was eating away at their defenses again, with his magic. No wonder he'd been able to break into the city and capture Erish.

Cleo, her second soul, coiled angrily around her heart. *We'll kill the Hunter King, someday. We'll watch him burn.*

"We certainly will," Rosalind whispered.

As she crossed the grasses, she reached down, plucking a bluebell from the grass. She wrapped the stem between her fingers. Miranda had loved these little blossoms, and they seemed to calm Rosalind's thoughts a little.

Unfortunately for her, the bluebells weren't going to cure the raw ache in her thighs. Caine had been running her ragged with his training, until her muscles burned.

He didn't seem to want her practicing too much magic, so she'd been using swords and axes, and learning to hunt him through the woods. But on her own, when Caine was occupied elsewhere, she spent her free time on the cliffs over the Astarte Sea, trying to master the gods' powers on her own.

The magic itself felt glorious, but she still couldn't control it. Every time she used too much power, the gods would begin to claim her mind, taking over until she'd find herself running wild through the woods, looking for something to kill.

And yet, with every spell, and every throw of a punch, she was one step closer to ridding the earth of the Brotherhood—assuming she hadn't already lost the war.

As she approached Caine, her heart thrummed. Even after everything they'd been through—even after he'd kicked her out of his bedroom for a twat named Esmerelda—she'd never get sick of the sight of him. Slowly, she took in his muscular form, and the starlit gaze that had an irritating tendency to rob her of the power of language.

With the silver magic winding through the air around him, Caine exuded pure power. If she hadn't been jacked up on the magic of seven gods, she never would have dared to fight him—even in training.

"Rosalind." The corner of his mouth twitched, and his eyes slid down her body.

He didn't even have to touch her. Just his gaze made her stomach flutter, and yet—she still didn't know what that woman had been doing in his room.

Esmerelda.

"Are you ready for this?" he asked.

"Battle magic?"

He took a step closer, now so close she could feel the heat coming off his body. "I want to see what you can do in hand-to-hand combat. I don't want you to rely on gods-magic alone."

"How did I know you were going to say that?"

"You've been using it too much. You shouldn't overuse it. You saw what happened to Drew."

"I'm not going to win this war by punching people. I'm gonna need to blow things up."

He arched an eyebrow. "You're not going to win this on your own."

She folded her arms. "Right, but I won't be any use at all without magic. You know that. So we practice both. We fight with our fists, and with the gods-magic that we both possess. Fair?"

Amusement danced in his pale eyes. "Aren't you imperious?"

"I learned from the best." She raised her hand, letting fire spark from her fingertips. Caine might be a demigod, but he wasn't immune to fire the way she was. She smiled at him. "Are you ready for this?"

Before she could work up a real flame, Caine flicked his wrist, freezing the air around them and snuffing out her fire. "You'll have to do better than that, Rosalind."

She closed her eyes, letting the power of the storm god flood her body. Thunder rumbled over the horizon, and electricity charged the air. Ancient rage sang in her blood, and she opened her eyes again, ready to inflict some damage—

Caine was already gone. Storm clouds seethed above. The air was thick with moisture, and she scanned the darkened landscape, searching for the whorls of Caine's silver magic. Pale light shimmered by a blackthorn grove, and she shadow-ran to the spot, letting Nyxobas's magic flood her body.

She arrived, breathless, but Caine's magic was nowhere to be found.

CHAPTER 2

The storm clouds she'd created began to unleash their rain, hammering her skin with fat droplets. Beneath the churning storm, an unkindness of ravens circled. Was Caine among them?

With her gaze fixed on the birds, she almost missed the silver aura curling around her. Caine's strong hands slipped around her, pinning her arms to her sides. He leaned in, whispering, "You're going to have to move faster."

Her body thrilled at his touch, her desires warring with the battle fury. She moved her hips against him, just enough to throw him off guard. Then a quick shift to the side, and she pumped her elbows back into his chest, breaking his grip. Pivoting, she threw a punch, but he caught her fist in his.

His grip was crushing, and he forced her hand down. It took a fraction of a second for him to pin her other wrist. His pale eyes bored into her.

Rain poured from the sky, soaking her clothes.

She let the vernal power of Druloch rush over her skin. She had to control Druloch's power. The forest god was a god of true chaos, and who knew what he'd unleash if she gave in to his will entirely.

Druloch's magic whispered of savagery and orgies, mob rage and lust-crazed lovers fucking against tree trunks. She clenched her jaw, determined to stay in control this time.

While Caine gripped her wrists, she focused on the blackthorn behind him. Willing Druloch to do her will, she forced the boughs to reach for Caine. But as they did, another emotion heated her body.

Visions burned in her mind: The first time she'd kissed Caine in the Salem woods, straddling him in the dirt, fingertips digging into the mud. The feel of his bare skin on hers, his hands on her thighs, the embers burning hot inside her when she kissed his perfect mouth. That was what she should be doing. Why didn't she just do what she wanted? Druloch would set her free.

She focused on the blackthorn boughs, drawing them closer to Caine. She'd root him in place, then make him hers. It was what Druloch wanted—what *she* wanted. The blackthorn branches snaked around Caine's waist, thorns cutting into his skin in streaks of crimson.

He dropped his grip on her, and she moved in closer, pressing against him. She licked her lips, letting her gaze linger over his powerful body. Then she slid her mouth over his rain-slicked neck.

"Rosalind," he said. "This will not be an effective strategy against the Hunters."

She ran her fingertips over his muscled chest, down to his waistband, listening to his sharp intake of breath. Leafy magic whirled around her. She wasn't Rosalind anymore—she was one of Druloch's nymphs.

Caine flexed his muscles, breaking through the ropes of plant that encircled him. The feel of his aura caressing her skin, stroking her thighs, sent shivers of pleasure through her body.

He spun her around, pinning her arms to her waist again. "Rosalind," he whispered. "You're letting the gods take over. This is why gods-magic is dangerous."

Her pulse raced, and his body felt amazing pressed against hers, but she tried to gather her thoughts. She tried to remember what she was supposed to be doing.

"Fighting," Caine said, as if hearing her thoughts. "You were letting Druloch take control."

Druloch's earth magic still pulsed through her body, and the rich scent of the Edin Woods enveloped her. She leaned back into Caine, arching her neck. "I can learn to control it. Tell me how you control it?"

His grip on her softened, and he ran his fingertips over her waist, his touch now slow and lazy. "The gods are like clinging vines. The more you resist them, the tighter they grasp."

"So I need to give in to them? That seems… dangerous."

"Druloch is the god of trances and liberation. You can't resist him too strongly, nor the others." He moved his fingertips to her arm and extended it, before folding her arm to bend at the elbow. She watched, entranced, as he guided her hand into his. "You have to learn to bend to the gods, too. Let down your defenses a little. Yield to them, because if one unyielding force meets another, one of you will break. And it won't be the god."

His loamy scent distracted her. "Right," she said. "I guess I need to work on that."

He pulled away from her, sitting beneath the low boughs of the blackthorn tree.

Rosalind joined him, leaning against the trunk. After the glut of gods-magic, her body hummed with a strange mixture of exhaustion and excitement.

Caine gazed at her. "And that's why you need to take care. Before you know it, you can lose yourself in the insane minds of the gods."

"Like Drew," she said. "I get it. You've said this before."

"I don't want to see you turn into your parents."

She frowned. "Don't be ridiculous. I'm nothing like them." She plucked a spray of grass, and tossed it at him. "You don't really think I'm evil, do you?"

He shook his head. "Of course not. It's not that simple. But it's like you said before you drank the ambrosia: humans weren't meant to wield gods-magic."

"How do you know? It's not like there's a book about this." A sigh slid from her. "Why do I get the feeling you're trying to keep me from becoming powerful because it makes you uncomfortable?"

"You already are powerful."

"Not the way I need to be."

"You're perfect the way you are."

She smiled. "A rare compliment from Caine. But the truth is, I have to do this, even if it means burning myself out. I have to kill Drew, for Miranda's sake. There's nothing left for me, apart from that. I can't have a normal life as a normal person. That dream is dead."

"What exactly is a normal life?"

"I suppose if you've been living in a vampire realm for centuries the concept of normality would be a bit confusing." She bit her lip. "I guess my vision of a normal life is the same as Miranda's dream. She wanted us to live in a protected world—like Lilinor, but full of life and light. One where we could all live in the sun, and feel the rainwater on our faces. Where we could pluck wildflowers, bake bread, read by the fire. All that normal stuff."

"It sounds idyllic," he said. "But I suppose idylls are rarely real."

"So you've never had just a normal, human-like life with a family and... I don't know, normal family meal times, walks in the park?"

"Not really."

She frowned. "Where were you born, anyway? Maremount?"

His jaw tightened. "No."

"Silly of me to think you'd actually answer a personal question."

"It's not important." He pushed his rain-soaked hair off his forehead. "What's important is that with every victory Drew wins for the Brotherhood, they are able to absorb more humans into their cult. Every Brotherhood victory and glorious new building signals that Blodrial is all-powerful, a god who will bestow success and wealth on his followers."

"Oh, believe me, I'm familiar with their P.R. tactics."

"And worse, Drew is using Erish to create demons that have not walked the earth for centuries. Storm demons, uridimmu, wraiths of famine... and that's just the start, if we aren't able to stop Erish from creating more. There could be no end to Drew's power, and we will find ourselves in the midst of a true apocalypse. Considering Drew is slightly fixated on you, I'm guessing Lilinor will be his first stop with his new legions of the damned."

Rosalind hugged herself. Her clothes were sodden. "How do you know the specifics?"

"I have a spy among his people—someone who can shift into human form and disguise her magic."

"Who?"

"Esmerelda."

"Oh. Right. The unpleasant woman you had a dinner date with."

He took a deep breath. "I allowed you to think it was a dinner date, but it wasn't. She was reporting to me."

Her eyebrows rose in surprise. "First a compliment, then an open admission. I'm starting to think the apocalypse is upon us already."

The corner of his mouth twitched. "Perhaps. It is one of the seven signs, I believe." He reached for her face, then tightened his fist again and pulled it away, his expression darkening. "I think I should go alone to get Erish. You should remain in Lilinor with Malphas."

"No." She swallowed hard. "We should stick with the plan I've been working on for weeks."

"The one that I think is a terrible idea?"

"I'll be fine," she said firmly. "Don't underestimate me."

"I hate this idea," he said fiercely.

"It's my decision."

He held her gaze for a long time, a look that stripped her bare. "We'll need more time to get ready," he said, sounding as if he was trying to reassure himself more than her.

"I'll be fine. Now, if you don't mind, I'm going to finish my lunch." She started to leave, then thought better of it and turned back to him. "Are you going to admit why you wanted me to think you and Esmerelda were having a little romantic evening?"

He shrugged. "Because I was angry with you."

"You're over that, right? You understand now, surely, that it wasn't me who slept with Ambrose? It was Miranda."

The rain had slowed to a drizzle, but a chill rippled through the air. "It wasn't Miranda who kissed my brother."

She shook her head. "No. That was Cleo. She was controlling my mind."

He smiled wryly. "Just Cleo, was it?" Abruptly, the amusement left his expression. "I'm not sure what bothers me more: the fact that you kissed my brother, or the fact that you're unable to take responsibility for things you've clearly done."

Above, the clouds began to thin, letting in shards of moonlight.

"And why is this so hard for you to understand?" she asked. "I've heard all about the fact that you did something terrible when you got your second soul. I kissed Malphas—big deal. I'm guessing you did something worse. What was it?"

His frigid aura snaked from his body, icing the air around them. "Much worse. But I don't blame it on my second soul."

"Maybe you should. Then maybe you could ease up on the self-loathing and relax a little."

His body had gone completely still, and shadows slid across his eyes. "A second soul is not entirely a foreign entity. It brings out your true nature, your true desires."

"That's not a real thing. You just made that up." She cocked a hip. "And what are you suggesting my true nature is?"

"I'm not suggesting it's anything," he said. "Only that your true nature has chosen Malphas—and of course it would. It's destiny that you should choose him."

CHAPTER 3

Cold rain slid down Rosalind's skin, chilling her to the bone. "Why would you say that?"

"It's not important."

"What did your second soul bring out in you, then? What's your true nature?"

For just a moment, darkness crept over his eyes like pooling ink, giving her a dizzying glimpse into the void. "You're kidding yourself, little girl, if you think you don't already know."

A shiver snaked up her spine, and she let out a long breath. "You're going to have to stop calling me that, when I'm wielding the power of seven gods. Perhaps that's the real obstacle for you, isn't it? A woman with power greater than yours?"

"No, Rosalind." His eyes brightened to silver again. "But the important question is, are you sure you're ready for what lies ahead, even with your power of seven gods?"

Her stomach flipped. She wasn't ready—not at all. But she wasn't about to tell Caine that.

"Of course I'm ready," she lied. "And I need you to make me a promise: When I go into Cambridge, you can't come after me. I need you to trust that I can do it on my own. Don't underestimate me, okay?"

He stared down at her, and she was certain the starlight dimmed in the sky for a moment. "If that's what you really want."

She turned to walk away from him, dread blooming in her chest.

Perhaps this would be a good time to get herself acquainted with Cerberus.

* * *

The light rain continued to fall, and Rosalind rubbed her arms for warmth as she walked down the cobbled path to Cerberus's bar. Drew and the Brotherhood had the upper hand in every way, creating dreadful armies and palaces, recruiting new converts with the promise of wealth and riches from a benevolent god. Her cousin would be sitting on a marble throne, presiding over the kingdom he'd always wanted… and planning how to capture his queen.

Cleo's aura roiled restlessly in Rosalind's chest. Rosalind wanted a few hours off, but, as ever, her second soul was hungry for bloodshed and vengeance.

Kill the Hunters, Cleo sang.

"I will," Rosalind whispered. "You and I will kill them together."

Rosalind's footfalls clicked over the stones. There was a time when she had no chance in hell of walking through these streets unscathed, but since she'd been using gods-magic, the vampires had begun to ignore her.

The street curved down to a steep-roofed stone building, a grimacing, winged gargoyle looming over its entrance. *Cerberus's.* Perfect. With any luck, a few hours there would mean a few hours where she could forget about Drew—and perhaps forget about Caine's bizarre proclamation that she and Malphas were destined for each other.

She pushed through an arched wooden door into the bar. As the breeze filtered in, candles guttered over the shadowy stone walls. In alcoves around the bar, vampires hunched over silver cups, barely registering her arrival.

Faint moonlight streamed through multi-paned windows, onto an oak bar. A man stood behind it, his jowls as formidable as his velvet suit.

Rosalind crossed the stone floor to him, raising her eyebrows. "Cerberus?"

"Yeah?"

"Looks like I'm in the right place." She took a seat between two vampires—a woman casually dressed in a T-shirt, and a distinguished, silver-haired gentleman in leather pants and a frilly white shirt.

Cerberus leaned on the bar. "What'll it be?"

Rosalind scanned the offerings. Crooked stone shelves were crammed with bottles of blood, and amber and clear alcohol. Two large barrels with taps hung above the bar, simply labeled *Red* and *White.*

"Red wine, I guess. No blood. Just the wine."

"Suit yourself." Plucking a silver goblet from behind the bar, Cerberus shuffled off to fill it.

Rosalind peered at the young woman to her left, whose dark hair had been dyed purple at the tips. On closer inspection, she was surprised to find her wearing a *Count Duckula* T-shirt, jeans, and frilly bunny slippers.

The woman sipped her drink, then caught Rosalind's eye and raised her glass. A faint sheen of blood glistened on her lip.

Cerberus slid Rosalind's wine across the bar, and she lifted the goblet to the purple-haired woman before taking a sip. The clear, fruity taste danced on her taste buds.

"Rebecca!" The older man on her right leaned over her to yell at the woman in the T-shirt. "Must you bring down the tone of the place every evening with your ridiculous clothing?"

She scowled. "First of all, I go by Becca now. Second of all, I am two thousand years old. I remember when Caligula made his horse into a consul, because I was there. I will wear what I want, Duke Ricard, and I want to be comfortable."

Duke Ricard sniffed. "Vampires are supposed to comport themselves with a sense of dignity. Bunny slippers and Count Duckula T-shirts do not qualify as dignified."

"Says the man in leather pants." Becca rolled her eyes. "Honestly, Ricky. The *nouveau mort* are the worst."

The Duke's lips pressed into a thin line. "You do not have permission to call me Ricky. I am the Duke of Death and Rain. Furthermore, I have impeccable taste. You have wine stains on your shirt. Mine is spotless." He gripped his cup so hard he crushed it. "You take back what you said."

Becca swiveled on her chair, then leaned back on her elbows, curling her lip. "I stand by it. *Nouveau mort.*" Despite her pink bunny slippers, she managed to inject her voice with some serious menace.

The Duke rose, his eyes darkening to midnight black. Snarling, he revealed his fangs. Rosalind turned to watch the action unfold. She was about to witness one of those bar brawls Aurora had mentioned. She'd come to forget about Drew and Erish for an hour or two, and she would not be disappointed.

In a flash of pinkish light, Becca leapt over the bar and plucked a bottle of vodka from the shelf. On her way back over the bar, she shattered the bottle against the oak, splashing Rosalind with vodka.

"You need a weapon, do you?" snarled the Duke.

Becca's lip curled, and she lunged for him. He dodged back, and soon they were caught in a wild dance of lunging and whirling, striking and ducking, the Duke always just out of reach of her broken bottle. He managed to land a wild haymaker, but Becca followed up with a jab of the broken bottle. Streaks of crimson stained the front of his shirt.

Okay. Time to step in.

Rosalind stood, stepping between the two vampires, just as the Duke was lunging again. Using silver night magic, she formed a shield. "Okay, this has been fun, but maybe let's just drink now, shall we?"

Becca, who had lost one of her bunny slippers in the fray, simply shrugged. "Sure. But I would just like to note that Duke Ricard's shirt is no longer pristine."

"Gutter vampire," the Duke muttered, taking his seat again.

Becca returned to her chair, smoothing her hair. She scowled at the Duke. "Come back to me when you hit five hundred years, and we'll see how much you care about dignity."

The Duke straightened, looking straight ahead. "I might not live that long, not with the Brotherhood gearing up to slaughter us at any moment. Bastards keep raising the sun in the land of night."

Okay. So apparently there was no escaping this current crisis.

Becca arched an eyebrow at Rosalind. "Aren't you that mage? You're not a vampire. And you're not human." She looked Rosalind up and down. "So you're the person who's supposed to save us."

Rosalind swallowed an enormous gulp of her wine. "I will have help."

"So what's the plan?" the Duke asked. "Aren't you supposed to turn us into daywalkers? Ambrose promised us."

This particular trip to the bar was about as relaxing as hip surgery. "We needed my sister for that. We had a bit of a setback—namely, she died."

"Oh, that's right," Becca said. "Sorry."

The Duke raised his glass. "To your sister." He knocked it back.

"So," Rosalind continued, "we'll find another way. But for tonight, I just want to drink wine."

"Fair enough," Becca said.

Rosalind finished off her wine in silence, half listening to Becca and the Duke bicker about shoes. When she finished, it suddenly occurred to her that she hadn't brought any money with her. She channeled the icy magic of Nyxobas to create three silver coins and dropped them on the counter.

CHAPTER 4

osalind spent another hour in the bar, drinking her way through a few more glasses of wine, before she returned to the fortress. As soon as she was inside, something compelled her to seek out Caine. She wanted to know exactly what he'd meant about the whole *You're destined for my brother* thing. Caine had been keeping secrets from her for too long now.

Rosalind's and Caine's lives were now completely intertwined, twin vines searching for light—and the secrets Caine carried were a blight that would rot them from the inside out.

Should she tell him that when she'd woken that morning, tangled in her sheets, she'd reached for Miranda's hand? And that when she didn't find her sister there, she'd been able to think of only one other person she desperately wanted to see.

Caine. Not his brother.

He needed to know that. But she also needed him to let down his defenses a little and actually tell her about himself. She wanted all of him—not just his beauty and grace, but all the dark, sharp edges. He was her blackthorn tree: dark, beautiful, and savagely spiked. She wanted him just as he was—assuming he could learn to trust her.

After all they'd been through together, he still wasn't telling her the truth.

In the high-arched hall, candlelight danced in the lanterns, casting writhing shadows over the floor, like half-living creatures. By now, her clothes had totally dried, though her hair still hung damp over her shoulder.

Her gaze landed on the portrait of Lord Byron outside Caine's room. Standing before his door, she took a deep breath, then knocked on the oak.

After a few moments, the door creaked open. Eerily, no one stood before it. Caine sat in a silver armchair, reading a large book by candlelight. He wore a black T-shirt, short-sleeved, showing off his muscles.

He arched an eyebrow. "We've already finished our training for the day. You were supposed to be resting. Eating. Whatever it is humans do." The breeze lifted strands of his dark hair. "If you'd like to bathe here, of course, feel free. I'll be happy to help."

She folded her arms. "About our conversation earlier…"

He closed the book, sliding it onto a small oak table. "Yes?"

"Why are you so certain that my true nature wants your brother, and that Malphas and I are destined for each other? I don't understand."

Caine looked at the window. "When I was locked up in your parents' house, there was one ray of light: Malphas. Unlike me, he wasn't chained. He could move from place to place. He'd come see me in the cellar. He'd leave, and travel through the fields, through the forest." He met her gaze again. "Always, when he came back to me, he was talking about one thing: Rosalind. Rosalind is brave. Rosalind led us on an adventure. You weren't the good twin, but you fascinated him. That's part of it, anyway."

Rosalind's heart tightened. "And what's the rest of it?"

Caine rose and crossed toward her, his movements smooth but precise, his hands in his pockets. His icy eyes—starlit on the inside, with a deep pewter ring around the irises—made her stomach swoop. She'd never quite appreciated their depth before.

As he stepped into her space, he pressed his hands against the wall on either side of her head, boxing her in. His powerful aura caressed her skin, lighting her body up. She glanced at the sharp tattoo on his forearm—the heart of his dark secrets.

Her breath hitched in her throat. She would ask him about his secrets, and he would dodge her questions. This was their eternal dance.

"In the vision of your life that I saw, there was a blond woman brushing her hair in a cracked looking glass."

Shadows flitted across his eyes. "And what does that have to do with you?"

"Who was she?" She reached up, touching the tattoo on his arm. "This was hers. The hairpin."

He flinched. "She's the real reason why Malphas is your destiny, and I am not."

Suddenly, her legs were trembling. Her pulse raced. So this blonde was another lover, perhaps. "Why? Who was she?"

Caine's eyes darkened, became black as the void. The candlelight in the lanterns guttered, and the temperature in the room dropped. An icy chill ran up Rosalind's spine.

"He's here," Caine whispered.

Dread stole Rosalind's breath. *Drew.*

Caine cupped her face, staring into her eyes. "It's too soon."

Rosalind glanced over Caine's shoulder as the rising sun had stained the sky blood red. A tendril of horror coiled around her heart. "We don't have a choice," she said. "We need to act now. Find Ambrose."

"I'll stay with you. We can defeat him together, now."

"Go." She tried to steady her voice. "See that the vampires are safe. I'll handle Drew. It's what I've been training for. You know this."

This was it. *This* was her actual destiny.

But Caine didn't respond to her command. Instead, he seemed to be searching her face for something, and every moment he wasted meant another vampire could die in sunlight flames.

Gently, she pushed at Caine's powerful chest. "He's going to kill again. He's going to kill every last one of Lilinor's citizens. Keep the vampires in their rooms. This is your duty now."

He clutched her waist, his fingers tightening possessively. "I've changed my mind. This isn't a good idea. I'll face Drew. You look after the vampires."

"Caine. I can survive sunlight. I can survive fire and drowning. I can call up fire and storms. The vampires are helpless against him; I'm not. You need to trust me."

He leaned in, his hard body pressing against hers, and kissed her hard. It was a desperate kiss, as if he thought this might be his last moment on earth. His fingers gripped her, and a wave of molten heat surged through her blood. Visions danced in her mind of Caine, cradling a blue-eyed baby.

Slowly, he pulled away, his eyes closed.

She touched his face. "I'll be fine. Cleo will take care of me."

"She'd better." Caine kissed her one last time, then disappeared in a flash of silver, a few whirls of his magic lingering like smoke.

Cleo's aura curled around her ribs, hungry for blood. *We're going to slaughter the Hunter King. I want to bathe in his blood. I want to light the corrupted Brotherhood's city on fire.*

"We will," Rosalind promised.

As Rosalind moved through the halls, Cleo's memories sparked in her mind. The night—centuries ago—when Ambrose had betrayed her. The Hunters had arrived for her, iron tools in hand. The field of bluebells and aster, stained in blood. The Hunters had locked her in a cell, cut her skin, broken her thumbs. Raped her. They'd burned her alive in the town square while her lover looked on.

And now, Rosalind was about to face the Hunter's king. She had to defeat him—not just for herself, but for her twin sister. For Lilinor, and for Cleo.

Amber rays from the rising sun slanted through the window, filling her with dread. Never before had she been so terrified of daylight. Long shadows crept over the ground, and between them the rising sun stained the floor red. Within the rooms, the vampires began to scream, desperate to hide themselves from the sun. At least they were awake this time, not completely defenseless.

It's time to face Drew.

She moved faster through the hall, shadow-running down the stairs. She needed to stop him now, before he slaughtered the entire city. Duke Ricard had been right—the vampires were vulnerable here, just waiting for the next slaughter—but she was not.

Like a phantom wind, she moved swiftly down the long hall toward the portcullis. Goosebumps rose on her skin, from a mixture of fear and anticipation. This was what she'd trained for.

As she approached the portcullis, she let the storm god's magic sing through her blood. Electricity sparked from her fingertips. With each step toward the entrance, her body charged.

She strode over the crimson carpet, an angel of death with storms in her blood, and Cleo's aura writhed around her body.

Let's kill the Hunter King.

CHAPTER 5

*E*ven from inside, she could feel the storm clouds gathering overhead, ready to unleash their fury. At the end of the corridor, she pulled a lever, and the enormous latticed doors creaked open.

There, in the center of the stone esplanade, stood Drew, dressed in white. At the sight of him, rage stole her breath—tinged with a little bit of fear. The expression on his face didn't quite look human, and whorls of magic snaked from his body in colored tendrils. Somehow, his body had grown in size, and his eyes blazed with pure flame.

For what he'd done—for what he still wanted to do to her—she wanted to rip his heart right out of his chest. He was here for her, and she was here to kill him.

She stepped into the cobbled esplanade, just as the roiling clouds began to unleash their rain.

"Cousin," she said. "I knew you'd come for me."

He flexed his fingers. "We're going to create our dynasty, Rosalind." His voice sounded distant, as if it were coming from a void. "It's your destiny."

The wrath of the storm god rippled over her skin, cold and vengeful. This was where Drew had murdered her sister, just twenty feet away, at the wooden stake. This was where Rosalind had felt the world end.

She lifted her hand, letting the magic surge to the end of her fingertips. *I want to watch you burn.*

When she flicked her wrist, a bolt of lightning shot from her fingertips to her cousin's chest.

The scent of burning flesh curled into the air. Drew arched his back, paralyzed, then fell to the earth. She took a deep breath. Maybe her plan wouldn't have to come to fruition at all. Maybe she should just kill him now...

Had she killed him? No—his chest still rose and fell slowly. She'd merely slowed him down.

Burn him, Cleo whispered.

Molten rage imbued her body, and the fire goddess's magic ignited her veins. But he'd been through Emerazel's inferno, and fire wouldn't burn him. *Could* he be killed?

Now, in his presence, something in the back of her mind whispered that he couldn't, that he was as enduring as the gods themselves...

She felt Mishett-Ash's electricity surge through her blood again, the ancient chaos of the storm god; she struck Drew again, in the center of his chest, with a stunning spear of lightning.

His body shook, convulsing, and smoke curled into the air. Yet he still breathed, his chest rising and falling.

Her mind whirled. *How do I kill him?*

He sat up, his eyes blazing with a fiery light, and Rosalind kicked him hard in the side of his head. His neck snapped backward, and she kicked him again. In the next moment, his body flashed with colored light, and he sprang up from the ground, his mouth bleeding.

Before she could strike him again, he lunged for her with the full force of a hurricane wind. He grasped her around the ribs, hurtling with her through the air.

Her breath left her lungs, and then he was slamming her against the wooden stake with one hand, his other tightening around her throat.

Her stomach churned. *This is where it happened. This is where he killed Miranda.*

As Drew squeezed her neck, she stared into his eyes, but she could see no humanity there. In his burning eyes, she saw the gods looking back at her.

At that point, she was certain of one thing: the gods weren't evil. They weren't loving.

They were simply insane.

Revulsion turned her stomach as she felt Drew's fingers crawling over her flesh, his magic claiming her body like an infection.

Panic stole her breath. How could she fight him, if the gods' fire and floods couldn't hurt him?

He squeezed her throat harder, pressing on her trachea until the pain ripped her mind apart. Her mind spinning, she closed her eyes.

This is how the world ends, in the darkness and the damp. Quietly, and utterly alone.

Her eyes snapped open again, and a flicker of movement in the corner of her eye caught her attention. Tammi stood in the entrance of the Ninlil fortress, rain soaking her thin white dress.

"Rosalind!" she shouted.

No! Rosalind's mind screamed. *Get out of here!* This wasn't how it was supposed to go. Tammi shouldn't be here.

"Rosalind," Drew whispered, his fingers inching up her flesh. "You belong to me now."

Rosalind wanted to scream to Tammi to rush inside, but Drew was crushing her trachea.

The song of the valkyrie rushed through her body, filling her with power. A burst of electricity surged through her, knocking Drew back on to the soaked cobblestones.

Drew's face contorted with rage as he sprang to his feet. Flames blazed from the tips of his fingers. "You need to understand. You won't be able to kill me. I'm a god now, and gods don't die; we create."

What the hell was he talking about? Was this true, or the product of an insane mind? "I think all that magic warped your mind, Drew. You sound like a lunatic."

"Using gods-magic changes you. It's changed me, and it will change you, too." Slowly, his movements reptilian, Drew shook his head. "I know your weaknesses, Rosalind. You're not scared you'll be hurt." He pointed to Tammi. "You're scared *they'll* be hurt. Your little friends." Rage flashed in his eyes, and his aura whipped the air around him. "Your *lover!*" He bellowed this last word, and the sound rumbled through Rosalind's gut.

A wave of horror washed over Rosalind, and she turned to Tammi. "Run!" She screamed.

Tammi's eyes widened, and she turned to flee. As she did, Drew turned to face the fortress, and hurled a ball of fire at the gate.

Icy wrath blazed through Rosalind, and she rallied her shadow magic, then hurled a stream of frigid shadows at the flames. The rush of silver magic froze his flames in the air.

Rosalind rushed for Drew, yanking an iron knife from her belt.

Kill him... Cleo whispered.

Rosalind brought the iron down toward Drew's chest. At the last moment, he dodged, and she pivoted. When she'd been a Hunter, she'd learned to anticipate her opponent's next move, and Drew tended to dodge to his left. The next time she lunged for him, she shifted lightly to the right. She plunged the knife between his ribs, pulling it out again for another strike.

But this time, Drew grabbed her wrist—twisting it, crushing her bones. Pain ripped through her arm.

She called on the power of Borgerith, Lady of Stone, and filled her body with the strength of the mountains. Already, her bones were healing where Drew tried to crush them.

I am the dark places under the earth, the cave and rock.

Rosalind ripped her wrist from Drew's grasp, following up with a hard punch to his jaw. Her body blazed with power.

When her fist connected, his bone crunched; he stumbled off course.

I am the things you want to forget. I am your guilt, the weight of the lives you've taken.

She rained blow after blow onto his head, each punch delivering the force of a ton of rocks. Drew stumbled back, and she pressed on, trying to break him.

I am Miranda's broken body. I am Cleo's tormented soul.

Drew fell back, and Rosalind leapt on top of him, pounding his face with her fists.

I am your judge, and your executioner.

Blood poured from his mouth and nose, and his eyes dulled. *Miranda.* Slam. *She died, she lived.* Slam. *She died again.*

Blood streamed from his face, mingling with the rain in rivulets through the cobblestones. Rosalind had broken every bone in his face, smashing it beyond recognition. Now, she needed to finish the job—if she could. Was he telling the truth? Was he really a god now? Was she?

She pulled another iron knife from her belt, gripping it high above her head. But as she brought her hands down to deliver the death blow, Drew caught her wrists, his grip vice like. Where had he found this reserve of strength.

"Rosalind," he rasped, his words slurred through his broken jaw. "You can't kill a god this way. Didn't your lover tell you?"

He snarled, his body glowing with golden light until the rays nearly blinded her. Tammi was long gone by now, but what sort of a blast was he working up?

I have to stop him.

Rosalind let the frigid rage cool her blood as she geared up for another strike of shadow magic.

Just as she wrenched her wrist away, an explosion of flame burst from Drew's body. The blast knocked her back into a stone wall, her back cracking. The earth shook, rock and debris raining around her. Screams ripped through the air. When she pushed herself to her feet again, pain splintered her body, and she stared in horror at the decimated fortress walls.

Drew stood before her, immense as a god, his back arched, body vibrating with white light, like the birth of a star.

From the skies, balls of fire rained, igniting rooftops all over the city. Everyone she cared about in the world was in this city.

Caine, Tammi, Aurora...

Her world tilted. Drew was going to murder everyone, and she wasn't strong enough to stop him.

This had gone on long enough.

"Stop!" she screamed.

Drew turned to look at her, his eyes blazing like hellfire. "My bride. Are you ready to give in, or do you want me to keep going?"

Her legs trembled. "Yes. I'm ready!" she screamed. "Stop the fire!"

In a flash, he was standing before her, grabbing her by the throat, thumb pressing into her trachea. In his eyes, she saw only the fractured madness of the gods.

"Tell me you'll agree to be my mate," he growled, his face mangled beyond recognition. "Or I will burn the entire city while you watch. You and I will live through the flames while you listen to their screams."

Through her half-crushed throat, she choked, "I agree." Revulsion turned her stomach. She didn't want to go anywhere near him, but this was the only way.

As he tightened his grip on her, the skies turned to a midnight black.

This is how the world ends.

Drew's smile was a thing of terror, his eyes dancing with light. He pulled out a set of iron cuffs, pinning her arms behind her back. Magic whirled from his body. The ground gave way beneath Rosalind's feet, and a flood of dark water rushed up. Drew dragged her into its murky depths.

CHAPTER 6

She plunged deeper into the portal, with Drew gripping her waist, her hands chained behind her back. She was sinking deeper underground, plummeting with him. Something sharp pierced her flesh below her ribs, and she looked down to see a syringe. Drew, his face mangled, was injecting her body.

And when he'd finished, she stared as he sealed her skin with his magic. This time, he was going to make sure Rosalind was unable to flush the iron from her system.

Panic ripped her mind apart—but only for a few moments—until the iron began to dull her thoughts again.

Now he'd be able to control her mind. The iron from the syringe was seeping into her body, polluting it. And yet, it wasn't working as quickly this time.

This couldn't be it—she wasn't going to end it this way, to make her grave in his palace, to live as a breathing corpse. Whatever it took, she would fight until she took her last breath.

She wasn't the same girl she'd once been. She'd seen too much death to remain unscathed, felt her own heart stop when Miranda's had. She'd lost a piece of herself, buried under the yew.

Drew dragged her deeper under the water, his hands rough

around her waist, and she detached her mind from the feel of his fingers on her skin. She'd told Caine to have faith in her, and she'd meant it. It wasn't over yet.

There'd been a time when this plunge into the water would have burned her lungs, would have pierced her muscles with the cold. Maybe Drew was right—maybe gods-magic had changed her. Her descent through the portal felt no colder than the icy dread in her heart. Was she transforming, too? Becoming a god?

According to Drew, this was her destiny. Seemed like a lot of people had ideas about her destiny, and none of them had bothered consulting her on the matter. *I'm not done yet, please gods, don't let me be done yet.* She had to write her own destiny.

She looked up at the murky surface. Golden rays of light streamed through the water.

Never before had daylight so unnerved her. Like a Pavlovian response, the amber rays of day now filled her chest with dread.

Drew pulled her up through the water's surface, dragging her onto a cold mosaic floor.

She lay flat on her back, staring at a ceiling painted to look like a blue sky, with astrological signs etched in copper.

Drew stood above her, staring down at her. Already, his face had begun to heal, his bones regaining a semblance of their former shape. The water seemed to have washed the blood off him.

Rosalind swallowed hard, standing to survey the enormous, octagonal room. Gold and maroon fabric hung draped over bone-colored walls, and chalice insignias had been embroidered all over the rich silks. In the center of the room stood a bed on dais—a gold, winged base, with platinum silk draping from a golden-crowned canopy.

Two demons stood in the corners of the room. Rosalind's mouth went dry as she looked at them. Their bottom halves looked like scorpions, with long, pointed legs, and enormous tails that curled high over their heads, twelve feet long at least. Their chests and arms were human-like, their torsos thickly corded with muscle, and each one gripped an iron spear. They stared at Rosalind through empty black eyes, and she shivered. When she turned to look at the other side of the room, she found two more blocking the door.

Slowly, the iron seeped deeper into her blood, weakening her senses, sapping her magic. She blinked, staring at the iron rings studding the room, protruding from the walls and bedposts. All the places Drew could chain her...

From the corner of her eye, she could see Drew's magic curling all over the walls in colorful strands. He'd created this entire palace, and it bore his signature like magical DNA. It felt corrupted, toxic.

Drew was studying her, and she wanted to get as far away from him as possible.

Her body was moving sluggishly now. Slowly, she stumbled to a set of French windows, staring out upon the transformed city of Cambridge. A vast courtyard stretched out before them—nearly a mile of grass surrounded by marble buildings, each one brimming with Drew's rotten magic.

As the iron's magic began to cloud her mind, she tried to clear her thoughts, forcing herself to focus. Besides the magic, there was something really *not right* about this place. As she studied the wall by the window, she noticed its surface seemed oddly smooth—and under the surface, it appeared as if a network of veins spread through the building. Somehow, the windows seemed to breathe, flexing gently in and out.

She swallowed hard, her mouth tasting of ash, trapped in Drew's kingdom of blood and bone. He'd made sure there was no way out. She blinked, searching for an exit route. Cold mists clouded her mind, but she knew it would be important later, that she needed to study everything here.

Around the city, marble walls closed them in, nearly a hundred feet high. And if she knew the Brotherhood, every inch of those marble walls was rigged with anti-demon weapons: iron dust, hawthorn stakes, flamethrowers. The place was impenetrable. Dimly, she could imagine herself standing on the other side of the walls, blasting them with magic, decimating them. She'd storm into the empire, blazing with fire, and burn down the city that never should have been. She'd... burn... *What was I thinking about?*

She pressed her forehead to the window, the glass cool against her skin. Morning sunlight blazed over the city, turning her blood to ice. *My new home.*

She felt Drew walk up behind her. He swept her hair out of her face, and leaned over her shoulder, breathing down her neck.

"What do you think of your new home?" he purred.

She shuddered at his touch. Something wasn't right. Her thoughts were muddied, but... "This isn't my home," she slurred.

"Rosalind, my little pet. You will learn your place." His fingers slid around her waist. "Tell me that you worship me."

She clenched her jaw, fighting the compulsion to say what he wanted her to say. His iron had infected her system, but deep in the hollows of her mind she could still form her own thoughts. *Dear gods.* How long would it be until she could get out of here?

Without warning, he spun her around, slamming her against the window. Her head smacked against the glass, and she winced.

"You are my queen," he said. "And you will treat me as your king. Did you know that I no longer need to drink the blood from Blodrial? The magic of the gods is simply within me now. I *am* a god. I *am* Azazeyl, and so are you. And the two of us—with gods-magic in our bodies—we will never die. You and I will live together forever, do you understand? And that is why I am your destiny."

Panic ripped her mind apart. He tightened his fingers around her throat, crushing the air out of her. Pain blazed through her body, searing her lungs. He liked this move—strangling her. He liked the control, like the pain he inflicted. More than that, she was certain he liked being close to her. He was desperate for human touch, and he had no idea how else to get it.

Her lungs burned. *How long until I can get out of here?*

"Rosalind," he purred. "I will make you behave. Looks like one injection isn't enough for you now. Not to worry—there's plenty more."

The needle pierced her skin, just between her ribs. His charmed serum would allow him to control her mind. And when he finished, he pressed his hand hard against her ribs, sealing her skin.

The charmed iron spread through her body; ice encased her mind.

As if watching from a distance, she saw Drew press a finger over her mouth. "There, there, my little queen."

All the anger had left her body. Now she didn't feel anything at all.

Drew stared down at her, his face still lumpy and red from the beating. "Now. Tell me what I want to hear."

* * *

HOURS PASSED IN A FOG, and Rosalind knew only that she'd been chained to a bed. Sunlight streamed in through the thin curtains, burning her eyes, and the iron shackles around her limbs and neck chafed her skin.

Sometimes, Drew would come in and force her to speak, to say the things he wanted to hear.

She'd feel her mouth forming the words, but she couldn't quite decipher the meaning—only that he seemed desperate for something, and that he'd tear out his hair with rage if he didn't think she was saying it right.

Glaciers slid across her mind, and her thoughts moved sluggishly beneath them like ice floes. Every now and then she'd catch a wisp of a feeling floating by... a fleeting stab of sadness, a spark of rage. And then, just ice and iron, and the burning sunlight.

For the first time, she realized someone had changed her clothes, dressed her in sheer wisps of white fabric that hardly covered anything. Goosebumps rose on her skin, and she shivered.

She closed her eyes; somewhere beneath the ice, images flitted through her mind: a girl who looked like her, pinned to a stake with a nail through her heart. A beautiful man with porcelain skin and gray eyes. And another like him, with sun-kissed skin and a dark secret...

The door to her room creaked open, and someone strode in, the strike of his heels echoing off the ceiling. It was someone *different* this time, not the cousin who called her "queen." A man with flame-red hair who made her skin grow cold… He stared down at her, a dark smile curling his lips. In another life, she'd known him…

Desperately, she tried to grasp a tendril of a thought. There was something dangerous about him.

"Do you remember me, Rosalind?" he asked. "I suppose you might not."

He wore an iron chalice pin on his lapel, and the sight of it sent a shock of panic through Rosalind, but she wasn't sure why.

"Allow me to reintroduce myself, now that you've been given that little brain-altering treatment. You once knew me as Randolph Loring. I was your leader, when you fought the witches and demons. Before you turned into their whore." He frowned, taking a deep breath. "I know what you're thinking—assuming you can think at all. I have surrounded myself with magic now, and this is never how I imagined it would all turn out. But you can't fight magic without magic. I know that now." He gestured at the building. "And all this— it's for the glory of Blodrial. The populace must know how truly dangerous magic is, and I'm teaching them." His eyes burned with the fervor of a fanatic. "When my work here is done, when the old ways have returned once more, then anyone defiled by the use of magic will feed my flames of righteousness."

Rosalind felt a chill wash over her, and for just a moment, she jerked against her chains.

The man wagged his finger. "Uh-uh-uh. Lie still, Rosalind." His forehead creased. "I'm not sure why he has you chained. It's not like you can go anywhere, not with all that charmed iron in your blood. But I suppose he likes the way it looks on you." He stroked the chain attached to her collar. "I can't fault his tastes. It *is* a good look on you." He leaned down, staring into her eyes. "You know, I would tell you to forget everything I've said, but I'm fairly certain I don't have to. But I'll be seeing more of you soon." He scanned her body. "A lot more."

He turned, walking out of the room. Rosalind couldn't quite figure out why, but a gnawing dread climbed up her chest.

CHAPTER 7

osalind stood by a bay window, squinting in the milky sunlight. Gauzy curtains, like moth wings, fluttered in a draft from the window. She wore a silky, cream-colored bathrobe, cool against her skin. Around the room, the scorpion men stared at her.

That painful, soul-sapping ice encased her mind, freezing her thoughts. As she stood by the window, she was dimly aware of servants bustling around her, stripping off her clothes.

This can't happen... a stray thought screamed under the ice. There was something she needed to return to—deep silver eyes, flecked with starlight. Golden skin. Cool and warm, dark and light. Soft lips on her neck...

She just couldn't remember who that was, or why she cared. As she stood, dumbly, a woman smudged blush on her cheeks, then painted her lips with a blood-red lipstick. Another woman stood behind her, braiding flowers into her dark hair.

Rosalind's hands hung limply at her sides. A servant with pale blond hair and gray eyes stepped in front of her and looked up, her eyes pleading. She held a piece of stuffed bread in front of Rosalind's face.

Rosalind's lip curled in disgust, and nausea turned her stomach. With all the glaciers in her mind, food seemed repellent to her right now. She didn't want to eat or drink. She wanted it to end.

A voice underneath the ice floes in her mind screamed, and yet all she could do was stand still, gaping at the soft light of the window, waiting for her own funeral. For the dirt that would cover her corpse. *I lived. I died.*

"Please." The girl's lip trembled. "I'm supposed to get you to eat."

Rosalind blinked, trying to clear the fog of her mind. Slowly, she shook her head. How could she eat when she wasn't truly alive at all?

The girl lifted a chalice of red wine, and Rosalind stared at it dully. "At least drink this." Fear glimmered in the girl's gray eyes, and Rosalind wanted to help her.

She didn't quite understand why, but this girl needed her to drink the wine. Rosalind nodded, and the girl brought the wine to her lips. Slowly, she tipped the cup, letting the wine flow into Rosalind's mouth. It tasted fruity and crisp, but Rosalind didn't want any more than a sip. For some reason, she was certain this entire marble palace was a mausoleum, and she didn't want to drink in a tomb.

The girl lowered the cup, shooting Rosalind a grateful look. The door creaked open, and footsteps echoed off the ceiling. The pale girl began shaking as she stared over Rosalind's shoulder. She turned to look at the new person.

It wasn't Drew, she thought—but the man with the bright red hair. A man she'd once known and revered. The one who called himself Randolph.

He crossed to the blond servant, who stared at him, wide-eyed.

Randolph looked the girl up and down. "You may leave."

Even through Rosalind's clouded thoughts, the girl's terror was palpable. When she moved to leave, she stumbled, spilling her wine onto Randolph's chest. Slowly, she raised her eyes to him, her entire body shivering.

Randolph's features darkened, and he stared down at the girl with barely controlled rage.

Something terrible is about to happen...

Randolph pivoted, his gaze sliding to one of the scorpion men, and he nodded curtly.

"No!" the girl shrieked. "Please!"

The scorpions moved closer, dark eyes locked on the girl, tails lowering.

Numbness spread through Rosalind, and she stared as Randolph backed away from the girl, letting the scorpions close in.

The girl screamed. Rosalind wanted to help her, to stop whatever was happening, but her body wasn't responding the way it should. She took a step closer to the girl. There was something she could do to help…

Randolph shot her a sharp look, his jaw clenched. "Stay where you are, Rosalind. Or there will be consequences."

At the sound of his command, her body slowed against her will. But the scorpions were closing in, and the girl's screams pierced the air. Rosalind needed to stop them.

Fighting against the ice in her mind, she forced her body to take another step—but she was moving too slowly, as if the weight of a thousand rocks pulled her down. She stared as one of the scorpions snarled at her. He looked older than the rest, his hair streaked with gray, and he lowered his tail piercing the girl's shoulder.

The servant's agonized screams slid through Rosalind's bones. As the girl fell to the ground, tears stung Rosalind's eyes. The girl's body convulsed, jerking and writhing on the floor as her muscles seized. Her pale face contorted with pain, her eyes pleading with the gods to end her torment. She rolled onto her side, vomiting red wine onto the floor again and again, until nothing but bile came up. Her mouth frothed with red and white foam. Under the glaciers in Rosalind's mind, a dark rage began to bloom.

The girl's agony seemed to go on forever, her body bucking and writhing, until at last she lay still. Wide open, her eyes gaped at the ceiling.

Rage curled around Rosalind's ribs like wisteria vines. She turned to look at Randolph, her body shaking.

Smoothly, he moved closer to her, and the sinister curve of his smile made the hair rise on the back of Rosalind's neck. He wore a black suit with an iron lapel—a chalice, decorated with rubies. That symbol had meant something to her once, long ago.

He reached for her, stroking her face, gently at first. Then, he grabbed her by the jaw, squeezing hard. He smelled of onions and ambrosia, and the combination turned her stomach. "I told you there would be consequences if you defied me." He pressed harder on her jaw. "Lucky for you, the iron in your blood stopped you before it could get any worse for you. I wouldn't want to have to mutilate a bride just before her wedding."

He leaned in, his voice sending ice through her veins.

"I know you've broken free of Drew's mind control before. I want to make sure that it's worked properly this time."

He dropped his grip on her, then smacked her hard across the face.

She fell back on the floor, and pain exploded through her head. While a cry of despair keened under the surface of her mind, she simply lay there, staring at the blond girl's corpse.

"Stand," Randolph commanded.

She felt her body respond to his commands, and she pushed herself up on her elbows and rose. Her face still throbbed where he'd smacked her.

Slowly, her gaze drifted to the scorpion men. They watched, unmoving.

"Walk closer to me," Randolph said.

Slowly, one foot in front of the other, she moved into the center of the room, where pale light streamed through a window.

"You've caused such problems for us, Rosalind. And I'm pleased to see Drew has tamed you. I wanted him to kill you, but he was so keen to keep you. And I need to keep him happy until I'm done using him."

The chill in the room went right to Rosalind's bones.

Randolph walked in front of her, looking her up and down. "In the ancient custom of the Brotherhood, the high priests have the right to a bride on her wedding night. In this case, I am the high priest."

Rosalind couldn't quite make sense of his words, but she began to shiver. She'd freeze to death in here.

"Perhaps a preview of tonight is in order," he purred. "Take off your robe."

Deep in the recesses of her mind, a vernal aura began to stir. And yet, she felt herself untying the bathrobe. She let it slide off her shoulders, and fall to the ground.

She had the sense that the scorpion men were looking on, that laughter danced in their dark eyes. She looked down at her trembling body, surprised to see that she wasn't wearing a bra. Someone had dressed her in white panties.

"I want you to kneel," Randolph said.

As a voice in the back her skull raged, she dropped, the cold tiles biting into her knees. That strange, green aura roiled around her mind, threatening to snap. One of the scorpion men cocked his head as he stared down at her, his lips curling in a wicked smile.

Randolph crossed to her, and he reached down to stroke her hair. "I never supported women as Hunters or leaders, but times changed. I guess I was right to have my reservations. Since your betrayal, we've begun to rid our ranks of women. Your place now is to serve us, as it was in the old days."

He stroked her face, then smeared his rough thumb over her lips. "You're lucky you're not in the dungeons with Erish."

At the sound of Erish's name, a flicker of recognition sparked in her mind. *Erish is important... The secret weapon.*

"You're going to be married in our amphitheater today. And when I'm ready to purge the demons and heretics from my city, you and Drew will burn there."

Dread bloomed in her chest, and she stared at the floor. Randolph raised his hand, smacking her once more, and pain burst through her cheek as she fell back on the floor. She lay on the cold tiles, her head throbbing, and Randolph stood over her.

"I'll leave you there for now," he said. "Someone will be in to dress you soon, but I look forward to our meeting tonight."

Her skin felt cold against the tile, and the floor seemed to pulse beneath her, throbbing with Drew's magic. *Erish is in the dungeons...* Magic stirred in Rosalind's ribs as she lay staring at the corpse on the floor. Such a strange thing when a building seemed alive but the girl on the floor didn't…

She wasn't sure how much time had passed before two girls came in, and pulled her off the floor, fussing over her as they pulled a corset around her, tightening the stays until she thought her ribs would crack. They dressed her in a white gown—a cage of lace, ribbons, and frills.

My wedding gown… Her heart tightened with dread.

One of the girls tied a bow just below her breasts. "Your groom will untie these later." She frowned. "Or the high priest. I'm not sure which comes first."

Rosalind's stomach lurched. She swayed slightly, as nimble fingers wove flowers through her hair.

Deep within her, a green leafy aura stirred, bringing with it the scents of the forest, of life. Rosalind's heart beat a little harder.

She wasn't sure why, but she turned to one of the servants, and felt her mouth form words: "Can you please tell me where the dungeons are?"

The girl's eyes widened in surprise. "Below the palace."

As if from a distance, Rosalind heard herself ask, "But how do I get to them?"

The girl frowned. "You're going to marry the emperor today. Why would you need to get to the prisons?"

Rosalind's lip curled. Something inside her mind didn't like this answer. Her hand shot out, and she snatched the girl's wrist, tightening her fingers. She would get the answer to this question, whatever it took. Her mind flickered with visions of the rowan grove, the silky dress that caressed Cleo's thighs—then the flames that seared her milky skin.

Gritting her teeth, she tightened her grip on the girl's wrist until she screamed. "Tell me, Hunter," she snarled, her voice laced with venom. "How do I get to the prisons?"

The girl's eyes widened, and she stammered. "There's a tunnel that connects to the prisons from the amphitheater where you'll be getting married today. Please don't tell your husband that I told you."

Rosalind nodded and dropped the girl's wrist. Once again, the icy mists returned to her mind, clouding her thoughts, and her muscles relaxed.

One of the women pulled a thin, gauzy veil over Rosalind's head, making the world even hazier, then grabbed Rosalind by the hand. As she led Rosalind into the arched hall, one of the servants turned to her, blinking. "I don't know why they wanted you there for this part of the ceremony. Drew wanted you to see it. After the prayers, the wedding begins with a sacrifice. It won't be pleasant."

Rosalind's heart slammed against her ribs. *A sacrifice.*

"Oh, don't worry," the girl said. "They're just demons and witches."

CHAPTER 8

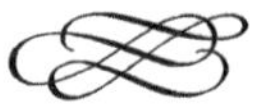

The girl led Rosalind through a long hall, and Rosalind's gaze trailed over the bony walls. Statues stood in alcoves, most of them depicting Drew with a crown. As her shoes clicked over the floor, she had the sense that shadows were flitting around the walls, watching her. A shiver snaked up her spine.

A breeze rushed over her skin, and at the other end of the hall, sunlight slanted in through an arch. She squinted at the light, that leafy aura curling around her ribs. Buried in the depths of her mind, a voice whispered *a tunnel from the amphitheater…*

The servants led her into the open air, and the hall opened into an imposing amphitheater, a sandy pit surrounded by a vast semicircle of stone benches. They moved on to a seat not far from the orchestra pit. In the center of the sand stood an iron altar, set with ruby-flecked chalices. And fanning out on either side of the altar were iron stakes, encircled by bundles of wood.

Her blood ran cold. *We start with a sacrifice.* Leafy magic licked at her ribs, and rage smoldered under the surface of her mind.

Slowly, Rosalind surveyed the space. Banquet tables had been set around the edges of the pit, laden with fruit, meat, and wine. A cool breeze rushed over the stone, toying with Rosalind's hair, and she shivered. Slowly, the wedding guests began to fill the rows, pouring out from arched halls, staring at their new empress. They'd come to watch a sacrifice. Embers of wrath seethed in the hollows of Rosalind's mind.

The afternoon sun dipped low, staining the guests with a lurid ginger light as they took their seats. Their bodies cast long shadows, and the guests' voices echoed off the stone.

Cleo's leafy aura churned in her chest, and she glanced to the right, where a tunnel opened directly into the pit. She couldn't remember why, but that tunnel was important. *The prisons...*

Slowly, the rows of seats filled with guests, most wearing the iron chalice insignias. All around the amphitheater's pit stood scorpion guards in iron armor.

Something moved in the corner of her eye, and she turned, her pulse racing. A man loomed over her, his eyes like flames. Tendrils of colored magic whirled from his body, staining the air with gold, green, and silver...

It should have been beautiful, but something about the sight of him filled her with dread. And under that, pure rage. *Drew.*

"Rosalind, my bride..." His voice wasn't quite human. It sounded like seven people speaking at once—feminine and masculine, old and young—and all filled with a strange, lonely sort of agony. She would have felt sorry for him if she didn't want to kill him.

A dark smile curled his lips. "I've so looked forward to this day. To making you mine. You do look beautiful." He cocked his head. "I like you when you're silent and still."

That delicious aura stirred in her chest. *I will watch you burn. I will sear your skin, melt your bones.* Rosalind smiled placidly.

Drew sat by her side, and grabbed her right hand, pulling it into his lap. His grip crushed her fingers, his nails piercing her skin, drawing blood. He wanted to hurt her. He knew she wouldn't cry out —she'd just sit there smiling numbly.

And yet, as magic stirred in Rosalind's mind, it began to eat away at those cold, icy mists. Slowly, the scorpion guards began leading chained men and women to the stakes. Rosalind's gut churned. A girl with short brown curls sobbed uncontrollably, and a young man with tattoos wailed to the skies. Their pain pierced Rosalind to the bone.

Drew pressed his fingernails further into her skin, letting her blood drip down her hand. He leaned into her, whispering, "Grooms are supposed to make their brides bleed on their wedding night, Rosalind."

His breath, hot on her neck, fanned the flames of rage burning in her chest. She'd beaten his face once, broken his bones. Smashed it to a pulp. Under the icy stillness of her mind, she wanted to break him again, to crush him like an unwanted doll.

A heavy silence enshrouded the crowd, and they stared at the line of sacrificial victims. Rosalind's gaze landed on one of the humans— a young girl with pink hair. She stood trembling in her thin, yellow dress, muttering to herself. She knew what was about to happen. She was about to burn.

Slowly, Randolph strode into the orchestra pit, and the sunlight lit his red hair ablaze. He wore a white robe, stained pink in the setting sun. The high priest of blood.

Rosalind needed to stop this somehow, if she could remember how to move. She scrambled to grasp at the strains of cloudy thoughts. *I lived. I died.*

Drew dug his nails further into her skin, moaning slightly. He was enjoying himself, drawing blood.

Randolph stood before the altar, and picked up a goblet. Raising it to the sky, he shouted, "Blodrial grants us power!"

The crowd roared back the same call. "Blodrial grants us power!"

Randolph began leading the crowd in a long, rambling series of prayers—prayers that Rosalind had once memorized as a novice in the Brotherhood. With the fog in her mind, it was hard to remember what they'd meant, but it was something about blood and iron, and ridding the world of evil.

As Randolph solemnly droned on, the guards chained the men and women to the stakes, and their panicked sobs and cries pierced the air. Rosalind's blood roared in her ears.

Randolph raised his hands to the reddening skies. "We require a truly stunning sacrifice today, in honor of the one true god!"

The girl with the pink hair shrieked, her screams unrelenting. The sound of her panic tightened Rosalind's heart.

By Rosalind's side, Drew mumbled, "Azazeyl is the one true god." He spoke in the voices of seven tormented gods. "Azazeyl rules the heaven and earth."

She glanced at the blood on her hand where he pierced her flesh. Deep in her skull, a green aura roiled.

Around the amphitheater pit, the scorpion guards began moving, snatching torches from iron holders. One by one, they lit the torches, and with each blaze of flame, the angry fire in Rosalind's mind burned hotter.

An image flashed in her skull—she was chained to a stake, and flames climbed up her body. She screamed for Ambrose, for Richard...

I can't watch this happen...

Her aura was ready to explode from her body. She needed to stop this, if she could only free her thoughts from this mist clouding her mind, filling her skull like an icy miasma. If she could only...

Without understanding why she was doing it, she clenched her free fist, piercing her own flesh with her fingernails until she drew blood.

While her betrothed muttered about Azazeyl, Rosalind's lips began moving, until she was muttering along with him. They weren't her own words, and she wasn't entirely sure what she was saying, but that vernal aura that was roiling in her skull, the one that smelled of oaks and moss, compelled her to speak, compelled her to pierce her own skin, making holes in her palm.

As she stared down at her hand, blackish blood flowed from the cuts in her skin. And as it did, the icy miasma clouding her mind slowly began to thin. Blood and iron poured from her hand, spurred on by the spell she'd just chanted, and it freed her from her icy prison.

I lived. I died. I lived again.

As the ice melted from her mind, clarity bloomed. Slowly, she looked around the amphitheater, at the guests who'd come to watch the sacrifices burn. Rosalind should bathe this entire place in fire, but she wouldn't. She'd come here for a reason. She'd risked the charmed iron, and infiltrated the empire—she'd endured Randolph and Drew and the scorpion men for one reason, and one alone. She was here to stop Drew from creating any more demons to fuel his armies.

Maybe Rosalind had been mesmerized the entire time, but Cleo hadn't. When she'd developed this plan, she'd been counting on her second soul. She swallowed hard, eyeing the scorpion guards as they moved around the edges of the pit, lighting torches while Randolph continued his lengthy preamble.

Her gaze flicked to Drew, whose fiery eyes were locked on Randolph. Even while Randolph chanted about Blodrial, Drew was muttering about Azazeyl, his voice growing louder, face redder. To him, this was sacrilege.

As her thoughts crystalized, she surveyed the amphitheater pit, where the prisoners stood chained to the stakes. The human witches among them screamed. The demons stood in stony silence, their bodies curling with colored auras, one of them a woman with a deep silver aura, like Caine's. *Caine.* As soon as she thought of his name, his absence felt like a hollow ache in her chest.

She scanned the rest of the sacrificial victims, taking in their aura. Besides the witch and the shadow demon, there were three valkyrie, two keres, and two hellhounds.

Slowly, she turned to take in the crowd. All around her, the wedding guests wore the iron insignias of Blodrial, their god. They smiled blandly, watching the guards chain the prisoners to their stakes, listening to the terrified screams. They'd come to watch a bloodletting.

Horror welled in her gut. This was supposed to be her wedding day, a gruesome slaughter. Later, Randolph planned to rape her. And who knew what horrors Drew had in mind.

But Rosalind had planned all of this—the drugging, the mind control. Infiltrating the Empire. For weeks, she and Caine had practiced, experimenting with charmed iron that clouded her mind, letting Cleo take over while Rosalind's body went numb. And it had worked.

Now, she had to stop this slaughter before it happened. And that meant channeling all the magic she could—without Drew noticing a thing.

Randolph finished his prayers, and held his hands to the skies as if he were some sort of god. *Prick. I will kill you some day. Not today, but some day I will watch you take your last breath.*

Bearing torches, the scorpion men crossed to the stakes. A young witch with curly brown hair and large glasses shrieked in terror, and the sound turned Rosalind's blood to ice.

She glanced at Drew. He clutched her hand in a death grip, but he wasn't paying her attention. She surveyed her surroundings. Here, in the open air, the Hunters didn't have a single weapon aimed at her. No iron powder or flamethrowers to stop her.

They'd underestimated her.

Drew closed his eyes, chanting about the seven gods. While he lost himself in the hell of his own mind, Rosalind let the power of Nyxobas flood her body—that cold magic, scented of lightning and peat. At the same time, she channeled the storm god's magic to surge through her blood. Her pulse raced as she watched one of the scorpion gods bend lower, touching his torch to the pile of wood beneath one of the valkyrie.

The valkyrie—an Amazonian woman with pale white hair—was staring directly at Rosalind, watching, as if she could sense the storm power building in Rosalind's body. Perhaps Rosalind could use the valkyrie's power, too. Subtly, Rosalind nodded at her. The valkyrie nodded back.

Now raw, electric power blazed through her blood.

First she needed to take out Drew. He was her biggest threat here, and he alone had the power to stop her magical assault.

Over the reddening sunset, dark clouds rolled in. Electricity began to charge the air, and the hair on the back of her neck stood on end.

After she immobilized Drew, she'd free the prisoners. Unshackled, they could slaughter the whole crowd of bloodthirsty Brotherhood wedding guests.

Flames began to ignite on the bottom of the valkyrie's pyre, smoke curling around the demon.

Rosalind glanced at the sky, narrowing her eyes, letting her body fill with Nyxobas's power, his speed. In a blur of cold shadows, she ripped her hand from Drew's grasp, then shadow-ran into the pit. In there, the growing storm winds rushed over her skin, tearing at the ribbons of her wedding dress. Surging with the power of the storm goddess, she whirled in the air, churning it. Before her feet touched down in the pit, she sent a spear of lightning racing directly for Drew. Once.

It struck him just as her feet landed in the dusty earth. Twice, another bolt for good measure. Dust clouded over her white dress.

Drew fell back, the scent of burning flesh filling the air. Her body sparking with electricity, Rosalind summoned the storm's power, and she struck Drew a third time. Around the amphitheater the crowd began screaming, now sounding a lot like the terrified witches as the stake.

Rosalind smiled darkly. *Where's your god now?*

CHAPTER 9

She couldn't kill Drew now, but the lightning would knock him out for long enough to get the real chaos going. Rosalind pivoted, flicking her wrist to send an icy stream of shadow magic at the pyre's flames, extinguishing their fire. She pivoted again, snuffing out the torches.

Then she let the power of the fire goddess burn through her veins, a molten inferno welling within her. She held out her hands, calling a ring of fire that encircled the wedding guests, trapping them where they sat. Screams rose to the darkening sky. The fire goddess in her thrilled at their cries.

Boil their blood, Emerazel whispered. *Melt the marrow in their bones.*

She searched the crowd for Randolph, but she couldn't find him in the chaos, and there wasn't much time to look for him. The scorpions were moving for her, but Rosalind shadow-ran away from them, rushing around like a phantom wind. As she moved, her attention focused on the prisoners, and she felt the power of the mountain goddess light up her body. As coppery magic spiraled from her chest, she focused on the chains, twisting them from the prisoners' necks.

I am the ancient mountains and stone, goddess of strength... I will bury you in your guilt. Images of Miranda's dead body flickered in her mind, and Rosalind's body tensed. *I will bury you under the rocks.*

Rosalind tried to block out the goddess's voice. She needed to stay focused.

As five scorpion-men closed in, running over the red sand, Rosalind summoned her fire magic, letting it build in her body. The good people of the Empire had come here to watch a massacre, and she couldn't disappoint them, could she? She lifted her hands, letting fire blaze from her fingertips, streaming in five perfect arcs into the scorpion-men's chests. Within moments, fire engulfed their bodies, and they writhed in the dancing flames.

Rosalind's lips curled in a dark smile at the scent of searing flesh, and the terrified screams filling the air. *Melt the marrow in their bones.*

The people in the seats were desperate, falling all over each other to rush from the amphitheater, shoving and screaming. She couldn't let them get away that easily, could she? Humans needed to learn that Blodrial wouldn't protect them.

She summoned the power of Nyxobas, letting it thrum through her body, ancient and cold. Silver streams of magic whirled from her fingertips, curling around the panicking humans, freezing them in place. Rosalind stared through the flames, a dark thrill rippling up her neck. The humans' skin glazed over with white webs of frost, their eyelashes peaked in frozen icicles, hair dusted with white.

Fire and darkness, flames and ice... such a beautiful combination.

Let them feel the cold. And now, let them feel the gnawing dread of isolation. She closed her eyes, letting wisps of the void stream from her body into theirs, streaming into their chests as they slowly froze.

Shadows whirled around her, and she rose into the air, staring down at them. "Where's your god now?" she roared. "Did he save you?"

From behind her, an electric power thrummed over her skin, and she turned to see one of the valkyrie rising into the air, filling the skies with her song, her eyes dark as death. The valkyrie struck Drew with another gleaming shard of lightning.

But the valkyrie wasn't the only thing taking to the skies. In the distance, helicopter rotors beat the air. The Brotherhood were sending in their troops.

As much as she wanted to stay and fight in the battle, she'd come here for one reason. She needed to get Erish from the prisons, and return with Drew's secret weapon to Lilinor.

Silver magic whirled around her body, scented of Caine, and she used it to propel her into the tunnel, her stupid wedding dress whipping in the wind as he ran.

She shadow-ran through the hall, and as she moved, the smooth sandstone gave way to dark, rough walls. Filled with the power of Nyxobas, she moved on the wind.

She wasn't Rosalind anymore—she was Nyxobas, ancient god of the void. The god of stealth and terror, death and the vastness of space...

As she moved, emptiness gnawed at her chest.

Focus, Rosalind. You're still Rosalind. As the air rushed over her skin, she turned a corner, finding one byzantine curve after another. This place had been built like a labyrinth, and she couldn't say how long Nyxobas's power would spur her on before she sacrificed her mind completely to the god of night.

She sniffed the air, scenting the seductive, jasmine scent of a succubus. Tendrils of black magic curled through the air toward her. *Erish.*

She followed the dark aura around another corner, and her gaze landed on the rows of iron cell bars. *Bingo.*

She slowed her pace, peering through the cells as she walked. Huddled in filthy corners were clusters of humans and demons, many so sick they hardly registered Rosalind's arrival. Rough stone walls enclosed the cells, the floors covered in mud and rats.

Rosalind swallowed hard, her pulse racing. She'd come here for one reason, and one alone: to bring Erish back to Lilinor. But she couldn't leave the prisoners here, either. Drew would burn them all in the amphitheater stakes.

First, she needed to heal them, and then she'd set them free. She wasn't leaving anyone behind her to burn.

Slowly, she paced between the cells, letting the healing power of Druloch thrum over her skin. Foxglove and oak, the medicinal strength of moss—Druloch's magic whirled around her. Green forest magic curled into the prison cells. And with it, curling around the green in strands of silver, Rosalind sent shadow magic to heal the pain.

Power ignited her body, and her back arched. *I live again.*

All around her, she could hear the prisoners rallying, shifting on the stone floors as they healed. She could even hear their hearts beating louder, stronger.

As she healed them, she moved from one cell to another, searching for Erish.

At last her gaze landed on the succubus, huddled in a corner in filthy rags. Erish was still beautiful, of course, her skin golden and her dark eyes captivating, but her body had transformed. In the prisons here, her body had become gaunt, her collarbone protruding. Her cheeks looked hollow, her lips thin. Once, long ago, Erish had been worshipped as a goddess. A pang of pity tightened Rosalind's chest.

"My old friend," the succubus rasped. "Have you come to bring me food and blankets again?"

Rosalind crossed to Erish's cell, wrapping her hands around the bars. "I've come to bring you back to Lilinor."

Erish narrowed her eyes. "From one prison to another. How tempting. Why should I go with you? Might as well stay in this festering cell, where I have company."

With all the power pulsing through Rosalind's veins, she could probably just *take* Erish. The succubus was halfway into the grave. Still, the journey would be much easier if Erish came willingly, and something told Rosalind she might actually need Erish's help at a later time.

She couldn't promise Erish much. The queen was still a traitor, and Ambrose wouldn't want her roaming freely around Lilinor, stirring up trouble. But she could promise *something.* "You'll still be imprisoned, yes. But we can put you in one of the palace rooms, with a guard outside. You'll have food, a bed, a bath." Rosalind surveyed

Erish's tattered dress, a filthy brown that had once been white. "You'll have clothing."

"When I arrive, I want a visit to my husband." She straightened. "After I have time to clean myself up."

"I'll make it happen."

"And why should I trust you, Rosalind Atherton?"

The magic of the gods rippled through Rosalind's muscles, and she cast a glance over her shoulder, to see if anyone was coming for her. Her grip tightened on the bars. She was quickly losing patience. "For fuck's sake, Erish. It's not going to get much worse than this. Randolph plans to use you to build an army. And when you've created all the demon species he could have ever wanted, he won't need you anymore. He'll simply breed them together, creating new breeds under his control. He'll keep you in rags, and starve you down here. And when he's done, he'll burn you at the stake."

Erish's cheeks blanched, and her body began to tremble.

"Don't you understand what a prize you are, Erish? You're a succubus. You were once worshipped as a goddess, and your power scares the shit out of them. It scares the shit out of most men, and they want to kill you for it." Rosalind clenched the bars so hard her knuckles whitened. "Do you understand? You can't count on them. We need to make our own destinies. If you come with me, you'll live. That's got to be better than this."

Erish stared at her, and something flickered in her dark eyes.

"Are you in or are you out?" Rosalind demanded.

Erish stood unsteadily, still chained to the ground. "Get me out of here."

"Good. I just have a few other prisoners to get out, too."

She stepped back from the cell bars, summoning the power of Borgerith. She lifted her arms, the magic of the goddess dizzying her, its power intoxicating. Copper magic spiraled from her chest, twisting around the iron bars.

Her body hummed with magic, until she no longer felt like Rosalind, but like Borgerith herself. *I am the icy winds over Monte Bianco. I am the fiery depths of Etna. And I will crush Drew with his guilt.*

Rosalind gritted her teeth, trying to control the goddess's raw strength. *I'm in control here.* And yet even as she thought it, the euphoria of power thrummed over her skin. She had an overwhelming desire to hunt down Drew and rip his spine out of his back. She'd draw and quarter him, sever his head and limbs and scatter them over the earth. Even for an immortal, that would be a difficult situation to recover from.

But she had to stick with the plan, had to get out of here, back to Lilinor. If she gave Drew another chance to capture her, it would all be over for her. He wouldn't make the same mistake twice, and she'd find her own body dismembered, impaled with iron spikes. A difficult situation to get out of, and Drew would find a way to control her, one way or another.

Coppery magic swirled from her body, curling around the iron prison bars. Around her, the bars groaned as they twisted and bent.

She glanced at Erish, whose iron chains fell from her body. "Let's get to the portal. We need to get to Lilinor."

A moaning noise from one of the cells caught Rosalind's attention, and her throat tightened. One of the prisoners had been left behind.

Erish stepped from the cell, rubbing her wrists. "Are you coming?"

"Go." Rosalind's heart thundered. "There's one more thing I've got to do. Get back to the portal before the Hunters track you down, okay?"

Erish nodded once, then disappeared in a blur of dark shadows.

There, in a shadowy corner, a hunched and huddled form. A child, by the looks of it, no more than three or four, and completely human. He looked too weak to move, untouched by the healing magic.

Rosalind crossed into the cell. "Hello?"

The child's ripped clothing exposed his spine, which protruded from an emaciated back. Rosalind crouched next to him, touching his back. Mossy green healing magic rippled down her arm, swirling from her fingertips, and curled around the boy. After a few moments, he heaved a deep breath, stretching his arms. He lifted his head, blinking large, brown eyes as though awaking from a deep sleep.

"What's your name?" she asked.

"Owen." He looked around himself, confused. "Where'd Mama go?"

A lump rose in her throat. Mama had probably died, but he'd been too sick to realize, or too young to understand. "Was she here with you?"

He nodded.

"Was she sick? Was she sleeping a lot?"

He nodded again, tears filling his eyes. "She wouldn't wake up." His face crumpled, cheeks reddened, and he let out a wail.

Rosalind reached for him, picking him up. Wailing, he wrapped his arms around her neck, tears streaming down his cheeks.

"Shhh… It's okay, Owen. We're going to need to run fast. Real fast. Are you ready?"

"Where's my mama?" His pained screams echoed off the walls.

Shit. It'd be hard to move inconspicuously with Owen in her arms, and if Drew caught them, they could both end up dead. But there was no way she could leave him behind now. Gripping him tight, she summoned her shadow magic, feeling its power thrum through her body.

But before she could break into a sprint, fear slammed her in the gut. There, snaking down the curve of the hall, the long tendrils of Drew's magic, curling closer, feeling her out like insect antennas.

She held Owen close, whispering *Shhhh…,* her pulse racing. The truth was, even without Owen's siren-like wail, Drew would seek her out. She knew how to sense Drew, and it worked both ways. He could smell and feel magic just like she could.

Still, she felt a sudden surge of protectiveness for Owen. If she wasn't able to get away from Drew, she wanted to hide Owen long enough that just maybe, he'd be able to find his own way out.

Nyxobas was the god of night, and the god of sleep, too. As Drew's magic moved closer through the hall, she stroked Owen's head, letting the magic of the night flow from her fingertips into his skull. Slowly, his body relaxed, his chest rising and falling slowly, until he was sleeping on her shoulder.

Her heart hammering, she hurried into one of the cells, tucking him in a dark corner. As she crossed out of the cell again, she called upon the ancient strength of the mountain goddess.

With the sandstone hall emptied, Drew's footsteps echoed off the ceiling. She glanced down at her hands, at the place where fingernails had pierced her palms. Already, the skin had healed over, leaving only a faint, white line. Perhaps she *was* immortal now, just like Drew. He could torture her, imprison her. Cut off her head. But he wouldn't be able to truly kill her.

In the distance, footsteps pounded through the hall, so powerful that the stone trembled. A faint layer of dust rained from the ceiling, and her heartbeat sped up, hammering against her ribs.

He's coming.

"Rosalind!" Drew's voice reverberated through the halls—the voice of many, of young and old, male and female, icy and hot. But one, clear emotion rang through the chorus: agony. "Rosalind!"

At the sound of his strange voice, her heart skipped a beat, and she thanked the gods Owen would be asleep for whatever was about to happen next. She wasn't sure exactly how this fight would end, but it would be bloody and brutal, and the poor kid was probably emotionally damaged enough as it was.

As Drew's magic strengthened around her, the seven gods' own thoughts mingled in her mind. She was going to face Drew, the architect of this living nightmare. A man who saw fit to imprison toddlers, to let them watch their mothers die.

As the gods-magic ignited, a cacophony of rage rang inside her skull. *He'll get what's coming to him.* She was going to get out of here alive. And she was going to take Owen with her.

Her fingers twitched with anticipation. When Drew came into view, the first thing she noticed was the iron nail in his fist. He wanted to hurt her the way he'd hurt Miranda—the way Caine had killed her parents.

It wouldn't happen. Drew had no idea how strong she was now, had no idea of the power coursing through her body. *I will drive that into his heart. I will hear the sound of his ribs cracking...*

Propelled by the gods of storms and night, she broke into a sprint.

When she reached Drew, she slammed a punch into his face, fist against bone. The crack reverberated through the hall, and his head whipped away, blood pouring from his mouth.

The next punch he was ready for, and he blocked it with his arm. His eyes burned with the madness of seven tormented gods, and his lip curled. "You should have been controlled, my wife."

"I was," she murmured. "But Cleo wasn't."

She let Borgerith's power flow through her veins, and she smashed her fist into his chest. She knocked him back into the dirt, the nail falling from his hand with a clang.

For just a moment, fear flickered across his features, and she lunged for him, hammering him in the head with one powerful punch after another, a punishing hail of blows—snapping bones, drawing blood.

Slam. Droplets of blood flew through the air as she smashed his teeth, and he staggered on his feet, eyes wide.

Destroy him.

She smashed her elbow into his temple—a move that would have killed a mortal man—and Drew's eyelids drooped. Dazed, he searched for the iron nail, fingers scrambling around him. He'd come here to torture her. Truly, that was his one burning obsession in life, to punish the woman who'd abandoned him—who'd humiliated him by loving his worst nightmare.

Slam. Her elbow struck him in the side of the head again. Now, somewhere under the fog of his pain, he was having second thoughts, a frightened animal ready to crawl back to his hole.

Slam. He grunted from the pain.

Desperately, he tried to block the blows, probably hoping for mercy. He wouldn't get it. Rosalind reared back for another blow to Drew's head, one that would truly crack his skull, and his eyes opened wide, flickering with flames.

Before she could land the next blow, silver magic exploded from his body, knocking her off him. Drew was gone, disappearing in a blur of silvery shadows, so fast the wind rushed over Rosalind's skin.

Give him what he deserves, Borgerith whispered.

She clenched her fists, torn by an overwhelming desire to hunt her cousin down, and the certainty that she should get back to Lilinor, and to get Owen to safety. The longer she stayed here, without backup, the greater the risk that she'd get herself into some kind of trouble, or end up buried in the cold earth with her sister. She couldn't die, but she could be buried deep under the earth…

At the thought of Miranda six feet underground, grief bloomed in her chest.

I need to return to Lilinor. I need to get Owen out of here.

A lump rose in Rosalind's throat as she turned for the prison cell. She crossed through the warped bars, swallowing hard. The kid looked so peaceful in his sleep, tears making clear tracks through the dirt on his cheeks.

But as she reached for him, someone violently yanked her head back by the hair, pulling her onto the floor. Her body slammed against the sandstone.

CHAPTER 10

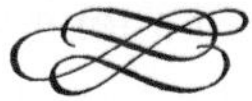

*R*osalind's back screamed with pain. Panic stole her breath as Drew climbed on top of her, straddling her waist. He tore at the front of her lace dress, trying to rip it off. She swung for him, but she hadn't had enough time to prepare. Borgerith's power no longer blazed through her body, and her blows weren't doing the damage she needed to do.

Drew pinned her arms, snarling. "My loving wife." Leaning down, he opened his mouth wide, biting deep into her neck like a wild animal.

Pain ripped through her body, and she thrashed beneath him, her screams echoing off the ceiling. She knew one thing for sure. If she didn't get out of this, it was all over.

She summoned the power of Borgerith, letting it explode from her body and into Drew's. He fell back, clutching his chest as if a great weight were crushing him.

Her pulse racing, Rosalind snatched Owen's sleeping body from the ground, trying to block out the pain splintering her body. Blazing with shadow magic, she clutched Owen tight to her chest, rushing through the hall at the speed of a hurricane wind.

But she was losing too much blood, couldn't keep moving this fast. She faltered, stumbling against the wall, still clutching the child.

Think, Rosalind. Cleo's aura bloomed in her chest. There was one way out of here: an Angelic spell. Holding the boy tight against her chest, she launched into the teleportation spell. At the final syllable, her body flickered away from Drew's until the world around her shifted, the sandstone floor giving way to a flooded crypt.

She was free, and she loosed a long sigh of relief. In one arm, she cradled the child, and with the other, she gripped her neck, trying to stanch the bleeding where Drew had torn out part of her flesh.

She'd better be immortal, or she'd be dead soon. Within minutes, she'd find out whether Drew had been telling the truth.

Blocking out the pain, she inched closer to the portal of water. She knew hardly anything about trying to swim with another person in your arms, except that it was supposed to be easier if that person wasn't thrashing and kicking. Was it better to leave Owen asleep? But then, perhaps, he'd drown. Gods *damn* it. Whoever had designed these water portals clearly hadn't thought about transporting babies and toddlers.

Perhaps awake was better. She waved her hand in front of the child's sleeping face, pulling the shadow magic from his body, leaving just enough to keep him relaxed. Slowly, he opened his eyes, blinking at her blearily.

"Owen. Have you ever been swimming?" she asked.

"Milk."

She gritted her teeth. "Have you ever been swimming? In a swimming pool?"

He nodded. "I go swimming. I'm a super super big super strong swimmer, like the Octonauts."

Good. Promising. "Do you know how to hold your breath under water? Like the Octonauts?" *Whoever the hell they are.*

He nodded. "I'm gonna need you to do that Owen, okay? We're going under water for a little bit. You need to take a deep breath, okay?"

He stared at her neck, concern flickering over his features. "What's that red stuff?"

She was still clutching her neck. "It's just paint, honey."

He seemed dubious, but didn't ask any more questions.

"I'm gonna hold you tight, Owen. And you're gonna hold your breath. Like the Octonauts."

Slowly, her body shuddering, she inched over to the filthy water. "Now, Owen. Hold your breath."

She watched as he took a deep breath, and she plunged under the icy surface. Blood poured from her wound as she drifted beneath the water, losing blood in the murk. A bone-deep chill spread through her body, and she began shaking uncontrollably, holding Owen tighter.

She needed to get out of here fast, but her body wouldn't stop shaking. Probably the blood loss. *Fight, Rosalind.* Just as her vision began dimming, she glanced up once more at the surface. This time, faint beams of light piercing the darkness—pearly light, faintly streaming. Moonlight—not sunlight.

Thank the gods. We're in Lilinor.

Her body burning with fatigue, she kicked her way to the surface, desperate to get Owen into the air again.

At last, her head breached the air, and she hoisted Owen out. He grasped for the fountain's edge, crying. She'd never been so happy to see the night sky in her life. "Hang on, Owen."

She hoisted herself over the fountain's edge, tumbling onto the cobbles. Then, she reached for Owen, pulling him out of the water. His teeth were chattering uncontrollably, and she held him tight, slipping down against the side of the fountain. She sat at the fountain's edge, wet clothing clinging to her body, heavy and cold, and shivers overtook her.

She held Owen close, cradling him in her arms. He was wailing, and she was beginning to question her choice of bringing a human toddler into a vampire realm. Still—it's not like she'd had a lot of choices.

"Shhhhh…" She cradled his head, summoning her soothing light magic, feeling his muscles relax. "Go to sleep, Owen."

Within moments, his eyes had closed, his limbs going limp. Now, she just had to summon the energy to walk up to the fortress.

As she listened to the sound of the water dripping from her sodden hair and clothes onto the stone, her eyelids slowly drifted closed. Somewhere in the distance, a raven cawed.

Rosalind wasn't sure how long she'd been lying on the stone when powerful arms scooped her up, a loamy, comforting scent enveloping her body. A soothing aura slipped around her skin, caressing her, warming her body, and Rosalind felt herself melting into an embrace. A rhythmic sound of beating wings filled the air, and the wind rushed through her hair.

As the healing aura wrapped around her, Rosalind's eyes fluttered open. She looked up at Caine, whose deep silver eyes peered down at her, bright as the starlight.

"Rosalind," he whispered. "What happened?"

Wincing, she reached for her neck, feeling the ragged wound.

"Seven hells," he snarled. "I knew I should have gone after you. What did he do to you?"

"I told you not to come—" Oh gods, it hurt to speak. *Shit.* What had happened to the boy? "Where's Owen?"

"Don't talk if it hurts." His powerful arms tightened around her, and she rested her head against his chest. "Owen is the child you returned with, I suppose? Tammi's up ahead with him. He woke, screaming for milk and for his mother. I'm not sure how you slept through that, but I need to finish healing you. Then, you're going to rest."

Her mind flashed with images of a palace full of bone, of walls formed from corrupted veins, a building breathing. The thought of being trapped in another room sparked a burst of dread. "Don't lock me inside again. I need to stay in the open air."

As Caine's magic whispered over her skin, soothing her entire body, her eyes fluttered closed, and she drifted again into a deep sleep.

CHAPTER 11

osalind woke wrapped in silky bedsheets, a floral breeze kissing her skin. For a moment, dread tightened her chest, until her eyes focused on Lilu, Caine's raven. The bird stared right at Rosalind, her head cocked, candlelight glinting in her black eyes.

Clearly, Rosalind was no longer in the Brotherhood's malignant palace. She pushed herself up on her elbows. Instead of a ripped, bloodstained wedding dress, she was wearing a silk nightgown. Black.

Caine dressed me.

She rubbed her eyes, clearing the sleep from her mind, then surveyed the room. It wasn't the room she'd been sleeping in before—the one she'd been sharing with Miranda before she died. This room was enormous, fit for a queen.

Through the open glass doors, she had a view of an enormous stone balcony lined with myrtle trees. Moonlight bathed the leaves in silver, and streamed through their leaves onto a small, round table on the tiled balcony. The wind toyed with delicate silver curtains, and she breathed in the fresh air. Caine had been paying attention when she'd asked not to be locked in a room. In fact, he'd found her the closest thing to being outside.

By the wall near her bed, a silver, domed tray sat on an oak table.

843

The smell of bacon made her stomach rumble. When was the last time she'd eaten? When she touched her stomach, she could feel her ribs protruding. Her memories of Drew's palace were hazy, but clearly she hadn't eaten much while she'd been there.

When she thought of the palace, nausea rose in her stomach. Disturbing memories flickered through her mind. The scorpion men, stinging a girl to death. Randolph, forcing her onto her knees in some sick sort of power play. At the thought of him and Drew, bile rose in her throat, and she closed her eyes, trying to clear her mind. *Lilinor. I'm in Lilinor now, in a city of lavender and jasmine, of eternal night. My new home.*

When she opened her eyes, her mind began adjusting to the dim room. In the far corners of the room, sleeping in two enormous velvet armchairs, were Tammi and Caine. Tammi lay curled up, her pale hair draped over Owen, who slept nestled into the crook of her arm. Somehow, they'd found a pink plastic sippy cup, and Owen clutched its handle in his sleep. Someone had dressed him in clean clothes that looked like they were from the 19th century—a velvet jumper with a lace collar.

A faint noise like a low, uneven growl filled the room. Across from Owen and Tammi, Caine slept, his powerful chest slowly rising and falling, his eyelashes a stark black against his golden cheeks. He wore a black T-shirt, its short sleeves exposing the severe tattoo on his arm —the hairpin she'd seen in his memory. His aura curled through the room, soothing and electric at the same time.

Between the two chairs, an enormous, silver-framed mirror hung on the wall. Rosalind straightened, gazing at herself in the reflection. Her cheeks looked gaunt, and purple circles darkened the skin below her eyes. How long had she been trapped in Drew's hellish fantasy? She shuddered. The next time she saw Drew, she hoped it would be the day he died.

As she watched Caine sleep, his chest rising and falling, his breath hitching slightly, she realized the source of the low growl. Caine—the demigod—snored lightly in his sleep, and his chest seemed to pause at the end of his inhale. In his sleep, he seemed strangely human, and

Rosalind felt a sudden rush of warmth for him. She'd never seen him sleeping before, and she had an overwhelming desire to curl in his lap and kiss his cheeks.

Even if she'd been in a hellish fog for her entire time in the Empire, somehow she'd felt his absence like a hollow in her chest, like she'd been missing an important part of herself.

She'd needed his smell, the feel of his skin against hers, the faint brush of his stubble against her cheeks, his fingertips stroking her thighs. She needed to feel her hand pressing over his heart, the blood rushing through his body. She'd wanted to tuck her head into the crook of his neck, to smell his deep, earthy scent, to feel her lips against his, his large hands on her skin.

Before she'd left, he'd told her that she wasn't destined to be with him. Something about a woman with blond hair—the reason she was fated for Malphas, and not Caine. It made no sense to her, and she had no idea what he'd meant by that. He must be wrong, because Caine felt like a part of her now—a part of her she'd never before known existed. If she lost him now, she'd never feel whole again.

As she looked at him, she traced her fingertips over her lower lip, imagining what it had felt like the last time he'd kissed her.

As if hearing her thoughts, his eyes opened, and her breath hitched in her throat. What would he say if she told him everything she really felt?

Within moments, Caine seemed completely alert, his silver eyes fixed on her. Apparently, he didn't need much time to gather his thoughts after waking.

He rose, walking to her, and sat at the edge of her bed, studying her closely. "How do you feel?"

"About what?" she asked, still slightly dazed. She wanted to wrap her arms around him, to pull him close, and she had to restrain herself.

"Your neck. How does your neck feel?" His fist clenched, and he traced his fingertips over her throat, pain flickering in his eyes. "Drew tore half your neck out. I can't understand how you survived that. It should have killed you. How were you able to swim back here? With a child, no less?"

She touched her neck. For the first time, she realized she'd nearly completely healed. Where a deep wound had been not long ago, now lay only a faint scar where Drew had bit her. "I feel fine, apart from the memories."

Shadows clouded his eyes, and the candles guttered as the temperature dropped. "What did he do to you?" Rage laced his voice.

Rosalind swallowed hard. "Did you know that you snore?"

"Don't change the subject." His jaw tightened. "And I absolutely do not." Caine took her hand in his. "What happened to you there? You look like they starved you."

"It wasn't pretty, but I did what I had to do. And just like I told you, Cleo looked after me. I've come back unscathed."

"Apart from the part where you had your throat ripped out and nearly died."

"About that," Rosalind said. "Drew claims that he and I are now immortal. He says that using gods-magic has fundamentally changed us, and that we are basically gods now."

Caine narrowed his eyes. "That sounds absurd."

"And yet, I'm here, alive, when I shouldn't be." She loosed a sigh. "The downside is that I failed to kill Drew, since he is immortal, too. Surely there must be a way around the whole immortality thing. What if I severed his head and buried it under the ocean? Or burned him to ash, and kept his cinders in separate vaults. I'm just trying to think creatively here."

"What do you mean you 'failed to kill Drew'? We discussed this." He studied her closely. "You weren't supposed to attempt to kill him. You were there only to retrieve Erish, which you did. You didn't fail at anything."

"How long was I gone?"

"Eight days. Did they starve you?"

She hugged herself, shaking her head. "No. I didn't want to eat, because I felt like I was already dead."

Caine looked deep into her eyes. "If Drew has become immortal, that might explain why he's lost his mind. Why your parents did. Humans were never meant to be immortal." He brushed his knuckles softly over her cheeks. "And yet, you seem sane."

Exhausted, she rubbed her eyes. "I told you I'd be fine. I managed to use Azazel's power without becoming overwhelmed by lust for power."

"For now."

She thought of the gods' voices, whispering in her mind when she used their power. "Admittedly, sometimes they compel me to destroy things. But they don't control me completely."

"If you're going to use their power, you need to yield to them just a little." He pushed a strand of hair out of her eyes. "The important part is you deprived Drew of his secret weapon. And, it seems, a horde of refugee prisoners who we now have to look after. I hope you realize the vampires will want the humans to donate blood in exchange for their stay here."

She swallowed hard. For a moment, hazy memories flitted through her mind—Randolph telling her to take off her robe, making her kneel before him.

Caine studied her closely. "What? Tell me what Drew did to you there?"

"I'm fine," she repeated. "I'll tell you this much. Randolph might be the real mastermind. Easier to kill, definitely. But also much, much smarter. I don't think Drew is in control of his own mind. He's too lost in the world of the gods. On our wedding day, he was muttering to himself about Azazeyl. The gods are mad, I think—and Drew is merely a puppet of their whims."

Caine's silvery aura whipped around his body. "I will relish the day I rip both their heads from their bodies."

Rosalind shook her head. "I think that's my privilege. But I'll let you watch."

Caine shook his head. "You won't be able to kill Drew."

"Why not?"

"If he's immortal like I am, there's only one way to end him. It's secret knowledge. It's not something immortals tend to pass on."

"Oh, I see. You have trust issues. You don't want me to know how to kill you."

He quirked a smile. "I would enjoy watching you eviscerate Drew."

She frowned. "Why do I get the feeling like that would be some kind of weird foreplay to you?"

He shrugged.

Rosalind glanced at the window, at the white flowers blooming in the moonlight. "You got me a room open to the air."

Caine had been locked up once, too. He clearly knew a thing or two about needing the open air, about yearning for freedom.

She pulled off the sheets and rose on unsteady legs, then crossed to the open doors. The breeze kissed her skin, and she hugged herself.

The balcony was enormous—thirty feet across. From the myrtle boughs hung small lanterns, their candles twinkling in the darkness. Sighing, crossed to the balcony's edge, gazing at the Astarte sea. From here, she had a perfect view of the shimmering phosphorescence, and the waves breaking over the rocks.

Caine came up behind her, his body warming hers. He pointed at the sea. "There, you can see the nippexies. The water spirits that flicker through the ocean."

The scent of moonflowers, orchids, and lilies hung heavy in the air, and underneath that, the briny scent of the ocean. Miranda's scent. "Are you the one who put me in this nightgown?"

With a sly smile, he shrugged. "Someone had to do it."

Rosalind's stomach rumbled, and she grabbed it. She had only hazy memories of mechanically eating dry pieces of bread, and drinking black tea. If it hadn't been for Cleo keeping her alive, she probably wouldn't have eaten a thing. "I'm starving."

He grabbed her hand, pulling her back into the bedroom. "That's why I ordered food for you." He led her to the oak table, and she plopped down in one of the chairs.

She pulled off the silver tray, finding a plate laden with bacon, buttered toast, and steaming coffee. Her mouth watered, and she piled a few strips of bacon on the toast.

The rich, smoky taste sent a shiver of pleasure through her body.

Caine reached for a bottle of wine and poured himself a glass, then one for her. "Do you remember anything from the palace that might help us when we go to war with them? Any weapons, or defenses we need to know about?"

Rosalind swallowed an enormous mouthful of toast and bacon. "He's built an enormous marble wall around the city. Since it's the Brotherhood, I'd guess they have it rigged with stakes, iron bullets, anti-magic dust… If I could get close enough, I could blow the damn walls up."

"Mmm. You're not going back without an army. What else did you see?"

"It's hazy." She took a sip of the wine. "They have an amphitheater, and I think they like to burn people there. Oh, Erish created scorpion men. They have the torsos of men, but the lower halves of scorpions. I watched them sting a girl to death. Punishment for spilling wine on Randolph."

Caine's jaw tightened, and he stared at her.

Rosalind finished the last of her toast and bacon, washing it down with wine. "What?"

"I shouldn't have let you go," he said quietly.

She leaned back in her chair. "And yet I got Erish back. And I saved a bunch of prisoners while I was at it."

Before he could reply, Tammi stretched her arms over her head, yawning loudly. Owen rolled over next to her, sticking his thumb in his mouth.

Tammi blinked, slowly awaking. "You're awake!"

Rosalind couldn't face more questions about what had happened in Drew's empire of nightmares. Time to change the subject. "I'm awake, and Caine was just about to tell me what's been going in Lilinor while I was gone."

"Caine was mostly waiting by the fountain, threatening to go through it to find you. And I would have gone with him, if Ambrose hadn't stopped us." Tammi frowned. "I can't believe you didn't tell me your plan before you left. Letting Drew poison you and counting on your second soul? That was insane."

"So I've heard." Her gaze flicked to the moon, and relief washed over her. She'd turned into a creature of the night, whether or not she wanted to. *Might as well join the vamps.*

Tammi crossed to the table, taking a seat. "You missed eight days of Caine snapping at everyone and terrifying the shit out of people. None of us slept the whole time, because we were all imagining the worst. Oh, and because he had us all sun-proofing the entire fortress. There are sheets of silver over every damn vampire room in the fortress, in case Drew decides to raise the sun again, and some sort of dome above Ambrose's open air bedroom."

"And we've been building sun shelters in open areas," Caine said. "Pity we don't have Drew to just magically create an entire city in a few hours."

"Beautiful work." Rosalind lifted her glass. "And now, we just need an army of our own. If only we had no sense of morality, we could turn thousands of humans into lethal demons, like Drew did."

Caine shrugged. "That's not a bad idea, honestly."

"I wasn't serious," Rosalind said. "We'll find a way to create the daywalkers, and invade with the army we have."

Tammi winced. "There's a bit of a complication."

Wonderful. "And what would that be?"

"Do you remember Bileth?" Caine asked.

Rosalind frowned. "The demon who I stabbed with a fire poker? The terrifying horned creature who has repeatedly tried to murder and mind-control me? Yeah, he left a bit of an impression."

"He's here," Caine said. "In Lilinor."

Rosalind's heart climbed into her throat. "Why?" She remembered seeing his portrait hanging over the hall, but she'd never known him to actually *visit.* And if she remembered correctly, Ambrose and Bileth seemed to hate each other.

"Bileth does not think Ambrose is in control," Caine said. "He plans to restore law and order to the vampire realm."

Rosalind's jaw dropped. "So, I probably need to find refuge elsewhere. We're not exactly on good terms."

Caine took a deep breath. "Supposedly, he has promised to leave you unharmed. He understands your importance to our army. Of course, I don't trust him."

She glanced nervously at the door. "Neither do I, and he could easily murder me in my sleep. He's a high demon and probably several millennia old."

"The plan," Caine said, "is that I keep you in my sight at all times. Maybe he won't protect you, but I will."

"I guess you're just gonna have to sleep together," Tammi said. "I mean, in the same room."

Rosalind thought back to her encounter with Bileth in Cambridge. "I don't understand. I found him working with the Brotherhood in Cambridge. He's literally working for the people who are trying to kill us. He said, 'the enemy of my enemy is my friend.' And his enemy, if I recall, is Ambrose. So how is Nyxobas allowing this to happen?"

Caine's brow furrowed. "Bileth has convinced my grandfather that he is simply spying for the enemy. Like you said. Bileth has been on earth for several millennia, and he's been closely serving the god of night for the entire time."

"So Nyxobas is blind to his faults." Rosalind asked.

Caine cocked his head. "Nyxobas is too lost in the void to understand what's happening in the real world. So, he's ordered that we accept Bileth as a temporary leader, until order is restored. And we just have to play along for now. Even I can't fight the god of night."

Something in the back of Rosalind's mind whispered. *And what if I'm a god, more powerful than the rest...* Her fingers tightened into fists, and gods' magic whirred through her chest. "I need to get back to Cambridge. I need to murder Drew and Randolph, and raze their cursed city to ash."

Tammi touched her arm. "Simmer down, girl. We just got you back. And now you apparently have a toddler to look after."

"Me?"

"You brought him back."

"He looked quite cozy with you there."

Tammi frowned at the child. "I'm gonna find some of those harem girls to help with this one."

Rosalind was still lost in thoughts of battle. She stared into her wine, her lip curling. She could envision herself flying over Drew's empire, fire blazing from her fingertips, melting the cold marble. "If I cut off the head of the snake, the battle will be over."

Caine shook his head. "No. It'll grow another head. There are plenty of Brotherhood fanatics to take Drew and Randolph's place. We go in together, when the army is prepared."

Destroy him, her mind whispered. Her back arched, desperate for the thrill of powerful magic. In the hollows of her mind, an image flickered—her own hand, plunging into Drew's chest and ripping out his heart.

"Besides," Tammi said. "I've been learning to fight, too. You're not going alone, because I'm joining your army."

Rosalind shook her head, the magic roiling inside her skull. "I can do it on my own. Slaughtering Drew is my destiny."

Caine was studying her carefully. "Rosalind." He leaned closer. "Be careful. If the gods' power claims your mind, we may never get you back."

CHAPTER 12

*R*osalind walked through the Gelal Fields, her long, silky dress sliding against her legs. The landscape had transformed, with three silver-domed constructions jutting from the grass. Some of the sun shelters the vampires were working on.

In the nearby elms, nightingales trilled, filling the night with their song. The air felt warm and heavy tonight, and the full moon bathed the fields in pearly light. As she walked, tall grasses and wildflowers tickled her ankles.

If she squinted her eyes at the moon, she could just see the sterling shield that protected the vampire city from Drew's invasion. Her stomach tightened. The shield appeared thinned in several places, which meant that at any moment, Drew and his Hunter friends could create a portal into the city. She'd escaped once—what would they do to her the next time they managed to capture her? And she couldn't ignore the possibility that Bileth would hand her over to his Brotherhood allies at any moment.

Rosalind took a deep breath, searching the dark field for Caine. Just ahead, by a lone rowan tree, Caine stood by his brother. Their stunning silvery magic curled to the heavens, spreading over the thinned parts of the shield. She breathed in, inhaling the electric scene, like the smell of burnt air after a rainstorm.

The Mountfort brothers didn't need to work alone anymore. Rosalind could use shadow magic nearly as well as they could, and her body ached to unleash the power of the gods.

As she moved closer through the dandelion-dappled grasses, Caine turned to look at her, arching an eye brow.

"I'm here to help," she said. "You should have woken me when you were coming out here."

"You needed rest," he said. "I've warned you about using too much gods-magic."

Irritation simmered. "I'm fine."

Malphas eyed her with concern, moonlight washing over his porcelain skin. A faint smile curled his lips, and for a moment, Rosalind had a vision of him as a wide-eyed little boy, standing by the edge of Atherton Pond, pushing his hand-made sailboat into the water. "Rosalind." He touched her shoulder. "When you were with Drew, it was hell. I'm so happy you're back. And my brother is right. You're not returning to Drew's empire without us."

She smiled at him. "We're going to have to work together to keep Lilinor safe until we get our army together. Okay?"

Caine turned to face the shield again. "Far be it from me to argue with seven gods." His aura snaked around his body, blazing from his chest. Malphas's curled into the air, rising toward the moon.

Rosalind took a deep breath, luxuriating in the feel of the powerful shadow magic that electrified her skin.

Then, she arched her back, letting Nyxobas's power surge, starting with her ribs and curling into the night sky. Her magic intertwined with Caine and Malphas's in a perfect stream of gleaming silver.

Her arm brushed against Caine's, and a shiver of pleasure ran over her skin. This was where she belonged. This was how it was meant to be.

For just a moment, she opened her eyes, meeting Caine's gaze. He was peering down at her, his skin glowing like a god's.

Their magic surged, streaming over the night sky. As the magic flowed between them, images flitted through her mind—running through the woods with Malphas, holding his hand, a carpet of mayflower petals below their feet, his laughter filling the air. Leading him into the forest to search for buried treasure—a toy soldier's torso, a rusty coin. Malphas held each treasure aloft in the chinks of honeyed sunlight that streamed through the hawthorn trees—each discovery was a jewel, a magic talisman to bless them with unimaginable powers. Every stick was a wand, every flower a transformed nymph.

They couldn't have known then that talismans weren't needed, or that powers came with a price.

Then Caine's memories whirled through her skull: the queen's dress fluttering in the night air, after he'd thrown her from the window. A beautiful woman with blond hair. Men were dragging her screaming from her house, blood trickling down her chin. Caine bleeding and nailed to a stake, the word *Stolas* on his lips. The first time he saw Rosalind, lying on the rainy sidewalk, her eyes wide, body shaking with fear at the sight of him. Until at last, an image of something beautiful—a vault of stars above a grove of cherry trees, a stolen cup of fresh milk.

Filled with the memories around her, she stared at the canopy of silver magic above them. Caine and Malphas: both demigods of the shadow realm, and yet one brother was shadow, the other light.

At last, a thick shimmer of silver magic covered the entire sky, and Rosalind took a deep breath, her magic retreating into her chest.

But as she finished her magic, a chill rippled over her skin. Another aura lurked nearby—black and scented of an old grave. Her heart skipped a beat. *Bileth.*

Just as the warning was forming on her lips, Caine's head whipped around, and the air around her thinned.

She turned, her pulse racing at the sight of the horned demon stalking through the tall grasses. He was still a hundred yards away, but even from here, she could smell the fetid magic snaking from his body. As he moved closer, anger simmered. Bileth had manipulated his way into this city, and she didn't trust him in the slightest. At the sight of him, goosebumps rose on Rosalind's skin.

As Bileth stalked toward them, she had the strange sense that the grasses were wilting around his feet, the birds fluttering from the trees, desperate to get away from him. Gray shadows whispered over his waxy skin.

Seven auras coiled through her bones, their essences as mad as they were ancient. Even if he was several millennia old, she was beginning to wonder if she could take Bileth on her own—with all that gods magic on her side. Her fingers twitched, body buzzing with explosive power.

Caine leaned close to Rosalind, whispering, "It's not the time to attack. Not yet."

Clouds rolled over the moon, and Rosalind shivered. Caine and Malphas might be related to the god of night, but Bileth seemed a true emissary of the void. At the sight of him, Rosalind could feel the valkyrie's icy rage rippling through her body.

With each of Bileth's footsteps, a distant war drum seemed to beat, the sound reverberating through Rosalind's core. Thunder rolled over the horizon, and a few fat drops of rain began falling from the sky.

As Bileth drew closer, he snarled, "Incubi. And the woman." The last word he spat like an insult.

Rain began to fall harder, streaming down Rosalind's skin, and she took a step closer to Bileth. "How lovely to see you here."

"I see you're toying with the magic of the gods," he growled. "Humans weren't meant for such powers."

Rosalind waited for him to continue. There was obviously a point to all this.

Lightning flashed, glinting off Bileth's pale horns.

The rain picked up, plastering her hair to her face, her dress to her body. "Demons," she said, "were not meant to roam the earth. And yet here we all are. Funny how life is."

Caine cocked his head. "None of us were meant to be. The angels were never meant to fall from the heavens. Humans were never meant to learn Angelic. Dead things were never meant to live again. And yet —as Rosalind says—here we all are, in a city of vampires."

Rosalind narrowed her eyes at Bileth. "The last time I saw you was in the Brotherhood's headquarters. You seemed to know the Hunters very well."

Bileth's eyes were empty pools. "As Nyxobas knows, I was there as a spy."

"Bullshit," Rosalind muttered. "Anyway, what do you want from us?"

His gaze slid to Caine. "You've been Ambrose's general for centuries. And where has it gotten Lilinor? An insane human terrorizes your kingdom. You hide behind a shield. This is not worthy of a son of Nyxobas."

Rosalind felt the air around her chill by twenty degrees. As the cold rain slid down her skin, her breath clouded around her face, and she hugged herself, shivering.

Malphas took a deep breath. "What brilliant plan do you propose to protect Lilinor, Bileth?"

Bileth's nostrils flared, and he pounded one of his fists into the other. "If vampires cannot fight mortals, then they do not deserve to live. We fight the Hunters as we are. Only the strong survive. The rest must give up their souls to the void. This is as it should be."

"And this is your plan," Caine said, his voice low and controlled. "Sacrifice the vampires to make a point about strength."

Bileth's lip curled. "Nyxobas does not need the weak."

Rosalind stared at him, thinking of what he'd said to her in the Chambers. *The enemy of my enemy is my friend.*

And for whatever reason, he'd been talking about Ambrose.

That ancient magic, the song of madness and power, whispered through her mind again.

Perhaps I could end this right here. "And what sort of leader are you, if you're willing to give up without a fight?" She tightened her jaw. *Rein it in, Rosalind.*

Bileth's lip curled. "One who will survive, when your vampire city lies in ashes. I will live, as I have done for a hundred thousand years on earth, and I will live long after your body has begun to feed the worms by your sister's side."

"Sounds like an interesting challenge," she said. She pushed past Bileth, stalking over the grass, her fingernails piercing her palms.

Bileth needed to die, but it wouldn't happen today.

CHAPTER 13

Flanked by Tammi and Aurora, Rosalind stalked through the hall toward Ambrose's bedroom. Ivory rib vaults arched high above them, and moonlight streamed in through tall, peaked windows. Just an hour before, a servant had arrived at the door, instructing her to wear a formal gown for a visit with the king. The servant—a tall man with thin features and green eyes—had suggested that she might want to wear the frothy chiffon gown he'd brought for her. It was the exact shade of crimson that the king most admired.

Instead, Rosalind had pulled on her leather pants and a tank top, and she'd zipped her tallest boots. Until Caine and Malphas started wearing frothy chiffon to military meetings, she'd wear whatever she damn well pleased.

Aurora's boots clacked over the tile. "Any idea what this meeting is about?"

Rosalind frowned. "My guess is Ambrose is getting desperate. Bileth seems ready to torpedo all his daywalker plans."

"Really?" said Tammi. "And Bileth seems like such a reasonable man. You know, apart from being a king of hell who kills people with his mind."

859

"And what are the plans Bileth is supposedly screwing up?" Aurora unscrewed the cap from her flask. "Who is this third human we're supposed to use for the daylight spell?"

Tammi bit her lip. "I would have volunteered myself, but I kinda lost my human status."

"I don't know," Rosalind said. "We're at a bit of a stalemate. Caine won't allow Malphas to do it, and Ambrose won't allow anyone *but* Malphas to do it. I'm just glad you both were willing to come with me. Maybe you can help us talk some sense into Caine."

At the end of the hall, a set of marble stairs led to an imposing set of oak doors, carved with wicked looking weapons. Two Viking guards with long, blond braids stood before them. As Rosalind and her friends moved closer, the guards shifted, pulling open the doors.

Inside Ambrose's room, Caine's silver aura sparked through the air. He stood with his hands in his pockets—a casual stance—but anger writhed in his darkened eyes.

And between the two Lilinor leaders, Malphas stood with his arms folded. Flames in lanterns around the room seemed to flicker and dim. Moonlight washed the room in cold light, gleaming over Caine's aura.

Aurora took a sip of her drink. "Well, this meeting looks like it's going well. Glad you brought me."

"Mmm…" said Tammi. "I always get the hint that Caine is annoyed when the air begins to frost, and darkness envelops the light. It all gets a bit apocalyptic. I'm not sure he'd do very well in a poker game."

Aurora nodded. "Not very subtle."

Caine's eyes had turned black as the void. "Find another human." He enunciated each word as if he'd said them a million times. Which, perhaps, he had.

Malphas stared at his brother. "The spell worked for you. I don't see why it shouldn't work for me."

Caine shook his head. "If you think it worked for me, you remember nothing."

There it was again—the reference to Caine's insanity after he'd been given his second soul. And she still had no clue what they were talking about. Irritation simmered. Caine knew all her secrets now, but he still kept his own closely-guarded.

Malphas's pale eyes blazed. "I remember everything, Caine. I was there. But who's to say it would be the same with me?"

At his words, a chill spread through the room, and the moonlight itself seemed to dim. Caine kept his hands in his pockets, and though his body looked relaxed, his silver aura whipped viciously around him.

His eyes were chasms of black. "And why would it be so different for you, Brother? We're both born from the same father. We're both tainted by his darkness. Or you do think there is another reason why I did what I did?"

"Is this really relevant?" Ambrose asked, his jaw clenched.

Rosalind's stomach fluttered. *Okay. So I'm witnessing some weird family drama.*

Malphas took a slow breath. "It will be different because we're prepared this time, and I have you to guide me."

Caine took a step closer to his brother. "Perhaps you should just say what's on your mind Malphas. We have the same father. But not the same mother."

Tammi wrinkled her nose. "We can come back later, if this is a bad time."

Ambrose paced over the flagstones, glancing at Rosalind. "I need a status update about Drew's army. What did you see?"

Rosalind shook her head. "Not much. I was in a fog the whole time. I saw guards, but nothing of their army."

Caine frowned. "I've been interrogating Erish. She isn't telling me everything, but my spies are feeding me more information. Your wife created legions of demons who haven't darkened the earth's surface for millennia. Ifrit, Pazuzu, Uridimmu, Asag... I'm still learning what else."

"What?" Rosalind asked.

Aurora leaned in, whispering, "Fire demons, plague demons, gruesome hounds, and... I don't know."

"Right."

"All waiting to attack," Ambrose said.

"Last night, some of my spies reported that a horde of Pazuzu were trying to break through the shields through a portal Drew had created."

"And what did you do about it?" Ambrose asked.

"It was daylight in the human world." Caine glanced at Rosalind. "Rosalind helpfully brought us a small troop of valkyrie who'd been imprisoned by Drew, and they're after his blood. I led them through the portal, and we fended off the attack. And moreover, the shield is holding for now. It won't last forever, but we have plenty of supplies. There are the women in the harem for blood, and Rosalind has brought us a fresh supply of humans."

Rosalind raised her hand. "I wouldn't call them *supplies*. If they give blood, it should be voluntary."

As Caine and Ambrose continued arguing, Rosalind turned to Tammi. "Who is Owen with?"

"He's in the harem. Those chicks are obsessed with him. And there's a fae warrior guarding him. He's fine."

Breaking off from his argument with Ambrose, Caine glanced at Rosalind for the first time. "You have the power of seven gods."

"You don't say."

"So perhaps we don't need a third human," Caine said. "When the first three mages conducted the spell, they had only human powers. They had extensive knowledge of Angelic and how to manipulate magic, but they were still mere humans. Rosalind and I have their magical knowledge, and we are gods."

"That's a bit much," Aurora muttered, giving Rosalind the side-eye.

Rosalind crossed to Caine. "It's worth a shot. I don't really understand Caine's objections fully, since he's never told me what exactly happened when my parents gave him that extra soul. But this journey with another soul hasn't been an easy ride. When Cleo first started inhabiting my mind, she kept trying to light me on fire. She could have killed me." She glanced at Malphas, thinking of their kiss. "And at times she has taken over my body completely. We don't know what Malphas's second soul would do to him."

"So you agree with me," Caine said.

"Not entirely." She cocked her head. "It's worth a shot to see if we can spare Malphas what we went through. But if it doesn't work, we've run out of options. We can't keep waiting around while Drew plans the next invasion. Even if you're protecting against the sunlight, his powers are growing. I could feel them."

Caine stared at her for a long moment. The air had gone so cold, that her breath misted before her face. "Fine. First we try on our own. If it doesn't work, Malphas gets the third soul."

Shadows darkened the air around Ambrose. "I've read the legends, the historical accounts of Alexander the Great's army. It won't work with two mages. You're wasting my time."

She suppressed the urge to roll her eyes. "We might as well try Caine's idea. What do we have to lose? It either works or it doesn't. Then we move on."

Ambrose stared at her for an uncomfortably long moment before straightening. After a moment, he snapped his fingers. "Kevin! Come closer."

Rosalind jumped, startled to realize that another vampire guard had been lurking in the shadows. A tall, thin man with long hanks of ginger hair lumbered into the center of the room, a silver pike in his hands.

Kevin. Rosalind frowned. They really needed some better vampire names around here. Mentally, she was renaming him *Vlad the Eviscerator.*

"Kevin," Ambrose said, interrupting her thoughts. "We're going to try an experiment on you."

Kevin—Vlad—furrowed his brow, his eyes widening. Clearly, he didn't like this idea, but he seemed to like the idea of arguing with Ambrose a little less. *Smart man.*

Vlad cleared his throat. His fingers visibly tensed on his pike, knuckles whitening. "What do you need me to do?"

Ambrose cocked his head. "Just stand there, I believe. We've never done this before." He turned to Rosalind. "I take it your second souls know the spells?"

"Let's find out," Rosalind said.

She stood next to Caine, staring at Vlad. Truth be told, she wasn't sure she was ready for this. She had no idea what would happen to Vlad. He seemed like a nice enough guy, and for all she knew, she was about to kill him with magic.

"Just give me a second." She threaded her fingers together, then flexed. "I just have to get in the right zone."

Caine quirked a smile, his body already glowing with silver light. "Certainly. You wouldn't want to pull something."

Rosalind closed her eyes, summoning Cleo's vibrations, that leafy, green power that curled through her body. *Cleo. I need to turn this vampire into a daywalker.*

Tendrils of Cleo's magic enshrouded her body like vines. In the next moment, she was whispering the words to an ancient spell, a song that spoke of light and darkness, day and night, a union of opposites. As she chanted, she could feel Cleo's aura mingling with Caine's magic, shadows entwining with life, birth with decay. She could feel Caine's body drawing her closer, like a magnetic pull, until her arm brushed his...

As magic unfurled from their bodies, she began to lose all sense of time and space. They were simply the night and the forest, the crows feasting on dead deer, the yews growing above graves, sun dappling their branches.

The whispers of the ancients whispered in her mind. Dizzy, she opened her eyes, staring at the stars, staring as the constellations shifted around the North Star, the slow waltz of Cassiopeia and Ursa Major.

She had the sense of shifting winds, shifting stars, time slowly passing while the words of the spell tripped off her tongue, over and over, while magic whirled from her body. As her magic whirled around the room, her body began to grow tired, her legs shaking. How long had she been chanting for? Since the beginning of time, perhaps.

The ancient song of magic knelled in her skull, the power of the gods, until her legs began to shake, and her breath grew ragged in her throat. And in the vault of stars above them, the night sky danced on —until shadows crept over the pearly light. She stared above her as a dark wind snuffed out the stars. At last, nothing remained but the darkness.

A painful void gnawed at her chest, and in the hollows of her mind, her sister's face flickered, eyes wide. Sorrow climbed up Rosalind's throat, and she sank deeper into the darkness. Caine's magic was overwhelming her, his shadows seeping into her body. And yet, she couldn't feel his presence anymore. She only felt alone. *Stolas.*

The void would suck her in, and never let her out again.

Light. I need more light. If she couldn't conjure the light, she'd die here, alone and insane.

And that's when the screams pierced her concentration. Her eyes snapped open, and she stared at Vlad, his clothes blazing like a torch, smoke curling through the open roof.

In the next moment, shadow magic surged from Caine's wrist, and he iced the flames, snuffing them out in cold shadows. Vlad's body shook, holes burned through the fabric of his clothes, and smoke curled through the open roof. The air smelled of burnt flesh.

Rosalind rolled onto her hands and knees, her body shaking. Nausea welled in her gut, and she suppressed the urge to vomit.

I guess that didn't work out so well.

Caine held out his hand to her. "Are you all right?"

She grabbed it, standing on shaky feet. Fatigue burned through her muscles. "I'm fine. More importantly, is Vlad alright?"

"Who?"

"I mean, Kevin." She turned to the vampire, who shuddered, smoke still rising from his skin. "Are you okay, Kevin?"

Mutely, he nodded, then shot a panicked look to Ambrose. "Do I have to do that again?"

Ambrose frowned. "Yes."

"No." Rosalind loosed a sigh, fighting the nausea that climbed up her throat. "I don't think this is a good idea. It didn't feel right. If the spell was meant for three mages, I don't think it will work. How long were we gone for?"

In the corner of the room, Tammi had fallen asleep in an armchair, and Malphas sat at the edge of a bed, sipping wine, watching them. Aurora had already left.

Ambrose shrugged. "Eight, ten hours. The servants have been supplying me with blood."

No wonder her legs were trembling. "You do know that humans need food and water, right?"

Ambrose frowned. "It sounds vaguely familiar."

"One more time." Caine ran a hand through his hair. "It didn't work that time, but we can try it one more time. I felt it working before Rosalind succumbed to the magic."

"Don't blame this on me," Rosalind said. "You were using too much magic. I could feel it overwhelming me."

Shadows thickened around Ambrose. "I don't want to wait any longer. Caine, fetch the sigil. It's time to grant your brother another soul."

"One more try," Caine said, the air chilling around him. "Then we use the sigil."

Dizzy, Rosalind faltered and Caine caught her by the elbow. He tucked a finger below her chin, looking into her eyes. "You don't look like you're ready to try again."

"I may have the magic of seven gods, but I still need to eat and sleep like a human. Whatever we're doing, I'm not doing it now."

Caine glanced at Ambrose. "She hasn't learned how to absorb the gods' power yet. If she uses too much at once, she'll become lost in the magic. It's already overwhelmed her. We won't be using the sigil nor the spell again until Rosalind has rested." Caine slipped an arm around Rosalind's waist. "I'll help you get back to your room."

She shook her head. "Thanks, but I'm fine. I can get back on my own." She pulled away from Caine, walking for the door.

"Rosalind," Ambrose called out before they got to the door. "Whatever you do, don't let Bileth know about this. Any of it."

She turned to look at him. "What's the story between you two? Why does he hate you so much?"

"That's none of your concern," Ambrose said.

"I'll find out, one way or another." As she began walking again, her eyes started to drift closed, but she fought against the urge to sleep, blinking to keep her eyes awake. She couldn't let her mind rest yet—not until she'd figured out a way to save Lilinor.

CHAPTER 14

osalind lay back on her bed, letting her muscles melt into the soft blankets. Her mind churned. Was Malphas really the only answer to this problem? In a world of magic, there had to be more than one way to achieve their goals.

A knock on the door interrupted her thoughts. Peeling herself off the bed, Rosalind rose. On the way to the door, she caught a glimpse of herself in the enormous, silver-framed mirror. Even now, her cheeks still looked gaunt and pale, her shoulders a little bonier than she'd like.

She pulled open the door—expecting Caine, but finding instead a young vampire, whose long black hair tumbled over a white dress. She held a domed tray, and steam curled from the top.

"The beautiful incubus said you'd be hungry. He sent me with dinner." A blush rose to her cheeks. "If he ever needs anything else from me, tell him he can ask me anytime."

"I'm starving. Thank you."

The scent of garlic and fresh fish wafted into the air.

"Where should I put it?" asked the vampire.

"I'll take it." Rosalind's mouth watered as she pulled it from the vampire's hands. "Thank you."

As she turned to walk to the balcony, the vampire propped open the door, adding one final request. "Like I said. If he needs *anything*, I'm available."

"Got it." Rosalind practically slammed the door in her face, then crossed to the balcony. She wanted the open air as much as possible.

She slid the tray onto the table. She took a seat, then pulled the dome off the tray, her stomach rumbling at the sight of salmon and garlic mashed potatoes, seasoned with rosemary. At this point, she was so hungry her entire body was shaking.

A corked bottle of wine lay out from the night before, and she pulled the cork, filling the empty wine glass on the tray.

It was peaceful out here, with flickering lanterns hanging from the myrtle trees, and the faint rhythm of the waves pounding the rocks below. She cut into the fish, spearing it with just the right amount of potato on her fork. The flavors melted in her mouth, and she closed her eyes as she ate. *Heaven.* The vampires had no idea what they were missing.

When she was halfway through her meal, someone knocked on the door.

"Who is it?" she called out.

"Malphas."

Interesting. "Come in."

He pushed through the door, crossing to the balcony. As he pulled out a chair for himself, he smiled. "I see you're making fast work of the meal I ordered for you."

"My hunger waits for no man." She smiled. "So *you're* the beautiful incubus."

His eyebrows rose. "As if you just noticed."

She giggled. "Where's Caine?"

"Busy scouring the harems. I believe that was once a favorite pastime of his."

"I don't want to know."

"Looking for a third human who Ambrose will approve of."

Rosalind took another bite of the salmon and potatoes. The rich, buttery food melted in her mouth. Lilinor's fae chef was amazing. "Do you want any of this food?"

"No. I've eaten already."

Good. She didn't particularly want to share.

The lantern-light wavered over his porcelain skin, flickered in his pale eyes. When she looked at him, she could see the boy he once was. She could almost hear his laughter filling the air, as they trampled over the mayflower petals, running through the hawthorn grove.

He poured himself a glass of wine. "Despite what Caine said earlier, he's still resisting allowing me to take on the soul."

"He's awfully protective of you."

"Do you think this spell will work, even if Caine finds another human?"

"I have no idea. It's not like we have a lot of information to go on." She took a sip of the dry red wine. "I don't suppose you're going to tell me why Caine is so determined to stop you from taking on this role?"

He loosed a long sigh, staring at the moon through the myrtle leaves. "Before you began using the gods-magic, you were human. You were human when you got the second soul. Caine and I are demigods. We're descendants of Nyxobas, the lord of darkness. He believes that we're tainted somehow. That darkness runs through us, and that with all this power, it will turn us into monsters. He believes that a second soul unleashes your true nature, and that because of who our father is… our true nature is malignant."

"And what is your father like?"

Malphas shrugged. "Neither of us really knows him, but he's on Nyxobas's council. Caine says he's a rapist."

"Oh."

"I don't think Caine really thinks we *are* the same, though." Malphas's gaze met hers. "He wants to think we are, but he's worried that we're not."

"What do you mean?"

"We were born several centuries apart, from different mothers. My mother was from the noble classes of Maremount." His eyebrows drew together, and he took a sip of his wine. "He doesn't talk about his own mother. Not even to me."

Caine was never as open as Malphas, and she was so fascinated she nearly forgot to eat. "Was Caine's mother from Maremount too? Is that where you both were born?"

He shook his head. "Caine is from South London."

How strange that after all this time, she'd never even known where he'd been born.

"Where is your mother now?" Malphas was close to her age. His mother might be in her forties or fifties.

"Dead. I never knew her. After my father seduced her or raped her or whatever he did, her reputation was ruined. Not long after I was born, she jumped from the Silver Tower of Throcknell Fortress."

"I'm sorry." Her heart ached for him. "If that's how they treat women, I'm glad to be out of Maremount."

He swirled his wine in his glass. "It's an unforgiving place. Or it was. Things might have changed now. The King was imprisoned, by his own daughter I believe."

"Your mother was nobility, even if her reputation was ruined. And Caine's mother...?"

Malphas took a deep breath. "I only know she *wasn't* nobility. Caine was born five hundred years ago, in a time when everyone believed that some people are better than others by virtue of their lineage. I think that concept stuck with him. I think that deep down, he thinks my mother's lineage made me different than he is. Purer, or something. He calls me *the good brother.*"

Rosalind thought back on the things Caine had said to Malphas in Ambrose's room. "He was trying to goad you into saying it. He wants to hear you say it out loud."

"But I don't believe it's true. I don't believe Caine's theory, that his second soul brought out his true nature. He is lying to himself."

Rosalind nodded slowly. "So when he said you can't handle a second soul either, it's because he needs that to be true. He's not trying to convince you. He's trying to convince himself. He truly believes that a second soul brings out your true nature. And if you could handle a second soul better than he could, what would that say about him?"

"That he's tainted through and through. At least, that's my guess."

Rosalind took another bite of her food, the salmon a perfect complement to the mashed potatoes. "It seems very astute to me." Since Malphas was much chattier about his personal life than Caine was, this seemed a perfect opportunity to find out more. "How did you and Caine end up with my parents in the first place?"

Malphas drummed his fingertips on the table. "You know some of my brother's history now, don't you? You know he killed the king and queen of Maremount, centuries ago."

"Ah yes, the Ravener threw them out the window. He told me. Considering they'd enslaved him for a year, I can't say I blame him."

"You wouldn't blame him, but others did. After he escaped Maremount, the King's son placed a bounty on his head. Parents told their children stories of the Ravener, the demon who slaughtered innocents in their beds. The monster who raped queens."

A chilly night breeze whispered over them, and the lanterns groaned, swinging the branches, their candlelight flickering.

"But that's not the way it happened," Rosalind said. "It was the other way around. I saw it in his memories."

"Well, Caine wasn't around to tell his side of the story, and no one would believe a shadow demon anyway. Especially not one with a father like Abrax."

Rosalind nodded slowly. "I get it. But that was centuries ago. Long before my parents were alive. How did he end up back in Maremount?"

Malphas traced his fingertip around the rim of the wine glass, the movement hypnotic. "One generation after the next, the mortal kings sought to bring Caine back to Maremount. They wanted to torture him publicly, to hang his ruined body in Lullaby Square."

"To keep Erish's sister company. Her petrified head decorates the fountain."

Malphas raised his glass. "Nothing can bring a city together like a demonic scapegoat. As you can see, the Brotherhood continues to use that strategy to perfection. It would have been a beautiful way for the king of Maremount to unify a city, to appease ordinary citizens with a show of bloodletting." He raised his hand like an orator. *"You see, peasants? We're not the monsters oppressing you, keeping you from learning magic. Keeping you in the dirt. It's the demons you should fear. And we're here to kill them for you. We are your protectors."* He shrugged. "So the kings of Maremount hunted my brother for centuries. What a boon it would have been for them to torture the Ravener in the town square."

"And Caine evaded them."

"The Throcknell family had no idea he was here, in Lilinor. They'd completely lost track of him. After Caine first escaped Maremount, he found his way to this shadow realm for safety. As a grandson of Nyxobas, he could claim sanctuary here. Ambrose took him in, gave him a place in his army. And in a short time Caine proved he was capable of leading it. He was fearless. He liked fighting. And men respected him."

A marine wind rushed off the sea, whispering over Rosalind's skin. "If no one knew where he was, how did my parents end up imprisoning him?"

"They had leverage on him."

"What?"

"Me."

Rosalind let the wine roll over her tongue for a moment before swallowing, and her chest tightened. "They found you after you were orphaned."

"It wasn't just that my mother had gotten pregnant outside of marriage. It was that the father of the child was a demon. One who'd produced the Ravener himself. You can imagine how much that would have impressed the rest of the king's court. After she gave birth, they locked the two of us in a tower room. For three years, it was just me and her. I was happy, I think. We played games. She told me stories about talking rabbits and dragons."

I swallowed hard. "So why did she jump out of the tower?"

His expression darkened. "I don't know, exactly. I remember that she cried a lot, and spent a lot of time just lying in bed. I think she had no one to talk to, besides me. And I could hardly talk."

Rosalind's throat tightened. "And after that, you had no one."

"Within an hour of her death, I was out on the streets, a beggar and an outcast. Half-brother to the Ravener. It was a wonderful opportunity for social climbers like your parents."

"What do you mean?"

"Your parents were smart. They knew Caine's weakness: family. They knew his history. And they believed they deserved a more powerful position in the city of Maremount. They wanted a prime spot in the Throcknell Fortress, on the council. They wanted more control."

A lump rose in Rosalind's throat. It was starting to become clear to her. "So they thought they would deliver a prize to the royal family. The Ravener. And you were the bait to lure him to the city."

Malphas shrugged. "It worked. Your parents sent ravens throughout the realms to deliver a message to Caine. They used scrying mirrors to prove that they had me. Anyone could tell by looking at my eyes that I'm a son of Abrax, a descendent of the shadow god."

"And Caine came for you."

"Your parents were waiting for him. He didn't come alone, of course..." He trailed off, clearing his throat. "Well, never mind that."

Rosalind leaned forward, the ocean wind toying with her hair. "What do you mean?"

"It's not important. The point is, when he arrived, they were holding a knife to my throat. From there, it wasn't difficult to control Caine."

"And they thought they'd present him as a gift to the king, so he could be executed."

"Tortured, yes. I'm not sure the royal family knew how to kill a demigod, so he probably would have been trapped, still alive, in amber, with his limbs cut off. Something like that."

Rosalind covered her mouth, nausea climbing up her throat. She no longer wanted any more of her meal. "That's what the Throcknells did to people?"

"I told you. It's an unforgiving place. Unfortunately for your parents, King Balthazar didn't care. He was caught up in his own machinations. Namely, he was busy having his wife executed to impress his mistress."

"So my parents had an incubus on their hands, and his little brother. And they weren't going to let the opportunity go to waste."

"This is how Caine tells it. If the king wouldn't give them more power, they would make *themselves* rulers of Maremount, by creating supreme magicians they could control. They summoned the spirits of the three greatest mages who ever lived, and trapped them in a sigil. First, they experimented on Caine. It seemed to go well. It didn't kill him. He didn't seem mad. They learned everything they could about magic. They learned of their own history, the rumors of Azazeyl. They believed themselves to be gods, and they moved in and out of the city, from Boston to Maremount, collaborating with the Brother-hood, drinking Blodrial's blood."

She arched an eyebrow. "Ah. That's where they got their blood."

"The blood drove them mad."

Rosalind took a deep breath. "Caine is certain that it will drive me mad, too. I guess, given the available data... My parents and Drew..."

"It doesn't look good."

"When you say that my parents went mad, what do you mean? What happened?"

"My memories are hazy. I wasn't much older than you at the time. I mostly know what Caine told me. They believed they were gods, and that they deserved worship. And that's when they decided what to do with their two other souls. They would have three powerful mages in their control, to build the empire of their dreams."

Goosebumps rose on Rosalind's skin. "But then something happened with Caine."

"That's not my story to tell." Malphas's eyes seemed to deepen to a dark pewter. "The stuff about your parents, that's for you to know. If Caine wants you to know what happened to him, he will tell you."

"I understand. But I saw him, how he was punished in the square. The iron nails through his arms and chest. The royal family got their Ravener after all, and they didn't want to let him get away that time." She shook her head. "So how did he get out?"

"In the dead of night, I freed him. And when he recovered, he went after your parents."

"For revenge," she said.

"No." Malphas leaned back in his chair, studying her. "Perhaps that, too. He knew they had two more souls, and that they planned to use them on other humans. He didn't know who. And he didn't know that it was already too late."

He'd never mentioned that before—that he'd killed them to try to stop them from ruining other people's lives. He kept secrets even when the stories would exonerate him. "Do you have any idea how Miranda and I ended up separated, and living with the Brotherhood?"

Malphas slid his glass across the table. "That might be a question for Caine."

"What do you mean?" Her pulse sped up. "*Caine* sent me to live with the Brotherhood?"

Malphas cocked his head, considering what to tell her. She'd never seen him looking quite this beautiful before, with golden light tinging his skin, the amber flecks in his eyes. She couldn't remember seeing him in the sunlight before...

At that thought, the world tilted beneath her. *Sunlight.*

Malphas turned, his jaw dropping. There in the sky—a winged demon, blazing with a fire so hot she had to shield her eyes.

CHAPTER 15

Rosalind's pulse raced as she stared at the sky. Around the flaming demon, cracks opened in the silvery shield. She gaped, watching the shadow magic disintegrate before her eyes.

The winged demon had enormous, curled horns and long talons. Silhouetted by the rising sun, his wings beat the air. Behind him, the sun began to rise, staining the sky a hot pearly rose, washing the world in lurid pink. Panic tightened its cold claws around Rosalind's heart.

He's coming. Drew is coming for me.

"I don't understand," she shouted, her heart hammering. "I can see the shield falling apart. Why? How is this happening?"

"I don't know. No one from the outside should be able to destroy it so quickly."

She swallowed hard, glancing at Malphas. Already, his black wings were growing from his back, his pale gaze locked on the fiery demon. Sunlight gilded him.

"It's an ifrit," he said. "They haven't walked the earth in thousands of years. One of Erish's creations. They come from her part of the world." Golden sunlight gleamed from his wings. "Unfortunately, they don't usually travel alone."

As soon as the words had left his lips, another demon emerged from the glaring sunlight, seeming to fly from the center of the sun itself.

From below, shouts pierced the air. The silver curtains should shield them, but clearly, some kind of attack was imminent. *Time to take action.*

Rosalind's body was still exhausted, but she closed her eyes, summoning her fire magic, letting it roil in her chest. *And the best way to defeat fire is with ice.* And with it, she rallied her shadow magic. Nyxobas's cold power rippled through her body. She and Malphas should be able to take down two demons together.

Malphas turned to her, nodding once. And in the next moment, he burst forth from the balcony, rising into the reddening sky.

Gods-magic rushed over her body, and she took flight, the wind whipping at her hair. She soared around one of the ifrit, circling him. His eyes blazed with the heat of a dying star, so bright she couldn't look at him directly. The ifrit opened his mouth, and with a gut-churning shriek, he spat out a ball of fire. In the air, Rosalind dodged, the sea winds tearing at her hair.

After going through the fire hell, fire would no longer burn her. But she saw no reason to waste a perfectly good outfit by letting it incinerate.

She circled the ifrit again. She could take one demon easily. *Let's see what Nyxobas's magic will do to him.*

Dark magic ran through her body like ice floes, and she flicked her wrist, sending a surge of night magic at the creature. The ifrit threw back his head, shrieking to the skies, his enormous body sizzling as her magic extinguished his flames. Writhing, he fell to the earth, and she glanced at Malphas. Malphas's black wings beat the air, his opponent already fallen.

But already, a third demon was coming for her, silhouetted in the sun as if the great star had birthed him. And behind him, a fourth, and a fifth. Her heart began to race. Within moments, a stream of the creatures headed right for them, flying for the fortress. Dread coiled around her. They were flying straight for the vampires—for the very flammable vampires.

Rosalind circled in a wide arc, summoning Nyxobas's magic. Shadows surged through her body, reaching for the sky in pearly tendrils.

"Strengthen the shield!" she shouted to Malphas. "We need to stop them from coming in!"

Immediately, a stream of night magic rushed from his body, spreading out in a dome above the sky.

Another burst of night magic surged—from below her this time. Caine was flying into the air, his black wings pounding the air like an angel of death. Thick coils of silver magic spiraled from his powerful body.

As the ifrit swarmed the sky, fire rained over the city. Caine and Malphas skillfully dodged it. Rosalind ignored it, no longer worried about her clothes. *Let them burn.* The flames warmed her skin, strengthening her body.

Soaring through the sky, Rosalind sent the icy magic of the void curling around the fiery demons.

And yet the creatures pressed on, swooping inexorably lower, landing on the rooftops and setting them alight. Terror ripped through Rosalind. The city would turn to ash if they weren't able to stop the ifrit.

As the fortress burned, the vampires would run into the open air— where the sun would light them ablaze. Aurora, Ambrose, the sassy chick in the Duckula T-shirt... all of them would die. As she swooped through the air, horror hit her in the gut. The ifrit were running into the fortress, dragging vampires out into the light. The scent of burning flesh curled into the air.

And at that, icy wrath flooded Rosalind's mind, until she could no longer hear her own thoughts. She only knew that she wanted to kill, to destroy. She wanted to send the ifrit into the center of the earth.

As the magic poured through her body in icy streams of silver, shadows claimed her mind, climbing up the walls of her skull, until she was no longer Rosalind. She was the god of night, of darkness and the void, cloaked in shadow. She was the beginning and the end of time, the universe without light.

Her body mercilessly slung night magic at the ifrit, and she listened to the hiss of their flames extinguishing. But while she fought on, her mind wasn't in Lilinor. Her mind lurked in the void, and she closed her eyes. Deep in the hollows of her mind, she walked through the inky night, swift as an astral wind. Nyxobas reached for her, brushing her cheeks with his icy fingertips.

Today, Rosalind was the god of death.

Her body blazed with cold magic, a whirling blizzard of power. As cold winds kissed her body, her eyes flickered—opening and closing—and she caught glimpses of the sky darkening, the stars gleaming, the sun silvering into the moon.

As darkness claimed the sun, a heavy snow began to fall, frosting her skin, until Nyxobas's emptiness whispered through her. A voice spoke through her mouth, *Slaughter them all. Send them to the void. I will keep their souls,* she hissed.

A vision of her sister's face flashed in her mind, and for a moment, grief pierced her to her very marrow. She couldn't quite remember what she was doing, and her body moved on its own, twisting and soaring through the frigid sky, until her feet landed on the earth again, inches deep in snow. The cold fog in her mind began to clear. Shivering, she looked up to find snow falling from dark clouds, Nyxobas's icy magic still freezing her blood.

Around her, the frozen bodies of the ifrit demons lay in the snow, frosted husks. Icicles hung from their horns. Her gaze flicked to the fortress, covered in webs of frost, the fires extinguished. *Holy shit.* Still, the air smelled of burnt flesh.

From above, Caine and Malphas swooped lower, their black wings beating the air. A dome of silver shimmered above them. While she'd been summoning a blizzard, the two brothers had been repairing the shield.

Shivering, she looked down at her naked body. The fire had burned all but a few singed scraps of fabric off her body, and goose-bumps covered her skin. Her teeth chattered; her legs shook. The magic had weakened her body, but her mind still blazed with icy magic.

In the snowy sky, Malphas circled her once before soaring away again, while Caine landed in the snow by her side, his wings covered in a layer of frost, and his silver eyes locked directly on her.

Too bad for him, the frigid wrath of Nyxobas still lit up her mind. "Your grandfather gave me the power of a god. He took over my mind."

"I saw. You killed them all."

Nyxobas's void ate at her chest. When she'd first met Caine, he'd looked down on her. Who was more powerful now? She took a step closer to him in the snow, her feet growing numb.

"You've kept so many secrets from me." Her body shuddered. *I should hurt him for lying to me.* "What happened after my parents gave you that second soul? And how did I end up with the Brotherhood?"

Caine's eyes slid to the sky, where Malphas had been flying. "I see you and Malphas have been talking."

Rosalind summoned her fire magic, letting the flames play about her fingertips, warming her skin, even if her heart felt frozen. With her sister dead, she had no family anymore, and she still couldn't quite trust Caine. "Tell me the truth. Fire doesn't hurt me. But I know it hurts you."

"I can see Nyxobas's darkness in your eyes right now. It's more than a bit unnerving to look at a beautiful, naked woman and see my own grandfather there. I'm not sure if I want to kiss you or run far, far away." He cocked his head. "In any case, this is what I warned you about. If you can't control your magic, you shouldn't use it."

Her lip curled. "Always lies and diversions with you. Tell me. Did you hand me over to those sadists—to the Brotherhood?" Flames burned higher from her fingertips.

"Yes," he said coldly, stepping closer, unafraid of her fire. "You were orphaned. And I needed to send you both to live with people who would control the insane spirits in your head. Who would stop you from ever using magic. I wanted them to keep you wearing the iron rings. You were just children, with unimaginable powers. You were a danger to yourselves and everyone around you. It wasn't until Ambrose decided that he needed the three mages together that I sought you out."

"Why did you separate us?"

Darkness pooled in Caine's eyes, and his magic whipped around his body. "So you wouldn't kill each other." Venom laced his voice. "Are we done reminiscing, or shall we go see who died?"

His last sentence snapped her out of her trance, and the cold night magic drifted from her body. The flames died at the ends of her fingertips.

"Right." Suddenly, the cold overwhelmed her body, and she began trembling. She still needed answers from Caine, but this wasn't the time. "We'll talk about it later."

Caine stepped closer over the snow, then wrapped his arms around her. "You're going to freeze," said Caine.

His body warmed hers, and her muscles began to relax as she rested her head against his chest, listening to the sound of his beating heart.

"Your feet are going to freeze." Caine reached down, scooping her up in his powerful arms. "Your power is impressive. I've never seen anyone kill that many demons at once."

"Where did the ifrit come from? Malphas said they hadn't walked the earth for centuries."

Caine held her close, folding his wings around her to shield her from the wind. "Erish would have known about them. She probably fought them, thousands of years ago, when she was a warrior."

"Erish created them…" she said, just as the seed of an idea began to bloom in her mind. "Maybe she can help us."

"How?"

"Maybe we've been approaching the daywalkers all wrong." She wrapped her arms around his neck. "I'll talk to you about it later. You were right. We need to check on the fortress. People might need healing from their burns."

He pulled her in tight, his dark wings beating the wintry air. In the next moment, they were lifting into the sky, soaring over the snowy fields, and she held him tightly.

The shield had recovered its silver sheen, the magic thick as the fortress walls. "You did a wonderful job with the shield."

"The question is: How was it weakened in the first place? Only someone from the inside should have been able to destroy it like that. And it wasn't Malphas or I."

Shivering, Rosalind looked up at Caine, at the snowflakes catching in his dark eyelashes. Her mind whirled with all he things she wanted to say to him—the questions about her past, how she'd ended up with the Brotherhood. The fact that despite it all, he was wrong about how Malphas was her destiny. She knew to the depths of her soul that she and Caine belonged together, that she loved his darkness and his thorns.

But it wasn't the time for that now, not when the smell of death and ash still hung heavy in the air.

CHAPTER 16

osalind had quickly dressed in jeans and a warm sweater, pulling on a pair of boots, and then she rushed through the stone halls, moving from one to another. In each hall, she'd found injured vampires, their skin blistered and burned, body parts shattered by falling stones as the building had burned. As she moved through the north wing, Caine and Malphas spread out through other parts of the building, using their shadow magic to heal the injured vampires.

She'd already reconnected with Aurora and Tammi, sighing with relief when she'd found them safe.

Both had been deep in the bowels of the fortress, near the armory, when the ifrit had come through.

And outside, as the snow continued to fall over the Gelal Fields and the cemetery yews, Ambrose and his soldiers had already begun burying the dead.

On one of the top floors of the fortress, an icy wind whipped through the ceiling, chilling her blood. Fire had eaten through the stone arches, and piles of snowy ash and soot lay all over the hall. Now, a thick layer of snow blanketed the flagstones. As she moved deeper into the open-air hall, icy wind had snuffed out the candles. Rosalind could hardly see where she was going.

She flicked her wrist, and with a burst of light magic, she created a ball of light. As soon as it sparked into existence, a scream tore through the silent air.

The sphere cast a warm, glowing light on a vampire who lay curled on the floor, her skin red and raw under the snow and soot. Her hair had been singed, partially burned off. One of her pink bunny slippers had turned black, and the air smelled of burnt fabric. The girl's entire body shook.

Of course, Rosalind had probably just terrorized the traumatized vampire with that burst of flame. "I'm sorry!" said Rosalind, hurrying over the vampire. "I'm here to help. It's okay. It's just light. The ifrit are gone."

The girl continued screaming, staring at the ball of light, pointing in terror.

Rosalind flicked her wrist, snuffing out the light. "It's okay." She knelt by the vampire's side. "We don't need the light."

The girl fell silent again, but Rosalind could still hear her frantic breaths. Slowly, Rosalind's eyes began to adjust to the dark, and she summoned the power of Nyxobas to see through the shadows.

"It's okay," said Rosalind. "The city is safe. I'm going to heal you." The leafy power of her tree god surged through her blood, and tendrils of leafy magic curled from her fingertips. She raked her fingertips through the air above the vampire's body, watching as the vampire's skin began to heal. Combined with the natural accelerated healing of a vampire, the girl's body would be healed in no time.

As her hair lengthened again, returning to its original brown and purple, Rosalind recognized her. It was the *Count Duckula* chick from the bar—Becca. As the healing magic curled around her body, Becca stopped shaking, sighing with relief. She shut her eyes, gently touching her own skin.

"Are you okay, Becca?" asked Rosalind.

Becca nodded. "I am now. At least, my skin seems to be healed. I think I'll be having nightmares for years."

Another scream echoed off the stone hall, just around the corner, and Rosalind's heart raced. "Go get some rest, Becca. I've got to go."

She rose, hurrying through the hall to the next victim. An enormous male vampire, his brown beard singed, crawled on shaking limbs through the hall. The fires had badly burned his body, and he groaned. His hands and knees left bloody streaks through the snow, the skin burned off. Rosalind couldn't imagine where he was going, but he seemed to be driven by some primal instinct to move.

She ran to him. "Wait! I can help you!"

Grunting, he paused and turned to her, his face contorted with pain. Already, the healing magic of Druloch was spiraling from her body in whirls of green, curling around the vampire's enormous muscles. As her magic took his pain away and healed his burnt skin, he closed his eyes, leaning back against the wall. His singed beard began to grow again, his body relaxing.

His eyelids fluttered, and a sigh slid from him. "Thank you, human." Slowly his eyelids opened again, and he stared at Rosalind with something like awe. "Not human anymore."

"Maybe not. Are you okay now?"

He stared at the ravaged ceiling, the crumbling walls. "I'm fine. Not sure about the fortress."

Crossing her arms, Rosalind walked further down the hall, inspecting the damage to the building. Nearly the entire roof had burned. If she hadn't frozen the fires with the cold snap, the rest of the fortress would have gone down with it. She listened for more sounds of distress, but the hall had fallen silent. The only sound was her boots crunching through the snow.

Now, her muscles ached from the power she'd used today, her thighs trembling with fatigue. She had the strongest urge to curl up in the snow and drift away to sleep.

Still, she wouldn't be getting much sleep in a fire-ravaged building, and neither would anyone else. As she walked further through the snowy hall, she felt a familiar magic thrum over her body, scented of peat and thunderstorms. She turned to see Caine, walking through the hall, his wings now gone. If he weren't so staggeringly beautiful, he'd almost look human.

"I liked what you were wearing before better," he said.

"It was a little chilly."

"Did you find any more dead?"

She shook her head. "No. Everyone I'd found was still alive. Just barely, but they made it."

"That means that thanks to the storm you created, only three vampires died, a fifteen-hundred year old man named Ælfwine, a young vampire named Lucia, and a woman we called Kitty."

"Gods damn it."

"They were all trained soldiers in Ambrose's army, and they died fighting for their city, blessed by Nyxobas. Their souls are free now. We hold their death feast tomorrow."

"Are there any more injured?"

"No." He touched her shoulder, rubbing it gently with his thumb. His touch sent a surge of warmth through her. "Which means you need to get some rest now. You expended an enormous amount of energy—both from the failed daylight spell, and from the storm you created. You need to sleep. I don't want to have to see my grandfather's eyes staring out at me from your face again."

She glanced at the ceiling. "There's a bit of a hole in the roof. And over half the fortress, to be honest."

"We can fix that." Caine closed his eyes, and he began chanting in Angelic, his aura bursting from his body.

Rosalind stared at the ceiling as stone began to form and arch over them. Closing her eyes, she joined in with him, and their auras curled together, licking at the walls and ceiling of the ancient fortress. And as their magic mingled with the building, blending into its very fabric, she could feel the fortress's history—over a thousand years of it: the city's founding, by a vampire warrior with long blond hair and tattoos on his face. He ruled the city until Ambrose arrived and slaughtered him in single combat. An ancient, primal battle of kings, with Ambrose the victor. The things these walls had seen...

At last, she could feel the fortress walls healed, the stone walls and ceiling restored. She opened her eyes. Once again, stonework arched above them, and she ran her fingers over the walls.

Exhausted, she faltered, leaning against the wall for support.

Caine slipped his hand around her back. "Come. You've done enough for one day. We're not far from your room."

By his side, she walked down the hall, her boots sinking into the snow. She leaned into Caine, resting her head against him as she walked, just trying to keep her eyes open.

But she still wouldn't be able to sleep today—not until she had more answers. "I need to know from you what happened—when you sent me to live with the Brotherhood."

"Oh. We're going to talk about that, are we?"

"Yes." Irritation simmered, and she straightened. "We're going to talk about that now."

Silvery magic licked the air around him. "I was chained in your parents' cellar. They thought to use me, to curry favor with the king."

"Malphas told me this part. They were social climbers and it didn't work. They used Malphas to lure you there and control you."

"It was the first time I learned I had another younger brother. They threatened to cut off his fingers, one by one, until I chained myself to their cellar wall."

She frowned. "What do you mean *another* younger brother?"

His pale eyes slid to her, shadows thickening around him. "Slip of the tongue. The point is, that was the first I learned I had a younger brother. When I arrived at your family's estate, I wanted to kill them."

"Naturally."

"But as soon as I entered, I saw that they were holding a knife to Malphas's throat. He only came up to my knee. He was terrified, his eyes wide. His face dirty. He was too skinny, and they really hadn't been looking after him. With the knife to his throat, he started crying. They nicked his skin, and he let out a loud wail, panicking. It broke my heart. They'd told him he was my brother, so he was just yelling 'brother, brother!'—desperate for me to help him. And that's how your parents were very smart. It wasn't the iron that controlled me—iron probably couldn't have kept me in the cellar. It was Malphas."

Rosalind's fingers tightened into fists. She truly was descended from monsters. "I'm so sorry."

"It's not your fault. You're nothing like your parents." He took a deep breath. "As you can imagine, I did what they wanted. Which was to march willingly to their cellar, where I let them chain me with iron. They kept Malphas as a servant. I supposed they thought he was harmless enough."

She stopped as she got to her door, and she turned the knob. Here, too, a thin blanket of snow covered the ground, but the roof had since been restored by their magic. Outside, in the snowy landscape, lights flickered in the tree branches, and she caught a glimpse of Lilu circling over the myrtle branches, his wings dusted in snow. A cold wind filled the room, and she closed the balcony doors.

Caine sat at the edge of her bed and flicked his wrist, lighting candles in the sconces on the wall. "When they started drinking from the blood of the Brotherhood, that's when they really started to lose their minds." He scrubbed his hand over his mouth. "After they imbued me with a second soul, and I was nailed to a post in the square, Malphas saved me."

Exhausted, Rosalind dropped onto her bed next to Caine. He'd skipped right over whatever he'd done to get himself locked in the town square, but she wasn't going to press him on that.

"I was half out of my mind," he continued. "I knew your parents had two more spirits. I didn't want them to damage anyone else the way they'd tormented me. Not to mention the fact that this sort of power was dangerous for someone unprepared for magic. I hunted them down. I found them, heading west with both of you. Your father had been ranting about founding his own city."

Rosalind nodded. "Drew's castle in Maremount is the continuation of their work."

"I believe so." Shadows slid through his eyes. "I left you both there, in the mud and the rain. I left you there screaming. I'd killed your parents in front of you, and I left you there, undefended, spattered in their blood."

A lump rose in Rosalind's throat. "And how did we end up with the Brotherhood?"

"For the next few nights, I'd wake up every night, hearing your screams. Miranda and you. The sweet sister, and the other one. After the rage I felt at how they'd treated Malphas, and I'd left you in the wilderness. I was sure you were dead. I had my spies in Maremount check on you, and they told me something almost as bad. You were alive, orphaned. But you had been given the extra souls, with no one to train you or help you. So, I did what I needed. I took from your parents' treasure. I used the money to pay for your care."

"Why did you care?"

He sucked in a deep breath. "Your parents were no longer in good standing with the king. You had no money. Do you know what would happen to two little orphan girls in Maremount, with no money?"

"I can guess."

"And moreover, you had powers beyond your controls. You would have killed. Slaughtered each other, possibly destroyed the world. Who knows. Or maybe you'd have grown into insane tyrants like your parents."

"So you sent us to live with the only people who would suppress our magic."

"Yes." His sleeve had ridden up on his right arm, and she caught a glimpse of his tattoo—the sharp blade of black ink. Just like the hairpin she'd seen on a table, when she'd glimpsed a vision of his life.

"My parents threatened to kill Malphas. Like the queen threatened to kill someone you loved years ago. That's how people control you. Love is a liability, right?" She pointed at the hairpin on his arm. "Why do you have that tattoo?"

The candles guttered, and he pulled down his sleeve. "I've told you your secrets. There is no reason you need to know mine."

Fatigue mingled with the flickering sparks of gods-magic that lingered in her chest. "Why?" she demanded. "Why are you so terrified of telling me about yourself?"

His silver aura whipped the air around him. "I'm terrified of nothing, Rosalind. Count yourself as fortunate I've told you as much as I have."

"Only because Malphas began the conversation with me. I tortured him in a prison, and he trusts me more than you do."

Caine leaned back on his palms. "Of course he's trusting. He's the good brother. I'm not. Go to sleep, Rosalind. You've been awake for far too long."

"Nice evasion." Even as she mumbled the words, she was crawling under the covers, her body drawn to the soft bed. Caine blew softly into the air, snuffing out the candles with a stream of silvery breath.

Rosalind curled up in the bed, her muscles burning with raw fatigue, and she stared at the balcony. Outside, flurries of snow were drifting on the breeze, sticking to the window.

In the warmth of the blankets, her body began to relax, her eyelids drifting closed. "Tomorrow, I need to find Ambrose."

"Shhhh…" Caine's body warmed hers as he crawled into bed by her side. "Sleep."

And at his word, calm washed over her like a blanket of snow.

CHAPTER 17

$\mathcal{R}$osalind couldn't say how long she'd slept, but when she'd awoken to a fresh pot of coffee and buttered toast, her body no longer ached, and her mind had cleared. Caine hadn't been by her side when she'd woken, but the sheets still smelled of peat and lightning-seared air.

After eating her breakfast and dressing, Rosalind had rushed off to find Ambrose. As soon as she'd awoken, a plan had begun percolating in her mind—a solution to their daywalking problem. Ambrose had reluctantly agreed to join Rosalind outside.

Now, as they walked through the Gelal Fields, her breath still frosted the air. The cold snap she'd created hadn't yet abated. And just below the silvery sheen of magic that protected the city, northern lights tinged the air with wild swirls of green.

Rosalind found a wool coat to wear out into the night air, and she pulled it tightly around her. "Thank you for meeting me out here, Ambrose."

"How could I refuse someone with your powers?" He gestured at the snow. "It seems you have changed the seasons in my city."

"You did a wonderful job clearing up the ifrit bodies," she said.

"Pity the shield you three created wasn't any stronger."

She frowned. "Caine and Malphas seemed to think someone inside the city must have weakened it."

His green eyes pierced her. "And what do you think?"

"If it was anyone inside the city, I would assume it's Bileth."

Ambrose arched an eyebrow. "So would I. But what brings you to that conclusion?"

"He once referred to you as his enemy. What's the deal? You're both shadow demons. You should be on the same side."

Ambrose narrowed his eyes. "When I agreed to meet you out here, you'd promised me a plan. Are you here to dwell on history, or do you have something to propose?"

"A little of both. But if I'm going to help fight in this war, I'm gonna start needing answers to questions."

Shadows pooled around him. "What is your proposal?"

"I'm going to need you to seduce your wife."

He glared at her. "For what purpose?"

"Maybe we've been approaching this daywalker task all wrong. We've been trying to use Angelic to convert them, depending on the power of three mages. Maybe that's not the only way. Erish has been turning humans into demons."

"Maybe so. But I no longer consider her my wife. She tried to have me killed."

"Okay, but maybe she can turn demons into... other demons. Maybe she can change your species. Vampires are the only type of demon vulnerable to sunlight."

Ambrose shook his head. "The vampire city would no longer be full of vampires. What would we become?"

"Whatever you wanted—keres, valkyrie, oneiroi... We could mount a surprise attack on the Brotherhood, one they'd never expect, just as the sun was rising. Drew could no longer attack simply by raising the sun here. If your soldiers chose different species, you'd have different vulnerabilities. It would make you harder to defeat."

"I'm not sure my soldiers would agree to this."

Her fists tightened, and she tried to marshal her patience. "Maybe not. But what are you going to do about Bileth? You can't allow him to stay here if he's attacking you from the inside."

"You don't understand. It's a long and complicated story."

"Tell me, then."

"Bileth and I go back a long way. To when I was first turned. Unlike other demons, vampires were humans once. Apart from hellhounds and Erish's abominations, we're nearly unique in this way. Our human lives continue to shape who we are today."

"And what is your story?"

"You don't need to know the whole story. Only that Erish is the one who turned me, centuries ago."

Understanding dawned in Rosalind's mind. When she'd been in the Brotherhood, she'd learned that vampires who'd been turned by high demons were more powerful than the rest. This would explain how Ambrose ended up as a king.

"She wanted me to live forever," Ambrose continued. "She seduced me, convinced me to drink her blood. She slit my throat, performed a spell. And I rose from the earth as a vampire."

Rosalind hugged herself. "And what happened between you and Bileth?"

"He was in love with Erish. Always has been. She's nearly the last succubus, and her powers of seduction are legendary. Erish's love for me sparked his rage, and so he got his revenge."

Rosalind's blood chilled. "How?"

"He locked me in a wine cellar, and sealed it off, chained me with iron." For just a moment, Ambrose's expression was unguarded, and raw pain flashed in his green eyes. "He starved me of blood for weeks. Bileth took the chains off eventually. But not until he locked my entire family in there with me."

Horror slammed Rosalind in the gut. "You killed them."

"They didn't stand a chance. And that is why I escaped to Scotland."

"Where you met Cleo," said Rosalind.

"As you can imagine, I don't think fondly of Bileth. I have made several attempts to kill him, with no success. I'm fairly certain

Nyxobas doesn't care if I live or die. Bileth is one of his twelve lords. Bileth was with him in the Great Fall, a hundred thousand years ago. That's all that matters to him."

"We've got to act quickly, then. Bileth will be trying to destroy us from the inside. And the Brotherhood will be trying to kill us from the outside. And there's no one to help us." She paused, grabbing Ambrose's arm. "So will you do it? Will you convince Erish to help us? I know she still loves you. She is thousands upon thousands of years old, and she chose you. That must mean something."

"She committed treason and waged a war against me. That means something as well."

She tightened her grip on Ambrose's arm. "Look, every relationship has its problems, but you've known each other for centuries. Before the treason thing, what did you love about her?"

His cold gaze slid to Rosalind. "Everything." He shrugged, looking away. "It doesn't mean I didn't love others as well."

"All you have to do is have dinner with—"

"—No."

Clearly, this wasn't getting anywhere. She'd have to find another way to persuade Erish to pass on her wealth of magical knowledge.

"Fine," said Rosalind. "I'll persuade her on my own, even if I have to glamour myself as you and seduce her myself."

Ambrose quirked a smile. "That sounds like something I'd enjoy watching."

She turned to walk away before he could see her eyes roll, and she began walking back to the Ninlil fortress, its dark stone walls bathed in silver.

Surely she'd built up goodwill of her own with Erish at this point. Rosalind had brought the succubus food and blankets in the dungeons. She'd freed Erish from the Brotherhood dungeons, and convinced Ambrose to give her a luxurious bedroom with a bath instead of a rat-infested cellar.

Maybe Erish owed her a favor at this point.

Rosalind shivered as she walked, her mind whirling with visions of the story Ambrose had just told. Was there anything crueler than forcing someone to kill their family? The thought of it made her sick. Apparently, it had become a favorite tactic of Drew as well. No wonder Bileth and Drew got along so well, bonded in depravity.

Drew had tried to do the same to her, to force her to murder her sister. Here, she wasn't far from the cemetery, where her sister lay buried between the roots of a yew. Tonight in the cold, her sister's resting place seemed especially grim. The air smelled like the bottom of a grave, and the breeze had died. Not a single leaf or blade of grass twitched in the wind. In fact, as she walked past the abandoned temple of Nyxobas, her footsteps crunching in the snow, a dark power thrummed over her skin.

Still as the dead. Her skin grew cold.

Shivering, she pulled her coat tighter around her. A shiver snaked up her spine. This wasn't just the cold magic seeping from ancient graves, or the temple of Nyxobas. A living being lurked in the shadows, his magic dark and powerful.

She whipped her head around, searching the cemetery shadows. Inky magic pooled around her, and as its power curled around her limbs, she realized that smell—that dank scent—wasn't the cemetery at all.

It was Bileth. Perhaps she could fight him on her own, but not if she didn't know where the hell he was right now. The bastard had cloaked himself with magic.

Her pulse raced. *Probably best to just get out of here for now.* Rosalind summoned her magic, letting it thrum over her skin. Her body began to blaze with the ancient power of the valkyrie.

As the storm winds filled her blood, she started to soar into the air, but a rough hand grabbed her ankle, pulling her back to the earth. Her body slammed against the frozen ground. As her back slammed against the snow, pain ran up her spine. She still couldn't see Bileth.

Run, her mind screamed. Frantically, she kicked at him, catching him in the jaw with her heel—she thought. On her hands and knees, she scrambled to get up, but Bileth grabbed her by the back of the hair, yanking her to the ground again.

She reached for the dagger in her sheath, but in the next second, she felt his weight on her, crushing her ribs like a ton of rocks. She still couldn't see him, but if she could just summon her fire magic—

Bileth hammered her with a hard punch to the back of her head, and pain exploded through her skull. In the next moment, Bileth was flinging her onto her back, climbing on top of her.

Anger wound through her. Frantic, she thrust her hips upward, knocking Bileth off her. She turned, slamming her elbow where she imagined his head would be. A stroke of luck—it connected with a loud *crack.* She hooked her leg over his enormous body, raising her blade above her head.

"I know what you did to Ambrose, you sick fuck." Nyxobas's power ignited her body, and with it, she started to see Bileth's silhouette, a dark chasm, like the opening of the cave.

Clenching her jaw, she brought the knife down, aiming for his heart—but Bileth gripped her wrists just in time.

He let out a low snarl, tightening his fingers around her wrists in a death grip.

He'd crush her bones. "Like I said. I will live long after you begin to feed the worms by your sister's side."

"What do you want from me?"

"What I've always wanted from your kind." He tightened his grip further, until she cried out with pain, dropping the knife. "Submission."

Fury stole her breath. *I need Borgerith's power.* Pushing out the excruciating pain in her wrists, she closed her eyes, imagining a mountain.

Ancient, coppery magic sang through her body, strengthening her bones, lending her power. And with it, she summoned the flames of the fire goddess.

She opened her eyes again, staring at Bileth, power rippling through her body.

Bileth's body had begun to smoke. "I see you're toying with gods-magic," he grunted.

She ripped her hands free from his grasp. With a roar, she slammed her fist into his face—once, twice, three times, listening to his skull crack, smelling the searing of his flesh, watching the flames flicker around his silhouette.

But as she reared back for another punch, two gunshots rang out, and pain seared through her gut. She shrieked, clutching her bleeding stomach. *Iron bullets.*

Already, she could feel the gods-magic weakening in her body. Bileth had brought a gods-damned gun.

As her magic dampened, her body began to tremble. She rolled off Bileth, weakened, nausea welling in her gut.

Run. Without magic, she didn't have a chance in hell against an ancient demon in a fight. She pushed herself to her feet, and pain splintered through her core.

Gritting her teeth, she broke into a run, her breath ragged in her throat. With iron searing her insides, she wouldn't be able to fly, or even sprint, but she had to get the hell away from him. Right now, she was closer to the forest than to the fortress—if she could find her way within those towering, gnarled oaks. *Thirty more feet.*

She could lose him in there, maybe run into Ambrose. The vampire king would help even the odds in this fight. *Ten more feet.*

As she ran, her blood roared in her ears. At last, she reached the forest's edge, her feet pounding the deadfall. And slowly, she felt Bileth's dark magic creeping over her skin, curling around her body like an invasive vine.

Her heart threatened to gallop out of her chest. *Why hasn't he caught up to me yet?* The pain from her bullet wounds split her in two.

She just needed to focus on the running. If she could lose in him in the shadowy forest—

Bileth's hand grabbed her by the hair, yanking her back. His other hand slipped around her stomach, gripping her hard, pressing into her bullet wounds. Pain screamed through her body, and she thrashed against him.

He chuckled in her ear. "How amusing to watch you try to run from me, as if you had a chance."

She kicked at his shins, but he held tight to her, enjoying her agony. "I told you what I wanted from you. Submission."

He pulled her to the ground, and in the next moment, he was climbing on top of her, his body now fully visible. "But let me revise my requests. I want submission, and then your death. And I will enjoy both equally. I don't need Ambrose using you as a weapon, though right now you don't seem so powerful."

He clawed at her jacket, ripping it open. Frantically, she grasped around her for something—any kind of weapon. Bileth reeked of death.

Bearing his fangs, Bileth leaned in, biting her throat. Pain ripped through her neck, and a scream tore from her throat. *He's going to eat me alive.*

She could feel the blood rushing from her body, just as her fingers grasped a rock. She slammed it into Bileth's head—once, twice, three times. Dazed, he fell back onto the ground. As her vision dimmed, she grasped for the gun in Bileth's belt. She pulled it out, pointing it at him. She fired it, aiming right for his chest, and he let out a roar. Then, his body thinned to a black smoke, and floated away on the wind.

Her entire body shook, and she crawled along, over the roots and moss of the forest floor. She had to find her way back to Ninlil fortress before the bullets poisoned her. If only her world weren't going black...

CHAPTER 18

$\mathcal{P}$ain wracked Rosalind's body, so sharp she thought her mind might rip apart.

She drifted in and out of a fevered sleep, dreaming of Maremount —of Malphas, leading her by the hand through a field of seagrass, to Athanor Pond—of Miranda, waiting to practice magic by the shore. Miranda had made wands out of mayflower wood, and she'd held them up proudly, bathed in milky light.

The memories came so clear now, burning in her mind like the sunlight glinting off the pond.

All these years, she'd stored these memories deep under her mind's surface, not wanting to remember. Trying to shut out the painful, gnawing loneliness she'd felt when Caine had left her and Miranda by the river's edge, the darkness so profound she thought she'd never find her way out of it. She'd closed it all away, deep under the surface. But along with her terror, she'd robbed herself of her beautiful memories, too.

Her vision rippled, giving way to another, darker memory—she and Miranda, walking down the damp stone stairwell to the cellar, hearts beating fast, hands clammy with sweat.

Malphas had said that she was fearless. She hadn't been, though. It was more that she *liked* being afraid, liked the rush of adrenaline, and the pounding of her heart. She'd known then, that something terrifying lurked in the cellar—a monster. She'd heard the chains rattling, heard the roars of rage.

It had been her idea to lead Miranda down the cellar stairs, and her sister stopped partway, unwilling to go on.

For just a moment, Rosalind's eyes snapped open again in her bedroom in Lilinor. Agony shrieked through her body. What was happening to her? Surely, this was more than just bullet wounds. Her body was on fire. Something was very wrong. She was supposed to be immune to fire.

Pain clouded her mind, and her vision dimmed again, until she was walking down those stairs once more, back in her parents' wine cellar, cold water dripping down the stone.

Her parents had constructed a cell for him down there—a dungeon of sorts, with three stone walls. As she'd moved closer to the sound of those rattling chains, fear had raked its claws up her spine. But she'd pushed on anyway, her own nerves exhilarating her.

And when she'd rounded the corner, deep in the cellar, she'd seen him—the inhuman monster with black eyes, the powerful body that towered over her, capable of ripping a human to shreds in seconds. Someone had impaled his wrists with iron spikes, pinning him to the wall, blood seeping down his fingers.

And yet still, he held something in one of his hands—a sharp, iron hairpin. The one tattooed on his arm.

Trembling, she took a step back from him, cowering in the shadows. And just then, her gaze darted to a figure lurking in the shadows.

The monster wasn't down there alone. There were *two* monsters.

In Lilinor, Rosalind gasped, her eyes snapping open. The air sparked with the scent of electricity, and Caine's silvery presence curled around her.

Her stomach clenched, and she leaned over the edge of the bed, vomiting a clear liquid onto the floor. She clutched the bedsheets, dry-heaving.

Grimacing, she wiped the back of her hand across her mouth. "What's happening to me?"

Caine brushed his hand down her back. "Ambrose found you. We took the bullets out, but you have a toxin running through your system. I think I know who did this to you."

"What's your best guess?"

"Bileth."

She nodded weakly.

"When he bit you, he filled you with his demonic venom."

Her muscles seized, her stomach tightening. "I saw you in the cellar," she whispered. "My parents' cellar. You weren't alone."

Agony rippled through her bones, and darkness claimed her mind again.

* * *

She woke, clutching the damp bedsheets, her body soaked in sweat.

Her mouth had gone dry, and her stomach tightened in pain.

"Rosalind," Caine said softly. His silver magic blanketed her body, soothing her limbs.

He lifted a silver cup to her lips, and she took a sip of cool water.

She looked up at Caine, her vision blurred. Even through her haze, she could see his silvery eyes blazing.

"You weren't there alone," she whispered. "In my parents' cellar. You were with another person."

He traced his fingertips down her collarbone, his touch soothing. "Was I?"

"You were holding the hairpin."

He brushed the backs of his fingers over her cheeks. "It was my mother's hairpin."

"Your mother, from London," she muttered. "Malphas told me you were from London."

"She's the woman you saw in your memories. The one with the blond hair. I'm the son of a South London whore. I grew up in a whorehouse, in a tiny room. And when her clients came in, she'd close the filthy curtain between us. When I wanted to get away from the city's filth, I'd flee the city walls, to the fields to the east, where the cherry trees grew." He began brushing his fingers over her ribs again, so gently she could hardly feel it, just the soothing thrum of his magic.

She tightened her fingers around his hand. "I saw the cherry trees in one of your memories."

"My mother took me there sometimes, too. Her name was Jane, and she died young. So you see, I'm not from the same sort of stock as Malphas, even if we're brothers."

"Coming from *good stock* is a bit of an archaic concept, don't you think?"

"Perhaps you haven't noticed, but demons don't live in the modern world." He traced his fingertips from her shoulder down her arm, and with every inch he covered, he took a little more of her pain away. "Are you feeling better?"

She swallowed hard. "Only when your hands are on me."

"Happy to oblige, as always."

Dizziness overwhelmed her, but she had so many questions she wanted to ask him. "The hairpin belonged to your mother. I saw it in your memories. But there was someone else in that vision. A baby."

The candles flickered in the sconces, nearly snuffing out, and Caine caressed her skin. "My little brother. Not Malphas. Stolas."

Stolas... She'd heard that name before, in a vision. But before she could ask another question, her mind spun, and her vision went dark.

* * *

The sound of a knock on a door pulled Rosalind from her sleep. Slowly, she opened her eyes.

Caine still sat at the edge of her bed, frowning at the door. "Who is it?"

"Malphas."

"Come in." Caine looked down at Rosalind, pushing a strand of hair from her eyes. "She's awake."

The door creaked open. Slowly, her gaze shifted to Malphas.

His clothes were soaked by rainwater, and he ran a hand through his wet hair. "He's gone. I might not be as skilled as Rosalind at sensing magic, but his aura is powerful enough that I'd feel it. He's left Lilinor."

"Of course," Caine said. "He knows that the next time I see him, I will slaughter him, no matter what Nyxobas thinks. And I'm one of the few people who actually knows how."

Rosalind's throat felt like sandpaper. "Why did Bileth try to kill me?"

"One," said Caine, "He's hated you ever since you impaled him. Two, he wants to destroy Ambrose and claim Erish for himself. After what you did with the ifrit, he knows just how powerful you can be."

Malphas took a step closer to her. "Did you get the poison out?"

Rosalind winced, her muscles burning. "It doesn't feel like it."

"The venom is out, Rosalind," said Caine. "But it will take you three days to recover."

"Three days until I can take on a legion of fire demons again," said Rosalind. "Let's hope no one else attacks between now and then."

"We'll handle it," said Caine.

Rosalind licked her dry lips. "Not without me, you won't. You need me now."

Malphas frowned at her. "I think I liked you better when you were incompetent." He turned, heading for the door. "I'm going to change out of these clothes. Caine, while I'm gone, please do your best to contain Rosalind's ego." He closed the door behind them.

Caine's silvery gaze met hers. "You're not wrong, though. You *could* be more powerful than we are. As long as you don't let the gods take over and try to murder me." He traced his thumb over his bottom lip. "Though if I am going to die someday, I might as well go at the hands of a beautiful woman."

"And if I'm not going to gain control, I need to give a little control, right?"

He lifted Rosalind's hand and curled it into a fist. Slowly, he brought their two fists together. "If a strong force meets another without yielding, both will break. Bend to the gods' will, just a little, and you can mold their power."

"Is that what you do with shadow magic?"

"I can't ever totally give in to Nyxobas. His spirit runs too deeply in my blood. But you're different. You're human. You can set yourself free, and create like the gods. Just not until you go a few hours without puking over the side of the bed."

A small smile curled her lips. Already, she could feel her eyes drifting closed again, her mind claimed by dreams of the seagrass by Athanor Pond and the waves gently lapping at the shore.

CHAPTER 19

*R*osalind leaned over the balcony, staring at the fields of bluebells that blanketed the ground, bathed in moonlight. Lilu cut lazy circles in the sky, the moonlight glinting off her wings. The snow had melted, and whether through magic or sheer persistence, Lilinor's wildflowers had survived the cold snap she'd created.

A briny breeze kissed her skin, rustling through the tall grasses below her window. Even now, a dull pain throbbed in her thighs—the remnants of the poison—but she'd made a nearly complete recovery.

Caine stepped onto the balcony, his gaze raking slowly over her body. "You look like you're feeling better."

"I'm getting there. Tell me I missed some good news while I was unconscious."

"You did."

"Care to share?" she asked.

"We've managed to kill a few hundred of the Brotherhood's soldiers—humans and demons. I've been sending vampires through the shields at night, and they've been luring the hunters out of the gated empire with reports of demon and witch sightings in the suburbs. The vampires have been attacking from the shadows, and returning back through the portal before the sun rises."

"Very clever."

He frowned. "But we won't be able to use the same tactics forever. Even the Hunters will catch on eventually."

"And what about Bileth?" Rosalind bit her lip. "How do you plan to kill him, if he's immortal? I rammed a poker through his chest and it barely even slowed him down."

"Like I told you, there is one way, but I'm the only one among us who knows how. Even Ambrose doesn't know."

"And you still don't care to share?"

He stared into the streams of moonlight. "It's forbidden for this knowledge to be shared. You can imagine why. Immortals don't exactly want this secret getting out. It makes us vulnerable."

The wind rippled over her skin, raising goosebumps. When she shifted closer to Caine, she could feel the warmth radiating from his body. "If we manage to kill Bileth, what will Nyxobas do?"

Caine's gleaming aura slashed the air around him. "He cherishes strength above all else. There's a chance he'd be proud." He gazed at the moon. "Besides. I can't have Bileth working with the Brotherhood. They'll learn all our weaknesses, if they haven't already."

"Weaknesses? I thought you didn't have any?"

"Not me, of course." He shrugged. "The vampires. Shadowy bastards catch on fire all too easily."

She leaned against the balcony ledge. "I may have a little way around that. I'm not sure Ambrose is keen on it, but I think it's our best bet."

"What?"

"We forget about the daywalker spell from centuries ago. And we try something new. We try converting vampires into different types of demons."

Caine arched an eyebrow. "I'm not sure the vampires would go for that."

"They'd be able to walk in the daylight. They wouldn't have to drink blood anymore. What's not to love?"

"Maybe you haven't noticed, but vampires *like* drinking blood and being creatures of the night."

"So persuade them. You're their general. They look up to you. Anyway, I'm sure they can keep drinking blood if they want. The point is, you'll have an army who can march in the daylight. They can remain shadow demons if they're so fond of Nyxobas. Oneiroi, or keres, or—you know more shadow demon types than I do."

He shoved his hands into his pockets, looking unimpressed. "I'll take your opinion into consideration."

"You just don't like it because I thought of it and you're supposed to be a leader."

He shot her a hard glare. "Don't be ridiculous."

"Tell me again how I'm stronger than you are."

"That's not even remotely accurate."

She cocked her head. "Mmmm. I think I heard you say that I'm more powerful than you."

"You have the potential—with magic only. I still have several centuries of fighting experience over you."

She narrowed her eyes, widening her stance. "All right, old man. Prove it."

He never took his hands from his pockets. "You can't be serious."

She smiled wickedly. "Are you afraid of getting hurt?"

His aura whipped around his body. "I'm afraid *you'll* get hurt."

She kicked him, aiming for his shoulder. He blocked it with his arm. Shifting her stance, she kicked again, this time hitting him in the chest, hard enough that she knocked him back a foot.

He smiled slyly. "Any excuse to touch me."

When he stepped closer, she lunged, hooking her foot around his ankle. She pulled his leg toward her, knocking him off balance—but only for a moment.

Quickly, he righted himself, then hooked his leg behind hers, giving her a shove. She fell to the ground, and in the next moment, he was on top of her, his body covering hers. His silver aura caressed her skin, distracting her.

Okay, perhaps it had been an excuse to get her hands on him. Caine slid his hands up her arms, sending a shiver of pleasure through her body. She bent her knee, sliding it up his leg, arching her back. Slowly, Caine lowered his mouth to her neck, his teeth grazing her throat. Molten heat warmed her core, and she tilted back her head.

Caine's knee pressed between her legs, his fingers laced through hers. "Do you still believe you're more powerful than I am? It seems I have the upper hand."

With a smile, she lifted her hips, flipping him off her. She slid a leg over him, straddling him, gripping his hands. His silver eyes flashed, and she breathed in his rich, loamy scent. Electricity rushed over her skin.

She leaned in to kiss him, her lips crushing against his. And when her tongue brushed against his, the earth seemed to rumble…

No—the earth *was* rumbling. Stone dust was shaking from the walls.

Caine's body tensed, and she turned, looking through the stone columns of the balcony. There, in the fields, oak leaves trembled as heavy footfalls boomed over the fields. A bell began to toll from one of Ninlil Forest's towers, signaling an oncoming attack. Rosalind rose, staring at the shaking forest.

In a blur of silver, Caine rushed into the bedroom.

She glanced up at the magical shield, reassured by the thick, pewter sheen rippling over the sky. "The shield is in place." *Boom.*

Caine returned from the bedroom, strapping his sword and scabbard around his back.

Boom.

"The shield is in place now," he said. "But perhaps something came through when the ifrit arrived. It's a large kingdom, most of it wilderness. We wouldn't have noticed monsters lurking far outside the city."

Boom.

She gripped the edge of the balcony. There, in the distance over the oak trees, copper magic curled over the treetops. *Boom.*

And as it moved closer, she saw what was coming for them. Rustling through the oak forest, copper wings breached the forest canopy—fine-boned, their tips so thin that moonlight shone through them.

"Something is coming for us." Her breath left her lungs. "A giant with copper wings."

As the creature moved, it seemed to wilt every tree in its path, turning the leaves black, the branches withering. The reek of carrion wafted through the air.

"Copper wings, and it kills all the living creatures in its path," he said, his jaw tight. "A creature that hasn't walked the earth for thousands of years. Another of Erish's creations from the old world that she knew, tens of thousands of years ago."

"What is it?" asked Rosalind.

"The Asag." Caine turned to her. "He won't be alone. Turn away. Just the sight of him will stop your heart. Even if you're immortal, one look at him will turn you to stone."

"Copper magic," she said. "Borgerith's magic. You forget, Caine. The mountain goddess is inside me. Her magic won't hurt me."

"I hope you're sure, because the vampires won't defeat him. Only the gods-magic will vanquish a monster like this."

CHAPTER 20

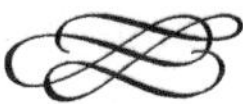

half mile away, the creature breached the forest's edge, and Rosalind's breath left her lungs.

The monster that emerged on gnarled limbs curdled her mind. He must have been a hundred feet tall. Scars marked every inch of his naked skin, and sharp teeth glinted in the moonlight. And he wasn't alone—a small army of rock demons swarmed around his knees— creatures that seemed to be made of gray bone, their eyes a milky white.

But it was the giant's enormous eyes, gleaming in the moonlight, that stopped her heart. Not just two eyes, but dozens. Images flitted across them, and even from this distance she could make them out— nightmarish visions of brutal violence, of humans slaughtering, raping, torturing each other.

"Careful, Rosalind," Caine touched her cheek, pulling her gaze from the monster. "Don't look into its eyes. I don't care if Borgerith is in you. You'll get lost there."

She shuddered. "I can see that. Are you ready to help me kill it?"

The Asag and his army were heading for the Eastern Wing—where Tammi and Aurora slept. She didn't have any time to waste.

Against her will, her gaze turned again to the Asag, locking on his eyes. Deep within his dark irises, an image blazed—a woman burning at the stake, her blonde hair ablaze, her skin blistering... *Cleo.*

"Rosalind!" Caine shouted.

She snapped her gaze away, catching her breath. *Okay.* Even with the power of Borgerith flowing through her veins, the Asag would drive her insane. She understood that now.

Caine's icy aura snapped from his body, and his black wings sprouted from his back, unfolding behind him. "I'm going to lead the vampires from below against the rock demons. I need you and Malphas to fight the Asag. Okay? But you need to fight him without looking into his eyes."

"Any idea what his weakness is?"

Caine shook his head. "His skin is hard as rock, and swords will do nothing to him. I can kill the rock demons by finding their livers. The Asag is impenetrable."

"Magic it is."

The army of rock demons marched onward, shaking the ground with their footfalls.

Below, vampires began pouring into the field, silver armor and swords glinting in the silvery light. They were waiting for Caine to lead them.

She let her eyes lift just enough that she could see the creature's three gnarled, gray feet clawing into the ground, a hundred feet away. "I understand. Go get your soldiers. I've got the Asag."

Caine climbed onto the balcony's edge, crouching for a moment before leaping into the air, his aura frosting the air around him.

A moment later, he landed in the field, in the front line of the phalanx of vampire soldiers. Raising his sword, he shouted an order, leading the charge of vampires.

A movement overhead caught her attention, and she looked up at Malphas, soaring through the sky, his black wings beating the air, already heading for the Asag.

Rosalind closed her eyes, summoning the power of the mountain goddess, letting it whisper through her blood, mingling with the wrathful fury of the valkyrie. Power surged, and she leapt into the air, her body blazing with the ancient magic of the gods.

The night wind rushed over her skin as she took flight. High above the charging armies, she followed the trail of silver magic that Malphas had left behind him, trying to keep her gaze off the Asag's eyes.

She caught sight of Malphas, circling above the giant, and tendrils of silver magic unfurled from his body, enclosing on the demon. She took care to look only at the creature's feet.

Good. They could start by binding him with magic, until they could figure out a better strategy.

Below, vampire swords clashed against the rock demons. The demons were slamming the vampires with their powerful fists, trying to crush them. Rosalind blocked out the carnage of the battle below, focusing only on the feel of shadow magic welling in her chest.

As she soared around the Asag, binding him with magic, she resolved to give in to Nyxobas, just enough to keep him happy.

She inhaled deeply, letting her mind drift into the void as silver magic whirled from her body. The night god's power rippled through her body, and icy magic curled around the demon's wings.

The creature snarled, and Rosalind widened her arc, flying out of reach. The night wind whipped at her hair, and she looked at the ground, catching sight of Aurora, driving her sword into a rock demon's liver.

She swooped again in another wide arc, crossing paths with Malphas, and her heart tightened as her gaze strayed once again to the battle below. Tammi had joined the fight, inexpertly wielding a sword in the middle of the fight. Tottering, she swung the sword at a rock demon, and it bounced off his arm with a *clink.* Apparently, Tammi hadn't been joking when she'd said she was learning to fight. She just hadn't gotten very far with her training.

Whatever the case, Rosalind needed to end this now. There was no way Tammi would last more than ten minutes in a sword fight.

Rosalind swooped a little tighter around the Asag, directing her magic in silver spirals around its body, binding him tighter.

The beast threw back its head, shrieking. As if lured by a magnet, something pulled her gaze to the Asag's eyes once again.

There, flickering in the depths of its many eyes, dozens of images of Caine—nailed to the wall, blood pouring from his wrists, clutching his hairpin. The giant's magic invaded her mind, like a disease rotting her from the inside out.

With a roar, the Asag burst free from the tendrils of shadow magic, grasping for Rosalind. The monster tightened a long, taloned hand around her, the tips of his claws piercing the skin near her spine. Its breath reeked of rotting corpses.

And in the Asag's eyes, she saw Caine, gripping that iron hairpin and ramming it into someone's heart, over and over... The breath left her lungs.

Don't look, Rosalind. She closed her eyes. If this bastard was made of rock, maybe she could melt him. But fire would probably do more damage to the vampires than to the rock demons.

So maybe I fight you with your own god.

She envisioned a stark, snowy mountain shimmering with copper magic. And she opened herself to the power of Borgerith, letting the goddess's power pulse through her veins. Borgerith had the power of magnetism, total control over rocks.

Rosalind felt herself directing the goddess' magic into the Asag, as though she were becoming part of it, melding with it, letting herself dip into the dark abyss of its mind, where humans slaughtered and tortured each other in an orgy of violence.

As her magic melded with the Asag, an image blazed in her mind: Azazeyl, falling from the heavens, his perfect, godlike body splintering into seven pieces. Shrieks rent the air, the unrelenting agony of being fractured into pieces. Perhaps this was how Drew had gone mad.

And yet even as Rosalind's mind split apart, the gods-magic invaded the Asag's body, surging through its veins. Rosalind arched her back, trying to drown out the screaming of the gods as her magic penetrated every inch of the monster.

"Expand," she breathed.

And with a terrifying boom, the demon exploded into a billion particles of dust.

Rosalind hurtled through the air, slamming against the earth, the air leaving her lungs, bones cracking. Pain ripped through her body, and dust rained down on her. Coughing, she rolled onto her stomach. With the fall, her teeth had pierced her tongue. Blood poured from her mouth, staining her shirt. In the depths of her mind, the gods' screaming subsided.

Yet still, her mind felt nearly as fragmented as her body. The seven fallen gods screamed in the hollows of her skull, lamenting their fall from grace, the last time they'd felt whole.

Slowly, she pushed up onto her knees, rubbing the dust from her eyes. Her bones felt like they'd broken in ten places. They probably had.

She surveyed the scene around her, finding it still. As soon as she'd destroyed the Asag, the rock demons had fallen to the ground, lifeless.

She blinked, trying to clear her mind of the pain that ripped through her body.

In the next moment, Caine was by her side, his aura washing over her skin, snaking around her limbs. Gently, he touched her back, his touch soothing. As his aura kissed her skin, whispering through her bones, the pain ebbed from her body.

She leaned back, sitting on her heels, catching her breath.

Caine brushed the hair from her face. "That was dramatic, but effective."

She stared up at him. "And how many more times does this have to happen before Ambrose decides to do something dramatic? I need you and Ambrose to listen to me. We can't just stay here in Lilinor, cowering in terror as one demon after another invades the city. You realize we can't keep this up, right? Just being defensive, never attacking?"

"I know," said Caine. "I want to murder the Hunters as much as you do."

She rose on shaky legs, still hearing the echoes of the gods' screams, the raw terror of Azazeyl when he plummeted to earth.

"Good. Because we're going to get Erish on our side, convert the vampires into something else, and invade Cambridge. We're going to murder the Hunters."

He narrowed his eyes. "Who is leading this army, you or me?"

She stood, brushing the dust off herself. "I am now. But I'll take your advice into consideration."

CHAPTER 21

Covered in dust and blood, Rosalind stormed through the halls, heading straight for Erish's bedroom. As she walked through the hall, her boots echoing off the stone arches, the visions replayed in her mind: Azazeyl, falling to earth, splintering into seven pieces, his agony excruciating.

She pushed the image deep into her mental vault, and strolled up to Erish's oak door, carved with a silver snake on the front. Rosalind pounded on the wood.

She waited for a moment, hearing nothing inside.

She banged on the door again. What she really wanted to do was to kick the damn thing down, but she wouldn't do a very good job of persuading Erish to help her if she began the conversation that way.

"What?" Eventually, Erish's languid voice pierced the wood.

"It's Rosalind. I need to speak to you." She swallowed hard. "I need your help, Queen Erish." *Still need to get used to those formalities.*

"Come in."

Rosalind opened the door to find Erish sitting in a golden armchair. Candlelight danced over her warm skin, and her black hair tumbled over a pearly gown.

Iron chain, studded with diamonds, encircled her wrists and ankles, binding her to her chair.

"To what do I owe this visit?" asked Erish.

"I missed our conversations."

"So you showed up, covered in blood and dirt, smelling like a corpse."

Rosalind cocked her head. "Perhaps I should have showered."

"I thought I heard a battle. Pity I couldn't see any of it." She lifted her wrists, and light sparked off the gems in her shackles.

"Maybe you don't need to stay in here," said Rosalind. "If you could prove your loyalty to us again, maybe I could free you."

Erish arched an eyebrow. "You could free me? Did Ambrose die and crown you?"

"No, but I'm taking matters into my own hands. I want to end this war as soon as we can."

"And how do you want me to prove my loyalty?"

"I stole you back from Drew because you were his secret weapon. You were creating armies of demons for him, converting humans into demons."

"And?"

"I just fought one of your demons. An Asag. You've been creating creatures that haven't walked the earth for millennia." Rosalind took a deep breath. "So I'm fairly confident you could convert vampires into something that walks in the daylight. Am I right?"

"I suppose." Erish tilted her head, her dark eyes gleaming. "And then what? I was once queen here. I was feared and respected before Ambrose cast me aside, his eye straying from one human whore to another."

"You were a queen. And now you're the most powerful weapon we have. That commands respect, too. You can be more than a wife, Erish. You can be our salvation. We will take down Bileth's portrait in the entrance hall, and replace it with yours."

A small smile curled Erish's lips. "That would gratify me."

"Are you on board?"

Erish sniffed. "Fine. But I'll need a larger room, with more servants, and I will need them to worship me like a goddess twice per day. And of course, I'll need ambrosia."

"The gods-blood. I have a small vial in my room."

Erish narrowed her eyes. "Don't you need it for yourself?"

"As Drew so helpfully informed me, I don't need to keep drinking it. As a descendant of Azazeyl, I only need to drink it once. Using gods-magic has transformed me already. And now, Blodrial lives inside me."

"So you've become a demon, like the monsters you once hunted," said Erish. "How does that feel, Hunter?"

Rosalind's lips curled in a smile. "Powerful." *And terrifying.*

Erish returned her smile. "Now you understand. But I'm not doing anything unless Ambrose knows about it. You may have gods-magic, and I may be a traitor, but Ambrose is still my king."

* * *

By Erish's side, Rosalind walked the meandering path that led to the abandoned temple of Nyxobas. A full moon hung in the dark sky like a jewel, and she breathed in Lilinor's intoxicating scent of jasmine. In her right hand, she clutched the tiny vial of ambrosia. Although she didn't need gods-blood for her magic anymore, she still had to fight the overwhelming urge to drain the vial herself, to feel the gods-blood surge through her veins. Something in the back of her mind urged her to drink it, to heal the splintering in her mind, to quiet the faint screaming of the gods.

A strange energy electrified her body as the gods clamored for a release from their torments.

She pushed the thought from her mind, glancing at Erish. "Are you ready to see your husband again?"

Erish looked at her sideways. "You haven't told Ambrose I'm coming, I suppose."

"No. I thought it might be better to catch him off guard. Especially with you dressed like that."

Erish wore a sheer gold gown that hugged her curves, and her dark hair gleamed in the moonlight. Apart from the iron shackles binding her wrists, she looked every inch the goddess.

"And the vampires I'm supposed to experiment on," said Erish. "Will they be here?"

"Assuming Aurora has found them."

At the bottom of the hill stood the forgotten temple of Nyxobas, its crumbling walls bathed in pearly light.

"I can teach you," said Erish. "If we're supposed to convert the entire army, I wouldn't mind a little help."

"I'd be delighted."

At the bottom of the hill, she crossed through the threshold into the old stone ruin.

There, Aurora leaned against a wall, sipping from a silver flask. Tammi paced the grass, a sword hanging from her hip.

And in the shadows stood two skeletal male vampires, bound in thick chains, stringy hair draped over bony shoulders.

"Hello, my friends," said Rosalind. "Where's Ambrose?"

"On his way with the incubi brothers," said Tammi. "They don't know why they're coming, but I just said you were ordering it."

"I'm sure that went over well," said Rosalind.

Tammi shrugged. "At least it united Ambrose and Caine in their irritation with you."

Rosalind nodded at the prisoners. "I see you brought us two victims. What were they imprisoned for?"

"Raping girls in the harem," said Aurora. "Caine has a thing about that."

"Glad to know someone has a moral code here," said Tammi.

"Rapists?" Rosalind eyed the vampires. "Good. Now I don't have to feel bad about doing this without your permission."

The vamps stood glumly, hardly looking up from the ground. One of them, a man with thinning blond hair, said, "Aurora promised us fresh blood."

Aurora frowned at Rosalind. "Those bastards haven't had blood in months. Why aren't they trying to drain you right now?"

Erish smirked at Rosalind. "Little girl, you're not human anymore."

"It would appear not," said Rosalind.

Tammi bared her pointed teeth in a smile. "She's an abomination. Just like the rest of us."

Rosalind looked at her friend. "If Erish and I can do this successfully, would you want to be human again?"

Tammi stroked her long, silvery hair. "To tell you the truth, Rosalind, I've never felt more like myself."

Aurora sipped her drink. "We better hope Rosalind is immortal. On a scale of punching to evisceration, how violent do you think Ambrose will get when he learns she's been plotting with his wife to mess with his army?"

Erish shrugged. "If I know my husband, he's awfully fond of decapitation."

"Everyone relax," said Rosalind. "No one is decapitating anyone tonight." She glared at the two prisoners. "Unless I get the spell a bit wrong with the rapists."

Erish quirked a smile. "And what makes you think you can control an ancient vampire lord?"

"He wants to destroy the Brotherhood. So do I. And maybe you and I can give him what he wants. Victory. What's there to get angry about?"

Tammi twirled her hair around her finger. "Maybe he'll let you off with a light spanking. If it helps, I'd be willing to make the sacrifice of taking the punishment for you."

Rosalind clutched her heart. "That's my girl. Always so generous."

The sound of footfalls over gravel turned Rosalind's head. Flanked by Malphas and Caine, the vampire king strode over the path. His shadowy aura curled from his body, darkening the air around him, his emerald eyes locked on his wife.

Slowly, his cold gaze slid to Rosalind. "Why have you released this traitor from her prison cell?"

Rosalind straightened. "This traitor is going to help us make daywalkers. She was the Brotherhood's greatest weapon. That's why I risked my life to get her out of there. And now she can be our greatest weapon."

Erish examined her nails. "I am awfully good at creating demons."

Caine's aura curled the air around him. "We've noticed that, since you have so successfully created the armies that attack us every few days. Thank you for the Asag, by the way. If Rosalind hadn't stopped him, we'd have lost half our army."

"But you had Rosalind, so I don't know what you're complaining about," countered Erish. "I don't think she's as fragile as when I first met her. I'd advise you not to underestimate her."

"I'd never do anything so stupid." Caine leveled his icy gaze on Rosalind. "Especially not when she seems to be conspiring to take over Lilinor's army."

"Divide and conquer." Shadows pooled around Ambrose. "Pit Caine and me against each other. Is that your strategy?"

"The Hunter scents weakness, and goes in for the kill." Caine closed in on her, studying her intently. He stopped just inches from her, staring down into her eyes. Gently he lifted her chin, peering into her eyes. "I can see the magic of the seven gods flickering in your eyes."

She could feel them, too, still screaming in the hollows of her mind.

CHAPTER 22

She stepped away from Caine, ignoring him, and looking at Ambrose. "I'm not taking over your city, Ambrose. But we need to act now. We don't have time for the two of you to decide who will take on the third soul. I have another solution, and we need Erish's help."

"I was the Brotherhood's most dangerous weapon," said Erish. "And I can be yours, too. I'll help you destroy them. And when I'm done, you can let me out of my chains."

Ambrose glared at the two chained vampires. "And why have you dragged two rapists into the Temple of Nyxobas?"

"We're going to try a little experiment," said Rosalind. "We'll turn them into..." she frowned. She didn't want to convert them into anything more dangerous than they already were, so they could go around terrorizing more women. "We'll turn them into wood sprites. Just to see if demons can be converted into other demons."

Caine nodded. "Perfect. I've always wanted to lead an army of three-inch-tall wood sprites."

"It's just an experiment. We'll turn the rest of your army into valkyrie, or dragon shifters, or incubi, or—"

"No succubi," said Erish. "But anything else is fine by me, as long as they're capable of killing. The succubi are meant to be worshipped as goddesses, and I'll not have any little vampire strumpets filling that role."

Caine stared at Rosalind. He seemed to have gone silent, but she could see the disapproval in his eyes, and she knew what he was thinking. She was turning into her parents, and she'd go mad with the power of seven gods. Humans were never meant to wield gods-power, and so on. She'd just have to ignore his disapproval for now.

Malphas shrugged. "It's worth a shot, isn't it?"

She took a deep breath. "It's just two prisoners, and no one even cares if they live or die."

"I do!" one of them called out.

"Once we see if it works," said Rosalind, "then we can decide what to do with the rest of the army. All I'm doing is giving you more information."

"And you expect my soldiers to agree to this?" said Ambrose.

Rosalind shrugged. "I have complete faith that Caine will be able to convince them."

Ambrose gestured at the prisoners. "Show me."

Rosalind turned to Erish. "Shall we?"

Erish nodded, and they crossed through the long grasses to the two prisoners.

The one with blond, stringy hair stared at her. "Did you say wood-sprite?"

"It was the first thing that came to mind."

"Will you turn us back into vampires again?" asked the other.

"No," said Erish. "But we'll let you free in the woods. Seems a fair trade. You won't need to starve, and we don't have to worry that you'll attack anyone else."

"What if—" the blond began, but Rosalind silenced him with a flick of her wrist. A burst of shadow magic sealed his mouth with a thick layer of skin. He'd get his mouth back when he was a wood sprite.

The other vampire began shaking, his chains rattling.

Erish thrust her hand before Rosalind. "I'll need the ambrosia."

Reluctantly, Rosalind handed it over, even though the gods' voices in her mind desperately wanted her to drink it, to feel whole again. *All seven, together in one...*

Nevertheless, she forced herself to drop the vial into Erish's hand, and Erish's dark eyes sparked with excitement. She pulled the cork from the top of the glass vial, then emptied the blood down her throat, moaning as she drank. Her dark aura flared, rushing over Rosalind's skin in waves of silky pleasure.

"Ahhh..." Erish licked her lips. "Delicious." Magic pooled around her, in wild tendrils of copper, blue, and green. Her dark hair began to snake around her head, writhing in the air, and her eyes darkened to deep, black pools. "The One who is All fills me with his power, he of the seven gods." Her finger trailed down her chest. "I will teach you the spell, Rosalind. But you must listen. Hear the call of Azazeyl, deep in your bones. Let him fill you. Azazeyl, the One who is All, gave the gift of language to the beasts. And from language, the beasts created meaning. Through words, the beasts became gods." Her words were coming out in a frantic rush. "Gods or devils, fated to heaven or hell—which, I cannot tell you, only that it is Azazeyl who gives you the gift of creation."

The hair rose on the back of Rosalind's neck. Somehow, these words rang true in the dark chambers of her mind.

Erish stepped closer to the mouthless vampire, whose pale eyes snapped open wide with terror. He seemed to be trying to scream under that layer of skin. The succubus gripped his skull, her magical aura curling around his body like colored vines. The vampire's eyes widened further, his body shaking.

Erish turned to Rosalind again, her eyes two fathomless pits. "Listen, child, to the words of Azazeyl. The One who is All. Listen and remember them."

Erish threw back her hand, and launched into a spell, the words as old as time itself. And somehow, Rosalind understood them: Erish was weaving a spell of renaming. *Light turns into dark, dark into light. Earth turns to sky, and up to down, pain to pleasure.* Erish revoked the title of *vampire,* and bequeathed a new one: the angels' name for *wood sprite.*

And at the final word, the vampire's body seemed to vibrate with light, and the sound of cracking bones pierced the air. His skin hardened, becoming wood-like, his fingers like spindly twigs, legs like gnarled, slim branches. Widened with horror, his eyes turned yellow, and a spray of leaves sprouted from his skull. A mouth appeared—one like a hollow in a tree. Finally, his entire body constricted, snapping down to the size of a mouse. Yelping, the tiny creature scampered through the long grasses.

Erish's lip curled in a wicked smile. "It seems that demons can be converted. Just like humans."

The other vampire's mouth hung open, and he stared at Rosalind. "No. I don't want to be a wood sprite. I'm a vampire. I—"

The voices of the gods rang in the back of Rosalind's mind. She swished her hand, slamming the vampire with a spell that covered his mouth with skin. His screams died in his throat.

Caine stepped closer, watching her closely.

Rosalind turned to him, taking a deep breath. "What was the name of the girl he raped?"

"Vanessa," he said.

"Thanks." She stared into the vampire's terrified eyes. "This is for Vanessa."

She stepped closer, placing her hands on the vampire's head, trying to ignore the greasy feel of his hair.

From behind her, Erish said, "Think of the One Who is All. Think of his true name. His blood runs through your veins."

Rosalind closed her eyes, mentally repeating the name *Azazeyl*. As she felt his power percolate in her ribs, her body tensed. It felt *too* powerful, like he could overwhelm her. She wanted to clamp down on it, the way she had with Cleo's magic, to keep it under wraps. But Caine had said that she needed to give in to the gods, to allow them to take over just a little if she wanted to use their power.

She arched her back, relaxing her muscles; as she did, an image burned in her mind of an angel, falling to earth. Bronze skin, dark hair and eyes, a face so beautiful it hurt to look at him. He tried to fly, but his wings were like lead, dragging him to earth. Down was up, and up was down. Light was dark. With his wings dragging him to the earth, the world no longer made sense. He screamed to the heavens, for his brother who'd betrayed him, for the loss of everything that made him whole.

Had he really deserved this? He'd given humanity a gift—that was all. And for his sin, he'd suffer eternal torment.

But he hadn't felt the worst of it yet—not until his mind began to fragment. As his magic rippled through her body, Rosalind felt his pain, the indescribable agony of ripping apart, until he no longer knew who he was anymore. Slowly, as Azazeyl fell closer to earth, he shattered into seven tormented pieces, each one trapped—in the mountain and sea, the skies and trees, the inferno and the void. And after him, fell the lesser angels, transforming into demons of shadow and light.

And Blodrial—the final insult—coursing through the blood of the beasts themselves. If Azazeyl loved the beasts so much, let him suffer there.

From one angel came seven warring demons, with no memory of their past, no understanding that they'd ever been united. They only knew that every moment was an exquisite agony, and that they yearned to join the heavens once more, to be whole again.

Rosalind's eyes opened again, and she stared at the vampire before her. The magic of Azazeyl swirled around him, filling the temple of Nyxobas, and the vampire's eyes opened wide. As if sensing something terrible might happen, Erish and Caine had stepped away from her.

I can do this. I have the power of Azazeyl.

Rosalind tightened her grip on the vamp's head, bringing to mind the spell Erish had woven. And when she opened her mouth, the words tumbled from her lips as though she'd always known them, as if they were a part of her. And perhaps they were.

When she chanted the final word—the Angelic name for *wood sprite*—she felt magic coursing from her own body into his, invading his cells and his veins, melding them to her own will. The vampire's skin hardened, turning to bark, and an array of leaves grew from his head. Within moments, his entire spindly, arboreal body constricted down to a few inches, and the wood sprite ran off through the grass.

Rosalind turned to the others, who stared at her warily.

"What?" she asked.

"You look a little scary," said Tammi. "Your hair has gone a bit medusa."

Aurora grimaced. "Yeah and your eyes are doing that chasm of terror thing. Like Erish, only creepier."

"I'm sure it will wear off," said Tammi.

Malphas smiled slyly. "I find it oddly attractive."

Caine glared at him, shadows flitting in his eyes. "Right. Rosalind has made her point. She can create wood sprites."

"This is potentially a brilliant plan," said Malphas. "If we had an entire army of valkyrie—"

"Not valkyrie," said Ambrose. "I won't have any army entirely made of women. I don't need to be outnumbered to that degree. Not to mention that valkyrie are demons of light. We belong to the shadows. I realize that doesn't mean anything to you, Rosalind. But it means something to us."

Erish cocked her head. "I don't feel especially loyal to Nyxobas. He fathered an incubus, but he's not particularly fond of incubi and succubi like us. I think he'd rather we all died."

Rosalind's mind burned with the vision of Azazeyl plummeting to earth, fracturing into seven parts. "Light and shadow demons are just an illusion. We all come from the heavens, and all the earthly gods come from one angel." She shouted the words, desperate to make them all understand. "We're all one, infinitely powerful. Don't you see?"

"Right," said Aurora. "I was wondering how long it would take till she completely cracked."

"What?" asked Rosalind.

Tammi grimaced. "Your hair is still doing that thing, and you sound kind of like an insane mystic."

Rosalind threw up her hands. "Fine. But the point is, let's not worry about allegiances to shadow and light, or to gods who really don't care if we live or die. Our allegiance is to Lilinor, right? I don't even come from here, and neither does Tammi, but we've got no other home right now. So this is our home, and we will fight for it. And it doesn't matter if we are vampires, or keres, or insane mystics. We're all abominations. Let's embrace it, shall we? And let's kill the mother-fucking Hunters so they stop invading our home. And maybe when we're done, if you're all still worried about being vampires, we can change you back."

Malphas smiled. "I like the new Rosalind."

Ambrose folded his arms. "And what demon type do you suggest we convert my soldiers into, Rosalind?"

"Why not let them choose?" she asked. "They can be whatever they want to be, as long as they can kill."

"I like being a vampire," said Aurora. "I'm a creature of the night, and I like drinking blood. But you know what I like better than being a vampire? Not bursting into flame every time the sun rises. I could perhaps see myself as a valkyrie. I've always wanted to fly."

"Good," said Rosalind. "Because we know that this works. We could give Malphas another soul, and wait for however long it takes him to regain his sanity long enough to perform the spell with us. We could wait to see if the spell even works, since this theory is based on nothing but three-thousand-year-old legend. Or we could do something now, before we all die at the hands of one of Erish's monsters."

Ambrose stared at her. "You make a compelling case."

Aurora lifted her flask. "I like the option that doesn't involve death by fire."

Rosalind smiled, and the voices of the gods quieted in the back of her mind. "Good. Tomorrow, we assemble the vampires."

"And I'm supposed to convince them," said Caine. "I understand your logic, but you'll be using intense gods-magic for several days straight. Is that really a good idea?"

Rosalind's mind roared with the voice of Azazeyl. *I fell to earth, shattered into seven tormented pieces, each one trapped—in the mountain and sea, the skies and trees, the inferno and the void.*

Rosalind nodded. "I know you will. You know it's the right thing to do. And when they're convinced, they just need to choose a new identity. Erish and I will transform them, one by one. If we attack at sunrise, Drew will never see us coming, and he won't expect to be fighting creatures who can fly. The Brotherhood's defenses will be down, and we will have a tactical advantage."

Ambrose nodded slowly. "I promised my army they could walk in the daylight."

"And they will," said Rosalind.

Ambrose turned to Caine. "Convince them." He turned, his footsteps crunching over the gravel.

CHAPTER 23

*R*osalind sat in a throne on a dais before a blood-red hall, the stone walls bedecked with a terrifying array of weapons. Several thousand vampires had crammed into the Great Hall, all of them staring at her and Erish. She wore a long, black gown, dripping with silver jewelry she'd borrowed from Aurora. If the vampires were going to assent to her transformations, she probably needed to at least look like she belonged here.

Despite her outfit, the horde of vampires standing before her didn't look particularly thrilled to be here. Rosalind tightened her grip on the throne's armrests, waiting for Caine to arrive.

She scanned the crowd, looking for a friendly face, and she relaxed a little when she spotted Tammi and Aurora standing near Becca, who wore a cartoon vampire T-shirt that read *Vampires Suck.* Perhaps Rosalind had overdressed.

At last, the enormous wooden doors at the back of the hall swung open, and Caine stood in the doorway, dressed in his black military gear, a sword slung over his back. Even now, his otherworldly beauty took her breath away.

The hall fell completely silent, and the entire legion of vampires parted for him, making way. He strode across the red floor, his silver eyes locked right on Rosalind, his aura whipping from his body in vicious silver curls. She could feel the tension in the room. The vampires respected him, but they feared him, too. And with his eyes boring into her, she couldn't help but feel that he was studying her, judging to see if she was transforming into her insane parents.

The man knew how to make an entrance, she'd give him that.

He ascended the stone steps, then turned to face his army. "Like me, you're creatures of Nyxobas. We dwell in shadows. We thrive in darkness. The void terrifies us, but it's also part of us. But you don't need to hide in the darkness to be a shadow demon. I'm a creature of night who sometimes walks in the daylight. I know you want this, too. You want to fight in the daylight, kill in the daylight. Maybe fuck in the daylight."

"Hell yes!" someone shouted from the back.

"Drew's greatest weapon against us has been the sun, which he controls. It means we haven't even been able to attack his empire at night, because he can easily raise the sun against us, and burn the entire army to ash in an open battle field." For the first time, he turned to Rosalind. "Rosalind, our mage, wants to help you walk in the daylight."

Murmurs erupted over the room, and Caine held up a hand to silence them. "But not as vampires."

The crowd fell silent again, and the air in the room seemed to cool. She could feel the vampire's auras thickening the air.

Caine turned to her. "Rosalind. Would you care to explain?"

She took a deep breath, rising from the throne. Okay. Maybe she should start with the truth. "Look. Ambrose wasn't lying to you. There's a three-thousand-year-old legend about daywalking vampires in Macedonia. There's a chance that three mage souls could get you there. We've got two mages right now. But the truth is, when Drew murdered my sister, he killed the best chance we had of making that happen."

Caine faced the vampires again. "Of course, we can imbue the soul into Malphas. We could wait for however long it takes for Malphas to recover his mental state, and hope that it doesn't break him. And while we're waiting, Drew could break through the shield, send his legions into Lilinor. He could send more ifrit to rain fire upon us. In the last attack, we buried three people. Before that, it was two, and before that, twenty-seven. Here's the thing about being a creature of Nyxobas. It doesn't simply mean we're shadow demons. It means we value strength. It means we act on the offensive to destroy our enemies."

Another murmur rippled through the hall.

"Rosalind and Erish can transform you into different types of demons. You can choose to be a shadow demon if you want. An oneiroi, or a ker. An Incubus, if that suits you. Something that can walk in the light. Or you become something else, a creature of another god. A valkyrie. A hellhound. A fae—unaligned, but powerful. Maybe your appearance and your magic changes, but the important things that make you a citizen of Lilinor remain the same: strength, dominance. A home in the shadows."

As he spoke, shadows seemed to writhe and dance around him.

"As daywalkers, we can attack the Brotherhood in their own city, in the daylight. When they're not expecting us. When Drew's greatest weapon against us—the sun—will have no effect."

Aurora pushed through the crowd, climbing onto the dais. "The Brotherhood captured me, and eight other vampires. They dragged us into the sunlight." She turned, exposing her backless dress, the one that showed off the burn marks on her back, then turned back to the crowd. "And that's why I'll happily live as a valkyrie, or a shadow demon, or whatever. At least for as long as it takes to kill the fuckers."

Rosalind nodded. "Let me put it this way. You can stay as vampires and probably die terrible, fiery deaths. Or you can transform into another kind of demon. And we destroy the Brotherhood together."

The mood in the room seemed to have shifted, and she saw heads nodding, a bit of interest sparking in the vampire's eyes.

From the front, a muscular vampire stroked his beard. "If it's temporary, I'd like to become a woman." He looked around him nervously. "Just to see how it feels."

Aurora raised her arms to the ceiling. "I'm turning into a valkyrie. Who's with me?"

Slowly, one after another, hands began to raise around the hall. Relieved, Rosalind smiled.

* * *

Rosalind sat in one throne, Erish in the other—her own throne, in fact. Rosalind scanned the crowd. "Who wants to be the first to volunteer?"

Someone was pushing through the crowd, forcing them to part. At last, Becca climbed the steps, nervously toying with the hem of her *Vampires Suck* T-shirt.

Rosalind smiled encouragingly at her.

Shyly, Becca returned her smile. "Do you think you could turn me into a hellhound? I'd like to be able to light people on fire, and watch their skin burn."

Rosalind's smile faded. Apparently, Becca had a bit of a dark side. *A bit brutal, but this is a war.* "Okay. Hellhound it is."

Becca knelt, and Rosalind placed her hands on her purple hair. Azazeyl's magic pulsed down the length of her arms, burning through her fingertips.

As Rosalind chanted the Angelic spell, she drifted into the world of Azazeyl, feeling the terrifying rush of his fall to earth, the wind whipping over his skin as his leaden wings pulled him to earth. When dark was light, and up was down, and nothing meant anything anymore.

The power of seven gods dizzied her. As the magic flowed, it felt as if the ground had been torn out from under her feet.

Just as she felt Azazeyl's soul fracturing, she opened her eyes again, staring at the red-eyed hellhound before her. Becca held up her hand, smiling, and flames sparked from her fingertips.

At the sight of fire, panicked screams echoed through the hall.

Rosalind held up her hands. "Easy, Becca. Let's save the fire until the battle, okay?"

Suddenly, Becca's eyes widened, and a look of pain contorted her face. She clutched her heart.

Shit. Rosalind held out a hand. "Are you okay?"

Her skin pale, Becca shook her head. "There's something wrong with my chest."

Concerned murmurs rippled through the crowd.

"What does it feel like?" asked Rosalind.

Becca swallowed, her face pained. "Like a pounding in my chest. Like a thumping… things moving…"

Rosalind loosed a breath. "That's your heart. You're feeling your heart beat again, pumping blood around."

Relief washed over Becca's features, tinged with confusion. "Oh. Yeah." Muttering to herself, she turned and walked down the steps.

Next, Duke Ricard ascended, adjusting the flounces at his wrists.

"What have you decided on?" asked Rosalind.

"A fae lord."

Rosalind frowned. "I'm not sure that I can make you a lord, per se—"

"—A fae lord," he repeated, kneeling.

"Fae lord it is," she said.

She touched his head, and the vision of Azazeyl burned in her mind—the dizzying fall, the screams the angels ignored… Azazeyl's mind began to fracture into seven pieces, and Rosalind's eyes snapped open again.

Before her stood a formidable fae warrior with long, silver hair and pale blue eyes. For a moment, confusion clouded his features, and he gripped his stomach. "What's this feeling?"

Rosalind leaned forward. "What feeling?"

"I feel… empty. Like I need something. In my stomach."

"Ah. That's hunger. Actual hunger, not blood hunger. You'll need to find the fae chef. And I hope his fae magic allows him to make food for five thousand people at once, because we're gonna have a lot of hungry soldiers."

Duke Ricard's lip curled with disgust. "You want me to eat… a meal of food?"

"You'll love it. Trust me. Ask him for corn dogs."

"Corn dogs," he repeated slowly.

"It's an American delicacy. Fit for a fae lord." Her stomach rumbled. When was the last time she'd eaten? Just part of a baguette hours ago. "And while you're at it, could you ask him to send some corn dogs this way? Like, three of them."

The Duke sniffed as he rose. "I suppose I could try them." He strode down the steps.

One by one, the vampires climbed the steps to the dais. They knelt before her, and she touched their heads, letting the magic curl around them, transforming them into woodwose, keres, shadow demons, valkyrie... Azazeyl's magic rattled in her skull, splintering her mind every time she transformed a creature. Time seemed to slow down, her body burning with fatigue. With each spell, she felt a little emptier, more fragmented, but she kept going.

Just as a leggy redhead got ready to ascend the stairs, she held out her hand, pausing the line of vampires.

Exhausted, Rosalind leaned back in the throne, her mind whirling with the screams of the gods. Fatigue sapped her strength. According to Drew, at some point this magic would no longer tire her, but for now, she felt ready to burn out. Each time she performed the spell, Azazeyl's torment felt a little more vivid.

She glanced at Erish, who'd just finished transforming a male vampire into a long-fingered woodwose, covered in hemlock leaves.

Erish's eyes had darkened to black voids, her dark hair writhing around her head. Rosalind cringed. *Gods below. Is that what I look like?* She touched her hair, feeling it snake around her head like a living thing. *Yep, that is what I look like.*

From the crowd, Caine pushed through, then climbed the stairs. His glacial aura cooled the air around him, and sent shivers over her body. "You don't quite look like yourself anymore. This might be a good time to stop."

The gods whispered in her mind, *make me whole again,* and their agony put her on edge, angering her. Someone needed to pay for what had happened to Azazeyl.

She glared at Caine. "Why do I get the feeling you're a little threatened by this?"

The air seemed to cool. "I was born a demigod. I'm not threatened by anything."

"I can feel your disapproval. You've been standing there in the shadows staring at me like I'm some kind of monster."

"I'm watching you change before my eyes into something I've seen before. I can see the anger in your eyes." His aura sliced the air around him. "You don't know how the gods work. Their vengeance knows no bounds, and they exert their wrath on one generation after another."

Okay. He's lost me. "What are you talking about?"

"The gods don't forgive the sins of the father. And they punish us by dooming us to repeat their sins. You can't fight fate. And now, when I look into your eyes, I see your parents."

His words hit her like a blow to her chest, and she tightened her grip on the throne's armrests. "You think that everyone is destined to fulfill a tragic destiny, just because you did something terrible? You're certain that you're cursed. And you want to drag the rest of us down into hell with you, don't you? Then maybe your despair won't be quite so lonely."

A heavy silence fell, and the lights in the hall seemed to wane and flicker.

When Caine walked away, an icy chill washed over her body, until another aura began snaking over her skin.

She looked up into Ambrose's emerald eyes.

Intrigued, she leaned forward, blinking the tears from her eyes. "So what would you like to be?"

"An incubus."

CHAPTER 24

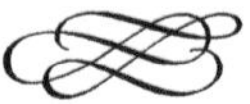

*D*izzy, Rosalind threw herself on her bed, her boots hanging over the edge. She'd spent the past several days converting vampires into Lilinor's new army. And that meant days of reliving Azazeyl's torment, falling to earth over and over with leaden wings, her mind fracturing in seven pieces that could never reunite.

Now, nausea climbed up her throat, and she clutched her stomach. She still didn't have much time here to rest—just an hour or so before she had to get back to the hall, converting more demons.

A sigh slid from her. Where was Caine? With Bileth gone, he no longer needed to sleep in her room, but she missed his company. Since she'd started converting the vampires, he'd been avoiding her completely, as if he couldn't stand to look at her with the gods-magic pooling around her body. Did she really remind him so much of her parents? The thought horrified her.

It hardly seemed fair. She wasn't a power-crazed maniac after her own glory. She was trying to save this city. By Erish's side today, they'd worked their way through scores of demons, converting them into valkyrie, fae, shadow demons…

And when she closed her eyes, she felt herself falling, the wind tearing at her skin and hair. She bolted upright. *Okay. So maybe the power is screwing with my head.*

She rose from her bed, eager to take her mind off Azazeyl's agonizing descent. Taking a deep breath, she crossed to the door.

She wanted one person right now: Caine. Her muscles aching, she walked the halls, entranced by the wavering candlelight that danced over the flagstones. The strike of her heels echoed off the ceiling.

Caine had said the gods cursed people with the sins of their fathers, dooming them to repeat their parents' worst transgressions. So how had the gods punished Caine? It was something to do with his father, Abrax. She didn't know much about Abrax, only that he was Nyxobas's son, and that he was a monster.

If Caine had a theory about her, she wanted to hear it. Did he know something he wasn't telling her? As she walked to his room, images flickered in her mind—those leaden wings, dragging Azazeyl to earth as his mind shattered.

At last, she stopped by the portrait of Lord Byron—Caine's bedroom. She knocked twice on the oak, listening for the sound of footfalls on the other side of the door.

He opened the door, and her gaze lingered over the muscled panes of his chest. Candlelight bathed his brutal, spiky tattoos in warm light. Caine—her blackthorn.

He leaned against the doorframe. "Rosalind."

He wasn't about to welcome her in, but she pushed past him anyway, stepping into his room.

"Tell me what happened to you," she said.

He turned to her, shutting his door, and arched an eyebrow. "This is your new imperious side, isn't it? Queen Rosalind."

She sat on his bed. "I guess you'll just have to get used to it."

"Don't you remember?" he shoved his hands in his pockets. "Don't you remember what happened to me?"

What? "No. I remember walking down into the cellar, and finding you there. There was someone else there. I remember now, the hairpin in your hand. I remember that you terrified me."

"In the vision you saw of my life, you saw a woman with long, blonde hair, and a baby. The woman was my mother. And the baby was my younger brother, Stolas."

Stolas. The word she'd heard, the name on his lips when he'd been impaled. The terrible thing Caine had done. "And what happened to Stolas?" she asked. But with a sinking feeling, she thought she already knew.

Caine cocked his head, and the air chilled. "Do you really want to know what happened? Because it seems you've worked very hard to forget your past. The things your parents did. Miranda remembered, but you didn't want to."

She shook her head. "I didn't want to remember. I wasn't ready for it before. I am now."

"Centuries ago, when the king and queen enslaved me, they used my brother to control me. Stolas. He was only a few years younger than me, but they'd managed to capture him, and imprisoned him with iron. They threatened to kill him if I defied them."

"And my parents knew your weakness. Family."

He nodded, almost imperceptibly. "When your parents sought to control me, they had two brothers to use against me."

His silver aura chilled the air, and he stepped closer to her, hands in his pockets. His eyes had turned dark as the void, and he seemed to be lost in the hell of his own mind.

Icy dread bloomed in Rosalind's chest.

Caine moved closer, looking down at her, his eyes icy cold. "After they imbued me with the spirit, in that dark cellar—your parents' cellar—I lost my mind. I could hear my second soul's voice, screaming in my skull. I didn't know what he wanted, only that his agony, his rage, blinded me. And he hated shadow demons."

"He watched his lover burn to death." Rosalind's skin felt cold, and she hugged herself. "He blamed Ambrose for betraying her."

"You want to know what I did?" Caine reached for her face, brushing his thumb over her cheek. "I'll show you."

His silvery aura curled around her body, thrumming over her skin, his power raw, frightening. And in the next moment, a vision rose in her mind—

Caine stood in her parents' cellar, his arms nailed into the stone wall, blood dripping down his wrists. Across from him, another man who looked just like him, only slightly slimmer, not quite as powerful. Stolas. Just like Caine, Stolas's limbs had been nailed to the wall with iron nails, and dark blood seeped down his body.

Caine looked at his brother, agony etched on his features. He clutched the iron hairpin in his fingers, stroking it gently. "I'm going to get us out of here."

"What about Malphas?" Stolas asked.

"I'll get him out of here, too. We can't stay here, Stolas. Something terrible is going to happen. I can feel it."

Stolas frowned, his pale eyes piercing the darkness. "What about the spell they wove? The soul they put into you? What did it do?"

Caine shook his head. "I don't think it worked. I can't even feel it. I feel the pain from the iron nails, but that's it. It's just this feeling, that the world is about to end. Our world is about to end."

Stolas raised his brow. "Are you sure about this?"

"I'll get us out of here," said Caine.

Caine gritted his teeth, ripping his arms free from the wall. An animalistic growl rose from his throat as his tendons tore, blood pouring from the wounds.

And then, a horrible silence enshrouded the cellar. Caine's brow furrowed, and his eyes darkened. Black, feathered wings appeared behind his back.

"Caine," said Stolas.

But Caine didn't seem to hear his brother. He clutched the iron hairpin in his fingers, seemingly oblivious to his ravaged limbs. Silver magic sliced the air around his body.

He growled, gripping his head, falling to his knees. "She burned," he muttered in a voice not quite his own. "I watched her skin burn. Then they came for me." A choked sob rose from his throat—a sound she'd never heard from Caine. "The shadow demon turned her in. She trusted him."

Stolas's brow furrowed. "Caine? What are you talking about? Who are you talking about?"

Caine gripped his hair tighter. "The shadow demon never really loved her. Monster. They're all monsters."

"Caine!" said Stolas.

Caine's muscles tensed, and he looked up at his brother. Slowly, he rose, gripping his mother's hairpin between his fingers.

Stolas looked into his eyes. "Stay with me, Caine. Stay with me."

Caine shook his head. "That's not my name," he snarled.

Stolas's fingers curled into fists as his body tensed. "Caine. Stay with me. It's you and me, brother."

A low snarl tore from Caine's throat. He cocked his head and began speaking in a hiss, chanting ancient Angelic words, a spell that Rosalind understood—one that spoke of turning angels into beasts, trapping them in dying bodies. Azazeyl's lament.

Stolas's eyes opened wide, gaping as his brother pulled his immortality from him in a gleaming stream of silver light, until the stunning light left Stolas's eyes.

Panicking, Stolas started to pull himself from the wall, but it was too late.

Gripping the iron hairpin, Caine reared back his arm and slammed it into his brother's heart, pushing it in until the tip was completely submerged in Stolas's chest.

Stolas's pale eyes snapped open, and a choking noise rose from his throat.

"Shadow demon," Caine snarled, turning away from his brother. "Demons betrayed us..." His sentence trailed off, and he stared down at his bloodied hands. "Demons betrayed us. That was our mother's. That was our mother's hairpin. I kept it all those years. Don't you remember, Stolas?" His voice broke. "I looked after you when she was working. You'd cry unless I took you outside."

Thick streams of blood dripped between his fingertips, from his ruptured veins, from his brother's heart, but he seemed oblivious. Oblivious, too, to his brother's silent torment, just a few feet behind him, to the dimming of Stolas's eyes, the fluttering of his eyelids.

Caine fell to his knees, blood pooling around him.

And in the next moment, tendrils of colored magic curled into the room— sinister undulations of copper, gold, and blue. And following the magic, two humans, their eyes black, hair writhing around their heads like snakes. Eye sockets empty as voids.

Rosalind's parents.

Pain coiled around Rosalind's heart. When she opened her eyes, Caine was sitting next to her on the bed, staring down at his hands.

Raw pain ravaged his features, an expression she'd never seen on him before—one he'd kept well-hidden. "So now you understand. I lost my mind, and the beast in me came out. I'm the sort of demon who murders his own kin."

Rosalind touched his arm. "No, you're not. You've always looked out for them. You didn't kill Stolas. Richard did. Your second soul. I saw it happen."

"Do you really think it's so easy for me to absolve myself? I was born from a monster, the incubus Abrax. Even Nyxobas hates his own son. The beast lies dormant in me." His eyes flashed with fierceness. "You must have seen it when I fight. I *like* killing."

Rosalind tightened her fingers on his arm. "You're thinking about it all wrong. You're not a killer. You're a warrior."

His gaze slid to her. "It's just a different name."

"It's a different concept. You fight for a cause, for loyalty to your home. And you're not like your father. You don't think Malphas is a monster, do you? He has the same father you do."

"But not the same mother. I watched my mother kill a man, using the same iron hairpin I used. And after she finished, I watched her hang at Tyburn. A common whore and a murderess." His silver gaze met hers, beautiful and brutal. "So if there is good in me, where would it come from?"

A pang of grief tightened her chest, as she thought of the little boy standing in a hostile London crowd, crying for his mother as the hangman killed her. He would have been all alone in the world.

She leaned in to him. "I told you. Being born from *good stock* is an archaic concept. Forget about it." She stroked the stark tattoo on his forearm. "You tattooed her hairpin on your arm. And you kept her hairpin with you all those years. You loved her."

He lowered his gaze, and she could see the ghost of his dark wings behind him. "I did."

In that moment, he reminded her of Azazeyl, her broken angel, and she could almost feel his dizzying fall, the wind rushing over his skin. The blind terror.

"So she wasn't a monster," she said. "She loved you. She loved Stolas, I'm sure. Anyone can snap if they're being abused. I can't imagine it was an easy life being a London prostitute in the 1500s. Right? Maybe she needed to fight back. Is this really why you think Malphas is better than you?"

His silver eyes met hers, and she was struck again by the agony there, and that no one else ever saw this side of Caine—not even Malphas. How long had he kept his armor up?

He looked at his hands again, as if searching for traces of blood. "Malphas had to free me from Lilitu Square. Your parents found Stolas's body. They found me covered in his blood. They thought their experiment had failed. A demon like me couldn't hold two souls, my blood was too polluted, poisoned by Nyxobas. They turned me in, had me dragged to the town square, where they nailed me to a cross. I didn't object. I was supposed to die there, but Malphas saved me anyway. He was only five."

"Richard took over your body. I saw his pain, through Cleo's eyes, when she was executed. I saw his rage. And that's what filled your mind when the second soul took over. When I first took off the ring, Cleo completely dominated me. She didn't kill anyone else, but she wanted to kill me for being a Hunter. She made me feel like I was on fire. Remember? I was completely out of control."

"I remember."

"Our second souls have had their revenge. They took out their rage on a Hunter and a shadow demon. The closest beings to the people who betrayed them." He wasn't meeting her gaze, and she wanted him to look at her again. "What happened after they killed your mother in London?" she asked. "You had no mother and father. How old were you?"

"Seven. Stolas was three."

"And how did a three-year-old survive with no parents?"

"I looked after him," he said softly. "I did whatever I needed to."

"Caine, you looked after him because you loved him. You

protected him in Maremount when the queen enslaved you. Your love for your brothers was strong enough that it could be used to control you." *Love is a liability,* he'd once said to her. "You were their protector. Richard killed Stolas. Not you."

His gaze drank her in. "You don't believe we're doomed to pay for the sins of our fathers."

"If we are, then I'm fucked. You can't really believe that I'm like my parents, can you? That I'd nail people to walls, and use children as bait?" Her fingers were digging into his arm now. "You can't possibly fucking believe that about me."

He studied her closely, looking strangely lost. "When I first met you I was sure you were like them. You've slowly been changing my mind. I had to wonder, when you came back for me in Maremount, when I was nailed to the stake. You came back to save me, and you didn't need to."

"That's because we're not destined to become our parents. That's a fiction. You write your own story, Caine."

He wrapped his hand around hers, looking at her as if he were drowning in his own history, as if her touch was his lifeline.

She leaned in, kissing him on the mouth. "I have to go, Caine."

His hand slid down to her waist. "Why?"

"I need to finish creating the army we're going to use to slaughter the Brotherhood. Are you still worried about me turning into my parents if I use too much of Azazeyl's power?"

"No. You're nothing like your parents. I know that. I just didn't want to lose you to the hell in your own mind. You already have two souls. The voices of seven gods are a lot to contend with on top of that. But perhaps if anyone is strong enough, it's you. Go. I'll meet you in your room when you've finished."

CHAPTER 25

After the third day of transforming vampires, Rosalind strode back to her room, her silky white gown gliding against her thighs. She and Erish had finished transforming each vampire into a new species. And for three days, she'd felt Azazeyl's tormented fall to earth, each time her own soul splintering just a little bit more. An emptiness nagged her chest.

Despite the unease in her mind, the longer she used Azazeyl's magic, the more powerful she felt. Now, a preternatural surety filled her limbs. The moment she looked at another creature, she knew exactly what she'd need to do to kill them.

This time, when she went into battle against the Hunters, she'd destroy them with Azazeyl's power blazing through her bones.

When she opened the door to her room, she found Caine, sitting on her bed, eyes downcast—her fallen angel. Through the windows, the breeze played with candle flames, and shadows danced over the stones.

Caine looked up at her, his gaze uncharacteristically unguarded. Just now, it struck her that the vision he'd shown her had given her the key to his mortality. He'd showed her the spell, the one that turned

946

angels into dying bodies. Now, she knew exactly how to kill him, even if she wanted nothing more than to protect him.

She glanced at herself in the reflection, relieved to see her eyes had returned to their normal brown hue, and that her hair was no longer snaking around her head.

"What's the news from your spies?" she asked.

"The news is that tomorrow is our day to attack. We sent out a small troop of hellhounds and valkyrie to Hadley in Western Massachusetts. They've been wreaking havoc, terrifying the humans. So the Hunters have sent half their human army in to control the demonic outburst. My spies tell me that right now, the emperor's palace is as vulnerable as it ever gets."

"Tomorrow." Apprehension prickled over her skin. She crossed to him, standing so close she could feel the heat from his body. Slowly, she ran her fingertips over his heart, feeling his powerful pulse. "Does anyone else know how to kill you?"

"Malphas, of course. Bileth does, I'm sure." A breeze filtered in from the window, toying with his hair. "He has been an immortal for far longer than I have."

"I'm going to kill him."

Caine quirked a smile. "Will you be my savior?"

"If I need to."

His expression darkened. "Maybe you should stay in Lilinor tomorrow."

"You've got to be kidding me. Why?"

"You're the primary target of both Bileth and Drew. As soon as we get to Cambridge, they'll be coming for you. You're our most powerful weapon, and Drew's intended bride. He has powers like yours, but he's been using them longer. He's stronger than you. It's too much of a risk, and I don't want to let him capture you again. I should have never let you go the first time."

Rosalind shook her head. "No way. Drew and Bileth will be trying to kill you too. And anyway, didn't you just say half the Hunters were gone? This is our chance."

"*Half* the Hunters, yes. But not the demons. My spies have told me what awaits us tomorrow: an army of phantom edimmu who can inhabit bodies, and feast on souls. There are the pazuzu: the demons of famine, and storm demons who haven't flown the skies in millennia. Gruesome hounds. They've created armies like the world has never known."

Rosalind sucked in a deep breath. "So, our chances aren't good. But I'm not letting you go without me. We're going to fight them together."

A desolate look crossed his eyes. "I don't want anything to happen to you. I can't risk losing you."

Rosalind wrapped her arms around his neck. "Then if we have to die, we'll die together. I'm not letting you go without me."

He pressed his forehead to hers. "Rosalind."

He ran his hand down her silk gown, and she stood on her tiptoes to press her mouth against his. As soon as his lips touched hers, heat ignited her body. Her pulse raced, breath shallowing.

Caine grabbed her silk dress and pulled up the hem of her gown. "You're wearing too many clothes," he whispered. As he exposed her skin to the cool night air, goosebumps rose over her skin.

Rosalind's heart pounded hard. She slipped her hands under his shirt, her fingers brushing against his perfect abs, and she pulled his shirt off. Her gaze slowly roamed over the dark, brutal tattoos covering his muscled body.

Slowly, she slid her arms around his neck, letting her silky bra graze against his bare skin. He leaned down, kissing her, his tongue brushing against hers, sending fire through her veins. He cupped his hands under her thighs and, in one fluid movement, lifted her as she wrapped her legs around his waist.

Gripping her tight, he carried her to the wall, pressing her back to the stone. The cold wall chilled her back, while every brush of his fingers singed her with heat. His eyes blazed with starry light, and he unhooked her bra, pulling it off. The feel of the cool air over her bare breasts sent a thrill through her.

Lightly, teasingly, he began brushing kisses over her neck, his tongue gently flicking against her skin. She arched into him, thrusting her fingers into his hair. Slowly, his lips moved lower, his warm mouth covering her breasts in kisses. Gently, he grazed a hint of teeth over her skin, and she groaned slightly, grinding her hips into him, throwing back her head.

Rosalind's world narrowed to the thrill of his mouth on her skin. Right now, nothing else existed apart from Caine and the heat roaring through her body, the rest of the world forgotten.

Caine pulled away from her breasts, and raked his gaze over her bare skin, his expression purely carnal. "In the future, I want you permanently naked in my room."

"You too." She unwrapped her legs from him, and slid down his body. Hungrily, she grabbed for his belt, unbuckling it, then pulled off his pants.

Caine moved in closer, one hand on her naked waist, the other pressed against the wall, boxing her in. Gently, he trailed his hand up and down her waist, tracing the curve of her hipbone, lazily stroking just above her silky panties, making her back arch. She slipped her arms around his neck, trying to pull him in closer, but he held back. He wanted to draw this out. He leaned in again, kissing her, his tongue flicking against hers.

He moved lower, trailing kisses down her neck again, his breath hot on her skin.

"I want to hear you say you love me," he said, his fingers teasing the hollow of her hips.

"I love you. But I also want you, and you're moving too slowly."

He gripped her hips tighter and brushed kisses down her breasts, her abdomen, and at every brush of his lips, a hot thrill blazed through her core.

He moved onto his knees, fingers teasing the rim of her panties. Gods, she needed him now. He hooked an arm under her leg, lifting it, his mouth moving up the inside of her thigh. She threaded her fingers through his hair, desperate for more of him. She could see herself in the mirror, chest flushed, her breaths deep. Caine brushed his fingertips between her legs, and she groaned as he slowly teased her. Waves of pleasure washed through her.

"Caine," she breathed. She wanted him *now*. She pulled her leg out of his grip, then thrust her fingers into her panties, pulling them all the way down to her ankles. When she rose again, Caine's eyes were slowly taking in every inch of her bare skin, moving over her bare breasts, her stomach, between her legs, his breath hot on her skin.

Caine's measured restraint seemed to slip, and his fingers tightened on her hips, no longer gentle. Shadows darkened his eyes, and his silver aura viciously cut the air around him. He rose, staring into her eyes.

Rosalind reached for him, pulling off his underwear. "I need you."

Caine reached down, grabbing her thighs, and she hooked her legs around him, her back against the wall. She was moaning his name as he thrust into her, and her fingers raked viciously down his back. Neither of them was being gentle now, driven by pure hunger and need. She moved in rhythm with him, kissing him until pleasure claimed her mind. And with that moment of release, her fractured soul began to heal just a little.

Rosalind woke in Caine's arms, reveling in the feel of his smooth, bare skin against hers. She didn't want to leave this bed. She wanted to stay in here, exploring his perfect body for the next week.

Sadly, it wasn't going to happen. The longer they waited to attack the Brotherhood, the greater the chance they'd lose the upper hand.

Moonlight streamed into the bedroom, and she glanced at the clock—four a.m. Her body tensed. *Nearly time.*

In just a half hour, they were going to gather in the Gelal Fields. Together with Malphas and Caine, Rosalind would create a portal large enough for the entire army of Lilinor to plunge through.

The Brotherhood would never see them coming.

Reluctantly, she pulled herself from Caine's embrace, sniffing the air, her mouth watering at the smell of bacon and coffee wafting into the room. She rose from her bed and pulled on a bathrobe. Then she crossed to the door and pulled it open to find a tray of food on the floor.

Good. She and Caine would need to fill their bellies for what lay ahead today. As she carried the tray back to the table, Caine sat up, his body suddenly alert. He didn't really seem to have a waking-up period —just deep sleep or total alertness, like he was ready to kill.

He glanced at the clock. "Almost time." He rose from the bed.

Rosalind let her eyes roam over his naked body. "If we win this battle, will your former vampires be able to restrain themselves from rampaging through the city and slaughtering everyone in their paths?"

"I'll give them strict instructions not to rape and pillage the city of Cambridge." He sat in a chair across from her, pulling the dome off the tray.

"Tell me the plan again," she said. They'd been over this already with Ambrose, Malphas, and Aurora, but she needed to hear the details again.

He poured himself a cup of coffee. "The plan is that we divide the army into cohorts to maximize their offense capability. Aurora and the valkyrie can attack from above and fight the pazuzu and edimmu demons. The hellhounds will be on the front lines, to ignite the Hunters and demons with hellfire. Winged cohorts can also attack the land-bound demons from above."

"Becca will enjoy that," she said. "Anything else?"

"I'll hold the shadow demons back. Some of the keres, and the oneiroi, so we can draw the Brotherhood's forces into a trap and surround them."

Rosalind heaved a sigh of relief. "Good. So Tammi will be out of the main action."

"Some of the keres will be in a flying cohort, Tammi among them. The other shadow demons will need to use their powers of stealth. They can move through the shadows the easiest, can go unnoticed. When we've lured Drew's forces into that courtyard, the shadow demons will flank them. They'll surround them and cut them down from the outside in."

Rosalind's stomach was already clenching with dread, and she couldn't quite imagine Tammi swinging her sword in the middle of a melee. "Okay. While that's going on, I've got to break off from them and hunt for Drew."

Caine poured her a cup of coffee, shaking his head. "You can't go in there alone."

She took a sip of the strong brew. "You and Malphas will need to stay with the rest of the army. It's not like we have a ton of demigods on our side, and the soldiers will need your leadership. You're their general. Besides, I can handle Drew on my own."

"He's been using these powers longer than you have."

"True. But he's insane."

"I suppose you have a slight advantage in that regard." He frowned at her. "If you need me, call to me."

"And what if I'm nowhere near you?"

"Remember when you borrowed my magic?" he said. "I felt it. I knew you needed it. Use my magic again, and I'll come find you."

She crossed her legs. "And what if you need me?"

"I'll do the same. I'll ask to borrow from your power. We're linked, you and I." A smile ghosted across his lips. "I quite like the idea of having Azazeyl's power at my fingertips."

She knew she should eat, but with her nerves buzzing, she didn't have much of an appetite. In fact, she kind of felt like she wanted to throw up. Regardless, she bit into the crisp bacon. "Anything else I need to know?"

"Kill anyone you meet, as long as they're not on our side."

"Okay. Good strategy. Sophisticated."

Her body buzzed with nervous energy, and after a few bites of bacon, she rose, unable to wait any longer. She crossed to the wardrobe and pulled on her best fighting clothes—steel-reinforced leather pants and corset, her weapons belt, and a crap-load of blades.

She'd mostly be using her magic, but it never hurt to load up with weapons.

As she dressed, Caine pulled on his own clothes, though he didn't bother with reinforced leather or any sort of armor. She supposed that when you've spent five centuries as an immortal, it was hard to feel vulnerable.

Nervousness tightened her stomach as they walked through the shadow corridor, the general and the assassin.

* * *

Rosalind and Caine stood on the shores of the Astarte Sea, listening to the waves break and crash over the rocks. Already, the army of demons had begun to gather, their silver armor and weapons gleaming in the moonlight.

Caine had organized them into cohorts, roughly sorted by demon-types. The shadow demons, the hellhounds, the fae, the creatures who could fly. Tammi stood in the middle of the shadow demon cohort, her pale hair draped over her armor. Ready for battle, her silver wings were on display behind her shoulder blades. Rosalind sucked in a breath. She'd never seen Tammi's wings before, but like Caine, they emerged when she was ready to fight.

At the front of each cohort, soldiers carried enormous shields. Ambrose stood on the other side of Caine, facing his army, resplendent in his silver armor. As an incubus, his skin no longer had that unearthly pale hue, now a little more golden, nearly matching his hair. Charcoal-gray wings arched majestically behind his back.

Rosalind had her own weapons—a sword, some daggers. But most importantly, she was bringing with her the iron nail that she planned to ram into Drew's heart, right after she stole his immortality from him. She stroked her fingertips over the long nail in her pocket, trying not to think of what would happen if she failed today, but the fears invaded her mind anyway. If Drew and the Brotherhood were ready for this attack, Rosalind would end up imprisoned again.

This time, she was certain she wouldn't break free. Drew would find a way to use her for breeding, then he'd cut off her head, burn her body. Make sure she couldn't rise from the ground.

Caine and Malphas would be slowly tortured for the rest of their long lives—just like the Throcknell family had once wanted. Lilinor would be destroyed. That little boy, Owen, and all the prisoners she'd freed would probably die. Total destruction of the city, of the civilization here. Dread tightened its grip on her heart. They couldn't lose today.

Despite her fears, Rosalind felt a strange thrill as she stared out over the cohorts, the soldiers all looking at Caine and Ambrose. Her heart thundered like a war drum.

Among the valkyrie, a clean, gray aura whirled from Aurora's body—the magic of the storm gods. And embedded within the shadow demons, Tammi wore chainmail, and gripped a spear.

On the shore of the Astarte, silence reigned, and tension thickened the air. A marine wind rushed off the waves, raising goosebumps on her skin. Soon enough, Rosalind would warm the skies.

As the last of the demons took their positions in the cohorts, Rosalind stared at the magic wafting off them, the stunning tendrils of gleaming gold, silver, bronze, grey and black—and blue, too. The color of her sister's magic. Their auras pulsed over her skin, smooth and briny, clean mountain winds, icy electricity. Azazeyl's magic coiled together under the night sky. Here, it almost seemed as if the seven gods were reuniting once more.

She glanced at Ambrose, waiting for his command. He gripped a battle-ax, and his eyes shone with the same stunning, starlit color of Caine's gaze. His knuckles went white as he gripped his axe. "I have missed the thrill of battle." For just a moment, apprehension flickered across his beautiful features, but then he tightened his jaw. "Raise the sun. I want to feel it on my face again."

Rosalind glanced back at the glistening ocean, the waves undulating under the night sky.

Caine leaned in, his breath warming the side of her face. "Dazzle them."

She turned, walking to the ocean's edge, her toes dipping into the frothy spume. Dagon lurked in these waters, but the god of the depths no longer scared her. He lived within her now, with the other gods, all vying for wholeness.

She closed her eyes, envisioning Emerazel, the goddess of fire. Heat ignited, erupting through her veins, until her body burned like the fires of Etna.

She opened her eyes again, her breath catching at the sight of the sky. Crimson sun rays bled into the sky, and behind her, her soldiers gasped, a few shrieking. A crown of deep honey light rose above the waves, gilding the Astarte Sea.

The army of the Night God stood beneath a sky of hot amber and pumpkin, streaked with buttery light. The sun warmed Rosalind's body, and she turned back to the soldiers. Some squinted into the sunlight, while others gaped at their hands, marveling at the sunlight on their skin.

Rosalind glanced at Aurora, resplendent, a golden goddess in her armor. The sunlight washed over the banners of Nyxobas, the midnight cloth flecked with silver stars and crescent moons.

This might be a motley crew of demons standing in the morning sun, but they were still loyal to the god of night.

An eerie silence had fallen over the crowd, and Rosalind glanced at Tammi, who stood rigid, a proper soldier. In the wind, her silver hair whipped over her face. And at the front of the shadow demons' cohort stood Malphas, the sunlight gleaming off his silver armor, and he waited for her to speak.

Ambrose's gaze slid to Caine. "General. Your speech."

Caine climbed a jagged rock, surveying the army. "The Brotherhood will have everyone believe that humans must fear the world of magic. They teach that we're all monsters who should be burned, that the safety of the human species relies on our destruction."

Caine held out his hand to Rosalind, beckoning her onto the rock. "Perhaps you'd like to explain."

As she climbed the rock, the waves crashed against the shore, spraying her with spume. "Your general is right. The Brotherhood is very convincing. I believed them once, though now I no longer fear you at all. I've learned to live among you, even love some of you." She glanced at Caine, heat blooming in her chest. "Now, I put my faith in you, the demons—the abominations, like me. I want to live among you all, and some day die among you all. It's my sincerest hope that that day is a long way off." Tears stung her eyes, and she nodded at Caine again.

He turned back to the legion, and his voice boomed as he spoke.

"This is our home. And anyone who dares to invade it should fear us —not because we are monsters. But because we want what anyone wants—to keep our home safe." This time, his gaze slid to Rosalind. "To protect those we love." He raised his hands to the sky, and the sun rays ignited him from behind. He looked to her like he'd fallen straight from the heavens. "Let the tyrants fear, not us. It's their cruelty that is monstrous, not us. When the tyrants of the Brotherhood threaten us, we will defend our home. And it begins today, in the light of day."

The crowd roared, raising their weapons. And over their shouts, Rosalind yelled, "We could not have hoped for a more worthy general than Caine, or a more worthy king than Ambrose. I am proud to fight by their side, and by yours. And before the sun sets again today over Cambridge, we will defeat the enemies of Lilinor. We will defeat the enemies of those we love."

From the shores of the Astarte Sea, the ground rumbled with the roars of the demons, the sound sliding through Rosalind's bones with a dark shiver of pleasure.

Caine descended from the rock. "It's time to make a portal."

Rosalind followed him, crossing over the jagged rocks to the ocean's edge, until the water soaked her toes. Seawater misted the air, and Malphas joined them at the ocean's edge. When they'd all lined up together, shoulders nearly touching, Rosalind summoned her shadow magic.

A hollow opened in Rosalind's chest, and from it, silver magic spiraled into the ocean, a vortex of starlight that churned over the sea's gleaming surface, spreading over the undulating water. The portal had been opened.

Caine turned back to the legion, lifting his sword until it sparked in the light. He shouted an order in Angelic, and the ground rumbled as the legion moved.

Flanked by Caine and Malphas, Rosalind walked into the breaking waves, the water chilling her skin.

When she'd plunged in up to her knees, she turned to Malphas.

"Do you remember what you told me when you were training me to use Dagon's power?"

"We're walking into the place where life began."

"And so our new life begins."

CHAPTER 27

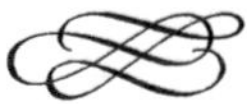

osalind crawled from the Charles River, her clothing drenched, clinging to her skin. As river water sloshed over the grass, Rosalind crossed onto the path, surveying the city.

From here, she could see the city's landscape had changed drastically, the squat brick buildings of Harvard's campus replaced with towering white marble, blinding in the rising sun. And behind her, the rest of Lilinor's army began crawling onto the river's bank, coughing and spluttering, some of them hurling up river water.

Rosalind stepped onto Memorial Drive. At five a.m., there were no cars on the road, but they'd be arriving soon enough. She needed to clear a pathway for the army. Behind her, Caine was shouting orders, organizing the legion into the proper cohorts again, hellhounds at the front.

Rosalind held out her hands to either side. She let Druloch's magic spiral through her body, calling to the sycamore trees, her aura becoming one with the bark, the roots. As the vernal magic whirled from her body, she forced it around the rows of sycamores. With a flick of her wrists, she tugged at the boughs, until they groaned and lengthened, slammed against the pavement, snaking over the road. She'd formed blockades on either side of a quarter-mile path.

That should stop the cars for a while.

Behind her, the soldiers had formed orderly lines, and from the front, the hellhounds sparked with golden fire.

Caine shouted an order, and the legion began marching from the river, bodies dripping with water. She moved ahead to make room, then fell in line with Caine and Ambrose in the vanguard. As they marched down JFK street, she blended into the frontline of hellhounds.

On either side of the road, classical buildings loomed, marked with chalices of Blodrial. The city of Cambridge slept, and no one had sounded an alarm yet.

She pulled a sword from her scabbard, glancing at Caine. He lifted his sword, then shouted an Angelic word—the word for *Charge.* Around her, the hellhounds began running.

Gripping the hilt, she broke into a run. The soldiers' footfalls pounded the pavement, and they thundered through the narrow streets of Cambridge, heading for the heart of the Brotherhood.

As they ran, an alarm began tolling over the city, and screams began piercing the air. By the time the Brotherhood's towering marble gates came into view a quarter mile down the road, the sky was darkening with a cloud of swarming locusts. At the sight of them, a chill rippled over Rosalind's skin.

"The pazuzu," said Caine. "Demons of famine."

As the demon legion stormed toward the Brotherhood's gates, the locusts swarmed overhead, whirling in wild eddies. Caine's entire body was rigid with tension as he waited for the right moment to strike. His black, feathered wings appeared behind his back, and his eyes darkened with shadows. Long, black talons grew from his fingertips, a growl rising from his throat.

Caine's voice boomed, rumbling through Rosalind's bones, as he shouted for the winged cohorts to take to the skies. His black wings beat the air, and he lifted into the skies at the front of the attack.

Rosalind summoned her storm magic, and it surged through her body. Within moments, she lifted into the air after Caine, the wind rushing over her skin. Blazing with the power of the storm god, she felt the phantom wings spread from her back, and she gripped her sword. And all around them, the cohorts of valkyrie and keres swarmed the air, heading for the locusts, who were weaponless. But Caine had already told her what terrors awaited them with the pazuzu...

As Lilinor's army surged closer, a hundred feet in the air, the locusts shifted into larger, winged demons, with leonine faces and fingertips ending in large talons. Ribs protruded from their emaciated chests, and they glowed with a sickly, gray light. At the front of the legion of demons, one of them wore a thorny, copper crown. The pazuzu king.

Blazing with pale auras, the valkyrie and keres raced toward them, wind whipping at them.

The pazuzu king's eyes landed on her, and her stomach clenched.

The two forces met in the skies, and Rosalind swung her sword into a locust's neck, slicing off its head. Dark blood arced through the sky, staining her clothes. Around her, the pazuzu tore into Lilinor's army with their talons.

Electrified by the ancient power of storms, Rosalind's sword found its mark in one locust after another, slicing through limbs, hacking off heads. And yet the locusts kept swarming, heading for the land-bound soldiers below.

Rosalind glanced down at the army of Lilinor. Horror bloomed in her chest. She rushed through the air, darting and weaving to avoid the locusts while she took in the scene. There, on the streets of Cambridge, the locusts who descended seemed to be sucking the life out of Lilinor's army. With each stroke of their long talons, the Lilinor demons seemed to wither before her eyes, their muscles shriveling, bones jutting from stretched skin. And all around her, keres and valkyrie were raining from the sky, bodies drained. Embedded within the hellhounds, at the front of the battle lines—Ambrose was hacking into the locusts.

Caine shouted an order for the winged cohorts to retreat to the rearguard, to the back of Lilinor's legion. The hellhounds were going to fight the locusts with fire now, and their own troops needed to clear the way. Good thing Rosalind couldn't burn.

Rosalind and the rest of the flying cohort swooped lower. As she neared the vanguard, a locust slammed into Rosalind, knocking her to the ground. She crashed into the road, her sword clanging against the pavement.

Above, the unending swarm of locust-demons darkened the sky, writhing and pulsing like a living thing. These things would destroy the entire legion if they didn't burn them fast, but Caine would wait until the flying cohort had fully retreated to the rearguard. Otherwise, they'd be igniting their own soldiers.

As she reached for her sword, another pazuzu slammed into her, teeth bared, knocking her to the ground. Her head slammed against the pavement, the wind rushing from her lungs. She blinked, trying to clear her vision, and grasped for her sword. The locust bent over her, his body blazing with sickly gray light, the color of a corpse's skin. Grinning, he reached for her with a long, black talon.

No! She gripped the hilt of her iron sword and swung for the demon, cutting into his side. He threw back his head and shrieked, the sound agonizing and otherworldly.

The pazuzu fell to the ground, but already chaos reigned around her. She gaped at the tormented faces of Lilinor's legion. Those who'd been touched by the locust demons seemed to be withering away—just as Caine had said they would. Some gnawed frantically at patches of grass, trying to fill their stomachs, their cheeks smeared with green. Others, ravenous, pounced on each other, tearing into flesh. She glanced at Caine, who hovered above the fray, cutting into the locusts as they approached, but they were getting dangerously close, even to him.

Rosalind rose to her feet and heard a screech behind her; she turned, slicing her sword through a locust's throat. Dark ichor oozed from its neck.

As another locust swooped down, Rosalind drove her sword up, stabbing it through the gut. The creature fell to the ground with a thud, and Rosalind pulled her sword from it. Dark blood stained her blade.

"Rosalind!" Malphas shouted.

She whirled to find a locust's talon just inches from her body. But before she could even strike the creature, Malphas's sword pierced him from behind, protruding from the creature's chest. The locust fell to the ground, and Malphas nodded at her before returning to the fray.

"Get to the vanguard, Malphas!" She shouted. "We'll be lighting up the air with fire any minute now!"

She glanced at the sky, and her pulse raced at the sight of the creatures dropping to earth, bodies glowing with that sickly gray light, the color of a corpse. There were just so many of them...

"Caine!" Rosalind shouted, her sword slamming into a locust demon. "Get to the back!"

A shadow darkened overhead as Caine lifted into the air. His command boomed across the city, so loud it seemed to ring in her skull, to come from her own mind. He was giving the order for the hellhounds to unleash their fire.

All around her, fire blazed, hot as the infernos. A fireball rose into the air, igniting the pazuzu.

Just as she was summoning her own hellfire, a bony hand gripped her arm, and her stomach dropped. She turned to find—not a locust—but one from her own army. A ravening hellhound who'd been touched by one of the locusts, her face gaunt, eyes hollow.

The hellhound opened her mouth wide, revealing a sharp set of teeth. "So hungry..." In the next moment, she was leaping on Rosalind, teeth in her neck.

Pain ripped through Rosalind's throat, but only for a second. Becca came up behind the emaciated hellhound, her body blazing with flames.

Becca pulled the creature off her, and in one fluid movement, snapped its neck. "She's not one of ours anymore."

Rosalind looked at the sky, where the locust bodies blazed like torches. Some of them were plummeting to the earth, bodies blazing.

Caine roared the command for fire again, and the angelic word rang deep in their skulls. The hellhounds unleashed another brutal blast of fire, aiming for the heavens. Fire blasted the skies, and shrieks rent the air. Some of the pazuzu began to retreat, flying away from the flames, ragged bodies blazing.

Caine's voice boomed in her mind, speaking in Angelic. *Fire and storms,* he commanded. This was his command to her alone—the one here who could withstand fire, and call the storms of Mishett-Ash.

She lifted into the air, ducking the plunging bodies of burning locusts. As she flew, she summoned the power of the storms, letting the gods' ancient power ignite her veins.

The gods' magic lifted her into the air, the wind whipping at her hair, and she cast a glance back at Caine. He was flying high above his army, sword drawn. His dark clothes glistening with ichor and blood, an angel of death. She nodded at him, and he flew lower over his army, sword ready for battle with the land-bound locusts.

Rosalind rose into the air. Rushing at the speed of a hurricane wind, she swooped beneath the locusts, her body charged with electricity, with fire.

Caine's Angelic command boomed in her mind, rumbling over the horizon. *Flames.*

Rosalind and the hellhounds below her unleashed a wild burst of flame, searing the air. Fire billowed all around her, igniting the skies.

Shrieking, the locusts retreated higher into the air, bodies flaming. As they crashed into each other, chaotic, panicked, the fires spread from one creature to another.

Again, from far below, Caine's voice rumbled through her mind. *Flames.*

Together with the hellhounds, Rosalind summoned hellfire. *I am the goddess of the volcanoes, of molten rage. I am the flames of Pompeii...*

Flames exploded from the hellhounds, from her body, curling high into the skies.

Storms, boomed Caine's voice.

Before all these flaming torches plummeted onto Lilinor's army, it was time to move them elsewhere. Ancient currents danced through her body. Lightning seared her veins, and hair rose on the back of her arms.

First, I bring the winds...

She closed her eyes as she flew, riding on the wind, becoming one with the storm. All around her the winds picked up speed, carrying her faster, harder. Her body was exhilarated.

Dark clouds moved in, roiling and churning, darkening the horizon.

She swooped higher between the flaming locusts, expertly avoiding their toxic talons. And as she flew through the air, she focused on building the storm, until it rattled the rooftops and windowpanes below her, and ripped off tree branches.

She was at one with the storm, and the storm with her.

Far below her, she caught a glimpse of Caine slicing off the head of a locust, his speed breathtaking in a blur of silver and black. *Winds,* his voice boomed.

In the driving gales, the locusts struggled to control their flight. Screeching, the burning creatures scrambled to stay on course, knocking into each other.

Hard gales whipped through the skies, slowly driving the creatures south in frantic whorls.

Flames, Caine commanded.

Another explosion of fire from below, but this time, Rosalind was working on the winds.

She swooped again, soaring beneath the locusts, and electricity charged her body.

Flying on phantom wings, she arched her neck, and slashed her wrists at the iron-gray storm clouds. A spear of lightning ignited the sky, striking a cluster of locusts. The creatures screeched, some falling to earth, smoke curling from their bodies.

Rosalind struck again, calling down twin shards of lightning from the heavens. Forked lightning touched down in the cloud of locusts, and the creatures writhed, smoke rising from their bodies. Frantically now, they were fleeing the storm and the flames. Rosalind soared below them, the storm's power thrumming through her veins, and she built the wind's power. One by one, burning, charred bodies plummeted to the earth, smashing cars, roofs.

She swooped back again, heading for Lilinor's army. As she flew she surveyed the damage below her. Among Lilinor's ranks, famished soldiers were gnawing the bark off trees, shoving dirt into their mouths, and worst of all, trying to eat through each other's flesh. Most of the locusts had been slaughtered, but too many of Lilinor's army had been transformed.

Rosalind scanned the crowd until her gaze landed on Caine, who was driving his sword through a locust's chest. She heaved a sigh of relief to find him unharmed.

She landed next to him, and his silver gaze met hers. "We need to heal them. All the soldiers touched by the pazuzu—we need to heal them with shadow magic." An emaciated ker stumbled forward, grasping for Caine, who slammed a hard punch into his face. The creature fell to the ground, unconscious.

"Malphas!" Caine's voice boomed, the command of a god.

Instantly, Malphas was at his brother's side, their bodies blazing with silvery magic, brilliant as the stars. Caine threw back his head, as if in a strange sort of ecstasy, and his stunning magic snaked from his body. Without realizing it, the ravening soldiers cleared space around the incubi, as if they instinctively knew they were in the presence of gods.

Rosalind's shadow magic built in her ribs, then curled into the air, mingling with Caine and Malphas's magic in perfect tendrils. Shadow magic caressed the sickened soldiers, gently coiling around their poisoned bodies. She could almost feel the pain ebbing from them, all that agony, evaporating into the darkened sky.

After a few minutes, she looked around again, catching her breath. They hadn't managed to save everyone. Some of Lilinor's soldiers had been too far gone, and they lay on the road, their mouths smeared with dirt and grass. Others had been eaten alive, and Rosalind's stomach turned at the sight of them. Blood stained the ground, and charred demon bodies smoked among the starved, the ravaged.

"Rosalind," said Caine.

She clenched her jaw, trying to tear her eyes away from the carnage.

"Rosalind!" he said, meeting her gaze. "The real battle hasn't begun yet. Stay with me."

CHAPTER 28

*E*mbedded in the vanguard, Rosalind marched for the Brotherhood's towering marble gates, the ones she'd stared at from the window of her decadent prison. Colored magic swirled around the wall, a relic of Drew's magic, and a few rays of sun pierced the clouds, glimmering off the magical wall.

When she'd been imprisoned, she'd spent so long trying to make sense of those gates, to imagine someone coming to rescue her over the wall. Under the ice floes of her mind, she'd pictured herself on the other side of them, or running freely through the long, narrow court-yard that spread out before the palace.

As she stood now, on the other side of the gates, her stomach clenched. If they failed here, it wouldn't be death for Rosalind—it would be much worse. The thought of Drew's hands on her made her sick.

Worse, it wasn't just she who had a lot to lose here. If they lost the battle, it could mean the end of the army of Lilinor. The Brother-hood's power would grow after a victory against the dark forces—the evil demons they needed to torture to death. *Don't you see, Americans? This is why we must torture and burn.*

Just like the old days they wanted to bring back.

Rosalind wasn't about to let any of that happen if she had any control over it.

As they marched closer to the wall, Caine's voice rang in her mind. *Flames.*

Rosalind—and the hellhounds—were going to blast through the walls with their fire power. To her right, Caine lifted his sword, shouting a command for the hellhound cohort to march forward, while the rest of the army would remain behind.

Rosalind and the hellhound vanguard marched up to the wall, halting when Caine shouted the order—about twenty feet from the marble wall. At this range, exploding marble would slam into them, but the hellhounds had shields, and with Borgerith's protection, Rosalind would emerge unscathed.

Summon the flames. Caine shouted the command in Angelic.

Rosalind lifted her hands to the heavens, thinking of her imprisonment in that tower room—of Drew's crazed eyes, Randolph's commands that she undress. She thought of her ex-boyfriend, Josiah, coercing her to torture Malphas. As rage and fury simmered, Rosalind thought of what she'd once been, and who she'd once served.

As these images blazed through her mind, Emerazel's fire surged, hot and wrathful. Combined with the power of the mountain goddess, her entire body hot and powerful as molten rock.

Fire! Caine commanded in Angelic, his voice rising in her skull.

With a snarl, Rosalind slashed her hands at the gates, and missiles of fire shot from her hands, slamming into the walls. A blast of fire burst around her, flames blazing from the entire line of hellhounds. On impact, the marble exploded in a hail of fire and white dust.

The explosions shook the earth, and the boom nearly deafened her. All down the marble wall, explosions erupted from the line of hellhounds, blasting the marble to pieces in a fiery storm. Hot blasts rushed over her skin, like solar winds.

When the explosion settled, Rosalind wiped the dust from her eyes, and brushed herself off. She gazed at the sky, where storm clouds still darkened the horizon, and she called to the clouds. The skies unleashed a torrent of rain, soaking her clothes.

The rain hammered against the explosion's flames. It dampened the fires over the rubble, and black smoke curled into the sky. She heard Caine boom a command to the shadow demons, ordering them to break off from the rest of the legion when they entered the courtyard. He barked another order, and the legion began marching. Caine and Ambrose remained further back, with the valkyrie and fae—the flammable land-bound fighters who formed the middle ranks.

The army pounded over the rubble, pouring into the Brotherhood's courtyard, an enclosed city of marble buildings. Silence enshrouded the city. Where was the Emperor's army, his demon courts?

Even as the storm clouds thinned, lightning cracked the dark sky, glinting off the white, columned buildings. They marched past a temple of Blodrial, its doors open, and Rosalind glanced inside to see an enormous font of the god's blood. Inside the temple, human bones lined the walls—or more likely, a mixture of human and demon remains, relics of the poor souls the Brotherhood had tortured to death. The sight chilled her to the core.

She tore her gaze away, marching on among the hellhound front lines. Caine's plan for what would happen next was brilliant, but it didn't stop the fear snaking up her spine. And none of them knew which of Drew's demon hordes would be coming for them next.

Marching on, her heart thundering to the beat of the heavy footfalls, she gripped her sword. Why hadn't Drew yet shown his face? They swarmed into the courtyard before the palace. A set of stairs led to an imposing building, with towering stone columns and long, narrow windows. On the top of the upper story, where Rosalind had been imprisoned, a statue of Blodrial dominated the roof. The marble god held out his wrists, which appeared to spurt real blood.

For just a moment, Rosalind felt a pang of sympathy for him, for his pain. She knew the agony of the gods when they'd splintered into seven, fractured souls that could never feel whole.

Blodrial, the god of repentance and guilt, believed he could reach the heavens through a complete denial of that original sin—the gift of magic to the human realm. If he expunged magic from the earth, he could feel complete again. And that was the gods' real hell—not the torment of being trapped in the blood of beasts, or hell fires, or the void, but the agony of incompleteness.

A chill rippled over Rosalind's body. Here, in the gleaming city of Blodrial, the air hung thick and still as a grave. And as she looked closer at the palace, she realized why. A thick shield of shimmering magic, in green, blue, copper, silver, and gold, shone over the white marble. Drew had protected the palace with his magic. No wonder he hadn't bothered to step outside to fight them with his magic. He felt perfectly safe in there.

Caine and Ambrose were marching behind the hellhounds—so they wouldn't get burned when Caine gave the order to release their flames.

She pushed her way through the ranks, her eyes on Caine's gleaming silver aura, curling from his body. She'd know it anywhere. When she shoved through the lines of hellhounds, Caine's darkened eyes landed on her. Apparently, his demonic form took over while in battle.

"Caine! Ambrose! Drew's got a shield up." She pointed at the writhing matrix of colored magic. Drew had been able to break down the shields they'd created. She just needed to figure out how he'd done it.

Caine's dark eyes were cold, otherworldly. "Do you know how to break through it?"

She shook her head. "I have no idea. But Drew did it to our shields, so there must be a way."

His brow furrowed, dirt smeared on his cheek. She lifted her hand to wipe the muddy smudge off his face before stopping herself.

A battle-hardened general wouldn't allow his lover to clean off his face before battle. As she looked up into his silvery eyes, she was struck by the sudden realization that she would give her life for him. Without thinking twice she would step in front of a sword to save him.

"I'm going to see if I can break through the shields."

Caine opened his mouth to speak, then closed it again. For once, she sensed some hesitation from him, as if he wanted to keep her close.

Ambrose's emerald eyes locked on her. "Go. Work on the shield."

Without waiting for a response from Caine, she pushed through the ranks of warriors again, heading for the palace. As she walked, she heard Caine shouting orders to the hellhounds, getting ready for the next demon onslaught.

Rosalind broke through the lines of warriors and crossed to the palace steps, glancing at the third story, where her room had been. Her stomach clenching, she climbed the steps, slowly moving closer to the undulating waves of magic. Tentatively, she reached out, touching the shield. The power of it sent shockwaves through her body, and nausea climbed up her throat. When she'd first met Drew, he'd had only a few tendrils of copper magic curling off his body. Practically an ordinary human. And now, he created like a god, with a power no human was meant to possess.

When she touched his magic, it felt toxic, as if it were poisoning her blood. She shuddered, trying to push the disgust to the back of her mind. If she could force herself to interact with the shield, to bond with it, she'd have the best chance of destroying it.

She touched it again, reeling at the shock of his magic slamming into her body. Dread and revulsion climbed up her throat, but she kept her hand on the shield. As she stood there, visions from his mind whirled in her skull.

She saw herself through his eyes, chained to the wall in his room. She felt his possessiveness of her, as if he were staring at his favorite doll. He ran his finger down her throat, then grabbed her breast, squeezing it. Rosalind fought the sickness clouding her mind, and the image swirled.

Drew strode onto one of the palace's balconies, where a roaring crowd greeted him.

When he looked down, Rosalind kneeled before him, gazing up at him with worshipful eyes.

She opened her eyes, tugging her hand away from the magic. She turned, retching.

After touching the shield, her body felt corrupted, sickened. She just barely managed to keep down the coffee she'd drank earlier. Rosalind wiped the back of her hand across her mouth, glancing back at the lines of soldiers.

The sun had brightened over the courtyard, and Rosalind squinted in the bright rays. Only moments ago, her storm had been dousing the entire city in torrents of rain. Now, the sun burned like a hot coal, sucking the moisture from the air.

As the sun burned hotter, Rosalind squinted into the sky. The weather was changing eerily fast, and if she looked close enough, she could see the shimmer of Drew's magic snaking through the sky. *Drew* was bringing out the sun, and it blazed hot off the soldiers' silver armor. What creatures required sunlight?

Before she could finish her thought, a stream of demons began pouring from the palace rooftop, a river of winged creatures swooping overhead, bodies the color of desert sand, their eyes a dull gray. The scent of death whispered through the air, and Rosalind's heart thrummed in her chest. *The edimmu.*

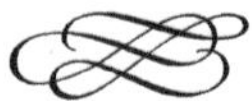

Caine shouted an order that boomed over the courtyard, and the hellhounds fanned out, allowing the middle ranks to shift through. From what Caine had told her, fire wouldn't hurt the edimmu. But beyond the traditional swords and axes, no one knew what killed the edimmu. Shuddering, she crossed the marble steps, clutching her sword. She only knew that the edimmu were capable of inhabiting other people's bodies.

Hell. She already had two souls. What was another?

Rosalind gripped her sword, staring at the vortex of demons above them. The sun seemed to blaze hotter, and her palms began to sweat on the hilt of her sword. Why would Drew need to raise the sun like this?

Her gaze sliced to the eerie horde darkening the skies, and her knees began to tremble with the familiar rush of battle fury. There were so many of them… Caine's spies had told him of the edimmu, but they had no idea how many of them Erish had made. And Erish had been unwilling to part with all her secrets lest she run out of bargaining chips.

She summoned the power of the valkyrie, hastening over the pavement to the rest of Lilinor's army. Caine and Ambrose stood at the front, swords drawn. Caine's dark wings spread out, and Ambrose's charcoal wings rose behind him. The two leaders took flight, and Caine boomed out an order that rang across the city, echoed in the soldiers' minds. *Winged cohorts, rise.*

Just as the edimmu began to dive for the earth, she took flight into the skies with the winged cohorts. In the blazing sun, a sense of surety surged through her limbs.

The edimmu shrieked as they dove, and the sound curdled Rosalind's stomach. As Lilinor's winged cohorts rose higher, the horde of edimmu plunged to the earth, mouths open to expose pointed teeth, naked bodies pale as sand. Their milky, white eyes were locked right on Lilinor's army.

Their shrieks rent the air, and Rosalind gripped her hilt hard, her palms sweating. As an edimmu swooped for her, Rosalind swung her sword, slicing through its neck. The creature's head tumbled to the ground. Instead of blood, a cloud of dust puffed into the air, its body crumbling, desiccated.

The edimmu were pouring into the legion, attacking without mercy.

In the air, the winged cohort's swords met the edimmu's dusty flesh, slicing through limbs and necks. But there were just so many of them, surging onward…

Aurora was at the front of the winged horde, carried on her gray valkyrie wings. Her sword flashed through the air as she swung, her skill breathtaking. Caine and Malphas fought side by side, their movements stunningly graceful in the air. Carried on gray wings, Ambrose's golden skin shone in the sunlight. While Caine and Malphas fought with grace, Ambrose was brutal, vicious. With each swing of his sword, he unleashed a chilling war cry. If it hadn't been for the endless sea of edimmu approaching, this would be an easy fight.

Rosalind's body surged with adrenaline, and she soared higher, hacking through another edimmu's neck. Battle rage spurred her on, and she moved like the wind, slicing through the enemy lines.

There, in the center of the aerial melee, Tammi was holding her own, her pale silver hair flying wildly in the wind. She sliced her sword through an edimmu's neck in one clean arc.

Then, an edimmu soared into Tammi's body from behind, disappearing within Tammi's flesh. Tammi's body went rigid. *Oh, hell no.*

Rosalind flew closer to her friend, fighting her way through the oncoming demons. High winds carried dust through the air as she hacked through their bodies, her body shaking with battle fury. Edimmu dust sprayed into her eyes, and tears streamed down her cheeks as she fought her way to Tammi. When she flew close to her friend, Tammi turned to her, and a tendril of fear coiled through Rosalind's chest. Tammi's jaw hung open at an odd angle, and her skin looked oddly dry. She curled her lip, snarling, her silver wings beating the air.

Gripping her sword, Rosalind scanned the winged cohort. Around her, soldiers of Lilinor were beginning to turn on each other, their skin suddenly dry and chalky. It had all happened faster than she'd expected. Time to retreat before the edimmu infected everyone. She'd just have to take Tammi with her until they could sort out this demonic possession situation...

As if reading her mind, Caine's voice echoed through the skies, reverberating in her skull. *Retreat.*

Just as Rosalind was grabbing for Tammi's arm, she felt something slam into her from behind and seep into her body. A hot, dry power crawled around the inside of her body, claiming territory in her ribs, her skull, desiccating her gut.

Desert winds seemed to race through her mind, whispering of death, of ancient ruins half buried in desert sands. *Death.* She needed to kill, needed to dominate and claim her territory for the gods of wind and fire. Ancient enemies of the darkness. Fury rippled through her body, hot as the desert sun.

Hot winds rushed around her skull. *Slaughter the sons of Nyxobas.* Next to her, the demigods were the most powerful creatures here. Rosalind turned, searching for the incubus. She recognized him by the beautiful silver blazing from his body, curling into the air like smoke.

And she knew how to kill him, now. She knew the Angelic words that would make him mortal. For a mortal man, just one cut of the sword...

Her chest clenched. Something was wrong. Her mind felt dry as bone.

In the skies, as Caine led the retreat, a crowd of edimmu surrounded him. His magic burst from his body, trying to fend them off, but they kept coming for him, until one of them leapt into his body from the back. His arms shot out to the sides, back arching as if he were in pain. His sword glinted in the sun as it tumbled to the ground. *Defenseless. Now is the time to attack.*

She flew closer to him, the wind whipping at her hair. As she approached, sword in hand, he turned to look at her, a dark smile on his lips, black wings beating the air.

Slaughter the sons of Nyxobas. Darkness is the enemy.

Caine soared closer, racing for her in a blur of silver. Their bodies met in the air, slamming against each other. Before she could attack, he was at her throat, hand tightening around her neck. She unleashed a burst of electricity from her body, knocking Caine away. Dark smoke coiled around his perfect body like a caress.

He curled his lip in a snarl, circling her. "Rosalind."

When she'd first met him, she'd been completely defenseless against him. Not anymore.

But why did her mind feel so dry, as if all the life had been sucked from it? Her mouth was like sawdust, and a strange torment ripped her mind apart, the agony of a fractured soul.

It didn't matter. What mattered was that she knew how to take Caine's immortality from him, and she needed to slaughter him, to rid the world of his darkness. *All will be arid sands and light...* She lifted her fingers, launching into the spell. Caine's eyes, black as the void, opened wide as he recognized the words. *Slaughter the sons of Nyxobas. Darkness is the enemy.*

Dread curled around her, and a hollow bloomed in her chest as she chanted the spell that would kill him.

Something isn't right.

Druloch's magic craved life, water, and fresh soil. Cleo's presence coiled around her ribs like thirsty vines, unfurling from her body, green and calming. Slowly, her second soul bloomed—seeking life, seeking water. Slowly Cleo forced the edimmu from Rosalind's body, and she gasped with relief, her thoughts clearing once more. Had she nearly been about to kill Caine? The horror of it ripped her mind apart. Caine—her blackthorn. Her love.

Still, he stared at her with a chilling rage, his fists clenching. His black wings slowly beat the air, and around them the winged cohort turned on each other, minds claimed by desert winds.

As Caine stared at her, his silvery aura sliced through the air, sharp as thorns.

First, Rosalind had to find a way to get Lilinor's general back. If she took her eyes off Caine for even a moment, he'd attack. Then, she'd work on the edimmu.

Slowly, talons appeared from his fingertips, and Rosalind's stomach dropped as she watched him shed his humanity. He wanted to rip her to pieces.

At any moment, if she made a wrong move, he'd be thrusting a powerful hand into her chest to rip her heart out.

"Caine." She held out her hand to him, beckoning him closer. An invitation, not a threat.

Light flickered in his dark eyes, but he let out a low growl, glaring at her like a wild animal about to attack.

Slowly, gently, she reached for him, touching his arm just above where the hairpin tattoo marked his skin. The soft contact seemed to confuse him, and she moved in closer—close enough that she could feel the heat from his body.

She reached up, stroking the sides of his face. She tilted his head down to look at her, her body brushing against his. She stared into those fathomless, black eyes, searching for his second soul.

"Richard. I need your second soul to help. Get the edimmu out of Caine's body. Cleo and I need your help."

Caine snarled, gripping her hard by the waist, his fingers digging into her flesh.

She brushed her thumb over his cheek. "Caine," she whispered. "Richard. Anyone."

He grimaced, but in the next moment exhaled with relief, his fingers finding their way to her waist. For just a moment, he bowed his head.

Then, without opening his mouth, his command boomed through his army, *Retreat.*

Rosalind glanced at the skies—some of the winged cohort were obeying the command, but too many had already been claimed by the edimmu. Drew had perfected the art of using an army against itself. Rosalind's heart leapt into her throat. In the dry, blazing sun, she searched for her friends—Aurora, Ambrose, and Malphas remained unscathed, leading the retreat. But Tammi still zigzagged wildly through the skies, her body dry as sand, eyes wild.

As the others obeyed Caine's command, flying for the earth, Rosalind raced for Tammi again. As she approached, she commanded her magic to unfurl from her fingertips in a line of vines that coiled around Tammi's body. Snapping her wrist back, Rosalind pulled Tammi closer. As her friend thrashed and bucked in the restraints, Rosalind wrapped her arms around Tammi, holding her close to fly with her to the earth.

Caine's command bellowed again. *Retreat.*

After him, Ambrose shouted the same command, his deep voice booming through the air.

He was ordering the army back over the rubble—the long portion of shattered wall, and the edimmu were flying in close pursuit. He wanted to fight them on the ground.

As Rosalind raced through the air with Tammi in her arms, Drew's aura curled around her, heating the sky, blazing like a hot star. Blinding sunlight glinted off the soldiers' silver armor as they retreated.

At last, Rosalind reached the ground, landing hard with Tammi in her arms—outside the empire's gate. They rolled over the hard earth on the pavement, the army of Lilinor retreating toward them. Rosalind unfurled the vines from Tammi—left bound, she'd be too vulnerable. She left her on the empty city streets, then took flight into the air again, soaring over Lilinor's retreating army to rejoin Caine. She touched down between Caine and Malphas, just at the edge of the destroyed wall. As she landed, her body brushed against Caine's, and for just a moment, his darkened eyes flicked to her, his body rigid. He'd recovered his sword, and now clutched it tight.

As Lilinor's forces retreated, Rosalind stared at the oncoming horde of edimmu, who swarmed over the courtyard, spreading out over the grass and pavement.

A perfect trap. The edimmu had nowhere to run. Rosalind closed her eyes, summoning the wild fury of the storm god. These dry, desiccated creatures hated the dark. Hated rain and water. And Rosalind was going to hammer them. How powerful would they be when their arid bodies felt the force of Dagon?

From her right, Caine's command boomed into the minds of the soldiers. *Encircle, flank all sides.*

Moving from the shadows, the cohort of shadow demons crept from their hiding places, encircling the edimmu, swords drawn. Soon, the rest of Lilinor's army would close in again, moving back over the rubble to trap their prey. Caine had outmaneuvered the demon horde.

But Rosalind had already seen what the edimmu could do, had felt their arid presence in her body. The sun was *powering* them.

"I'm going to call up a storm," she said.

Caine nodded, his powerful aura snaking over her skin. Battle seemed to imbue him with greater strength, and his magic felt intoxicating, a vortex of power.

As they began their march back over the rubble, Rosalind unleashed a wave of Mishett-Ash's magic, summoning the storm clouds. As the army marched forward, dark, roiling clouds raced in, drawing shadows over the skies.

Drew's magic seemed to pulse in the air. He could sense what she was doing, and knew she was trying to create a storm. Caine shouted the order to attack, and all at once, Lilinor's army closed in on the edimmu, swords drawn.

As Rosalind charged, her sword ready, she channeled the magic of the sea—her sister's magic. They reached the line of edimmu, and Rosalind whirled like a storm wind, cutting into the edimmu before they got the chance to possess her.

As she fought, Dagon's power flooded her body. All at once, she smelled Miranda, that rich, briny scent, and a pang of longing pierced her. She felt as though Miranda's magic were rushing over her skin, cool and wet. And in that moment, she felt her sister's presence surrounding her.

In the darkening skies above, Dagon's magic merged with the storm god, the sky now dark as a cauldron.

She whirled, striking through another edimmu. As she fought in a fury of ducking and whirling, the ground rumbled, and she could feel Miranda's god approaching. She imagined him, Dagon, the god of the depths, and called him to her body. *Dagon, you can find wholeness again with me.*

From the nearby Charles River, she could feel Dagon rushing toward them, until a wall of water breached the Empire's fallen gates.

A wave slammed over the courtyard, forcing Rosalind to the ground, knocking the breath out of her. In the muddy water, she scrambled to get up, finding the water up to her knees. She gasped.

With the wave's arrival, the storm clouds unleashed their full fury, battering the courtyard with a hard rain.

She scrambled around in the mud for her sword, and snatched it from beneath three feet of water. As soon as she gripped the hilt, she looked around her. All around the battlefield, the edimmu bodies were soaking up the water, and those who'd been possessed by the edimmu seemed to have recovered, their eyes no longer empty. *Good. Tammi should be recovered.*

Lilinor's forces closed in, hacking through the damp, limp flesh of the edimmu, weakened by the water. Already, some of the edimmu bodies floated face down in the shallow, muddy water. Rosalind glanced at Caine and Ambrose, who moved in a blur of silver and black. Fury still electrified Rosalind's body, and she moved just as fast, her sword swinging through the air, legs shaking with the roar of battle.

Now it was just a matter of finishing off what they'd started. As the rain hammered down over the battlefield, Lilinor's army worked their way inward, slaughtering their prey. Rosalind lost herself in the fury of fighting, her limbs trembling.

As Lilinor's army hacked through the last of the edimmu, Rosalind sheathed her sword, her hands shaking. She stood, knee-deep in the mud, searching for Tammi. She caught a glimpse of Tammi, crossing over the rubble again, her silver hair plastered to her head. *Thank the gods. She's fine.*

A powerful, silver aura turned her head. Caine was striding toward her through the muddy water, sheathing his sword. When he reached her, he touched her arm. Instantly, his touch soothed her, and his silver magic caressed her skin. The shaking in her limbs began to abate, and she took a deep breath.

She shoved her hand in her pocket, gripping the iron nail, the one destined for Drew's heart. Now she just needed to find a way to break through his shield.

CHAPTER 30

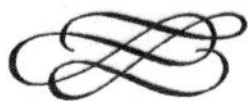

*R*osalind climbed the steps once more, narrowing her eyes at the shield. She rammed her hand into her pocket, gripping the rusty iron nail like it was her lifeline. Filthy water soaked her clothes, and her footsteps sloshed up the stairs.

She traced her fingers over the shield, and Drew's aura thrummed over her body. As she touched the shield, one word rang in her skull: *dominance.* The real heart of Drew.

Her mouth went dry, and she let herself fall into the hellscape of his mind...

Flickering through Drew's magic were images of Rosalind's parents, their bodies hanging limply from the stakes where Caine had killed them. A phantom, golden crown glowed on her father's head. From the shadows, Drew approached, pulling it from her father's head.

Rosalind forced the image from her own mind. Could Drew see into her mind, the way she could see into his when she touched his magic? Maybe the way to defeat him was to slam his rotten skull with images of her own.

What really bothered him? She knew one thing that seemed to drive him crazy...

She thought of herself, climbing on top of Caine, wrapping her legs around him. She leaned down, and whispered into his ear *I love you, Caine.*

At once, the image began to ripple and tremble. A vision slammed her back—Rosalind, naked and on her knees, kneeling before Drew. She pulled away from the shield, bile rising in her throat.

Through his magic, an overwhelming feeling of malice washed over her, turning her stomach. Sweat beaded on her forehead, and she lifted her hand, getting ready to touch the shield again. She'd been getting somewhere...

Just then, a rumbling noise pulled her from her task. She turned, surveying the grassy courtyard and the vast army spread out before her. Something in the distance was making the muddy earth tremble, shaking the leaves. Whatever it was, it was coming from the opposite side of the courtyard, and the low rumble was sending a shiver of fear up Rosalind's spine. A low growl raised the hair on her neck, and turned her stomach. *The gruesome hounds.*

From the battlefield, Caine boomed an order that rang in the minds of his soldiers. *Hellhounds to the front! Form the wall!* Caine and Ambrose shifted behind the front lines.

Quickly, the legion shifted, and the hellhounds marched to the front, holding their large, silver shields in front of them. From one of the wide avenues that adjoined the courtyard, a horde of beasts charged at the legion. Rosalind gripped her sword, her heart hammering, and rushed for the front lines. She landed next to Becca, who nodded at her, eyes burning with hellfire.

They looked like dogs, except for their strangely human eyes. Apart from their powerful jaws and sharp teeth that glinted in the sunlight, they had strangely humanlike faces, and the pale, blue eyes of men. As they drew closer, Rosalind could see that these beasts were not the size of dogs. They were closer to the size of horses.

They pounded the earth on all fours, kicking up mud, drool dripping from their fangs. Caine barked an order, and the front lines shifted, forming a tight wall with their enormous, silver shields.

Snarling, the hounds charged for the ranks of soldiers.

When they were in close range, Caine's order boomed through her mind. *Fire!*

Rosalind and the hellhounds unleashed a wild, explosive burst, and anguished howls rent the air. *Fire!* Caine shouted again. The creatures' yelps and screams filled the air, and yet they kept coming, moving forward into the flames as if they had no sense of self-preservation.

Any second, the hounds were going to break through the wall of shields and start tearing into the soldiers.

Caine's command boomed again. *Winged cohorts, rise!*

An icy wind rushed over Rosalind's skin, and the storm god's aura sparked through her veins. But just as she prepared to lift into the air, the beasts broke through the shield wall. A hound lunged for her, knocking her to the ground. Within an instant, the hound's teeth were in her shoulder, and pain ripped through her body. As its claws tore into her, she scrambled for her sword, but it was too large to get a good swing in—she needed a dagger to kill at this distance. The hound shook his head, tearing at her tendons, and she shrieked.

The magic of the valkyrie rippled through her body, a hot electrical charge, and she sent a flash of lightning through the hound. He yelped, and the scent of burnt flesh filled the air. Ignoring the pain in her shoulder, she scrambled to get out from under the hound before its enormous body collapsed on her.

She rushed to her feet, and snatched her sword from the mud beneath her. Blood poured from her shoulder, but she could ignore the pain for now.

She glanced at Becca, who was driving her sword through a hound's chest.

Propelled by the storm god, Rosalind lifted into the air along with the winged cohorts. Soaring above the battle lines with Aurora and Tammi, Rosalind flinched at the scale of the attack. From here, they could hack into the hounds' bodies from above, slicing through their heads.

Already, the incubi were circling over the hounds, swords arcing through the air as they brought death from above. If Rosalind could steer clear of her allies, she could blast the hounds with fire.

"Move back!" She shouted at Caine.

His gaze met hers for an instant, and he ordered the winged cohorts further back, out of her way.

Rosalind gritted her teeth, blocking out the pain that ripped through her shoulder blade, and she summoned Emerazel's fire. Molten power surged, and she circled over the hounds. As she swooped over the demons, flamed sparked from her fingertips. When she flicked her wrists, fire shot from her hands, exploding into the horde.

The beasts shrieked, and she hammered them again and again until they scattered from the impact site, and she circled again. She slammed them with another ball of fire, and they scrambled to retreat—running straight for the winged cohorts, who hacked into them from above. But as the battle lines became more enmeshed, she'd need to strike with more precision.

As the battle raged below her, an electrical charge burned through her nerve endings, and the ancient winds of the valkyrie caressed her body.

Rosalind sent electrical charges at the hounds, lighting up their bodies. The smell of charred flesh filled the air.

Rosalind arced again, catching sight of Aurora. Carried by her valkyrie wings, she drove her sword into a hound's neck, severing its spine.

Rosalind circled the battle again, charged with battle fury. The storm winds whipped at her hair. *Mishett-Ash, god of storms, help me strike at my enemies.* A cold gale rushed over her body, and her blood charged with electrical power. She took in the crowd below her, taking note of all the hound locations. When she'd committed them to her memory, she unleashed a surge of lighting, striking for the gruesome hounds.

She opened her eyes, gratified to find she'd hit ten of them at once, their bodies now collapsed into the mud.

She circled again, striking a second time, taking out a dozen more hounds.

At the back of the horde of hounds, Caine was driving his sword through a hound's spine. Lightning glinted off his blades, and his black wings beat the air. All at once, an enormous hound leapt into the air for him, clamping its jaw around Caine's leg. The creature dragged him to the ground.

A crowd of hounds surrounded him, and Rosalind's heart skipped a beat. A wave of protectiveness washed over Rosalind as she rushed for him. The hounds had marked him as the leader, and they wanted to tear him to pieces.

CHAPTER 31

Hounds surrounded Caine, one of them tearing at his wing. Rage lit up Rosalind's body. With Caine so close to them, she couldn't strike them with lightning.

She swooped lower, gripping her sword, and landed just behind the melee. Within moments, she was swinging her sword through one of the hounds' necks. An arc of blood sprayed into the air, and Caine hacked into another, snarling like a beast. His powerful aura washed over her in waves.

One of the hounds leapt on him, claws on Caine's face, and he stumbled back. Four red slashes marked his cheek.

Hot anger surged, and Rosalind lifted her sword for a strike. But before her sword could find its mark in another hound, an agonizing pain splintered her leg. A beast pulled her to the ground, then leapt on top of her, claws digging into her skin. Panic began to claw at her chest. As her pulse raced, she kicked her leg into the hound's gut, then his chest. She knocked the creature off her, then leapt to her feet, plunging her sword through its neck.

The beasts all seemed to be heading right for Caine now. Of course, they understood him as the alpha. Adrenaline lit up her body, and she channeled the power of the valkyrie and the night god, moving like Caine in a silvery blur of power. Her sword whipped through the air, cutting through flesh, and she fended off the oncoming hounds.

But even with the power of the gods blazing through her body, her wounds were slowing her down. As she thrust at an oncoming hound, agonizing pain ripped through her leg.

She fell to the ground, sinking into the muddy water, and a beast leapt on top of her, jaws open to bite her neck. Frantically, she fought to clear her head above the water, kicking at the hound above her, but she couldn't get the right angle. *Slam.* At last, her foot hammered the hound's chest, and for a moment, she forced her head above the mud, gasping. Mud spattered in her mouth, and in the next second, the hound was forcing her head under the muddy water again, teeth at her throat. *Fuck fuck fuck.*

Just then, the dog's bite went limp, its heavy body collapsing on top of her. Summoning the raw power of Borgerith, she forced its body off of her, and scrambled out of the muddy water. Caine stood before her, covered in mud and blood, his sword dripping with crimson, black wings spread out behind him.

Rosalind surveyed the battlefield, now littered with the bodies of hounds and edimmu. Lilinor's forces were blazing and cutting through the last of the gruesome hounds. Rosalind's body shrieked with pain, and she winced.

Caine was by her side in the next moment, staring at the wound in her neck. "Where else are you hurt?"

"My legs." She looked him over. "You're almost completely unscathed."

"I've had more time than you to get used to being a god. I'm better at it."

Her body felt like it was fracturing, and for just a moment, she thought of Azazeyl's fall. "Just heal me please, and let's move on."

He pulled her close to his powerful chest, his hands startlingly gentle on her lower back, behind her neck. He curled his enormous wings around her like a protective shell, and let his soothing shadow magic caress her body, kissing her skin, and she melted into him. Slowly, his magic pulled all the pain from her body, and her back arched in response to him. She ran her hands up his chest, folding them around his neck. For just a moment, she leaned her head against his chest, listening to his heart beat.

She knew she had to break away in a moment, but she needed just this moment with Caine, to savor his life and his body.

So quickly she nearly missed it, Caine leaned down and brushed his lips over her forehead. "You're ready to fight again."

Reluctantly, she forced herself to pull away from him, and he tucked his wings behind his back.

She turned to the battlefield, the action now stilling. Demon bodies littered the courtyard, half sunk in muddy water, blood mingling with the mud.

Among the bodies, Malphas sheathed his sword, dripping with blood, and Aurora was cradling a ravaged arm. Bite wounds covered her body, but as a valkyrie, she should heal quickly.

Ambrose's battle-ax dripped with blood, his body glowing with dark light. Somehow, he had managed to get through the battle without becoming soaked in mud, and she had the feeling that he *loved* this—slaughtering in the daylight.

Rosalind began carefully stepping through the carnage, and her throat tightened at the sight of a crumpled hellhound, six inches deep in muddy water. Her armor had been torn off, and her throat ripped out. Blood stained her *Vampires Don't Sparkle* T-shirt. Rosalind's throat tightened. *Becca.*

By Caine's side, she moved among the dead, her stomach churning. When she caught sight of Tammi, she exhaled. Tammi was wrapping fabric around bite marks in her arm.

She glanced at Caine. "We're in a vulnerable position here. Drew will keep sending in legions of his archaic demons until we break through to that palace.

"How long till you break through the shield?"

She swallowed hard. "I'm close, I think. I just need to mentally break Drew."

"That doesn't seem like it would be hard."

She frowned at him. "Harder than you'd imagine."

"You need to stop joining us in battle. Just work on the shield. When the next demon horde comes for us, your job is to break through the shield. Understood? We'll be fine. Tammi will be fine. And I'll protect you while you're delving into the shield."

She nodded. He was right—the shield was their priority now. "Let's go."

"Fast," he added.

She summoned her shadow magic. Together, they shadow-ran across the battlefield in a blur of dark magic, the wind rushing over her skin. The scent of death filled the air.

On the palace steps, Rosalind slowly approached the shield, her mouth going dry at the thought of entering Drew's mind again. Slowly, she ran her fingertips over the shield, and Drew's sickening energy coursed through her. He slammed her with a series of images, of herself kneeling before him, telling him that she worshipped him.

What was Drew afraid of more than anything else?

"Rosalind."

She snapped away from the shield. Caine was pointing across the courtyard again. On the other side of the carnage, another legion was coming for them. Faint colored filaments coiled from their bodies. Even from here, she could recognize them as human, modified with Drew's magic.

All except for one, clad in silver armor. Shadow magic poured from his enormous body, and a flash of lightning glinted off his horns. *Bileth.*

The army of humans came armed to the teeth, laden with machine guns. A helicopter rotor beat the air, and dread tightened its grip on her heart. She was running out of time.

"Keep working," he said. "I'm going to make sure nothing happens to you while you're concentrating."

She grabbed his arm. "Caine. If I get through this shield, you need to stay and lead your soldiers against this army. But I'm going into the palace if I can get in. If I can murder Drew, maybe this will all be over. I can go in on my own."

Shadows flickered in his eyes. "He's too powerful." He gestured at the city. "Look at all this. He's been using his power longer than you."

"I'm powerful, Caine, and your army needs you. You need to lead the battle against Bileth and the Hunters, and if I break through the shield, I'm going in."

Caine stared at the helicopters. He wasn't as familiar with fighting humans as he was with demon warfare. "Tell me what the Brotherhood carries in those machines."

"Missiles and iron dust. You don't want them to get any closer. And the Brotherhood might have flamethrowers. You'll need to use your shadow magic to neutralize it."

Rosalind turned to the shield, tuning out the sounds of Caine's commands ringing in her mind, his deep booming voice that commanded the winged cohorts to rise.

Rosalind touched the shield's rippling surface, and Drew's corrupted magic seeped into her body, bringing with it images of Rosalind chained to the wall, telling Drew that she loved him. These were no longer fantasies. This was what had actually happened when she'd been trapped in the palace. He was trying to break her, but his images only stoked her rage. Right now, she wanted to tear his fucking head off and throw it to one of his hounds. *Soon enough.*

She gritted her teeth, trying to concentrate. What was Drew afraid of—what was *anyone* afraid of? A pointless existence in a dying body. A soul trapped in a corpse, rotting into the forgotten riverside— painful isolation for eternity.

Okay. How could she show this to Drew?

Perhaps Caine—not Rosalind—was Drew's greatest weakness. Caine was more to him than a simple rivalry. After all, Caine murdered Drew's heroes, the king and queen who should have beaten death and achieved immortality. *Caine* was Death, a god from the underworld, come to drag Drew into the void.

She envisioned Drew, walking over the muddy riverbank in the rain, just before three wooden stakes. Tendrils of his colored magic snaked into the air around him. And as he trudged through the mud, silver magic writhed around the oaks like a living thing. The forest's shadows grew heavier, pooling like ink. *Death is coming for you, Drew. Let's invite Caine into this vision.*

He appeared, his black wings protruding from his shoulder blades, eyes dark as caves. In his black talons, he gripped a long, iron nail. He stalked closer to Drew, who stumbled back through the mud. A hard rain battered their faces.

Drew raised his hand to strike Caine with a spell, but Caine rushed for him in a blur of silver and shadows, slamming Drew hard against the stake with a growl, black talons piercing white skin.

Caine began chanting the spell to steal immortality—the one she'd gleaned through his memory. She mixed it up a little, changing some of the words. There was no way she was giving Drew knowledge of the real spell. Still, she left in just enough of that spell that he'd recognize the intent.

Drew's colored magic flowed from his body, leaving him slumped, his skin wan and gray, dark circles beneath his widened, green eyes. Completely mortal.

The shield shuddered.

In the vision, Drew lifted his hands defensively, and Caine slammed a nail into his chest, piercing him against the stake like a butterfly specimen.

Drew's body slumped, his eyes widened in shock. And Caine—his angel of death—simply slipped away into the shadows.

Drew's shield began to crack, but Rosalind wasn't finished yet. She showed Drew a vision of his body pinned to the stake, his skin turning gray and corrupted. Slowly, nature claimed his body, as the forest's vines snaked around him. Alone, forgotten, his body rotted into nonexistence.

As she finished her brutal vision, the shield ruptured. With a loud report, like a ship's cannon, the shield splintered and cracked around her. Before Drew could raise it again, she rushed through, her feet pounding up the palace steps.

As she raced up the steps to the towering maroon doors, she hurled an explosive spell at them, breaking them open.

When she ran into the vast, marble hall, a line of empty-eyed scorpion men blocked her path. Good. She'd been hoping to kill some more of them.

CHAPTER 32

osalind stepped into the cold, marble palace, staring at the line of scorpion men who blocked her path.

In here, Drew's chilling magic snaked over her body, curling inside her ribs as he tried to rebuild the shield. Since he'd built this place with magic, his aura tainted nearly everything around her, making it hard for her to focus.

His magic filled her with a gnawing emptiness, and visions flickered in her mind—Drew and her, sitting on iron thrones. Her eyes were vacant, her jaw slack, and her belly swollen with his child. Drew's fantasy.

She didn't want to linger in this hellhole any longer than she had to. She needed to search for Drew, and slaughter the bastard. And when he was dead, the magic sucked dry from the walls, this place would be nothing more than an empty, marble skeleton. She'd blow the fucking thing to smithereens.

First, she just had to put these scorpion men into the ground. Sucking in a deep breath, she summoned her battle rage, until her legs trembled with anticipation. She gripped her sword hard, remembering the scorpion men watching her in her prison room. They'd enjoyed her humiliation. Most of her time in captivity had been a blur, but she remembered vividly the scorpion man ruthlessly slaughtering that gray-eyed servant girl, and the girl's pale body writhing and convulsing on the ground before her, mouth foaming.

Right now, she could only hope the scorpions were wildly underestimating her power.

One of the men stepped closer to her, his clawed legs clacking on the marble floor, footsteps echoing off the ceiling. Their tails and stingers shone in the light. Rosalind's pulse raced, and sweat beaded on her forehead.

She arched an eyebrow, daring him to move closer. If she was going to defeat all five of them, she'd need to move fast—inhumanly fast. On top of the battle fury, she'd need shadow magic on her side.

Nyxobas's magic pooled in her chest, and she submitted to it, bending to the god of night, to the vast and empty chasm. She didn't have to fear the void anymore. This was Caine's magic, too, and he was her home.

When the scorpion took another step over the marble, she was ready for him. She shadow-ran to him, leaping into the air at the last moment and slicing her sword through his neck. Blood arced into the air. *One.*

For just a moment, her feet touched down on the ground, and she leapt in the air again, moving like a phantom wind. Before the scorpions had a chance to react, she whirled, cutting her sword into the next scorpion's neck. *Two.*

A scorpion's tail was reaching for her through the air as she touched down again. She dodged, running for the wall. At the speed of a hurricane wind, she let her feet climb the wall, then bounced off it, flipping through the air until she landed before the scorpion. She bounced off the marble floor, leaping again to hack her sword into the next scorpion's neck. *Three.*

Immediately, she pivoted, leaping, swinging. A scorpion head rolled across the floor. *Four.*

She looked up at the final scorpion, who stared down at her. Slowly, he began backing away, fear sparking in his eyes. It was one she'd remembered—the one with gray patches in his hair. This one she'd saved for last. She wanted to see the fear in his eyes, just like she'd seen the fear in the blond servant's eyes.

"Remember the girl you killed?" asked Rosalind. "I remember. I don't know her name, but I remember her. I want you to think of her now, as I'm coming for you. I'm your angel of death, Scorpion, and I want you to remember her."

He opened his mouth wordlessly, then closed it again. Rosalind's footfalls echoed off the ceiling, and the scorpion backed away. Shadow magic rushed through Rosalind's body like an arctic wind, and she rushed forward, sword drawn.

The scorpion man lunged for her, suddenly on the attack, his tail ready to sting again. He wouldn't get that far. As she ran for him, she leapt into the air. Whirling, she sliced her blade clean through his neck.

His head tumbled off, rolling over the floor in a spray of red.

Five.

Now she just needed to find Drew. And while she was at it, she was going to slaughter that bastard Randolph.

CHAPTER 33

Scorpion men poured into the hall behind her, and Rosalind's pulse raced. How long would it take her to kill all of them? The longer she spent in here, the worse her chances got. She just needed to put distance between herself and the scorpions.

She shadow-ran over the marble, and as she moved the shadows seemed to climb the walls around her. As she moved deeper into the enormous palace, the walls seemed to change—no longer smooth marble, but now made of vast expanses of ivory bone, as if she were moving through the skeleton of an expansive creature. Around the halls stood statues—some of Blodrial, his veins spurting blood. Some depicted Randolph and Drew. Carved into the bone around the halls, the letters *R&D*, intertwined. *Rosalind and Drew.* She wanted to puke.

The further she moved into the building, the more the walls began to change. A network of dark veins throbbed beneath the walls' surface, like thin, pale skin. The shadows grew, shifting between the statues.

Energy reverberated through this building, pulsing like a heartbeat. She felt as if she were running through a living creature, as if the walls themselves pulsed with life.

She slipped her hand into her pocket, running her fingers over the old iron nail. *This thing needs to find its home in Drew's heart.*

From the shadows, figures emerged from crouching positions, their wispy bodies thickening and solidifying. The three creatures wore cloaks, though beneath their hoods she could see that the creatures had large, dark eyes. The lower halves of their faces were simply a mass of wrinkled, gray flesh. At least until their lips parted, revealing a chasm of black interrupted by a few spiked teeth. Smoky auras undulated from their bodies, and iron-gray wings curved from their shoulder blades.

A chill snaked its way up Rosalind's spine, and she readied her sword. An emotion tinged their magic, but to her surprise, it wasn't anger or menace. It was despair. It rolled off their bodies, staining the air with stark melancholy. It wrapped itself around her muscles, freezing her in place, and as the force of it hit her, her sword drooped in her hands.

She had the sense that these creatures had once been something different—something majestic, from a past so distant they no longer remembered it at all, yet still they lamented its loss.

One of them stepped forward, tapping his sharp teeth together. "Rosalind." *Tap. Tap.* "Our queen. Reign over us in the Desert of Anguish." *Tap.* He pointed an elongated finger at her chest, his nails gray and sharp. *Tap. Tap.* "Queen Rosalind," he hissed. *Tap.* "Rule us." *Tap. Tap.*

Sorrow coiled around her heart, tightening its grip, and a dry wind seemed to rush over her skin, calling her to the Desert of Anguish. *Tap. Tap. Tap.*

An iron crown appeared on her head, weighing heavy on her skull, and her grip loosened on her sword. What was she doing here? Why fight? Miranda had bled out on the cold stones, an iron nail in her heart, and Rosalind hadn't been able to help her at all. Raised from the grave, her soul splintered.

Rosalind's body began to sway to the rhythm of the palace's heartbeat, as the demons lulled her into their spell. *Tap. Tap. Tap.*

Miranda's body, cold and alone, buried deep beneath the earth.

Queen of Anguish... She had no family. She'd let her sister die. Her parents had been monsters who'd ruined Caine's life, forced him to slaughter his brother.

"Join us," said the creature. *Tap. Tap. Tap.*

Her soul was corrupted, tainted by the sins of her parents. She was a solitary monster...

She gritted her teeth, trying to focus. Closing her eyes, she forced the images from her mind—her desert throne, her iron crown. Cleo's magic whirled within her, forcing out the despair.

She hadn't come here to become a queen. She'd come here to kill. She tightened her grip on the sword again, forcing their smoky magic from her body. "I'm sorry. You've got the wrong girl."

She swung, cutting through one head, then two. She pivoted, cleanly slicing off the third head. The three creatures slumped to the floor.

She stared at their withered bodies, their dark blood staining the floor. "It's for the best. Someone needed to put you out of your misery."

Rosalind stalked the halls, listening for footfalls. The place was surprisingly empty. Apparently, Drew and Randolph had sent all their soldiers to the battlefield outside, depending on Drew's shield to keep them safe in here.

Rosalind frowned, not entirely sure where she was going. Drew's magic was all around her, so it was hard to trace it to a particular source. She seemed to be in an endless hall of veiny bones.

Where would Drew be hiding out? It's not like she'd been given a tour of the palace when he was keeping her chained to the wall in her room, and these halls seemed to go on forever.

Drew was obsessed with dominance, with supremacy, with ruling as an emperor. She supposed he'd be in the most grandiose room in the palace, one that gave him a view of his entire domain. When she thought of her view from her prison room, she'd been on the third floor at least. She imagined Drew would have kept his own chambers near hers.

She needed a stairwell. At last, a door interrupted the smooth, bony walls. She pushed through it, finding a twisting stairwell that spiraled upward like winding ribs. *I'm on the right track now.*

She ran up the stairs, heart pounding. When she got to the third floor—the top floor—an enormous iron door barred her way. With the power of the mountain goddess strengthening her body, she kicked through it, knocking it open onto another hall.

Inset into the wall directly across from her was a set of oak doors, carved with chalices and crowns. Iron barred the doors. *Someone* was clearly in there, hiding. What sort of sad coward locked himself in a room while his city was under siege?

Based on the ornate doors and the iron, it looked like a room fit for a king, and if her calculations were right, this was the center of the palace, the high point from which an emperor could look out over his entire kingdom. *Bingo.*

She crossed to the oak doors, running her fingers over the wood, feeling for a surge of Drew's magic. If he were inside, she would feel his magic like an intense vortex.

Yet, she felt nothing here. At least, nothing more than the same low thrum of corrupted magic that covered the whole palace.

A room for a king. Perhaps Drew wasn't the real king anyway. He believed he was the emperor, and needed that illusion to sustain him, but he wasn't the true ruler. He was too mad for that, too enraptured by his own fantasies.

Randolph, on the other hand…

Randolph is the one who'd threatened to find her on her wedding night, to rape her first before Drew had the chance.

Iron barricaded the door. A safe room—just the place a coward like Randolph would hide.

When she'd been imprisoned, her mind encased with ice, a dark rage had bloomed in her chest, curling around her ribs like dark vines. Now, it thrived.

"Randolph," she whispered. "You sick fuck. Are you in here?"

She took a step back from the doors, whispering a spell in Angelic —the one for bending iron. Slowly, the iron creaked and groaned, contorting until it fell to the ground with a heavy *clang* that echoed off the walls.

She let the rage flow through her body like shadow magic, then she kicked through the oak doors.

They splintered into a million tiny shards of wood, opening the way into an enormous octagonal hall. Randolph sat at the back of the room, guarded by three scorpion men.

An oblong table stood between her and Randolph, who leaned back in a leather armchair.

For just a moment, she saw a flicker of fear in his eyes, but the satisfied smirk on his face told her that he had no idea how quickly she could kill the scorpion men. Before the oval table, the scorpion men stared down at her, their dark eyes locked on her like prey.

"Hi, Randolph," she trilled. "If I'm not mistaken, you wanted to rape me and then burn me alive. I do believe we have a score to settle."

His face paled. "You can still repent. If you don't, you will find yourself in one of the earthly hells after you die instead of fractured into seven."

She took a step closer. "You must be fucking joking, Randolph. I don't need to repent, and I don't need to worship Blodrial. The gods are in me. Do you understand that? I know their secrets, better than they know their own. I saw their birth. I know what they fear, and I know what makes them suffer. So I will not be repenting to Blodrial. But I will make a little sacrifice to him." She took a slow step closer to him, smiling slyly. "Do you know what I'd like to sacrifice, Randolph? I'll be serving them up a fresh coward today."

His throat bobbed, and he no longer looked convinced the scorpion men would win in a fight against her.

Randolph shot a nervous look at the scorpions, then nodded at them—his signal to kill.

Rosalind readied her sword. "You, Randolph. In case it wasn't clear, I'm going to sacrifice you."

Shaking, he stood. "I had understood the implications. But perhaps you forgot what my scorpions did to that servant girl."

Battle fury ran through Rosalind's body, making her legs tremble —and with it, shadow magic whispered through her blood, filling her muscles with a preternatural surety.

The scorpion men clacked over the floor to her, their tails extending closer to her. A dark smile curled her lips, and she rushed into action, shadow running for the table. From the oak surface, she swung her sword, cutting through the first scorpion's head. *One.*

His muscled body slammed to the ground, blood spurting from his neck.

A scorpion swung his tail for her, and she ducked out of the way, moving like the night wind. From a crouching position, she thrust her sword into the scorpion's chest. He lurched back, and she sprang up again. Whirling, she cut through another scorpion neck, listening with a grim satisfaction as his head thudded on the ground. *Two.*

The injured scorpion swung his tail again, and she dove, touching down on the floor for just a moment before springing up again. She carved her sword into his neck, hacking through it.

His head rolled on the floor, his enormous body slumping. *Three.*

She turned, her gaze landing on Randolph. The coward was trying to run for the doors. She flicked her wrist, slamming him with a blast of shadow magic that froze him in his tracks.

Slowly, she walked closer to him. "Randolph. Remember when I was frozen, and you came into my room? Remember when you forced me to my knees?"

Slowly, she circled him. "How does it feel, Randolph, to be completely at my mercy?"

His mouth opened, only a choking noise rising from his mouth.

She stood in front of him, grabbing his jaw, hard. "I believe you wanted to burn me, Randolph. How many demons have you burned at the stake? I was supposed to be one of them. My sister Miranda would have been one of them, if Drew hadn't killed her first. Maybe you need to feel what it's like to burn. Do you think?"

Randolph's body began shaking, and his pale eyes opened wide. His face had gone completely white.

"You're not like some of the others. You're a true believer, but the Brotherhood was never supposed to use magic," she continued. "You thought you could use it just long enough to get what you wanted, that the ends would justify the means. But you tainted your soul for nothing, and I want you to die knowing that you failed. I want you to die believing that you'll suffer eternal torments in one of the hells."

As the power of the gods flooded her body, they spoke to her in whispers. They spoke to her of their torment, of fragmenting into pieces, of needing to be whole again. They whispered of rock and fire, storms, and the darkest depths of the oceans. The gods didn't want repentance from her or Randolph or anyone. They were simply broken.

As their power flooded her body, she tried to force out their voices. They were overwhelming her, and her own thoughts clamored to be heard.

Rosalind slid her hand around his neck, squeezing. "There is no way for you to repent, Randolph, because the gods don't care."

Power flooded her body, the auras of the seven gods. As they whispered in her skull of all the ways she could kill the man who'd hurt her. Fire, perhaps, or peeling off his skin. Lightning to roast him. Rip his blood from his veins…

Molten rage ignited her body, and the voices of the gods blared in her skull.

She lifted her fingers, letting flames dance from her fingertips, then touched them to Randolph's black shirt. As smoke curled into the air, his eyes widened in fear. The scent of charring flesh wafted into the air as his skin burned.

She tightened her jaw. No—they were the gods' desires, not her own. She wanted Randolph dead, but she wasn't a sadist like he was. With icy shadow magic playing about her fingertips, she flicked her fingers, freezing the fire.

Randolph's body shuddered, and Rosalind eased her mental barrier to the magic, letting her body relax.

She took a deep breath. She didn't need fire or magic to kill this man. She lifted her sword. Swift as a lunar wind, she ran it through his heart. His eyes opened wide, and a stream of blood trickled from the corner of his mouth.

She pulled her sword from his chest, cocking her head.

Humans. So fragile.

Randolph crumpled to the ground. Now, she just needed to find Drew.

CHAPTER 34

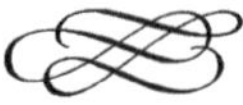

$\mathcal{R}$osalind stepped out into the bone-walled hall, her fingers gripping the iron nail in her pocket. In here, tall windows interrupted the vast ivory expanses, and rain hammered the glass. The valkyrie were channeling a storm to battle the helicopters.

Outside, the battle raged, and she pressed her fingertips to the window. Lightning cracked the dark sky, illuminating Caine, flying through the air, directing the winged cohorts. He moved in a terrifying maelstrom of silver and black, his shadow magic curling around a helicopter. Rosalind scanned the crowd for Tammi, her heart skipping a beat when she caught sight of a Hunter aiming his gun at her. But Tammi was fast—she blasted him with two shots to the head from her own gun before he could pull his trigger.

Rosalind loosed a sigh of relief.

She turned, stalking through the hall again. On the top floor, silence reigned, and the stillness sent a shiver crawling up her spine. A powerful, corrupted magic snaked over her skin. Drew's magic.

Her heart pounded hard, rattling her ribs. He was here—not far now. She just had to follow his aura. Her footsteps echoed off the high ceiling, and she gripped her sword. Randolph's blood dripped onto the ivory floor, leaving streaks of crimson. As she moved through the hall, Drew's magic grew stronger, pulsing over her skin.

She could see it now, weaving through the air in tendrils of silver and gold, copper and gray.

"I'm coming for you, Drew," she whispered.

He had to know she was coming. He could sense her magic, just as she could sense his. That meant he'd be waiting for her, totally prepared while she had no idea what she'd be bursting into. As much as she wanted to blow his doors open and rip his spine out of his neck, she needed to act carefully.

Cold sweat beaded over her skin as her gaze homed in on an oak door at the end of the hall. This door was different—no chalices or Latin inscriptions. This one bore the mark of Azazeyl—that sharply pointed sigil enclosed within a circle. Apparently, Drew didn't see the need to hide himself. No iron barring his entrance, and a giant bullseye right on his door. Thick magic coiled into the air from the door.

Of course, he didn't need to hide. He was one of the most powerful beings on the planet, and he sure as shit wasn't scared of Rosalind. But maybe he should be.

Drew had taken her sister from her, and she *needed* to kill him. She was wrath, born of blood, ice, stone, and flames. Born of the forest's shadows, where civilization fell away and nothing remained but the will to live.

As she moved closer to his room, images flickered in her skull like a grainy old film: Drew slamming Miranda against the stake, ramming a nail through her heart. Miranda's limp body, lying on the floor, rain drenching her clothes. She'd seemed so cold. Sorrow ate at Rosalind's chest like a cancer. Abominatonia—Miranda's dream. The little house in the woods, a family at last. Rosalind wanted to kill Drew extra slow for taking that from her sister.

She moved closer to the door, nearly overpowered by Drew's magic. She stood outside his door, flexing her fingers.

She took a few steps to the side, then kicked the door, splintering it into tiny flecks of wood. Immediately, she dodged to the side, just in case. Waves of magic burst from the room.

Rosalind peered around the corner, and her heart skipped a beat.

Drew lay in the center of a circular room draped with gold and scarlet. Shirtless, he reclined on a cherry-red chaise longue. His aura formed a halo around his head. He wore nothing but a pair of white linen pants, and he sipped from a chalice.

He didn't give a fuck about the battle raging just outside his palace, nor that Rosalind had come here to kill him. Tightening her fingers on her sword's hilt, she stepped into the doorway.

Amusement danced in Drew's emerald eyes, and his lips curled in a smile. From sharp iron sconces, candlelight wavered over his bare skin.

"Ah. Rosalind," he breathed. "I knew at some point, you'd come right to me. Do you know why?"

She heaved a sigh. "Yeah. Because we belong together. Oh, no—wait. Because I'm going to kill you."

Almost imperceptibly, he shook his head. "No. You're going to submit to me, once and for all." He sat up, his body pulsing with magic. "It's your destiny."

"You're so full of shit, Drew."

Drew's eyes bulged for a moment, then he swiped his hand through the air. The movement sent a shock of pain through her skull, and she fell to the floor. Her sword clanged on the marble.

The metallic taste of blood pooled in her mouth, and she struggled to stand. Maybe she needed to freeze the fucker, just like she'd done to Randolph.

She rose, letting her mind fill with Nyxobas's void. She gave in to the god's will, and it rippled through her body.

From the ground, she blasted him with a burst of shadow magic, but Drew instantly unleashed a burst of fire from his body, burning away the tendrils of silver magic. An incendiary power rippled over her body, and if her skin could have burned, the magic would have incinerated her. Around her, the silks caught ablaze, and the marble floor reddened. Slowly, Rosalind pushed herself up.

He slashed the air again with his fist, and pain splintered her mind as she fell back against the floor. *He's going to bash my head in, without getting up from the sofa.* Panic clawed at her heart. She needed to gain control of him.

Gritting her teeth, she stared at Drew from the floor. This is where he wanted her, wasn't it? She didn't want to give him the satisfaction. The magic of the dark god filled her body again—Caine's magic. Before Drew had a chance to react, she shadow-ran to him, touching down just behind him.

She gripped his head, ready to snap his neck. Before she could twist, he gripped her arms, pulling her over his head.

He slammed her onto the floor, and her body cracked the marble. She clenched her jaw, trying to block out the pain. At least she could heal quickly.

Pushing up to her elbows, she cocked her head. She couldn't seem to hurt him, but maybe she needed to try something different. Something he wouldn't expect.

He stood above her, towering over her, his green eyes flashing. She closed her eyes, imagining a cool mountain wind—the power of Our Lady of Rock, and of Blodrial, his veins spilling open. She'd just bleed him out.

She stared at his veins, calling his blood to her. Drew's eyes bulged, his body shaking. In the next moment, blood began to spurt from his wrists. She could feel the power seeping from his body, and fear flashed in his eyes.

With a bestial roar, a flare of magic burst from him. He slashed at the air with his fist, and a wave of magic slammed into her with the force of an oncoming train. Her body went hurtling back, slamming against the wall. The crack of her bones echoed through the room. Her body shrieked with pain. In a blur of colored magic, Drew shifted across the room, his hand gripping her throat before she had the chance to get the next words out, squeezing. Her lungs burned.

This was impossible. No matter what she did, Drew seemed to have the upper hand. Clearly, Drew had perfected his gods-magic more than she had. And yet, she had something in her arsenal that he didn't. She knew how to fight without magic.

In the Brotherhood, she'd been trained to manipulate, to confuse—to use anything around her as a weapon. Iron sconces hung on the walls. Maybe if she got enough iron into him, it could weaken him.

Mentally, she merged with the goddess of stone, her body surging with the power of magnetism. She felt herself connecting to the iron around the room, as if tied by an invisible cord, and she pulled the iron sconces—sinking them right into Drew's back.

He screamed, dropping his grip on her; Rosalind crumpled to the floor, her body broken. For the first time, she seemed to have actually hurt him, and blood poured from his back. She blasted him with shadow magic, and his back arched as she froze him. She blocked out the pain wracking her body, and raised her hand, summoning the magic of Borgerith.

Drew slammed into her, crushing her into the wall. In the next moment, his powerful hand was around her throat again. This was his favorite move. He liked the intimacy of choking her, liked the control it gave him. The dominance. He wasn't going to kill her from afar. He wanted his hands all over her when she died, wanted his breath on her face.

He crushed her throat, threatening to snap her spine. The pain was unbearable, dizzying. Starved of oxygen, her mind dimmed as Drew pressed harder. Her throat spasmed. Glimmers of Drew's wrathful eyes flashed into her vision, then darkness. With Drew's hands around her neck, she drifted into the void, sinking deeper and deeper.

In the darkest hollows of her mind, she embraced the emptiness. This was Nyxobas's world, and Caine's, and as she plumbed its depths, she felt Caine's silver magic whisper over her skin.

What had he said to her that day in the sycamore grove? *If you bend, you're less likely to break. Let down your defenses.*

There's strength in vulnerability. If she could just come out the other side of this darkness...

Drew's tight grasp on her neck lessened, and he let in a little bit of air. She gasped for just a moment, before he pressed on her throat once more.

He leaned in, whispering, "I told you, Rosalind. You can't die. We're gods now, and I can kill you over and over again, for the rest of eternity, but you'll come back every time. If only you'd given Miranda some of Blodrial's blood, and let her become a god like us. She'd still be alive now. It's your fault she's dead."

Pain ripped Rosalind's mind apart. She could hardly focus on Drew's words. Any minute, he'd snap her spine.

He whispered, his breath hot on her cheek. "I'm your king, Rosalind. I've always been your king. Perhaps if I cut out your tongue, you'll find it a little difficult to defy me."

Panic blazed in her mind as her vision dimmed again. Slowly, she drifted into the void. Images flickered in her mind, like an old film strip showing flashes of her life: setting a tiny, flaming sailboat into Athanor Pond with her sister. Holding hands as she, Malphas, and Miranda walked into the forest, searching for adventure. Her adoptive father, red-faced, a vein popping in his forehead as he screamed at her. Lying back in the grass at Thorndike University between classes with Tammi, their bellies full of sandwiches and hard cider.

And then Caine—his hands on her skin, his breath warming her ear as he whispered, *Let down your defenses.* The pain etched on his features when he told her about Stolas. At last, he told her, and she couldn't have loved him more.

Caine's aura caressed her skin. And with his magic, his arms slipped around her. Sometimes, strength required vulnerability.

Drew loosened his fingers, and Rosalind sucked in a ragged breath. She needed Drew to think she was completely defeated, vulnerable.

Drew smashed her head against the wall again, and Rosalind let her body go limp. But with her free hand, she reached into her pocket, curling her fingers around the iron nail.

Drew growled in her ear. "You were supposed to be mine. And I haven't broken you yet."

Even as her muscles went limp, gods-magic blazed through her body. The strength of Borgerith, the fires of Emerazel, the darkness of

Nyxobas. Her magic pooled inside her, blazing through her veins. As the magic burned through her, more powerful than she'd ever felt, it worked through her body, healing it. The gods knit her bones together, soothing her pain.

If Drew hadn't been so blinded by his thrill at having her at his mercy, he would have noticed the magic roiling around her body.

He gripped her face, and she let her head loll as if she were unconscious. "Rosalind. If I just keep hurting you enough, you'll submit."

She half-opened her eyes, giving Drew a dazed look. *Let him think you're weak.* She reached up, limply hitting him, missing. She made it look as pathetic as she could. She needed him to let down his guard.

Drew had two things he relied on when he fought her. One was strangling. The other was running away as soon as she got the upper hand. She wasn't letting him get away this time.

She let her eyes glaze over, and he grabbed one of her thighs. "Oh Rosalind. Rosalind. I like you when you're like this."

Anger erupted. Just then, she tightened her fingers around the nail and slammed it into his chest, cracking through his bones.

Drew's green eyes snapped wide open in shock, and he fell back.

"*Uggae Lalartu Dalkhu Mitu Wussuru Telal.*" As fast as she could, Rosalind rattled off the spell for mortality. As she spoke, Drew's immortality curled from his body, staining the air around him in wisps of silver, blue, green, and copper. Horrified, his skin paling, Drew stared at the magic leaving his body. The tendrils of magic floated into the air, disappearing like smoke on the wind.

Drew fell back on the floor, his head cracking against the marble. Clutching his chest, he gaped at her. Blood poured from the wound, and the magic escaped him.

Rosalind rose, standing above him. His jaw trembled, and his body looked oddly withered.

"I think it's time you learned your place, Drew." She kicked him hard in the chest, cracking his bones.

Humans. So weak.

"Your place, Drew, is in the ground."

The last of his magic curled from his body. And when it disappeared into the air, Drew rasped his final, rattling breath.

CHAPTER 35

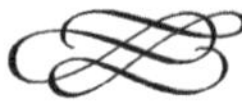

Rosalind picked up her sword, moving for the doorway. With Drew's final heartbeat, the sheen seemed to wear off the palace walls, giving the ivory a dull, gray cast. That reverberating power she'd felt all over the palace dissipated, and the walls no longer seemed to breathe. Now, she walked through a carcass. Before she left the place, maybe the Brotherhood's empire was due for a cremation.

As she moved through the building, Rosalind felt at one with the seven gods, and their magic mingled within her, merging into a white light. She lifted her hand, staring as ivory plumes curled from her fingertips.

Outside, the battle still raged, and the Hunters fired into the crowd of demons. Caine, seemingly dodging bullets at a stunning speed, cut through the lines of Hunters, hacking through their bodies. She traced her fingertips on the window, leaving trails of frosty white.

Here he was, her king, breathtaking in his savage beauty, his body blazing like starlight. She sucked in a deep breath, steeling her resolve. The battle wasn't over yet, and Lilinor needed her. She turned, then rushed through the halls in a gust of shadows, and slipped down the winding stairs, onto the ground floor. This palace, this corrupted carcass, never should have existed, and it was time to end it all.

A line of Hunters had entered the palace, searching for her. They trained their guns on her, and she didn't need to be told that iron bullets filled their guns. Still, they weren't shooting, yet. They knew who she was—their emperor's intended queen. They just had no idea what she could do.

She closed her eyes, arching her back as she walked, and liquid fire pooled in her veins. She burned like the inner core of the sun, and when she flung out her arms to either side, flames licked along her arms, surging down her wrists, and exploded from her fingertips.

White hot flames seared the air, and the impact rumbled through the walls. Around her, fire bloomed like a wildflower, claiming the hunters, the walls, the palace in an inferno.

Screams pierced the air, and the walls crumbled around her. Fragmenting marble rained around her, but she continued striding through the halls, until she stepped out of the hellfire, into the courtyard. Dark smoke billowed into the air. Explosions ruptured the building, and she stepped onto the marble steps. Caine whirled, his magic dancing around his body. Through the smoke, his silver eyes pierced her.

For just a moment, the fighting had stopped as everyone gaped at the exploding building, the Hunters' empire destroyed. The filaments of colored magic that had coiled from the soldiers had all but disappeared, gone with their leader. A hail of bullets ripped through the air, and Caine whirled again, blasting icy shadow magic at a line of Hunters.

Slowly, she stepped down the stairs, her body blazing with white light, and surveyed the carnage. She searched the crowd for Tammi, and her heart clenched as she found her friend crawling through the mud, legs bleeding. Any minute, one of the Hunters would finish her. Rosalind glanced at Malphas, one of his wings damaged, half of it blown off. His movements were labored. The winged cohorts had entirely taken out the helicopters, but Lilinor's forces were in rough shape.

In the center of the melee, Ambrose was stalking Bileth, their dark auras curling around both of them. Ambrose swung with his battle-ax, and Bileth dodged. Lilinor's king—the new incubus—had the upper hand here. Still, as much as she wanted to watch him hack into Bileth, he wouldn't be able to kill him without knowing the right spell. And moreover, she needed to end this battle now, before anyone she loved got hurt.

A rush of white magic murmured over her skin. The humans had nothing left but their weapons, and she could take those. She raised her hands before her, her fingertips sparking with white light, and she felt for the magnetic pull of metal, an invisible cord that tied her to the guns, the shields, the swords. Lifting her fingers, she pulled the weapons into the air, while the Hunters frantically tried to cling on to them. Without their weapons, they had no chance. A few of them clung to their machine guns twenty, thirty feet in the air, until they dropped to the ground with a hard *thud.*

The demons got to work with their hands and teeth, snapping necks, biting into veins. Apparently, vampire habits died hard in the fog of war. Panicking, a stream of Hunters began running for the shattered wall. But Rosalind's gaze was locked on Bileth, his powerful body curling with that shadowy magic of his. He and Ambrose circled each other, gripping their weapons. Even with Ambrose's formidable lethal power, he needed the right spell.

Magic electrified her body, and she descended the stairs. As Rosalind moved, white magic coiled around her. Unconsciously, the crowd seemed to part for her, and she headed straight for Bileth. His dark gaze landed on Rosalind, but he looked away again, uninterested. He *still* didn't see her as a threat. It was best that way.

Gripping an iron sword, Bileth lunged for Ambrose, who deftly dodged. Rosalind glided closer to them, picking up her pace, and when she was close enough, she rushed forward, punching him hard in the throat, with the full force of the mountain goddess. Bileth staggered back, eyes widening in surprise, and she followed up with two brutal punches to his skull. Dazed, Bileth staggered. While he tried to reorient himself, Rosalind chanted the spell to steal his immortality.

She watched the light flow from his body, disappearing on the wind, and Bileth's dark eyes stared at the escaping aura. Slowly, his muscles slackened, his skin turning to ash gray. A layer of matted fur covered his body, and his horns cracked. His eyes yellowed, muscles slackening.

Bileth stared down at his hands, his body trembling.

Rosalind nodded at Ambrose. "The coup de grâce is yours."

Horror washed over Bileth's features, and his body trembled. It took only a moment for Ambrose to slice through his neck with his ax. Bileth's headless body fell to the ground, and Ambrose closed his eyes, whispering a prayer to Nyxobas.

Rosalind whirled, joining the battle, or what was left of it. The Hunters had once been her tribe, but not anymore. Not since she realized what they truly were—history's monsters.

She moved like the wind, a frantic whirlwind of sword against flesh, cutting down the Hunters, her sword dripping with blood. Just as Caine had said—if you cut off the head of this snake, it'll just grow another head. The Hunters would always exist. But their defeat today would deliver a message—the gods were not smiling on The Brotherhood, and Blodrial would not bestow riches and luck on his followers. In fact, the gods did not care at all. The gods were insane.

CHAPTER 36

Rosalind stood in the blood-soaked field as the smoke began to clear, the rain mingling with the rivulets of blood and dirt. An eerie silence shrouded the battlefield, raising the hair on the back of her neck. Deep inside her chest, the gods-magic had mingled into one pure powerful core of light, and the screaming of the gods abated to a low, melodic hum.

Across the courtyard, bodies littered the field. The bloated carcasses of the waterlogged edimmu and the bleeding bodies of the hounds stained the fields. She swallowed hard, her gaze roaming over the dead. Lilinor's soldiers were gathering the corpses of their fallen comrades, hoisting the bodies over their backs. Ambrose was barking out orders, his silver armor glinting in the light. Each fallen soldier would have to be carried home again, and laid to rest in the earth with a feast of the dead.

Caine crossed to her, his body glowing silver. He reached out, touching her arm.

Blood and dirt smeared his cheeks, and at that moment, she had an overwhelming desire to wash his skin clean and kiss him all over. She trusted him with her life, as he trusted her with his, and she wanted to lie curled in the crook of his arm, smelling his skin, kissing his neck for the rest of their lives. She wanted to lie in bed as night blended into day and back, to stroke his waist and kiss his mouth until their skin glowed, to feel his warm lips on hers.

She was struck by the feeling that their bodies belonged together, endlessly intertwined. But more, that *they* belonged together, two orphaned monsters who glowed like starlight in each other's presence. When she'd first met him, he'd been such a mystery to her, and now she knew the darkest depths of his soul. She knew what he feared, and what hurt him. She'd seen his nightmares, and knew what could kill him. She knew that he was loyal and protective, that he dreamt of cherry trees under the stars. She even knew that he snored lightly in his sleep—that part of him was deeply human.

If he'd died today, she'd be lost again—left with nothing but the indifferent forest where she'd make her home among the rocks and moss. If Caine disappeared, she'd hollow out. She'd need the quiet darkness of the yews to let her sleep.

"What?" he said, pushing a strand of hair from her face.

Tears stung her eyes. "Nothing. Just—I'm happy you're okay."

He cupped her face, and pressed his forehead against hers. "We survived it. And now, I want to build a world with you, of stars and cherry trees in full bloom."

He slid his hand around the back of her neck, and kissed her gently on the lips.

She pulled away, looking into his eyes, her hands on his face. "I want to get home and wash the filth off you."

"Did you honestly think for a second I wouldn't be okay?" He looked almost hurt.

"I worried."

A faint smile ghosted over Caine's lips. "I like your parting gift. Blowing up the building. Dramatic."

"It needed to die."

His eyes darkened, and a wicked smile curled his lips. "I've never found you more attractive." He grabbed her hand. "I want to take you home to Lilinor."

"There's just something I need to do first," she said.

* * *

Taking to the air, Rosalind swooped over the burning building, the heat from the flames warming her body. Acrid smoke curled into the air as she flew, soaring over the palace remains to the amphitheater. In the center of the pit, iron stakes protruded from the ground. The earth around the ground had been blackened, a relic of the people they'd burned in the center of the pit. By Drew's side, she'd stared at these stakes, with a dull horror throbbing beneath the ice floes of her mind.

She didn't know how many people had died here, but because she had Cleo's memories fluttering in the back of her mind, she could imagine the terror they'd felt, the indescribable pain. Randolph had wanted to burn her here, when they'd finished with her. After they'd forced her to bear Drew's children for the empire.

This place needed to die, too, and the Brotherhood's followers needed to see once and for all that Blodrial's cult was not the answer, that he protected no one.

As she soared, she rallied the magic of Azazeyl, letting it vibrate over her skin in white light. For a few glorious moments, she felt the seven gods uniting within her, whole again. The seven merged in the air—the rocks and sea, storms and forests, darkness, fire, and blood—mingling together once more.

She swooped lower over the pit, magic bursting from her body, streaming from her fingertips into the center of the amphitheater. The pit, the iron stakes, the stone—they exploded in a blaze of light. Fragments of rock and dirt rained around her, clouding into the air.

Rosalind soared through the debris, leaving the ruined pit behind her until she swooped through the clear air above. She was heading back for Caine, just as rays of amber sunlight pierced the clouds.

She'd take him home now—back to Lilinor, where her sister lay beneath the earth. Where the sun could rise, and Rosalind could sleep safely in Caine's arms, listening to his heart beat.

She found him waiting for her on the battlefield, his silver eyes piercing the clouds of smoke, standing by Malphas's side, each holding the body of a fallen soldier. She landed hard on the muddy earth, her magic flickering in her gut. She leaned down, scooping up the body of a slain soldier—a fae with a long, golden beard and silver armor. She heaved him over her shoulder. Between Malphas and Caine, she walked toward the river, back toward their home.

When she reached the edge of the Charles, the three of them summoned their shadow magic, opening the portal to their home. Their shadow magic coiled together in silver streams, and Rosalind felt Lilinor pulling her in, like a gravitational force. Gripping the body of the fallen soldier, she leapt into the portal, plunging deep beneath the icy water.

She drifted beneath the surface, her mind rolling over images of the girl she'd once been: the lost girl, at the river's edge, watching her parents die. The Hunter, lured in by the promise of ridding the world of evil. What would that girl have thought of the woman today, who'd slaughtered Hunters by the droves?

Clutching the fae's body in her arms, she sank deeper into the river. Was she really human at all anymore? She wasn't sure if it mattered at all.

CHAPTER 37

*I*n Lilinor, the sun streamed through the yew's boughs, dappling the cemetery grasses with dancing flecks of gold. Rosalind breathed in the lush scent of spring—somehow, it was always spring in Lilinor, the grasses always blanketed in bluebells and cowslips.

Further over the gentle hill, Lilinor's demons were laying out a feast across the Gelal Fields. Only a few of Lilinor's soldiers wanted to return to their vampiric form after the battle. The rest, it seemed, had enjoyed the sunlight and the corn dogs too much to revert to their vampire forms—at least for now.

So while a handful of vampires stayed in the depths of the fortress during the daylight hours, the rest of Lilinor strolled through the tall grasses in the sun, eating and drinking under the silvery shield of shadow magic.

Rosalind leaned back among the bluebells, breathing in the fresh spring air. She plucked a wildflower from the ground, twirling it in her fingers. Cleo had been lingering among the wildflowers the night her world had ended, when she'd been waiting for Ambrose. With a flicker of surprise, Rosalind realized that Cleo had gone quieter recently, melding into her own mind as a part of her. Somehow, even with two souls and the magic of seven gods, Rosalind felt whole again.

A breeze rustled the yew leaves, toying with the bells, and through their chimes, Rosalind thought she could hear her sister whispering through them, telling her all the things she wanted. We'll make our own tiny little kingdom, the three of us. *We'll get a little house by the water, and we'll build a magical shield around it...*

Footfalls crunched over the path, and Rosalind turned to see Tammi and Aurora walking toward her through the tall grass, weaving between gravestones. Aurora wore sunglasses, shielding her eyes from the glaring light. She wore a shimmering blue dress, her gray valkyrie wings trailing behind her. She *really* made a stunning valkyrie.

Tammi's silver hair cascaded over a red dress, resplendent in the morning light, and she carried Owen on her hip. The little human child, his cheeks now full and round.

Rosalind smiled. "Hello ladies! And Owen!"

Aurora plopped next to her, a flask in her hand. "We thought you might be here."

Tammi sat next to them, and Owen stood, staring at the tree.

"I was just paying Miranda a visit," said Rosalind.

"Why?" said Owen.

Rosalind took a deep breath. "I don't know. It just makes me feel better."

He stared at her. "Why?"

She shook her head. "I don't know, Owen."

Tammi reached up, brushing her fingers over the shimmering ribbon that read *Miranda*. "This was sort of her dream, wasn't it? A safe place, shielded by magic, where she could make a home with us."

Tears stung Rosalind's eyes. This *had* been Miranda's dream. Abominatonia, a sunlit city of demons and freaks. "If Drew hadn't killed her, she'd have everything she wanted now. Everything she deserved."

"You're still alive," said Tammi. "And we both have very long lives ahead of us. We will just have to make the most of them."

"And how do you intend to do that?" asked Aurora.

Tammi cocked her head. "I'm going to start with seducing the fae chef who made those hush puppies I ate this morning."

Aurora unscrewed the top of her flask, before sighing and closing it again. "I don't think I can keep drinking whiskey all day. It doesn't feel quite right in the sunlight, especially with the kid here. And I don't think my valkyrie body fancies it as much."

"So what will you do with the daylight hours?" asked Rosalind.

"I was thinking of forming a goth band, with black and white clown makeup." Aurora scratched her cheek, mulling it over. "Do you think a valkyrie can be a goth?"

"Anyone can be a goth," said Rosalind, her voice deadly serious. "You just need lots of fishnets, I think."

Aurora nodded, frowning. "I'm learning to play synth."

Tammi sighed. "I can't plan beyond the fae chef, to be honest. Since this all began in May, everything seemed to happen so fast. I feel like, one minute we were at Thorndike's campus, getting ready for a party. The next thing I know, we're living in a vampire city with a demon army. And I kind of like it." Tammi pointed at Rosalind. "Plus, you're apparently a goddess, with a lover who happens to be the hottest man who has ever walked the earth."

Rosalind shook her head. "Don't call me a goddess. I'm going to get a big head."

"Well then you'd be a perfect match for Caine. Speaking of which, I think he was looking for you."

Rosalind rose, brushing the dust off her black pants. As she walked through the grass, some of Caine's memories flitted through her mind —Stolas in his arms, Malphas pleading with him for help. The starlight gleaming through the cherry trees.

She swallowed hard, thinking of the day when her parents had died. The place where Tammi began the story at Thorndike wasn't the *real* start. It had begun in Maremount, that terrifying and beautiful place where she'd started her life. It had begun in blood and madness, in the darkness and the rain when Caine had killed her parents, and it ended here in the quiet light of day. Across the Gelal Fields, demons milled around in vibrant colors, gilded in the sunlight. They were feasting on an array of foods: barbecued chicken, mashed potatoes, chocolate cakes. No wonder they hadn't wanted to become vamps again.

As Rosalind walked deeper into the Gelal Fields, she caught a glimpse of Erish and Ambrose, striding side by side by the blackthorn grove. Erish looked at her husband with an expression of absolute worship, touching his cheek. *Looks like they're no longer trying to kill each other.*

She found Caine standing by Malphas, by the lone sycamore tree where they'd once stood, summoning their shadow magic to build the shield together, where their memories had seeped into her mind.

As she moved closer, she studied the two brothers—the dark and the light. Malphas had once said of Rosalind and Miranda that he'd loved them both, and that's how she felt about these two brothers. She loved them and needed them both, in different ways, but Caine truly had her heart.

Malphas turned as he saw her approaching, and his silver eyes met hers for a moment. He bowed to her, then walked away, taking her approach as his cue to leave.

Caine watched Rosalind walk over to him, his eyes lingering over her body, the way they always did.

She smiled. "I heard you were looking for me?"

He shoved his hands in his pockets, sunlight bathing his skin in amber. "It's nothing urgent. It's just that I believe we agreed to a plan, whereby if we survived the battle, we would spend the rest of our days naked in my room."

Rosalind nodded. "I don't remember that plan."

"I'm sure we made it." His face grew serious. "I told you, I want to make a home with you."

"Cherry trees in the stars."

He nodded. "Will you miss being human?"

She shook her head. "I feel human when I'm with you."

"Funny that. I thought the same thing about you."

Rosalind stared into his eyes—the irises pale silver, rimmed by a deep pewter, the black lashes framing it all, and in them, she could see his darkest memories still flickered there, still haunted him. She cupped his face, breathing in his delicious scent of peat and lightning storms.

His breath warmed the shell of her ear. "So what's next for us?"

"Maybe we need to free ourselves from our old memories, and make new ones. We need to make our own world." She wrapped her arms around his neck, moving in close enough to feel his heart beating against her chest.

"Yes," he whispered. "We make our own world. We write our own stories."

Rosalind stood on her tiptoes, letting her body brush against his. Whatever happened to them next, she would follow him to the ends of the earth, and into the seven hells. And she knew he would do the same for her—the two orphaned monsters whose bodies glowed like starlight when they embraced.

* * *

THANK you so much for reading the Vampire's Mage series. If you would like to see more of Caine, he plays a role in some of the future books.

The next books in the Demons of Fire and Night World come from the Spy Among the Fallen novels.

DEMONS OF FIRE AND NIGHT: BOOKS 9-11
A SPY AMONG THE FALLEN
C.N. CRAWFORD